MAYBEL

MAYBEL

E. D. JUMPER

Erika Danielle Jumper

Maybel
by
E. D. Jumper

Catherine, would you like some lemonade?" Bernard asked.

"Yes," Catherine smiled.

Our rose garden was in full bloom and it was Catherine's birthday. Mommy and daddy held a small party in Catherine's honor and our new neighbors from down the street were invited. They had recently moved in, and their son, Bernard, was Catherine's age, and he seemed to like Catherine.

Catherine had insisted that I wear a pretty dress with frills and lace, and a stupid, pink ribbon in my hair to match the stupid, pink ribbon around my waist. Catherine dressed me up like one of her dolls, with whom she said she was now too old to play.

"Maybel," Catherine called to me, "come meet our new neighbor."

I skipped over to Catherine. "Maybel, this is Bernard."

"Hello Bernard, do you want to play with me?" I asked him.

"Maybe later, Maybel," he smiled politely at me.

Several of Catherine's schoolmates were in attendance, as were Granny and Grammpy. Mommy's sister, Aunt Mary, came with our cousins, Daisy and Shanna, and daddy's brother, Michael, came with our cousin Gerald.

Samuel, another boy in attendance, handed Catherine a glass of juice. Samuel had always asked to carry Catherine's school books to class and had always been very keen on sitting near her at church and festivals.

Bernard brought Catherine a slice of her birthday cake.

Samuel handed her a napkin.

Bernard then pulled a chair out for Catherine.

I played in our pond while Catherine and her friends chatted and ate cake. There were several boys and girls at Catherine's party, and I was Catherine's little sister. Nobody really talked to me much, but I didn't care. Catherine played piano, our cousin Daisy took ballet lessons, and I liked making small bowls out of mud for tea parties with my dolls. Catherine and her friends weren't that much older than me in years, but they liked boys now, and I still liked playing hopscotch.

The fish in our pond came to my ankles thinking I had bread for them. "Gertrude and Sylvia, you must wait for dinner," I told the bossiest of the fish. "It's not dinner time yet." Our fish weren't allowed names until they survived at least one winter and Gertrude and Sylvia had survived three.

I bent down and scooped some mud into my hands because my dolls needed new teacups. Their last set of teacups were smashed to bits when the boy down the street pulled my pigtails and I angrily set him straight.

I set the handful of mud on a nearby bench. There weren't too many stones or muck in this batch, so I was happy.

"I like pottery too," a boy said as he walked over. I was annoyed at his disruption. "It's not pottery, it's mud. I'm going to make teacups," I told him.

"Yes, that's what pottery is," he said. "You take mud and make things out of it." He came closer and put his hands on my mud pile.

"Stop!" I shouted. I flung a piece of mud at him and hit his cheek. Blood poured out. The boy touched his face, and as he pulled back his hands, he saw his blood-stained fingers and began crying.

"I'm sorry!" I pleaded. "I didn't mean to hurt you!"

The boy ran toward Catherine and her friends. The girls gasped.

That new boy, Bernard, immediately took charge and wiped the blood off the boy's cheek with his napkin. "Paul! What happened?" Bernard asked as he dabbed at Paul's cut and held an ice cube from his drink to the boy's cheek.

"That mean girl hit me!" he pointed at me.

Everyone turned to look at me. I stood there by the bench with muddy ankles and mud up to my forearms.

"Maybel! What's wrong with you?" Catherine yelled at me.

"I meant to hit him, Catherine, but I didn't mean to make him bleed!" I yelled back.

Catherine glared at me. Catherine's friends glared at me. Paul looked embarrassed that he'd been leveled by a girl, which made me smile internally, and Samuel looked at me like I was a dumb kid. The only person who didn't look at me like I was bad, was that boy Bernard, who liked Catherine. I decided to make Bernard a teacup for not looking at me with annoyance.

Mommy came outside. "Why did you hit him?" she asked me.

"He was trying to steal my mud!" I said angrily as I glared at him. "I didn't know there was a pebble in the mudball I threw at him!"

"Maybel," mommy said sternly, "Go wash up right now."

I kicked stones with my bare feet as I walked inside and everyone in attendance at the party watched me leave.

When I returned, the partygoers were playing some sort of big kid version of tag or something. I didn't know, and I didn't really care. The boy I hit was sitting on a bench by the roses. Mommy had told me to apologize. I walked over to him.

"Hi," I began. "I'm sorry I hit you."

I paused and took a deep breath and drew a circle in the stone path with my big toe.

I fidgeted. I took another breath. "I didn't realize there was a pebble in the mud, and I'm sorry I hit you."

"I wasn't stealing your mud," he said. "I just wanted to play with you. I've made a bowl out of mud before. Want me to show you?"

That sounded more fun than the stupid game Catherine and her friends were playing.

"Yes," I said.

"My name is Paul," he reached out his hand.

I took Paul's hand. "I'm Maybel," I said.

Paul was my age and we both liked playing in mud. I was delighted to finally meet someone who liked playing in the pond and climbing trees as much as me. Catherine used to like those things, but now she liked dancing, and dresses with matching bows, and boring indoor things, and really, I just missed Catherine a lot.

I was surprised at how much fun Paul and I had that day. Paul said he was Bernard's cousin from out west. He had come with his family to visit and help them get settled in their new home.

"Roll the mud like this, Maybel," he said, "between your palms."

He showed me how to make a really nice bowl by mushing together ropes of mud we rolled in our palms. We signed our names on each other's bowl. He told me it was called sculpting and that his grandmother taught him. I was actually sad to see him leave with Bernard when the party ended. Also, I felt really bad about the small gash I left on his face.

"Paul," I yelled as he walked away with Bernard, "will you come play with me again?" I asked.

Paul smiled, "I can't wait!"

Several days later, Bernard came by to see Catherine. Catherine was upstairs getting ready, so I relished in my time with a playmate.

"Where's your cousin, Paul?" I asked Bernard.

"He and his family returned to their home out west," he said.

"When are they coming back?" I wanted to play with him again. There weren't many children my age close by.

"Probably not for a long time, Maybel. They live out west," Bernard replied.

"Catherine doesn't want to play with me anymore. She likes dresses and playing the piano. I finally met someone who wanted to play and jump and climb trees."

Bernard saw my disappointment. "Why don't you show me the bowl you made the other day with Paul. I'm sure it's dried out thoroughly enough to paint now."

I went to my bedroom to retrieve my bowl. It was resting on my window sill on top of a rag. I brought it to Bernard, who'd been waiting in the garden.

"Have you any paints?" he asked.

"Mommy has some in our drawing room," I replied.

"Well then, let's bring the paint out here. It's a nice day," he said happily.

I did as Bernard asked. I brought the paints from the drawing room to the bench where he sat.

Catherine was still in mommy's and daddy's bedroom trying to tie her hair up in braids just as perfect as the ladies in the newspapers from Boston and New York looked. Mommy was fruitlessly trying to help Catherine, but the printed pictures did not come with instructions.

I placed the small vials of paints in their wooden stand. "Here, Bernard, would you like to paint first?" I asked him, handing him a paintbrush.

"No, Maybel, this is your art. My grandmother always tells us to let our hearts guide us, so which color does your heart tell you to choose first?" Bernard sat next to me on the garden bench. His legs straddled the bench so that he faced me. I was sitting in a polite position because girls weren't allowed to spread their legs when they sat. That's what mommy said.

"I want to use red first because the roses are in bloom now and the red ones are my favorite." I began by dipping my brush into the small container of red paint and swiping red around the rim.

Bernard grabbed my hand, "If you paint the top first, you'll have nothing to hold onto while you paint the bottom, and you'll get paint all over your hands. May I show you a different way?"

"Yes," I said. He seemed nice and didn't yell at me when I made a mistake.

Bernard stood and came around to sit behind me on the bench. He put his arms around me and held my bowl in front of me.

"There now, see?" He wrapped his arm around my shoulder to guide my hand holding the paint brush around the bottom of the bowl. His other hand held the bowl steady in front of me so I could paint. I chose yellow next, and then he helped me finish painting the rim red, and we painted the inside of the bowl orange.

"You do alright painting," I said.

He chuckled, "Thank you, my grandmother has taught Paul and me to appreciate art, and this bowl now looks like a sunset, don't you think?"

"Yes," I said. "Paul signed his name on the bottom of my bowl, see?" I showed him Paul's signature.

"I signed my name on his bowl, too." I paused and looked at my painted bowl. "I liked playing with Paul. Will you ask him to play with me again soon?"

Bernard looked at me with pity. "I will include your request in my next letter, Maybel, but I don't think he'll return soon. It's quite the long journey."

"Do you want to play in the pond?" I asked with wide eyes and hope.

"I'm sorry, Maybel, I have my good clothing on as I'm about to take your sister for some custard at the candy store."

"Will you climb a tree with me?" I pleaded. "Your clothing won't get wet," I begged.

Bernard sighed, he paused and contemplated. "How much longer will your sister be?" he asked.

"Likely another hour," I lied. I had no idea. I wanted someone to play with desperately.

"Alright, Maybel, I'll climb a couple limbs, but no more."

We went to my favorite tree which was nearest to my bedroom window. I shimmied up quickly, and when I reached the top, I looked down at Bernard. He looked taken aback at my athleticism.

"Maybel, I certainly can't climb that far nor that fast in my good clothing," he said.

"It's ok, so far only Samuel has been able to," I lied. I'd never climbed trees with Samuel.

I could see the mention of Samuel made this competition more interesting. His face with resolve, he climbed to me with more speed than I'd anticipated. I was genuinely surprised by his agility and strength.

"Wow! You're really fast and strong!" I exclaimed.

"Certainly better than Samuel, and you be sure to tell that to your sister!" he grinned at me. "Come now, let's climb down."

He had no trouble climbing down, but I was much slower, and that embarrassed me. Before just now, I thought I was the fastest tree climber ever. I was certainly faster than Catherine, and that had given me more than a little pride.

Once on the ground he dusted himself off. "Does your sister usually take this long?" he asked.

"Not at all," I replied. I curled my lips into a smirky grin. "She usually takes a lot longer!"

Bernard laughed, "You certainly have quite the sense of humor!" he smiled at me.

"Tag! You're it!" I screamed and ran around the fountain.

"Maybel, I mustn't get sweaty." he called to me.

"I'm faster than you!" I ran around a row of tall lilac bushes.

Suddenly Bernard cut through the line of bushes and met me head on. "Got you! You're it!" He ran back toward the house and behind the fountain.

He was so much faster than me, and my pride shrunk. I had been faster than Catherine for a year now, at least! I ran to the fountain, and every time I ran around one side, he ran even faster in the opposite direction. I was breathing heavily now. I couldn't catch him.

"Do you give up?" he laughed.

"No!" I shot back. My cheeks were hot and my lungs struggled to keep up with my running. Thankfully, Catherine entered the garden.

"You two look like you're having fun!" she smiled.

"Catherine you look beautiful!" Bernard said.

He wasn't even out of breath, I thought begrudgingly. I could not believe he wasn't breathing even a little heavily, I thought angrily.

Catherine smiled at me. "She's quite fast and strong!" Catherine said proudly.

"And can't catch her breath," Bernard winked at me.

His gentle chiding really made my blood boil! I huffed and furrowed my brow and stared in silence.

"Would you like some custard, Catherine?" asked Bernard.

"Yes," she replied.

They turned and began walking side by side toward the gate, not even saying goodbye to me. They were too entranced with each other to notice anyone else.

I went inside. Mommy had been watching out the kitchen window. She smiled kindly at me, "There, there, sweetheart. I am a little sister, too."

She wrapped her arm around me and led me into the family room to have tea and cookies. "It will be ok," she said as she rubbed my back.

Some weeks, maybe a month had passed. There was a knock at the door. "Can you get that, Maybel?" mommy asked. "It's probably the fabric I ordered for our new kitchen curtains," she called to me with an air of glee.

I skipped over to the door, excited for the postman, who always had a small lollipop for Catherine and me when he brought mommy or daddy packages.

It was Bernard. "You're back already from boarding school?" I asked, surprised.

"Hello, Maybel, yes, I'm back a day early." He handed me a package and two lollipops. "The postman and I arrived at the same time and I told him I would carry your mother's package to the door."

"It's a cherry lollipop this time!" I squealed with delight. I took mommy's package and skipped into the kitchen.

"Mommy, Bernard brought your package and cherry lollipops from the postman." I handed her the brown paper package. I put one lollipop in my mouth and kept Catherine's to give her later.

"Where's Bernard?" Mommy looked over my shoulder.

"I don't know," I replied. "Probably still in the foyer."

Mommy looked annoyed. "That's not how you treat a guest, Maybel," she huffed as she walked toward the foyer.

"Bernard!" she called to him when she saw him still standing by the door. "I'm so sorry Maybel left you here! I'll have to speak to her about manners," she turned to glance at me with piercing eyes.

"Oh, I'm fine, Mrs. Wyndham," Bernard smiled politely, "I know my presence is unexpected, but I was excited to see Catherine. May I see her?" he asked.

Mommy's face looked concerned. "Well, yes, of course," she stammered and fidgeted with her hands. "It's just that, well, she's not here right this moment, but I will tell her you dropped by, dear."

Mommy had already begun opening the front door. "Please give my best to your mother. The cake she made for our quilting group last week was absolutely delicious," she smiled brightly as she held the door open for him.

"Mommy, can Bernard stay and play with me until Catherine and Samuel return?" I asked.

If I thought mommy's eyes were icy when my lack of manners left Bernard in the foyer, I had been mistaken, for the levels of how icy her stares could become were multi-tiered. I stood there with my lollipop and stared blankly back at mommy. I had no idea how mommy's eyes went from icy to frigid like that, but it was quite the look to behold.

Bernard's face suddenly became solemn.

Mommy quickly spoke, "They went to school to help Mrs. Andrews clean up the school room for autumn break, dear. They will receive an extra credit toward their final grade for assisting their teacher."

Bernard looked relieved but I had no idea why. A smile replaced the sorrow that had been on his face. "I understand, Mrs. Wyndham. Please give my best to Catherine, and if it's ok with you, may I drop by again tomorrow at this time?"

"Wait! Mommy! Can I show Bernard my dolls, and can we play tag, and can I show him how to row our boat on the pond?" I screamed while jumping in mommy's face.

"I'm sorry, dear. I'm sure Bernard has much to do to unpack and get settled in. It's quite the journey from his boarding school," mommy said as she again moved toward the door.

"Not at all!" Bernard said excitedly. "Perhaps Catherine will arrive home before we are done playing!" Bernard playfully scruffled my hair. "What shall we do first?"

"I finally have someone to play with!" I jumped up into Bernard's arms and wrapped my legs around his waist and my arms around his neck to hug him. He seemed surprised but laughed at my silly antics.

"You remind me of baby koala bears in Australia," Bernard laughed at me. "They hold onto their mothers like this."

"Maybel, dear, you're getting too old to jump on people like that," mommy said. "Perhaps try a gentle pat on his arm with a polite smile to show your happiness."

Bernard had already begun carrying me through the house toward the back door and yelling to mommy over his shoulder, "It's ok, Mrs. Wyndham, she's lighter than all my little cousins!"

I giggled as he whisked me out the back door.

Bernard let me down and I immediately screamed, "Tag! Race you to the pond!"

I ran as fast as I could toward our pond. To my surprise Bernard did not gain on me. I pumped my legs as fast as I could wanting to show off. Bernard's long legs were easily moving to keep up with me. We arrived at the edge of the pond and while my lungs were on fire, he glided to an easy stop a couple steps behind me without so much as a huff or puff escaping his lips.

"Hey!" I shouted, "You let me win, didn't you?"

"I get the feeling you are a bit competitive, Maybel, and I didn't want to upset you," he winked at me. "Besides, your speed has noticeably improved since summer."

"Really?" My eyes gleamed with delight.

"Really," he said. "Now let's see, who here will give me a rowing lesson?"

"Me!" I shouted. I scrambled inside our little row boat.

Bernard took off his shoes and socks and climbed inside. I hadn't been wearing shoes because it was a warm autumn day and shoes were confining. Bernard sat on the seat facing me and grabbed two oars.

I held my set of oars. "Ok," I used my most teacher-like voice. "I'd like for everyone to please pick up their oars and do everything I do.

"Yes, Miss Maybel," Bernard smiled. He did as I instructed and put the oars in the water and together, we pushed off the bank.

"Miss Maybel," Bernard teased, "where are we going?"

"To that small island, Mr. Bernard," I giggled.

With every stroke, I pulled back as hard as I could, and pushed through the water with all the might I could muster. We moved slowly.

Then with every lazy stroke Bernard pushed and pulled, we soared through the water, the boat cutting through like a warm knife slicing butter. I watched Bernard's eyes. They were pure green, like the emeralds I saw in the city at the fancy jewelry store. Bernard smiled back at me. He seemed nice, I thought.

There were some trees on our small island and I showed Bernard the tallest. "I can climb all the way to the top but Catherine can't."

I started climbing but was going slower than usual because my arms were tired from rowing.

I reached the top and Bernard was close behind. When he reached the top, he sat beside me on a strong branch. "Wow!" he exclaimed. "You can see everything from here!"

He looked all around and out toward where the skyline met the trees. He turned and looked at the small foothills far away in the opposite direction. "This is magnificent, Maybel! I've never seen a more picturesque view! I wish I could paint these colors but I'd never be able to do this scene justice!"

"The fall colors will be more dazzling in two or three weeks. Will you come back with me?" I asked.

"Certainly!" Bernard said, still gazing with awe at the scenery.

I was happy at how happy Bernard was. We began our descent. After jumping off the lowest branch, we looked around the little island. I showed him all the places Catherine and I used to play. I told him about all the games we used to make up.

"You miss her, don't you?" Bernard looked down at me kindly.

I had a sudden flash of memories dance around behind my eyes. Once when I was five, Catherine had me dress up and hold flowers while she, in a white dress, held a bouquet of roses from our garden. I did whatever Catherine told me to do. I was her doll and she dressed me, flaunted me around to relatives at reunions, and I loved every second of her attention.

I looked back up at Bernard. "Yes," my eyes began to tear up. I wiped them and looked down. I changed the subject quickly. "Do you want to wade out a little and catch crawdads and minnows?"

"Sure," Bernard said sweetly. "You lead the way."

I showed him the rocks and logs a few feet from shore where all the biggest crawdads liked to stay.

"I've never met a girl unafraid of crawdads before," he smiled at me. "You are quite unique, Maybel," he winked at me as he suddenly pulled up the biggest crawdad I'd ever seen and threw it at my feet.

I squealed in terror when I felt it skittle across my toes and then drag its large tail up to my ankle. I screamed again and grabbed hold of Bernard's shoulders and hoisted my legs up and around his shins and thighs, whatever I could get my legs around, and away from that sea monster.

Bernard reached down, grabbed my waist, and threw me over his shoulder like a sack of flour, laughing the whole time.

He carried me onto land and gently put me down. He was still laughing at me. I was unamused. "Oh, come now, Maybel, you have to at least agree that your reaction was a little funny!" he continued in hysterics.

"I guess it was a little funny," I smiled at him. "It would have been funnier if I'd thought of doing that to you first!"

It was getting late in the day. I'd hardly felt time pass while playing with Bernard. We got in the little boat and began our trip home. Halfway along, my arms gave out. I'd been struggling until that point, and then my overworked arms gave out completely. "I'm sorry," I told Bernard, "I don't normally row, climb, then row again. My arms hurt."

Bernard put his oars in the boat and laid on the bottom of the boat. "It's a good time for a rest, anyway. Lay down beside me. I want to tell you about the stars and planets above."

I looked up, and to my surprise, there were already a couple shiny stars above us. "It's not that late, is it?" I exclaimed.

"No, it's not," he smiled, "but you can already see a couple stars peek through."

I clumsily attempted to lay down beside him and came terrifyingly close to capsizing our boat. Bernard's strong arms caught and steadied me. I laid beside him while he pointed to several stars and gave them names. "You'll soon see more stars peeking through and together some of them will form various constellations."

I turned my head to the side to watch him speak. He seemed really smart, I thought.

"Look, Maybel!" he pointed excitedly. "That is Orion! Do you see the three stars there? That's Orion's belt."

"Is this what you do every day at your boarding school?" I asked.

He chuckled, "Not every day, no. My grandfather used to take me camping and he taught me all about stars and how to use them to navigate through lakes at night."

"So I wasn't teaching you how to row then was I?" I grinned.

"No, I'm afraid not, but you were, nevertheless, a great teacher," he winked at me.

We continued rowing back to shore. Mostly it was just Bernard rowing, and me making little effort to help. My arms still hurt.

Once we pulled the boat halfway onto land and secured it, we set off toward home. I saw mommy scurrying around in our kitchen preparing dinner. I yelled to her, "Is Catherine home yet?"

She reached her head out our kitchen door and yelled back that Catherine must still be helping Mrs. Andrews.

Bernard looked sad. I walked him to our front gate. "I have to help mommy cook dinner, but you can try the duck pond in town," I said. "They usually end up there when they spend time together. Catherine likes to feed the ducks. Will you play with me again tomorrow?" I asked hopefully.

"Do Catherine and Samuel often spend their days together?" He looked angry, and that confused me.

"I don't know. She doesn't play with me hardly ever anymore is all I know."

"Maybel, I've had a lovely time with you. Thank you. I'll be heading home now. Take care," he said briskly before suddenly turning to leave. He walked away abruptly.

"Will you play with me again tomorrow?" I called after him, but his long, quick strides had already taken him halfway down the block.

Several days passed without Bernard coming to our house. Catherine sat with mommy and me at the sewing table in our family room. "Did he say anything else?" Catherine asked me for the twentieth time.

"No," I said. "He came looking for you, but you were cleaning Mrs. Andrews' room with Samuel, so we rowed to the island, climbed that tall tree you and I used to play in, then came home. He seemed annoyed when you were not here at home, and left." I repeated my account of what had transpired. "And really, I don't understand why you're upset, Catherine. We've been having lots of fun together, me and you, haven't we?"

"Yes, lots of fun," Catherine looked sulkily at the kitchen curtain she was sewing.

"Catherine, I'm sure he's tired from school and traveling," mommy reassured Catherine. "Why don't you take Maybel into town for a custard or sweet bread?" Mommy handed Catherine money from her apron.

Catherine sulked all the way to the candy store. I tried cheering her up with fanciful stories I'd made up in my head. It almost seemed like it was working when suddenly Catherine stopped in her tracks and looked angrily into the candy store window. There sat Bernard with Catherine's friend Edith.

"Do you see what I'm seeing, Maybel?" Catherine screeched in a pitch almost too high for human ears to detect.

"Hey! Bernard and Edith are here!" I ran excitedly into the candy store and up to Bernard.

"Bernard, you never came back to play with me! Do you want to come play with me at my house now?"

Suddenly, Catherine's hand gripped my shoulder like I imagine an eagle grips its prey after snatching it from its slumber and carrying it off to its hungry young.

"Bernard's clearly busy, Maybel!" She sunk her fingernails into my shoulder and dragged me out with her talon, like the way I imagined only a hungry eagle could do.

I wondered from where this strength had come. She could barely throw a ball to me, and now I felt like she could hurl me through the glass window if I showed any hesitation in leaving.

We were a good block away before I dared ask her what was going on. As though I accidentally kicked the top off an exploding volcano, she railed in a shrieking voice how Edith was never to be mentioned again and Bernard was a two-timing, double-crossing, bad, no-good person.

I didn't understand what Bernard did wrong. Catherine had custards with Edith all the time, so it probably wasn't the custard. I decided to keep quiet then recount the story to mommy later and ask for her to explain to me what just happened.

We arrived home and Catherine stomped up the stairs to her room. Mommy and daddy watched after her with puzzled expressions.

I sat next to mommy and began telling her what happened. When I got to the part where I said we saw Bernard and Edith at the candy store, daddy got up from the sofa. "Ok, I'm up to speed. I'll be in my office until Bernard returns to his boarding school." Daddy took his newspaper and closed the office door behind him.

"Maybel, Catherine is jealous because Bernard is spending his autumn vacation with Edith and not Catherine," mommy explained.

"Why?" I asked mommy. "They were just eating at the candy store. Besides, Catherine goes to the duck pond with Samuel. They're all friends passing boredom," I reasonably explained to mommy.

Mommy smiled at me, "Sometimes when you like someone, and I mean really like them, more than just a friend, you don't want to see them with someone else."

I just stared at mommy. "I eat custard sometimes with Della from school, and I saw her just last week with Leah at the candy store, but I didn't go dragging anyone out like eagle prey."

"Trust me, Maybel, you will understand when you get older," mommy said.

The next day Catherine moped around and alternated between crying into mommy's arms and yelling angrily that boys were unintelligent, unreliable, and she would never again let her heart be broken. I had never seen anyone with so much angst. It was like watching one of the plays mommy took us to see in town at the opera house. One act of bitter sadness followed by another scene full of rage. I lost count of how many times the curtain closed and a new character emerged. Who would be onstage this time? I mused to myself. Would it be Catherine the victim, or Catherine the executioner?

Daddy entered the room briefly, took in the scene, muttered something about growing up with his sisters, then exited stage left.

It was mommy who finally was able to calm Catherine enough to make her listen to reason. I sat waiting with interest and enthusiasm, wondering if this play would be a tragedy.

"Catherine," mommy said tentatively, "If you like Bernard and want to stay friends with him, you owe it to yourself and to him to at least talk to him and ask him if he wants to be friends, or perhaps more than friends, and how Edith fits into this triangle."

"It's more of a square, really," I accidentally said out loud.

"What?" Catherine flashed her angry eyes at me.

"Well, that day he was here, he waited for you, but you were with Samuel. So that makes four people involved, which would make all of you a square, not a triangle," I said.

"I was cleaning the school room with Samuel!" Catherine raved. "That's hardly a date! How could he be so assuming? What kind of a lady does he think I am?"

"You assume he was on a date with Edith," I said.

Catherine bore a hole through my skull with her angry eyes. "When someone is angry and irrational, Maybel, you let them be as angry and irrational as they want!"

"Ok," I squeaked. I decided not to poke the hornet's nest that was Catherine.

"Let's go tell Bernard that Samuel is only a friend," I said.

"No! Then he'll tell me he's dating Edith and I'll be standing there like a fool!" She stomped her feet then crumpled into a ball in mommy's arms.

Daddy walked in holding a sandwich, looking like he was about to ask mommy where she kept something, then left just as quickly.

As much as I loved the theater our family room had become, I loved Catherine more. I decided to ask Bernard if he was in love with Edith or Catherine.

Love could not be this confusing or difficult, I thought.

Catherine always made things better for me by offering guidance on how to navigate the school-yard, and what to say to my friends when I didn't understand what had happened between us, so now it was my turn to help her. She would thank me because I would make this all better. I took my lightweight coat off our coat stand and I walked to Bernard's.

I marched up to Bernard's door and knocked. Bernard's family was the richest family in town now. The VonHerrings used to be the richest family in town until Bernard's family moved here. When Bernard's mansion was being built, daddy said the owner must have deep pockets. When I met Bernard's father at the hardware store, I stared at his pockets then told him I had thought his pockets would be much deeper. Bernard's father laughed loudly but daddy's face turned red from embarrassment. Daddy later told me it's impolite to speak of wealth.

Bernard's butler greeted me when I knocked. "I'd like to speak to Mr. Bernard Charleston please," I said in my most grown up and polite voice. He looked surprised, and a little, amused smile played along his lips.

"Well then, won't you please come in then miss...." He trailed off, allowing me to finish the sentence.

"Miss Maybel Wyndham," I said, giving him my hand.

His smile widened as he politely took my hand. "One moment, please."

He gestured inside, "Won't you please wait here?"

"I'll be happy to," I said, still using my most polite manners I'd learned from watching mommy.

Mrs. Charleston entered the foyer with an air of curiosity on her face. "Hello, Miss Wyndham, how may I help you?"

"Hello, Mrs. Charleston. I'd like the honor of speaking to Mr. Bernard Charleston," I said, my posture straight, my head held high, and my voice with an air of dignity and professionalism. I was polite, but I was not asking to see Bernard, I was kindly telling her that I will be seeing Bernard.

Mrs. Charleston smiled at me. She seemed to be amused with me, but I didn't know why. "Bernard is in the stables tending to the horses. May I take a message?"

"I respectfully decline to leave a message, Mrs. Charleston. This matter is of utmost importance and must be resolved immediately."

Mrs. Charleston stifled a laugh, bringing her hand to her lips to hide her mounting amusement.

"Well then, if it's a matter of utmost importance, then I shall take you to Bernard myself." She had a gleam in her eyes. She took her shawl from the coat stand beside me. "Follow me, then, Miss Wyndham," she motioned.

We walked to the stables and Mrs. Charleston called to her son. "Bernard, dear, you have a visitor."

Bernard turned and saw me standing beside his mother. His brow squinched together in sheer puzzlement.

"May I present Miss Maybel Wyndham," Mrs. Charleston said, with an extra flourish, sweeping her arm around and curtsying.

Bernard stared in amazement. "Mother?"

"Miss Wyndham has a matter of the utmost importance to discuss, Bernard. I suggest you pause your work and listen to her," she winked at Bernard, and with a theatrical spin causing her skirt to twirl, she held her chin high and walked with prominence back home.

Bernard stared at me like I was some little kid who had just escaped from a mental hospital.

"Bernard, do you like Catherine?" I asked bluntly.

He continued to stare at me for a moment. "Yes," he said. He still looked puzzled.

"And do you also like Edith?" I continued my inquisition.

"What?" he asked, looking surprised.

I raised my eyebrows and repeated my question, this time with a stern stare.

"What do you mean?" Bernard asked. "Do I like Edith as a friend, or am I dating Edith?"

"Are you romantically involved with Edith?" I asked.

Bernard shook himself free of his stunned amazement at my blunt approach.

"What is going on, Maybel?" he asked, appearing irritated with me. "Why are you here, and why are you asking me these questions?" he demanded.

"Bernard, we saw you on a date with Edith and now Catherine has been crying, and I came here to sort this out."

"Catherine has been crying?" he seemed shocked.

"You cheated on her! Of course she's crying!" I shot back angrily.

"I wasn't cheating! She was!" He was now very angry.

"She was not!" I practically snarled. I stood my ground. I wasn't going to budge an inch until I gave him all my fury. "Catherine shall be avenged!" I screamed angrily.

"She was with Samuel all day and you said they often feed ducks together," Bernard said with a mixture of anger and sadness.

"So what?" I shot back. "You were with me all day, that very same day, and frankly, I don't know why Catherine worries so much about you and Edith!" I placed great emphasis on Edith's name, almost growling when I said it.

"Is Catherine dating Samuel?" he asked bluntly.

"No," I replied. "Are you dating Edith?" I asked equally as bluntly.

"No," he answered.

"Do you want to date Catherine?" I asked.

"Yes," he responded.

"Then go tell her! Why can't you two just talk instead of being this way?" I asked exasperatedly.

Bernard's shoulders relaxed. "I was jealous."

"So was she," I said.

"How do I make things better, Maybel?" He held his hand to his forehead and snorted, "I can't believe I'm asking for relationship advice from a child."

"She's really, really explosive right now. You should explain to her, from a distance, that you were not dating Edith, and that you would like to take her on a real date. But," I paused, "you're going to have to be really, and I mean really, grand with your gesture. And mind your distance until after the part where you tell her you were not romantically involved with Edith. That last part is very important!" I stressed.

"Ok," he said slowly, "And where and when and how do you suggest I do this? You seem to know her better than anyone."

"Take this carriage," I pointed to the carriage behind him in the stable. "Do you have any roses? Maybe not this time of year...." I pondered out loud.

"I have a necklace I bought for her on a weekend trip to the city while I was away at school!" he excitedly exclaimed. "I had intended to give it to her during this autumn break."

"That's perfect!" I squealed.

Bernard was grinning ear to ear. All the consternation he'd had at the beginning of our meeting immediately evaporated and he was now happy and carefree.

"Well, what are you waiting for?" I shouted, "Let's go!"

"Wait!" he yelled, "I must go collect the necklace!"

We ran giddily to his house. His mother and butler had been watching us intently from the kitchen window.

"Bernard, everything ok?" his mother asked as she watched us barge in.

"Yes, mother! I'm going to win Catherine's heart with the guidance and support of this little lady right here!" he beamed at me.

Mrs. Charleston turned to me as Bernard dashed up the stairs. "It appears your matter of utmost importance has been resolved then," she smiled at me.

"Yes, Mrs. Charleston, I'm quite happy with the result of our discussion," I smiled back.

"Please, call me Anna," she winked at me. "I think I'm going to like having you around."

I returned her wink, which made her giggle.

Bernard came dashing down the stairs with a small box yelling, "Hurry up, Maybel! Let's go!"

We ran back to the stables and Bernard harnessed a large, brown horse with a big, swishy black tail.

He climbed into the front and I was about to do the same when he reached down, and with one swoop, he pulled me up and sat me on the bench next to him. "No time to waste," he said.

"Wow!" I looked down. "We're really high up!"

"Are you scared?" he taunted.

"No!" I said, and grabbed the reins. "Why, yes, I'd love to steer your carriage, Bernard!"

"You're quite funny, Maybel. Let me steer the horse safely onto the road and maybe, if you're ready, I'll help you steer a little."

We headed into the street. Bernard wrapped one arm around me and pulled the reins up toward my hands. I held onto them and yelled, "Go horsey! Go now! Onward and westward!" I screamed the words from my favorite book about the Wild West that daddy read to me and Catherine in the evenings.

"Whoa there," Bernard laughed. He was still holding the reins with me. "You gently tug this way if you want to move left, and you gently tug this way if you want to go right."

It was difficult for me to reach over Bernard's lap to gain control of the reins, so I crawled over his legs and sat on his lap. "Bernard, how did you learn to make the horse go where you want him to go?"

"Mother has always loved horses. She trains them and breeds them," he explained. "Here, grab the reins like this, and with both hands, lightly slap both reins behind his head." Bernard slapped both reins and yelled, "Hyaw, Big Ben!"

The horse moved forward with a faster pace. "You named your horse Ben?" I giggled, amused at a horse with a human name.

"My mother named him. She's had him forever, since he was a foal. It's short for Benjamin, which is her father's name."

We trotted along the streets and toward my home. It was a bright, sunny day with crisp, autumn air. We rounded the corner and I saw my house in the distance. Big Ben began swishing his tail happily and trotting faster. Suddenly Bernard tensed up and shoved me off his lap and back onto the bumpy wooden driver's seat next to him.

"Almost there!" he squirmed and readjusted his sitting position. He had almost an uncomfortable grimace, and his voice cracked. He pulled at his pants awkwardly.

He must be getting nervous, I figured. I wanted to steer though. "Hey!" I shouted, "I wasn't done steering!" I attempted to hold the reins and climb onto his lap again but he shoved me, this time forcefully, back onto the bench.

"Ow!" I yelled at him.

"I'm sorry, Maybel, it's too dangerous for you to try and control Ben now. I have to stop and tie him to a post and he might buck if you don't hold his reins properly." Bernard's body was stiff and his voice stern.

"Fine!" I pouted. "But I'm very unhappy about this!" I crossed my arms and stomped my foot. I apparently looked amusing because Bernard relaxed and even giggled at me.

"You're quite funny when you're mad," he laughed. "We'll ride again sometime, Maybel."

Catherine came running outside. "What are you doing here?"

I couldn't tell if she was happy or angry, but before she had a chance to possibly express her wrath, I quickly interjected, "Good news, Catherine! Bernard wasn't dating Edith, and you weren't dating Samuel, and Bernard wants to date you!"

Catherine stood in awe trying to process my information. Again, I couldn't tell if she was about to explode with happiness or anger, but either way, I sensed an impending explosion.

Suddenly Catherine began crying. I hadn't expected that reaction, I thought. She was like a magician, pulling handkerchiefs out of her hat and you never know which color of handkerchief would pop out next.

Catherine came toward the carriage still crying. "Bernard, I've missed you," she cried.

"I've missed you too, Catherine," Bernard said.

I carefully climbed down and Bernard followed. Catherine ran into Bernard's outstretched arms and they held each other.

I began walking to our front door. Mommy and daddy were both peeking out our foyer windows.

"Maybel," Catherine called.

"Yes?" I turned around.

"Thank you," she smiled gratefully.

I smiled back then left them. I went inside and watched them nervously smiling and talking to each other from the windows by our front door.

I had always hung onto Bernard from the time we met. I adored Bernard. I sat in his lap and always ran to sit beside him on the sofa before any of Catherine's friends could sit beside him first. I loved being around him. I thought he was the most amazing big brother. And Bernard indulged my every wish. He let me come to his house and we ran and played. He and daddy taught me how to shoot a gun and how to fish. Whenever I asked for custard or a cookie, Bernard gladly obliged. I loved laying with him under trees while he read to me and Catherine. I batted acorns with a big stick while Bernard read from thick, leather-bound books to me and Catherine. Catherine didn't much enjoy playing now that she was older, but she never minded if Bernard indulged me in a game. He taught me to ride a bicycle. Catherine and I didn't have bicycles, but Bernard was rich and had two. He taught me how to throw a baseball farther, and how to kick balls in a way that would confuse the opposing team as to which way I would next run. Catherine often sat and watched us, not wanting to mess her beautiful hair.

"Bernard the trees have turned colors. Remember when you said you'd climb to the top of the tallest tree on our island? Will you keep your promise?" I asked Bernard. We were sitting on a log feeding ducks at my pond while waiting for Catherine to return from her piano lesson.

"I'd love to Maybel, but I'll be going back to boarding school soon and I need to pack."

"Oh. Ok." I looked down at my feet, which were barefoot and dirty. Today would likely be last warm day of autumn and then months of being cooped up inside during the cold, winter months.

"I say, Maybel! I've never seen a more sorrowful sight! Alright," he sighed, "do you think you can row-climb-row now, or will I be rowing for the both of us again?

I looked up at Bernard, my eyes wide with excitement, and squealed as I jumped into his lap and hugged him.

"This must be a quick trip, you understand?" he told me more than asked me.

Bernard was eager to get back for Catherine's return. He rowed with great strength. It was no wonder he could climb trees so well, I thought. His arms were really muscular. I looked down at my little, twiggy arms. I had muscles too, I thought, somewhere.

"Here!" Bernard yelled.

"Already?" I looked up, surprised.

"Yes, already!" he laughed.

"Ok, Maybel, I know how you get when you lose so I'll give you a head start."

"I do not need a head start!" I said hotly. "You've been rowing. There's no way I'm going to lose this race to the top!"

"Ok, then!" Bernard laughed at my gumption.

"Ok, get ready!" I shouted. I got into position. "Go!" I screamed.

Bernard took off and beat me to the lowest limb. I wasn't far behind him though. We were on opposite sides of the tree and climbing rapidly. I was breathing hard.

"Ow!" I yelled.

Bernard stopped climbing. "What's wrong?"

"Stupid splinter," I said, "but I'm fine!" I yanked out the splinter, gritted my teeth, and continued upward, even gaining the lead!

I reached the top first! I was panting and holding my palm as Bernard peeked through the top a split second behind me.

"Congratulations, Maybel! You win!" He smiled at me.

"You're not even panting!" I was annoyed because I knew he let me win.

"Stop letting me win, Bernard!"

"Actually, I didn't." Bernard winked at me.

"I don't believe you, but I'll still tell everyone I won anyway!" I laughed.

"Maybel, you weren't kidding!" he gasped as he looked around. "This view is incredible! The forests all around look like they're on fire!" he awed. Bernard breathed in deeply. The crisp, fall air was exhilarating.

"I like this time of year," I said. "Daddy says there's a sadness because all the colors will fade and then leave like a memory, but daddy also says it's just to allow for more colors and memories in the spring."

"That's a remarkable thing, Maybel!" He looked around, taking in all the vibrant colors.

He looked back at me and when his eyes met mine, I leaned over and kissed him. It was a light peck on his lips.

Bernard stared at me surprised. "Maybel," he pushed me away, "Why did you do that?"

"I like you," I said simply.

"I like you too, but don't ever kiss me again." His voice wasn't angry, just plain and direct.

I was hurt. "Why can't I kiss you?" I asked, genuinely confused. "When people like each other, they kiss," I told him.

"No. Married people kiss," he stated firmly.

My eyes welled up. "Mommy and daddy kiss like that," I cried.

"They're married. We are not even courting. Do not go around kissing people," he lectured me. "You will get a bad reputation."

"I've never kissed anyone before!" I said incredulously, shocked that he would think I would go around kissing boys. "I just like playing with you, Bernard. I like you. That's why I wanted to kiss you," I cried. "Why don't you want to kiss me?"

"Because you're a child, Maybel. Because I want to kiss Catherine, not you," he stated bluntly.

I was hurt by how easily he dismissed me. I had thought we were friends.

"You and Catherine kiss and you aren't married," I said, anger creeping into my voice.

"I said I want to kiss her, not that I had kissed her," he said.

"I know you've kissed her!" I cried.

"Why do you think we kissed?" he asked incredulously.

"Because I saw Catherine last night in her room by her dressing table mirror kissing her fist," I said. "She's been practicing."

Bernard stared at me. "Does Catherine practice on her hand a lot," he seemed very curious now.

"I don't know. Does she kiss like she's been practicing on her hand all day and night?" I asked sarcastically.

"We've never kissed," he said sheepishly. "I've never kissed anyone," he said quietly.

"Oh," I said. "I haven't either."

His voice softened. "It's ok, I'm not mad at you. I feel like I'm your big brother, Maybel. You are just a child. I'm trying to protect you from the boys who will try to take advantage of you. Do not kiss anyone you aren't going to marry, is a good rule in which to live your life."

I sat atop the tree quietly watching him.

He sighed, "Maybel, stop looking at me like I just broke your heart! Maybel, please!" His voice was pleading. "Look, you're a nice kid, and you'll find a boy your own age someday when you're much older."

I continued watching him in silence with tears streaming down my cheeks.

Bernard sighed, "Let's just get back to your home. Catherine will arrive soon."

"Is Catherine going to be mad at me?" I suddenly thought of the ramifications.

"If I told her, yes, so forget this happened. You're just a child so you don't understand these things yet. There's no need to cause a rift between you and Catherine. Besides, she might not want me around anymore if she knew, so forget what just happened."

He began climbing down and I slowly followed.

We got into the boat and I never once looked up at him while he rowed us both home. I didn't understand why kissing was a big deal because mommy and daddy kissed just like that.

However, what Bernard had said made sense. Maybe I shouldn't kiss anyone I wasn't going to marry. I didn't see people walking down the street kissing, or sitting in church kissing, and I'd never kissed my schoolmates, so perhaps there were rules, and like Bernard said, I hadn't quite figured out those rules.

We arrived at the shore. "Bernard!" I suddenly became excited. "Will you take me to the library and show me which book explains who I'm allowed to kiss and when?" I was happy to have found a solution to my problem.

"What?" Bernard looked at me as though I were ridiculous.

"You must have read a book about this, and that's how you know what not to do, and what not to say. I need a book about etiquette, or how to behave, or whatever it was you read."

Bernard just looked at me the way I used to look at our dog when I tried to teach him tricks. He looked at me like I was a dumb puppy.

"There is no book about who you can kiss and not kiss," he told me. "You just watch and observe other people, and do, or don't do, whatever it is they're doing, or not doing."

"What?" Now I looked at him like he was the dumb puppy.

I considered Bernard's words though. Bernard made sense, but I still had questions. "If you're always mimicking other people, how do you know you're not doing something wrong?" I wondered. "Maybe the person you're copying is doing it wrong. Beatrice Shaw used to sit beside me at school and I saw her copying my geography answers, so I began writing the wrong answers. We both got bad marks, but it really was worth it to see her face scowling at me when we failed, and she's never done it again."

Bernard continued staring at me. He finally spoke. "I don't know how to react to that. I want to laugh, but you do make good points."

Catherine's voice called from the distance.

Bernard turned back to me. "Look, Maybel, this is very important: Do not kiss me again, and from this point forward, you forget you ever kissed me."

"Well, how can I remember not to kiss you again if I can't remember you telling me not to kiss you?" I asked sarcastically.

"Maybel!" he growled.

"Ok, Bernard!" I growled back.

Catherine finally reached us and hugged Bernard. Bernard returned Catherine's hug affectionately. "So good to see you again, Catherine."

I pried them apart and hugged Catherine exaggeratedly hard. "So good to see you again, Catherine," I chirped in my cutest singsong voice.

While still hugging Catherine tightly, I turned my head around to smile smugly at Bernard. He was not amused.

"What's going on between you two?" she asked, puzzled.

"I can't remember," I smiled sweetly at Bernard.

"Nothing, Catherine, but when I get home, I'm going to thank my parents for not giving me a little sister," he smiled exaggeratedly back at me.

I let go of Catherine and she and Bernard began walking hand-in-hand back home. I caught up to them and grabbed Catherine's other hand. "Maybel, what's gotten into you? You're acting so strangely."

"I'm just watching what everyone else does and copying. I've heard it's a good way to make sure you're behaving properly and using good manners." I looked over Catherine's shoulder at Bernard and raised my eyebrows and winked.

"Yes," he said lowly, "and it's such a good thing there are no people jumping off cliffs right now. Would be a shame if you copied that," he said slyly.

"Ok, you two!" Catherine shook her hands free from both of us. "Whatever irritations you have with one another stops now."

"I'm sorry, Catherine," Bernard apologized. "I'm not used to children or their annoying games. I'll try harder to be a more patient person."

"I'm sorry too, Catherine." I stuck my tongue out at Bernard behind Catherine's back.

We arrived home and I went inside, leaving them alone. I felt rejected, like the broken toys at the toy store that worked a little, but didn't do what they were supposed to do, so they sat in a bin that said their prices were significantly reduced. Bernard didn't want me to kiss him, and that hurt my feelings. I wanted Bernard's attention.

I sat beside Bernard in his kitchen. Mommy and daddy were off to town doing things and allowed me to stay with the Charlestons. Catherine would come get me later. In the meantime, Bernard and I ate sandwiches he made for us. His mother and father were sitting at the kitchen table with us drinking tea.

"Bernard?" I nudged his arm next to me.

"Yes?" Bernard pushed a napkin to me. I was messy when I ate.

"When are we getting married?" I asked him.

"What?" Bernard looked over at me puzzled.

"When are we getting married?" I repeated.

"Maybel, you and I are not dating," he said.

"Ok, but when are we getting married?" I asked again.

"We're not getting married," Bernard said.

"Why not?" I asked. I was surprised Bernard thought we would not marry.

"Because I'm with Catherine, not you," Bernard sighed with irritation.

"Why aren't you with me?" I asked.

"Because you're too young, Maybel."

"We're not getting married?" I asked for clarification.

"No, Maybel," Bernard said as plainly as if he were telling me the grass was green.

I suddenly felt very sad. "I thought we were getting married someday."

"I thought so too," Bernard's mother spoke up.

"Mother, please!" Bernard sighed.

"Bernard, you know I'm always right about these things," Mrs. Charleston said.

"That's true, son," his father said. "Your mother is always right about these sorts of things."

"Father, mother, please stop! I don't want to talk about this now!" Bernard looked agitated.

"Mrs. Charleston, do you want to play?" I asked her.

"I'd love to dear," she smiled warmly at me. "I've always wanted a daughter just like you."

"You can come play with me anytime," I told her.

"Thank you, Maybel," she looked happily between me and Mr. Charleston.

"Why didn't you have a daughter?" I asked her.

"After Bernard, we just never had another baby," she looked really sad when she said that.

"Well, when Bernard and I have a baby, you can play with our baby whenever you want."

Mrs. Charleston smiled sweetly, "Thank you dear, I look forward to that."

"I'm not having a baby with you, Maybel," Bernard said. He seemed annoyed.

"Why not?" I asked.

"Because I'm with Catherine!"

"Ok, but why can't you have a baby with me?" I asked again.

"Yes, son, why not?" Mr. Charleston chuckled. His eyes were smiling as he watched me and Bernard.

"Father, please!"

"I want to name her Isabel, and we'll call her Belle, like my name, Maybel."

"That's beautiful, Maybel," Mrs. Charleston smiled happily. "I can't wait!"

"I do like the idea of grandchildren, Bernard," Mr. Charleston winked at Bernard.

"I'm not having a baby with you, Maybel! You're a child and I'm with your sister!" Bernard seemed even more annoyed now.

"But I want to have a baby with you, Bernard!"

"You don't even know what that means, Maybel!"

Mr. and Mrs. Charleston giggled.

"Yes, I do Bernard! We're going to get married and have a baby!"

"Sounds wonderful to us," Mrs. Charleston smiled. "I'd love a granddaughter named Belle."

Me too," Mr. Charleston said with a broad smile and a chuckle. He seemed very amused as he watched me and Bernard.

"Our other daughter, we might have twins Bernard, but I haven't decided yet, will be named Anabel, after you Mrs. Charleston. I think we'll call her Annie. Do you like her name?" I asked Mrs. Charleston.

Mrs. Charleston smiled so happily and looked positively giddy.

"You don't even know how to make a baby, and I'm with Catherine, and this entire conversation is very odd!" Bernard huffed.

Mr. and Mrs. Charleston laughed.

"How do we make a baby?" I asked Bernard.

Mr. and Mrs. Charleston both watched Bernard as they giggled.

"We don't, Maybel! Look, you're very young. Just don't worry about it now."

"What do you want her middle name to be? Bernadine? Like Bernie? You know, like Bernard?" I pondered.

Mr. and Mrs. Charleston laughed harder.

"Maybel, come here. Let's go do something. Do you want to paint or play cards?" Bernard changed the subject.

"Paint," I answered.

We left Mr. and Mrs. Charleston still laughing in the kitchen.

I followed Bernard to the art room where we did a lot of our painting and playing.

Bernard sat at the table and got our paints ready. He seemed tired of me already.

I sat on his lap. I turned around and hugged him and kissed his cheek. "I love you."

He sighed, "Ok, Maybel, I love you too, now let's paint. Catherine will be here in an hour."

"Bernard, I think Isabel is a good name."

"Maybel, please don't talk like that around Catherine. It will upset her."

"Ok, Bernard."

I continued sitting on Bernard's lap as we drew and painted. "I'm always going to love you, Bernard."

"Maybel, don't talk like that around Catherine. It will make her angry and sad."

"Why?"

"Because Catherine loves me."

"I love you too," I said.

"Maybel, it's different. I love Catherine in a different way."

I turned around and wrapped my arms around Bernard's neck. "I still love you," I whispered.

Bernard sighed, "I love you too, now please stop."

The next time I saw Bernard was when his family invited us to a Christmas Eve party. I heard mommy and daddy talking one evening in our family room while I was trying to learn to sew a straight line in a dish rag mother had brought me.

"Have you seen this invitation to the Charleston's Christmas Eve party?" Mommy was giddy. "Just look at the paper and embossed script!" she exclaimed, holding the card only an inch away from daddy's nose.

"The lettering is finished in gold print!" she squealed. "I'll need to order fabric from Mrs. Suffolk's shop in the city! And flowers to put in the girls' and my hair! There's so much to do!" Mommy chattered on as I sat by the fire with my dish rag, my needle, and my thread.

I was watching daddy as mommy scurried to the kitchen. Daddy saw me watching him. "Maybel, don't grow up on me too fast," he said to me. "I enjoy your level-headedness. Will you promise me you will always keep your stubbornness? It's your stubbornness and level-headedness that I truly enjoy."

He paused, his pipe near his lips, "I don't enjoy your stubbornness when you do something I don't want you to do, but overall, your stubbornness will do you well."

He put his pipe between his lips and puffed while still watching me.

"Yes, daddy, I promise to always be level and stubborn," I smiled at him and he smiled back.

Arriving at the Charleston's house was like reading a book, except I was in this book, and all the merriment was real. From the number of waitstaff to the smaller details, like monogrammed napkins, and more forks and spoons by my plate than I knew what to do with, the Charlestons did not know how to be subtle.

I stayed by mommy and daddy while Catherine danced with Bernard. The old people talked about how lovely the decorations were and sipped drinks that I was not allowed to taste from long, crystal, champagne flutes.

A boy across the room was playing with a wooden toy. Finally, something fun to do, I thought.

I approached him. "Hello, I'm Maybel," I said.

"I'm Archie," he replied. "Do you want to play with me?" he asked.

"Yes!" I happily answered. I was glad to do something fun. Dancing and talking about the president and which cigars make the finer blend of tobacco bored me.

Archie pointed to a small, wooden toy. "My grandmother got this for me," he said. "It's from France."

"Sounds brilliant," I said. I had no idea why a wooden toy made in France was any better than the toys made by Mr. Collingsworth at the lumber yard. Archie's toy looked the same as the toy Mr. Collingsworth's daughter showed off last summer at her sister's sixteenth birthday party ball.

Archie then showed me his other games and random cars and trucks his grandfather gave him for Christmas this year. "I've just opened these today!" he exclaimed! "I've not yet properly played with them but I'll let you have the first go with this train," he told me, expecting me to feel grateful.

"Thanks," I said. I pushed it back and forth. I found this kind of play a little boring but it was still more fun than trying to keep a conversation going with the dull partygoers.

"Do you want to play hide-and-seek?" I asked. "I bet there are lots of hiding places here in this big house. Will you show me?" I hoped Archie would want to play something else more interesting.

"Sure!" he shouted. "There are lots of closets and cupboards and all sorts of places!" he said excitedly.

We ran upstairs because Archie said there were more hiding places up there. "Ok, that's Aunt Anna's and Uncle Byron's bedroom. We should stay away from there. Over there's grandmother's bedroom when she visits, and that's Henry's and John's room when they visit."

Archie continued to name which room was whose. There were a lot of rooms, and two long hallways that intersected.

"That's Bernard's room when he's home from school." Archie pointed to a large end room.

"Ok, now that you know where everything is, I'm going to go in Aunt Ethel's room and count to thirty while you hide.

As soon as he walked into Aunt Ethel's room, I bolted down the corridor to a pink room several doors down. There were lace and ruffles everywhere. I didn't remember whose room this was, but it looked a lot like one of the rooms in Catherine's doll house that she played with when we were younger; there was a lot of pink and ruffles.

I cracked the closet door then I hid under the bed, a trick Catherine taught me back when she still wanted to play.

Several moments later Archie tiptoed in. "Come out, come out, whenever you are!" he sang.

He first looked in the closet. I laughed to myself. He's such a child, I thought. Probably never played hide and seek with a big kid, I chuckled softly.

Suddenly he flopped to the floor beside me. "Found you!" He reached under the bed and tagged me.

We both giggled uncontrollably. This was turning out to be a fun night, I thought.

Next was my turn to count. I could hear Archie's footsteps clodding along the wooden floors like a horse on cobblestone. I finished and yelled, "Come out, come out, wherever you are!"

I ran to where I thought Archie's hoof stomps stopped. It was a room with quilts, lots and lots of quilts. Quilts on the walls, and a particularly colorful quilt on the bed.

I looked at the wall with the windows and rolled my eyes. This child has got to be joking, I thought. There was a quilt decoratively displayed on the wall with two feet protruding out the bottom.

I ran toward the two-legged quilt and poked Archie's belly. "Found you!" I yelled.

"That was a good hiding spot, wasn't it?"
he asked proudly.

"The best!" I cheered.

"Ok, my turn to hide," I yelled.

Archie pulled the quilt back over his face and began counting.

I rolled my eyes again. This was still better than talking about boring things with boring people downstairs, I decided.

I entered a room with a large, wooden, walnut bed with matching nightstands and dressers. It was beautiful, actually. I wondered whose room this was.

I could hear Archie reach twenty, so I scrambled into the closet. He'll think I'm under the bed, I chuckled to myself, beginning to realize the benefits of playing with a little kid. I relished the idea of teaching him all the tricks to hiding that Catherine had taught me when she used to like playing with me.

"Archie, it's time for cake." I heard a woman's voice call.

"Yes, mother." I heard Archie's little, hooved feet scamper away from the doorway.

Did he just leave me here in someone's closet? I fumed. I could not believe he just left me in the middle of a game to go eat cake! I seethed.

I put my hand on the closet door, about to storm out, when suddenly, I heard voices that were giggling and whispering, enter the bedroom.

"Catherine, you are so beautiful" I heard Bernard say.

"You are quite handsome yourself, Bernard."

They held one another and they spun around and landed on the bed. Catherine sat on the edge of the bed next to Bernard. She was giggling.

Bernard looked awestruck with Catherine's beauty. "May I kiss you?" Bernard asked Catherine.

My eyes were as wide with curiosity and fear of getting caught as they could possibly get.

"Bernard," Catherine suddenly looked solemn. Her voice wavered. "I've already been kissed by someone," she said, almost wincing in pain.

I could not believe my own sister didn't tell me about her first kiss!

Bernard looked surprised.

"I'm so sorry! I didn't want to kiss him! He kissed me and I didn't want him to," Catherine cried.

"Who was it?" Bernard grew angry. "Whoever it was should not have kissed you without your permission!"

"It was Samuel that day we cleaned Mrs. Andrews' room," Catherine cried harder. "It was at the duck pond and it happened so fast. I told him not to speak to me again and he hasn't!"

"I'm going to find him and level him!" Bernard's face turned red and his neck veins protruded.

"Bernard, please, he has left me alone since, and I do believe it was an honest mistake. I was spending too much time with him because I was lonely for you. I don't think he meant to upset me. I'm only telling you this because I think you should know I've been kissed."

"Catherine, I don't care. I really like you." He held Catherine's cheek with one hand and her hand with another.

"Bernard, may I ask you a question?" Catherine's voice was tentative.

"Yes," anything he said.

"Have you ever kissed anyone?" she asked.

"No," he replied.

Catherine smiled happily.

"Would you like to kiss me?" she asked shyly.

"Yes," he said, and bent forward and lightly kissed Catherine's lips.

Catherine gasped and smiled.

Bernard smiled back.

They kissed again, a little longer.

Bernard stood up with Catherine in his arms, "Come now, Catherine, people will be missing us downstairs."

They left. I remained seated in the bottom of the closet.

I waited until I could hear no more movement, then I went back downstairs. I saw Archie at a table in the dining room with his precious cake. "Hi Archie. Did you forget I was hiding?" I asked sarcastically.

"No. I wanted cake. Do you want cake, too?"

He had two pieces on his plate. Ah, that's sweet, I thought to myself. Archie was waiting for me with cake.

I watched him sitting there at the table stuffing cake into his mouth and smiling at me.

"Sure. Why not?" I said. Archie seemed happy. Maybe cake would make me happy, too.

"The cake is in the kitchen," he said, and pointed to a table full of desserts through the doorway and across the kitchen.

"Thanks," I said dryly.

I went into the kitchen and found a plate. I took a slice of chocolate cake and stood by the far wall and ate alone.

"Hello," a boy said as he was passing by.

"Hello," I said, my mouth completely full of chocolate cake.

The boy stared at me.

"What?" I asked him. He just stood there looking at me.

"Would you like to put together a puzzle with me in the drawing room?" he asked me.

"I'm eating cake," I replied dryly.

"Bring it," he smiled.

"Ok," I said shoving another forkful into my mouth.

There was a puzzle started on the large oak table. "Are you good at puzzles?" he asked.

"Yes," I said.

I sat down and began separating all the pink and purple pieces. "I'll take these," I told him. "You can have the orange and green ones. I don't like those colors as much." I was tired of people tonight and was ready to go home.

"What's your name?" he asked me.

"Maybel," I answered. I continued sorting my puzzle pieces into edges and middle pieces.

"Don't you want to know my name?" he asked.

"No," I replied. "You're probably one of Bernard's cousins from out west and I'll never get to see you again or play with you again after tonight."

He looked sad.

"I'm sorry," I said. "I'm in a bad mood and I didn't mean to upset you, and I'm sorry."

"I understand." He still looked sad.

"Do you want to play tag?" I asked. "That always cheers me up," I smiled weakly at him.

"That sounds fun!" he instantly seemed happier.

"What's your name," I asked.

"Michael," he smiled.

"Hi, Michael. Sorry we got off to a bad start. I'm usually happier." I shook Michael's hand.

"Me too," he said. "Maybe we can cheer each other up," he smiled at me.

I tapped his shoulder, "Tag! You're it!"

I ran around the table. He ran around too. Suddenly he dropped to his knees, out of sight behind the large table. I was puzzled.

In an instant he popped up right in front of me! "Tag! Now you're it!"

I laughed hard at Michael.

Michael ran through the kitchen and into the conservatory, which held all kinds of plants, a few trees, and herbs and flowers.

I quickly gave chase. I wasn't far behind, but he'd already hidden somewhere.

"Scared you!" He popped out from behind a large tree with big, fat leaves.

"Ahh!" I screamed with surprise and glee. "You're fast!" We were laughing hysterically now.

"Can't catch me!" He laughed as he ran back through the kitchen and back into the drawing room.

I ran quickly behind him trying to keep up, but he was like a little jack rabbit! Aside from jack rabbits, I'd never seen this impressive level of agility.

Inside the drawing room, I looked behind the large, oak desk, behind the sofas with big, stuffed cushions, and underneath the table. He was nowhere to be found.

"Here I am!" Michael came flying from behind the overstocked coat rack.

"Got you again!" he shrieked. We laughed together.

I liked him a lot. He had made tonight so much more enjoyable.

"Maybel, what is that behind your ear, in your hair?" He moved close to my face, peering behind my ear.

"Michael!" Bernard angrily yelled. We both jumped. I looked up shocked.

Catherine was behind Bernard standing in the doorway. Bernard came to me with concern.

"Maybel, are you ok?" Bernard grabbed my shoulders and lightly shook me. I saw fear behind his eyes. "Did he kiss you?"

"What? No!" I said, stunned.

"Bernard what are you doing? We were playing tag!" Michael yelled.

"Michael, leave now before I tell your parents you were taking advantage of Maybel!"

"He was not!" I yelled. "There was something in my hair and he was helping me get it out!" I was so mad now!

"There's nothing in your hair, Maybel! He was trying to take advantage of you!" Bernard angrily watched Michael.

"I was not Bernard! I was not!" Michael angrily yelled.

"Go!" Bernard's face was red and he pointed to the door for Michael to leave.

Catherine stepped to the side to let a visibly shaken Michael pass by.

Bernard's voice calmed and his face was no longer bright red. He grabbed my shoulders again and led me to the bench by the fireplace.

I was scared now because Bernard was angry and Michael left and I didn't understand what was going on.

Bernard hugged me tightly. "Maybel, I saw his face right next to yours and his lips were so close to yours. I thought he was going to steal a kiss. I'm sorry I overreacted."

I returned Bernard's hug and cried into his neck. "You scared me, Bernard," I cried. "I was bored and I finally made a friend and you chased him away."

"I know. I'm sorry, Maybel. I don't know what came over me." Bernard kissed my forehead. "I'll talk to Michael. I'll apologize."

Bernard left and Catherine sat beside me and held me. She stroked my hair. "Bernard will make it right," she said soothingly. "He has begun to think of you as his little sister."

Bernard, followed by Michael, entered the room. "Catherine, Maybel," Bernard began, "I explained myself to Michael and apologized."

He nodded toward Michael then toward me. "Michael, Maybel, please continue enjoying your evening and I'm sorry I interrupted and overreacted." Bernard seemed genuinely embarrassed by his overreaction.

"Catherine, would you like to continue dancing?" He held his hand for Catherine and they headed onto the dance floor.

Michael sat next to me on the bench in front of the fireplace. For what seemed like eternity, we sat in silence. Gradually, I began to relax a little.

"Well, that will make for an interesting story down the road." I made a feeble attempt at laughing.

"Yes," Michael said, "I suppose so."

There was more silence. Finally, Michael turned to me. "Would you like to finish that puzzle?"

"Yes, I would," I smiled.

We continued to work on the puzzle, barely speaking to one another for the rest of the night, which was actually only another hour or so. It was now very late. Mommy and daddy came to get me.

Daddy appeared to have had a lot of Christmas cheer and was quite chatty. "Maybel! It's after midnight, darling! Merry Christmas!" He kissed the top of my head. "Time to go home!" he happily beamed. "I trust you've enjoyed your time?"

I looked at Michael. "Yes, I truly have!"

Michael returned my smile. "Me, too, Maybel."

"Well then, shall we?" Daddy wrapped one arm around me, and his other arm around mommy. We met Catherine in the entryway and returned home by carriage.

During spring vacation, Bernard returned from boarding school. He came to see Catherine, but I, as usual, begged him to play with me.

"Bernard, remember when I kissed you?"

Bernard swallowed hard.

"I'm sorry I kissed you," I said.

"Maybel, stop. I don't want to talk about it." Bernard seemed irritated.

We were on my back porch playing cards. "Bernard, I'm sorry."

"Be quiet, Maybel. I don't want Catherine to hear," he whispered.

Bernard laid his cards down. "I win!" he exclaimed, then stood and walked toward the porch door.

"Where are you going, Bernard?" I asked.

"To be with Catherine," he said as he walked inside.

I sat on the floorboards of the porch and collected my cards, and then Bernard's cards. I stacked them together.

"Catherine, would you like to come with me to the spring concert tonight?" I heard Bernard ask.

"Yes! I'd love to!" she squealed. And then she lowered her voice. "Let's leave before Maybel finds out where we're going." They giggled and I heard their footsteps as they ran through the kitchen and out the front door.

I finished putting the cards into their cardboard box. And then I sat there, on the floor of our porch, just watching the trees and the flowers with their newly-forming buds.

In my mind, I created scenarios where I had friends. My imagination was so vivid that the friends I created were real to me. And when I was hurt, I could envision any outcome I wanted onto my imaginary friends.

I was hurt by Catherine and Bernard. In my mind, while sitting like a pathetic, little, sad girl, I imagined, in great detail, the kind of life I'd lead once I was grown. By then, Catherine and Bernard would be married, and I'd be a teacher, writer, and archaeologist who traveled the world with my pelicans. Catherine told me pelicans did not make good travel companions, but I told her since she had never met a pelican, she was not an expert on the matter, and should only advise me on things in which she was well-versed.

I leaned against the porch post. I rested my head on the wooden, painted post, and watched the hot air balloon in my mind float to China, carrying me inside.

In my mind, I could control the outcome. In my mind, nobody whispered plans to desert me. And in my mind, I was the popular one who had friends and was invited to parties.

"Maybel, what are you doing there," mommy asked.

"I was just thinking of China, mommy," I said.

Mommy chuckled, "Oh, my dear, sweet, Maybel," she kissed the top of my head, "I do enjoy your imagination!"

I rested my head on the porch post again, and stared out at the clouds until they changed from white to yellow, and then orange, and finally red.

"Maybel, dinner is ready," mommy called.

slowly got up and went inside.

As the tree buds formed leaves, the sun warmed, and the grass began to grow lush and tall, Catherine and Bernard spent more time together. I begged them to take me wherever they went.

Today, we were home, and Catherine played on the piano while I skipped around pretending to dance.

Bernard laughed, "You've almost mastered the waltz, Maybel."

"Really?" I asked excitedly.

"No," Bernard laughed even harder.

I frowned.

"Oh, come now, Maybel, let me help guide you." Bernard grabbed me by my waist and spun me around.

"Ok, hold your hands up like this." He stood straight, with excellent posture, and his head held regally. He held one of my hands in his own. His hand was twice as big as my hand and enveloped it entirely.

"Put this arm around my shoulder, or you can pull closer and place your hand gently around my neck." he instructed.

"To strangle you?" I laughed.

"Ha, ha, Maybel, funny," he laughed sarcastically. "Now pay attention. You can only pull a man close and wrap your arm or hand around his neck if you are courting. Do not let me catch you dancing at the next Christmas Eve party with your body pressed against some no-good boy!"

And with that he effortlessly tossed me up into the air, grabbed my waist, and spun me around.

I laughed and shrieked with happiness. "Do the airplane, Bernard! Do the airplane again!"

He bent his legs and rolled backward onto our small dance floor then pushed his feet upward while clasping my hands. I squealed with joy.

I looked down at him. "Now do the air turbulence!" I screamed. He clasped my hands tighter and rapidly bounced his feet up and down, eliciting even louder shrieks from me.

Catherine laughed at us. "You two are funny!" she grinned. "Shall I play some vaudeville music for your crazy antics?" she laughed.

"I have a better idea!" Bernard returned me to my feet and stood up. He glided to Catherine and lifted her up and onto her feet. "Let me take you to my house for hot cocoa? We can sit by my fireplace and play cards."

"You can do that here, too," I piped up. I stood there with a hopeful gleam in my eyes and my hands clasped in front of my chest, visually begging them.

Catherine and Bernard turned to look at me. "I'm sorry, Maybel," Catherine began, "I love being with you, I truly do, but I think I would like some time alone with Bernard. You understand, don't you?"

"Ok," I said. My tightly clasped hands dropped to my sides.

"Why don't you ask one of your little friends to play a game?" she asked soothingly.

"Ok," I said.

They turned and walked to the foyer. Bernard took Catherine's coat for her and helped her put it on. Then they left me.

It was now time for the spring festival. After long months of being stuck inside, the townspeople were brimming with excitement because the weather had warmed, and now we could pass time outside with each other.

The park was filled with music and laughter. Games, food, and flowers filled the park, and every storefront had their doors propped open to allow fresh air inside.

At the spring festival, I ran to sit beside Bernard on the bench in the park before anyone else could sit beside him. I held his hand and leaned against his shoulder. "Bernard," I kicked my feet back and forth, "What do you want to do today?"

"Catherine and I are going to listen to the band about to play."

"After that, what are you going to do?"

"I'm not sure. She's over there talking to friends so I imagine we'll be doing something with them later."

I was bored and fidgety. I played with Bernard's hand and swung my feet back and forth in boredom. I looked up at Bernard. My head was still on his shoulder. "When you're done with that, are you coming back to my house?"

"I don't know, Maybel. Can't you ever sit still? You move around constantly."

I let go of his hand and wrapped my arms around his chest and looked up at him. "Pleeeese play with me! I'm so bored!"

"Maybel, I can't. I'm going to watch this band's performance, then do whatever Catherine is planning for us to do."

I sighed. I held his hand again and fidgeted with it while I leaned my forehead onto his arm and rolled my head side to side. "I'm soooo bored!" I sighed.

"Maybel, stop fidgeting. Can't you sit still for just one minute?"

"I don't know. I've never tried," I said.

Bernard stood up and pulled me along with him to where Catherine stood. "Catherine, what are our plans for today? Your sister is like a puppy and starts being annoying when she hasn't been played with and exercised enough."

I smiled widely at Catherine as I held Bernard's hand and I swung around him like a ribbon on a May pole.

Catherine sighed and rolled her eyes while her friends giggled at my antics. She asked Bernard with annoyance, "Would you mind taking this annoying puppy on a walk to let it play off some of its pent-up energy?"

I smiled even wider, "Thank you, Catherine! I love you! You're the best, big sister ever!" I reached up and wrapped my arms around Bernard's neck and squealed, "Piggyback!"

Bernard leaned over and kissed Catherine's cheek. "This may take a while. I think she's eaten a lot of sugar and needs to run it off," he chuckled.

Catherine looked even more annoyed, "See you later, Bernard."

"Ruff ruff?" I smiled at Catherine.

"See you later, puppy," Catherine mumbled and turned back to her friends.

Bernard swung me around and over his back for a piggyback ride to the edge of the park.

"I'm so happy I get to play with you, Bernard!" I squealed as I hugged his neck.

"Me too, Maybel."

He let me down and we entered the wooded area by the park.

"On guard!" I held a stick to Bernard's chest.

"On guard!" He skillfully swatted my stick to the ground with his stick, and then put his stick to my belly button. "Don't move, pirate!"

"Arrrr ye matey! I shall avenge my father's cruel fate!" I grabbed his stick and pulled.

Bernard pulled back hard, so I pulled harder, then he smiled wickedly and let go. I sprung backward and landed in mud. "Bernard!" I screamed.

Bernard laughed so hard he could barely catch his breath.

"I demand a duel do-over!" I yelled.

I picked a larger stick off the ground and held it like a baseball bat.

"That's not how you duel, Maybel!" He picked up a stick and held it like I saw an actor do in a play I'd seen last year.

"This isn't how you duel?" I swung my bat, narrowly missing his arm.

"No, Maybel!" He laughed and poked my back with his stick as my bat swished past him again.

"Are you sure?" I swung again. "I'm pretty sure this is how you fence," I laughed and swung again.

"It's not, Maybel," he took his stick and poked my stomach laughing.

"Well then I'm improvising!" I giggled.

Bernard lunged forward and spun me around and pulled my big stick hard against my chest wedging me against him. "I'm improvising too," he laughed.

"Aye matey! I shall never give up me ship!" I tried to pry the big stick off but I wasn't as strong as Bernard, so I turned around facing him and tickled his stomach and armpits.

"Maybel!" He laughed and dropped the stick. He tried to grab my flailing arms but I was more agile than him and tickled his waist and legs and when he bent down to pick me up, I tickled his armpits again and he let go.

"Get off me ship you pirate!" I roared.

"Ok, Maybel, you win!" he laughed. Then suddenly pushed me to the ground and tickled my ribs. He was on top of me and I laughed so hard tears began streaming down my cheeks.

"Bernard!" I breathed through tears of laughter, "Please stop!"

"Ok, I suppose you give up your ship now!" he smiled at me.

I sat upright, wiping the tears away and breathing hard. "No!" I screamed, and pounced on him. "I've got you now!" I straddled his waist and tickled his armpits. He pulled me down on top of him and pinned me with one arm and with the other he tickled my ribs and I writhed around on top of him squealing and laughing so hard that I couldn't breathe or ask him to stop. I lost control of my bladder and peed on him.

Bernard suddenly stopped. "Did you just pee on me?"

I struggled to regain my breath and rolled off of him crying, this time from embarrassment.

I covered my face with my hands crying hard. "I'm sorry Bernard! I couldn't talk to tell you to stop because I lost my breath!"

"Let's pretend this didn't happen. We'll go to my house to change."

"I don't have any clothes there," I cried. I had dirt on my face and leaves and twigs in my hair from rolling around being tickled.

"You can wear my mother's dress until we get to your house."

"Ok," I cried, sounding pathetic.

Bernard pulled me up off the ground. "Let's walk around the festival so no one sees us."

"Ok," I whimpered.

When we arrived at Bernard's home, he grabbed my hand and pulled me around the corner and up the stairs quickly to his bedroom.

I went into his bathroom and ran the water.

"Shut the door, Maybel!" Bernard yelled to me.

"Bernard, I can't get the water the right temperature."

Bernard came into the bathroom. His head was down and he looked very embarrassed. I wasn't even naked. I still had my underwear on.

He twisted the knobs in his bath, adjusting the temperature. "There," he said and left quickly, closing the door behind him.

I got into the bath and washed myself. The soap he used for his hair smelled like exotic spices and I breathed in its smell while I washed and rinsed my hair. When I finished, I wrapped a towel around myself and went into Bernard's bedroom where he laid on his bed in his robe.

He went into his bathroom and closed the door. I laid on his bed with the towel over me. His pillow smelled like the spices in his soap.

Bernard finally finished and came out of his bathroom wearing his towel around his waist.

"Cover your breasts, Bernard!" I giggled.

"Very funny, Maybel." Bernard was not amused.

"Your bare breasts are scandalous, Bernard! It's causing a controversy!"

Bernard just looked at me as though he were annoyed. He went to his closet and pulled a shirt over his head then to his dresser for underwear and pants and headed back into the bathroom to dress.

He returned from dressing, then left his bedroom, I assumed to find a dress for me. I looked around his bedroom for a hairbrush. He certainly didn't have the dressing table amenities that Catherine had strewn about her dressing table.

I went to the bathroom to find his hairbrush. It was on the sink. I began brushing my hair in the mirror. The towel around my body fell to the floor when I raised my arms to brush my wild mane, but I continued brushing my hair. There was still a tiny twig in my hair. I'd thought I'd gotten all the nature out of my hair, yet there was still a speck of a leaf behind my ear. I suddenly noticed Bernard's reflection in the mirror watching me. I continued brushing the tangles out, wondering why he liked watching me brush my hair. I finished and set the brush back down on the sink. When I turned around Bernard was no longer there. I picked my towel back up and wrapped it around me. When I went into Bernard's bedroom, he was laying on his bed.

"You can wear that dress," he nodded to the dress on the chair beside him.

I took the dress from the chair and pulled it over my head. "Maybel! You can't dress in front of me!" Bernard snapped.

"Catherine says you think of me as your little sister."

"You're not really my little sister!" Bernard said with exasperation.

"You treat me like your annoying, little sister," I said. "And Catherine and I change clothes in front of each other."

I looked in Bernard's standing mirror. I looked very odd in Mrs. Charleston's dress. "Bernard, I look strange," I whined.

"Since when do you care what you look like?" he laughed. "Come, Maybel," he grabbed my hand, "Let me take you home."

"Bernard," I said just before I opened his bedroom door, "Please don't tell anyone I peed on you!" I begged.

Bernard looked down at me sympathetically and hugged me. "I won't tell anyone, sweetheart." He kissed the top of my head.

Luckily, I didn't live too far away, and everyone was at the festival, so we didn't pass anyone on the way to my house.

Bernard held my hand as he walked me home. I jumped and skipped and sang songs I made up. Bernard smiled at me, "You've quite the imagination."

I sang, "Bernard, I love you; you look like candy and I love candy too! Bernard, I love you! You are pretty, and you play with me. I'm gonna marry you!"

We arrived at my house and I went upstairs and changed my clothes. I brought his clothing I borrowed back downstairs to him. "Bernard, I forgot my other dress at your house."

"I'll have our maid wash it and the next time you're over, you'll probably get dirty again, and need something to change into," he smiled and pecked my cheek. "See you later, Maybel." He looked embarrassed, and like he wanted to get away from me as fast as he could.

"I'm sorry about that, you know, that thing that happened. Are you mad at me?" I asked.

"No, honey. Everything is fine." He still acted like he wanted to get away from me.

"Will you still play with me tomorrow?" I begged.

"We'll see. I have to get back to Catherine. See you later." He turned and left quickly.

"See you later, Bernard," I whispered. I ran upstairs crying and hid under my covers in embarrassment.

A couple weeks had passed. I had been gardening earlier that morning with mommy, daddy, and Catherine before it got too hot. Daddy was now at the hardware store and mommy and Catherine were in town.

There was a knock on the front door. It was Bernard.

"Catherine's at the store with mommy. You can wait for her if you want, Bernard." I hugged him and playfully held onto him, stepping on his shoes with my bare feet, making him hold onto me as I leaned back giggling.

"Bernard! You smell like chocolate! Did you bring me candy?" I asked excitedly.

"Of course, sweetheart!" He laughed as he held me. He made wide steps into the family room with me giggling and trying to stay atop his feet.

"Where are they?" I squealed. I shoved my hands into his pockets and found them inside. Bernard sat on the couch and I climbed into his lap. "They're all for me, right?"

"No," he laughed, "Some are for Catherine, your mother, and father."

"Aww, Bernard!"

"Now Maybel, if you eat too much your belly will hurt," he playfully tickled my tummy.

"You're my favorite boy in the whole, wide world," I said as I placed a small chocolate in my mouth.

"Your favorite?" he laughed. "I'd better be the only boy in your life. You're too young to date."

"When can I date?" I playfully tugged his shirt buttons and ran my hands through his hair as I sucked on the candy. I pulled his hair gently to see hard I could pull before he told me to stop.

"You like to see how far I'll let you go before I tell you to stop, don't you!" he laughed, and tugged a lock of my hair.

"Ow!" I pretended it hurt, but I was giggling uncontrollably.

"When can I date then?" I again asked.

"Never," he laughed. He held my hands and playfully pushed me backward and side to side and I giggled. I loved when Bernard played with me.

"I'm going to have either four or a hundred children, so I'll have to date someone to get married."

"Oh really? Four or a hundred children? There's no in between?" Bernard laughed.

"No. Four or a hundred!" I giggled.

"That is not how it works, Maybel!" he said laughing.

"How do I get babies?" I asked him.

Bernard blushed, "I don't know, Maybel. Don't think about that until you're older."

"How many babies are you going to have?" I asked.

"I don't know. I hadn't really thought about it."

"How many does Catherine want?"

"I don't know. I've never asked her."

"Don't you think you should ask her? If you want one and she wants a hundred like I do, then you'll have to settle for fifty. Are you going to be ok with only fifty?"

Bernard laughed, "Well, firstly, good work dividing a hundred by two. And secondly, no one has fifty children, much less a hundred!" he laughed at me. "I do love your mind, Maybel! You always keep me entertained!"

Bernard took a piece of chocolate from my hand as I was about to eat it.

"Bernard!" I yelled.

The chocolate was warm from having been in my fist and squished through his fingers.

"Ha! That's what you get, thief!" I laughed at him.

"You're so messy!" Bernard said, annoyed. "I need to wash my hands!"

"No! Don't throw away my chocolate!" I shrieked.

Bernard started to stand but I quickly grabbed his hand and licked his fingers. Bernard looked at me like I had gone crazy. I put his fingers in my mouth and licked between them with my tongue and sucked the chocolate off. Bernard suddenly shivered and sucked in air.

I licked and sucked his other finger and he suddenly froze and bent over. I thought he was in pain. "Maybel! Please stop!" His voice was low and begging. He moaned and he pushed me off his lap. He ran to the bathroom and slammed the door. A few minutes later he returned. His face was flushed red.

"Did you vomit?" I asked, concerned?

"No."

Bernard sat back down on the couch and put a pillow over his lap. "It's just a stomachache."

"Were you constipated?"

"No, Maybel!" He sounded annoyed.

"Daddy makes grunting noises when he poops sometimes, too."

"I am not constipated, Maybel! Can I just sit here for a minute? I'm really tired!"

Bernard leaned back and closed his eyes and exhaled deeply. I climbed into his lap again but his eyes shot open and he pushed me off onto the floor.

"Ow! Bernard!" I sat on the floor and looked up at him hurt.

"Maybel, I think you are getting too old to sit on my lap."

"No, I'm not!" I sprung up and pushed myself back into his lap.

Bernard shoved me back off onto the couch. "You're getting too old!" he said, his voice raising.

I was angry and hurt and started crying.

"Maybel, stop crying!" he said, irritated.

I didn't understand why I could sit on his lap a few minutes ago but not now. "I was just sitting on your lap, Bernard! I haven't suddenly grown up in the last ten minutes!"

Bernard sighed. "I'm sorry, Maybel. I just don't want you to sit on my lap right now."

"Can I later after your stomach feels better?"

"I don't know, Maybel."

I curled up next to Bernard and rested my head on his chest and he wrapped his arm around me.

"Don't you love me anymore?" I asked.

"Of course I love you, Maybel." He breathed out deeply then patted my arm.

It was a hot and rainy, summer day. Bernard and I sat together on his bed lazily passing time, waiting for the rain to stop. Catherine had gone to the kitchen to get us snacks. I rested my head on Bernard's chest while he read to me.

"Maybel, move your head," Bernard said.

"No," I replied.

"Maybel, I need to get up to pee," he said.

"Fine," I sighed. I moved my head and he stood up and went to his bathroom.

We had been waiting for the rain to let up for what felt like hours.

Bernard returned from his bathroom excited. "Maybel, there's a double rainbow! I bet we can see it better from my parents' bedroom!"

I followed Bernard to a large room with a beautiful view. There were two rainbows over the trees in the distance. "Wow!" I exclaimed. "They're beautiful!"

"I thought you'd like them," Bernard smiled.

"Can we go outside?" I asked excitedly.

"Now? It's still raining," he said.

"Let's slide down that hill in the mud, the one we slid down last summer." I took his hand and tugged him toward the bedroom door.

"I don't know, Maybel, it's muddy, and we'd have to bathe afterward, and it seems like a lot of work to have a little fun."

"Where did your sense of adventure go, Bernard? You may as well be an old man. Do you need to borrow my grandfather's cane?"

"Ha, ha, Maybel. Come on, let's go back to my room. Catherine has probably returned."

"I bet you have to eat prunes so you can poop, old man."

"Funny, Maybel, ever the joker."

"I bet you have gray hairs already." I jumped on his back and ruffled his hair.

"Ok, fine, Maybel, we'll go play in the mud."

"Yayyyy! I love you again, Bernard!"

"Love you too, even though you are annoying," he sighed.

I smacked his head lightly when he called me annoying, and then I giggled. He carried me on his back and we returned to his bedroom where Catherine sat with our snacks.

Catherine wrinkled her nose in disgust at the idea of playing in mud. "You two go ahead. I'm going back downstairs. Your cousin Henry is here, Bernard. While you're outside getting muddy, I'll talk to Henry in the study with your parents. He has just returned from Paris and I want to listen to his stories."

"Just don't fall for his charm, Catherine," Bernard said, with what I thought was perhaps a whiff of anger, or maybe fear.

"Which one is Henry?" I asked.

"John's brother," Bernard said.

"Who's John? Have I met them?" I asked.

Bernard pried me off his back and set me down on the floor. "Henry is the one with a new girlfriend each week," Bernard said dryly. "And John, too, enjoys sowing his oats."

I held Bernard's hand as we went downstairs to the study. I wanted to see this farmer, Henry, who had lots of girlfriends.

"You've met him before, Maybel," Catherine told me.

"I have? When? Where?" I tried to recall a Henry and a John in my memories.

"They have come to Bernard's house several times for parties," Catherine said, trying to jog my memory. "Henry is the more handsome of the two, although they are both good-looking."

I felt Bernard tense up beside me as we walked down the long corridor to the study.

Catherine opened the door to the study and Mr. and Mrs. Charleston, a handsome, young man, and some other, older people, were sitting on leather chairs and drinking from thick, crystal cups.

"Ah, Bernard! Hello, cousin!" The young, handsome man stood and smiled at Bernard. He came to Bernard and shook Bernard's hand.

"Hello, Henry," Bernard said.

"Hello, Maybel," Henry smiled at me. I hid halfway behind Bernard. Henry was beautiful! My mouth became dry and my heart beat faster.

"Hello, again, Catherine," Henry smiled at Catherine.

Henry looked familiar, but the Charleston's parties were always filled with so many people that I never bothered to remember who was who, or how they were related to Bernard.

Henry looked older than Bernard, so I had likely ignored him at parties, because old people talked about boring things.

"You're the prettiest farmer I've ever met." My voice cracked from nervousness as I spoke to Henry.

Henry appeared amused. "I am studying to be a businessman," Henry smiled. "What made you think I was a farmer?"

"I heard you sow a lot of oats," I said.

Henry blushed while the room erupted with laughter.

"I'm taking Maybel to play outside," Bernard said quickly. "Good to see you, Henry." Bernard pulled me out of the study and closed the doors.

"Come, Maybel, let's go." Bernard held my hand as we walked outside.

The rain alternated between sprinkling and pouring. The sun shined, though, so the double rainbow shone beautifully, almost glowing, against the dark, gray, storm clouds.

"Dance with me!" I yelled over the pattering rain.

Bernard looked down at me and smiled. He picked me up and spun me around in the rain. I held my arms out wide and gleefully laughed.

We splashed through puddles and slid down the hill on the edge of the lawn and down to the stream.

Bernard held my hand as we waded in the stream. I stooped low to see if any fish were enjoying the splashing rain. Little fins swirled around my ankles.

"Maybel," Bernard pulled me into his embrace. "I really like playing with you. I'm glad my parents and I moved here. You're my best friend, you know."

"You're mine too," I smiled up at him.

Catherine, Bernard, and I sat together in our garden. I braided dandelions into a crown for Bernard. "Look, Bernard! You're a king!"

"Thank you, Lady Maybel," he smiled.

"Queen Catherine, would you like a royal crown?" I asked her.

"Yes, m'lady," she giggled.

I braided her a crown while I sat in between Bernard's legs. We were on the grassy field outside my house. King Bernard and Queen Catherine held hands and kissed.

"Why do you like to kiss?" I asked them.

"It makes me happy," Catherine blushed.

"I like touching you with my lips," Bernard smiled at Catherine, who giggled and blushed deeper. I didn't understand their attraction.

I leaned back into Bernard's arms as he turned his head and kissed Catherine.

Bernard wrapped his arms around me and the three of us watched the sun set.

"Are you cold, Maybel?" Bernard asked me.

"No," I answered.

"Your arms feel cold," he said.

"I'm not cold," I said.

Bernard pressed me against him and rubbed my arms. He kissed the top of my head.

"Maybel, let's get you inside," he said.

We walked into our kitchen and when I turned around, Catherine and Bernard were slipping back outside to be alone.

"They always try to get rid of me!" I cried to mommy.

"They're young, Maybel. I know your feelings are hurt now, but you'll understand when you're older." Mommy wrapped her arm around me and led me into the family room to sit between her and daddy.

I joined the Charlestons on Mr. Charleston's business venture in the Midwest. They had family there too they wanted to visit, but I suspected they had family everywhere. At every party the Charlestons hosted, there were always cousins.

Catherine was supposed to come with us, but backed out at the last minute saying she had a migraine, so it was just me accompanying the Charlestons. Bernard seemed disappointed to be stuck with just me, but he nevertheless hadn't conveyed aloud his disappointment that his girlfriend was not coming, and that he was stuck entertaining his girlfriend's little sister.

I was excited, but very nervous because I'd never left my parents before. I clung to Mrs. Charleston. She must have sensed how scared I was and led me through the train talking to me and trying to sooth me. I was grateful. She held my hand and occasionally pointed out the window and explained various landmarks and the different kinds of trees and wildlife we passed. She had great knowledge of plants and flowers too. She pointed out medicinal plants as we passed them, and explained how they could be prepared by boiling and straining, or dried and ground into powders. Her knowledge of which plants, flowers, and even tree bark could be used, and for which maladies, greatly impressed me.

We saw Mr. Charleston enter the car where we were seated by a large window. "Dear," Mrs. Charleston said, "I need to speak with Mrs. Winters about some business matters. Look after Maybel will you?"

It wasn't really a question to her husband, as she caught Mrs. Winters' gaze and waved to her, then she and Mrs. Winters left, leaving me with Mr. Charleston.

He looked uncomfortable. "Well, dear, I don't have any daughters. What do ladies your age enjoy doing?"

"We mostly gamble and tell lewd jokes," I said with a straight face. Mr. Charleston roared with laughter.

"Well, honey, let's go find some mischief to get into before Mrs. Charleston returns. She never lets me gamble or tell lewd jokes. Such a fuddy duddy!" he chuckled.

I held his hand at looked up at him. He looked surprised I took his hand, but not upset. I wondered if Bernard's family held hands and hugged and kissed as much as my parents hugged and kissed Catherine and me. They always held our hands, too. I had never really thought to watch other families to see what they do.

Mr. Charleston led me to a room with sofas and chairs. He sat in a chair and without thinking about it, I sat on his lap. He reminded me of daddy. He shifted uncomfortably. "Do you and Catherine sit on your father's lap?"

"I do, but Catherine doesn't as much anymore because she's older, but she does sometimes when daddy tells us stories. And she lays her head in his lap when he reads to us, but only if she gets there first. I usually beat her there, and we fight over who gets to be on daddy's lap."

Mr. Charleston chuckled, "And who usually wins?"

"I'm stronger so I push her off, but she gives daddy this cute, little, sad face that he has never been able to say no to, so daddy makes me scoot over and let Catherine cuddle up too."

Mr. Charleston smiled, "I never realized how much I wanted a daughter until now," he smiled weakly. There was a pain in his eyes. "Your father is very blessed."

"I think so too," I giggled.

I leaned back into Mr. Charleston's arms as he began telling me stories about his family and Mrs. Charleston's family. He also added some stories about Bernard as a child, which I thoroughly enjoyed. Mr. Charleston made me promise I would only recount to Bernard those embarrassing stories at only the most inappropriate and inopportune moments. I liked Mr. Charleston's sense of humor, and he seemed to truly enjoy mine.

The first night in the train I was very scared. I'd never been away from home before, and I was now away from my home and my parents. Bernard's and my sleeper cars were adjoining, so I opened the door between our compartments, and went to his bed. I climbed in beside him and curled up next to him.

"Maybel, what are you doing?" Bernard asked, surprised.

"I'm scared," I said.

"There's nothing to be scared of. Go back to your bed," he grumbled.

"Can I stay here please? I've never been away from my parents before and I'm scared." I was also scared Bernard would make me leave.

"Maybel," Bernard sighed.

"Please!" I started crying.

"Ok, Maybel, but just this one time. You'll see that there's nothing scary, and you can sleep in your own bed tomorrow."

"Thank you," I sniffled.

Bernard let out a loud and annoyed sigh. "Come here, Maybel." He pulled me onto his shoulder and wrapped his arms around me. "Stop crying and go to sleep," he said. He sounded irritated with me, but I was too scared to be offended.

In the morning I awoke still clinging to Bernard. I looked over at him and he was awake. "Oh, you're awake?" I yawned.

"I didn't want to wake you. You were sound asleep when I woke up, so I let you sleep."

"What do you want to do today?" I asked excitedly.

"Pee. I really need to pee. And then I don't know."

"What kinds of games do we play on a train?" I asked excitedly.

"Card games."

"What else?"

"That's it. We sit and talk, and play card games, and read books, and wait for our train to arrive."

"Ok, let's play cards," I suggested.

Bernard sighed. "Let me out of bed, Maybel."

I rolled out of bed, letting Bernard out. "Maybel, go back to your room. I need to get dressed so I can go to the car with the toilet."

I went to my car and closed the door and got dressed then went to find the toilet too. There was a line. By the time it was my turn I really had to pee.

After I finished, I knocked on Bernard's car. He opened his door, "What now, Maybel?"

"When do we go eat breakfast?"

"I'll be ready in just a minute," he sighed.

I followed him into his car. He put his shoes back on, "Ok, let's go, Maybel."

We entered the dining car and saw Bernard's parents already eating breakfast. I skipped over to them. "Good morning!" I said happily.

"Good morning dear, come sit," Mrs. Charleston smiled.

Bernard and I sat across from his parents and I immediately began recounting the dream I'd had.

"I dreamed last night that our train, whenever it made a stop at a station, we were in a different time. At the first stop, I got off the train with Bernard and I was an older woman with blonde hair, and Bernard was older and had blonde hair too, and we were married with three children, two girls and a boy. We got back on the train and at the next stop we were Chinese! Can you believe it!" I giggled.

Mr. and Mrs. Charleston smiled at my retelling of my dream, and Mrs. Charleston winked at Bernard, who looked either embarrassed or maybe a little annoyed.

"When we were Chinese, I continued, we wore really odd robes and they were colorful and silky. We were getting married so we hadn't had children yet, but I felt we ended up having five boys and one girl. Then we got back on the train and at our next stop we got off the train and we were speaking to each other in a different language, but it was a dream, you know, so somehow, I understood Bernard when he told me in that other language that he had to leave me, and I didn't want him to leave because I knew he was going to drown on the ship, but he didn't believe me, and he left and I never saw him again."

I picked up a piece of toast and took a bite and then a sip of tea.

Mr. and Mrs. Charleston were watching me intently. Even Bernard was interested. "Well, what happened next?" Mr. Charleston asked. They seemed to really care about my dream.

"I woke up crying Bernard died and I was sad," I said plainly.

They kept watching me as though I had more to say, but I was hungry, and the jam on the toast was really tasty, so I took another bite.

"That's it?" asked Mr. Charleston. "I was hoping for a longer dream."

"That was quite the dream, Maybel!" Mrs. Charleston beamed. "Would you mind writing that down? Bernard says you're an excellent storyteller."

I swallowed my bite of toast. "Sure, Mrs. Charleston. Also, at the train station where Bernard drowned, later I fell in love with and married Catherine, but she was a man at that train stop, not a woman, and not my sister. We had twins, a boy and girl, and the twins are my parents right now. What a strange dream, right?"

"Maybel, darling," Mrs. Charleston asked, "Will you write down all the dreams you've ever had that you remember, and start writing down every morning all the dreams you dreamed that night, before you forget them?"

"Yes," I said, finishing my delicious strawberry jam and toast.

"There were many, many more train stops. Some I don't remember clearly. And some were ahead of me and I woke up before the train could get to those stops. I think at one stop I was an Indian chief out West but I don't think that place is there now, and also I was a man."

They continued listening to me, very fascinated with this dream I was telling them. I was surprised because my family was never this interested in my dreams. They were interested, but not as much as the Charlestons were right now. Perhaps that was because my family was used to me talking about my dreams, I reasoned.

"Mrs. Charleston, at one of the train stops, you were there, and you looked like you do now, except you were a little girl, and a woman who looked like you, but was old, said to tell you that yes, she sees you every day, she likes the Christmas decorations, she's taking care of the baby girl, and she likes the green dress, so stop worrying about that."

Mrs. Charleston's eyes filled with tears and they streamed down her cheeks but she did not make any crying sounds. "Thank you, Maybel," she whispered. She smiled gratefully at me.

I became scared that I'd made her cry and I looked to Bernard for guidance in what to do next.

Bernard put his arm around my shoulder. "It's ok, Maybel. Mother is happy."

"Yes, dear, I am." Mrs. Charleston reached her hand across the table and held mine and squeezed it. Her hand was shaky. "I'm going to go freshen up." She excused herself and Mr. Charleston followed.

"What happened?" I asked Bernard.

"Mother likes your dream. It made her happy." Bernard rubbed my back. "Are you still hungry or do you want to play cards now?"

"Hungry!" I smiled.

"And what would you like?"

"Ice cream."

"For breakfast?"

"You ate pancakes with syrup, Bernard. That's like cake and frosting."

Bernard laughed, "You do have a point. I don't think they serve ice cream for breakfast though. Would you like cake and frosting?" he laughed.

"You mean pancakes and syrup? Yes! I would love that!"

Bernard and I played card games and then I wrote down my dream for Mrs. Charleston. By then it was dinner time and I really wanted to stretch and climb something, run somewhere, or do something in fresh air.

Bernard and I sat with his parents again for dinner. I handed Mrs. Charleston the papers containing my dream. She smiled and came over to me and hugged me and kissed my cheek. "Thank you, sweetheart."

I was surprised at how much she liked my dream.

A small quartet played softly in the dining car. It was relaxing. Mr. and Mrs. Charleston talked to Bernard about school and his cousins. I watched all the people dining. I wondered what they were like when they were behind closed doors. There was a lady wearing a gigantic hat, and I wondered what was underneath that hat. She looked so prim and proper, but I wondered if she farted after a big meal.

"Maybel, please pass the cream," Bernard's voice shook me out of my daydream.

I passed him the cream.

"Do you want any of my fruit?" Bernard asked me.

"Yes, the raspberries and blueberries. You can have the grapes," I said.

Bernard seemed more like a boring adult around his parents. He smiled less, didn't laugh much, and spoke of boring topics like the economy and France.

I wondered what the Charlestons were like in their home when no one else was around. Did they loosen up and tell jokes? Did Bernard used to sit on his father's lap and call him daddy? Did Bernard's mother rub his tummy when he was sick, or did he have a nanny to rub his tummy since they were rich?

I didn't want a nanny for my children. I wanted to rub their tummies myself.

"Maybel you prefer tea, don't you?"

Again, Bernard brought me out of my daydream. I looked at him startled. "What?"

"What do you want to drink?" he asked, annoyed that my mind had not been present.

I turned to our waiter. "Whiskey neat. Unless you have scotch, then scotch on the rocks, but not the bottom shelf swill, top shelf only, please."

Our waiter stared at me shocked while Mr. Charleston roared with laughter.

"Or just hot tea with lemon," I said.

"Very well," our waiter said, then left.

"Maybel, you have your father's sense of humor." Mr. Charleston was still chuckling.

"Mommy is funnier. She once told me to practice math during my summer vacation."

Mr. Charleston again laughed heartily, "I'm very glad to have met your family."

"I am too," I said.

After dinner Bernard went to wash up and brush his teeth. I sat in my car wondering what my parents and Catherine were doing. I missed them. I didn't know how Bernard could go away to school for such long stretches of time. I decided my children were not going to attend boarding schools and weren't leaving until college.

After I washed myself and brushed my teeth, I returned to my car and put my nightgown on. I hesitantly knocked on the door between Bernard's and my rooms.

Bernard opened the door, "Stay in your bed, Maybel."

"I don't want to be alone," I pleaded.

"You're not alone! There are dozens of people around you!"

"Can I sleep at the foot of your bed? I won't take up much room, I promise!"

"I'll leave the door to our rooms open. It will be just like we're in the same room."

I stood there looking up at Bernard, silently begging him.

44 - E. D. JUMPER

"People will think we're sleeping together. You're too young."

"I'm too young to sleep with you? How old do I have to be to sleep in the same bed as you?" I asked.

"What? No. You're too young to sleep with a man."

"You're not a man, you're just my brother."

"I'm not your real brother."

"You're not a man yet. You're a boy."

"I don't think you're understanding me. You are too young to sleep with anyone," Bernard said.

"I sleep with Catherine all the time. I have bad dreams and crawl into her bed."

Bernard sighed, "You're too old to sleep in my bed."

"You just said I'm too young!"

"You're too young to sleep with someone, and too old to sleep in the same bed with me!"

"I have absolutely no idea what you are saying, Bernard!"

Bernard grabbed my arm and yanked me into his room. "Just get in bed and be quiet!"

I got into his bed. "Why are you so mad at me? What did I do wrong?"

"Nothing Maybel. I'm not mad, now be quiet."

I inched closer to Bernard and put my head on his shoulder and reached for his hands to hold. Bernard sighed and wrapped his arms around me and rested his head against mine.

I felt safe and immediately fell asleep in his arms.

The next morning, I awoke first. I watched Bernard sleeping. I could imagine his face as a toddler. I could imagine his face as a young boy, too. Bernard opened his eyes.

"I swear I felt you watching me, Maybel. Also, why were you watching me?"

"I was thinking I could imagine what you looked like as a toddler and a young boy."

"I was handsome then too, right?" he laughed.

"Yes," I said.

Bernard blushed, "Time to change and go to breakfast," he said quickly.

Breakfast consisted of more delicious fruit jams and toast. Mr. Charleston laughed and asked me if I'd like my whiskey neat now. I politely declined and said I was more in the mood for coffee.

"Absolutely not!" Bernard interjected. "You have more than enough energy as it is!"

"Have you any dreams to report?" Mrs. Charleston asked.

"I don't remember dreaming last night. I slept really well and can't remember waking up once."

"I'm glad to hear you are rested, Maybel," she smiled. "We'll arrive soon and we'll be able to take in the beauty and fresh air of the Midwest."

"Oh good! I really need to run around and stretch my legs!"

"I've never seen Maybel stay this long in one place, actually," Bernard smiled at me.

We arrived at our destination and exited the train. "Maybel!" a voice called. I was surprised to hear my voice being called and turned around only to be hit by a small ball of mud on my arm.

I was about to retaliate and picked up the largest rock I could find on the ground when a boy charged me shouting. "I'm sorry Maybel! It was a joke!"

"Paul?" I asked astonished.

"Yes, Maybel!"

He ran to me and hugged me and I happily returned his hug. "Maybel!" he kissed my cheek, "I've missed you! Let's go play!"

"Ok!" I carried my bag with me, and without considering the Charlestons, I ran off with Paul.

"Sorry, Maybel, let me carry your bag," Paul reached for my bag but I pulled it away from him.

"I'm strong Paul! I can manage!"

"I know you're strong, Maybel, but a man is supposed to carry a woman's bag!"

I smiled and handed him my bag.

"Maybel! Stop!" I heard Bernard call.

I stopped and turned around. "Yes, Bernard?"

"You can't just walk off a train and leave! Where are you going?"

"I don't know. This is Paul, Bernard! Remember Paul?"

"Yes, Maybel, he's my cousin," Bernard said dourly. "Come back here, the both of you!"

We walked back to Bernard sulking.

"You can't just run away like that! We need to know where you are so you don't get lost."

"We're not lost, Bernard," Paul said, "I know where I am! This is my home!"

"Can I go play with Paul, Bernard? Please?" I clasped my hands in front of me, begging Bernard to let me go.

"Paul, bring Maybel to your house in one hour. Maybel hand me your bag."

Paul and I scampered off as fast as we could before Bernard changed his mind.

"Bernard is really annoying," Paul said when we were out of earshot.

"I figured he'd be happy to get rid of me," I said. "My sister was supposed to come, but she didn't, and I think Bernard has been annoyed having to take care of me."

"Don't worry Maybel, we're going to have fun now!"

"Oh, I'm so happy!"

Paul and I ran away as fast as our legs could carry us. We wound up in a stream in a forest. "This is where I get the mud for my sculptures," Paul pointed to a bank on the other side.

"Oh, Paul! I still have the bowl you made me! It's on my shelf in my room!"

"I have the bowl you made me too, Maybel! It's on my dresser," he laughed and grabbed my hands. "Maybel may I kiss you? I wanted to kiss you at Catherine's birthday party, but Bernard told me I was not allowed."

I giggled, "Well, Bernard is not here!"

We stood in the shallow creek and Paul leaned over and very lightly kissed my lips. "I've been wanting to kiss you forever, Maybel!"

"I like you too, Paul!"

"Here's my scar. This is from the rock that was in the mud you threw at me."

I suddenly felt embarrassed. "I'm sorry, Paul. I never meant to hurt you, and I'm sorry I did that."

"It's ok, Maybel, I tell people Cupid hit me with his arrow and that I'm going to marry the girl who gave me this scar!" He laughed and then looked a little shy as he slowly leaned toward me again, kissing me gently, and a little longer than our first kiss.

"I like you, Maybel."

"I like you too, Paul. Can you come live with Bernard so we can play together every day?"

"I wish I could Maybel, but my parents have businesses here."

"Oh," I said sadly.

"But we can play together today and tomorrow!"

"Yes!" I giggled, and then I leaned in and kissed Paul because I felt that I'd known him forever and I felt safe with him.

Paul and I grabbed handfuls of the mud from the opposite bank and began walking back to the other side of the stream.

The water was crystal clear and came just past our ankles. I could see the pebbles on the stream bed. There were tiny minnows and crawdads scuttling over and tickling our feet.

Paul led our way to his house. Bernard met us in the field between us and what I assumed was Paul's home. "Where have you two been? It's been three hours!"

"It has?" I asked surprised.

"Yes, Maybel, and I was worried!"

"Bernard," I said excitedly, "we saw minnows and crawdads and we got this mud!" I showed him my fistfuls of mud. "And we saw deer, rabbits, a coyote, a white wolf, a black wolf, and a cougar!"

"You could have been killed!" Bernard screamed at us.

"No, Bernard, they were far away!" Paul said.

"They run faster than you both! Be thankful they weren't hungry!"

Bernard grabbed my shoulder and led me toward the house in the distance.

"Bernard, we really were safe!" Paul pleaded.

Bernard ignored him and kept his hand on my shoulder, sternly guiding me toward the house.

As we got closer, I realized it wasn't a house. It was a stone and wood mansion.

"That's your house?" I asked Paul.

"Yes," he answered.

"Are you rich like Bernard?" I asked.

"That's what the kids at my school say. They tease me sometimes," he said sourly.

"I get teased too, but not for being rich," I admitted shyly.

"What do you get teased for?" Paul asked.

"For not being as pretty as Catherine, or as good as her in school, or at piano, dancing, and sewing." I paused to think, "And cooking. And I'm not good at small talk at parties like she is either. And I'm sure there's more," I sighed.

"I like you better than Catherine," Paul said.

I smiled at him. "Thank you, Paul. I like you too."

Bernard's grasp on my shoulder became more claw-like.

"Easy on my shoulder, Bernard! You have a hand, not an eagle's talon!"

Paul laughed.

We arrived at Paul's house and Mr. and Mrs. Charleston were on the porch along with about a dozen other people who looked like Bernard and Paul.

"Come on, Maybel, let's take the mud to my workshop behind the house."

I followed Paul and thankfully Bernard went to the porch.

"Maybel, Bernard likes you," he whispered.

"He's nice. I like him too."

"No, Maybel, Bernard really likes you."

"Yes Paul, I really like him too. He's going to marry my sister. He's going to be my brother."

"If you say so, Maybel," Paul said in a way I didn't understand. It was like he wasn't quite patronizing or condescending, but it was like he was disagreeing with me. I was determined to remember his reaction and think about it at a later time to understand what exactly it meant. But right now, we had sculptures to make.

Paul was an excellent artist. I could not create a replica of a cardinal like him but my bird had its own merits. It looked a little like a bird. And the wings didn't fall off. And those were its merits.

Paul and I went inside the backdoor to get washed for dinner. "My mother doesn't like when I drip mud everywhere so we have a room in the back where I can hose myself off. We can rinse the mud off there."

We went to the back room and there was a hose for us in this room and a drain in the floor.

Before I was done taking in the modernness of the room, Paul sprayed me with the hose. He laughed and hosed me down while I giggled and tried to take the hose away.

I yanked the hose away and sprayed his chest. He raised his arms and turned around in circles laughing.

When we finished, he told me to leave my dress on the hook and the maids would clean my dress for me. I had an undershirt and shorts underneath my dress so it seemed reasonable to me. Paul undressed down to his undershorts and I peeled off my heavy, wet dress.

We walked through the back of the house, avoiding the common areas and up the back stairs. "This is your room, Maybel. Your bag is already here. I'll come get you after we dress for dinner."

I took my wet clothing off. I didn't know where to put it so I set it in the corner of the room and would ask Paul what to do with it later. I dressed and combed my hair and used pins to sweep it up into a bun since it was wet and I didn't have time to dry it.

I heard a knock on my door. "Maybel," Paul called, "I'll take your wet clothes."

I opened the door. "I was wondering what to do with my clothes." I retrieved them from the corner and handed them to Paul. "Thank you, Paul," I said.

Paul smiled sweetly at me. He kissed me. "You're beautiful."

I blushed.

"I've wanted to see you ever since I first met you," he said.

"Me too. But Bernard said you lived out west and that you probably wouldn't visit again. I was sad."

"I'll visit you again, Maybel. I don't know when, but I will. I like you."

"I like you too," I swallowed hard. I was nervous but I kissed Paul's lips.

He smiled and reached for my hand. "Let's go to dinner."

I sat beside Paul, and Mr. Charleston was on my other side. Mr. Charleston seemed to like my humor. I liked his too. Bernard sat across from me. He seemed less happy than he was on the train.

Paul and I were completely glued to each other. We talked about the town where he lived and he told me stories about the townsfolk. I told him about my town, Catherine, my parents, and Charlie the owner of my favorite store, the candy store.

After dinner, Paul escorted me up to my room and stayed for a little while because he wanted to hear me tell more stories.

"I love your stories, Maybel."

"Thank you," I replied.

"Maybel, I'm down the hall in my room if you need anything."

"I might. I sometimes have bad dreams," I said.

"Do you want me to stay with you?"

"Yes, but Bernard says boys and girls are either too old or too young to sleep in the same bed. I'm not really sure what he was saying to be honest."

"Then we'll sleep on the floor in my room! It's not a bed and I have blankets and sheets that my other cousins and I use as a fort when we tell scary stories to each other."

I became very excited. "Oh! That sounds fun!"

I followed Paul to his room and we set four chairs in a circle and draped blankets over them. Paul had a candle that he lit and we laid under the fort and proceeded to tell ghost stories.

Paul went first. "Once there was a young girl buried alive because her pulse dropped and everyone thought she was dead. The cemetery caretaker was tending to the lawns when he noticed the dirt above her grave was sunken. Fearing a grave robber, he contacted the police and they exhumed her body. Her face was contorted and her fingertips were bloody and broken from trying to dig herself out of the wooden box. She broke through the box but was suffocated by the heaps of dirt that filled her coffin."

I laughed hysterically and Paul stared at me like I'd lost my mind. "What a bunch of idiots!" I laughed. "They didn't think to put a mirror to her mouth and nose and check for respiration?" I continued laughing hard.

"My God, Maybel! If you think that story is funny, what terrifying ghost story do you have hidden away in that mind of yours?"

"Ok, let me think of something."

"No, wait, I have another one!" Paul exclaimed. "This will terrify you! There was a demon named Buttingsworth."

I started giggling.

"What in the world is making you laugh now?"

"A demon named Butt," I giggled harder.

"Buttingsworth!" Paul corrected me.

I couldn't stop laughing. "I call upon the Great Demon of Darkness of the Superior Echelons of Hell, Butt, to come forth and grant me three wishes..." I trailed off giggling.

"Demons don't grant wishes! That's a genie you're thinking of!"

I laughed even harder. "I need to go pee, hang on, I want to hear all about the great demon, Butt, after I go pee!" I laughed all the way out of Paul's bedroom.

I returned and Paul was still sulking. "Ok, I'm sorry, Paul. Please tell me about Butt the demon," I bit my bottom lip to keep from laughing.

"Buttingsworth," Paul reminded me, "was the demon of grievances. When you had a grievance with a neighbor or politician or in this case the pastor of your church, you called upon

Buttingsworth to settle the grievance. A man named William had moved to a town not far away from here and married a woman named Francesca. Frannie was devout and attended church and bible study religiously. Her pastor was a young man from the south named Kildare. Frannie bore William three daughters, all of whom were beautiful and intelligent. Pastor Kildare was handsome and charming and convinced Frannie he could offer her daughters a better education by tutoring her daughters after school. The pastor was wicked and one day after church he cut off their heads, and when Frannie called upon Buttingsworth, he commanded Kildare to push a sword through his own chest."

"I like this Butt demon. He rid the world of that bad guy," I said.

"Should I rename the demon something scarier, like Demon Chiphellingaard?"

"Yes, Demon Chip is a lot scarier," I bit my lip harder.

"Ok, your turn Maybel."

"There were two Russian twin brothers, Morris and Boris, who moved to America a long time ago when they were newborns, and they had a very special talent. As they grew from babies to toddlers, they never spoke. As they grew into young children, they never spoke. Yet, when they were asked questions, they nodded yes or no. It seemed they understood their Russian parents, and their English-speaking teachers and classmates at school, but they refused to speak. They began playing card games in the park with each other when they were quite young and had earned a reputation around their neighborhood as being talented and scrupulous players. It was common for the twins to make facial expressions to one another as though they were having a conversation or disagreement or just talking about what was around them. It was as though they were conversing in their minds, and this interaction fascinated those who knew them. They became accomplished card players on an international level, and their wealth grew by millions. When they played cards, one stood on the side, while the other played against competitors. The brother standing on the side spoke to the brother playing at the card table telling him which cards his opponents had, but he did so in his mind, and no one knew that they were using their special powers. Boris became greedy. He began saying, "Kill yourself!" in his brother's mind every night while Morris slept. Boris wanted to abscond with their amassed wealth with a Spanish woman with whom he'd fallen in love. One morning, Morris awoke and in a dazed and confused act, he came into the breakfast nook where Boris sat, and turned around and closed his eyes, putting a gun in his mouth and pulling the trigger. The bullet passed through Morris' throat and into Boris' right eye, coming to a stop in his brain, killing them both instantly."

"Wow," breathed Paul. "That's quite the story, Maybel! When did you write that one? Bernard says you write a lot of stories."

"I just now wrote it in my head."

"Impressive, Maybel!"

"You create sculptures in an instant. You're quite impressive too, Paul."

Paul smiled at me. "Do you want to kiss again?"

"Yes," I giggled.

Paul moved closer and was laying in front of me. He kissed me and I kissed him back.

"You're lips still taste like ice cream from dinner," he said smiling, then kissed me again.

"Yours taste like the chocolate you had on your ice cream," I giggled. I kissed him again.

"Maybel, lay beside me tonight."

"Ok," I smiled. I put my pillow beside his pillow and laid next to him. He smiled and held my hand.

"I feel like I've known you forever," I told Paul.

"Me too, Maybel," he kissed me again and his lips lingered on mine.

We rested our heads on our pillows and faced each other and fell asleep holding hands.

In the very early morning, I awoke to Bernard picking me up and carrying me to my room. I was still half asleep when he put me on my bed. "Sleep in your own bed." Bernard left.

I fell back asleep for a little while then woke up and dressed. I went to Paul's room. He was not there. I went downstairs and found him sitting glumly at the breakfast table picking at his toast.

"Be careful sitting next to me, Maybel. Bernard is angry about us sleeping together last night."

"Why?"

"I don't know. He told me boys and girls are not supposed to sleep together. I don't think we did anything wrong. I told him my other cousins and I build forts and tell ghost stories."

"Let's leave the house after breakfast. We can play together again," I said.

"Ok, Maybel," I like that idea.

Paul and I slipped out as quickly and quietly as we could. We returned to the stream. I liked the feel of the little pebbles under my toes. Paul and I skipped stones and played in the tall grasses of the field near his house.

"I want to show you how well I can climb trees," I told Paul. "Where are your good climbing trees?"

"They're over this way, at the edge of the field."

We walked through the grasses, and when we came upon the tall oaks and maples, I shot up.

"Wow, Maybel! You're really fast and strong!"

Paul climbed up beside me, albeit much slower and more clumsily. "Maybel, look how beautiful!"

"It really is gorgeous here, Paul!"

"I meant you, Maybel; you are beautiful."

I blushed and Paul kissed me. We sat for a few minutes in the tree kissing and giggling.

We heard Paul's mother call from the back porch that it was lunch time. Reluctantly, and only after another peck on the lips, we climbed down and went inside for lunch.

I sat beside Paul and ate. We talked about classmates at school, and we learned we both hated math.

After lunch, we went outside to walk around the land surrounding Paul's house. "This is such a beautiful place, Paul. You are so lucky!"

"I really am not, Maybel. I'm always alone. No one lives near me."

"I'm always alone too," I said. "My friends don't live in town near me."

"Do you want to stay with me during the summers?" Paul asked.

"Yes, but I can't because I'll miss my family."

"Do you want to stay with Bernard during the summers?" I asked Paul.

"Yes, but I'd miss my family too."

"Maybe we can visit each other when we're older?" I smiled at him.

"I'd like that, Maybel." He held my hands and kissed me. We giggled at each other and blushed.

We explored all afternoon and talked about everything we could think about. Paul wanted to be an artist but his father wanted him to be a doctor. I wanted to be a school teacher or nurse. Paul's favorite color was green, like his eyes, while I liked light pink. Paul and I both loved freshly baked bread with strawberry jam and we both loved chocolate. We both had dark, wavy, untamable hair.

It was getting a little dark, so we began walking home to dinner. Paul held my hand. "Maybel, I want to marry you when we get older, but I think Bernard is going to marry you."

"Bernard wants to marry my sister, Catherine."

"Maybel, Bernard loves you, and he lives closer to you, so I think you will marry him instead of me, but I really wish you would marry me instead."

"I might not marry anyone. I haven't decided."

"Well if you did marry me, would you move out here?"

"Can my parents and sister come too?"

"Yes, my house is big enough."

"Ok, then I would move out here."

"I'd like that, Maybel." Paul stopped walking and pecked my lips and blushed. I giggled and kissed him back.

Paul held my hand again and we continued walking. "Why do you think Bernard wants to marry me?"

"The way he looks at you, Maybel." Paul said it like it was obvious. "He looked at you that way at Catherine's birthday party too, you know. You would have noticed if you weren't so busy throwing mud at me. And this morning before breakfast, I told my mother that Bernard was upset that we slept on my floor and she said that Bernard's mother told my mother that Bernard secretly loves you. And Bernard's mother feels inside her that you and Bernard will marry, not Bernard and Catherine."

"I've seen the way Bernard looks at Catherine. He looks at her like she's the only girl in the room, and I've seen them kiss." My eyes widened and I stared into Paul's eyes to make sure I had his attention. "Paul, they touched their tongues when they kissed!"

"Ew!" Paul made a disgusted face.

"I know! But it's true! They put their tongues in each other's mouths!" We laughed at how disgusting that was.

We arrived at Paul's home and washed up and sat next to each other at the dining room table. Paul and I didn't talk to the grownups because they were boring. We were the youngest people at Paul's house so we preferred to sit together and talk about interesting things, like what would happen if humans had large eyes like deer, and were spaced widely apart too. Would there be a blank space directly in front of us where we could not see? Would we have to constantly move our heads back and forth so we could see predators directly in front of us? Paul and I laughed at the funny things we imagined. His imagination was quite good!

After dinner, I again snuck into Paul's bedroom and we talked and giggled for a long time.

"Maybel, I've been thinking about what you said, about Bernard and Catherine touching their tongues. Do you want to try? Just for a second, to see what it feels like?"

"Well, maybe just one second. But I bet it will feel gross."

"Yes, it will probably feel gross," he agreed.

We hesitated.

"So, how do we do it?" Paul asked.

"They opened their mouths and then they touched their tongues."

"Like this?" Paul opened his mouth very wide, like he was going to scream, then stuck is tongue out as far as it would go, and I laughed so hard I almost cried!

"No, not like that," I said through giggles, "Your mouth has to be open," I couldn't stop laughing, "but only parted a little, and it's only the tip of your tongue that you touch, I think."

"Ok, show me how wide to open my mouth."

"Like this," I opened my mouth as wide as I could and stuck my tongue out as far as I could and shoved my face in Paul's face and laughed hysterically. Paul laughed too, "Ok, that does look really funny, Maybel!" He was laughing as hard as me now.

"Ok," I said trying to compose myself and stop my giggles, "let's be serious now."

Paul started giggling again, then I stared giggling again, and we just couldn't stop laughing and sticking our tongues out at each other with our mouths wide open.

"Ok, ok," Paul breathed, "Ok, I can't look at you if I want to stop giggling!" He turned his head away, still trying to catch his breath from laughter.

I turned around too until I could catch my breath.

"Are you ready, Maybel?"

"Yes."

"This time just a regular little peck on our lips, ok?"

"Ok," I said.

We turned and faced each other and leaned toward each other slowly. We pressed our lips against each other's lips and sat there looking in each other's eyes.

"Ok now what?" Paul mumbled as our lips were smooshed against each other.

"Open just a tiny bit," I mumbled, our lips still squished together.

We opened our lips just a tiny bit, still smooshing our lips together.

"Ok, now we stick our tongues out," I mumbled.

We both pushed out our tongues and immediately leaned backward wiping our mouths. "Ew!" we squealed.

"That felt so weird!" Paul laughed. "Let's try again!"

"Ok!" I giggled. "Wait, maybe if we stick our tongues out first, then lean in, it might work better."

"Ok," Paul said.

We stuck out our tongues and leaned toward each other until our tongues touched. His tongue felt warm and wet and squishy. We leaned away from each other quickly, giggling hysterically. "Maybe we're not doing it right," Paul laughed. "It feels weird."

"It does feel strange," I giggled. "We can stop."

"Maybe we just need more practice?" Paul smiled.

"Maybe," I grinned. "Bernard and Catherine just had their faces together, and their lips weren't far apart, and their tongues weren't all the way into each other's mouths."

"Ok, let's try again, but keep your tongue inside your mouth until we touch lips, and then just touch with the tips."

"Ok," I said.

We moved close together and gently touched lips, then gently parted them. I felt him breathing nervously. Our tongues lightly touched and I very gently moved my tongue against his. We closed our lips and kissed, then opened them again and Paul held my cheeks gently while he carefully pushed his tongue against mine. We looked into each other's eyes then continued gently exploring each other.

Paul and I practiced kissing for a little while until we heard movement in the hallway outside his bedroom. We quickly sat far apart. "Is the weather always this nice, Paul?" I asked as Bernard opened the door.

"Maybel, it's time for you to go to sleep in your room."

"I don't want to, I get scared. We're staying far apart on this blanket. We're not touching."

"Come, Maybel, I'll take you to your room."

I pouted. "Fine! You never let me have any fun! You're such a fuddy duddy!"

Bernard led me back to my room with his hand firmly on my shoulder. He opened my door. "Stay here."

"You act like a father. I'm not your child, Bernard!"

"Then don't act like a child and I won't have to treat you like a child!"

"This is why I only see you as a brother."

Bernard stared at me. "What?"

"I only think of you as a brother because you treat me like your little sister."

Bernard just stared at me looking confused.

"Maybel, I'm trying to protect you. I am keeping you safe."

"That may be, but when you treat me like a little sister, I only see you as a big brother."

Bernard looked at a loss for words. He turned and left, closing the door behind him.

I sat on my bed and felt lonely and scared. I laid under the covers but I couldn't sleep. I wondered why was I just now realizing how loudly the night animals screamed.

I imagined a coyote on the north side of the house screaming to his wife, "Are there any rabbits over there?"

The wife, on the south side of the house answered, "No, but there's a nosy fox nearby!"

"What?" the coyote husband screamed.

"A nosy fox!" the coyote wife repeated.

"You found a box?" he screamed back.

"Horace, you need your ears checked!" the wife screeched and yipped.

I wondered why the bird on the tree branch outside my window sounded so angry. Why were the crickets so noisy? Suddenly I heard yips and howls and a white wolf was pawing at my window! I darted down the hall and jumped into Bernard's bed and hid under the covers.

"Maybel, what's wrong?"

"The wolves are trying to get into my bedroom window!"

Bernard laughed, "This is why I treat you like a baby! You act like one!" he laughed again.

"They were right outside my window, Bernard! They were going to eat me!"

"Ok, baby, you can sleep here tonight, but you don't have to lie."

"I am not lying!" I wailed.

"Go to sleep Maybel. We leave in the morning."

"If we're still alive!"

"Baby!" he laughed.

I crawled closer to him and shoved my face into the back of his neck.

"Maybel are you cold?"

"No."

"You're shivering!"

"I'm scared, Bernard!" I began crying.

Bernard rolled over and faced me. "Maybel, what has you so upset?" He looked worried.

"There was a white wolf trying to get into my bedroom window, Bernard! I told you already!" I shook and cried.

"Come here, Maybel," he sighed and pulled me against him. "I've got you. I won't let anything hurt you, sweetheart." Bernard's voice was soothing as he stroked my hair. I began to stop shaking and slowly fell asleep in his arms.

I awoke the next morning still clinging tightly to Bernard. I hadn't slept well. "Bernard," I whispered. "Are you awake?"

"No," he whispered back.

"Bernard, do you want to get up now?"

"No," he whispered.

"It's morning," I said.

"The sun's not up yet."

"There's a little light."

"Go to sleep, Maybel," he rested his head on mine and stroked my hair. I felt myself relaxing and I fell back asleep.

I woke up again to Bernard lightly shaking my shoulder. "Maybel, it's morning. You're still alive," he chuckled.

I opened my eyes and watched Bernard. "Thank you, Bernard."

"You're welcome, little baby," he winked at me.

I wrapped my arms around him and hugged him and he kissed the top of my head. "Come Maybel, it's time for breakfast and then we go home."

"You're excited to see Catherine again, aren't you?"

"Yes," he smiled. His head rested on his pillow and his hair was tousled and messy.

"I'm leaving Paul and I'm very sad." I laid under the warm blankets and I didn't want to get up.

"I'm sorry, Maybel, but who knows, maybe you'll see him again next year, or in a couple years. You'll be fine."

"Easy for you to say. The love of your life lives just down the street from you"

"Yes, she does." Bernard smiled at me.

"Paul lives two nights away," I sighed dramatically.

"Paul is the love of your life?" Bernard asked sarcastically.

"Yes," I said definitively.

"You barely know him."

"How long until you knew Catherine was the love of your life?"

"Let's just go eat breakfast, Maybel. You're too young to fall in love."

"I love you," I said.

"You have made it quite clear you only love me as a brother," he said, looking annoyed.

"Aren't you going to say you love me back?" I pouted.

"I love you too, Maybel," he sighed and pulled me into a hug.

"If things don't work out with me and Paul, I'll marry you, Bernard." I rolled over on top of his stomach.

"I'm your second choice?" He looked annoyed again.

"Well, if you must know, you were my first choice, but Catherine seems to really like you, so I guess I'll let her keep you." I looked down at him and rested my forehead on his forehead and giggled.

Bernard laughed, "Very kind of you." He tickled my waist.

"I'm a good sister." I tickled his neck.

"Come, Maybel," he spanked my bottom lightly, "It's time to go eat, then go home."

"Ok," I groaned and rolled off him and slowly slid myself off the bed and onto the floor. "Ohhhh," I whined dramatically, "I'll miss you Paul!" I made kissing noises with my lips.

"You better not be kissing anyone," Bernard got out of bed and went to his dresser. He only wore undershorts.

"How were you not freezing last night if all you wore to bed were undershorts?"

"Because you clung to me all night long like a hot, little blanket that wouldn't stop snoring!"

Bernard dressed while I stretched and rolled around. "I think you're right, Bernard, I can't sit still."

"No, you absolutely cannot!" Bernard bent down to pick me up then threw me over his shoulder and took me to my bedroom. "Get dressed," he said as he closed my door then left.

I dressed and skipped down to breakfast. I ran to sit by Paul. "Hi, Paul!" I smiled.

"Maybel! Did you know there were wolves outside last night?"

"I know! A white wolf pawed at my window trying to get inside!"

"Really?" Paul's eyes were wide. "Let's go see if it left paw prints below your window!"

The house was partially built into a hill so that the second story bedroom where I slept was by the top of the hill. "Maybel! There really are wolf prints under your window! There're huge!"

We ran back to the dining room and Paul couldn't wait to shout out what had happened. Everyone looked amused until we led them to the bedroom window where I'd seen the white wolf.

"See, Bernard! Look how big that paw print is! I told you I saw a white wolf pawing at my window!"

"A white wolf? Really?" Bernard's mother asked.

"Yes!" I said excitedly. "It was howling at me and pawed at my window!"

"Well, that's quite interesting, Maybel, sweetheart. Indians believe that indicates the white wolf is your protector."

"She tried to eat me, Mrs. Charleston!"

"She was saying 'hello,'" Mrs. Charleston giggled and hugged me.

"Maybe next time she can say 'hello' with less teeth!"

Mrs. Charleston giggled again. "I absolutely adore you, Maybel," she held my hand. "Let's finish breakfast, shall we?"

After breakfast I went to Paul's room with him. We closed his door and giggled as we kissed and touched tongues again. We giggled and kissed for several minutes until we heard Paul's mother calling us downstairs.

After one last kiss we went downstairs. I boarded a carriage along with Bernard and his parents. Paul and I waved to each other until we could no longer see each other. Bernard had been watching me. I rested my head back on the seat and watched out the window quietly until we arrived at the train station. I felt lonely and sad.

I sulked in a chair by myself in a common area in the train.

"Ah, there you are," Mr. Charleston sat in a chair beside me.

"I miss my daddy," I said, as I went and sat on his lap. He put an arm around me and pulled me into a hug. "I'm sorry, sweetheart, you'll see him soon." He kissed the top of my head.

"You and my nephew Paul seemed to get along well. Are you sad that you've left him?"

"Yes," I said, my lips were pouty.

"I'm sorry, honey. It's not fair that things change."

"And Bernard doesn't like me. He always says I'm annoying and my hair is messy and that I'm a tag-along," I fought back tears.

"Oh sweetheart," he chuckled, "I used to tease Bernard's mother like that. It wasn't right. I shouldn't have done it. I suppose looking back, I didn't know how to tell her I loved her. I hope Bernard hasn't inherited my inability to express myself honestly."

"Can I just sit here with you?"

"Yes, of course sweetheart," he kissed the top of my head again.

"Mr. Charleston, did Bernard sit on your lap when he was a boy?"

"Yes, he did."

"Did he call you daddy when he was young?"

"Yes, he did. I miss those days more than he'll ever know." Mr. Charleston's countenance took on a sadness as he stared out the window at the passing trees. His breath slowed and I felt a deep longing inside him for a past long gone.

"Did his mother rub his tummy when he had a tummy ache?"

"Yes, she did," he still stared out the window but he was really looking inward.

"That's good. Bernard has good parents."

"Thank you, honey." Mr. Charleston patted my shoulder.

I wrapped my arms around his neck and fell asleep on his lap.

I awoke to Mrs. Charleston rubbing my back. "Maybel, dear, it will be dinner time soon. Why don't you go get washed up?" she smiled at me.

I looked around still half asleep. I looked at Mr. Charleston. He was asleep with his arm still around me holding me.

I patted his shoulder and he awoke and saw me still sitting on his lap and smiled kindly.

I sat up and steadied myself. I must have been in a deep sleep. "I didn't sleep well last night Mrs. Charleston. The wolf scared me."

"I know sweetheart, you're safe with us."

I stood up and hugged Mrs. Charleston and she wrapped her arms tightly around me and kissed my cheek. "You're a good girl, Maybel," she kissed my cheek again.

"You're a good mommy," I said. She smiled at me sweetly.

"I'm going to go get ready for dinner." I left but before I was out of sight, I turned and saw Mrs. Charleston wipe a tear from her eye then sit in the chair next to Mr. Charleston and they held hands.

I went to my car and brushed my hair. I put a bow in my hair. I checked my fingernails for dirt and I looked in the mirror to make sure my face was clean.

I heard Bernard moving around in his room but I didn't knock. I decided to go to the dining car without him. He would probably be happy to be rid of me soon, I decided.

I stepped out of my room and walked to the dining car. I saw Mr. and Mrs. Charleston. I smiled and waved to them and sat down across from them.

"Is Bernard not coming?" Mrs. Charleston asked.

I heard him getting ready in his car but I came without him.

"Oh? Are you two in an argument?"

"No, but he thinks I'm a baby, and I have messy hair, and I'm an annoying tag-along. I think he's just tired of babysitting me."

Mrs. Charleston put her hand to her face and giggled loudly. "Oh, I'm sorry, Maybel, Bernard should be nicer to you. It's just that it reminds me of Bernard's father!"

She turned to look at Mr. Charleston who started laughing loudly. "It is like me, isn't it dear!" he laughed.

"You were so mean and I thought I hated you!" she giggled uncontrollably.

"I'm so sorry, my dear," he kissed her sweetly and she giggled again.

"Maybel I do believe Bernard simply doesn't know how to show his affection. I think it must be a Charleston male trait." Mrs. Charleston suppressed a giggle and patted Mr. Charleston's hand.

"Paul was very kind and expressive," I said.

"He's not a Charleston honey, that's probably why he's nice," Mrs. Charleston giggled as Mr. Charleston grumbled.

"He's not a Charleston?"

"No dear," Mrs. Charleston said. "He's my sister's son."

"Oh. What's his last name?"

"Cambridge."

"Paul Cambridge?"

"Yes, honey."

"Your last name used to be Cambridge?"

"No, honey, it was Fox. My sister married a man with the last name Cambridge."

"Oh, I love the last name Fox. If I could pick any last name it would be Fox because I love foxes!"

"I do too, sweetheart," she smiled at me.

"I thought Paul was a Charleston because he said his grandmother loved art, and Bernard said his grandmother loved art, so I assumed they had the same grandmother."

"Both my mother and Mr. Charleston's mother love art," Mrs. Charleston explained.

Bernard arrived finally. "I looked all over for you!" Bernard huffed angrily as he sat beside me at our table.

"Well, not all over. You didn't check the dining car until just now," I said.

Mr. Charleston laughed as he buttered his toast, "She has a point, son."

"Why did you leave without me?" Bernard unbuttoned his suit jacket and put his napkin in his lap.

"I figured you had babysat me long enough."

Bernard looked at me and then at his parents. "Alright then."

He seemed annoyed at me. Bernard always seemed annoyed at me these days. He used to never get annoyed at me.

As we ate dinner a violinist played not far away. Her music was beautiful. I couldn't stop staring.

"You like the violinist, Maybel, don't you?" Mrs. Charleston asked.

"She's amazing," I awed.

"Mother plays violin," Bernard said.

"Can I hear you play sometime?"

"Of course, Maybel. I'll let you play it, too."

"Oh, I don't know how to play."

"You'll learn if you want to learn," she said.

I smiled at Mrs. Charleston. "I really like you," I said.

Mrs. Charleston giggled and looked at her husband and back at me. "I really like you, too, sweetheart."

After dinner Mr. Charleston asked Bernard and me what we'd like to do before it was time to go to bed. "I'd like to learn how to gamble," I said.

Mr. Charleston laughed, "Oh would you now?"

"Yes," I said.

"You can't gamble, Maybel, you're horrible at math," Bernard said.

"Why do I need to be good at math?"

"Because that's the foundation on which card games are built," Bernard said. Bernard, as had become customary, seemed annoyed at me.

"Bernard, when you lie, your right eyebrow goes up. When you are eager about something, you're left thumb twitches."

"That's not true!"

"Your right eyebrow just raised!" Mr. Charleston slapped the table with his hand and roared with laughter. "Son, playing cards is about math, but it's also about tells."

"What are tells?" I asked.

"You understand people, Maybel. You can see their tells. You see what they are accidentally telling you without realizing they are telling you."

After dinner I went with Mr. Charleston to the car where the grownups played cards. I sat on his lap and picked which poker cards to play.

We won one thousand dollars. The other players became angry. "You all have tells," I said.

Mr. Charleston chuckled, "She can see every tell you make, fellas."

"I have no tells!" An elderly man with a long, white beard and mustache said indignantly.

"When you bluff you tap your left foot lightly."

"I have never done such a thing, young lady!"

"Actually George, you have," said another elderly man.

"And when you get happy like you are about to win something, you lick your lips," I told that other elderly man and he looked miffed.

"Alright, fellas, you can have your money back if my little girl here doesn't win the next round. If she wins, though, she keeps the money."

There were nods and grunts around the table.

I picked the cards Mr. Charleston should use. He was hesitant about the last card, but I won.

"You looked unsure about the last card," I whispered to Mr. Charleston, "but you weren't unsure. You only acted that way to confuse the fellas."

Mr. Charleston chuckled and kissed my cheek, "My God Maybel, I adore you, sweetheart!"

We kindly accepted our earnings and Mr. Charleston took me to my car and handed me the money. "Put this in a safe place, dear. You earned it," he kissed my cheek. "Have good dreams, honey."

I hugged him and went into my car. The door between Bernard's and my room was open. I went to Bernard. "Why is our door open?" I laid next to him.

"To save you the trouble of knocking, and me the trouble of having to get up and open the door."

"Well, I'm sleeping in my bed tonight!"

"Ok, Maybel," he continued reading without looking up at me.

I went back and started to undress.

"Close the door Maybel!"

"No! Just keep reading! I haven't grown any breasts anyway, so it's not like you'd see anything!"

"I'm not your real brother," he reminded me.

"Well, you sure act like it!"

I dressed in my nightgown and went back to Bernard's bed. He didn't look up. "Why are you here? You said you were sleeping in your bed tonight."

"I am."

"Then go."

"Do you want to come with me?" I asked shyly.

Bernard laughed, "I knew you were a baby!"

"Bernard," I whined, "please?"

"No."

I laid next to him. "Can I stay here then?"

Bernard looked up from his book. "Why are you scared?"

"I don't know." I played with the bed sheets. "I just am."

Bernard sighed, "You can sleep here." He went back to reading.

"Bernard?"

"What, Maybel?" he asked, annoyed.

"Why are you always annoyed at me nowadays?"

"Because you're young, and immature, and a baby, and I'm not used to having to babysit you all day, every day. You're tiring."

I sighed and laid next to him.

"You used to be nicer," I finally said.

"Well, why do you keep thinking I'm your brother? I'm not."

"I thought you were my brother because you were really nice to me and you were dating my sister. Now you don't seem to like me very much and you think I'm annoying and a tag-along and you make fun of my messy hair."

"Maybel, I like you."

"Then act like you like me."

"I don't know how to act like I like you without people thinking I'm in love with you!"

"Who thinks that?"

"Catherine thinks I love you."

"I love you, too."

"No, Maybel, Catherine thinks I am in love with you."

"Are you?"

"No! You're too young!"

"You raised your right eyebrow."

"Just go to sleep!" he yelled at me.

"Bernard?"

"What now Maybel?" He seemed really angry.

"Will you hold me?"

"Brothers don't hold sisters, Maybel! And since you only think of me as a brother, I can't hold you!"

I laid on my side and rested my head next to his shoulder. "What are you reading?"

"A book about medicine."

"Did you know your mother knows about plants that heal?"

"Yes."

"She's really smart."

"I know."

"Have you asked her to teach you about the plants? When you're a doctor that will be helpful."

"Yes, Maybel, now go to sleep!"

I played with my fingers making different shapes, and with Bernard's hair, trying to comb it with my fingers. I read a page of his book. Then, being extremely bored, I began narrating everything Bernard did.

"The boy reads a book, he looks interested, yet, he is unsure of the contents of the book. It confuses him. He furrows his brow. He looks over at the girl next to him."

"Maybel! Shut up!"

"He yells at her to shut up, but deep down he wants to play with her. He wants to wrestle. Yes, wrestling would be fun, he thinks. He furrows his brow again."

"Maybel! Shut up!"

"He again tells the kind, little, peasant girl to be quiet. The girl is sad. She wonders why he doesn't like her anymore. He used to be nice to her, she muses. But now everything she does annoys the boy."

Bernard turned his head and looked at me. "Are you done?"

"Yes," I pouted. I put my head on Bernard's shoulder and wrapped my arm around his chest. I kissed his cheek. "I love you, Bernard" I whispered.

Bernard paused and breathed in, "I love you too, Maybel," he exhaled, "even though you are exasperating." He let his book fall to the floor. He reached up and turned off his lamplight then wrapped his arm around me. "Goodnight."

The next morning I awoke clinging to Bernard. I'd had a bad dream that Bernard and I were running toward each other, and we were so happy to see each other, then a bullet struck his chest and he died in my arms. I woke up clinging to Bernard feeling like I was losing him all over again.

"Bernard," I cried. "Don't die! Please don't die!"

Bernard opened his eyes and looked at me. "What?"

"I love you and I never got to tell you I loved you, and I never got to kiss you either!"

"Maybel, what is going on?"

I cried and held Bernard.

"Maybel, I'm right here. I'm ok!"

"Bernard, I didn't get a chance to tell you I love you! But I do love you! And I never got a chance to kiss you!"

"Maybel, it was just a dream! You're awake now. I'm alive. You're alive."

I looked at Bernard next to me. "You have to understand that I love you, Bernard."

"I love you too, Maybel." He wrapped his arms around me and rubbed my back gently. "Shh, sweetheart, I'm ok. I'm ok. I'm alive." he whispered over and over.

After Bernard calmed me down, I told him my dream. "It was so real," I said. "It was real."

I looked into Bernard's eyes as he laid next to me. "It's really important that you know I love you, Bernard."

"I love you too, Maybel."

I leaned forward and kissed his lips. "I didn't get to kiss you back then."

"Maybel, let's go to breakfast and you'll start to shake off this dream and wake up."

The rest of the day on the train I followed Bernard around like a puppy. I knew I was being silly, but my dream had felt so real that my soul still felt sad. I didn't want to be apart from Bernard.

Fortunately, Bernard was not too annoyed at me for gluing myself to him. He was more understanding and sympathetic than other boys his age.

I held Bernard's hand and he led me to a car with sofas and chairs and when he sat down in one of the large, overstuffed chairs, I sat on his lap. "I'm fine Maybel, I'm not about to be shot."

"I just want to be with you, ok."

"Ok, Maybel," he sighed.

"Why do girls always watch you?"

"What girls?"

"Every girl we pass, and every girl that walks past us, stares at you."

"Do I have food on my face?"

"No."

"Then I don't know," Bernard said. He looked out the window.

"It's not just today. It happens every day and everywhere we go."

"That's funny, Catherine says the same thing."

"Do you know them? Are they your cousins?" I asked. "You seem to have a lot of cousins."

"No, I don't know them."

"Then why do they watch you?"

"I don't know, Maybel. Catherine says they're attracted to me."

"Well, you do look nice. I wouldn't stare at you, but you are attractive."

"You look nice too, Maybel."

"Then why don't boys stare at me?"

"Probably because I'd punch them."

"Oh," I paused, "Should I go punch those girls?"

"No, please don't."

"Why would you punch boys if they stared at me then?"

"Because I don't want boys to look at you."

"Why?"

"Because I don't want boys to flirt with you."

"Boys don't flirt with me. They all like Catherine."

"Yes, I've noticed," Bernard said drolly.

"Do you go punch the boys who stare at Catherine?"

"No."

"Why not?"

"Catherine is older than you, and a lot less naive about the world. She can protect herself better than you."

"So you are trying to protect me?"

"Yes."

"See, you treat me like your little sister."

"I suppose I do," he paused and thought about his response. "Maybel, when I protect you, do you then see me as your big brother?"

"Yes, I suppose. I like when you protect me though, Bernard. It means you care about me."

"That I do."

"Bernard, do think of me as your little sister then?"

"No, Maybel. I don't."

"I don't understand. You treat me like your little sister, but you don't think of me as your little sister?"

"I don't mean to treat you like my little sister. You think I'm treating you like a sister, but I'm not. I'm looking out for you and protecting you, but I don't do that because I think of you as my sister."

"Then how do you think of me?" I asked.

"I'm confused about how I feel. I don't know," he said. Bernard looked agitated and uncomfortable.

"When will boys look at me the way they look at Catherine?"

"They probably do now, but you don't seem to see what is right in front of you," he said sourly.

I leaned back into Bernard's chest and sighed. "I like being with you, Bernard. Tonight is our last night together."

"I hope not," Bernard said softly, kind of like he was in a daydream.

"Do you want to spend the night at my house tomorrow night?" I asked him.

"I'm certain I would not be allowed."

"Then can I spend the night at your house? I like being with you," I told him.

Bernard laughed, "I'm absolutely certain your parents would not allow that."

"I've really enjoyed sleeping with you these past several nights." I turned my head to look up at him as I laid back against his chest.

"Sleeping in the same bed, not sleeping with me," Bernard corrected me.

"What's the difference?"

"I'm sure your mother will explain it soon. You're getting old enough to need to know those things."

"Why can't you tell me?"

"It's something your mother will talk to you about," Bernard said.

"But you're going to be a doctor. You can tell me like I'm your patient, can't you?" I asked hopefully. I didn't understand nuances and I wanted to understand everything everyone said and did.

"I'm sure your mother will tell you soon."

"Well, I want to know now."

"Maybel, just sit here and relax. Some quiet time would be nice."

"Fine," I pouted.

I rested my head on Bernard's shoulder.

"You smell good." I turned my head back around and smelled Bernard's neck.

"Stop sniffing me," Bernard laughed, "That tickles!"

I slowly blew my breath at his ear. Bernard closed his eyes. He was ignoring me.

I blew on his neck. His eyes were still closed. He's still ignoring me, I thought.

I played with the waves and curls in his hair. I wound the curls around my finger then another finger. I fidgeted with Bernard's shirt buttons. Finally, I bored myself to sleep.

"Wake up, Maybel," Bernard rubbed my arms. I halfway opened my eyes.

"Let's go back to our room. This chair isn't as comfortable as our bed."

I held Bernard's hand and we went back to our room. I stumbled several times as I was still half asleep. Bernard laid down and reached for me. I crawled in beside him and he wrapped his arms around me.

"I'm glad you didn't get shot today," I said.

"Me too."

I snoozed in and out of sleep for a short time, then got out of bed. I stretched and yawned.

Bernard looked up at me. "It's probably time for dinner. We should get ready," he mumbled, still trying to wake up.

I went to my car and undressed.

"Close the door! I'm not your real brother!"

"There's nothing to see! I told you, I don't have breasts yet! Have you seen Catherine's? They're huge! Mine are barely there."

"No! I have not seen Catherine's!" Bernard yelled from his room.

"When will mine get big like Catherine's?"

"I don't know, Maybel! Why are you asking me such questions?"

"Because you're going to be a doctor! You should know these things!" I yelled back to him.

I finished putting my nice dress on and sat to brush my hair. I fixed a ribbon in my hair. I noticed Bernard had been standing in our doorway watching me.

"You can come in, Bernard. I'm completely dressed. You can barely see my ankles in this long dress."

Bernard sat on the bed beside me and took my hairbrush. He began gently brushing my hair. It felt really relaxing having him brush my hair. I smiled at him. He smiled softly back. "I'll miss you when we return home tomorrow," he said.

"I thought you were tired of babysitting me."

"No, you're fun to be around to be honest," he said.

"Come to my house tomorrow night."

He chuckled, "I really will get shot in my chest then, by your father."

"Climb the tree by my window. We can see each other and tell ghost stories and you can show me more constellations through my bedroom window."

"I would love that, but I can't."

"Ok," I said moping.

"Come," he held my hand. "Let's go to dinner."

"Can I sleep with you?" I asked.

Bernard was reading in his bed. We had finished dinner and were now dressed in our night clothes and ready for sleep.

"Why do you even bother asking?" Bernard didn't bother looking up from his medical journal.

"I'm polite," I said, and climbed in bed beside Bernard.

Bernard continued reading. I watched his eyes move as he read. Left to right, down, and repeat. Suddenly they looked right at me and I jumped slightly. "What?" Bernard asked, annoyed.

"I was only watching your eyes move."

"Why?"

"They went left to right, then down, then left to right, then down,"

"I know how reading works, Maybel. Stop staring at me."

"Why do you and Catherine touch tongues when you kiss?"

"What?" Bernard looked shocked.

"You and Catherine open your mouths and touch each other's tongues. Why do you do that?"

"When did you see us kissing?"

"I don't remember the day. Two, three weeks ago?"

"Why were you watching us?"

"I didn't go out of my way to watch, but when I saw you, I didn't stop watching," I admitted.

"Maybel," Bernard said irritated, "don't watch us kiss."

"Why do you want to use your tongue to touch Catherine's tongue?"

Bernard shifted uncomfortably. "I don't know, it's just how you kiss when you get older."

"It feels weird though, like a wet, warm, squishy sponge."

Bernard looked angry suddenly. "And how would you know?"

"I'm just guessing." I said sheepishly.

"Did Paul kiss you with his tongue."

"No."

Bernard relaxed.

"He kissed me with his lips. It was my idea for us to touch tongues."

Bernard looked really angry now.

"I would have punched Paul had I known."

"That's why I didn't tell you."

"Do not kiss boys, Maybel!"

"I just wanted to know what it felt like. You and Catherine seemed to really enjoy licking each other's tongues."

Bernard's face grew bright red.

"Your face is red. Are you mad or embarrassed?"

"Both!"

"I didn't care much for touching tongues. I liked kissing lips better. I can't say I'm fond of either though."

"Well, maybe it's because you don't know how to kiss since you're both babies!"

"I know how to kiss!"

"Obviously not! If you didn't like it, you were probably doing it wrong! Just wait until you're older and know how to use your body."

"How do you use a body?"

"Never mind, Maybel! Just stop talking or go to your own bed! You're annoying!"

"Fine! You're more annoying than me!"

Bernard laughed, "You don't even realize you just called yourself annoying!"

"No, I didn't!"

"You said I'm more annoying than you!"

"Well, you are more annoying!" I told him.

"No that's not, you know what, I'm not even going to continue this stupid conversation!"

Bernard continued reading and I continued watching his eyes.

"You'll eventually tire of staring at me." Bernard turned a page of his book.

"You obviously underestimate my anger, stubbornness, and sheer will." I continued staring.

Bernard slammed his book shut, but I didn't jump. He rolled over and faced me. He stared at me. I stared back at him.

We continued staring intently into each other's eyes.

"I enjoyed kissing Catherine with my tongue!" Bernard stared at me.

"Paul and I kissed over and over again until we figured out how to touch our tongues the way I saw you and Catherine do." I stared at him.

"You have dry lips, you slobber, and your hair is messy." Bernard crossed his arms.

"You have dry lips, you slobber, and your hair is messy," I said. I crossed my arms.

"Can't come up with your own insults, Maybel? Have to steal mine?"

He hasn't blinked yet, I thought to myself. He's good, I mused.

"Paul liked it when I flicked my tongue." I stared intently.

"I'm sure you drooled on him." Bernard stared intently.

"And I liked it when he kissed right here on my lips!" I puckered my lips.

"You look like a fish!"

"You're not a good kisser, Bernard!"

"Better than you!"

"Not anymore! I practiced a lot the past several days!"

"I'm sure you are nowhere nearly as good as Catherine!"

"I'm sure Paul is more sensitive with his touch than you!" I gritted my teeth.

"I'm sure Paul better not have touched you!" Bernard growled.

"Blink, Bernard!"

"You blink first, Maybel!"

I moved my face closer to Bernard's and stared.

Bernard moved his face closer to mine and stared.

I licked the tip of Bernard's nose.

"See, slobber."

I flicked his nose with my tongue.

"You drool."

I moved my face as close to Bernard's as I could possibly get without actually touching his lips and I stared widely into his eyes. "Blink, Bernard!"

Bernard moved closer and his lips lightly brushed mine and his gaze was just as unflinching as mine. "You blink, Maybel!"

I pressed my lips harder against his lips.

"See, you have dry lips Maybel."

"You have dry lips, Bernard."

Our lips remained pressed against each other's lips as we stared into each other's eyes.

I very slowly opened my mouth just a tiny bit.

Bernard slowly opened his mouth just a tiny bit.

I gently flicked my tongue along his upper lip.

Bernard put his hand on the back of my neck and pushed his tongue gently into my mouth and lightly flicked my tongue with his. He kissed me and pulled me close and gently explored my mouth with his tongue. I began breathing hard and then he kissed my neck and I moaned.

Bernard pulled back, "Maybel, I'm sorry!"

"That was so much better than Paul!" I breathed deeply.

"I've had more practice."

"It shows," I swallowed hard. "I'm not as good as you. I didn't know where to put my tongue or how far to push."

"You'll learn," Bernard breathed hard too.

I looked over at Bernard and I really wanted to kiss him again.

"Maybel, you don't understand what happens next. We have to stop."

Bernard placed a pillow between us.

I felt very confused. I didn't know what to say. I didn't know what to do. I had never felt the way Bernard had just made me feel.

We continued watching each other in silence. I felt awkward and didn't know how to make things normal again.

"Maybel, I'm so sorry," Bernard whispered. "I let things get carried away."

"I did too," I whispered back.

We watched each other a while longer, then Bernard reached over and turned off the lamp and there was complete silence.

We arrived safely home and the Charlestons took me to my house by carriage. I saw Catherine and Bernard together the next day. I was sitting outside in the garden reading when I saw them stroll by hand-in-hand. They were laughing and whispering to each other.

Bernard held her gently around her waist and kissed her. He pushed his tongue into her mouth.

I looked down at my papers. A teardrop fell onto my handwriting. Another teardrop fell and splattered, smearing my letters.

I kept looking down. I wasn't writing.

"Maybel," Catherine called, "I didn't realize you were here!"

I stared downward and hoped they hadn't seen several more teardrops fall. Seeing Bernard kiss Catherine made me shake with anger and sadness. I didn't know which emotion I felt most as they both bubbled to my surface and vied for dominance.

I tucked my chin deeper into my chest. I didn't want them to come closer and see me shaking, or the tears dripping onto my papers.

I heard them giggling again and walking away.

I couldn't move. I hadn't decided if I was crying because I was mad or sad, but I cried hard.

I ran to my room and cried. I didn't understand why I was so upset. I'd seen Bernard kiss Catherine before.

I didn't understand how Bernard had made me feel so special yesterday and then today it was like I had never existed.

I laid in bed crying. Whenever I felt a buildup of emotions that I didn't understand and couldn't sort, I wrote.

I began my story about a boy I named Bad. Bad stole and hurt. He was handsome and everyone liked him but he was full of lemon juice inside. The lemon juice came out when he cried. And since Bad was too bad to cry, the lemon juice began eating away at his insides. He had stomach aches. He thought it was because he overindulged in sweets and custards. He could never satisfy his hunger or thirst and kept eating chocolates and candies while his insides rotted away.

I was so angry at Bad. I wrote that he slowly and painfully dissolved into a puddle that I then splashed in, kicking about the remainder of his guts. Then, slowly, the lemon juice began peeling away the flesh on my ankles and shins. My toes dissolved and my body slowly sank and dissolved into the puddle where Bad pooled.

This is a stupid story, I thought, and balled up my paper and threw it at my door!

I was so angry but I couldn't understand why. I really wanted Bernard and Catherine to go away forever! Then I felt guilty. I didn't want to feel guilty. I wanted to bash Bernard's skull in with a rock but I couldn't pinpoint exactly why.

I decided to row to my island and stay until I could sort out these feelings that I couldn't understand.

I barged downstairs. No one was in the kitchen. I grabbed bread to take with me in case it took a long time to figure out why I felt so angry and confused.

I walked to the little row boat with my bread, but the geese I fed thought the bread was for them, and charged me. These evil, little, winged demons I'd fed since they were but babies chased me and bit my thighs and bottom. I ran toward my house vowing never to feed the little Hell Spawn again!

Catherine and Bernard rounded the corner of the garden to see what commotion was unfolding. I threw the loaf at Bernard's head and he instinctively caught it. The biting, little demons swarmed Bernard, making appetizers of his legs. He tripped, and they bit his ears and neck. Catherine screamed as they nipped her pretty, little legs and fingers as she batted them away. And to my thrill and delight, Bernard unsuccessfully battled his demonic swarm of hellions. He had bloody little bite marks on his hands and forearms.

I ran inside and up to my room, slamming my door. I felt vindicated, but also guilty, and then happy, too.

I heard Bernard and Catherine slam the front door, and then I heard Catherine's shrieks. "Maybel!" she screamed. "Why did the geese attack us?" she demanded.

"I think they were mad about something, Catherine!" I screamed back at her.

I heard gun shots. I looked out my window and saw two geese fall from the sky. Bernard had murdered two of my little, winged demons! I now wished I would have had more bread to throw at him. I was angry he shot them, but happy to see blood trickling from his neck.

I hoped he formed scars because Catherine was too consumed with appearances to let him shove his tongue down her throat then!

The geese bites were superficial and no one sustained any long-lasting injuries. I was still angry though. After much thought, and writing many, angry stories wherein a boy gets beaten, I deduced that I was angry at Bernard for kissing Catherine after our trip out west because it was as though I no longer mattered. I'd seen them kiss before and had never gotten upset. I was confused, and my confusion simmered into anger, and then sometimes sadness.

I began writing more. Writing helped me get my anger and confusion out of my mind and onto paper where it wouldn't hurt me anymore.

I wrote about a girl named Maude. Maude drank from a well that tapped into the underground water supply that ran underneath a chain of mountains. The well water was clean and pure and had no distinctive taste. One day, Maude went to the well, and the trees at the foothills of the mountain chain began to talk to her. Maude had always wondered what trees talked about.

"Maude," one large pine addressed her, "don't drink from this well. A wicked witch poisoned the water. You should look elsewhere."

There was no other place from where to draw water, Maude thought, so she drew water from the well.

"Maude," a large oak tree spoke, "You will slowly dwindle if you drink this water."

Maude drank the water. Nothing happened. Maude smirked up at the trees, "I always thought trees would talk about interesting things, not give warnings to little girls," she said.

"Maude," a maple tree warned, "You'll slowly go away. You'll slowly disappear. Go find your sustenance somewhere else."

Maude drank from the well and continued drinking from the well until one morning when she went to town, no one responded to her pleas for help. Maude looked down and could not see her feet or hands or belly. Maude had indeed dwindled and waned until she was but nothing. She was invisible. No one could hear her or see her.

After I finished the story, I reread it. I wasn't sure I liked it. It seemed too plain. I liked the talking tree part and I thought about how to incorporate that into a future story.

I stayed away from Catherine, but mostly because she was always with Bernard, and Bernard was the one toward whom I directed my wrath.

I didn't think I wanted to be Bernard's girlfriend. I kept seeing in my mind how he kissed me, then immediately took up with Catherine as though his kiss with me never happened. He erased me. And now I was unseen. That was what upset me. I felt better after having deduced and pinpointed the cause of my ire.

I also realized, after having written a story wherein two sisters killed each other by stabbing each other with six-inch hat pins, that I was more mad at myself than anyone else for having kissed my sister's boyfriend. I was a very bad sister.

I wanted to confess to Catherine, but I loved Catherine, and didn't want her to never speak to me again. I imagined telling her what happened and she locked me away in a tower, never speaking to me again. She stayed with her Prince Bernard, and the only one to suffer for transgressions was me. I saw myself thrown from the tower and locked away in the dungeon to be spat on by Catherine and Bernard and their children. I could not imagine, in my great and vivid imagination, a story where I was not labeled a loose woman, a bad sister, or a damned soul. I couldn't understand how Bernard's transgressions would have no consequences. And mostly, I was hurt that in none of my mental scenarios Catherine would side with me instead of Bernard.

After we had returned home, I immediately missed Paul. All my school friends lived way out in the countryside. Paul was so much like me, and I missed him greatly.

"Can we return to Paul in the fall?" I asked Bernard. We were in Bernard's drawing room where he and Catherine had been sitting in front of the fireplace. There was no fire as it was a warm day. Catherine had left to get tea and cookies for us.

"No, we are not returning in the fall." Bernard barely looked up from his science book.

"Spring?"

"No." Bernard's voice was low and droll.

"Next summer?" I asked, hopefully.

"No, Maybel! Trips like that take time and money! It will be years before we even consider returning!"

"Catherine says you're rich," I said. "She says you have been to Europe more times than you can remember. You can afford a train ride to Paul's house."

"Maybe I can," Bernard seethed, "But you cannot afford it, and I'm not paying for you to go kiss my cousin with your tongue again!" Bernard slammed shut his book and when he stood up, his chair fell backward to the floor.

"I'm saving my money, Bernard! I'm going to go back to Paul!" I said.

"Do you really think Paul will want you then? By the time you save up enough money and return, he'll have moved on, as should you!"

"You're mean!" I yelled at Bernard.

"I'm only bringing you truth. You are too idealistic."

"I don't like you anymore, Bernard!" I cried.

Catherine came into the drawing room and saw me crying. "What's wrong, Maybel?"

"Bernard says Paul won't want to be with me." I felt heartbroken because I had not considered Paul not wanting to see me when I had saved up enough money to travel to his house.

"Why would you say that?" Catherine looked puzzled.

"By the time Maybel saves up her money to visit Paul, he'll have a girlfriend. I told Maybel to move on." Bernard had picked up his chair from the floor where it toppled and sat in it again. He watched me and he didn't look happy.

"Maybel," Catherine said kindly, "if he loves you, he'll wait."

Catherine turned to Bernard, "Do you, or do you not, wait for me all those long months in your boarding school?"

"I wait for you, Catherine. I don't cheat while I'm away at school."

"Do you cheat when you're not away at school?" I asked. I had heard Catherine speak to our parents, and she always worded everything carefully. Catherine didn't lie, but she certainly didn't tell the truth.

"No," Bernard said through gritted teeth.

"I read about half truths, Bernard. Have you read about half truths, Catherine? It's when someone tells you something that's true, but they word it to veil a lie." I watched Bernard as I spoke because we both knew he was lying about kissing someone who was not Catherine.

Catherine looked flushed. "I'm sorry I went with Rebecca instead of going out west with you, Bernard. I wanted to try my independence. I know I hurt you, and I'm sorry. I didn't kiss anyone there."

"Let's just go," Bernard said as he furrowed his brow at me. Bernard and Catherine left.

I walked home, kicking rocks and acorns all the way. I helped mommy prepare food then sat at the table in the family room and wrote.

Just before dinner was ready, Catherine and Bernard came home. Catherine went upstairs to brush her hair since one, single hair was astray.

"Maybel," Bernard sat beside me at the table.

I ignored him.

"I know you're mad at me."

I ignored Bernard and continued writing about attack squirrels. I figured geese were terrifying, but squirrels could squeeze through cracks in roofs and get into places where people could not. Squirrels would indeed make better attack animals.

"I'm sorry about kissing you on the train," Bernard whispered.

I wrote that the trained squirrels were commanded to go to the bed chambers of the king. They carried tiny, little knives the blacksmith had forged himself after the king took his daughter. The knives were fastened in tiny, little crocheted holsters made by the blacksmith's wife. She dearly missed her daughter.

"I love you Maybel, I do, it's just that I made a mistake. You aren't much younger than me in years, but it feels like emotionally, physically, and where we are in our lives, we are in two different phases. I'm sorry I hurt you."

"I hope you get stabbed by a squirrel!" I slapped Bernard across his face and made it sting good.

"Get away from me now, and do not ever talk to me again, Bernard! I hate you with every fiber of my being! Go burn in Hell with the geese and attack squirrels!"

I stared at Bernard icily. He looked at me like I was insane. He stood up and left.

I felt a lot better, I thought. I didn't need to continue this angry story. I balled up my papers and tossed them in the fireplace. I couldn't believe how much better I suddenly felt.

Catherine came downstairs. "Where's Bernard?"

"He had diarrhea and went home," I said.

The next evening, when I was up in my bedroom reading, I heard someone climbing the tree outside. I opened my window and held a bat I kept nearby. Figuring it had to be Bernard looking for Catherine, I screamed, "Bernard! I will murder you tonight!"

"Catherine?" An unfamiliar voice asked.

"Wrong tree!" I screamed.

"Which tree leads to Catherine's room?"

"She doesn't have a tree outside her room because daddy cut it down a long time ago when he realized how problematic she would be!" I screamed, hoping daddy would barge into my room with a gun.

"Is Catherine home?"

"Why don't you knock on the front door like a good boy and ask my daddy," I continued screaming, "He'll be the tall, angry man carrying a gun!"

I heard the boy scrambling down the tree branches. "She's at her boyfriend Bernard's house, if you must know! You should go visit! He lives in the very large mansion down the street and around the corner! You can't miss it! Have a good evening," I continued screaming as he ran through the courtyard, "I'll be sure to tell her you dropped by for a visit!"

I heard loud and fast footsteps coming up the stairs. I hoped daddy brought his gun with him.

"Maybel!" Catherine pushed my door open, sending it banging into the wall. "What the hell are you doing?"

"Oh hello, Catherine." I said sweetly. "You had a visitor. It wasn't Bernard."

"Maybel, shut up right now!"

"Where's Bernard?"

"You shut up this instant, Maybel!" Catherine was angrily, but quietly, hissing at me. I wondered why she was trying to be quiet.

"Where's daddy? I thought the angry footsteps coming up the stairs was daddy carrying his gun."

More loud footsteps clodded quickly up the stairs.

"Daddy!" I screamed, "a boy tried breaking in my window!"

"Do not say a word!" Catherine's eyes narrowed like a serpent about to strike venom into its prey. If she had a tail it'd be curled up rattling right now.

"What is going on?" Bernard yelled angrily.

I pressed my lips tightly together.

Catherine did not turn to look at Bernard. She stared unflinchingly at me and I stared back.

"Catherine! There was a boy running past your family room!" Bernard yelled angrily.

Catherine was as still as a statue staring at me.

Bernard suddenly went from angry to deeply concerned. "Maybel, I heard you screaming and you called your father saying someone tried to break into your window. Are you ok, sweetheart?"

Bernard came to my bed and put his hands tightly on my shoulders. "Did he hurt you?" Bernard's face was bright red and the vein in his neck was bulging.

"Maybel!" he shook me, "Did he hurt you?" Bernard looked terrifying. I instantly became more scared of Bernard than of Catherine.

"I will kill him!" Bernard pulled me into his tight embrace, and I felt like while Catherine stared at me like a rattlesnake, Bernard was squeezing me like a constrictor snake.

"Maybel," he tried to soften his voice but he still sounded and looked like he just rode out of Hell and was bloodthirsty. "What did he do to you?" Bernard shook with rage.

I was too scared to speak so I looked at Catherine. I didn't know what I was allowed to say to Bernard.

"It was a boy looking for me, Bernard," Catherine said quietly.

"What?" Bernard's head snapped around to look at Catherine.

"He is Rebecca's boyfriend and came to pick me up for a party at her house. I wanted to go without you, Bernard, but I'm not dating any other boys. I just wanted to go to this one party alone. I'm not dating anyone else."

"You're not dating me either!" Bernard said angrily. His head snapped back toward me, "Maybel, did that boy hurt you?"

I shook my head no.

"Bernard!" Catherine pleaded.

"Goodbye, Catherine!" Bernard stood up and went to my bedroom door.

"Bernard," I finally found my voice, "don't be angry at Catherine, she's just in a different phase of her life than you. You understand, right? It's not a big deal, so you shouldn't be angry."

Bernard looked like he wanted to tear my head off. His face went from protective to loathing. He turned and stomped downstairs.

"What was that about?" Catherine asked.

"Go to your party, Catherine. I'll tell mommy and daddy that you went to Bible study at Rebecca's."

"I don't feel like a party now. I need to go talk to Bernard," Catherine pouted.

"He looked angry. You may want to let him cool down," I suggested.

"Why were you screaming at Rebecca's boyfriend?" Catherine suddenly looked irritated at me. "You knew Bernard would hear." Catherine looked upset that I had yelled at a strange boy for trying to enter my bedroom at night.

"Catherine!" I shouted, "I didn't know Bernard was here! I thought mommy and daddy were downstairs and I didn't know who the boy was. I thought a stranger was trying to hurt me!"

Catherine's shoulders shrunk and she looked sadly mistaken for getting angry at me over defending myself. "Mommy and daddy are at Aunt Doris' house," Catherine said softly. They'll be home later tonight. I will take you up on your offer to cover for me, Maybel. I'll be home in a couple hours."

"Catherine, wait, if you were going to go to the party, why had Bernard stopped by?"

"He wanted to spend time with me. I wasn't expecting him."

"Are you two breaking up?" I asked.

"I don't know. I think he has another girl in his life anyway. I don't know what will happen."

"Don't you love him?" I asked.

"Yes," she said and left.

I thought for a moment about Catherine and Bernard. They think my stories are crazy, but the stories they are writing in real life are crazier. I continued reading a book and tried not to think about them.

After an hour or so, I went downstairs for a snack. I spread jam over bread and took a couple cubes of cheese. I went back upstairs to my room. The house was quiet as I nibbled my cheese. I wondered why Catherine said she loved Bernard but wanted to go to a party without him.

I heard knocking at the front door. I ignored it. The knocking continued.

"Maybel!" I heard Bernard's voice below my window. I ignored him.

He continued shouting my name. I opened my window. "What?"

"I've been knocking on your front door for ten minutes!"

"Ok," I said, and closed my window.

"Maybel!" he continued yelling. I continued ignoring him.

I saw branches sway and leaves jiggle outside my window. "Maybel!" Bernard's stupid face popped up above the roof.

I popped another cheese cube into my mouth. I cupped my hand to my ear showing him I could not hear him. I shrugged as though I couldn't understand him.

"Maybel!" He climbed onto the roof and came to my window. "Let me in please!"

I opened my window. "What?" I asked, annoyed.

"I need to speak to Catherine."

"Ok," I said. I laid back down on my bed and continued reading.

Bernard climbed in and went to the hallway and into Catherine's room. He returned to my room. "Where's Catherine?"

"At the party."

"What?"

"You broke up with her, remember?"

"She left?" Bernard looked surprised Catherine wasn't home sulking about their breakup.

"Yes, it appears she didn't take the breakup as hard as you have."

"I can't believe her!" Bernard said angrily.

"She's in a different emotional, physical, and overall different place in life than you. I'm sure you, of all people, Bernard, understand."

Bernard looked like he wanted to wring my neck, and that made me inwardly happy that I had upset him so much by throwing his insensitive words back at him. He left my room and I heard his footsteps down the stairs. I hoped he never returned.

A couple hours later, when Catherine returned, she was crying and ran upstairs. I knocked on her door. She said Bernard broke up with her because he needed time to be alone and to sort out his future. He also needed to study more and some other stuff that I couldn't understand because Catherine was sobbing so loudly.

The next evening, I ate dinner with my parents while Catherine was having dinner at Rebecca's. "Mommy, why didn't Catherine come to Paul's house?"

"Catherine had a headache."

"Yes, but she then stayed with Rebecca."

"Catherine felt better later in the day, so she left with Rebecca's family to their vacation home just south of here."

"I'm glad she felt better, but I wish she would have come to Paul's house with us," I said.

Mommy smiled at me, "I'm sure she missed you, dear."

Daddy was anxiously awaiting dinner. He watched us as if to hurry our conversation forward to the part where he got to eat cake.

"Is the vacation with Rebecca's family why she didn't come with Bernard and me?" I asked, wondering if Catherine purposefully stayed behind.

"I don't think she planned it that way," mommy said. "When she felt better, she went to Rebecca's and was then invited on their vacation. Now eat up. Your cake is getting cold," mommy smiled.

"I can eat my cake before dinner?" I asked wide-eyed.

Mommy kissed my forehead. "I've missed you, sweetheart. You went out west, and soon enough, you'll move away and I'll be heartbroken."

"I've missed you too, honey," daddy said. "Pass the cake, sweetheart," daddy smiled like a cat eyeing a mouse.

I told mommy and daddy about the white wolf, and that Paul was the boy who came with Bernard to Catherine's birthday party. I showed them the bird I made from Paul's river mud. The wings were still a little bit attached. I told them Mrs. Charleston knew all about medicinal plants. I did not tell them Mr. Charleston taught me how to gamble. I decided that was more of a need-to-know situation.

I enjoyed having my parents' full attention. I imagined Bernard must enjoy being the only child. After dinner, Bernard came by looking for Catherine.

"She's not here," I said. I wasn't sure where Catherine spent most of her days now that she liked boys and pretty dresses. She didn't spend time with me, of that I was sure, and it made me very sad.

Bernard looked confused. Mommy took over the conversation. "Bernard, dear, her friend Rebecca asked her over for dinner. They will then spend a couple nights in the city with Rebecca's parents. She'll return in a couple days, honey."

"Can Bernard come in for cake?" I asked.

"Of course. Bernard, honey, would you like cake?" mommy asked him sweetly.

Bernard looked sad.

"Bernard, why are you sad about cake? It's cake! Mommy's cakes are the best!" I exclaimed.

Bernard hesitated. I grabbed his hand and pulled him toward the dining room. "Bernard, I told mommy and daddy about the white wolf. I showed them the bird I sculpted with Paul."

Bernard sat politely, but he didn't seem too happy. I tried engaging him in stories but he seemed distant.

"Bernard, do you want to come to my room and play cards?" I asked him.

"I'm sorry, Maybel, I should be getting home," Bernard said. He looked down and saddened.

"Oh," I said, disappointed. "Will you come over tomorrow?" I asked.

"I'll check with my mother and father to see which chores I have, and if I have any engagements they want me to attend." Bernard stood up and pushed his chair in.

"You're not coming over, are you?" I asked sadly.

Bernard smiled weakly, "I'll check with my parents, Maybel."

The next day I helped daddy sweep his workshop and fix one of the drawers in the kitchen. Then mommy and I washed clothing and made lunch. There was a knock on the door and I was surprised to see Bernard.

"Bernard! You came!" I jumped up and wrapped my arms and legs around him tightly.

"Yes, Maybel," he smiled, "I've finished helping my mother with the horses and father with some business."

"What do you want to do today?" I asked excitedly. I was quickly planning our day in my mind.

"Well, I suppose we can do whatever you want," Bernard said.

"I want to go to the stream near your house. It has a nice feeling there," I told him.

"That's funny, my mother says the same thing," he smiled at me.

"Mommy, can I go with Bernard? Please!" I begged.

"Yes, dear. You've been very helpful to daddy and me today." Mommy kissed my cheek. "Go have fun, sweetheart."

"It was nice seeing you dear," mommy kissed Bernard's cheek. "Please give my best to your mother and father."

"Yes, Mrs. Wyndham," Bernard smiled.

Bernard walked while I ran and skipped.

"Bernard, I really had fun with you on vacation!"

"Me too, Maybel."

"Why do you seem sad?" I asked.

"I'm sad Catherine left," he answered.

"She'll be back in several days," I said, not understanding why Bernard was sad about Catherine being on vacation.

"Yes, I know. I don't understand why she left though."

"She went to the city with her friend," I said. I thought Catherine's reason for leaving was obvious.

Bernard sighed. He looked sad.

"Can I have a piggy back ride?" I asked. My hands were already reaching for his neck, anticipating him saying yes to carrying me.

Bernard bent down and I got on his back and wrapped my legs around his waist and my arms around his neck.

"Will you take me to the candy store now instead of the stream?" I thought that might be a good way to get Bernard's mind off thinking about Catherine, and also, I wanted sweets.

"Sure, Maybel."

Bernard set me down and lightly held my hand as we strolled through town. His mind seemed elsewhere but he nevertheless tried to perk up from his sadness. "Would you like custard this time, Maybel, or a candy stick like last time?" Bernard squeezed my hand and smiled at me.

"A candy stick!" I squealed. "But I want the cocoa-flavored one this time!"

"Very good choice," Bernard said, leading me by my hand into the candy store. I rushed to the counter to choose my candy stick while Bernard followed at a slower pace.

"Good day, Maybel!" greeted Charlie, the owner of the candy store.

"Good day, Charlie! May I have a cocoa candy stick please?"

"Good choice, sweetheart! And for you, young man?" Charlie asked Bernard.

"I'll have the same, please."

"Very good," Charlie smiled.

I circled my arm with Bernard's arm on our walk home.

"Maybel, don't push and pull on your candy stick when you suck on it," Bernard said.

"Why?"

"Just don't," Bernard answered.

"How do you suck on it then?"

"Put it in your mouth, but don't twist or push or pull on it."

I breathed out deeply, "Ok, Bernard." I thought Bernard's request was silly.

"I know you don't understand why, just trust me. I'm trying to teach you, and keep you safe from boys who will take advantage of your naivety."

"Ok, Bernard," I sighed dramatically and rolled my eyes. I put the candy stick in my mouth and crunched down on it instead of sucking it.

Weeks passed without Bernard. He returned to boarding school without a goodbye. He then returned home for his school break but we did not see him. I wondered why. I missed him.

I finally went to his house and knocked on his door. His mother answered.

"Hello, Mrs. Charleston. Is Bernard sick?"

Mrs. Charleston looked puzzled. "No, dear. He's in his room. Would you like me to take you to him?"

"Yes, please. Oh, Mrs. Charleston?"

"Yes, sweetheart?"

"Why hasn't Bernard come to see me?" I asked. I felt sad because I missed him.

"I'm afraid he's been moody, honey. I'm sorry. Sometimes children go through phases when they're sour and upset and in a bad mood. He'll be ok. He just needs time."

Mrs. Charleston led me to Bernard's room and knocked on his door.

"I'm busy," he yelled.

"You have a visitor," Mrs. Charleston announced.

"Who is it?" Bernard sounded annoyed and angry.

"It's me, open your door or I'll climb through your window!" I kicked his door for added emphasis.

"Go away, Maybel!" Bernard bellowed.

"Wrong answer!" I kicked his door harder.

"What?" Bernard yelled at me when he flung open his door.

"May I interest you in snake oil?" I asked. Mrs. Charleston let out a laugh.

"What?" he grumbled.

"Snake oil. It's the latest trend," I batted my eyelashes.

"What do you want?" Bernard asked. Bernard looked like a troll living under a bridge.

"Snake oil cures angri-itis," I said. "That's when your grumpy for no reason."

Mrs. Charleston again suppressed a giggle.

I kicked his door open and ran and jumped onto his bed. "I'm in here! There's nothing you can do to get me to leave!" I yelled and laughed maniacally.

"I'm reading, Maybel. You can stay as long as you are quiet," Bernard went to his desk and sat in his chair.

Mrs. Charleston closed the door as she left.

"You know I can't be quiet, Bernard!"

Bernard sat at his desk and put his head down in the palm of his hand while he read. His elbow rested on his desk. He looked like he hadn't bathed in a day or two.

I laid on his bed watching him. "Bernard?" I asked softly. "Why don't you like me and Catherine anymore?"

"I do like you, Maybel!" He said angrily. "I just can't be with you."

"Why?"

Bernard took a deep breath then faced me. "Because I kissed you! Because I want to kiss you again!" Bernard seemed agitated.

"I've missed you," I said meekly.

"I've missed you too! I can't date Catherine because I cheated on her with you, and if I don't date Catherine, I don't get to see you!" Bernard looked troubled.

"You see me now," I said.

"Maybel, I'm so sorry. I shouldn't have kissed you like I did."

"I liked it," I whispered.

"I did too! That's why I can't be around you! I want to kiss you every time I see you!"

"I don't understand why that upsets you. You don't want to kiss me?" I wondered if Bernard was embarrassed of me.

"No, I don't want to kiss you!"

"Why? Because I'm not pretty like Catherine?" I felt my lower lip quiver.

"Because you're a child!"

"I'm not!" I argued.

"You're two, almost three years younger than me and you don't even know where babies come from!"

I felt my eyes begin to sting with tears but I didn't want to cry.

"You're not even in high school yet!" Bernard added.

"I will be soon enough!" I felt my lower lip pout and tremble and I couldn't stop it, and that made me angry.

Bernard took a deep breath and wiped his face with both hands. He got up and sat next to me. "I really like you, Maybel, and it's tearing me apart! I feel bad that I want to kiss you. I can't be with Catherine because I want to kiss you."

I laid my head down on Bernard's pillow and watched him. "You aren't mad at me or Catherine, then?

"No! I like you both! But I really liked sleeping with you in bed, holding you, and kissing you, and I feel very guilty about that."

"I liked it too," I said.

"Don't say that," he whispered, then stood up and returned to his desk with his head buried in the palms of his hands.

"I liked being with you because I was scared to be alone and you made me feel safe," I said.

Bernard sat silently at his desk.

"Bernard, I miss you. I haven't seen you in months. You left without a goodbye. You returned without a hello. If you don't want me around, I'll leave."

Bernard did not move. He stared at his book on his desk.

I got up and walked to his door. I was sad because I missed playing with him.

I closed the door behind me and walked downstairs. Mrs. Charleston was in the kitchen cutting vegetables. "Hello, Maybel," she said.

"Bernard doesn't like me anymore," I said, and sat at the table.

"I'm afraid he doesn't like me or his father right now either, honey. He's going through a difficult time, and I wish I could help him, but he won't talk to us."

"Do you want to play with me?" I asked.

"What would you like to do?" she smiled.

"Can we go fishing?"

"Yes, honey, that sounds fun." Mrs. Charleston smiled at me. She looked like a girl when she was happy.

We left out the kitchen door and went to their shed and got fishing rods then we walked to their pond.

Mrs. Charleston took a stick and began digging into the mud. "We need worms."

"I can dig with just my fingers," I said.

"May I join?" Mr. Charleston asked with a smile?

He came to his wife and kissed her.

"I'm all dirty!" she squealed. "Don't kiss me now!"

Mr. Charleston laughed, "I don't care if you're covered in mud or chocolate! You're gorgeous!" He kissed her and hugged her.

Mrs. Charleston blushed, "We were just getting ready to fish, honey. We're digging for worms."

"Oh, let me help," Mr. Charleston winked at his wife. "I'm good at wallowing around in mud," he laughed heartily.

Bernard appeared from behind the weeds and brush, beyond the edge of the pond. He didn't smile or talk, but he came toward us, and squatted beside me, then started digging for worms with a stick.

"Hi, Bernard," I smiled.

"Hi, Maybel," he whispered while looking down at the mud.

"Do you want to fish with me?" I asked.

"Yes," he said.

Mr. and Mrs. Charleston watched us. They looked happy that Bernard was with us.

I took a worm and put it on the hook but it fell out of my hand. I again tried to spear its skin with the hook on my fishing line. The worm squiggled away.

"Here, give me the hook," Bernard said softly.

"No, I can do it," I protested.

"I'll do it," Bernard said.

"No," I said.

"Fine, we'll do it together. I'll help you." Bernard pulled me down beside him onto the fallen tree by the shore and sat me between his legs. He wrapped his arms around me and took the hook and a worm and speared the worm in front of me.

"This is how you hold the hook," he said softly. "Do you want to cast the line, or do you want me to cast it?" he asked.

"I want to!" I smiled.

Bernard stood up and pulled me up. "Go ahead," he said.

I cast the line but it didn't go far.

Bernard came to me and stood behind me and told me to reel it in. I did, and he held his hand over mine and cast out the line again. It went much farther.

Bernard continued to stand behind me. He told me about which fish were in the pond and how big they get and if they tasted good.

I liked leaning back into Bernard. I tilted my head all the way back and looked up at him smiling. He leaned over and smiled back at me.

"Which fish do you think you'll catch?" he asked me.

"The one bigger than yours," I smiled.

Bernard laughed.

Mr. and Mrs. Charleston sat together holding hands watching us.

"Bernard," Mr. Charleston said, "thank you for fishing with us. Your mother and I have missed you."

Bernard looked like he didn't want to delve into that conversation. "You're welcome," he said hastily.

Bernard held my wrists. "When you cast, it's all in your wrists. You flick your wrists. Don't worry about how hard you can throw."

"Ok, Bernard," I said.

I leaned back into Bernard's chest and waited for the fish to bite.

"Bernard, do you want to go swimming?" I asked.

"It's too cold," he said.

"How about wading?"

"I just want to sit here with you, Maybel."

"Ok, Bernard," I said.

"Maybel, I'm sorry I haven't talked to you in months." Bernard whispered so his parents wouldn't hear. "I just didn't know what to say. I missed you though," he whispered into my ear.

I tilted my head back and looked at him upside down. "I missed you, too. You spent a lot of time missing me when I was down the street waiting for you."

"I couldn't come. Catherine would think I wanted to see her."

"Don't you?" I asked.

"I missed her, but I really missed playing with you. I really like spending time with you."

I relaxed back into Bernard's chest. The air was cool and wisps of fog floated over the pond water.

"Bernard," Mrs. Charleston called, "would you like to come inside with Maybel and drink hot chocolate?"

"Yes!" I answered for Bernard.

"Can we wait a little bit before we come inside? We haven't caught any fish."

"Yes, sweetheart. We'll be inside." Mrs. Charleston took Mr. Charleston's hand and they walked back to the house.

I stood up and turned around and sat back down on the tree trunk facing Bernard. "Will you kiss me again like you did on the train?"

"No, Maybel," he whispered. "I can't."

"You're not dating Catherine anymore," I whispered back.

Bernard looked to his side then back at me. He looked unsure. "Ok," he whispered.

"I liked when you kissed me. I liked how gentle you were." I leaned toward him and he leaned toward me and we kissed. It was just a quick peck on our lips. I turned back around and leaned back into Bernard's chest while we fished.

Bernard leaned down slowly and kissed my neck, below my earlobe. I closed my eyes and breathed in.

"Maybel, this is why I shouldn't kiss you; I keep wanting more."

"What's more?" I asked.

Bernard dropped his head. "You don't even know what 'more' is," he muttered to himself.

Bernard stood and reached his hand down and pulled me up. "Let's go get hot chocolate," he said.

"I love chocolate!" I danced around Bernard.

"This is why I can't kiss you, Maybel. You still act like a child."

"I do not!"

"You are dancing around, happy at the prospect of getting chocolate. You're still a child, Maybel, and I'm a horrible person for wanting to kiss you."

"I'm not a child, and I like kissing you!" I put my hands on my hips in defiance.

"Oh Maybel, you are a child."

"I am not!" I protested.

"Oh come on, let's go get hot chocolate."

Bernard held my hand as we walked to the shed to return our fishing gear. "Maybel, what should I do about Catherine?"

"I think she has a boyfriend. Or maybe he's just a friend. I'm not sure if they are dating. They went to the park together one day."

Bernard was silent. I looked up at him. I could not read any emotion on his face.

"You can ask her on a date if you want. Maybe she still likes you," I told him.

"Wouldn't that bother you?" Bernard crinkled his forehead.

"Why would it bother me? If you date her, I can see you and play with you more often."

"If I ask Catherine on a date, we'll kiss. Won't that bother you?" Bernard asked me.

I looked up at Bernard there in the shed as we lined our fishing poles against the wall. "I've seen you kiss Catherine before."

"I wish you would be jealous," he muttered, "but you don't yet understand anything about love."

"I have no right to be jealous," I said. "And if I don't yet understand anything about love, it's because you have confused me!"

"I know, Maybel, and I'm sorry!" Bernard took my hand and led me out of the shed, then closed the door. He slid a wooden plank across the door to keep it shut during windy days.

"Bernard, I was really angry when you kissed me on the train and then the very next day you shoved your tongue down Catherine's throat. You acted like you hadn't cared about our kiss and that hurt me. I was also upset with myself because I shouldn't have kissed my sister's boyfriend. I love Catherine and I don't want to hurt her."

"Our kiss did mean a lot to me," Bernard whispered.

"We were in very different places emotionally and physically," I said with sarcasm dripping heavily in my voice.

"I didn't want you to know how much I liked it," Bernard said shyly.

I fidgeted with my hands. I wasn't sure what to say.

"Oh Maybel, come here," Bernard came to me and hugged me. I have missed you so much." Bernard looked up at the sky and breathed in. He looked back at me. He looked sad.

"Let's drink our hot chocolate then I'll take you home," Bernard sighed.

Bernard left early to return to boarding school and did not say goodbye. He just never showed up again, and later mommy said that Mrs. Charleston said Bernard had returned to school early to study. She said he was taking a lot of advanced math and biology classes and needed more time to study.

I didn't know where to go. I was sad and lonely. The candy store was always welcoming, so I went there. "Hello, Maybel," Charlie slid from behind his office door.

"Hello Charlie, can I join your poker game?"

Charlie was shocked, or at least he pretended to be. "This is a candy store, Maybel, would you like custard, cookies, or chocolates?"

"No, I'd like to gamble, Mr. Charlie. Can you please ask Mr. Charleston if I can join? He'll vouch for me."

Charlie looked surprised but also curious. "I have no idea what you're talking about Maybel, but let me see which custards I have in my storeroom."

Charlie disappeared behind his office door.

There were roars of muffled laughter.

Charlie returned. "Maybel, I do have chocolate custard in my storeroom if you'll kindly follow me."

I looked down so Charlie couldn't see me rolling my eyes. Chocolate in the storeroom? I'm not stupid, I thought, and also, he twitches his nose when he lies. I found his tell to be likely useful in the future.

I walked into his office and down some steps into his basement. I smiled at Mr. Charleston, who sat in a chair sipping whiskey and puffing on a cigar.

"Maybel?" A surprised voice to my right called out.

It was daddy!

"Oh, Charlie," I said, as I began walking back up the steps, "there doesn't seem to be any chocolate custards down here. I'll come back next week to see if you have restocked."

"Maybel! Come here this instant!" daddy bellowed.

I solemnly sulked over to daddy.

"How do you know about this place? Have you been gambling?" he asked angrily.

Daddy looked very upset. He sat and drank whiskey and held a cigar in his hand, which he put down when he saw me staring at it.

"No daddy, I wouldn't say I've been gambling because that implies a chance at losing and I never lose," I said, still scared of his reaction.

Mr. Charleston and the other men roared with laughter. I did not laugh, however, and neither did daddy.

"Are you going to tell mommy?" I was worried.

"No, of course not! She'll know I've been gambling and be mad at me! Maybel, do you really know how to gamble?" daddy asked.

"Yes."

"And who taught you?" he asked me angrily.

I didn't want daddy to get mad at Mr. Charleston so I evaded his question. "I learned by watching other people."

"Where, Maybel?"

"I snuck into a train car once." This was true; I did do that. I didn't offer any more details that could implicate Mr. Charleston.

Mr. Charleston once told me lawyers found loopholes and joked that I could be a lawyer. I asked him what that meant, and he explained loopholes and half-truths. I told him I couldn't be a lawyer because mommy made me attend church, and I wasn't sure if people who found loopholes were allowed in church. Mr. Charleston laughed.

Daddy puffed his cigar and his eyes narrowed. "Maybel, can you win?"
"Yes, daddy."

"Come sit with me, Maybel," daddy said.

I went to daddy and he pulled me onto his lap. "Which cards shall I play?"

"I don't know yet. I have to watch everyone for a round before I know their tells."

Mr. Charleston's eyes twinkled and he winked at me when daddy wasn't looking.

"Ok, sweetheart, let's see if you can gamble." Daddy didn't believe I would win; I could tell by his tone.

For one round I watched the men. I learned their tells.

The next round daddy let me hold the cards and I sat on his lap and played. For three rounds straight, I won. I lost the next two rounds because, as Mr. Charleston once told me, 'sometimes the dealer gives you shit.'

And then I won the next four rounds.

The men became angry but I had become used to angry men who weren't good at gambling.

"Maybel, how do you know which cards to play?" daddy asked.

"I know when someone is bluffing."

Daddy sipped his whiskey and watched me closely. "Is that how you knew I had bought you that large dollhouse for Christmas when you were seven?"

"Yes, daddy. You told me that I wouldn't get a dollhouse for Christmas unless I swept the floor. I was being a baby and didn't want to sweep the floor and I could tell that you were lying when you said I wasn't getting a dollhouse."

The old men chuckled. Mr. Charleston delighted in watching me and daddy.

"Alright then, Maybel, what's my tell?"

"I don't want to say. If I say, then you'll stop doing it, and then I won't be able to know when you're lying about my Christmas presents."

Again the old men laughed.

"Alright then, what will you do with your winnings?" he asked.

"Well, I didn't gamble, because that's bad, so I haven't won anything." I moved the pile of cash to daddy. "They're your winnings."

All the men chuckled.

"And what would you have me do with my winnings?"

"Buy mommy all the fabric she wants and a better sewing machine."

"We don't have quite enough money for all that."

"We will once I'm done cleaning up," I said.

Mr. Charleston laughed loudly.

"Alright Maybel, I'll teach you a lesson about gambling. If you win the next round, you keep everything, and if you lose, these men get their money back."

"Yes, daddy."

"I want you to understand how a person shouldn't put all their eggs in one basket. You've just let everyone here know you read their tells. They'll stop showing you their tells. And now there's a very real possibility you will lose everything."

I proceeded to win and I never doubted my ability.

"Maybel," daddy asked, surprised, "how did you win? Horace stopped touching his chin when he got a good hand, and Anton stopped leaning his head to the right."

Both Horace and Anton looked up surprised. "We don't do that," they said in unison, while everyone else laughed because they clearly did do that.

"People have more than one tell daddy, and anyway, those weren't their most honest tells. Everyone has tells, and then they have really, really accurate tells. There are levels of tells."

Daddy watched me, intrigued.

I handed him my large stack of cash. "Mommy gets the best sewing machine in the store."

Daddy nodded.

I jumped off daddy's lap and kissed his cheek then bounded upstairs before he could ask me more questions. What I really wanted to do was talk to Mr. Charleston. I wanted to sit and talk to him and tell each other stories. I'd have to wait for another day.

The next weekend, I skipped to the Charleston's house. I really wanted to ask Mr. Charleston a question that had been on my mind. Vincent, my most favorite of the Charleston's staff, opened the main door and I hugged him. I gave him a piece of candy and he winked at me. I liked Vincent.

Mr. Charleston was in his office on the main floor. It was large and imposing and had two fireplaces, every imaginable liquor available for business associates or visiting physicians, a marble floor, and tall, wide windows with long, red velvet drapes held back by golden cords. Mr. Charleston liked opulence.

"Mr. Charleston, how much of who we are is our body, and how much is our soul?" I skipped down the marble steps to his enormous, carved walnut desk. He sat in his chair, but stood up when I entered, and motioned for me to come to the sitting area by one of the fireplaces.

I climbed onto his lap. "What percentage of our personalities is because our bodies are either whole and healthy, or broken or maimed?"

"Well, that's quite the question, Maybel. What brings you to ask such a question?" Mr. Charleston watched me with an amused expression.

"I was wondering about these bodies we're in, and how much of our personality is because of the condition of our body?"

"Maybel, I'm not sure I follow your line of thinking. Perhaps if you provide some context, I might be able to provide a better answer," he said.

"I was thinking about writing a story like Frankenstein, but I was wondering about the soul. How much of our personality is within our tissues, organs, and limbs? Frankenstein was created with different people's parts. Would Frankenstein then act like the people whose parts he used? Would he dislike the taste of broccoli if the original owner of his tongue disliked broccoli?"

Mr. Charleston watched me with great interest. I sat on his lap and looked up at him. He was quite imposing if you were on his bad side, I was sure. I was not on his bad side, so he was a big, stuffed bear of a man who treated me like a granddaughter, not a daughter. He spoiled me with reckless abandon when it came to ice cream, chocolates, and stationery. He knew my weaknesses.

I continued, "I have more questions. If I got hit in my head and couldn't speak, I'd still be me, but I might not be able to express myself, so nobody would know I was still me."

Mr. Charleston thought about my questions. "Maybel, I haven't an answer for you because doctors and scientists have been pondering those questions for a millennium or more."

"That's a long time," I said.

"Yes, it is."

"Then why has no one found an answer after such a long time," I asked.

"Those are extremely difficult and advanced questions, Maybel. We don't know how much of a person is their physical body and how much is their soul. We don't yet know where the line between body and soul is drawn."

"When will you know?" I pressed.

"I don't know that anyone will ever know. We will always theorize, but we won't know the answer to such a complex question."

"What makes it complex? We are at the mercy of our bodies, aren't we?

"I suppose so, Maybel, go on," he urged.

"My Uncle Ronald was really smart and worked as an architect and built a lot of buildings. One day a hammer fell on his head and he was never the same after that. When we visited him, his personality was different. He acted more like a child. He was angry, frustrated, and acted a little like an immature child. It was really strange. He fought with me over who got to sit on the little rocking chair daddy made for Uncle Ronald's children back when they were little. It felt like Uncle Ronald was no longer there in his body. He seemed like a different person and it really confused me. Mommy and my aunt cried about how differently Uncle Ronald acted after his accident. I guess I always wondered if he was still the same deep inside, you know, like where his soul is. If he had been born with damage to his head, he would have grown up acting like a child his whole life and no one would have ever known that deep down inside him, he possessed the ability to calculate math quickly in his head and design and build large buildings. The fact that he was able to do that, then lost that ability when a hammer hit his head, means we all have the ability to do great things, but some of us have bodies that don't work right and brains that are like Uncle Ronald's and don't work like they're supposed to. Do you agree? Do you have any books about this sort of thing?"

"I do not have any books about that, honey, but I sure wish I did," Mr. Charleston watched me with interest. I could tell his brain was thinking about all the things my brain had just told him. His expression was amused, but not at all condescending, as he waited for me to continue.

"I have another question. How much of my personality is shaped by the way others see me? I am a girl. You are a tall man. So, maybe I learn to be more careful with my words and behavior, but you don't have to worry so much about what you say to people, because if you offend someone, and they try to punch you, you can easily beat them up.

Mr. Charleston laughed, "Well honey, I cannot beat up everyone; we must never underestimate our opponents, but I will say that I can take on just about anyone, sweetheart, and I'll never let anyone hurt you." He kissed my cheek. He made me feel safe.

"I am not a big man, so I have to choose my words and actions more carefully than you," I told him. "I think that shapes my personality because I have to be more polite. I have also noticed men and women look at me like I'm just a defenseless child, and treat me as such, but everyone treads carefully around you, because you are tall, and have very large muscles, and a low, baritone voice."

Mr. Charleston nodded, but didn't say anything. He let me talk through my thinking.

"If you were in a woman's body, don't you think you would be treated differently? Wouldn't that shape your personality and behavior and make you act differently when you interact with other physicians and business associates?"

"You're smart, like my mother," Mr. Charleston smiled. "She has said the same things. She is petite and gets treated unfairly because of her short stature and kind and gentle disposition. Like I said before, it's never good to underestimate someone. My mother is small, but fights like a badger. Her aim with a pistol is second to no one. You'll like her, Maybel. And I know she will love you."

Mr. Charleston hugged me and patted my back. I liked when he hugged me. "You remind me of my grandfather." I felt sad remembering my grandfather because he always held me like Mr. Charleston held me.

"I'm not that old honey, maybe a little old, but I'm not old enough to be a grandfather," he chuckled.

"I know, Mr. Charleston, you don't have hardly any gray hairs. I only meant that you hold me like my grandfather held me, and you treat me like I'm your granddaughter, not your daughter."

"Oh? How so, honey?"

"Well, grandpa said he could spoil me and Catherine because that's a grandpa's right, and he said he had lived long enough to get to spoil us, and that was his reward. Mothers and fathers have to be more strict and teach good manners. If I were your daughter, would you let me gamble?"

He chuckled, "No, Maybel, I suppose not."

"But you let me gamble and have ice cream because you're more like my grandfather than my father because you don't have to teach me good behavior. You just get to enjoy me, that's what my grandpa said."

"Yes, Maybel, I enjoy our talks a lot." He hugged me tightly and kissed my cheek. "I always look forward to my conversations with you. You have the most interesting way of looking at things."

"Since you're like my grandpa and not my daddy, can we eat ice cream together now?"

He chuckled, "Of course sweetheart. Let's go to the kitchen."

"Mr. Charleston," I held his hand, "when did you realize you loved Mrs. Charleston?"

"I knew immediately, but I didn't know how to express myself honestly, so I tormented her relentlessly and teased her, and I'll always feel bad about that."

"You should make her a bowl of ice cream too," I suggested.

"You know Maybel, I think I will! Should I put a cookie on the side?"

"Yes, I would definitely put a cookie on the side."

We held hands and walked across the marble ballroom floor on our way to the kitchen.

"Mr. Charleston?"

"Yes, dear?"

"Can I have a hug? I miss my grandpa."

He smiled sweetly and picked me up in his strong arms and hugged me tightly.

Catherine was away at piano practice and I was bored. I decided to visit Mrs. Charleston after I finished helping mommy add embellishments to a dress she was sewing for a rich lady in the next town over.

"Maybel, honey, take a loaf of bread we made this morning to Mrs. Charleston and tell her I look forward to our quilting bee at the end of the month."

"Yes, mommy," I said and dashed into the kitchen to retrieve the bread. "I won't be long, mommy."

I hopped and twirled then skipped to the Charleston's, using the long loaf of bread as my imaginary dance partner. The bread didn't have feet to step on, so I danced more gracefully with it than I did with Bernard. His toes hurt after a dance with me.

I knocked on the Charleston's door and expected Vincent to answer.

"Yes, Maybel?" Bernard answered the door.

"Why are you here?" I asked Bernard. I thought he would be away at boarding school.

"I live here, Maybel. Why are you here?"

"I'm here for your mother," I said, lightly knocking the loaf of bread against his forehead and giggling.

"Why?" Bernard looked confused.

"She's teaches me about plants."

"Why?" Bernard looked over my shoulder, I presumed to see if Catherine was with me.

"Because we're best friends now, Bernard, and you're never here at home so I'm the favorite child now," I smiled and batted my lashes. "She asked if I wanted to learn about plants that can heal, and I said yes. She's really smart. She's already taught me about a lot of plants already."

"When?" Bernard followed close behind as I skipped toward the kitchen.

"When you were away at school. You left early without saying goodbye, you know. You need to work on your manners," I shoved the bread into Bernard's chest and ran past him and into the kitchen where Mrs. Charleston sat.

"Hi, Mrs. Charleston!"

"Hello, Maybel! Good to see you! How was your piano recital last weekend?"

"Terrible," I laughed. "I'm not as good as Catherine."

"If you weren't comparing yourself to Catherine, then how would you rate yourself?"

"I'd say I did ok," I answered.

"Well then, stop comparing yourself," she winked at me.

"Mrs. Charleston, I wrote a story for you. It's about a woman who talks to horses."

Mrs. Charleston stood up and kissed my cheek and hugged me. "Thank you, sweetheart. Let's go walk around the gardens, shall we?"

"When did you two become best friends?" Bernard entered the kitchen and handed his mother the loaf of bread.

"Bernard, dear, would you like to accompany us on our walk around the fields?" Mrs. Charleston asked her son.

"Not really, but I don't have anything else to do."

"Bernard you have lots of bunnies around," I said.

Bernard looked at me like he wondered why he should care.

I held Mrs. Charleston's hand and we went to the field by the horses. Bernard followed, but he dragged his feet and didn't seem interested.

Mrs. Charleston and I inspected the plants and the bee hives. We looked in bird nests. We found indentations where bunnies had been sleeping in the tall grasses. After taking note of what had changed and what remained the same in the fields, we returned to the kitchen for tea and cookies.

"This is my favorite part, Mrs. Charleston. I like tea and cookies while we chat."

"I believe it's my favorite part too," she winked at me.

After chatting about the story I wrote for Mrs. Charleston, Bernard said he would walk me home.

I hugged Mrs. Charleston. "I'll see you soon, Mrs. Charleston."

"Yes, Maybel, I look forward to it." Mrs. Charleston kissed my cheek, then Bernard and I set off for my home.

I held Bernard's hand as we walked to my home. "Bernard, your mother is really nice."

"Yes, she is."

"I like being with her," I said.

"Me too."

"When did you and Catherine start dating again?" I asked Bernard.

"We haven't," he said.

"Then why are you walking me home? You might see her. Will it upset you if she's studying with friends from school and one happens to be a boy?"

Bernard let out a long sigh. "I don't know," he grumbled.

We arrived home and Bernard left me at my gate. "Have a good afternoon," he said, then left.

I walked inside. Daddy was reading the paper. I sat next to him and rested my head on his shoulder. Daddy wrapped his arm around me. He never needed to say anything. He just gave good hugs.

"Bernard, please take me with you, please, please, please?" I stood barefooted on his shoes and clung onto his shirt. My fists were balled up, grabbing onto his shirt.

"Maybe, I don't know. We'll see." Bernard put his arms around me to steady me and held me close.

"You don't have to cling so tightly," he said softly.

"I don't want you to leave me," I stared up at him pleadingly.

"I'll take you, honey," Henry came and stood beside us.

Bernard pulled me tighter against his body. "No, I'll take you, Maybel."

"You will?" My eyes brightened.

"Yes," Bernard said, and picked me up in his arms and I wrapped my arms and legs around him and kissed his neck.

"Thank you, thank you, thank you!" I squealed. "I love you, love you, love you!" I kissed his neck as I clung to him.

Bernard carried me into one of their many parlors and sat me down in his lap. "You need to find your shoes. Where did you put them?"

"I don't know," I shrugged.

"Maybel, you're such a child. Even my littler cousins remember where they left their shoes."

I held Bernard's cheeks in my hands and squished them.

Bernard laughed, "Be serious." He attempted to straighten his face.

I squished his cheeks in my hands again while pretending to speak for him. I made my voice lower like his voice. "I love you sweetheart, come to the toy store and I'll buy you lots and lots of toys."

Bernard laughed again even though he tried to stop himself. "Maybel, I'm trying hard to get you ready so we can go."

"You're really going to take me with you?"

"Yes, honey," he pressed his forehead against mine. "You wore me down, as usual."

Bernard held my cheeks and rubbed my nose with his nose. "This is called an Eskimo kiss."

I smooshed my lips onto his lips. "This is called a Maybel kiss," I giggled.

Bernard laughed softly, "You shouldn't kiss me, but that was cute." He smiled sweetly at me.

I grinned.

Bernard looked to his side and his smile faded. He leaned back in his chair, "No more kissing," he whispered into my ear.

Henry stood way back in the hallway talking to a pretty woman, but watched Bernard and me.

"Henry doesn't want us to kiss?" I whispered to Bernard.

Bernard sighed, "Henry thinks you and I are too comfortable with each other, that we are too friendly with each other. We were just playing anyway. We weren't kissing like the way Henry kisses girls."

"How does Henry kiss girls?"

"He holds them close and tickles them!" Bernard tickled my sides until I couldn't breathe.

"You're fun," I giggled.

Bernard cupped my cheeks again then rolled his head side to side playfully while staring wide-eyed at me. He made me burst into giggles.

"We should find your shoes now, Maybel. I'll take you to the pastry shop to pick up mother's order for the party tonight."

"You'll sneak me a pastry, right?"

Bernard scruffled my hair. "Yes, sweetheart." He kissed my hair and stood up. I was still bare-foot standing on his shoes. He walked with me on his shoes to the hallway where Henry still stood talking with the pretty girl.

"Good afternoon, Maybel," Henry smiled kindly at me.

I hid halfway behind Bernard because this was Bernard's cousin who was by far the most handsome man in the world. I smiled a little, shy smile.

"Maybel, hello," another handsome man touched my shoulder lightly. I looked up at him. He looked familiar.

"Do you remember me? I'm John."

I smiled politely. I still clung tightly to Bernard, my arms locked around his waist, because Bernard was my favorite person in the whole world, and I didn't know Bernard's cousins well enough to be my usual, chatty self.

"We're going to pick up mother's pastry order," Bernard told them.

The pretty girl stood close to Henry and her hand rested lightly on Henry's arm. I watched her. Her breasts were big and she wore a ruby necklace that accentuated her lip color.

I smiled up at her. She politely gave a quick, but small smile. She looked bored. "Henry, dear, let's go upstairs, shall we?" She winked at Henry, and John chuckled as he playfully slapped Henry's shoulder.

"What's upstairs that's fun? Are you going to play hide-and-seek?" I asked.

John laughed, "Yes, Henry enjoys playing hide-and-seek with his bone."

Henry shot John an angry look.

"She's too young to understand," John smiled at me.

"Can I play hide and seek with your bone too, Henry?" I asked.

"You two need to behave yourselves!" Henry glared at John and Bernard, who were both erupting with fits of laughter.

"Come along, Maybel," Bernard laughed, "Let's go pick up mother's pastry order."

Bernard held my hand and we walked down the hallway and wound our way through his big mansion. My shoes were under the grand piano.

"We're you playing piano?" Bernard asked.

"No," I shrugged.

"Why were your shoes under the piano then?"

"I have no idea," I replied.

I skipped alongside Bernard as we headed through town.

"Where's Catherine?" I suddenly realized I hadn't seen her in a while.

"I don't know," Bernard sighed. "She was talking to the son of one of father's business associates earlier."

"Why aren't you with her?" I skipped and twirled around him.

"Because I'm with you."

"You like me better," I squealed.

"No, Maybel, I like small talk at parties less."

"Does it make you sad to see Catherine now?"

"Maybe a little, but she upset me when she stayed home instead of coming out west. I think she pretended to have a headache because she wanted to go with Rebecca. Rebecca has an older brother, and I think Catherine likes him, and anyway, she said some things that upset me."

"Like what?"

"I don't want to talk about that. Maybe someday I'll tell you, but not today," Bernard huffed. He had become irritated thinking about Catherine.

"Bernard, I love you!" I hugged him. "Get happy again, ok?"

"I love you too, and I'm happy. Now please be good in the pastry shop."

"I'm always good!" I said indignantly.

Bernard led me inside the pastry shop and paid for the pastries with a large stack of dollar bills he took from his pocket.

I tugged on his shirt and smiled widely.

"Yes, Maybel, you may have one now," Bernard winked at me.

I took a pastry and held it up high to Bernard's mouth. "Would you like the first bite, dear?" I giggled.

"Thank you," Bernard laughed and took a bite.

I took the second bite as I held the door open for Bernard, who carried a tall stack of boxes filled with delicious pastries.

"These pastries taste better than the ones at mother's and my favorite pastry shop in Paris," Bernard told me.

"They are delicious," I agreed.

At Bernard's house, more guests had arrived and we had to carefully wind our way through the crowd. Bernard put the boxes in the kitchen for the wait staff to place on polished, silver platters.

"Come, Maybel, let's go upstairs. I really don't want to be social today. I'd prefer to sit quietly and read."

"Can I play while you read?"

"Sure," he said.

We climbed the stairs and went to Bernard's bedroom. He laid down on his bed and I went to the large, carved chest by his dresser and opened it. There were toys from all over the world sent to Bernard by his grandparents.

"Why don't you play with these anymore?" I asked.

"Because I'm not a child anymore."

"I'm not a child either," I stated defiantly.

"I suppose I still played with some of them a couple years ago, maybe last year, even, Bernard admitted. He opened a book and laid on his bed.

"Bernard, I've seen you kiss Catherine."

"Yes, Catherine and I kissed." Bernard continued reading.

"How did you kiss Catherine differently than you kissed me? You said earlier there were different kinds of kisses, like the way Henry kisses girls. How did you kiss Catherine then?"

I walked over and stood by his bed. He had taken off his tie and undone the top buttons of his shirt. His shoes were under his bed.

"I held her differently and kissed her with more, I don't know, affection. I'm not sure. It was just different." Bernard continued reading.

I climbed over Bernard and laid next to him on my side facing him. I was curious about what made kisses different.

I propped my head up on my hand and leaned over and pressed my lips onto Bernard's. "Now what?" I mumbled, as my lips were smooshed against his.

Bernard started laughing. "You're such a child, Maybel, and you don't yet know how to kiss!"

I leaned back and furrowed my brows. "Don't make fun of me," I pouted.

I leaned in again and pressed my lips onto his lips. I pulled away and looked at Bernard for his reaction.

Bernard laughed at me. "Ok, that's enough," he laughed again.

"Teach me," I insisted.

"No, Maybel, go play with my old toys."

"I like kissing you," I said. "I wish we were married so we could kiss every day."

"I wish you were a year or two older," he said, "because you still think my toys are fun."

"They are. Kissing you is more fun though," I smiled at him.

Bernard smiled back. "I like you, Maybel. You're just immature for your age, but maybe in a couple years, you'll act more mature and less like an immature child."

I crossed my arms angrily. "I am free-spirited! That's what mommy and daddy say! Daddy says I dance to my own music, and my wonder and amazement with the world, combined with my imagination, is refreshing!"

"It is, Maybel," Bernard said gently, "and that's why I missed you when I broke up with Catherine. You didn't come here to ask me to play with you, and that made me sad. I like being with you, it's just, I'm confused about how I feel about you."

Bernard watched me for a minute then sighed, "Let's go down to the party." He stood up and walked toward his bedroom door as he put his necktie back on and buttoned the top two buttons on his shirt.

I followed him. "You said you didn't want to be at the party."

"If we stay here, I'll kiss you again, and I'm very unsure how to behave around you these days. Your body is growing up, but you still like to play, and I don't know what to do about that."

"Ok," I pouted. "We'll go downstairs, but I really want you to know I'm not immature. I'm creative and have a passion for living life unconventionally."

Bernard chuckled, "Did your mother and father tell you that?"

"No, my grandma did."

Bernard put his hand on my shoulder as we walked down the hallway. "Your grandma sounds wise."

"She is. I told you she thinks I'm smart. That's because she recognizes the greatness in me. Smart people see each other, and we admire each other."

Bernard chuckled, "I adore you, sweetheart."

Daddy took me to the hardware store Saturday morning. I hated the hardware store. That was where old men sat on old paint cans and sacks of sand or leaned against the old wooden pillars with peeling paint and talked about which screws worked better with which hardwood. Only the most boring conversations were had here. It smelled like oil and sawdust. The corner, where lamps and heaters were, sold smelled like kerosene and gasoline. The old grease-stained counter where Mr. Gibbs took our money smelled like coffee and cigarettes. Every corner of the hardware store smelled like something distinct.

Today Mr. Charleston was there talking to the other men. I sat on a small, wooden chair against the wall and leaned back, ready for a long morning that would likely last until lunch time.

I stretched out my legs and looked up at the ceiling. The last time I was here with daddy, there were three hundred and seventy-one nails in the wooden beam above me. I decided to see if there were still three hundred and seventy-one nails there as there was nothing more interesting to do.

I counted to fifteen when I heard Mr. Charleston joking with daddy about a hostess at the train depot who had apparently taken an interest in daddy. Daddy whispered and they changed the subject. I guessed daddy had mentioned my presence. I sat behind a large bookcase full of shelves with different types of nails and hinges.

I heard Handsome Henry's voice. I really wanted to peek around the shelves and see him. I wanted to be able to gaze lovingly and longingly at him without him noticing. I could stare at his beautiful face all day, every day.

Next, I heard Mr. Gibbs' voice. "You mean you haven't taken a jab at her yet, Henry?"

The other men laughed.

I wondered why the men wanted to hit the woman at the train depot. I wanted to see this woman. She had apparently liked daddy and the men wanted to jab her. I wondered if they wanted to jab her with a stick or their fists. I wished Catherine were here to explain the innuendo, because it felt like they were speaking in riddles.

I had learned long ago to keep quiet in the hardware store and barbershop. Catherine said to pretend we were invisible so the men would talk more and we could hear more gossip. She taught me to pretend to read a book so daddy would think we were oblivious to the gossip.

It proved to be a useful way to gather information. I learned I'd be getting a doll for Christmas when I was nine. It proved to have detrimental consequences, too. I learned the reason for my puppy's death when I was seven was because when I let her out to pee, she got trampled by a horse carriage. Daddy had told me she passed peacefully but she didn't. And then I learned Catherine's bunny accidentally ingested rat poison our neighbor, Mrs. Mills, had left out. Before Bubbles died from rat poison, Mrs. Mills shot her and ate her, thinking she was a wild rabbit and not realizing Bubbles had just consumed poison. It was the most grandiose funeral I'd ever attended, as Mrs. Mills was quite wealthy.

"Hello, Maybel," Handsome Henry said as he walked past me to refill his coffee mug.

I stared at him.

"Still don't want to talk to me?" Henry smiled.

I couldn't talk to Henry easily. He was so beautiful my mouth dried up when he spoke to me, and the few times I tried to speak to him, my dry tongue stuck to the roof of my dry mouth and to the sides of my dry cheeks. I sounded like I had a wad of cloth stuffed inside my mouth.

I went back to counting nails.

Henry passed again on his way back to talk to the men. "Would you like coffee Maybel, or are you still too young?"

If Bernard had said that, it would have sounded insulting, like he was calling me a baby. Henry, however, sounded honest and was genuinely being kind.

I shook my head no.

"Alright then," Henry smiled and walked around out of sight behind the shelves of nails.

The back door opened and closed and Mr. Gibbs offered his assistance finding whatever his customer needed. A woman's voice asked for help finding the necessary things to repair a gate. "I have a list," she said. Her voice sounded young, not old, like thirty.

Mr. Gibbs escorted her to the back where he stored paint cans. The men began gossiping like my friends on the playground. I heard one man suck in air and whisper something. The others laughed. I opened the book I brought for such gossip and pretended to be deep in thought, reading about whatever was in this book. I hadn't actually started reading it yet so I had no idea what filled its pages.

The men had apparently temporarily forgotten I was there. I heard Mr. Charleston say whoever wore her thighs like a scarf was a lucky fella. Daddy, to my astonishment, agreed with Mr. Charleston. I took my pencil and wrote 'wore thighs like a scarf' in the margin of my book so I could ask Catherine about its meaning later.

And then, to my even bigger astonishment, daddy asked Mr. Charleston if he wanted to tickle her thighs with the beard stubble he'd recently grown.

I didn't understand what joke they intended, but I knew Catherine would appreciate the subtlety and explain it to me.

Mr. Charleston replied that he was about to shave it off after his wife couldn't stop laughing the night before. All the men laughed.

I wondered why Mrs. Charleston thought Mr. Charleston's beard was funny.

"I tickled her 'til she screamed for the Good Lord," Mr. Charleston continued. All the men roared with laughter.

I wondered if Mrs. Charleston accidentally peed from being tickled too much because that's what happened when Bernard tickled me. I accidentally peed on him because he wouldn't stop tickling me when I told him to stop.

I wrote down 'tickled thighs with beard' in another margin of my book.

"Leave her to me," I heard Henry say. "I'm the young buck here in this crowd of old, married men. I'll see if she needs a ride home."

"How have you not been shot yet?" A man's voice asked.

Another voice echoed that sentiment. "Yes, Henry, I cannot believe the bullet of a husband, father, or brother, hasn't landed in your back. Hell, even the bullet from a son! You have 'em all ages!" The men laughed.

"My reputation precedes me, I see," Henry laughed. "Most stories you hear about my escapades are blatantly false," Henry paused, "though not by much," he chuckled.

The woman returned. I heard the clicking of her heels on the wooden floor. They click-clacked over to the counter to pay Mr. Gibbs.

"Does your husband have an account here, Mrs....?" Mr. Gibbs paused, waiting for her to speak her name and the name of her husband.

I admired Mr. Gibbs' way of eliciting information in a seemingly innocent manner. I wrote that down too. 'Does your husband have an account Mrs....' That was a good and inconspicuous way of getting information.

If I add this dialogue to a future story, I'll have to remember not to let daddy read it so he won't realize how much attention I pay to the conversations here.

"I'm unmarried," she replied. "I'll pay with cash."

I crept to the shelves and peaked around them. She was young, slim, and wore a pretty, blue dress with a white scarf in her blonde hair.

"Yes, miss, thank you for your business," Mr. Gibbs said.

"Miss, may I help you to your automobile or carriage?" Henry asked her.

"Thank you, but I walked here," she smiled politely.

"I'd be happy to drive you home," Henry offered. "Looks like you have quite a heavy bag."

I crept back to my seat against the wall.

"Oh, you have an automobile?" she asked, her voice lifting.

"Yes, miss," Henry smiled. I couldn't see him smile from my place behind everyone, but I heard him smile.

"Thank you, sir. I'm Betty, by the way."

"Henry," I heard Henry say, and in my mind, I could see him politely kissing her hand.

The backdoor opened and closed, followed immediately by raucous laughter. "Lucky man," a voice said.

"Keep your daughters and your wives far away from Henry," another voice said.

"That won't be a problem for me," Mr. Charleston laughed. "He's my relation. The rest of you should worry though!"

I heard some mumbling and grumbling about Henry keeping his shotgun out of other men's sheds, and I wrote that down to ask Catherine later.

I also wrote a note to myself to ask Catherine from whom she learns her grownup expressions. It could be Bernard or Edith. I wondered how they learned what old people talked about. I wanted to ask the librarian to recommend a book but she would tell my parents I asked for a book on understanding expressions such as 'tickled her thighs with my beard.' I didn't know what that expression meant, but I knew it was naughty by the men's laughter.

The backdoor opened and closed again, and I heard a different woman's voice. She addressed daddy. "I figured you were here," she told daddy. "Would you be able to help me measure a cabinet I need replaced?"

"Perhaps another day, Eloise," daddy said. She made a noise like she was disappointed.

I snuck back to the edge of the shelves and peeked through a bare spot on the shelf. She was a pretty woman with black hair.

"It won't take long," she said, and touched his forearm as she spoke. "I'll only borrow you from your wife for just a few minutes."

I sat back down against the wall and pretended to read.

Daddy peaked around the corner. "Maybel, honey, I'm going to go measure a cabinet for someone. I'll only be a few minutes."

I pretended to be so engrossed in my book that I didn't hear him.

Daddy walked closer. "Maybel?"

I looked up with a very slight jump that Catherine taught me how to do. "Oh! You startled me! I didn't hear you approach."

"Honey, will you be ok here if I leave to measure a cabinet? I'll be gone only a few minutes."

"Oh, daddy, may I come with you?" I looked up at him with pleading eyes. "I get scared without you."

"Well, I suppose, it will only be a minute though," he said.

"Well, if it will only take a minute, you'll hardly notice me there. I'll be quiet," I said, standing up.

"Alright then," daddy said.

I walked around the shelves. Eloise did not like seeing me. "You brought your girlfriend here?" Eloise asked with anger and jealousy.

"This is my daughter!" daddy snapped back with even more anger.

"Oh, my, I'm so sorry," Eloise said. "I'm so embarrassed. I'm not involved with your father. I was just surprised because of your age. I fear you have the wrong idea," she stumbled. "I'm not romantically involved with your father."

"Oh, I know, ma'am. I imagine if he had mistresses, she'd be much younger and prettier than you," I smiled.

Daddy clasped my shoulder with vulture talons. "Let's go home instead," daddy told me through gritted teeth. "Lunch will be ready."

On our way home, daddy asked me to let him tell mommy. "Maybel, honey, it will be better if you let me tell mommy what happened. Your mother is a very passionate woman. She's most passionate about family. She loves you, your sister, and me with all her heart, and when someone threatens her family, she can become the most passionate woman that you will ever witness in your lifetime, and I don't want to have to go down to the jailhouse again with a bribe to set her free."

"Again?" I looked up at daddy.

"I know you see me as your old dad and mommy is just another old woman in your eyes, but really, honey, there are actually men and women who still find us at least somewhat appealing, and when another woman appears to like me, mommy can get a bit wild. She becomes quite expressive, like a howling beast from one of your stories."

Daddy stopped walking suddenly. "Do not tell her I said howling beast, Maybel, she'll hit us both with her frying pan."

"She may hit you, but she adores me," I said.

"Maybel, please forget the howling beast part!"

"Ok, daddy!" I said.

"I'm sorry, sweetheart, it's just I feel like I'm about to knock over a hornet's nest."

"Mommy doesn't get that angry, daddy."

"Honey, mommy makes us cookies and when we're sick, she sits with us all night making sure we are still breathing throughout the night. She's a sweet, compassionate, angel of a woman until another woman takes an interest in me, and then she transforms into something a bit different, a bit wilder. Honey, mommy is a sweet, caring, gorgeous woman, the most beautiful woman I've ever seen in my life, and also the most untamable. Some wild horses can't be broken. Mommy is a beautiful, wild horse who will kick the heads in of any other mares that think I'm the kind of stallion who will trot behind mommy's back and mount them."

"What does 'mount them' mean?"

Daddy groaned as he sought an explanation. "It means, to have a lovely evening with someone."

We arrived home and daddy skulked into the kitchen. "A woman wanted me to measure her cabinet and repair it, and I think she was a bit flirtatious. Please don't hurt her and wind up in the jailhouse. I love you, and would never cheat on you."

"Maybel, were you present?" mommy asked.

"Yes," I squeaked, suddenly realizing why daddy was nervous about telling mommy another woman liked him.

"And what did you see?" Mommy had turned around and continued chopping vegetables for dinner. I now wondered why daddy didn't wait until after mommy had discarded her knife.

"The woman wanted daddy to measure her cabinet."

"And?" mommy pressed.

"Daddy didn't."

"And?" mommy pressed further.

"That's all that happened, mommy," I whispered.

Mommy did not convey anger, but she terrified me with her calmness and precision cutting. The carrots were precisely severed in quarter inch pieces. I could swear to their measurements. If I had a ruler with me, each piece would undoubtedly be a quarter inch.

"Lunch will be ready in forty minutes," mommy said, her back turned to us.

"Maybel, watch the pot." Mommy looked at daddy, "May I see you upstairs?"

Daddy hesitated. "Yes," he said.

I stayed in the kitchen but I heard them upstairs. It sounded like they were moving the bed around and I guessed mommy didn't want daddy to sleep in their bed tonight. I thought she was mad at daddy. I heard them yelling and mommy screamed to God. I was scared they stopped loving each other, but when they came downstairs, they were holding hands.

"Are you getting a divorce?" My eyes were tearing up.

They looked at me surprised. "No, of course not," mommy said. "Why would you think that?"

"You were yelling at each other upstairs, you're both sweaty from all your yelling and fighting, and mommy was praying," I cried.

Mommy's and daddy's faces turned bright red. I thought they were angry.

"No, honey, we were talking. We're happy and love each other. I was making sure daddy understood what he would miss if he ever strayed," mommy said.

I stared at them. "Are you mad at each other?"

"No!" They both said in unison.

"Everything is ok, sweetheart," mommy said. "We talked. Daddy will never be with another woman, no matter how much that bag of trash flirts with him."

"I will not," daddy kissed mommy. "I have never, nor will I ever. Mommy is my one and only." They smiled at each other and kissed. They kissed a little too long. I felt uncomfortable. I turned back around and took the pot off the stove.

At lunch, mommy and daddy held hands and sat side-by-side. "Where's Catherine?" Mommy asked.

"She said she was mounting Bernard," I said, and sipped my soup.

"What?" daddy yelled angrily.

"She's having a lovely evening with Bernard tonight," I said, and looked at daddy, wondering why he objected to them having a lovely meal together.

Daddy stood up so fast his chair fell backward and busted on the floor.

"Why are you mad?" I asked timidly. "You said mounting means having a lovely evening together."

Daddy turned his head to the side and exhaled, laughing lightly. "Yes, Maybel, I see. Don't say someone is mounting another person anymore. It has a different meaning too."

"What is the other meaning?" I asked.

"Maybel, when you're older, you'll understand."

I was annoyed they kept secrets. I continued eating my soup. Daddy took another chair and moved it close to mommy and they continued holding hands and eating lunch together.

The next Saturday daddy left without me to go to the hardware store. I was disappointed because I wanted to hear more naughty things.

I stayed home with mommy. Mommy had friends over for card games and a quilting bee. I quickly realized the reason daddy took me to the hardware store on Saturdays was because mommy and her friends were naughtier.

Mrs. Charleston, Aunt Mary, Aunt Sadie, and two of daddy's sisters, Aunt Margaret and Aunt Nora, came to play cards and finish a quilt they had been making for two years. The reverend's wife, the baker's wife, two neighbors, and a lady from the next town over also attended.

I sat on the sofa writing. I pretended to write a story but I was writing questions to ask Catherine and Bernard. Mommy and her friends talked about their husbands. I had a lot of questions already and we were only twenty minutes into our gathering.

The first issue to discuss, in their apparently long list of items to cover, was adultery. Aunt Mary worried that Uncle Frank was cheating.

My ears were so finely tuned I could hear Aunt Mary's breath from my place on the sofa while she sat at the sewing table in the next room.

"He's been distant," Aunt Mary complained. "And he goes to the barbershop every week."

"Perhaps he's trying to look handsome for you," Francine, the reverend's wife, consoled Aunt Mary.

"He's bald, Francine!"

"Oh, well then he's cheating," Francine said while quilting a baby blanket for her granddaughter.

Aunt Mary moaned, "I just don't know what to do."

"Well, you don't yet know he's cheating," mommy said. Mommy was the smartest of all these hens. Daddy called them hens.

"Well, then, what would you do, Mirabel, if Daniel went to the barbershop every week even though he were bald?" Francine asked.

"I keep a brick by the bed. He thinks it's for robbers but it's also for cheating husbands," mommy cackled and all the hens followed suit, cackling and hollering.

"If Byron cheated, I'd feed his carcass to hogs. They eat everything," Mrs. Charleston said.

"I'd make fertilizer out of his dead and dried penis," the reverend's wife said. She didn't even look up from the baby's quilt she sewed.

A round of agreeing murmurs went around.

My eyes were wider than the tea cup saucers on which those old hens set their tea cups. I wasn't even pretending to write. I stared at my papers while listening intently. I had no idea it was acceptable to talk about murder as long as you were knitting and quilting.

This was the best entertainment I'd ever experienced, far better than any play I'd ever attended.

"Do you have sex with Frank every night?" Aunt Sadie asked.

"No! That's what newlyweds do!" Aunt Mary retorted.

"How often do you have sex?" Aunt Sadie asked.

"Oh, I don't know, once or twice a month," Aunt Mary replied.

"You should have sex more often," Aunt Sadie said.

There was another round of agreeing murmurs but also several dissenting tongue clicks.

"Well, how often do you have sex, Sadie?" Aunt Mary became defensive.

"Once a week, at least." Aunt Sadie looked pleased with herself.

Mommy snorted at her sisters.

"What, Mirabel?" Aunt Mary asked, annoyed. "Speak up if you have something to say!"

"Danny and I have sex every other night," Mommy said proudly.

I did not know what sex was, but mommy and daddy kissed, so I figured it had something to do with kissing. I didn't mind seeing Catherine and Bernard kiss, but watching mommy and daddy kiss was a bit disgusting because they were old. I involuntarily gagged while the women gasped at mommy's admission.

Mrs. Charleston was the only one to take mommy's side. "I do as well," she said. "When you have a good lover, you enjoy every minute until his cock expires." And at that the women erupted with laughter.

"Oh, Calvin's penis expired forty years ago," our old neighbor, Ethel, said. "Enjoy it now, young ladies," Ethel continued. "If I knew penises had expiration dates, I would have climbed on more often!" Ethel continued knitting her great grandson's baby booties. All the hens cackled. I thought my eyeballs were going to pop out of my skull.

"Who wants wine?" mommy asked.

An almost deafening round of crowing filled the room. Daddy was right, they really did sound like hens.

The women continued talking about other women, newspapers, fashion, and plays they'd seen, but after that first glass of wine set in, it was as though all the filth we learned a about in church landed in my family room and expanded, growing, doubling in size and fed by the naughtiness of mommy and her friends.

I had thought Catherine's and Edith's gossiping got out of hand at times, but Catherine had a long way to advance before she reached mommy's and our aunts' level of gossip.

"I couldn't orgasm last night," Aunt Sadie said.

"Which position were you in?" mommy asked.

I wrote down 'position' in the margin of my paper. Catherine didn't always answer my questions, but I knew Bernard would always be honest with me.

"He was behind me," Aunt Sadie said.

I wrote down 'behind me.' This sounded important so I drew a star next to it. I didn't understand what it meant for Uncle Frank to be behind Aunt Sadie.

"Didn't he reach around?" mommy asked.

I wrote down 'reach around.'

"No," Aunt Sadie said. "Would that be better?"

"Yes!" The hens cackled loudly.

"He needs to touch that joy button," Ethel said, her dentures sliding around in her mouth. The hens crowed.

I wrote down 'joy button' with a big question mark.

"Just a second ladies," I heard mommy say.

I put a clean piece of paper over the one I was writing on and put my head down on top of it, pretending to be asleep.

I heard mommy's footsteps come closer and she looked down at me to make sure I wasn't paying attention.

"Ok, ladies, let's continue," mommy said, satisfied I wasn't listening. "I forgot Maybel was here today, but she's sound asleep, so let's get going."

Get going? I wondered. I had thought they were going full throttle already.

"Well Robert likes my mouth more than anything," I heard our neighbor, Arlene, say.

"They all do," Ethel said. I was beginning to like Ethel more and more. Her age made her candor amusing.

"I don't like doing that," Arlene said. "I want to be pleasured, too."

"Just do it for a couple minutes then get on top of him and please yourself," Mrs. Charleston said. "Always make sure you get pleasured before he goes soft."

"Amen!" Ethel said. I peeked back over the back of the couch at Ethel. Her thin white hair was in a bun and she was almost done knitting her great grandson's baby booties. She looked frail, but after listening to her, I thought perhaps she was much less frail than I'd ever realized.

"May I ask a very personal question?" Aunt Sadie asked.

"Oh yes!"

"Yes!"

"Certainly!"

"That's what we're here for," Ethel said, beginning another knitting project.

"Stephen is a good size, I think, well, I'm not sure. I've never had sex with anyone else. I sometimes feel like he's not all the way inside. Sometimes," Aunt Sadie blushed, "I wish he were longer, but I'm not sure how long other penises are. What is the average size?"

"Well how long and how wide is your husband?" Ethel asked. "If he's long and skinny, that can be nice. If he's short and fat, well, that has its benefits, too. And if he's long and thick, well, you should be very, very happy!" Ethel cackled. I decided Ethel was going to be my surrogate grandmother. She was hilarious.

"He's around five inches," Aunt Sadie said. She looked around at the ladies timidly.

"Oh...."

"Hmmm..."

"I'm sorry...."

"Is that little?" Aunt Sadie asked.

"Is he thick?" Ethel asked.

"Not particularly, I don't think. I mean, I don't know. I've never seen another penis."

"Is he rich?" Ethel asked.

"He has invested well and we don't want for anything," Aunt Sadie answered. "He bought us a vacation home in Maine."

"Oh, well then, he's fine," Ethel said.

I suppressed a giggle.

"Daniel is eight inches," mommy said.

"Byron is nine inches," Mrs. Charleston smiled.

I saw mommy roll her eyes but her face was turned so that Mrs. Charleston couldn't see mommy's jealousy.

Aunt Mary chimed in. "Frank is seven inches. That's probably why he goes to the barbershop every weekend." Aunt Mary sounded sad.

"Oh, now, you don't know he's cheating," mommy said.

"He's a really good lover." Aunt Mary looked down at the part of the quilt she'd been working on for two years. I had wondered why they'd been working on the same quilt for two years and now I knew why; none of them actually quilted.

"Why don't you just confront him?" Aunt Sadie asked.

"I'd go find a lover with thick hair," Ethel said. "Nothing makes a man work harder to make you scream than being replaced by a man with a full head of hair."

I decided Ethel was my new favorite person. She was blunt like me. Ethel was ninety. If being blunt and honest made you old, I'd live to be a hundred and ninety.

"There is a man in my church who always says hello to me," Aunt Mary admitted.

"He's being polite," Aunt Sadie said. "Don't confuse politeness with flirtation."

"I agree," mommy said.

"Should I accept his invitation to have coffee together?" Aunt Mary asked.

"No," both mommy and Aunt Sadie said.

"Yes," said Ethel. "It's coffee, not bourbon on a steamboat down the Mississippi while your parents aren't paying attention."

The women stared at Ethel.

"I'm ninety. By the time you're ninety you have a past. And in my case," she cackled, "you have several pasts!"

I loved my new grandma Ethel.

"Don't go," mommy said. "Talk to Frank first."

"You didn't talk to Danny first that time you went to that whore's house," Aunt Mary said.

"What's all this then?" Ethel asked.

"Nothing," mommy snapped.

"Mirabel found out a woman flirted with Daniel and confronted the whore," Aunt Sadie said.

"Oh, hush, Sadie and Mary, the both of you!" Mommy snipped.

"And Mirabel went to her house with a horse whip," Aunt Mary added.

"A horse whip?" Ethel asked.

"Yes, a horse whip," Aunt Mary said.

"I once went to a whore's house with a gun, but I guess a horse whip would be alright in a pinch, if you didn't have access to a gun." Ethel continued sipping wine and knitting.

"I thought Byron cheated on me once," Mrs. Charleston admitted, "so I put poisonous herbs in his morning coffee, but I dumped it into the sink when Bernard came into the kitchen talking about the wonderful time he'd spent with his father the night before. I realized Byron had been with Bernard, not some whore."

Mommy looked surprised at Mrs. Charleston.

"Oh, it wouldn't have killed him. It would have given him awful diarrhea though," Mrs. Charleston laughed.

"Well did he cheat?" Ethel asked.

"No. He's smart. He wouldn't ruin everything we've built over some dumb slut," Mrs. Charleston laughed.

"So, there was another woman who caught his eye then?" Ethel asked.

"I suppose you never know the truth, but I don't think there was anyone worth worrying about. I don't think he's ever cheated. That's why he's alive," Mrs. Charleston snorted.

Mommy kept her head down. She didn't laugh with the others.

"Mirabel, what's wrong?" Aunt Mary asked.

"Well, I don't think Danny has ever strayed, but like Anna said, one never knows the truth."

"Oh, honey, this is the wine talking," Aunt Mary took mommy's glass of wine away.

"None of that matters when you're old like me," Ethel said. "The only people that matter are the people you drink wine with. If I could have another glass of wine with Calvin, I would, no matter whether or not he strayed. He had the best sense of humor."

The women were quiet for a moment. I continued peeking over the sofa at them. They all looked like they were reflecting on their husbands and their fidelity and whether or not loyalty mattered.

"Don't get me wrong, I'd kill Calvin a second time for having sex with that dirty whore, it's just that after twenty years and six feet under, sometimes I miss the bastard."

"Maybel," Catherine called as she opened my bedroom door. "Bernard wants to know if you want to come get custard with us?"

"No thank you," I replied without looking up at her.

I laid in bed reading about trees. Catherine and Bernard had resumed taking strolls together, and recently attended a birthday party of one of Catherine's friends. I didn't know if they attended the party as a couple or just as friends.

"You've been turning down our invitations the last two weeks. Are you angry?" Catherine stood by my door wearing a pretty blue dress and heels. She wore a beautiful necklace given to her by Bernard when they first started dating.

"No, I'm not angry," I continued reading my book about trees around the world.

"Then why don't you want to spend time with us anymore? I rather think Bernard misses you. He keeps asking for you."

"Why?" I asked. "You two call me an annoying tag-along."

"I've never called you annoying," Catherine protested.

"You both make me feel unwelcome," I said. I continued reading my book. I liked trees, and I was just about to start a chapter about ancient yew bushes.

"Maybel, I'm sorry. Come with us."

"No thank you. I have plans," I told Catherine.

Catherine giggled, "Oh really? Becoming a socialite Maybel?"

Catherine left. She giggled because she didn't believe I had any friends. I did have friends, but they lived far out in the country. They aren't who I'd been spending time with though.

After I heard Catherine and Bernard leave, I set off to meet Danny. He was my new best friend. Bernard always chased boys away and I didn't want a big brother anymore, so I didn't tell him about Danny.

I met Danny at our usual spot in the woods by the park.

"On guard, Danny!" I screamed as I approached him from behind.

Danny turned around smiling. "I could hear you coming ten minutes ago, Maybel!" he laughed.

"No, you didn't!" I giggled.

"Yes, I did! I was tracking you!" he laughed.

"Prove it!" I shouted.

"Ok, you stopped to pick up a rock ten minutes ago and put it in the right pocket of your dress," he smiled triumphantly.

I smiled and pulled the rock from my pocket. "How did you do that?" I asked, genuinely curious.

"My mother taught me!" he grinned.

"Let's play!" I shouted with glee.

We battled each other with sticks while trying to maintain balance on a log. Danny was much better at balancing and using a stick like a sword than me. He let me win sometimes though. He put up a good fight, but I knew he let me win from time to time.

We played until dinner time. I was getting hungry and the mosquitoes were beginning to bite.

"Do you want to come to my house for dinner?" I asked Danny.

"You hadn't invited me before. I thought you were embarrassed of me," he said rather timidly.

"No, it's because my sister's stupid boyfriend chases away any boy that talks to me. He thinks he's my big brother protecting me, but it's annoying and angers me!" I became angry just thinking about it.

"It's ok, I don't want to eat anything my mother can't eat anyway. You can come to my house, Maybel, but we don't have much food." Danny looked down and was embarrassed and afraid of my reaction, I could tell.

"I don't care about any of that! I told you that already!"

Danny sighed, "Ok, you can come." He furrowed his brow and looked pained. "It's just, we don't have money, and most people I try to be friends with make fun of me when they find out I don't have money," he said, shyly.

I could see from his posture and voice he was scared and embarrassed. "Then you should make better friends," I said. "I'm not going to make fun of you."

"Maybel, we live on the east side." He looked down at his bare feet.

"I don't care! I already told you that!" I was exasperated with Danny's constant embarrassment. I had never been through the east side, but I could tell from passing by along the main road that it wasn't as pleasant as where I lived.

Danny led me to his house. We walked past the town stores, past the bank and post office, past the boarding houses, and past the barbershop, where all the men go to secretly drink alcohol then return home, unkempt, unshaven, and hair still ungroomed.

Danny led me quickly to the other side of the street just as two men stumbled from the barbershop, fists raised and yelling obscenities.

"Don't look at them," Danny whispered. "It's best if you keep your head down."

I did as Danny instructed until we passed the commotion. We turned two corners then passed a house where women sat on the porch fanning themselves in dresses that had very low necklines.

"Don't stare, Maybel," Daddy whispered. "The man that owns the place beats them, and he'll beat us too if we look too long."

"He beats them?" I gasped. "Why?"

"Because he can, Maybel," Danny said simply.

The women sat in rocking chairs and stood by the porch posts calling sweetly to the men passing by.

"Ruthie?" I suddenly recognized my friend from church from when we were but five or six years old. I barely recognized her through the heavy makeup and jewelry. She wore a tight cream and black dress that showed her tiny breasts far too immodestly.

Ruthie was surprised to hear her name called. She saw me wave and looked terrified. A man opened the door and whispered in her ear. She suddenly smiled exaggeratedly and waved back. "Hello, I'm doing well. Have a lovely evening." Her smile was plastered in place. It was fake.

"Maybel, walk faster, please!" Danny begged, "And keep your head down!"

I did as I was told but I felt really strangely. I was scared.

We arrived at Danny's house. It was one of several dozen one to two-room shacks lined up side-by-side with only some boards separating dwellings. Danny led me inside and it was dark and smelled moldy. The floor was dirt and the dust made me sneeze.

"Excuse me," I apologized, and promptly sneezed again.

"Maybel, this is my mother, Hannah." Danny introduced me to his mother. She was beautiful, with long, straight, black hair. She looked troubled, though.

"Hello, nice to meet you Mrs...." I turned to Danny, "I'm so sorry, I don't know your last name."

"Stronghorse," Danny answered.

"Oh, I've never heard that surname before. I like it," I smiled. "It's nice to meet you, Mrs. Stronghorse." I shook her small, limp hand.

"It's nice to meet you, Maybel. Danny talks about you often." Danny's mother spoke so softly I could barely hear her. She seemed extremely shy.

Danny's mother offered me a piece of bread. I didn't accept it saying I wasn't hungry, though after all the stick sword fighting, I was very hungry.

Before leaving I made plans to meet Danny the next day, then told Danny and his mother goodbye.

"Maybel, I have to walk you back to town so nobody hurts you. Just keep your eyes down."

"Ok," I said. I didn't know what to make of this area of town. Everyone was scared.

Danny walked me past that house with all the women and I quickly glanced over but didn't see Ruthie.

We arrived to the edge of the good part of town.

"Are you really going to meet me tomorrow?" Danny asked.

"Yes, of course. Why?"

"You didn't accept our food. Is it because you don't like our food?" Danny looked sad.

"I didn't want to take your food because you said you don't have much, Danny. If I took your food you wouldn't eat tonight."

"Whenever I make friends, they leave me when they see we don't have much," he said sadly.

"I'll see you tomorrow, Danny."

"Ok, Maybel." He didn't believe me, because in his eyes, he said a final goodbye to me.

The next day after breakfast I washed my dishes and tidied the kitchen. I took a loaf of bread and a jar of jam and put it in the bag in which I carried my papers and pencils.

Mommy stopped me as I opened the front door. "Maybel, where are you going?"

"To the park to write stories," I said.

"Catherine is hurt you no longer spend time with her," mommy told me.

I laughed and snorted. "That's funny mommy, she's always tried to get rid of me."

"I think she realizes now how much she enjoyed your presence. Perhaps the space you've put between you and Catherine has made her realize she enjoyed your company all along."

"I want to go write stories, mommy," I pleaded.

"Can you please do one thing for me? Spend one hour with Catherine," mommy asked sweetly.

"Doing what?" I asked.

"Talking, playing, I'll even give you money to buy a cookie at Charlie's if you take Catherine."

I narrowed my eyes. "Mommy," I watched her carefully, "did you used to give money to Catherine and make her take me with her?"

"Yes, dear." She smiled and patted my head. "Sometimes love and bonding need a little extra nudge. But look at Catherine now! She enjoyed your time together so much she is sad now with your absence!" Mommy kissed my cheek and brushed my hair back.

I took the coins mommy had been holding in her palm because she knew I couldn't say no to her.

"Catherine!" I screamed upstairs. "We're getting cookies! Hurry up!"

"Good girl, dear," mommy kissed my forehead.

I wondered how many times, and in how many ways mommy had manipulated us. I wasn't mad; I was envious of her manipulative abilities.

We were almost to the candy store when Bernard yelled, "Wait up!"

"Great," I mumbled.

"Can I join you ladies?" he asked jovially. He wore a green shirt, making his eyes appear to glow in the sunlight.

"No," I said.

"Maybel!" Catherine frowned at me.

I frowned back at Catherine, "Mommy says you're sad without me and paid me to bond with you. By the way, she admits to paying you to take me when I was younger."

Catherine looked embarrassed. "Maybe sometimes I didn't want to take you, but I always ended up enjoying our time together."

"I'll pay for our treats, and Maybel, you can keep your money, that is, if you let me come," Bernard smiled.

I was about to say no, but then realized I could use mommy's money to buy Danny and his mother cookies.

"Ok," I agreed.

"Who is this friend of yours I keep hearing about?" Bernard asked, as we sat down in the candy store.

"Just a friend," I replied.

"Do you have a boyfriend, Maybel?" he teased, but I could tell he wanted to scare away another boy who dared talk to his little sister.

"No," I said dryly.

"What's your friend's name, Maybel," Catherine asked.

"Danny." Luckily, I'd learned from Catherine how to lie to adults and used the same quick thinking she used on mommy and daddy. "It's short for a girl's name, but I forget what it's short for."

"Danielle?" Bernard asked.

"Sure," I said, "I mean yes," I quickly added.

"She's French?" Bernard asked.

"She speaks English," I said.

"Danielle is a French name," Bernard said.

"Then I guess she's French," I spoke through gritted teeth. "Anyway, I don't care where she or her mother are from. I like them," I said.

"I'm supposed to meet Danny soon, so I really need to be going now." I stood up and ordered two cookies for Danny and his mother.

"Maybel, brush your teeth when you get home so your teeth won't rot from sugar," Catherine called to me as I stood at the counter.

"Yes mommy," I said, sarcastically. I didn't bother explaining they weren't for me.

I hadn't realized how much time had passed until I reached the woods and Danny wasn't there.

I went to his house and his mother answered.

"May I please speak to Danny?" I asked her.

His mother paused. "Yes," she said, "he's here."

Danny came from the back and his face was dry and appeared pleasant, but I could tell he had been crying.

"I'm sorry, Danny, mommy wanted me to spend time with my sister. I didn't realize how late it had gotten."

"I thought you didn't want to see me again," he said.

"I like playing with you, Danny. I'm sorry I was so late getting to the woods. Look! I brought cookies!"

I gave them to Danny's mother and she gave one to Danny and hungrily ate the other.

Danny ate his quickly, too.

"My mommy likes giving gifts to people. Please accept this bread and jam," I smiled. Danny's mother cried and thanked me. I was surprised to see her cry when I handed her the bread.

"Maybel, don't come here alone ever again," Danny said in a very serious, almost stern voice. "It's not safe for you to walk alone here."

"Ok," I said meekly. "I'm sorry."

"Maybel, you're my friend, and I'm trying to keep you safe. I'm sorry if my tone was rude."

"It's ok, I understand. I'll be more careful," I said.

Danny gestured for me to sit on the ground. He and his mother sat on the ground beside me hungrily eating bread and jam.

After Danny and his mother ate, Danny and I went back to the woods to play pirates and cowboys and Indians.

"Danny, teach me to do that thing where you know I'm coming from a mile away," I asked.

"It's called tracking. You have to be very quiet and listen to what the wind tells you."

"Ok," I said.

"I mean extremely quiet. You have to quiet your mind and breath and heart."

"Ok," I said.

"Maybel, I really like you, it's just, well, you're never quiet, at all, ever."

I laughed. "So I've heard from many others," I laughed again.

Danny told me about tracking. He fascinated me. I liked him a lot.

"My people used to hunt like this," he said.

"What does that mean?" I asked.

"We hunted animals for food," he answered.

"No, I meant, what does 'my people' mean?" I was curious.

"My mother's tribe," answered Danny.

"What's a tribe?" I asked, even more curious.

"We're Indians, Maybel. That's what we call our family. They're our tribe," Danny said.

"You're Indian?" I asked, surprised.

"You didn't know that?" Danny asked, even more surprised.

"How would I know if you didn't tell me," I asked Danny.

"My skin is darker than yours, Maybel, and my mother's skin is even darker." he said.

"I know," I said.

"That doesn't bother you?" he asked.

"No," I said.

"Oh." Danny looked surprised.

"Do you want to play in the creek?" I asked.

"Yes," he said.

"I'm sorry I was late getting here. Mommy wanted me to take my sister to the candy store to spend time with her. And my sister's boyfriend came," I frowned.

"You don't like him?"

"I do, but he doesn't like when I talk to boys. He thinks he's my big brother," I explained.

"Does he like you?"

"We get along," I said.

"I meant, maybe he is jealous when you like other boys?" Danny suggested.

"I don't think so. I think he's just protective of me. That's what my sister says. My sister says Bernard, that's her boyfriend, is protective and brotherly toward me. Catherine has always said Bernard calls me his little sister when he refers to me while talking to Catherine's friends."

"Ok, Maybel," Danny said, and continued along the path we'd cleared to the creek.

I didn't like Danny's response. He didn't believe me. I could tell.

We arrived at the creek in the woods. It wasn't deep.

"We have a pond at my house. There are a lot of fish there. Do you want to come to my house?" I asked Danny.

"No!" Danny said, then changed his tone. "I'm sorry, Maybel, it's just people aren't nice to me or my mother, or to anyone where I live."

"Why?" I asked, confused.

"We don't have money," he said.

"We can still have fun here," I said and waded in.

Danny followed.

We spotted minnows. "They're fast!" I laughed.

"Yes," Danny laughed.

"There's a crawdad by your foot, Danny," I whispered.

Danny bent down to pick it up. He held it up for me.

I spotted one by my foot. I bent down and it skittered away. "Hey! Get back here!" I yelled at it.

Danny laughed, "You have to move with nature, Maybel. You can't fight the wind, you just let it take you."

"What?" I asked, confused.

"You have to relax, clear your mind, and move like water," he explained.

"What?" I asked again.

"Be faster, Maybel," Danny simplified.

"Oh, ok." I swooped down and didn't catch another crawdad.

Danny bent down and caught another one.

"Well, now you're just showing off!" I laughed.

Danny laughed, "I've had a lot more practice than you, Maybel. Just close your eyes and imagine what you want. Now imagine if you don't get it, your mother will go hungry another day. That mindset is good motivation to get what you want."

"Do you really not eat some days?"

Danny shook his head yes. He didn't speak because then he'd cry, so he kept his mouth shut. I knew that's what he was doing because I'd been like that before.

We continued wading through the creek. I carried my shoes and my toes squished in the muddy creek bottom. Danny didn't have shoes.

"Maybel," Danny began, "what's your family like?"

"They're nice," I said.

"That's nice," he said.

"What's your family like?" I asked.

"It's just me and my mother. My father left us," he answered, neither sad nor angry.

"You don't seem sad or angry. Why?" I asked Danny.

"There's nothing I can do to make him stay with me and mother. I was sad at first, then angry, but it didn't matter how I felt, he is still gone. That is just how it is sometimes."

"I'd be mad if my father left," I said.

"And in a year, or two years, you'll still be angry, and your father will still be gone," Danny said.

I watched him curiously. "May I ask why he left?"

"He couldn't find work. Nobody would hire him because he was married to an Indian. He figured he could get a job if he moved somewhere where nobody knew his wife and son were Indians."

"He sends money to you then?" I asked.

"No," Danny said, again, neither sadly nor angrily.

"I'm sorry, Danny," I said. I stepped closer to him and patted his back.

"We'll be ok, Maybel. Thank you."

Danny paused, "You know Maybel, you're the first white person I've met that's been nice to me."

"Well, you're the first Indian I've ever met and you're really nice too," I giggled.

We continued wading through the creek.

"Will you show me the hawk nest again?" I asked.

"Yes," he smiled.

He led me to the hawk next and I looked up, hoping to get a glimpse. It was a large nest of twigs high up in the tree branches.

"You like hawks, don't you?" Danny asked me.

"I don't know. I've never seen one," I replied.

"What kind of animals do you feel closest to?" Danny asked.

"I've never been close to any wild animals, well except for racoons and opossums and deer, animals like that," I told him.

We continued walking. I put my shoes back on, but then when Danny stepped on a twig that pierced his skin, I felt guilty for having shoes. I started to take my shoes off but he stopped me. "There's no sense in us both getting bloody feet," he smiled, but he was in pain, I knew.

"Which animal, of all animals, is your favorite?" he asked with a curious smile.

"Well there was a white wolf that terrified me not too long ago, but she was beautiful. Scary, but magical. Nobody believed me until we saw wolf prints outside the bedroom window where I slept."

"Here in town?"

"Oh, no, I went westward with my sister's boyfriend's family," I explained.

"That's your spirit's animal, Maybel," he smiled broadly.

"What's that?" I asked.

"Your spirit's animal guides you."

"And then what happens? Where do we go?" I asked.

"Your guide protects you, leads you, and helps you," he said.

"Well, she scared me," I said, "but she didn't hurt me, and she was the most beautiful animal I've ever seen."

"My animal guide is an owl. My mother's is a fox."

"What are the differences?" I asked.

"Well, I can see truths, and I feel like you can too, and my mother just wants to disappear. That's what our guides show us," Danny explained.

"I saw an owl outside my window. Maybe it was your guide?" I said.

"Maybe," he laughed. "Let's go further down the creek."

The woods became denser and darker because the trees and bushes were closer together.

"I've never been here before. Have you?" I asked Danny.

"Yes. You can see the animals and trees better here because there are less people."

"Danny, are we on people's land?"

"No, I don't think so. I think this is part of the town park," he answered.

"There are men over there. Are we on their land?" I became nervous.

"No, they don't live here," he said.

"Danny, those men look angry. I think we're on their land."

"Maybel! Run!" Danny screamed as they began running toward us.

Danny grabbed my hand and yanked hard. "Run!" he screamed.

We ran, but another man came from behind a tree and grabbed Danny.

"Run, girl!" The man snarled at me.

I didn't run. I stood terrified, watching the man raise his fist and punch Danny. Danny's lips bled.

"Run, Maybel!" Danny screamed.

I froze. I couldn't move and felt cold and scared.

A man grabbed me from behind. "You got a boyfriend, little girl?"

I couldn't breathe, my lungs felt bound.

"Well, you do now!" he laughed into my ear. His mustache bristled against my earlobe as he laughed.

"No!" Danny screamed. He kicked his captor between his legs and came to me. He picked up a branch from the forest floor and gouged the man's neck and I was released.

We ran and I couldn't feel my body anymore. I only saw twigs and brush along the forest floor. I had no feeling anymore and then the ground came toward me quickly and hit my face hard.

One of the men had struck me. He turned me over and his fist was raised but he was hit on the back of his head with a large branch and fell over next to me, eyes wide open.

Danny picked me up. He looked as terrified as I felt. "Run, Maybel! Please run!"

We ran. I didn't remember much but glimpses of forest and screams. We ran to Danny's house and a black boy came to help us.

He picked me up and we went into Danny's house.

I sat in a corner on the dirt floor breathing hard. I couldn't feel my hands, which made me breathe faster.

Danny and his mother were speaking to each other but I couldn't understand.

The black boy seemed scared to approach me. "I'm Isaac," he whispered. He cautiously handed me a ladle of water. "It's water," he said. "I won't hurt you."

"What happened?" I whispered.

"They don't like our kind," Isaac said. "Indians and black people. I don't know why they would go after a white girl. Somebody will miss you."

I could only stare at him. I was too scared to cry.

"Listen, you need to go home before you bring us more trouble," he said.

"It's not her fault Isaac!" Danny yelled.

"If she stays here," Isaac said, "her family will miss her and start looking for her. What do you think will happen when they find her here with Indians and black folk? They'll blame us and we'll hang!"

"We didn't do anything bad!" Danny screamed, "They attacked us!"

"Maybel, please leave," Danny's mother pleaded. "I'm so sorry! I'm just scared!"

"Mother!" Danny pleaded.

"Isaac is right. We'll hang. They won't care why a white girl is here. They'll see us and not ask questions."

I ran to the door and opened it. "I'm so sorry, Maybel!" I heard Danny scream behind me.

I ran home and went to daddy's workshop to dry my eyes and calm down enough to breathe. When I recovered, I went upstairs to bathe and dress for dinner.

The Charleston's were here. Daddy and Mr. Charleston spoke of business and politicians. Mrs. Charleston sat near mommy. Bernard and Catherine were holding hands.

I hadn't spoken to anyone. My thoughts were still racing.

"Maybel, what's wrong," daddy asked as he took another piece of bread from the platter.

"Nothing," I said quickly.

"You seem upset," he said.

"I'm fine."

I looked at my plate. There was so much food. I never realized how much food I had before Danny's mother was proud to offer me a slice of bread.

Daddy grabbed my wrist when I reached for a slice of pie. "What is this, Maybel?"

I suddenly and vividly remembered the man yanking my arm. I felt cold inside.

"Maybel!" Daddy screamed. He stood up holding my wrist.

Mommy told daddy to calm down.

Daddy didn't listen. He grabbed my wrist harder. "Who hurt you?"

"Men in the woods. They chased me and Danny." My words were barely a whisper, and flashes of men chasing me were so strongly in my mind that I could not focus on daddy.

Daddy's eyes went dark. Mr. Charleston stood up beside daddy.

"Where are the men?" Daddy snarled.

"The woods by the park," I whispered, terrified.

"Take me!" Daddy said angrily.

"No!" I cried. "I'm not going back!"

Mommy smacked daddy's hand and he let go of me.

"Then take me to your friend's house. I need to speak to her father," Daddy ordered.

I sat terrified.

"Maybel! Take me to your friend's house!" Daddy bellowed.

"Stop it right now!" Mommy screamed.

"Danny is a boy. He's my friend, not my boyfriend," I said, "and people are mean to him and his mother because they're Indians. Don't hurt them!" I cried. "They're nice!"

"Take me to his house!" Daddy commanded. "I'm not going to hurt him. I'm going to find the men who hurt you!"

"I'm fine! It's just a bruise!" I cried. I sat in my chair numb and scared.

"Maybel," daddy said with a cold and careful calmness that terrified me, "take me to your friend's house."

"Danny saved me from the men that chased me," I could barely whisper. "Danny protected me and hit the bad men. Don't hurt Danny. He's nice."

"I won't hurt him," daddy said calmly. He wasn't calm though.

Mr. Charleston was standing at daddy's side and buttoned his jacket. He looked angry, too. Bernard left with his father and daddy to get the Charleston's automobile.

Mrs. Charleston was quiet and stared at the table without blinking. Mommy and Catherine sat on either side of me.

Mr. Charleston arrived with his car. He drove and I gave directions. Bernard sat in the back and wrapped his arm around me protectively.

We quickly arrived at Danny's house.

"Danny, I'm Maybel's father. We're not here to hurt anyone. We only want to know who hurt Maybel and we'll be on our way."

Danny cracked opened the door only a whisper. "They live beyond the woods. They live in the white farmhouse. Don't tell them we told you," Danny whispered.

"They won't bother you again," daddy whispered very quietly.

Mr. Charleston gave something to Danny. "See to it you and your mother eat, you hear?"

Danny looked behind daddy and Mr. Charleston to find me. "I'm sorry," he whispered, then quickly shut his door.

Daddy took me home, then left with Mr. Charleston. Bernard stayed with me and mother, Catherine, and Mrs. Charleston. Bernard held a gun.

"What were you thinking!" Catherine whispered to me. We sat together on the sofa in the family room. "You know that's the bad side of town!"

"They're poor, Catherine, not bad!" I crossed my arms. Catherine sat close to me and seemed very distraught.

"I know they're not bad, Maybel! But there're more bad things that happen in that part of town!"

"Danny and his mother are good!" I said.

"You could have been hurt badly!" Catherine looked more scared than mad.

"I could be hurt anywhere I go!" I said.

"But the chances of being hurt there are higher!" Catherine countered.

"Danny's a good person and so is his mother! Danny saved me from those men! He could have left me but he didn't!" I told Catherine angrily.

Mommy was crying. "Please, stop! Please!" she sobbed.

"I'm sorry, Maybel." Catherine said quietly. "I just don't want anyone to hurt you. I love you."

"I love you too, Catherine. Danny didn't hurt me. The men who don't live in the bad part of town tried to hurt me. Danny saved me."

Mrs. Charleston still sat oddly stiff and still and her eyes were glassy and withdrawn. Bernard watched his mother as he gripped his gun tightly.

"Can I go to bed now?" I asked mommy. "I just want to lay down."

"Yes," mommy still cried.

Bernard stood behind his mother and held her shoulders. She reached up and squeezed Bernard's hand. Bernard had been whispering to his mother all evening and watched over her protectively.

"Maybel, I'll sit with you upstairs until your father gets home," Bernard said.

"I don't need a babysitter," I told him.

Bernard followed me upstairs and into my bedroom.

"I'm going to change into my nightgown now so either turn around or get ready for a show," I said.

Bernard blushed and turned around.

I laid down in bed. Bernard took a book from my bookshelf. "Would you like me to read to you?"

"Like you would read to a child?" I angrily responded. And then I sighed as I laid my head down on my pillow. "Yes," I admitted. "I might like you to read me a story."

Bernard sat at the foot of my bed and leaned against the wall and began reading. It was a book my grandmother bought me for my eleventh birthday just before she died. She wrote a note to me inside the cover telling me she would read all my wonderful stories in Heaven and to always keep writing.

Bernard paused halfway through the first short story. "Maybel, may I ask you a rather personal question?"

"Danny didn't kiss me."

"No, I want to know if the men touched you or kissed you?"

"No. One said he was my boyfriend now and then he grabbed my arm," I showed Bernard the bruise, "but Danny hit him with a branch."

"I'll have to thank Danny," Bernard said. "Maybel, you said Danny was an Indian?"

"Don't you dare say anything bad about that Bernard! I don't care if he's Indian! He's been my best friend this summer!"

"I would never say anything bad about Danny being Indian. I wanted to know more about him and his parents."

"His father left because he couldn't find work, because nobody wanted to hire him, because he married an Indian," I told Bernard.

"His father isn't Indian?"

"He's white," I said.

"And you don't mind Danny being Indian?"

"No! Why does it matter? Why does everyone think I should stay away from people with Indian blood?" I angrily yelled at Bernard.

"Everyone? Who tells you to stay away from people with Indian blood?"

"Well not everyone, just Catherine," I said, "She's so concerned about what people will think. She told me not to tell anyone if I kissed Danny because no boy is going to ever kiss me if they found out I've put my lips on an Indian."

Bernard just stared at me sadly. "Catherine said that?"

"Yes. She says Danny might very well be nice but I shouldn't kiss him because my reputation will be ruined and no boy will want me after having kissed an Indian, but I disagree. I told her not everyone is as concerned as she is about being high society."

Bernard just watched me with sadness.

"Why are you sad, Bernard?" I was confused about why he was sad suddenly.

"You are one of only two people in this world I know who are the strongest and most fearless people I've ever met. The other is my mother," Bernard told me.

I carefully considered his compliment. "Thank you, Bernard."

I sat quietly watching Bernard, who sat at the foot of my bed, in silent retrospection.

"Bernard," I asked, "If I kissed Danny, and then met you, and told you I'd kissed an Indian, would you still want to kiss me?"

"Yes."

"Catherine says you're rich and a part of high society. You would still kiss me?"

Bernard came over to me and sat beside me. He held my face gently in his hands and kissed me sweetly.

"I love you, Maybel."

"I love you too, Bernard."

"Will you be ok if I leave you alone for a few minutes?" he asked me.

"Yes, I'm fine. It's just a bruise. I'll be ok," I said.

Bernard left and I continued reading the book my grandmother had given me.

I heard angry voices in the yard below me. It scared me until I recognized the voices as Catherine's and Bernard's.

"I'm being practical, Bernard! If she kisses an Indian, people will ostracize her!"

"People like you!" Bernard countered angrily.

"Bernard! My family doesn't have enough money to stand firmly against society's rules! You can do whatever you want because you have the money to be righteous."

"Not being wealthy is not an excuse to be a coward! That's a choice you make!" Bernard yelled angrily.

"Look! I'm being practical! Most people have to abide by society's rules. If you marry an Indian you won't find work and then you'll starve. Some stores won't sell to black people. Some boarders won't rent to non-white people. I disagree with society's rules, but I don't have the money to break those rules. You do though! So you go change the rules because people like me would be ostracized and be forced to watch their family slowly starve as punishment for breaking the rules."

Both Catherine and Bernard stormed off in opposite directions. Catherine came into the kitchen and Bernard walked around to the front door.

I drifted off to sleep. I couldn't bear more problems tonight.

I awoke crying. It was dark in my bedroom. The moon was still up.

"Maybel, what's wrong?"

I jumped, startled by Bernard sitting in the chair beside my bed.

"Why are you here?" I asked him.

"To protect you." He came and sat beside me. He held me and stroked my hair.

"I had a bad dream," I said.

"I'm right here, Maybel. I won't let anyone hurt you."

"Bernard," I cried, "are Danny and his mother going to be ok?"

"Yes, Maybel."

"What's going to happen to them?"

"Mother and father will see to it Danny gets an education and his mother has shelter, food, and employment. They will do the same for the other boy, Isaac, and his family."

"Do you promise?"

"Yes, Maybel. You have my word."

"When can I see Danny?"

"I don't know, Maybel."

"Why were you and Catherine fighting?"

"I broke up with her," Bernard said without emotion.

I looked up at Bernard in the darkness. "I'll never see you again," I told him.

"We'll still be friends, Maybel. I'll still see you."

"No, you won't. I won't see you. You won't come here, and I can't come to your house because Catherine will feel betrayed," I told him.

"I'm here right now." He laid next to me in bed and kissed the top of my head.

I cried myself to sleep on Bernard's chest as he held me.

In the morning, I awoke next to Bernard. My bedroom was full of sunlight and the birds were already singing. I put my head back on Bernard's chest and he rubbed my back.

"You're awake?" I asked, startled.

"Yes," he said. "I've just been thinking."

"About what?"

"Catherine. I know she is a good person, and I know what she said made sense, but it still angers me."

"Are you going to get back together?" I asked him.

"I don't know. I need some time to think."

"I'm hungry," I changed the subject. "Can we go eat now?"

"Yes, sweetheart."

"Oh Bernard, if you and Catherine don't get back together, can I still come to your house tonight and swim and have a campfire with you? Maybe Catherine won't mind if I tell her I am still scared and need your protection."

"Yes, of course. You don't think that will upset Catherine though?"

"Oh," I paused, "I don't know. I guess she won't want me to go to her ex-boyfriend's house." I sighed and my shoulders slunk down. I really wanted to continue having Bernard in my life.

"Come over anyway," Bernard winked at me. "We can still be friends, Maybel."

We went downstairs to breakfast. "Good morning Maybel, good morning Bernard," mommy greeted us. She was flittering around the kitchen like a hummingbird.

"Good morning," we said to mommy.

"Maybel," mother hugged me and kissed my cheek, "how are you feeling, dear?"

"I'm fine, mommy, where're daddy and Catherine?"

"Catherine left. She's upset about your break up, Bernard. And daddy is still with Mr. Charleston."

"Daddy didn't come home?"

"No," mommy looked worried, but she smiled and pretended to enjoy making breakfast while daddy was missing.

"Can I go to Danny's house to make sure he and his mother are ok?"

"No, dear, it's not safe. Let's wait for your father and see what has happened."

"Bernard would you like pancakes or oatmeal?"

"Pancakes, please."

"Maybel?"

"Pancakes, of course!" Who would choose oatmeal over pancakes, I wondered.

"Mrs. Wyndham, I'm sorry I hurt Catherine. I need some time to think."

"I was young once, I remember break ups," mommy mixed batter while the pan popped with hot butter.

"You and daddy broke up before you got married?" I stared, shocked.

"Oh, no, honey, I was engaged to another man until I met your father. Your father swept me off my feet." Mommy laughed as she reminisced. She continued making pancakes like she hadn't just told me something important.

"You've kissed another man?" I asked mommy, feeling completely taken aback.

Mommy laughed, "Maybel, have you kissed a boy?"

I blushed.

"I'll take that as a yes," she laughed.

"And are you going to marry him?" mommy asked me.

"I wanted to," I said shyly. "but he didn't want me. He wanted someone else."

"That's his loss," mommy assured me. She flipped the pancakes and brought plates down from the cupboard.

"Mommy, do you remember that girl I used to play with after church named Ruthie?"

"Yes," mommy said.

"What happened to her?"

"Her mother contracted an illness and died. She and her father moved away last I heard."

"I think I saw her in town," I told mommy.

"Oh? I wonder if she and her father moved back?"

"Where did they move after Ruthie's mother died?" I asked mommy.

"I really don't know, Maybel. They just up and left after the funeral." Mommy stacked pancakes on our plates and set them in front of us.

I sat eating my pancakes next to Bernard. I wanted to tell mommy the truth, that Ruthie lived with women in a part of town I never knew existed, but I was scared to admit I'd been to places I'd been forbidden to go.

After breakfast, Bernard and I helped wash dishes and tidy up. Mommy let me walk to Bernard's house with him. She said she knew Bernard would keep me safe.

Bernard reached for my hand on the street.

"Bernard I'm fine, I don't need a babysitter."

Bernard started to pull his hand away but I held it tighter.

"I didn't realize you were so in love with Paul," Bernard said quietly.

"I was talking about you, Bernard."

Bernard smiled at me.

After spending some time with Bernard putting a puzzle together, roaming the gardens, swimming, and having tea, Bernard walked me home. I was anxious to know what daddy would tell me. I was worried about Danny and his mother. I asked Bernard to stay until daddy returned.

Bernard walked me home and stayed with me until daddy got home. Catherine had come home and seemed annoyed that Bernard was sitting in our family room.

"Hello, Catherine," Bernard said when she came into the family room. Bernard was not thrilled to see Catherine, but was polite.

And Catherine, to her credit, did not stab Bernard in his neck with her hat pin. "Hello Bernard, she said coolly."

Catherine walked into the kitchen and talked in a hushed, angry voice to mommy, who sounded like she was trying to soothe Catherine's irritation.

I had been sitting on the floor writing while Bernard read some of my finished stories. I looked up at Bernard to see his reaction. He sat watching me.

"I'm ok, Maybel. She's still mad at me and I'm angry about the way she talked about Indians."

"Do you want to leave?" I asked him. "You're probably uncomfortable being here."

"I'd like to stay here and see to it our fathers arrive safely," Bernard said. He continued sitting on the sofa staring at the ceiling.

I stood up and brought my writing over to Bernard and sat beside him. "I know Catherine has a kind heart," I said, "and I understand where she's coming from. I disagree with her, but I do understand that it's more difficult for us common people to break society's rules and survive through being ostracized."

"I know, Maybel. I'm angry at her though. I just need time." Bernard crossed his arms angrily and stared upward.

Daddy and Mr. Charleston came in through the front door in a hurry. "Maybel, are you ok?" daddy asked as he quickly came to me and hugged me tightly. There was dried blood around his nostril and he smelled like soil and campfire.

"Yes," I said.

Daddy picked me up and held me and kissed my cheek. "How are you feeling?" Daddy asked gently. He seemed very worried about my wellbeing.

"I'm fine, daddy. Are Danny and his mother ok?"

"Yes, Maybel. We took them away and put them with people who will get them on their feet," daddy assured me.

Mr. Charleston stood behind Bernard and put his hand on Bernard's shoulder. "Danny will receive a good education, Maybel," Mr. Charleston told me. "Isaac will, too. You have my word," Mr. Charleston said with a strong voice and honesty in his eyes.

"When can I see Danny?" I asked. I wanted to make sure Danny and his mother were safe.

"I'm sorry Maybel, you can't," daddy said firmly. "They will be staying away from here. It's not safe for them here."

"I'll never see Danny again?" I was heartbroken.

"No, Maybel. Trust me, please, sweetheart," Daddy hugged me. He hugged me so tightly I thought he was afraid I would disappear if he let me go.

Daddy bent down to look me in my eyes as he spoke. He looked so intensely into my eyes that I was scared to say anything. "Danny, his mother, and Isaac are safe, and those men will never bother you again. And Maybel," daddy held my cheeks and stared intently into my eyes, "this is really important baby, do not ever talk about Danny, his mother, Isaac, or those men to anyone, ever. Do you understand?"

I stared, scared.

"Do you understand?" Daddy repeated.

"Yes," I whispered.

"Daddy," I whispered again, "you have blood in your nose. Are you ok?"

Daddy wiped his nose with the handkerchief in his pocket. "I'm fine, honey, don't speak of this to anyone again."

I nodded. "Ok," I whispered, and daddy kissed my forehead.

Mr. Charleston motioned for Bernard to come quickly and took him home in their automobile. Daddy went upstairs to bathe.

That evening the Charleston's again came to dinner. The mood was tense. Daddy and Mr. Charleston spent much of the evening in daddy's workshop where he kept nails, garden tools, and his special cider. Daddy liked to make furniture in his spare time and sometimes people came from far away to buy his handicrafts. I slipped quietly to daddy's workshop while Mrs. Charleston admired the dresses mommy had designed and sewn.

Daddy and Mr. Charleston were speaking about the men that chased me and Danny. Daddy held a shovel and Mr. Charleston put clothing into a bag and set it on daddy's workshop table next to the kerosene can. I couldn't hear all they said but what I did hear, I didn't understand. It sounded like the men were gone for good.

Mr. Charleston rolled up his shirt sleeves and there was a gash on his forearm. He took the bag of clothing and the kerosene can and placed it in daddy's wheelbarrow.

Bernard whispered behind me, "Come now, Maybel. Do not make a sound."

He startled me. I went with him because he looked very nervous and his voice was stern and commanding.

"Don't listen in, Maybel. You need to forget everything and never speak of this to anyone." Bernard looked troubled as he led me quietly away. "Don't tell anyone you eavesdropped."

"I didn't hear anything," I said.

"Good."

Bernard took me back inside. Catherine was in mommy's sewing room helping mommy with her dresses.

I followed Bernard to the family room. He sat quietly on the sofa. His face was solemn.

"Why are you scared?" I asked him.

"I'm not scared. I just need some time to think about everything," he said.

"About Catherine?" I asked.

Bernard looked up confused. "No, about what happened last night between our fathers."

I sat beside Bernard. "Do you want to put a puzzle together or take a walk? Maybe you'll feel better?"

"I don't know, Maybel." Bernard leaned his head on his hand and slouched on the sofa arm.

I got up to go see what mommy was doing but Bernard reached his hand out to me. "Sit with me, Maybel? Please?"

I curled up next to Bernard. "Do you want to hear a story?"

"Yes," he patted my arm.

"What do you want it to be about?"

"Indians," Bernard said. "Tell me what you know."

"I don't know much. Just a little," I told him.

Bernard leaned back and wrapped his arm around me. He closed his eyes and took a deep breath.

I thought about what kind of story I could tell about Indians. A made-up story about cowboys and Indians, or something Danny had told me about his tribe.

I took a deep breath and began my story. "Danny first realized the significance of his darker skin when his father took him to town on a hot summer day and made him wear a long-sleeved shirt and long pants, and he was told to keep the brim of his hat low.

Danny's father needed to buy flour and took Danny into town because his mother had to stay home and dig his baby brother's grave. Danny was too little to help dig.

No one would sell food to Danny's mother because she was Indian, so Danny's father had to leave his wife to dig their baby's grave in order to get to town in time to buy food. Danny sat in the hot sun in his winter clothes while his father convinced the shopkeeper to sell him food. The shopkeeper was reluctant because he wasn't supposed to sell to Indians, but he sympathized with Danny's father for having just lost his baby son, so he sold Danny's father the flour on the condition he not tell anyone the shopkeeper had sold food to Indians.

Danny and his father returned home and his baby brother had been buried. The preacher wouldn't give the baby a funeral because he considered Indians godless heathens, so Danny's father did the best he could with prayers. And then they soon moved away. They moved from town to town often because people didn't want Indians to live in their towns.

Then Danny's father left Danny and his mother because no one would hire him because he married an Indian.

In the last town they lived in, Danny came home to find a man beating his mother and trying to tear her clothes off so Danny hit the man with a brick from the wall of their crumbling house and the man laid unconscious on the dirt floor. He was white so they fled town because they would have been killed for hitting a white man, Danny said."

Bernard stared at the ceiling. He wasn't crying but the lamp beside the sofa shown on the tears collecting in his eyes.

Mrs. Charleston had been standing in the doorframe crying, and mommy and Catherine were behind her, tears falling down their faces.

"Bernard, when you become a doctor will you give medicine to Indians?" I asked him.

"Yes, of course, Maybel," Bernard choked back sobs.

"Danny's baby brother died because the doctor refused to treat Indians. When you become a doctor, you'll be good to everyone won't you?" I asked.

"I will, Maybel." His voice was strained.

Bernard continued staring at the ceiling, then he stood up and went to his mother and hugged her.

I sat and spoke, more to myself than to the others. "Danny's really nice, and he says his family is called his tribe, and he taught me how to track people and animals. His last name is Stronghorse and he says my spirit's animal is the white wolf I saw at Paul's house. Spirit animals help your soul on its journey. I guess they're maybe like angels."

I stared at our fireplace. There was soot all around the mouth of the chimney. Little wooden chips lay strewn about the hearth.

"Danny lives in a two-room shack on the east side of our town. It's past a house where women live together and they wear dresses that show a lot of their skin. My childhood friend Ruthie lives there now because mommy said that Ruthie's mother died. I don't know what happened to Ruthie's father. The man who lives with all those women beats them. I'm really worried about Ruthie."

I felt I spoke to myself because there were no breaths of air in my house, only the absence of sound. Mrs. Charleston was not crying anymore. I looked at her, with Bernard holding her against him. Nobody moved and I could not hear their breaths or their silent sobs. I stared at Mrs. Charleston and then to Bernard. Mommy held Catherine in her arms. If I had a child, I would have held him or her too, because I would never want to see my baby die. I would never want to see other people watch my baby die with their dead hearts and emotionless stares.

I turned toward the fireplace again and closed my eyes, trying to make my mind stop thinking. I could never make my mind stop showing me pictures, so I stared at the soot and hoped I would fall asleep soon, and without too many thoughts bouncing around in my mind.

Daddy and Mr. Charleston left again that night and Bernard stayed with us. I asked mommy if Bernard could sleep in my room on the chair and she said yes.

Bernard slept in my bed and we laughed quietly and whispered to each other. I was thrilled to have Bernard stay with me.

"It tickles when you whisper in my ear," I told Bernard.

"Like this?" Bernard whispered unintelligibly into my ear as he held me.

I giggled, "Yes!"

I turned my head and whispered into his ear. I whispered, "I like being with you and I wish you would be with me forever."

Bernard whispered back, "I will."

The next morning after breakfast, Bernard whispered to his mother and she nodded.

"Come, Maybel, let's go on a stroll," Bernard took my hand and led me out the front door.

He didn't speak to me as we walked down the street. He was in deep thought and his brow furrowed in consternation.

Bernard took me to his house. We walked up his long courtyard flanked by towering trees and flower gardens.

"Why are we here?" I asked. "Everyone is at my house."

"I need to show you something, Maybel." Bernard was still deep in thought.

Bernard took me up to his bedroom and sat me on his bed. He went to his closet and from deep within, he pulled a beautifully carved wooden chest.

"Maybel," he said quietly, "this is very important to me." He set the chest on his bed and sat beside me. It had intricate hand carvings on all sides. The top was carved with a beautiful horse in the center with other animals carved around the horse. "Open it," he whispered.

I opened the wooden chest, and prominently displayed, was a photograph of an Indian wearing a long hat of feathers and necklaces of beads adorned his chest.

"Wow! Bernard! I didn't know you knew any Indians! Look at the beads! How do you make such jewelry?"

Bernard smiled shyly, "This is my grandfather, Maybel."

I stared at Bernard. He looked nervously at me. "Maybel, I'm Indian," he said quietly.

I laughed.

Bernard pulled back and looked hurt. "Why are you laughing, Maybel?"

"You know how some people prefer only blondes and some prefer only brunettes? Apparently, I like Indians!" I giggled. "I've only kissed two boys and they're both Indian! I've never kissed a white man yet!" I giggled harder.

Bernard looked relieved. "Oh Maybel, come here." Bernard hugged me tightly and kissed my cheek and looked into my eyes.

"Bernard, you don't look Indian."

"This is my grandfather. He's actually half Indian, like Danny. And he married my grandmother, who is white. And my mother looks more white than Indian."

I smiled at Bernard. "Bernard, I like you because you're a good person. You could paint yourself purple and be from the moon and I'd still be proud to love you."

"Maybel, may I kiss you?"

"Yes," I smiled.

Bernard kissed me sweetly. "I love you, Maybel."

"I love you too, Bernard."

"Maybel, nobody knows about my mother and me except of course my father. My mother's family lives out west. We don't tell anyone because some people won't do business with Indians."

"I'm not ashamed of you, Bernard. I love you and your mother."

"We're not ashamed, Maybel," he sighed, "It's that ancestry can be bad for business and money-making."

"I won't tell anyone Bernard, but I'm not embarrassed of who you are."

"We're not embarrassed, but we don't tout our ancestry either. And," he sighed, "not telling people we're Indian can be very useful in finding out whether or not a person is good or bad."

I watched Bernard. He looked down at his grandfather's picture. Bernard's expression was sad. "Catherine said no boy will kiss you after having put your lips on an Indian, Maybel." Bernard looked pain-stricken.

"I'm sorry, Bernard," I whispered.

"Don't tell her I'm Indian. I have only told people I love and trust completely and whole-heartedly."

"Who else have you told?" I asked.

"You. Only you, Maybel," Bernard said.

"Maybel," daddy said, "would you like to come with me to town today? We can go to the lumber yard then I'll take you to the candy store."

"Ok, daddy." I liked the idea of spending time with daddy. I really liked the idea of spending time with daddy at the candy store and hoped there'd be gambling involved.

I held daddy's hand as we walked into town.

"You know, Maybel, I'll always want to hold your hand." Daddy looked at me and he looked a little sad.

"Me too, daddy."

Daddy smiled.

When we arrived at the lumber yard, Henry was leaving with a load of lumber carefully stacked in his car.

"Hello, Mr. Wyndham, Maybel," Henry nodded at both of us.

"Your uncle has you busy, I see," daddy said.

"Yes," Henry smiled. "I'm rebuilding a store on the east side. It will look grand when I'm finished."

"Great," daddy smiled. "I look forward to toasting its opening."

Henry nodded and left.

Daddy and I walked into the office of the lumber yard. The owner was pouring over paperwork while his sons were sitting on chairs.

"Nolan, please," daddy told one of the sons. The son got up slowly and went to his father's office. He seemed annoyed he had to get up and do something.

Nolan came out and shook daddy's hand. "What can I help you with Daniel?"

"Oak shelving, maple boards, and pine wood, Nolan."

"Got a big order, I see," Nolan smiled.

Nolan yelled at his sons to get off their asses and get to work.

"Pardon the language, miss," Nolan said to me. "My boys don't understand subtlety." He paused, "and they're lazy," he added.

Daddy and I took Nolan's horse carriage home with the wood and I helped him unload the boards.

"You're quite strong," daddy said to me.

"It's from climbing trees," I replied.

"I used to be the best tree climber around," daddy said.

"That was before I was born," I smiled. "Now you're second best."

"Alright then, let's have a little challenge, shall we?"

I smiled. "Yes!"

Daddy and I scaled the two trees nearest his workshop and daddy won. I was completely shocked.

"Daddy! I must get my agility from you!"

"Have you never seen mommy climb a tree?" daddy asked.

"No," I said. "She's always cooking or cleaning."

"Mommy's better than me!" Daddy tousled my hair.

"I'd like to see that," I said. "I've never seen her climb a tree."

"I suppose as we get older, we place cooking and cleaning above playing, honey, but I'll talk to mommy and see what we can do about a family race."

I smiled up at daddy.

We finished unloading the wood daddy bought then returned the carriage to Nolan. His sons were tossing rocks into a trash can when we arrived, competing with each other over who had the best aim. They were still tossing rocks into the can when we left.

"Are they slow?" I asked daddy. I thought maybe they had some difficulties learning in school.

"No, honey, they are second generation rich."

"What's that?" I asked.

"Nolan did all the work and his sons grew up with everything they wanted. Now they are lazy and complacent."

I thought for a moment. "Is that why Henry works harder than Bernard?"

Daddy chuckled, "Henry is older than Bernard. Give Bernard some time before you judge him too harshly."

We walked to the candy store and ate custard together. The candy store was empty, save for a young couple smiling at each other in the corner. They looked happy.

"Daddy, why did you want to spend the day with me?"

"Because I love you. I like being with you."

"I love you too, daddy."

"Maybel, how are you feeling today?" Daddy asked me as he took a spoonful of custard.

"I'm fine, daddy." I continued eating custard next to daddy. I watched him while we ate. "Your eyes look very browny greeny in the light coming through Charlie's store window."

Daddy chuckled, "Why thank you, honey, I made them myself."

I laughed.

My mind wandered to recent happenings. "Daddy, where is Danny now?"

"I don't know, honey. Mr. Charleston said he would pay for Danny's education."

"Can I see Danny to make sure he's ok?"

"We've left that night far behind, Maybel. Things happened that night. It's best we don't ever talk about it to anyone."

I ate my custard bedside daddy and made a bit of a mess. I noticed I held my spoon exactly like daddy held his. I liked noticing similarities between us.

"I'll ask Mr. Charleston about Danny," daddy said. "Don't talk about it to anyone though, Maybel. Things happened. It's in the past. Let it go."

"Ok, daddy."

We continued eating and watching out the window at passersby.

"Can you ask about Ruthie, too?" I whispered.

Daddy looked sad. "Yes," he said. "If I ever see Ruthie's father, we'll have ourselves another night we can't talk about." Daddy looked angry when he spoke of Ruthie's father.

Daddy and I returned home and mommy had lunch ready.

"Daddy says you can climb trees better than him," I told mommy.

"Daddy speaks the truth," mommy kissed daddy.

Daddy grabbed her waist and pulled her into a hug.

"Will you show me after lunch?" I asked mommy.

"Yes, dear," mommy kissed my cheek.

After lunch, mommy changed into pants. She only wore them when no one but us were around. Mommy and daddy stood at the base of two trees and when I yelled go, they bolted upward. Mommy won. Daddy kissed her at the top.

When they descended, I hugged mommy. "You did great!"

"Thank you, baby," mommy kissed me.

Daddy took mommy's hand and led her to his workshop saying he wanted to show her his wood. They held hands and giggled as they went inside.

I went inside our kitchen and ate peaches from a jar I had helped mommy can last summer. When mommy and daddy returned from daddy's workshop, they were out of breath and sweaty.

"Were you two climbing trees again?" I asked.

They paused and looked at each other. Mommy started giggling, "Yes, I climbed all the way up that wooden pole."

Daddy squeezed mommy's waist and kissed her.

"I'll fix us tea," mommy giggled and kissed daddy.

"I'll finish up in my workshop and be right back," daddy said.

Mommy hummed as she prepared hot tea. There was a knock on our backdoor.

"Hello, Henry," mommy smiled. "He's out back in his workshop," she said, then returned to humming and placing cookies on a plate.

"Take these to daddy and Henry, please." Mommy handed me the plate of cookies. "And tell Henry he's welcome to stay for dinner tonight."

I froze. "Oh," I said.

"Oh Maybel," mommy laughed, "do you still freeze up talking to Henry?"

"He's so handsome," I said.

Mommy just giggled softly as she washed vegetables.

"I'm a little better now though. I can say hello to him," I said proudly.

"Well, that's a step in the right direction," mommy giggled again.

"Maybe I'll just quickly tell daddy that I have cookies and that Henry can stay for dinner, but not look directly at Henry? Do you think that will work?"

"Maybe," mommy laughed. She was amused that Henry rendered me speechless.

I opened daddy's workshop door and quickly placed the plate of cookies on the stool by the door. "Tea is ready and Henry can stay for dinner tonight," I blurted out as I stared at the floor, then closed the door.

"Maybel," daddy called.

I opened the door just a crack.

"Yes?"

"Come inside please," daddy told me.

I went two steps inside and looked down at the floor.

"Maybel," Henry is here.

"I know," I said.

"Say hi," daddy chuckled.

"Hi," I said, still averting my gaze downward.

"Hello, Maybel," I heard Henry say. His voice sounded as attractive as his face was beautiful.

"Still shy around Henry?" Daddy's voice sounded highly amused.

"I said hi," I said. I was proud I could now make my voice audible around Henry.

"Come give daddy a hug," daddy laughed.

"Daddy," I whined.

Daddy laughed harder. "Oh, come on now, come give your old dad a hug!"

I looked at daddy and I knew my cheeks were as red as hot coal. Daddy burst out laughing even harder.

"Daddy," I stomped my foot, "can I go now?" I whined.

"Yes," daddy could barely talk, he laughed so hard at my awkwardness.

I shuffled quickly out of daddy's workshop and into the kitchen where mommy took one look at me and giggled.

"I did it, mommy!" I spun around dancing. "I talked to Henry again! I'm getting so much better at talking to the most handsome man in the world!" I continued spinning through the kitchen and out into the family room while mommy watched me and giggled.

It was November, and while we celebrated Thanksgiving, Bernard and his family did not. Catherine asked Bernard to come to our house but he declined. After I ate with mommy, daddy, Catherine, and daddy's sisters and their families, I went to Bernard's house. I knocked on the door, and after several minutes, Bernard finally answered.

"Sorry," Bernard said, "we're in my parents' bedroom and didn't hear the door and our staff is away celebrating."

"It's ok, I was about to break in," I said.

I followed Bernard to his parents' bedroom.

"Hello, Maybel." Mr. Charleston greeted me.

"Hello, Mr. Charleston, can I spend some time with you and Mrs. Charleston and Bernard?"

"Yes, of course, sweetheart, but isn't your family missing you?"

"No, they're all drunk, except for Catherine and my cousins who are older than me and enjoy talking about boys."

Mr. Charleston chuckled, "Come on then Maybel, we're playing chess. Do you know how to play?"

"No," I said.

"Would you like to learn?" he asked me.

"I suppose I could watch, but I'd rather ride horses, swing on your tree swing, or make cookies with you," I said.

"I've never made cookies," Mr. Charleston said as I skipped across the room and jumped onto the bed next to Mrs. Charleston.

"Hello dear," Mrs. Charleston said. "Checkmate, Bernard," she smiled at her son and Bernard furrowed his brow in anger.

"I should have protected my queen better," he mumbled.

I laid beside Mrs. Charleston. "Will you braid my hair again, please?"

Mrs. Charleston smiled at me. "Of course, honey. I always wanted a daughter with whom I could braid hair and put ribbons."

Mrs. Charleston went to the bathroom for a brush and hair ties.

"Bernard, why didn't you come to Thanksgiving dinner at my house? Catherine is talking about boys with our cousins and I was very bored."

"I wanted to be with my mother," he said. "Thanksgiving is not my mother's favorite holiday, and not mine either."

Mr. Charleston took his newspaper from his nightstand. I watched him as he leafed through pages. He looked more comfortable and relaxed with his family, resting bed with them. Usually, he looked like a stern professional at his medical practice, and a fierce force to be reckoned with when he met with his business associates.

Mrs. Charleston returned with a hair brush and ribbons. "Maybel, sweetheart, would you like pink or white bows?"

"Surprise me!" I giggled.

Mrs. Charleston laughed, "Alright then."

Bernard sat and watched his mother braid my hair. I felt like a princess with my hair strands intricately woven together.

"Where did you learn how to braid hair?" I asked.

"My mother and grandmother."

"Did you used to wear your hair braided?" I asked.

"My mother always braided my hair and my dear husband used to make fun of my braids, calling them messy, ugly, and tangled."

Mr. Charleston looked sad. "I'm sorry honey, I was such a stupid boy."

"That's true," she laughed.

"I loved them, you know," he said. "I just didn't tell you I loved them."

"Why don't you braid your hair now?" I asked.

"I've never been good at braiding my own hair," Mrs. Charleston answered.

"Bernard, you watched your mother braiding my hair. Can you teach me so I can braid your mother's hair?" I asked him.

"I didn't pay close attention," Bernard shrugged.

"Oh, well, I'll ask one of the maids to watch. I bet they can watch once and be able to braid. They're very intelligent like that I've noticed."

"I can figure it out," Bernard huffed, annoyed.

Mrs. Charleston winked at me and I winked back.

Bernard carefully brushed his mother's hair and attempted to braid it. "Cross the strands of hair like this, Maybel," he instructed me.

"And there you have it," Bernard said as he tied the bottom of the braid.

Mrs. Charleston immediately turned around and kissed Bernard's cheek. She looked so happy to have her son's attention.

"Thank you, baby," she said.

Bernard blushed. "Mother," he said, embarrassed.

"My mommy and daddy call me 'baby' too, Bernard. It's ok. That just means they love us."

"Your hair is breathtaking, my love," Mr. Charleston said.

"It's not tangled or messy or ugly?" Mrs. Charleston quipped.

Mr. Charleston leaned toward his wife and smiled so sweetly then kissed her lips. "You have the most beautiful hair of anyone I have ever seen," he said softly, then kissed her again.

Bernard smiled watching his parents.

"Bernard, will you play with me while your parents kiss?"

Bernard stood up, "Let's go, Maybel." He picked me up and I wrapped my legs around his waist facing him. Bernard walked with me like that back to his bedroom. He said it reminded him of koalas in Australia when I held onto him like that.

"What would you like to do?" Bernard asked me as he pried me off and put me down.

"Anything!" I replied.

"I'm sure you would like to go to the candy store, but I imagine they are closed today."

"We can make cookies here," I smiled.

"Alright, we will. But first, let's go outside. I have something I want to show you."

"A present?" I smiled wildly.

"No, not a present, but something fun we can both enjoy," Bernard smiled mischievously.

"What?" I exclaimed.

Bernard laughed, "Come with me." He took my hand and led me downstairs to the carriageway. There was a shiny, new automobile in Bernard's carriageway. I ran and crawled over the door and landed in the driver's seat.

Bernard laughed, "I'll drive us around the town square and back," he said.

Bernard opened the driver's door and pushed me over with his hips. "I have to drive Maybel, you're too young."

"How old do you have to be?" I asked.

"I don't know. My father said I can drive though, and he knows the sheriff, so it won't be a problem."

I defiantly jumped over on Bernard's lap. "I'm helping!" I said.

"Ok, Maybel," Bernard sighed. "You're as stubborn as my mother."

"I like your mother."

"I do too," Bernard said.

Bernard put one arm around my waist and held me close.

"I'm going to drive slowly, Maybel. I don't want you to get hurt."

"I won't Bernard!" I yelled. "I'm so happy!" I screamed.

Bernard laughed, "You're fun, Maybel."

We ever so slowly went along the road to the town square. Bernard's big hand held my stomach and he protectively told me to be careful not to stick my arm out the window.

I leaned back. "Bernard! I feel like I'm flying!" I said, mesmerized.

Bernard kissed my cheek. "Me too, sweetheart."

"Hey, there are Catherine and Norma and Stella," I pointed them out to Bernard.

"Those are your cousins?" Bernard asked, shocked.

"Yes. They're my father's sister's daughters."

"They look like sculptures!" Bernard murmured.

"Bernard! Don't stop!" I pouted. "I don't want you to like them more than me!" I whined.

Bernard stopped. "Ladies, care for a drive?" Bernard asked in an annoying, flirtatious tone.

"Oh! Bernard!" Catherine cooed. "I didn't know you bought an automobile! How fancy! These are my cousins!" Catherine introduced our cousins.

"Norma, Stella, this is my boyfriend, Bernard," Catherine said proudly.

"You're dating again?" I asked Catherine.

"Yes," Catherine said. She appeared annoyed at me for discussing their brief separation in front of our cousins.

I turned my head around to look at Bernard to gauge his reaction. Bernard looked uncomfortable. "I missed you both," Bernard said softly, "and you wouldn't come to my house out of respect for your sister," Bernard said even more softly as he whispered into my ear.

"Pleased to meet you," Norma and Stella swooned.

I crossed my arms as they climbed in.

Bernard's entire demeanor changed, which left me angry.

"Ladies, a pleasure to make your acquaintances." Bernard used his most eloquent voice and I rolled my eyes.

Catherine sat beside me and Bernard. Bernard let go of my stomach and held Catherine's hand.

"Shall I take us all to my house?" Bernard asked.

Catherine smiled. She looked back at our cousins. "Bernard lives in a mansion!"

"Ooh," they cooed.

When we arrived at Bernard's house, Bernard took Catherine's hand and Stella wrapped her arm around Bernard's other arm, much to Norma's chagrin.

I followed behind.

Bernard took them to the study to sit and chat in the large, leather sofas and chairs.

I sat in the kitchen sulking.

Mr. and Mrs. Charleston came downstairs holding hands and giggling like schoolchildren. "Oh, Maybel," Mrs. Charleston looked embarrassed and quickly changed into a more adult and boring demeanor. "I thought you and Bernard had gone."

I rested my head on my hand at the kitchen table. I rolled my head up to look at them. Mr. Charleston wore only undershorts, and Mrs. Charleston a slip. Their faces were flushed.

"He's in the study with Catherine and my cousins." I said drolly, then rolled my head back down to stare at the table.

"My nephew is here, honey, why don't you go upstairs to the blue guest bedroom and ask him to play." Mrs. Charleston suggested.

"Ok," I said, with no intention of doing so.

"Mr. Charleston and I came down for a quick snack, but we have more work to do. Why don't you play with Henry until we finish, and then you and I can do something together?"

"Isn't Henry the beautiful one?" I asked.

Mrs. Charleston laughed, "Yes, I believe most everyone calls him that."

"I can't talk to him. My mouth gets dry and he's just so pretty I cannot speak," I protested.

Mrs. Charleston laughed, "Well, you can ask Catherine and Bernard to play cards with you, or perhaps go boating."

"Ok," I said. I had no desire to play with stupid Bernard when he was acting like a rich boy who adored all the girls' attentions. I liked the other Bernard, the one that acted normally.

I turned to watch Mr. and Mrs. Charleston leave and Mr. Charleston smacked Mrs. Charleston's bottom playfully. She giggled and I heard them ascend the stairs, the floorboards creaking underneath their weight.

I went outside to the tree swing. I slowly swung back and forth, listening to the last of the birds who hadn't flown south yet.

I looked up at all the windows in the enormous house. They reflected back the sky and the couple of leaves still left on the tree branches above me. The reflections went up and down, up and down, as I swung.

"Maybel, come." Bernard came out of the kitchen calling me.

"Where?" I asked, not bothering to slow my leg pumps on the swing.

"I'm taking the girls on a drive."

"I'm staying here. Your mother is going to play with me when she's done working with your father."

"Working?" Bernard looked confused. "Oh," he said and rolled his eyes. "They'll be a while. I'm sure we'll be back before they're done working." Bernard stressed the word 'working' sarcastically.

"I'll just go home then and see what my parents and aunts are doing," I told Bernard.

"Ok, Maybel, do whatever you want." Bernard left.

I didn't go home though. I went upstairs. I wanted to plunder around in Bernard's bedroom. He had lots of trinkets from Europe and toys his grandparents sent him from all around the world.

My quest to plunder was thwarted. "Hello, Maybel." Henry was coming out of the blue guest bedroom. He looked and smelled freshly bathed and wore a plain blue shirt and tan pants. I had never seen him in anything but a beautifully-tailored suit. He looked normal now, still exquisitely handsome, but more human and less God-like in a plain, cotton shirt.

"I, um, bedroom Bernard," I stammered.

I became flustered and put my head down in embarrassment. I walked quickly toward Bernard's room.

"Maybel?" Henry called.

I stopped walking and turned around, but didn't look at Henry.

"Would you like to get custard with me? I am headed to the sweets' shop now."

"It's closed. Thanksgiving."

"Ah, not that one," he said. "There's another that I know will be open."

I really wanted custard but I also really wanted to not further embarrass myself by choking on my words.

"You don't have to talk to me the whole time," he smiled. "You can be as mute as you like."

"Ok," I said.

Henry outstretched his arm to indicate I was to proceed down the stairs first. He had more manners than Bernard, I thought.

At the bottom of the stairs, I let Henry go in front of me because I didn't know in which direction we were headed.

Henry went out the carriageway door, but instead of a carriage, there was another automobile. Henry smiled and opened the passenger side door for me. I slid in and Henry closed my door. Henry got inside behind the steering wheel and began driving us toward town.

"Where is Bernard today?" he asked. "You usually come to visit him."

I thought I didn't have to speak during our outing. I wanted to explain that Bernard traded me for three beautiful girls, but all that came out of my mouth was, "Mmmm," and a shoulder shrug.

"Ok then," Henry chuckled.

I felt my face flush with embarrassment.

Henry drove past the town square. It was empty because of the Thanksgiving holiday.

We continued into the countryside where the tall grasses were brown.

"Looks like all the grasses and flowers are dying," Henry uttered, more to himself than to me.

"Dying to be reborn," I whispered.

Henry looked over at me curiously. "Yes, I suppose everything has to die to be born again later."

"Spring," I said. What I really wanted to say was that we'll see the new growth and new life in spring.

"Yes," Henry agreed, almost as though he could fill in the gaps where my words could not.

Henry suddenly stopped the automobile and two deer ran from one tall patch of weeds through the dirt road and into the tall weeds on the other side of the road. One was a buck.

"Did you see that buck's antlers?" Henry said with awe. "There had to have been a dozen points!"

I often saw bucks chase does every fall and wondered why. Daddy said they were playing tag. Mommy said they were making baby deer for spring births. I told daddy what mommy said and he said no, they're playing tag. When I asked mommy again, she said she had been mistaken and that they were indeed playing tag.

We entered into the neighboring town and Henry took me to a store and unlocked the front door.

"Uncle owns this store and I have helped him with restoring the floorboards. He will sell it and split the profits with me," Henry smiled.

Henry went behind the counter and pulled from the ice box a container of custard. I went to Henry and stood beside him watching him scoop custard into bowls for us.

Henry handed me a bowl and took a spoon from the drawer for me. "Here, Maybel," he handed me the spoon then tousled my hair on the top of my head the way Bernard always did.

Henry must think of me as a child. Bernard never tousled Catherine's hair, only mine, and Catherine said that's what big brothers do to little sisters.

"Let's sit by the window, shall we?" Henry asked.

I followed Henry. Henry pulled out my chair for me. I smiled. I liked Henry's manners.

"Are you enjoying school this year?" Henry asked me.

"Yes," I said.

"I'm studying business," he said.

"Bernard tells me Catherine wants to be a schoolteacher. Do you as well?" Henry tried to keep our one-sided conversation going.

"Yes," I said. "Maybe."

"What else might you want to study?" He asked me.

"Nurse. Nursing." I stumbled.

"You enjoy helping people then," he observed.

"Yes," I said.

"One of my friends wants to teach science because he says he wants to be the science teacher he never had in school. I admire his dedication to bettering children's educations."

I smiled at Henry. Henry smiled back.

"Are you still writing stories, Maybel? I read your story you wrote from the point of view of a circus bear. I dare say I had a tear or two escape my eyes. I had never thought about what a circus animal sees and hears and endures. Your stories could persuade people, you know, Maybel, make them see actions and consequences through another person's perspective."

I smiled, "I want to help."

"The circus bears?"

"Yes, and everyone else, too."

"I admire that," Henry smiled. "If there's anything I can do to be of assistance, do not hesitate to call on me."

I smiled at Henry. He seemed nice. Mommy didn't care for all the women on his arms at social gatherings. Daddy told her Henry was young and just having fun, then mommy accused daddy of being jealous of the tomcat. I asked what a tomcat was and mommy looked startled and said she thought I was asleep in daddy's arms. Later, Catherine chided me for not pretending to be asleep longer because she wanted to know more about Henry.

"What's a tomcat?" I asked.

Henry almost choked on his spoonful of custard.

"What made you think of that?" he asked.

I shrugged my shoulders.

"It's a man who chases after lots of women."

I giggled.

"Who thinks I'm a tomcat?" Henry asked.

"Everyone," I giggled again.

"I don't chase after women," Henry said. "They chase after me, and I can't say I dislike the attention," Henry chuckled and leaned back in his chair.

"Maybel, back to your stories. You've left a lot of them laying around the Charleston's house. Why don't you collect them all and assemble them into a book?"

"Maybe," I replied.

"Again, I am happy to assist you in your literary endeavors. I will be able to say I knew you before you were a famous author," Henry winked at me. He looked even more handsome when he winked and somehow my mouth felt dry while swallowing custard. I blushed and looked down at my last spoonful of custard.

Henry stood and collected our bowls and spoons and I followed him back behind the counter where he washed and dried them. I only rarely saw daddy wash dishes. Henry seemed to be comfortable washing dishes and that surprised me.

"Shall we head home?" Henry asked as he put away our clean dishes.

I nodded.

"Do you want to drive us home?" Henry asked me and my eyes grew wide with excitement.

"I'm joking, Maybel. Your feet can't reach the pedals."

My smile turned to a frown.

"Sorry, love," Henry said. "It was perhaps a cruel joke."

Henry opened my door for me. I got inside still pouting about not being allowed to drive.

Henry took his seat as driver. "Oh alright, you can steer when we get onto the country road where there's nothing to crash into."

I jumped over and hugged Henry then realized I was hugging the most beautiful man in the world and jumped back to the passenger's side immediately and looked out the window in complete embarrassment.

Henry had looked surprised when I hugged him and now chuckled at my embarrassment.

I continued looking out the window at the empty streets and bare storefronts. I became more and more excited as the stores and houses were spaced further apart, because I knew that signaled that the edge of town was near.

We turned onto the dirt road that led back to our town and Henry slowed his automobile.

I leapt over onto his lap and gripped the steering wheel tightly.

"Oh," Henry shifted uncomfortably. "I meant you could sit beside me and place your hand on the wheel and help me."

My excitement plummeted. I turned my head around and looked at Henry then slowly slid off his lap and sat beside him.

"Now don't look so sad sweetheart, you're breaking my heart." Henry watched me.

I placed my hand on the steering wheel. I figured I could at least pretend to have excitement.

Henry sighed deeply and rubbed his forehead. "Alright, you can sit on my lap and steer."

I looked up at him with my big, excited eyes.

"But Maybel, please do not tell anyone I let you steer. Your father and my uncle would both punch me. Please keep this between us."

I nodded emphatically.

"I will drive very, very slowly and you have to keep both hands on the wheel, and if there is any other automobile or carriage ahead or behind us, you must sit beside me and let me do the steering."

I nodded again very emphatically.

Henry took a deep breath. "Please don't get me into trouble, Maybel."

I shook my head no very hard.

"If you get hurt, I will never, ever forgive myself."

"I won't. Bernard let me steer today."

"He what?" Henry exclaimed angrily.

"I sat on his lap today and steered through town. I can do this, I promise, and I won't get us hurt."

"You have got to be joking! That little...." Henry stopped himself from saying more.

"This is not a toy! He needs to be more careful with you!" Henry seemed genuinely concerned for my safety.

Henry paused, "You know Maybel, you spoke to me, quite a bit actually."

I suddenly froze. I hadn't realized I'd spoken so freely.

I looked up at Henry.

"Come on, Maybel, you may steer, but I'm going to go very slowly and carefully with you."

I climbed into his lap with a smile from ear to ear. I put my hands on the steering wheel and gripped tightly. True to his word, Henry drove slowly.

Henry drove painstakingly slowly. A frog not far ahead had time to hop from one side of the dirt road to the other side well before we neared. I held the steering wheel and watched him hop at a leisurely pace. He even stopped to stare at me before resuming his cantering hops to the other side of the road. I could have sworn that frog smiled and croaked at me, mocking our painfully slow pace. When we finally reached the spot where he hopped into the grass, I looked over and glared at him, but he had already hopped out of sight. He had probably hopped into town by now, I thought ruefully.

I sighed and kept my hands on the steering wheel. Henry held the bottom of the steering wheel with one hand and wrapped his other arm tightly and protectively around my waist.

After watching a goose waddle from behind us to in front of us, I sighed exasperatedly. "You can steer now," I said.

I started to slide off his lap. "Wait! Don't slide off my lap now, we haven't stopped yet!"

"We haven't? I couldn't tell," I said dryly.

Henry came to a complete stop and I slid off his lap so he could resume driving. We finally passed the waddling goose.

I sat beside Henry with my hand on the wheel but he was doing all the steering.

When we reached the town square, Bernard sat on a bench with Catherine on one side, her head on his chest and arm wrapped around his waist, and on his other side, Norma had apparently won the fight to sit next to Bernard as Stella was beside Norma with her arms crossed.

"Now that is a tomcat," Henry joked.

Bernard called to us. "Maybel? Henry are you with Maybel?"

Henry raised his hand as a greeting as we passed, but didn't stop.

He continued to my house. "Thank you for the lovely afternoon, Maybel." Henry stepped outside his automobile and I started to follow. "No, Maybel, a gentleman opens a lady's door." Henry closed his door and walked to the passenger's side and opened my door.

He held his hand out to me. "Remember, if a man does not get your door, he's not a gentleman and you, Maybel, deserve a gentleman."

I smiled and took Henry's hand. He walked me to my door.

"Wait. Mommy made pumpkin pie," I said.

Henry looked hesitant but followed me inside. "Henry, what brings you by?" Daddy got up from the sofa where he had been sitting with mommy and his two sisters.

"Sweetheart," daddy called to mommy, "we have a guest. Let's go to my workshop fellas," daddy said to his brothers-in-law.

"You're using Henry as an excuse to leave us, aren't you," Aunt Elizabeth teased.

"There's only so much about fashion and dresses I can tolerate before I get bored to tears," daddy fervently motioned for Henry and my uncles to quickly follow him before he had to endure more mundane chatter.

"Maybel, come sit," mommy patted the seat cushion next to her that had been recently occupied by daddy.

I wanted to go with daddy but he didn't like Catherine and me to listen to him and the fellas when they were drinking. I reluctantly sat beside mommy.

"Do you have a boyfriend yet?" Aunt Nettie asked.

"No," I said.

"Maybe next year dear," Aunt Nettie smiled at me.

"I was thirteen when I kissed Johnny Eldridge," Aunt Elizabeth giggled.

"Don't give Maybel any ideas," mommy said.

"What? You haven't kissed a boy yet?" Aunt Nettie exclaimed.

"Mommy, may I go back to Bernard's house and make cookies with Mrs. Charleston?" I pleaded.

"Yes, dear," mommy laughed.

"Did we scare you away, dear?" Aunt Nettie asked me as I bolted outside. I heard them all giggling as I ran down the sidewalk.

I saw tomcat Bernard driving toward my house with his gaggle of girls vying for his attention. There was a fence beside me so I couldn't duck out of sight and into the bushes.

"Maybel, where are you going?" Bernard called to me.

"On a stroll," I yelled back.

I continued walking. I could hear Catherine and my cousins whispering and giggling, probably at my expense because I didn't like to dress up and fix my hair like they did.

I arrived at the Charleston's. Vincent was probably still celebrating Thanksgiving with his family, I figured, so I didn't bother knocking. I walked into the main entryway and crossed over the marble floor, past the sculptures of scantily clad Roman men and women, and eventually arrived at the kitchen.

The kitchen was empty so I started making cookies by myself. I didn't really belong anywhere, and didn't fit in well anywhere I went, so I decided to make cookies at the Charleston's house alone. It was unusually quiet with the staff away for the holiday.

I mixed flour, sugar, and eggs, and whatever else I could remember to add without the recipe in front of me. I rolled out the dough, placed the cookies into the oven I'd heated, and sat at the kitchen table and waited.

When the cookies were finished, I returned with them to the table along with a glass of milk and sat alone.

"Maybel, dear," Mrs. Charleston came into the kitchen talking to me. She wore more than a slip now. She wore a pretty green dress. "I thought I smelled cookies. How delightful!"

I took a cookie from the plate and reached it to her. She smiled and sat down. "You're here all alone?"

"My aunts wanted to know if I kissed any boys yet and I got embarrassed and left."

Mrs. Charleston nodded her head. "I remember those days." She bit into a cookie. "It was an awkward time for me when I was your age. You are leaving childhood and entering adulthood, but you are neither a child nor an adult."

I nodded my head in agreement.

"These cookies are delicious, honey."

"Thank you," I said, staring at the cookie in my hand.

"How are your parents? Are they enjoying your family's visit?"

"Yes," I said.

Mrs. Charleston reached across the table and took my hand. "You're not having a good Thanksgiving, are you?"

"No," I admitted.

"Thanksgiving is my least favorite holiday," she squeezed my hand.

"Why?" I asked.

Mrs. Charleston looked like she was thinking about how to carefully word her answer.

"I suppose it's that I like Christmas and birthdays more," she smiled, but I didn't think she was all that happy underneath her smile.

"Where did you and Bernard go today? Another fun adventure?" Mrs. Charleston asked me.

"No, he's driving in his new car with Catherine and my cousins."

"Feeling left behind, are you?" She asked me.

"Yes, but they try to get rid of me often, so this is nothing new," I said.

"I spent most of my childhood alone too," she squeezed my hand again. "I liked to be outdoors like you."

"You were lonely a lot?" I asked, surprised someone so beautiful was ever lonely.

"Yes. I had my brothers and sisters, but I spent a lot of time in the forest alone. I suppose you and I are similar in that we don't need constant companionship."

I continued nibbling my cookie.

Henry came into the kitchen. "I thought I smelled cookies. Oh hello, Maybel, I thought you were at your house."

Henry went to Mrs. Charleston and leaned down and kissed her cheek. "Bernard was still at the Wyndham's house when I left, Auntie."

"What took you to see the Wyndham's?" Mrs. Charleston asked.

"I took Maybel for custard, then to her house, and Mr. Wyndham was delighted to see me because it gave him an excuse to leave for his workshop." Henry and Mrs. Charleston chuckled.

"Men don't care much for ladies' chatter," Mrs. Charleston laughed as she spoke to me.

Henry sat next to his aunt and I held out a cookie for him.

"Thank you, Maybel," Henry smiled.

Mrs. Charleston watched me and smiled. "Are you still shy around Henry?"

"Yes," I said.

"Henry's a good boy," she tousled Henry's hair.

"Sometimes," she added, and winked at him.

Bernard, Catherine, and my cousins came into the kitchen. "I thought I smelled cookies," Bernard smiled and kissed his mother's cheek.

"Thank Maybel, dear, she made them," Mrs. Charleston told her son.

"Thank you, Maybel," Bernard grabbed my cookie out of my hand and took a bite.

"Bernard, how rude," Mrs. Charleston chastised him.

"It's how Maybel and I tease each other, isn't that right Maybel?" Bernard reached over the table to mess my hair.

I glared at him.

"No witty remarks, Maybel? Oh right, you're mute around Henry so I can tease you without repercussions!" Bernard laughed.

"Behave, Bernard," Mr. Charleston told his son as he came into the kitchen.

"Ooooh cookies!" Mr. Charleston's voice suddenly changed from warning Bernard to behave, to high-pitched and happy. He bit into a cookie. "Delicious!" Mr. Charleston winked at me.

I winked back and he laughed.

"I'm showing these beautiful ladies around our house," Bernard nodded toward Catherine, Stella, and Norma.

Stella and Norma had been watching Henry the entire time. Catherine snuck glances at Henry too, I noticed. I had also noticed Stella and Norma nudging each other as they stared at Henry.

Bernard and the girls left to admire Bernard's mansion.

"My cousins stared at Henry the way I stare at birthday cake," I said.

"You can talk around Henry now?" Mr. Charleston asked.

"Oh," I mumbled. I hadn't realized I'd spoken aloud.

"Don't retreat back into your shell now," Henry teased me.

I bit into another cookie so I wouldn't have to talk.

"Well, Maybel," Henry stretched his arms, "I have nothing on my agenda today, as Thanksgiving is more of a European holiday, so would you like to go fishing or shooting or anything of that sort?" Henry asked me.

"Horses?" I asked.

"Sure, Maybel. Have you been riding before?" Henry asked me.

I shook my head no.

"That's alright. I taught my little cousins. I can teach you," Henry smiled at me.

I followed Henry out the door.

"Maybel, walk beside me, not behind me," Henry said.

I skipped ahead to catch up to Henry. He sure walked faster than he drove, I thought.

We arrived at the horse stables and Henry introduced me to Big Ben. "Ben is tall and strong, but as gentle as can be," Henry said.

I smiled up at Big Ben and he snorted a hello.

"Are you scared?" Henry asked me.

"No," I answered.

"I'll climb on first and I'll pull you up in front of me."

"Ok," I said.

Henry easily climbed atop Big Ben and reached down and swooped me up by my armpits. He was so fast and precise I froze. One second, I was on my feet, the next second, I was atop a horse in front of the most beautiful man I'd ever seen.

"Easy, Maybel, you're safe," Henry whispered behind me. "You're safe. I've got you."

"You were so fast!" My voice was shaky.

"I've had lots of experience teaching my little cousins. I'll go slower with you, ok? Take a deep breath and relax," Henry continued whispering.

My body was as stiff as a tree trunk. I had never been this high up on an animal before, and although Big Ben was calm, his every breath felt like tremors beneath me, and when he shifted his weight from one foot to the other, I saw myself falling in my mind's eye and the subsequent funeral attended by my mother and father crying as they threw the first handfuls of dirt onto my coffin.

"Maybel," Henry spoke louder. "I asked if you want to continue or get down?"

"Go," I breathed out as my lungs shrunk and tightened. I was not a person that gave up, ever. If I died, then I died trying, and not from something boring like consumption.

Henry told Big Ben to go, and Ben seemed to sense my fear and moved as slowly as Henry drove.

By the time we arrived at Bernard's carriageway, I could breathe finally without wheezing from terror.

I gripped big Ben's reigns and Henry's hand was over top of both my hands while his other arm encircled my waist.

"Very good, Maybel, you're doing great," Henry said softly.

"Maybel! You're not allowed to ride horses!" Catherine yelled at me.

"Yes, I am!" I yelled back.

"Daddy told me I wasn't allowed to ride!" Catherine crossed her arms.

"He's never said that to me!" I shot back.

"It was implied!" Catherine yelled angrily.

"No, it wasn't!" I yelled louder.

"Get down!" Catherine ordered me.

"Go away!" I ordered Catherine.

"Maybel!" Catherine screamed.

"Catherine!" I mocked her silly, shrieky voice.

"Are you really not allowed to ride horses?" Henry whispered to me. "Your father will put a bullet through my skull!"

"Catherine isn't allowed," I turned my head and whispered to Henry. "Daddy took me horseback riding once and made me swear to never tell mommy or Catherine, so don't worry, daddy won't be mad at you, but please, please, please, never tell a single person daddy took me riding! If daddy finds out you took me riding," I continued whispering, "he might pretend to be mad, but that's only for show because mommy doesn't want me to ride. Just whisper to daddy that you didn't realize it would be a problem since daddy had taken me riding before, and I guarantee he won't say another word because he doesn't want mommy to find out he took me riding."

Henry smiled at me sweetly.

"What?"

"You're talking to me," his smile widened.

I turned back around quickly.

I heard Henry chuckle softly behind me.

Catherine was still scolding me with her shrill voice, reminding me that mommy's little brother got kicked in the head by a horse and that mommy shouldn't have to bear any more horse-related grief.

"Ok fine, Catherine!" I snapped. "We'll go back to the horsey houses and I'll get off the damn horse! Just stop with your shrilly shrills!" I yelled.

"Stables," Henry whispered to me.

"I know they're stables!" I yelled. "I get flustered when Catherine uses her school marm shrieky voice!" I yelled.

Bernard was laughing. I knew he, too, disliked Catherine's school teacher voice. I was glad Catherine had decided to become a school teacher because her annoying shrieks would be useless in any other profession.

Henry and I returned to the hay bales by the stables where Big Ben enjoyed several apples.

"I suppose we should leave Big Ben in his horsey house now and return you to Catherine," Henry snorted.

"I know they're called stables!" I shot back.

"Not anymore," Henry laughed. "They will forever be called horsey houses from now on!"

I rolled my eyes while Henry snorted again.

We walked side-by-side back to the house.

I went inside to wash my hands. I had to go upstairs to wash my hands because Bernard was using the downstairs bathroom sink.

When I came out of the upstairs bathroom, Stella had Henry pinned to the wall kissing him.

I walked back downstairs in disgust at having seen my older cousin shoving her tongue down Henry's throat.

I sat down at the kitchen table and took another cookie. Bernard and Catherine were holding hands under the table and giggling.

"How was your horse ride with your handsome friend, Maybel?" Norma asked.

"Ok," I said.

"Looked like he was holding you tightly against him," she continued.

"I was scared at first because Big Ben is really tall. Henry was protecting me."

"He seemed to enjoy protecting you," Norma giggled.

Bernard looked angry.

"Oh, what's wrong?" Catherine cooed into Bernard's ear. "Maybel doesn't yet know about any of that. I'm sure Henry was a gentleman."

Bernard made an angry, huffing noise.

"Bernard is protective of Maybel," Catherine told Norma. "He looks at her as his little sister, isn't that right, Bernard?"

Bernard just watched me.

"What?" I asked Bernard. "Stop staring at me! Do you want this cookie too?" I threw my cookie at him and it hit his chest.

Stella pranced into the kitchen smiling.

I saw Henry start to enter the kitchen then turned quickly and went toward the study, or maybe the drawing room.

"Where's Henry?" Norma asked.

"Well, he was right behind me," Stella turned around looking for Henry.

I began eating another cookie and Stella and Norma went on about things I didn't care about.

"Well, you know that's not what I heard," Norma gossiped about something.

Stella made a dissenting click of her tongue.

Catherine said something about her friend Edith.

Stella laughed about something.

I took my napkin and began folding it. I had recently read about Japanese origami. I couldn't remember exactly how to fold my napkin so I took some guesses that turned out to be good guesses. I was proud of my crane.

"Look, Bernard!" I smiled.

Bernard had been watching me while Catherine and Stella talked.

"Where's Norma?" I asked.

"She went to look at the sculptures and paintings in the grand entryway," Bernard said. He was watching me, but holding Catherine's hand as Catherine chatted with Stella.

"Bernard, can I put my crane in your bedroom so nobody takes it apart?"

"Sure, Maybel. I'll come with you."

"No, Bernard, stay with me!" Catherine looked lovingly at Bernard.

"I know the way to your room, Bernard," I laughed. "I won't get lost in this big house again."

I went upstairs and on my way to Bernard's bedroom, I passed the big, blue guest room where Norma was being a koala on Henry. They were sitting on the edge of the bed. Norma's skirt was pushed up and she was being a koala on Henry while she prayed.

I ran downstairs. I wasn't sure why, but it felt like I saw something I wasn't supposed to see.

"Here, Bernard," I shoved my crane into Bernard's hand. "You can put it in your room later."

I started toward the door. "I have to go home now," I said. "I'm hungry."

"Maybel, are you ok?" Bernard asked. "I can make you a sandwich."

"No, thank you," I said. "I want to eat mommy's Thanksgiving leftovers."

"Maybel, stay," Catherine said. "We'll all walk home together later."

I reluctantly sat at the kitchen table across from Catherine, Bernard, and Stella.

Catherine continued talking about England and royalty.

"Bernard has met royalty," Catherine said to Stella with an air of importance, as though she had also met royalty through association with Bernard.

Norma came into the kitchen and looked wearily at me.

I looked down.

"Where's Henry?" Stella asked.

"Oh, I'm not sure," Norma said.

Norma sat next to me but did not look at me.

"I need to ask Henry about horses," Stella said. "I've always been curious about thoroughbreds."

That was a stupid excuse, I thought. She had been staring at Henry whenever he was near and I knew she wanted to go talk to him. I would have pretended to go observe art like Norma did. That would have at least been slightly less obvious.

Catherine began talking to Norma about Germany and Switzerland, making it known that Bernard often vacationed throughout Europe.

Norma was still flustered and glanced at me from time to time.

"Maybel, let's go to the study to get paper," Bernard suggested. "You look terribly bored. Would you like to write while the ladies talk?"

"Bernard, Maybel knows the way to the study," Catherine said. "Stay with me, Bernard," Catherine smiled and leaned in for a kiss.

Bernard looked uncomfortable but gave Catherine a peck on her lips while Norma giggled.

"Such an adorable couple," Norma cooed.

Catherine smiled happily while Bernard seemed nervous that we watched.

"Go on, kiss her again Bernard," I goaded him. "We're not watching or any such thing."

Bernard blushed.

"Maybel!" Catherine looked annoyed, "Don't be crass."

"You're the one kissing in front of an audience," I reminded her.

Catherine became more annoyed. "The paper on which to write your stories is in the study," Catherine said tartly.

I stood up and walked around Norma. I paused at Bernard's chair. "Catherine says you use too much tongue," I told him.

"I did not say that!" Catherine yelled at me.

Norma laughed.

Bernard looked a little hurt. "You should have told me, not them!" Bernard said.

"Oh, go away, Maybel!" Catherine yelled at me.

I continued to the study where Stella sat on Henry's lap. She was also being a koala on Henry. Her skirt was pulled up and she was also praying. I wasn't sure why everyone wanted to be Henry's koala.

I closed the door and returned to the kitchen. I knew something strange was going on. I wanted to ask Bernard about koalas again.

"Can we go home now?" I asked Catherine. "I'm hungry and tired."

"Soon, Maybel," Catherine said, annoyed.

"I'll walk you home, Maybel." Bernard quickly stood up and before Catherine could object, he told her he'd be right back as he grabbed my hand and pulled me to the door.

When we got to the street, I stopped. "Bernard, can I be your koala?"

Bernard hesitated and looked around. "You're getting a little too old to be my koala, Maybel."

"I was your koala just this morning!" I exclaimed incredulously.

"That was indoors. It's just, I know we're playing, and it's completely innocent, but out here people might be suspicious of what we're doing," Bernard said.

"Fine, Bernard! I don't need you anymore! Henry has been giving out koala rides all day!" I turned on my heel and started walking toward home.

Bernard grabbed my arm and spun me around so hard I lost my balance and fell into his arms.

"Henry holds you like a koala?" Bernard was suddenly very angry.

"No, he gave koala rides to Stella and Norma. Why are you angry?" My voice was meek and I didn't understand why Bernard's face was suddenly flushed red with anger.

"Oh!" Bernard looked surprised. He suddenly changed from angry to amused. "He gave them both koala rides?" Bernard chuckled.

"Yes," I said.

"Damn that lucky bastard!" Bernard stood with his hands on his hips shaking his head and smiling.

"Alright, Maybel," Bernard took my hand and we continued walking. "You're getting too old for koala rides, but you don't yet understand why. Don't be a koala with anyone anymore. I know you don't understand why, but I'm sure you'll understand soon."

"Stella and Norma are older than me and Henry gave them koala rides," I argued.

"Stella and Norma shouldn't go handing out koala rides until after they marry," Bernard cautioned me.

"What?" I was very confused now. "So you have to be either very young or married?"

"No," Bernard sighed. "Just don't go playing koala rides anymore. I'm sorry, Maybel, I can't get into details."

We arrived at my house. "Happy Thanksgiving, Bernard," I mumbled. "Goodnight." I was annoyed because everyone seemed to understand things but did not want to impart their knowledge to me.

"Goodnight, Maybel." Bernard left back down the street to his house and I went inside mine.

"Maybel, it's time to go," mommy called up the stairs to me.

I excitedly ran downstairs. "How long do I get to stay with Bernard?"

Mommy laughed, "Oh, you just adore that boy, don't you?"

"Yes, he's my favorite. Can I spend the night at his house?"

"No, honey, that's inappropriate for a young lady."

They have twenty-seven bedrooms. I wouldn't be in Bernard's bedroom; I would have my own bedroom," I pleaded.

"They have twenty-seven bedrooms?" Mommy's eyes were big.

"Maybe fifty-two," I said, "I'm not sure."

"If you stay in a separate bedroom then yes, you may spend the night, but only if Bernard says it's ok. He may prefer to be alone after having watched you all day."

I jumped up and down with absolute glee. I felt stars in my toes and twirled around yelling "thank you!" to mommy.

When we arrived at the Charleston's home, I jumped up into Bernard's arms and clung to him. "I'm spending the night with you!"

"Only if you want Maybel to spend the night, Bernard," mommy said. "Your parents and Mr.

Wyndham and I will return from the theater quite late, so if you're too tired from looking after Maybel all day, she can come home with us when we return."

"Please? Please? Please? I'll be your best friend forever!" I squeezed Bernard's chest tighter.

Bernard looked down at me clinging to his chest and I made the saddest and most desperate and pleading face I could.

"Alright, honey, you can spend the night. I can't say no when you look like that."

"Thank you! We're going to have so much fun together! I love you Bernard, I love you so much!"

"I love you too," he sighed.

Mommy, daddy, and the Charlestons left by horse carriage. Catherine was still at our cousin's house visiting. I was beyond thrilled to have Bernard all to myself.

Bernard and I played in the slate creek behind his house in the waterfalls. When I left the little waterfalls, I sat down on the grass beside the creek. My stomach hurt a little.

I held my waist and winced in pain and then saw blood on the grass underneath me.

"Bernard! I'm dying!" I screamed.

I watched the blood pool slowly underneath me and I screamed for Bernard again.

Bernard rushed over to me.

I held myself between my legs and blood trickled over my fingers. "I'm dying," I screamed.

"Maybel, lay down!" Bernard commanded me.

I did as he asked.

Bernard lifted my skirt and my underwear was bloody. "Maybel, did you cut yourself or fall down?"

"No!" I screamed. "I don't want to die!" I cried.

"I think you're just menstruating, Maybel," Bernard said to me.

"What?" I cried. "Am I dying right now?"

"Do you have cramps here?" Bernard touched my stomach, just above my vagina.

"A little," I cried. I looked at my bloodied hands and cried harder.

"Maybel, you've gotten your period. It's normal. There's nothing wrong with you," Bernard tried to calm me.

"I don't know what you're talking about," I sat up. I wanted to wipe the tears from my face but I couldn't with blood all over my hands.

"It's ok, Maybel. You're fine. Take a deep breath and relax. You're not dying." Bernard talked to me calmly and soothingly.

"I'm bleeding to death, Bernard!" I sobbed.

"Every girl menstruates. Hasn't your mother talked to you about this?" Bernard asked me.

"No," I sniffled.

"Hasn't Catherine talked to you about this?" he asked.

"Catherine bleeds from between her legs?" I asked, stunned.

"Yes, every woman does," Bernard told me.

"Have you seen her bleeding from between her legs?" I asked. "Because I have not," I told him.

"No, I have not, but,"

I interjected, "Then how do you know?" I cried.

"Because it's just what happens to every girl," Bernard replied.

"Why?" I asked, terrified.

Bernard looked embarrassed. "Just ask your mother.

"Why am I bleeding if I'm not dying, Bernard?"

"Ok, alright, I'm going to be a doctor," Bernard paced nervously. "This is good practice for me," he said, talking to himself more so than to me.

"Every girl, when they get to your age, bleeds from her vagina. It happens once a month."

"What?" I screamed. "Once a month?" I screamed at Bernard. "Why?"

"It is blood from your uterus," he said, looking awkward and uncomfortable.

"What's my uterus?"

"It's where, Maybel, it's inside you, and once a month the blood comes out, and if you have more questions, ask your mother," he blurted out quickly.

"I'm scared, Bernard," I began crying again.

He sighed, "You'll be ok, sweetheart," Bernard tried hard to pretend to be comfortable and console me.

"I'll take care of you. Let's get you inside and get some clean clothes on you." Bernard tried to sound soothing, but I knew he was really uncomfortable.

"I don't want to be a girl anymore," I cried. "Why don't you bleed?"

"Because men don't have babies, Maybel," Bernard said.

"What does bleeding have to do with me having a baby? Oh God, Bernard! I'm going to have a baby now? I'm not married! I don't even know who is going to be her father!"

"No, Maybel, no!" he laughed.

"Why are you laughing at me?" I began crying again.

"You are not having a baby. Women bleed, and after intercourse, have babies."

"What?" I screeched. "What do men do?" I looked up at him with my tear-stained face.

"Maybel, just ask your mother." He stood up. "Come, Maybel, let's go inside."

"No! Everyone will see my bleeding! I can't go inside!" I sobbed.

"No one's home. They're all in town at the theater, with your parents."

"I want Catherine," I sobbed, still sitting on the ground.

"Believe me, Maybel, I wish she were here right now too, but she's not. I'll take care of you, honey."

Bernard, I could tell, was trying very hard to say the right things to put me at ease, but all I really wanted was Catherine.

I stood up and wiped the snot from my nose with my forearm, since my hands were bloody.

"Why didn't you go play with your friends today? Why didn't you go? Then you wouldn't be here to see this!" I sobbed uncontrollably. I was embarrassed and did not want Bernard to see me like this.

"Because I'd rather be with you, Maybel," Bernard whispered.

"You like playing with me?" I asked, hopefully, through pathetic sobs.

"Well, don't look so surprised, Maybel. I've always enjoyed being with you. Let's go get you bathed and dressed. You can wear my old clothes if you want."

"You're too tall!" I cried shrilly.

"I'm sure mother has saved some of my old clothes for my little cousins. They might be a little loose on you, but we'll figure something out," he smiled at me.

I followed Bernard inside his house and up the stairs to his bathroom inside his bedroom.

"Go get in the bathtub, Maybel. I'll put your clothes in a bag and I'll look in my mother's bathroom for whatever it is that women use for this sort of thing."

I took my dress and underwear off, and wadded them into a ball, trying to conceal the bloody parts.

I bathed and dried off. I opened the door to Bernard's bedroom.

"Maybel! You're nude! Put some clothes on!" Bernard's face turned red in embarrassment.

"I don't have any. That's why I came out here," I replied.

"You're not supposed to be naked in front of men!"

"It's just you, Bernard. You're like my brother," I reminded him.

"But I'm not really your brother, Maybel! Put some clothes on!"

"I will, Bernard! As soon as you get me some!"

"Fair enough, Maybel. Here, I think this is probably what my mother uses." Bernard handed me something. It was a cotton, rag-like thing.

"What do I do with this thing?" I was scared of it.

"I think you put it in your underwear," he said.

"I don't have underwear." My bottom lip curled under and I began crying.

"Let me find something." Bernard rummaged through his closet.

"Here're some of my old underwear." Bernard shoved them into my hands while avoiding my nakedness.

"They look like short pants!" I cried harder. "I don't want to wear boys' underwear!" I felt my lower lip squish together in a pout and tremble.

"Here is a short-sleeved shirt," Bernard handed it to me.

I put on his old underwear and put the cotton pad inside. "Is this how I'm supposed to do it?"

"I have no idea," Bernard sighed. "I'm not ready for this." Bernard looked nervous and confused.

I put his old shirt on.

"Here are my old pants from several years ago," Bernard handed them to me.

I put his pants on.

I mustered some humor from my pathetic situation. "Bernard, do I look handsome like you?"

"Yes, Maybel," he laughed. "You look very handsome."

"Bernard, thank you for taking care of me." I spoke in a serious tone. Tears still stained my cheeks and my lips still quivered.

"Of course, sweetheart." He came toward me. "I'll always take care of you." He kissed my lips, then suddenly looked surprised.

"I'm sorry, Maybel!" he said, startled by his own actions. "I don't know why I did that!"

"I like you too, Bernard," I smiled.

"Bernard, what do you look like naked?" I tried to maintain a serious face, but I knew my lips were smirking without my wanting them to show my amusement.

"Ok, that's enough awkwardness for one day, Maybel," Bernard smirked back at me.

"Then will you show me tomorrow?" I asked.

"I can't tell if you're joking or serious, Maybel," he said as he pushed a belt through the loops in his old pants to keep them from falling down around my ankles.

"I'm joking, unless you'll show me?" I giggled.

"No, Maybel," he laughed. "Come now, let's go get something to eat."

"What are you going to make me?" I asked as we walked down the stairs.

"What do you want?"

"I don't know," I said.

"How about a sandwich?" he suggested.

"Ok. Thank you, Bernard."

"You're welcome, Maybel."

We entered the kitchen. I stopped and pulled on Bernard's hand. "Bernard?"

"Yes?"

"Do you really like being with me more than being with Catherine when she attends friends' parties?"

"Yes," Bernard said.

"Thank you," I said sincerely.

Bernard came to me and kissed my forehead and I smiled up at him and hugged him tightly.

"I love you," I told him.

"I love you, too." Bernard went to his kitchen counter and made my sandwich, and his too. We sat at the kitchen table and talked about out west, school, and everything else in our thoughts. I always felt so comfortable with Bernard.

Our parents had not returned from the theater and it was late.

"I don't want you to take me home, Bernard. Catherine isn't there. I don't want to be alone. I get scared."

"You can stay here, Maybel," Bernard took pity on me. He knew I was terrified of being alone at night. "Our parents are probably drinking and won't be home for a while. I'll take care of you. I already said you could spend the night."

"I know, but mommy said you might not want me to spend the night after a long day with me."

"I want you to spend the night. I actually have a lot of fun when I'm with you. We have certainly never had a boring moment together."

"Thank you, Bernard." I was sincerely grateful because I was scared of being alone at home without Catherine, and because I was scared about what was happening to my body.

Bernard wore shorts, but no shirt, because it was quite warm still. He was more muscular than when I'd first met him.

Bernard took my hand, "Let's go to bed," he said.

"Bernard, can I sleep with you?" This house is really big and scary at night when all your maids and butlers are gone."

"I know," he sighed. "I got used to it though." Bernard looked sad in the dim lights.

"Can I sleep with you, please?"

"Yes," he said. "I don't think your parents would approve though."

"Daddy likes to drink with your daddy," I said as we climbed the stairs.

"They'll be too full of drinks to wonder which bedroom I'm in."

"Maybel, when you have children, will you go to the theater without them?"

"No, I will bring them with me if I go," I replied.

"Me too," Bernard said as we entered his bedroom.

I jumped and landed in the middle of Bernard's big bed. "Will you read me a story?" I asked.

"No," Bernard said. "Tell me one of your stories you've thought up in that big imagination of yours."

"Do you want a happy story, or a scary one? I also have bizarre stories. Really, I have thought up every kind of story you could possibly want as entertainment."

"I do not doubt your imagination, Maybel. You have the most interesting mind of anyone I've ever met."

I paused. "Bernard, before I tell you stories, will you please tell me what is happening to me?"

Bernard laid on his bed next to me. "Maybel," he looked unsure of himself, "you should ask your mother."

"Will you tell me? I don't understand and I'm scared."

Bernard looked troubled. "I suppose," he began tentatively. "I will try very hard to answer your questions the way a doctor would answer your questions. This is very difficult for me, Maybel. I feel very uncomfortable, but I'm going to be a doctor, so I must learn how to separate my emotions and speak to you as a patient."

"Bernard, how long will I bleed?" I asked him.

"My medical journals say around four to seven days," he answered.

"Seven days?" I gasped.

"Your menstruation will come about every twenty-eight days."

"It will happen again?" I asked. I did not want this to happen again!

"Yes, every month," Bernard answered.

"For how long?"

"The medical journals say until you are around fifty or fifty-five years old," Bernard answered.

"Are you joking?" I asked incredulously.

"No, Maybel, this is what happens to every woman."

"Why don't you bleed?"

"I'm a man," he answered.

"Why don't men bleed?"

"Men can't have babies," he said.

"I don't understand why bleeding from my vagina has anything to do with having babies!" I was becoming frustrated. My frustration made me angry.

"You really need to ask your mother where babies come from." Bernard shifted uncomfortably under the covers.

"I have! She says to wait until I'm older!"

"How old was Catherine when your mother told her about bodily functions?" Bernard was trying to be professional, but I wanted answers, not professionalism.

"Catherine doesn't know either," I told Bernard.

"Catherine knows," Bernard said.

"She does?" I asked.

"Yes."

"How did Catherine find out? Did mommy tell her?"

"I assumed so," Bernard said.

"Catherine knows about periods and babies?"

"Yes, "Bernard said.

"I asked Catherine, and she said she didn't know!"

"She was probably hoping your mother would tell you," Bernard said.

"How do you know she knows?"

"I just know she knows," he blushed.

"Everyone knows about bleeding and how to make babies except me?"

"Honestly, I don't understand how you don't know. It's a normal occurrence within the human body. I don't understand why your mother hasn't told you."

"Bernard! Tell me how to have babies! It's not fair everyone knows except me!"

"If you don't know how to make babies it's because your mother doesn't want you to know."

"Tell me!"

"And what would you say to your mother? Oh, no worries, mother, I already know how to make babies; Bernard told me. They would shoot me!"

"I won't tell them you told me!"

"No, Maybel!"

"It's not fair that everyone knows except me!"

"I'll show you a medical journal. You can draw your own conclusions."

"Ok," I sighed. "I just want to know."

Bernard took me back downstairs to the study. He pulled a big, thick book from the beautifully-crafted, wooden bookcase. It was leather-bound and had clearly been read many times judging from the yellowed and worn pages.

I sat on the couch in the study next to Bernard. I held the book and carefully read about anatomy. It was a woman's anatomy that was drawn on the pages.

Bernard sat next to me with his head turned. He looked embarrassed.

"What's this?" I asked shocked.

"It's a man's anatomy," Bernard said. "Haven't you ever seen a man naked?"

"Of course not! What kind of girl do you think I am?"

"I meant, have you never changed a baby boy's diaper or perhaps seen your father step out of the bathtub?"

I looked at him shocked. "No!"

I looked at the picture of male anatomy again and then at Bernard's waist.

"Maybel!" He shifted uncomfortably.

"That's what you look like under your pants?" I asked, absolutely shocked.

"Maybel!" He turned his head. His face was red.

"That thing doesn't look like what I have at all!"

"It's not supposed to! I'm a man and you're a woman!"

"What do you do with this?" I asked, still staring at the absolutely ludicrous drawing.

"With what?" Bernard asked.

"What do you do with a thing like this?" I pointed to the male anatomy. "Where do you put it? Does it hang down in your undershorts?"

"Maybel, I feel very uncomfortable!"

"Is this what you use to pee with?" I inspected it more closely.

"Yes, Maybel!" Bernard now looked positively mortified.

"What's it called?" I tapped the illustration with my finger.

"A penis," Bernard said.

"The pee comes out the bottom here?" I pointed to the tip of the penis.

"Yes! I should never have shown you this journal!" Bernard sighed loudly.

"What are these?"

"They are called the scrotum," he answered.

"They look gross."

"Maybel, please!" Bernard huffed.

"What do they do?" I asked.

"Just read the book, Maybel!"

I began reading. "What is sperm?"

Bernard sighed and rubbed his forehead. "They are very small and microscopic and one of the thousands created will join with the woman's egg and together they create a baby."

I stared in shock. "I have eggs? Like a chicken? I'm going to lay an egg?"

"No!"

"Babies hatch?"

"No! God no, Maybel!" Bernard was exasperated. "Alright, I will very quickly explain the main points."

Bernard cleared his throat and attempted to regain his composure. "The penis goes in the vagina and sperm comes out, and the sperm go to an egg deep inside you that is so small you can barely see it, and a baby starts growing here in your uterus." He pointed to the uterus in his medical journal.

Bernard took a deep breath. "The baby comes out of your vagina after nine months and it's covered in the blood from your periods. It's not in an egg. You are not a chicken. When you have your periods, it means you are not pregnant. When you don't have your period, you are pregnant, and you won't have your period again until after the baby is born."

"I've never seen a penis," I told him.

"It's right here in the book," he tapped the drawing.

"I mean, I've never seen one in real life. When did you see a vagina?"

"I haven't!" Bernard looked taken aback.

"Then how do you know this picture is accurate?"

"Because it's in a medical journal!" Bernard said.

"You've never seen a vagina?"

"No! I've seen my mother walk from the bathtub to her closet, but I haven't seen inside like what this illustration shows!"

"Then you don't know if this drawing is accurate," I said plainly.

"Maybel, my God! I have never in my life met someone like you!"

"Is the drawing of the penis accurate?"

"Yes," he said.

"You really look like that?"

"Yes," he said exasperatedly. "Maybel, you won't see one until you are married."

"Why? Why are penises so elusive?"

"Men and women don't show each other their naked bodies until they are married," Bernard said firmly.

"You're saying this picture of a penis is accurate?"

"Yes," he said.

"And you think this picture of a vagina is accurate?"

"Yes," Bernard sighed.

"Where are my eggs in this picture?"

"Here, they begin in the Fallopian tube and move down to your uterus."

"Then these drawings are inaccurate!" I said. "There is no way this small penis can touch here in the uterus!"

"The sperm swim to meet the egg," Bernard said. He was by now beaten down by my questions and looked more than a little exasperated.

"Like fish? You have something like fish in you, and I have something like a chicken's egg in me?"

"No. Now you're just being ridiculous, Maybel!"

"I am not! This thing right here looks like an elephant's trunk and you're saying this tiny, little version of an elephant's trunk can touch up here? If that's true, this drawing is not to scale!"

"The penis gets bigger! It swells up and gets longer when a man is aroused!"

"What else aren't you telling me? It gets bigger? What other details aren't you sharing?"

"I think that's everything, Maybel! My God!"

"What does 'aroused' mean?"

Bernard's head sunk lower and he groaned. "A man is aroused when he kisses a woman."

"You kiss Catherine. Does your penis swell and get longer?"

"I am done with this conversation! I cannot continue!" Bernard held his forehead in the palm of his hand.

"So, if I kissed you, your penis would get bigger and longer?"

"No!"

"Why not?" I asked.

"I'm not attracted to you."

"Why not?" I asked.

"You're too young," he answered.

Suddenly we heard voices down the hall. It sounded like loud talking and laughter. "Sounds like our parents are home," Bernard said. "I guess you'll be going home then," he said, sounding relieved.

"I didn't get to tell you stories!" I whined. "Tomorrow can we have a campfire and I'll tell you stories?"

"I don't know, Maybel, I'm exhausted," Bernard stood up and held out his hand for me. "We'll see."

I walked home with mommy and daddy, leaving Bernard drained from his first lecture as a doctor-in-training.

The next day I went to Bernard's house. He was in his bedroom sitting at his desk studying. "Bernard, most boys would have teased me and been mean to me when I got my first period. Why weren't you mean?"

He put his book down. "I'm going to be a doctor, Maybel. What happened to you is just a part of being a woman. Don't be embarrassed."

"I know, I'm saying you weren't mean. Thank you."

"Maybel," he sighed, "come here."

I went to Bernard and sat on his lap and wrapped my arms around his neck. I kissed him.

"Maybel," he pushed me away, "don't do that."

"I'm sorry, I didn't mean anything bad."

"We're not supposed to kiss," he whispered.

"Ok, I'm sorry." I whispered back.

He sighed and pulled me into a hug. "It's ok. Sometimes I forget too, that we're not supposed to kiss. You're too young, but sometimes, my mind gets a little blurry, and I like you."

"I like you too, Bernard."

"Is Catherine home yet from visiting your cousins?" Bernard changed the subject.

I got off his lap. "No," I said.

I wanted Bernard to play with me and not think about where Catherine was or what she was doing. I walked angrily to Bernard's door.

"Where are you going?" Bernard asked.

"You don't care! You only care about Catherine!" I started to feel tears coming. I didn't understand why I was so mad. I ran home, kicking rocks the whole way.

"Maybel, come help me prepare bread and pies for dinner," mommy called to me as I ran through the front door.

"I hate boys! I hate bleeding! I hate chickens!" I screamed as I ran upstairs. I didn't hate chickens. Bizarre words flew from my mouth when I was angry. I had no idea why I said I hated chickens.

Mommy came upstairs and into my bedroom. She sat on the edge of my bed. I could smell the kitchen on her apron. She smelled like flour and grease and cinnamon.

"I'm sorry I didn't tell you about bleeding. My mother never told me. It was always something girls figured out for themselves. I know you're mad at me and Catherine for not telling you. It's not a conversation I ever had with my parents. I'm sorry, honey. I try to do better than my parents did for me, and when you're a mommy, you'll try to do better than me and daddy did for you. Please know that I'm truly trying to do the best that I can."

Mommy rubbed my back as I laid face down into my pillow. I cried. I was scared and confused.

Mommy left and returned to baking downstairs in the kitchen. I stayed in bed sulking and writing about a girl who was blindfolded and led to the middle of a cornfield and told to find her way home. She was too stupid to know that all she had to do was take off her blindfold so she shivered all night and died from the cold.

Bernard told me I had become too old to sit on his lap and that people would talk. I often cried to mommy about it, but she said Bernard was right; I was becoming too old to play with, and certainly too old to sit on Bernard's lap. I didn't think I was too old. And Bernard was like a brother, but as mommy and Bernard reminded me, he was not really my brother, and that was why I could no longer sit on his lap.

One day I decided to press my boundaries to see if Bernard was serious about his lap policy. I sat on Bernard's lap eating ice cream while he talked to his handsome cousin, Henry. They talked about business. Henry wanted Mr. Charleston to be a sort of teacher and help Henry learn how to be rich. Henry wanted to be an apprentice.

I sat there listening. I could talk to Henry now, but his face was so perfect, and I always became mesmerized by his eyes and lost track of what I had been saying. I leaned back into Bernard's chest eating my ice cream and looking up into the tree branches above where we sat on Bernard's front porch.

Henry watched me from time to time while he and Bernard spoke. I liked Henry, but I was not able to talk to him without stammering. He looked like a painting or perhaps a statue of a Greek God.

My ice cream dripped onto my neck as I sat in Bernard's lap and looked up.

"Maybel, wipe your chin and neck," Bernard said, annoyed.

I reached into Bernard's pants pocket and pulled out his handkerchief. It was white with his initials monogrammed on the corner in fancy script. I didn't have anything monogrammed and wondered what it was like to have your name or initials displayed prominently and proudly onto your clothing, carved into the oak double doors of your mansion, and on the wrought iron fence of your grandiose carriageway.

I wiped my chin with Bernard's handkerchief.

"Ladies dab, Maybel," Bernard criticized my way of wiping my face.

"Show me," I said.

Bernard took his handkerchief and dabbed at my chin.

"Let me try." I took his handkerchief and made sure the tuft of handkerchief I held was smeared with my ice cream drippings and dabbed Bernard's chin, getting sticky ice cream on him.

"Maybel!" Bernard furrowed his brows, "You're making me sticky."

"I'm sorry," I said, innocently.

Bernard sighed and rearranged his handkerchief so a clean portion was available to wipe his chin.

I leaned back and continued licking my ice cream cone.

"Stop licking like that," Bernard said. "Just pinch it with your lips or something. Don't use your tongue like that."

Henry suppressed a chuckle. I looked at him. Henry then averted his gaze.

"Why does it matter how I lick ice cream?" I asked.

"It just does!" Bernard said.

"Fine! I'll pinch it. How do you pinch it with your lips?"

I held my ice cream cone to Bernard's lips. He lightly put his lips around a small portion and pinched it off with his lips.

"You only got a tiny bit of ice cream. It will take you forever to eat this!" I said.

"You're not supposed to eat it in big gulps like a horse chomps down on half a carrot," Bernard told me. He sometimes acted like my older brother, which I found annoying. He told me not to think of him as my big brother, but he treated me like his little sister sometimes.

"Horses can eat half a carrot at a time?"

"Yes, but you are not an animal, so don't eat like one!" Bernard advised me.

I considered how a horse could fit half a carrot easily into its mouth. "I bet it's because they have long mouths," I told Bernard.

"It's because they aren't taught manners," Bernard chided me.

I wondered how far I could fit something into my mouth. I'd never wondered about that before and now I wanted to know the answer.

Bernard and Henry spoke of investments. Henry seemed quite curious and intelligent. I liked that he asked questions. Most people didn't ask questions for fear they'd sound ignorant, but Henry asked really ignorant questions, and he didn't even seem to care how stupid he sounded. I admired Henry's quest for truth. Only really smart people asked questions, not caring whether or not other people tried to make them feel stupid for asking. Bernard did not try to make Henry feel stupid, and I liked Bernard a little more for that.

I pushed most of the ice cream into my mouth. I attempted to say, 'Bernard! Look!' but I choked instead, and the ice cream fell out of my mouth onto Bernard's neck and shoulder.

"Sorry, Bernard!" I yelled, and dove into his neck to clean the ice cream from his skin.

Henry grinned at Bernard and stood up. "I'll leave you two be," he chuckled and left.

Bernard froze as I licked his shoulder up to his neck.

"Maybel," he whispered.

"I'm sorry! Don't yell at me or call me Messy Maybel!" I licked another drip of ice cream off his shoulder and neck again.

"Maybel stop, please!" Bernard's voice sounded strained.

"I'm sorry I spilled my ice cream on you," I said. I leaned down and sucked the last of it off his neck and Bernard breathed heavily. I looked back at him and his green eyes watched me differently.

"What's wrong?" I grew concerned.

Bernard pulled me close, holding me firmly against him and kissed my neck and shoulder. I felt tingles as he kissed me and held my waist. When he pushed his tongue inside my mouth and held me close to his chest, it sent shivers up my spine and made my nipples harden.

"Bernard?"

Bernard stopped and pushed me away hard. I fell sideways onto the porch swing where we sat and a splinter pierced my thigh.

"I'm so sorry, Maybel!" Bernard breathed.

I was confused and left quickly. I went into the study. Henry was there reading.

I sat in the chair behind the big desk. I looked down, and in my mind, I replayed every little nuance of what had just taken place. I wasn't sure what had happened and why.

"Maybel? Are you alright?" Henry asked.

I never talked to Henry because my words fumbled in my mouth at his beauty, but I managed to shake my head no.

"What happened? Did Bernard hurt you?" Henry looked angry and protective of me, which surprised me.

"No," I said.

Henry watched me.

"I don't understand what happened," I said. I looked down again. I took a pencil and put its tip on a piece of typing paper. I could not think of anything to write, and anyway, I only wanted to look busy so I wouldn't have to talk to Henry.

"Do you want to talk about anything?" Henry seemed genuinely concerned.

"No," I said.

"Would you like to sit here together while I read this intriguing article on economics?" he asked me.

"Yes," I said.

"It's not intriguing," he clarified. "I was attempting a joke."

"I know," I said. "It was so subtle I forgot to laugh."

Henry laughed softly, "Your stories are surely more interesting," he said. "May I read one?"

I nodded yes.

"Will you bring me a story, please?" he asked me.

I took a story I had written a year or two ago from one of the drawers of the desk where I sat. I walked over to Henry where he sat on one end of the sofa, and handed it to him, then sat on the opposite end of the sofa.

Henry wore dark blue pants and a white, button down shirt. His shoes were dark brown and shined. I loved watching him. He took as much care with his appearance as Catherine did with her appearance. They were both always polished to perfection, never a single hair astray.

Henry began reading my story aloud to me.

"I used to be a dog. A lady took care of me and we ate together at every meal. When she died, her daughter didn't want me, and drove me to the top of a mountain and left me there. I walked for five days and five nights back to where I once lived. I crawled into my mother's daughter's arms and died. And now I'm here. I did not like the latter part of my life, but I am at last reunited with the lady who loved me, and we play together once again in young and healthy bodies."

"Maybel?" Henry asked, "How did you come up with this story?"

"I just sit down and when my mind stops chattering, I see stories come together."

Henry looked at me with interest. "I've traveled through India," he said. "Your writing has a subtle tone, as though you've read books written by Indian philosophers."

I stared at him.

"I am speaking of people from India, not the Indians who are from here in the United States."

I nodded my head, indicating I understood. "It's just a short, stupid story I wrote when I was lonely because Bernard and Catherine were in Bernard's bedroom and wanted to be alone, so they locked the door.

"When I get sad," I continued, "I write sad stories. I also wrote a story about my grandmother raising a pig every year, then taking those pigs to slaughter. One year she got really attached to a pig named Charlie. Charlie followed grandma around wherever grandma went, so when it came time, grandma got her neighbor to take Charlie to slaughter. Granny couldn't eat Charlie's bacon or pork chops, even though everyone told her Charlie tasted better than any other pig at the fair and won first place. Her neighbors bought half of Charlie's carcass, and every Sunday for a year, they feasted on him, and every Sunday for a year, granny cried."

Henry stared at me half shocked and half sad. "Were you sad when you wrote that story? Had Bernard and Catherine been ignoring you again?"

"No, I was hungry," I replied. "I like bacon," I shrugged.

Henry chuckled, "I like your stories; they are so odd and fascinating, and your humor is quite unique. I wish you weren't scared to talk to me."

"I'm not scared," I said defiantly.

"Then why don't you ever want to speak to me?"

"I'm nervous around you," I replied honestly.

"Why?"

"I like you. You're the most handsome man I've ever seen," I blushed.

"You seem like a nice, young lady, Maybel," Henry told me.

"You too, I mean you as well, I mean you are not a lady." I turned away from Henry. My eyes teared up. I hated that I behaved so awkwardly.

Henry smiled warmly, "Don't be embarrassed, Maybel. I'm just a regular person."

I could not look at him. I was embarrassed. I took a deep breath and then paused. I winced because I felt pain in my heart and in my mind. "I don't know what's going on," I blurted out.

I started to tear up. "I don't understand what is happening to me. And my mother and sister aren't explaining anything to me. And Bernard is confusing me. And I don't know what to do about anything. I'm very confused all the time."

"I'm sorry, honey," Henry quietly said.

Bernard came into the study where Henry and I sat. "Maybel, would you like to go to the candy store? I'm hungry."

Bernard knew my weaknesses. I nodded yes. He came to the sofa and reached out his hand. I accepted his hand and we left together.

We walked along the brick sidewalk toward the candy store. "Maybel, I am sorry I kissed your neck."

"It's ok," I said.

Bernard looked troubled. "It's better that you do not lick a man's neck."

"Ok," I said.

"It's not something you should do."

"Ok," I again said.

Bernard held the door to the candy store open for me and I entered. It smelled like sugar. There were children running around, and their parents chased after them. I remembered running like that in here when I was a couple years younger. Catherine though, I remembered her as always being perfect; she never ran around wildly.

Bernard and I sat side by side inside the candy store. I leaned against him and ate my cookie. My head rested on his arm. He smelled like cookies, or maybe the whole store smelled like cookies.

Three girls came into the candy store. They were not Catherine's friends even though Catherine always smiled and said hi to them. For a long time, I did not know Catherine hated them, but I heard her speaking with Edith, and Edith called them false friends even though the two groups of girls had smiled and waved at each other whenever they passed on the sidewalk. I was still confused about whether or not they were friends with Catherine, but I was fairly certain they were not.

"Hello, Bernard," the leader smiled. Her name was Elinor. Catherine once called her Smellinor to Edith when Edith spent the night at our home.

"Hello," Bernard replied.

"Would you like to come with us? We're going to the park to sit and talk. You can bring your little sister."

"She's not actually my little sister," Bernard corrected Elinor.

"She sure acts like your little sister," Elinor smiled at me.

"This is Maybel. She's Catherine's little sister," Bernard explained.

Elinor smiled at me again. "I know. It's just that she seems like your little sister too, always following you around, looking up to you as a big brother."

Elinor then smiled at Bernard. "You look really nice," she said. "I like your shirt. It brings out the beautiful green of your eyes."

I looked at Bernard's attire. He wore an old, green shirt and light brown pants. His shoes were old and scuffed. He looked poor, but he didn't care that he looked poor. If I were richer than the president, I figured, I could dress like a homeless person and not care either. I watched Bernard talk to Elinor and realized his confidence stemmed from knowing he could buy and sell everyone he met. He knew it, they knew it, and that's why he could dress in old, worn clothes and not care.

Elinor leaned down and whispered into Bernard's ear, the ear farther away from me so I couldn't hear.

Bernard looked uncomfortable and blushed and the two other girls giggled.

"Please tell Catherine I said hello," Elinor again smiled at me.

"Ok, Smellinor," I said.

Smellinor looked angrily at me.

I smiled back.

The three girls left.

"What did Smellinor say to you?"

"She wanted to spend time together in the park," Bernard said.

"Why?"

"I don't know," Bernard shifted uncomfortably.

"Are you going to spend time with her?" I asked.

"No, of course not!"

"Why?" I was surprised Bernard so strongly objected to a walk in the park.

"I'm with Catherine," he answered.

"Elinor wanted to spend time with you in the park, not go on a date with you," I said.

"She wanted more than time," Bernard said.

"What did she want?"

"Maybel, I will not spend time with Elinor. Can we forget about Elinor?" Bernard looked uncomfortable.

"I can. Catherine will be angry, I'll bet." I took another bite of cookie.

"Maybel, let's go home," Bernard said. He seemed apprehensive.

Bernard held open the door for me and walked beside me along the sidewalk in front of the store windows. He exhaled loudly, "Maybel, I asked you here to talk to you. I thought about how naive you are, and I'm worried some bad person will take advantage of you."

"Why?"

"Because you didn't realize it was bad to kiss a man's neck," he said exasperatedly.

"I didn't kiss you!" I couldn't believe Bernard thought I kissed him!

"You sucked on my neck," he whispered.

"I did not! I spilled ice cream on you. I cleaned it up! That's not kissing!" I was indignant. I was absolutely infuriated Bernard thought I'd kissed his neck!

Bernard looked at me. "Maybel, I need to talk to you about men and women." Bernard was serious. He looked serious. His voice and his face were very serious. "I'm concerned for your well-being. I want you to be knowledgeable, because knowledge will keep you safe. You are naive, and have absolutely no idea what happened earlier when you kissed my neck."

"I did not kiss your neck!"

Bernard looked ill at ease. "There are things men and women do to each other, and kissing each other's neck is one of those things."

I stared blankly.

"Kissing passionately like that leads to other passionate things." Bernard watched me. He seemed to think I should understand.

"Ok," I said. I continued nibbling my cookie. I didn't know what he was going on about, but I hadn't kissed his neck.

Bernard sighed, "I'm trying to think of words to explain everything."

I looked into the storefront windows at their displays while I finished the rest of my cookie. I figured this was going to take a while because Bernard was going along at a slow pace.

Bernard sighed heavily, "Let's just go back to my house. I don't know how to go about this situation."

I held Bernard's hand as we walked back to his house. I paused while Bernard began walking up toward his house. "Aren't you coming?" he asked.

"I'm very confused right now. I need time to think."

"It's about intercourse," Bernard blurted out. "Kissing each other's necks makes a man want to have sex with a woman. It arouses men."

I stared at Bernard.

"Don't kiss boys' necks. They will want more than kisses," he said.

"Did you?" I asked bluntly.

"No," he looked very uncomfortable. "You're too young."

"But you liked it? I mean it made you aroused?"

"Yes, Maybel," he angrily whispered. "I'm sorry!"

"You said being aroused means your penis gets hard. Was that what I felt underneath me, your hard penis?"

"Yes!" he hissed in an angry whisper. "You are so unbelievably blunt! I'm embarrassed! Let's go inside if you want to discuss this further. I don't want anyone to hear!"

I stared at Bernard. I was now thinking very intently on the hard thing I felt underneath me. "Ok," I said, and followed Bernard inside.

Bernard led me to his room. I sat down on Bernard's bed. I was quite blunt. "You're supposed to put your hardened penis inside a woman's vagina, right?"

"Yes," Bernard said. He sat on his desk chair in front of me. He looked uneasy, but also like he was trying to approach this conversation as a doctor, not my friend.

Bernard used the medical terminology for anatomy, and he always answered my questions with a professional tone. He used words like 'vagina' and 'penis' instead of saying 'private parts' or 'down there.'

I, in turn, used medical terminology with him as well, and as usual, I was more blunt than he deemed comfortable. "How can you fit your big, hard penis inside me without it hurting? My vagina is much smaller than what I felt underneath me."

"You'll relax and loosen up when you're aroused, but the first time you have intercourse, it may hurt a little bit and you may bleed a little."

I stared at him.

"Do you have any more questions?" he asked.

"Did it hurt Catherine?"

"Catherine and I have never had intercourse."

"Then how do you know so much about a woman's vagina?"

"I'm going to be a doctor! I have studied medical books!" Bernard said exasperatedly.

"How do you know those books are accurate? Why do you trust a book? Wouldn't a good doctor find out the truth instead of trusting an author?"

"It's a medical journal! Medical journals don't lie, they are used in teaching medical students!" Bernard looked almost worn down. He wasn't completely worn down, so I decided to see exactly how far I could push, and how many questions he would agree to answer.

"Ok," I said. "If I were studying anatomy, I would look at anatomy. I wouldn't believe a book just because I was told to believe it."

"It's accurate, Maybel!" Bernard looked like he was irritated with me, but also like he was considering my reasoning.

"Every single detail in your medical journal looks exactly like your penis? The length, the width, and the testicles are all exactly the same?"

"Yes!" he said with aggravation, but he also looked unsure.

"Where is your book?" I asked.

Bernard took a book from his bookshelf above his desk. "Here, Maybel, see for yourself."

"I have seen it. I committed it to memory," I said.

"That's what a penis looks like," he said.

"Every single penis looks like that? They are all the exact same shape, length, and thickness with the scrotum being exactly alike? I doubt the veracity of this book. The author drew a worm with hairy cherries. I looked at my vagina with a hand mirror after you showed me this book. I don't look exactly like that."

"You don't?" I had clearly piqued Bernard's interest.

"I'm not a circus oddity, Bernard, it's just, I think every person has variations. It's like when mommy makes Christmas cookies, she uses a metal shape to cut stars and ornaments, but none of them are exactly the same. They are similar, but not identical."

Bernard kept looking at me.

"What?" I asked. "Why are you staring at me?"

"How exactly are you different than this drawing? Is the shape of your vagina different?"

"No, it's similar, it's just that it's not identical. You cannot truthfully look at the drawing of that penis and say you look exactly like that underneath your clothing."

"No, I guess not exactly like it," he admitted.

I was surprised Bernard agreed. I didn't think Bernard would agree with anything I said. We usually argued even the smallest points. "How are you different?"

"I don't know, Maybel, I'm not a circus oddity either!"

"Show me," I said.

"What?"

"We can show each other. We won't touch each other. I just want to see what you look like. I don't believe until I see with my own eyes."

"Ok," Bernard said.

"What?" I was completely taken aback with Bernard's agreeable nature.

"I'll show you," he said. "I won't touch you."

I suddenly felt nervous. I had not expected to show my vagina to Bernard. I had been certain he would say no. Bernard got up from his chair and sat beside me on his bed.

"I didn't think you would say yes," I said. "I'm scared," I confessed.

Bernard laid down on his back. "I'll show you what I look like. You don't have to show me anything unless you want to."

I watched Bernard unbutton his pants and then unzip his zipper. I felt my heart beat faster. I wanted to see, but I was scared.

Bernard put his thumbs inside his undershorts and pulled down his pants to his knees, then laid on his back and watched me. He looked scared, too.

I looked down at his waist. His penis was much larger in proportion to his waist and thighs than the penis in the drawing. He was longer and thicker.

"Are you finished looking?" Bernard asked me.

I had been completely absorbed in looking at this thing I had never seen before, and Bernard had startled me when he asked if I was finished looking.

"No," I said.

"What more is there to look at? It's just a penis."

"I've never seen one before." I could not stop looking at his penis.

"Maybel, I feel embarrassed, can I pull my pants back up now? This is very awkward."

I kept staring at his penis.

Bernard reached down and tugged on his pants and began pulling them up around his knees.

"Wait," I whispered.

"You've been staring at it a long time," Bernard continued pulling up his pants.

"I'll show you what I look like," I said softly. My heart beat faster.

"You don't have to," Bernard said, but he looked like he really wanted to see.

I laid down beside Bernard and slowly pulled my skirt up then pushed my underwear down. I lifted my knees up and my skirt fell back atop my stomach.

Bernard sat up and looked down at me. "I can't see," he whispered gently.

I slowly spread my knees apart and let them fall to my sides. I was now completely exposed.

Bernard sucked in his breath as he looked at me.

"Are you done?" I asked.

"Your labia are stuck together," he said softly.

"What? Is there something wrong with me?" I began to panic.

"Nothing is wrong," Bernard spoke gently. "Your skin is stuck together over your birth canal. I can't see everything."

"My birth canal?"

"Just take your fingers and gently pull apart your skin."

I put two fingers on my vagina and spread apart my skin so Bernard could see better. His penis was now fully erect. He was very long, very thick, and looked very hard.

"I can't fit that inside me," I whispered to him.

Bernard looked down at his penis and quickly covered it with his hands.

"I can still see it," I whispered.

"I'm sorry, Maybel. I've never seen a girl naked before."

I pulled my underwear back up. Bernard pulled his pants up and buttoned and zipped them.

"Is it ok that we looked at each other?" I asked as I pushed down my skirt and sat upright.

"We didn't touch each other," Bernard said.

"Don't tell anyone you know what I look like naked."

"I won't," he said. "Don't tell anyone you know what I look like naked either."

"I won't," I promised.

Bernard and I sat apart on his bed and neither of us could look each other. I wondered how long until I could leave without offending him. I didn't want Bernard to think I was disgusted by what I saw, but I felt nervous and wanted to leave.

"Do you want a glass of water or something to eat?" Bernard's voice cracked and he sounded as nervous as I felt.

"No," I answered. "I don't know what to do or say now," I confessed.

"Me neither, but I don't want us to be like this."

There was another brief moment of silence.

"Do you have any questions?" Bernard spoke gently.

"Do you want to have intercourse with Catherine?"

Bernard must have gotten at least a little more used to my bluntness because he didn't even pause when I asked such an intrusive question. "I've wondered what it would feel like," he admitted.

"Why haven't you asked her?"

Bernard shifted uncomfortably. "I think maybe it would make things more complicated and Catherine has never seemed to want to do more than kissing."

"If she began kissing you, and asked you if you wanted to do more, would you?"

"I don't know. Maybe I would want to, but I don't want to get her pregnant. We've never gotten to the point where we couldn't stop from going further. Sometimes when you are kissing someone, you think you want more, but you aren't thinking clearly, so it's better to just not let yourself get to that point. I've always been able to stop myself from doing more, and I just don't know if I want to do more right now, I mean, sometimes I think it would feel good, but I don't know, Maybel."

"How do you know it feels good though? Maybe people only have sex to have children. Maybe your parents only had sex one time and my parents had sex twice, a long time ago."

Bernard laughed, then realized I was serious. "It's enjoyable. People have sex often."

"What makes you think that?"

"I hear boys talking at school and I've heard my older cousins talking," Bernard said.

"Like Henry?" I asked.

"Yes."

"Henry has intercourse?" I was surprised. I thought it was a long-standing joke that Henry had sex. I didn't know he actually had intercourse.

Bernard let out a laugh, apparently thinking I was joking, then quickly became serious again when I didn't smile. "Yes, he does."

"I thought everyone was only joking about Henry having a lot of girlfriends because he is so beautiful. Henry has really had sex?" I asked, surprised.

"Yes, Henry has sex," Bernard said.

"Henry's not married. You said you can only have sex when you're married." Bernard, I felt, was not entirely truthful about the interactions between boys and girls. Bernard had kissed my neck, then told me not to kiss boys like that. I was confused about the rules.

"Henry has sex even though he is not married, but do not follow his example," Bernard told me.

I crossed my arms. "Are you making up rules?"

"Maybel," he exhaled, "relationships are complicated. Henry sets a bad example. Don't look at Henry as a role model. Some people like Henry have sex before marriage. The women he has sex with should not be having sex before marriage, nor should they be cheating on their husbands with Henry."

"You cheated on Catherine," I said quietly.

"I know." Bernard looked troubled and truly at war with himself behind his green eyes.

"Has Catherine kissed other boys the way you kissed me?"

"I'm not sure," Bernard admitted.

"I think you and Catherine have sex. You don't want to tell me because you want to set a good example for me."

"We do not have sex or anything resembling sex," Bernard said, agitated.

"Then why do you sometimes lock your door?"

"Sometimes we want to be alone."

"So you can have sex," I said.

"No."

"Then you're doing other things like kissing each other's necks," I pressed further.

"No, Maybel, sometimes we just don't want you around."

I felt my eyebrows lower suddenly, without my meaning to lower them. My lower lip protruded into a pout. There was a pang in my stomach. My feelings hurt.

"I'm sorry, Maybel. Don't you ever want to be alone with a friend?"

"Only if I were touching his hard penis. That's the only possible reason why you two wouldn't want me around!"

"No, Maybel, sometimes you talk too much, and ask questions, and say things that are blunt and uncomfortable. Sometimes we get tired of you constantly wanting to play. You're a child still, and sometimes it's annoying to have to babysit you. Sometimes we just want to lay quietly and read together."

I started crying. I ran out of his room, out of the kitchen, and home as quickly as my legs would carry me. I always pushed people too far trying to get the truth, and then I got hurt when they spoke the truth. I felt worse for having learned the truth. Catherine and Bernard considered me an annoyance.

Catherine was in her room. I heard her singing. I opened her door. She was applying color to her lips. "You should knock first, Maybel," she said.

"You never knock on my door," I told her.

"What do you want, Maybel?" Catherine sighed.

"Elinor was at the candy store with me and Bernard. She wanted Bernard to come with her to the park. Bernard said no."

"Thank you for telling me." Catherine went back to looking at herself in the mirror.

"You're not angry?" I asked.

"Bernard isn't attracted to Elinor. I'm prettier, anyway." Catherine held up two pairs of earrings trying to choose which went with her dress best.

"Henry spends a lot of time on his appearance too."

"Henry is at the Charlestons?" Catherine turned to look at me.

"Yes. Do you think he's handsome?" I asked, already knowing the answer.

"He looks well-groomed," she said, and turned back to her mirror.

"If I were married, I would have sex with him," I said.

Catherine fumbled with, and dropped her lip color onto her dressing table. "How do you know what sex is?" she asked me, shocked.

"A friend told me. Mommy wouldn't tell me. You wouldn't tell me. You said you didn't know how to make a baby, but you lied! Why wouldn't you tell me?"

"It's an awkward conversation. I figured one of your friends would tell you eventually," Catherine said nonchalantly, like my questions about making babies were unimportant. Catherine's tone was dismissive. It upset me that she didn't seem to care about my confusion. I wanted her to be more caring toward me.

"Who told you about menstruation and intercourse?" I asked Catherine.

"I saw daddy having sex once when I didn't knock on the door, so please be sure to knock," Catherine said. She delivered that surprising information in the same nonchalant manner.

"That's how you learned? But how did you know what they were doing?" I asked her.

"I was really young, like three or four years old or something. The memory stuck inside my mind, and when I got older, I figured out what really happened. And Edith tells me some things. She has an older sister who occasionally tells her things that she passes on to me," Catherine said while brushing her hair.

"Why would you not then pass those bits of knowledge on to me?" I yelled. "I have been completely naive for too long! It's not fair that everyone knows everything except me!"

"I'm your big sister. I didn't want you to hear those things from me. I'm supposed to shelter and protect you. I didn't want to be a bad influence. I was hoping mommy would explain it to you. It's just one of those awkward things that you have to find out about on your own. I assumed you would hear about it from one of your friends like I did."

I stewed in confusion and anger in my bedroom. When Catherine finally came out of her bedroom, she wore a different dress than the one she had on several minutes ago.

"What was wrong with the other dress?" I asked as she walked past my door.

"I didn't know Henry was in town," she called as she descended the stairs.

Bernard came to see me and brought his baseball bat and glove one day. He said he was sorry for telling me I was annoying. The next day, he brought his bicycle and let me ride back to his house where he had another bicycle, and we rode his two bicycles down to the old mill and back. He told me sometimes he and Catherine wanted to read together quietly, but he missed playing with me when we fought. And the day after that, I went to his house to play in the treehouse his father built for all Bernard's little cousins when they came to visit. After playing in his treehouse and fishing with Bernard in his pond, I watched Bernard studying on his bed. I was bored and when I got bored, I moved around more than usual.

"Sit still!" Bernard told me. "You're like an eel!"

Bernard was sitting in his bed reading a book about biology, or the heart, or lungs, or something.

"Are you almost done?" I asked impatiently.

"No."

I sighed. I rolled away from him, then did a summersault toward him, my feet landing on his shoulders.

"I can't concentrate, Maybel!" Bernard stared at his book, not acknowledging me, which made me want his attention even more.

I scooted closer to him and locked my feet behind his neck. My head was on his legs. Bernard pretended to not notice me, so I began humming.

"You are being tremendously annoying," he said, refusing to look at me.

I scooted my bottom up onto his chest and my head now rested on his thighs. I crossed my legs behind his back.

"Stop behaving like this, Maybel. It looks like we are having sex. If anyone were to open my bedroom door, that's what they would think."

"My vagina is nowhere near your penis!" I said incredulously.

"It doesn't have to be. There is more than one way to have sex."

My eyes bolted wide open. "What? You never told me that when you showed me that medical book about how to make a baby!"

Bernard sighed, "There are ways to have sex without making a baby."

I rolled off Bernard then sat on his waist staring intently at him with wide eyes and a piqued curiosity. "You can have sex without making a baby?"

"Do you not talk to your friends? Does Catherine not tell you things?"

"Catherine knows?" My eyes bulged.

"It's impossible for you to be this naive." Bernard went back to reading.

I knocked his book to the floor. "Tell me!"

"Ok, Maybel," Bernard sighed. "What do you want to know?"

"Everything! I can't believe you didn't tell me everything before! Why didn't you tell me everything before? I trusted you to teach me everything, and you said you would, so that I wouldn't be taken advantage of by boys with mal intentions!"

"Calm down, Maybel," Bernard laughed at my exuberance. "You act as though I've committed perjury."

"Tell me everything now!" I screeched.

"Ok," Bernard leaned his head back into his pillow. "A man puts his fingers inside a woman's vagina. A woman puts her hand around the man's penis."

"Is that supposed to mimic sex?"

"Yes," Bernard said.

"Does the man move his finger around in a circular motion, like he's stirring cake mix, or does he push his fingers in and out like he's pretending his fingers are his penis inside her?"

Bernard looked confused. "I think he pushes his fingers in and out."

"Why don't you know the correct answer?" I did not trust Bernard's confused face. I wanted less confusion and more confidence.

"I've never done it before!" Bernard said exasperatedly.

"Why not? You said you can't make a baby. That means you can do it whenever you want and you don't have to worry about making a baby."

Bernard looked annoyed at me. "You cannot do this whenever or with whomever you want!"

"You said you have to be married to have sex because sex makes babies. You aren't making a baby if you use your fingers. Do you enjoy making up rules and confusing me further?"

Bernard sighed deeply.

I stared at Bernard.

Bernard rubbed his forehead. He looked like he was trying to find the right words to express himself.

"Ok, fine," I sighed, "The man moves his fingers in and out. Is that all? That sounds like it wouldn't feel good. You just sit there with your fingers inside a woman and she's supposed to like it?"

Bernard laughed, "The man moves his fingers around, then after sufficient stimulation, the woman orgasms."

"What is that?" I asked.

"What is what?"

"Orgasm. What is that?" I asked again.

"When a man is stimulated long enough, his penis spasms, and sperm comes out. When a woman orgasms, her vagina squeezes tightly."

"Oh, then I've orgasmed before," I said.

"With whom?" Bernard suddenly looked enraged.

"I wake up sometimes at night feeling my vagina squeezing. I always wondered what that was. Do you ever wake up from a dream feeling that way?"

"I've woken up after orgasming," Bernard admitted. He seemed embarrassed.

"Do you have to get up and change your underwear?" I asked. "I do, because it gets wet."

"Yes," he said. "It's sticky."

"It's sticky?" I stared at Bernard. "Like ice cream?"

"Warm and sticky," he answered. "But then it gets cold on your stomach as you lay in bed."

"Mine isn't sticky."

"It's not?" he asked, surprised.

"No, when I orgasm it's just wetter and slipperier."

"Is it white?" he asked.

"What?" I was confused by his question.

"When you orgasm, is your orgasm white?"

"No, it's clear, like water, but slippery, like slime on a rock in the creek, but not green or gross. It's clear and slippery. Yours is white?"

"Yes," he answered.

I thought for a moment. "I get curious sometimes about everything that happens. How long do you orgasm? Do you shudder? I shudder. Sometimes I orgasm several times. Do you?"

Bernard watched me with wide eyes. "No," he said. His voice was quiet. "I have one orgasm."

"How long does it last?"

"Just a second," he replied.

"Mine last longer. I feel a squeezing feeling several times, one after the other. You don't do that?"

Bernard thought for a bit. "The semen squirts out maybe a couple times, so I suppose it's like the squeezing you said you feel."

"Anything else you forgot to mention?" I asked him. I didn't want any more surprises down the road.

Bernard sighed, "The other way to have sex is to use your mouth."

"Kissing?"

"No," Bernard paused, "Well, yes, I guess it can be called kissing." Bernard hesitated, "The man puts his mouth on the woman's vagina and stimulates her that way until she orgasms. The woman puts the man's penis in her mouth until the man orgasms."

I stared at Bernard. I stared quietly. And then, I began laughing hysterically. "You're playing a joke on me! That's the stupidest thing I've ever heard!" I continued laughing.

"It's true. People do that."

"Who told you?" I continued laughing at Bernard.

"I hear boys talking at school."

"Maybe they're playing a joke on you!" I laughed. "Maybe they want to see if you'll actually do that!" I laughed so hard I snorted.

"Ok, Maybel, I don't care if you believe me."

"Wait," I said, "do people really do that?"

"Yes."

"Do you think if a woman put your penis in her mouth it would feel good to you and you would like it?"

"Yes, Maybel, I imagine it would feel really good."

"How do you know?"

"Well, it feels good when I hold it with my hand, so I imagine a warm, wet mouth would feel much better."

I thought for a moment about a penis and something warm and wet. "Do you hold your penis in your bath water and make yourself orgasm?" I asked him.

"No! I do not want to bathe in my own semen! That's disgusting!"

"But your bath water is warm and wet. You said warm and wet would feel good. Why wouldn't bath water?"

Bernard looked like he was carefully considering my idea.

I continued analyzing this new thing I learned. "When a woman puts a penis in her mouth what does she do? Does she just sit there with a mouthful of penis or is she supposed to do something with it?"

"I don't know!" Bernard looked exasperated with me. "I imagine she pushes it into her mouth then pulls it out repeatedly. That's the movement you make for intercourse, so I imagine you would mimic that motion for oral sex."

"Ok, then what would a man do? Would he push his tongue inside her vagina?"

"I never thought about sex in this much detail, Maybel! My imagination is not as good as yours! I'm not sure what the man does exactly, but I suppose he might push his tongue inside her."

"Why haven't you thought about it in great detail? If you don't know what to do with a woman, you'll be a bad lover, and she will leave your bed unsatisfied. That's very inconsiderate of you, Bernard."

Bernard looked like he was thinking very hard about what I'd said.

"What do you suppose a vagina or a penis tastes like? Do you think it would taste good or indifferent?" I asked.

"I don't know!"

"You have never had any kind of sex with anyone?" I asked.

"No, I have not."

"Well, that's good. You don't seem to know what you're doing. You might want to think about what to do with a woman so she doesn't laugh at you."

Bernard looked angry suddenly.

"If I have to wait for marriage to make a baby, when can I do these things you just told me about? I assume before marriage since a baby will not be made."

"You should wait for marriage," Bernard said. He was looking more and more tired from this conversation. "You also need to be careful because you can get diseases from having sex. You shouldn't have sex with a lot of people because your chances of getting a disease increases."

"Is there anything else? Any other ways of having sex? Any other surprises you haven't told me about?"

"I don't think so. If I think of anything else, I'll tell you." Bernard breathed in deeply and stared up at his ceiling.

"I have another question," I said. "Sometimes I wake up at night and my vagina is wet and I feel like I need to move my hips and thighs around, and it feels good when I do, but it also makes me want more, and then I can't get back to sleep because my vagina is wet and tingly. What do I do to make that stop?"

Bernard stared at me with big eyes for a solid minute. "Masturbate," he said.

"What is that, and how do I do it?"

"Put your fingers inside your vagina and move them around until you orgasm then you can get back to sleep."

"Ok. Anything else?"

"No, nothing I can think of right now." Bernard looked tired. I was certain I broke him.

"Bernard?"

"What, Maybel?" Bernard's eyes looked glassy and unfocused, but he was not yet completely broken. I hoped he would remain unbroken for one more question.

"How fast does your sperm come out? Does it squirt out like when you turn on the faucet? Or does it leak out more slowly?"

"It squirts out."

"I don't have any more questions," I said.

"Thank you," he said, as he continued staring at his ceiling. He looked fully broken now.

I visited my cousins, stayed with my grandparents for a short time, and mommy took me to the city one day to see a play. Daddy took us to visit his sister one weekend. And then Bernard came over to see Catherine one day. I was excited when Catherine said Bernard was coming over.

"Eight, nine, ten! Ready or not here I come!" I ran to find Bernard. He and Catherine had been friendly toward one another, but I was never completely sure if they were dating. They seemed happy to take walks together. I saw them smiling at each other at dinner one evening when the Charlestons came over to celebrate mommy's gowns being featured in the newspaper. Catherine had also gone to a play with Rebecca's older brother not long ago, and I was not sure if they were simply friends, or something more. Whatever kind of relationship Catherine had with Bernard, I was grateful for a playmate.

I rounded the house and around the porch and stopped by the wheelbarrow against the trellis. I saw his foot. I crept silently then screamed, "Found you!"

Bernard laughed and jumped out and picked me up. "Got you!"

I giggled and hugged him. He held my hands and spun me around fast and we fell to the ground together.

It was a hot, summer day. I had spent the morning tending to the vegetable garden and helping mommy with her rose garden. I helped daddy move a barrel of wooden planks from the doorway of daddy's workshop to the opposite wall, by the windows. And now Bernard was here playing with me. He was sometimes nice and sometimes like a big brother who teased me relentlessly. Today he played hide and seek with me and I enjoyed every second.

"Bernard, I win! I got you! Now you have to say, 'Queen Maybel rules the land!'" I giggled. Bernard still held my hands as we laid on the hot patches of dirt and cooler patches of grass.

"Queen Maybel likes to eat bugs!" Bernard let go of one of my hands and held a beetle above my face and dropped it onto my nose.

I shrieked, "Bernard!"

Bernard laughed.

I moved myself over top of Bernard and I kissed him.

"Maybel," he whispered, "I told you not to kiss me."

"You kissed me not long ago," I reminded him.

"I know, but I shouldn't have," he said.

"I really like you," I said.

"I like you too," he said, but he looked guilty and ashamed, even troubled by his admission.

I kissed him again and he let me. I kept kissing him and staring at him with my eyes wide open. He watched me with his eyes wide open and laughed. I lifted my head and looked at him, wondering why he was laughing at me.

"You're not supposed to watch me with your eyes wide open," he laughed.

"Your eyes were wide open!" I said.

"I was watching you because you were watching me," he kept laughing.

I became angry and I kissed him again with my eyes closed and held my lips on his.

He laughed again, "Your eyes are closed tightly and you pushed your lips onto mine and didn't move them!" He chuckled and his face was full of amusement. "You're supposed to move your lips a little."

"Stop making fun of me!" I started crying. "I don't know how to kiss!"

"You're such a baby!" Bernard laughed and pushed me off his chest and I fell on my back on the grass. Bernard laughed at me and walked away.

I laid there crying on the grass. I rolled to my side, facing away from the back porch. There were clovers and bees and lady bugs next to my wide-open eyes.

Bernard returned. "Stop being a baby and come inside."

I rolled over to my other side and faced him. "You made fun of me," I sniffled.

Bernard looked confused. "I only told you that you couldn't kiss well."

"What if I told you that you kissed badly? Wouldn't that hurt your feelings?"

"No," he laughed. "You're a baby. I don't care what you think."

I rolled back onto my side facing away from him. I wanted him to go away.

"Are you still crying?" he asked me. His voice sounded annoyed.

"No," I sniffed.

Bernard sighed like he was extremely irritated at me. "Ok, baby. I'm sorry."

Bernard left and went back inside.

I laid on the grass sniveling for a minute or two. I got up and went inside. Mommy was in the kitchen. I heard Catherine and Bernard giggling in the family room. I hoped Catherine would get rid of Bernard and find someone nicer.

I sat down heavily and angrily on the kitchen chair.

"What's wrong, honey?" mommy asked.

"I hope Catherine gets rid of Bernard. I want her to find someone nicer."

"You don't like Bernard anymore?"

"No," I folded my arms in front of me.

"Do you think Bernard dislikes you?"

"He doesn't like me," I said firmly.

"I wonder if maybe you asked him to make cookies with you, he would help?"

"I don't think so. He's mean," I said.

"Can I ask him to help make cookies?" mommy asked me.

"No, I'll ask," I said, and went to the family room.

Bernard was playing some stupid game with Catherine. "Bernard," I asked softly, "do you want to help me make cookies?"

Bernard looked at me then at Catherine. "No," he said. "I want to be with Catherine."

I went back to mommy with my head hanging low.

"Maybel, why don't you go ask Nicky from down the street."

"I don't want to make cookies anymore," I pouted.

"Maybel, please go ask Nicky to help us bake cookies."

"Nicky is a year younger than me. He's a child, mommy!"

"Maybel," mommy looked at me over her coffee mug, "go ask Nicky to come bake cookies."

I sighed, "Ok, I'll ask."

I walked slowly to Nicky's house. I asked his mother if he wanted to bake cookies. "Yes!" Nicky ran outside and almost knocked me over.

"What kind of cookies? Chocolate chip?"

"I don't know," I said. "I didn't ask my mother."

"Maybel, do you want to race to your house?" Nicky asked me. Nicky acted like he had already eaten a lot of sugar.

"I'll win," I teased.

"Ready, set, go!" Nicky yelled.

I ran with all my might but I thought I had lost by just a hair. "We tied, Maybel!" Nicky yelled.

I didn't think we tied, but I was happy he thought we tied.

Nicky and I ran inside, past Catherine and Bernard, and into the kitchen.

"Hello, Nicky, how is your mother?" mommy asked.

"She's well," he replied.

"Would you like to take some cookies home to her?"

Nicky's eyes lit up. "Yes, please!"

Bernard came into the kitchen.

"Go away, Bernard!" I yelled, "I'm with my friend!"

"What are you two making?" Bernard asked.

"The cookies you didn't want to make!" I stuck my tongue out at Bernard.

"Come on, Bernard, let's finish our hand." Catherine pulled a reluctant Bernard back to their card game.

Nicky and I made chocolate chip cookies with mommy. Nicky was nice. He had more energy than me, I thought. He was fun to play with.

Mommy packed a basket of cookies for Nicky to take home. "Maybel," mommy said, "Please take these to Nicky's home with him. And Nicky, please give my best to your mother."

"I will," Nicky smiled up at mommy.

Daddy came into the kitchen. "Hello, Nicky. How's your father?"

"He's well. I heard him say something about that furniture stain you ordered. I can't remember what he said though."

"I'll come see him soon. Tell him hello from me, please."

"I will," Nicky smiled.

He grabbed my hand, "Come on, Maybel, let's run to my house!"

I giggled as he held my hand and we skipped the whole way to his house. I gave his mother the cookies.

"Thank you for helping us make cookies," I said. "Bye, Nicky."

"Bye, Maybel, see you later."

I walked home. It was still sunny. There were ants and grasshoppers in the road. I became distracted by a bunny I nearly stepped on. It scampered away. A robin flew down into my path and I stopped abruptly. "Hello," I said. It flew away. I took a stick that had fallen from a tree and moved a worm from the road and into the grass. I hoped I moved it to the side of the road where its family lived and not the opposite side.

I arrived home. Bernard and Catherine were sitting on the front porch. "Where's your boyfriend?" Bernard asked sarcastically. He seemed unhappy.

"I don't know, which boyfriend are you referring to?" I asked.

Catherine laughed but Bernard did not.

I went inside and told mommy that Nicky's mommy said thank you, and then I went out back to lay under the trees.

I counted three bluebirds. They stayed together and flitted back and forth from branch to branch. The one was a faded blue so I knew she was the girl bluebird. The other two were bright blue so they were boys. They appeared to be playing together.

"Maybel?" I heard Bernard's voice at my feet. He was staring down at me.

"Go away. You made me cry and I don't like you anymore. I hope Catherine finds a nicer boy."

"I'm sorry," Bernard said.

"Sorry you're so ugly?" I asked.

"I'm sorry I made fun of you," he said.

"You should be," I said. "One day, I'm going to leave here and never see you again, and I'll be happy."

Bernard sighed and went back inside the house.

Catherine reluctantly allowed me to come with her to Bernard's house. I wanted to be with Catherine. I liked being with Catherine. She was always fun.

Bernard opened his front door. "Oh, you brought Maybel," he said while looking at me with annoyance.

"Yes, sorry." Catherine apologized.

"Why are you sorry?" I asked.

"It's nothing, Maybel," Catherine said. "Bernard and I were going to study. You'll be bored."

"No, I won't," I said.

"We're studying math," Bernard said.

"Ok," I said.

Bernard looked annoyed at Catherine. "Fine, Maybel, come on then."

We went to Bernard's room. Bernard smiled as he pulled Catherine beside him on his bed. They held hands and kissed.

"You're supposed to move your lips more, Catherine," I said.

Bernard shot me an angry stare.

Catherine ignored me and pulled Bernard's face back toward her and kissed him again.

"Can I kiss Bernard?" I asked.

Catherine looked at me strangely. "Are you joking?"

"I don't know. Am I allowed to kiss Bernard?" I asked.

"No," Catherine said.

"Why?" I asked.

"Because he's my boyfriend, not yours," Catherine said, irritated.

"Oh," I said.

Bernard had kissed me. I had kissed Bernard. I didn't think kissing was a big deal anymore. I certainly didn't think kissing Bernard was worthy of a newspaper headline. Catherine looked annoyed at me, so I laid at the foot of Bernard's bed and drew flowers on a piece of paper.

Bernard kissed Catherine again. I could hear their lips smacking and it sounded disgusting.

"Bernard, do you want to kiss Maybel?" Catherine asked.

I looked up surprised.

"No," Bernard said.

"Bernard doesn't want you, Maybel," Catherine said. "You'll have to find your own boyfriend." They both giggled.

"I will," I said. "And he'll kiss better than Bernard."

Catherine snorted, "Bernard kisses wonderfully!" She pulled Bernard into another kiss.

"How would you know though?" I asked. "If you've only ever kissed Bernard, how would you know if he's a good kisser."

Catherine looked guilty.

"It's ok, I don't care about Samuel," Bernard said.

"Oh yeah, I forgot you kissed Samuel," I said. "Is Bernard a better kisser than Samuel?"

"Yes," Catherine said through clenched teeth.

"What makes Bernard better?"

"He's just better!" Catherine snapped.

"Well, if you can think of any details, let me know. I want to learn how to kiss better because the last boy I kissed made fun of me," I said, looking at Bernard.

"He sounds like a horse's ass," Catherine said.

"Oh, he definitely is!" I replied.

"Find someone nicer," Catherine told me.

"I will," I said.

Bernard's knuckles were white as he clenched his fists. "Maybe the boy you kissed was giving you constructive criticism."

"I don't see how getting criticism from a smelly ogre will help me. If anything, it will make me kiss worse if I take his advice," I said, while drawing another flower.

"Who is this boy, Maybel?" Catherine asked angrily. "He's a pig."

"Some boy I know from school. He's not important. There's a different boy I like more, and he doesn't smell like a pig's pen."

"Definitely find someone nicer, Maybel. If a boy makes fun of the way you kiss, he's not good enough for you. Bernard would never make fun of me," Catherine told me, as she lovingly smiled at Bernard.

"I don't have to. Your kisses are perfect." Bernard then sneered at me when Catherine looked away.

"Why don't you ask Nicky to play. He seemed nice," Catherine suggested.

"Yes, he is, but they're moving soon, and I don't want to get attached," I said.

"It's sad none of your friends live closer," Catherine said.

"Where do they live? I'd be happy to go get one and bring her back here to play with you so I can have a few minutes of time alone with Catherine." Bernard looked extremely irritated with me.

"Fine, Bernard! I'll go away and I'll never see you ever again!" I gathered my papers and started toward the door.

"Good! I hope I never see you again either!" Bernard yelled after me.

I stomped downstairs to Bernard's kitchen to see if there were any cookies on the table. Mr. Charleston was there at the table sipping coffee with Henry. My heart stopped. Henry was the most handsome man in the world. Mr. Charleston and daddy made fun of me because whenever I came into a room where Henry was, or whenever he came into a room where I was, I froze up and stared at him. The first time he said hello to me, I made an unintelligible noise and ran away.

I froze mid-step by the doorway staring at Henry. Mr. Charleston chuckled heartily, "Hello, Maybel, come say hello to Henry."

I managed to nod my head.

"Hello, Maybel," Henry smiled. His hair was black and his skin was suntanned to perfection. His eyes were green and brown and blue, a perfect mixture of all colors. The colors dazzled back and forth between green and brown in the sunlight, and there was a mention of blue nearer the edges of his irises.

I stood frozen.

"Maybel, come sit." Mr. Charleston pulled out the chair beside him. "Would you like a cookie?"

"Mmmmm!" I shook my head yes.

I unfroze long enough to awkwardly stumble to Mr. Charleston and stood behind him for strength. I gripped the back of Mr. Charleston's chair so tightly my fingers went numb.

Mr. Charleston asked Henry about the weather through which he'd traveled. Then Henry asked Mr. Charleston about some investments.

"Maybel, come sit beside me," Mr. Charleston asked.

It startled me to be addressed and I froze again.

Mr. Charleston turned around in his chair and gently held my hand. "Why don't you sit beside me, sweetheart?"

He gently pulled my hand closer and gestured toward the chair beside him but I hopped into his lap instead. Mr. Charleston chuckled, "Alright, Maybel, I'll protect you."

Mr. Charleston tickled my ribs. "Maybel can at times be shy, though very rarely. I've never seen you sit still or be quiet ever, except for the several times Henry has visited."

I only stared wide-eyed at the most handsome man in the world across the table from me. I sat on Mr. Charleston's lap and he held me with his big, bear arms. He patted my back. "Would you like a cookie now?"

I shook my head yes.

He reached for a cookie from the plate in the middle of the table and gave it to me.

I leaned back into Mr. Charleston's chest and ate my cookie.

Bernard came down into the kitchen. "Oh, hello, Maybel," he taunted me, "I thought you were leaving and never coming back?"

I glared at him and stuck my tongue out.

"What have you planned for today?" Mr. Charleston asked Bernard.

"I'm getting a snack for Catherine and myself. We're upstairs studying," he replied.

I rolled my eyes sarcastically. Henry laughed at my mannerisms and I realized he'd been watching me. My eyes shot wide open and I froze again.

"Henry, you're the only person who can make Maybel shut up for more than two seconds. What's your secret? How can I harness your amazing power?" Bernard asked sarcastically.

"Be as beautiful and charming as Henry and maybe I'd be quiet around you! But you aren't, and you're not, so I talk to your stupid face!" I snapped at Bernard.

Henry laughed, and I felt Mr. Charleston below me, his belly shaking with laughter.

Bernard leaned over me and took several cookies. His elbow purposefully bumped into my temple so I reached up and twisted his nipple.

"Don't forget to wipe off your drool after you're done kissing my sister with your chapped lips!" I said angrily.

"I don't drool! You do! And your lips are dry!" Bernard suddenly looked surprised at what he'd said and clamped shut. I figured he was embarrassed of kissing me and didn't want anyone to know. He angrily stomped upstairs.

I shoved the rest of my cookie in my mouth.

"What's your favorite color?" Henry asked me, trying to engage me and get me to do more than just stare awkwardly at him.

I shrugged my shoulders.

"I was hoping you were not so shy around me anymore. We seemed to have made progress in our friendship recently. I hope to be able to have a conversation with you one day," he said. "Perhaps today will not be the day," he smiled kindly.

"Light pink and purple maybe," I whispered.

Henry smiled, "Did you hear that Uncle, Maybel is talking to me!"

Mr. Charleston smiled, "You're warming up to Henry, finally, aren't you?"

I nodded.

I leaned back into Mr. Charleston's chest. If a teddy bear came to life, it would be just like Mr. Charleston.

Henry began asking Mr. Charleston for advice on real estate. Judging by Mr. Charleston's answer, I gathered Mr. Charleston owned businesses in other countries, too.

"Maybel, I'm rebuilding a barbershop and salon," Mr. Charleston looked down at me on his lap. "This will be good practice for Bernard to learn about business firsthand. It's just a small business. I want to see how Bernard fares, how his mind works, and how he handles his business. Which color should I use to decorate the salon side and which color for the barbershop side?"

"The barbershop and salon are in the same building, but have a wall dividing them?" I asked, intrigued by the creative aspect of design, and momentarily forgetting about Handsome Henry sitting across from me.

"The building is such that when you walk in, there will be an entry area with a clerk. To the left you will enter into the barbershop, to the right you will enter the salon," Mr. Charleston explained the layout of his newest acquisition.

"This entryway is open then? You can see both the barbershop and the salon from the entry-way?" I asked.

"Yes," Mr. Charleston said.

"Oh, no, that's no good," I warned him. "Women go to the salon to complain about their husbands. You can have a greeting area, but there must be solid walls with oak doors on either side so the women can't see the men, and the men can't see the women. Once when I went to the barbershop with daddy, Mr. Underton was complaining about his wife's sister until he realized I was on the bench waiting for daddy and he got embarrassed and shut up. And the women go to the salon to compare husbands. If you are easily offended, never step foot in a salon."

Mr. Charleston hugged me and chuckled, "You're right, Maybel, you make excellent points!"

"You should ask Bernard what he thinks. You'll see I have an eye for detail. Bernard is a boy, and after talking to him for an hour, you'll see his thoughts only consist of food he wants to eat, and when will he get to kiss Catherine next."

Mr. Charleston laughed and Henry smiled at me.

"Make the two rooms separate with sturdy walls so the men and women can't hear each other. As for colors, women like happy colors, like a light rose color, or pale purple, maybe a nice shade of lavender. Hang some paintings of flowers with beautifully carved frames. Daddy can make the frames for you. Lightweight and airy, white, lace curtains will be lovely. Your salon manager needs to be a kind woman, but not young or thin because bitter wives don't like young, pretty women."

Henry and Mr. Charleston had a good laugh at that.

"For the barbershop side, you won't need much. Men don't care about decorating. Men like darker hues and boring colors like black, brown, and gray. A light gray color, or a light beige color will be fine, it doesn't really matter, men won't notice anyway. What color are your bedroom walls Mr. Charleston?"

He thought for a moment. "I have no idea," he seemed surprised.

"They're white," I told him. "How long have you lived here? See, men don't care."

Mr. Charleston and Henry shrugged at each other.

"Don't hang up pictures of women. The wives won't let their husbands get their hair cut. Maybe frame a newspaper article of your favorite sports team winning something. Oh, and you should have male barbers. Men relax around other men."

"Catherine and mommy are better than me regarding colors and decorating, so you should definitely have them finalize any plans you make."

Mr. Charleston kissed my cheek. "You've quite the mind for business because you know what people want. Would you like to come with Henry and me to look over my newest business? He's learning about business too. I told his mother I'd take him under my wing," he nodded at Henry.

I shook my head no.

"You've gone mute again?" Henry asked me.

"No," I blushed.

"Will you come if Bernard comes?" Mr. Charleston asked.

I shook my head no.

"And Catherine? You said she has a mind for decorating. Will you come if she comes?"

"Yes," I smiled.

"Alright then. Henry, would you please go upstairs and get Bernard and Catherine?" Mr. Charleston asked him.

"Yes," he said and stood up. He wore a light blue button up shirt with his sleeves rolled up and dark blue pants. I watched him wide-eyed as he passed by.

I heard Henry's footsteps go up the stairs.

Mr. Charleston patted my back. "Why do you get nervous around Henry?"

"He's just so beautiful!" I gushed. "Every time I see him, my heart starts beating really fast, and my mouth gets dry, and I can't talk!"

Mr. Charleston smiled, "He's much too old for you."

"I don't want to date him! I just like staring at his pretty face! I just can't talk to him because he's so gorgeous and suddenly I forget how to speak!"

Mr. Charleston reached over and got another cookie for me. I split it in half. "Here," I handed it to him. "Cheers!" I knocked my cookie against his. "Down the hatch, boys!" I yelled and laughed.

Mr. Charleston laughed and took a bite of his cookie.

"Were you ever nervous around a girl?" I asked him.

"Oh yes, sometimes I couldn't speak either."

"So then, is it normal for me to act awkward?" I asked him.

"Yes, honey, attraction is a strange thing. It can make you do beautiful things, and can make you do stupid things."

"I would like to stop doing stupid things," I said.

Mr. Charleston patted my back. "You don't do stupid things, honey, you're young and nervous. You haven't quite figured out how the world works and how all the people within act. But you will. Just don't grow up too fast."

"That's what daddy always tells me." I imitated daddy's low manly voice, "Don't be in such a hurry to grow up, Maybel, and pass the salt, please."

Mr. Charleston chuckled.

Henry returned, followed by Bernard and then Catherine.

"Why is Maybel coming?" Bernard asked, annoyed.

"She has good business sense," Mr. Charleston replied.

"She can barely add figures together," Bernard sneered.

I narrowed my eyes at him.

"Maybel has other talents. She knows what people want," Mr. Charleston said.

"I wanted her to leave but she didn't," Bernard said.

"How about you leave and I stay here?" I snapped.

"You two used to get along so well. What happened?" Mr. Charleston asked.

"He started being mean to me and making fun of me and teasing me and he pushed me into mud last week!" I crossed my arms and watched Bernard.

"Tattletale," Bernard said angrily.

"I haven't tattled about a lot of things," I squinted my eyes at him.

"Let's go to the new building," Bernard huffed. "The sooner we're done, the sooner I can be rid of you!"

"Bernard, you're being rude," Mr. Charleston said sternly.

Bernard turned back toward me, "I'm sorry, Maybel, shall we go?" His voice dripped with insincerity.

We took Mr. Charleston's automobile. The backseat was large enough for Catherine, Bernard, and me, but we were squished together uncomfortably.

"My hips hurt," I groaned. I got up and sat on Bernard's lap, as I had often done.

"No, Maybel," Bernard pushed me off his lap.

Henry sighed, "Bernard, how about you sit up here and I'll sit in the back with Maybel on my lap?"

My eyes shot open and my heart began thumping.

Bernard looked at me and my excitement. "No, it's fine, get on my lap, Maybel," Bernard said angrily.

I was devastated. I almost got to sit on the lap of the most handsome man in the world.

"Thanks, Bernard," I said dryly, and Catherine giggled.

Bernard kept shifting uncomfortably as we turned and twisted through streets. He kept shoving me further away from his chest and I almost slid off his knees several times. "Bernard! Stop pushing me!" I yelled.

"Your bony behind hurts," Bernard complained.

"On the way home, can Maybel sit on your lap, Henry?" Catherine asked. "I'm tired of their arguing."

"No, I'm fine, I just need you to sit a little farther down my legs, closer to my knees," Bernard told me.

When we arrived, Bernard complained of motion sickness and said he needed to sit in the car for a few minutes before following us into the barbershop.

"Just think about baseball, Bernard," Henry said. Henry smiled at Bernard, but it didn't look like a sincere smile to me. I thought Henry was maybe making fun of Bernard, but I couldn't understand the meaning Henry was trying to convey. I didn't understand how baseball would be beneficial to Bernard's bellyache.

The building Mr. Charleston had bought was run down. The windows were broken and the wood trim was broken in places. The red bricks were pretty though.

I took Mr. Charleston's hand. "Are you scared?" he asked.

"This place looks like I might fall through the floor or the roof might fall on me," I told him.

"I assure you it's structurally sound, sweetheart. It does need your creative eye though," he squeezed my hand.

Mr. Charleston looked over at Catherine. "Catherine, honey, which color should we paint the trim?"

"White," she said. "It's neutral. A nice navy if it were for men, or a very light shade of pink if it were for women would be nice, but it's for both men and women, so I choose white."

"Excellent, Catherine, thank you, dear." Mr. Charleston patted her back.

Bernard joined us finally. "Bernard, what color are your bedroom walls?" Mr. Charleston asked his son.

Bernard looked at his father confused. "I have no idea. Why?"

"Catherine, what color are Bernard's bedroom walls?" Mr. Charleston asked.

"White," she said. "The wood trim is a lovely rosewood."

Mr. Charleston chuckled, "Very good, thank you, Catherine, honey."

I held onto Mr. Charleston's hand as we ascended the steps and entered the rundown building.

"Why did you want to buy this building?" I asked.

"Because Maybel, you buy low and sell high."

"You'll have to sell really high to get back all the money you'll have to spend making this place look good," I told him as I looked around at the fallen rubble by the walls.

"Oh, the labor will be so cheap some may even call it free," Mr. Charleston laughed as he looked at Bernard and Henry.

"Bernard is going to get his hands dirty?" I giggled.

"Hands, arms, legs, face…" Mr. Charleston trailed off laughing.

We walked through both the future barbershop and salon. I could hardly imagine this building as somewhere people would pay to be. Catherine, on the other hand, was animated and gestured widely. "White paint here, light blue here, and in the salon, use mirrors to bounce sunlight off each other and brighten the place up greatly!"

"Catherine, sweetheart, I'm impressed!" Mr. Charleston exclaimed.

"I am too!" Henry smiled at Catherine..

Bernard glared at Henry.

We returned to the Charleston's house. I sat in the study drawing the garden of flowers I'd started drawing earlier.

I heard footsteps approaching, then they stopped. I heard Henry's voice, then Bernard's. Bernard and Henry began quarreling just outside the door.

"Why are you so cruel to that little girl?" Henry asked.

"She teases me, too!"

"You're supposed to be the big brother that sets a good example. You're supposed to be mature enough to ignore her teasing and not tease her back."

"I don't like Maybel! I don't want her around!" Bernard said angrily.

I sat in my white dress with a red ribbon around my waist. I didn't put pretty bows in my hair like Catherine.

"Why?" Henry asked. "She seems kind and intelligent."

"She's annoying and never lets Catherine and me have a moment alone! I wish she'd just go away!" Bernard became agitated.

I looked down at my hands resting on my legs. I had dirt under my nails. There was dust and dirt on my skirt.

"Do you remember when you were little like her? You always begged John and me to let you come on our adventures."

"It's not the same! She's always covered in dirt and her hair looks like a rat's nest!" Bernard yelled.

"You weren't any better several years ago, Bernard," Henry reminded him.

I sat in the big chair under the lamp and next to rows of books on shelves. I looked at my bare feet and they were covered in dirt. I started to cry.

"She's annoying and I don't want her around!" Bernard yelled.

It didn't hurt as bad when Bernard said mean things to my face. Hearing him say mean things about me to another person hurt more because the mean comments carried more weight. I quietly cried alone in the study still listening to Bernard say mean things about me.

The study door flew open and Bernard walked angrily to the bookshelf. He took a book from the shelf and turned to leave, then saw me.

His face changed from anger to guilt in an instant when he saw me sitting there, tears and snot running down my face.

Henry was standing in the doorway staring at me with sadness and pity.

"Maybel, I didn't mean it," Bernard said softly.

I was too hurt to talk. I just stared up at him with silent tears and quiet sobs.

"I didn't mean what I said, Maybel! I was annoyed and spoke out of anger but I didn't mean it!"

My heart hurt. I only stared up at him with pain and a trembling lip.

Bernard turned and left.

Henry leaned against the doorframe watching me with such pity in his eyes. "I'm sorry Bernard is cruel to you. You deserve better, Maybel. I'll get Catherine to take you home."

Catherine seemed annoyed that she was summoned to care for me but her expression changed when she saw how pathetic I looked.

"Come, Maybel," she said. She put her arm around me and took me home.

I did not return to the Charlestons for months, nor did I come downstairs when I knew Bernard was picking up or dropping off Catherine.

Catherine said Bernard had apologized and was sincerely sorry for what he said, and that he didn't mean it, but I told Catherine he hadn't apologized to me in person.

"You refuse to come downstairs, Maybel. How is Bernard going to apologize to you when you refuse to see him?"

"Tell him to mail a letter!" I yelled angrily.

"Oh Maybel, give Bernard a chance to make it up to you," Catherine pleaded.

"You should break up with him! You deserve someone better! If he treats your sister like that, he'll treat you that way, too!" I raged at her. "And Catherine, you still date him after how he treated me!" I stared icily at her and paused until I had her full attention. "I wish I had a better big sister!" I said with cold consternation.

Catherine looked down for a moment. She seemed to be contemplating what I said. "The barbershop and salon will open in the next several weeks. If it suits you, you are welcome to come take a look, and see all your ideas that have now come to fruition."

"Will Bernard be there?"

"Yes, as will Henry, as this is supposed to be a learning experience for them both. Mr. Charleston is taking them through each phase of starting a business."

"I'll stay home," I said, and turned back to my book.

"You'll have to see Bernard sooner or later," she said.

"Later," I said dryly.

"Oh, come on, Maybel! All he said was you're dirty and have messy hair. He says that to you all the time!" Catherine exasperatedly attempted to explain away Bernard's bad behavior.

"I thought he was joking when he said it to my face. When he spoke to Henry, he wasn't joking. He was really mean, Catherine!" My lip started trembling again just thinking about it.

Catherine sighed again. "Stay here then." She left my bedroom and went downstairs.

Before the ribbon cutting ceremony to officially open the barbershop salon, Mr. Charleston summoned Bernard and me to his office. I had arrived at the Charleston's because daddy requested my help delivering an ornately-carved bench Mr. Charleston had commissioned daddy to make for Mrs. Charleston. It was of cherry wood and stained. At each end of the beautiful bench, were richly-detailed horse carvings. The manes flowed behind the horses as though they were running freely through fields. I helped daddy unload the bench and Vincent told me Mr. Charleston would like to speak to me in his office.

"Go ahead honey," daddy said, "I'll meet you back home."

When I entered Mr. Charleston's office, Mrs. Charleston was seated next to him behind the enormous, carved, walnut desk.

Mr. Charleston motioned for me to sit in front of him and Mrs. Charleston. Vincent announced Bernard's presence. My eyebrows lowered and I crossed my arms and huffed.

"Come, Bernard," Mr. Charleston said. "I have a story for you and Maybel."

The sounds of Bernard's expensive shoes making hollowed, echoing steps off the marble floor, getting ever closer to where I sat, made me want to bash his skull in with his father's stone paperweight.

Bernard sat in the plush, leather chair beside me. He sat with good posture and crossed one leg over the other like a gentleman who had been taught manners in an expensive boarding school. Even Bernard's face looked like he was ready for a meeting with rich executives in a tall, city building guarded by big, burly doormen. I felt poor when Mr. Charleston and Bernard acted well-bred.

"Hello, Maybel," Bernard politely addressed me. I watched rats chew his eyeballs and gnaw on his nose in my big, angry imagination.

"When I was a boy," Mr. Charleston began, "I knew my wife." Mr. Charleston reached over and gingerly took Mrs. Charleston's hand in his. "We met as children. I teased her relentlessly. I look back on the things I said to her, and the way I treated her, and I'm embarrassed. I am amazed at her ability to forgive."

"What did you do and say that was so bad?" I asked. "Did you say cruel things about her appearance behind her back? Did she overhear your comments and fantasize about vultures eating your entrails?"

"I don't think she did," Mr. Charleston spoke slowly and thoughtfully, as though those thoughts may very well have gone through his wife's mind, but he hesitated in admitting her bloodlust. "If she did, she, perhaps, would have been right to have such fantasies, though, I regretfully admit."

Mrs. Charleston interrupted him. "I didn't wonder about vultures; however, I did wonder how many arrows I would have to carve to shoot into your heart to make you fall down and bleed to death." Mrs. Charleston said.

Mrs. Charleston winked at me and I smiled.

Mr. Charleston continued carefully. "I was not nice to you when we were children," Mr. Charleston looked at Mrs. Charleston beside him. "And that torments my mind to this very day."

Mrs. Charleston took his hand and smiled softly at him. "We have a beautiful life together now, my love," she said.

Mr. Charleston swallowed hard and his voice was unsteady when he next began speaking. "When we were young, I made fun of my wife for being Indian."

Bernard looked away. He looked disappointed more than angry at his father.

"When her brother got a hold of me, he beat me. He came to me and hit me, and he kept hitting me. I let him. I knew I deserved it. No amount of physical pain could be enough punishment for my behavior, and I've never been able to forgive myself for what I said and did to her."

Mr. Charleston reflected. I saw him watching his memories inside his eyes. His eyes were glassy, and he truly looked tormented by whatever he said and did to his wife when they were children.

Mr. Charleston pointed to a scar above his right eyebrow. "This is my reminder to speak gently and treat others the way I want to be treated. As long as a person doesn't harm a child, the elderly, or beat an animal, I treat them with respect and compassion."

"What did you do to make Mrs. Charleston love you?" I was genuinely curious, because they were so in love, that I could not imagine a time when Mr. Charleston behaved rudely toward Mrs. Charleston.

"I watched her kiss another man. I realized I had lost her. I went to her brother and father and told them I loved her and that I'd been mean to her. I told them I didn't expect her to go on a date with me, but I would like their permission to ask. Her brother denied my request but her father overruled him. Her father laughed. It was a deep belly laugh," Mr. Charleston patted his stomach, "and told me to go ask her now."

"I did. I went to the horse stable where she tended to Big Ben's mother. I told her I had fallen in love with her and to please give me a chance to earn her trust. If she would give me just the smallest chance, I promised I would spend every day of the rest of our lives loving her and respecting her more than myself."

"And what happened next?" Mrs. Charleston leaned against the back of her chair and crossed her arms, smirking smugly.

"She opened the gate to let the horses roam throughout the pasture and then she let me know how she felt about me."

Mr. Charleston unbuttoned his shirt. "This scar was made by my wife's arrow."

"You shot him with an arrow?" I asked, shocked.

"Yes, that I did," Mrs. Charleston smiled.

"Her father took pity on me and dislodged the arrow and culturized my wound after he stopped laughing," Mr. Charleston said. "I almost bled out though, because her next arrow went high into the rafters of the stable and a hornet's nest fell at my feet. I hadn't thought I could run so fast with an arrow in my shoulder but you'd be surprised how fast a hornet's nest can light a fire under your feet. Anyway, I passed out running to her house and when I awoke, I had lost a lot of blood. It pooled around me. I begged her for one date."

"And that's how you finally became a couple?" I thought their beginning as a couple was fascinating, to say the least.

"Oh, God no, she refused to speak a single word to me for one year, but I never gave up. I slept outside her house. I begged her as relentlessly as I had teased her."

"I agreed to one date only because my father was tired of tripping over him in the dark when he went to the outhouse to pee at night," Mrs. Charleston chuckled.

"You actually slept at her doorstep?" I asked.

"Maybel, sweetheart, I was a spoiled, prideful boy. I knew I always loved her, but I had been embarrassed of my love because I listened to people around me when they spoke negatively about Indians. I pushed her away and I tried to fall out of love, but all I did was fall more deeply in love, while her heart grew cold toward me."

"What made you forgive him?" I asked Mrs. Charleston.

"On our first date, he gave me the leaf I had given him the day we met when we were nine. I had written my name on it and I gave it to him. He put it between the pages of a book and kept it all the years he spent teasing me. When he showed me the leaf after all those years, it was perfectly preserved. It now hangs between two panes of glass in a frame in our bedroom. I told him because he saved my gift, I would give him one more date. He continued to impress both me and my family, and eventually, I accepted his marriage proposal."

"Do you get along with your brother-in-law now, the one who beat you mercilessly for teasing Mrs. Charleston?" I asked Mr. Charleston.

"Yes," Mr. Charleston smiled, "we do get along now. And I consider his sons to be my sons, too."

"Who are his sons?"

"Henry and John. John stays out west more, but we see him several times a year. And Henry, as you know, is with me daily as I'm teaching him entrepreneurship."

"Is Henry's father as beautiful as Henry?" I giggled.

"Yes," Mr. Charleston said, "it runs in their family," he winked at Mrs. Charleston and she squeezed his hand and had such a loving expression on her face when she looked at her husband. Mr. Charleston was a big bear and Mrs. Charleston was a pretty, little doe next to him. I smiled watching them.

Mr. Charleston looked at Bernard. "You have always hated this story, Bernard."

"Of course I hate it! You were mean to mother!"

"You always told me that your mother shouldn't have forgiven me, but that you were glad she had more grace than you and forgave me, because it resulted in your life with us as your parents."

"Yes," Bernard admitted.

"I wonder, son, do you still feel that you would not have forgiven me if you were in your mother's place?"

"I would not have forgiven you, father."

Mr. Charleston watched Bernard. It was almost as if the tiniest bit of amusement played on his lips. "I hope you do not follow in my footsteps and treat your future wife the way I treated your mother."

"I will never," Bernard said resolutely.

"Very well, son. Very well."

Mr. Charleston patted Mrs. Charleston's hand. "Shall we walk together admiring the sunset, my love?"

"Always," she replied, and he kissed her.

After Mr. and Mrs. Charleston left, I watched Bernard. His brows were still furrowed in consternation. "Catherine doesn't like Indians, and I think my father was telling me, in a roundabout way, to be patient and forgiving until she realizes she loves me more than she is scared of Indians."

"That's what you think your father was telling you?" I couldn't hide my surprise and annoyance. I had interpreted it as Mr. Charleston telling Bernard to stop teasing me.

"Isn't it? You're the storyteller, Maybel. What was my father trying to tell me?"

I thought for a moment. "I'm not sure now. I thought I knew, but now I'm confused."

"Well, what did you think he was telling me?" Bernard asked.

"I thought your father was telling you to stop being a horse's ass to me, but maybe he was telling you to be patient with Catherine. I don't know anymore. People are confusing and unpredictable, and I don't understand anyone."

"I am sorry for being cruel to you," Bernard spoke softly. "I was frustrated because I've always loved you, but you didn't return my love. It hurt my pride that you didn't love me the same way I loved you. It still hurts, Maybel. I was angry at you for not wanting me the way I wanted you. I shouldn't have been so mean to you though and I truly am sorry."

"I have always loved you," I said. Bernard made no sense. I had told him I loved him many times.

Bernard sighed and looked down at his hands. He sat back in his chair and looked as though he were inwardly contemplating. He looked like he was thinking of a way to better explain himself. "I love you more than you love me and it hurts, Maybel."

I sighed with annoyance, "I love you. I've said so hundreds of times. I have to get back home to help daddy with the rest of his deliveries."

I left Bernard there in his high-backed chair, that sat on his marble floor, that was in his enormous mansion, and returned home to my much-smaller, and much-loved house, with my family, whom I adored.

I was curious about the building Henry and Bernard renovated, and what it looked like now. I walked all the way there. It took a really long time and I was very thirsty when I arrived. I approached the building slowly, listening for Bernard's voice. I didn't want to see Bernard. I heard nothing. The outside still had that lovely red brick. The trim around the windows and doors were a crisp white. The grass had been trimmed, and there were no clumps of weeds growing up against the walls anymore. The crumbled and broken bricks that had fallen to the grass had been removed, and the walls had been repaired with new bricks. The building looked remarkedly good.

I went inside. The entryway had a receptionist's desk of carved walnut. A large oval mirror was behind it on the wall. The floor was of large walnut planks.

I first opened the salon door. Beautiful large mirrors adorned the walls and reflected light so bright into each other that the room was aglow. The walls were a very pale pink and the window trim was a slightly darker rose color. White lace curtains hung from very tall rectangular windows.

I next went to the barbershop. "Oh!" I exclaimed, startled. Henry was finishing painting the baseboards a slightly darker gray than had been painted the light gray walls.

"Hello, Maybel," he smiled at me.

I froze up.

Henry sighed, "Do you dislike me?"

"I like you," I whispered quickly.

He smiled, "You spoke to me."

I smiled shyly back.

"Did you walk here?" he asked me.

I nodded.

"That's quite a journey from your house. Are you thirsty or hungry?"

I nodded.

Henry stood and went to his lunch pail and brought me a jar of water and a sandwich.

"Thank you," I said. I was still so enamored at his beauty I could barely mumble.

"Give me a few minutes to finish this and I'll drive you home, Maybel."

"Ok," I mustered a response.

Henry went back to painting the baseboard and I drank half of the water quickly and ate half the sandwich. I decided to save the other half for him in case he was hungry.

"Can I help?" I asked.

He seemed surprised to hear my voice. "Yes," he said, "if you'd like."

I took a paint brush and painted the trim with Henry.

"Thank you, Maybel."

"You're welcome," I smiled shyly.

"Has Bernard been nicer to you?"

"I stay home," I replied.

"You haven't seen him since that day in his study?" Henry asked, surprised.

"I saw him not long ago when Mr. and Mrs. Charleston told us the story about how Mr. Charleston used to be mean to Mrs. Charleston. Bernard thought the story was about him and Catherine though. I thought Mr. Charleston was telling Bernard to be nicer to me."

"I'm sorry, Maybel. I spoke with him again. I think he is sorry for what he said, although that doesn't excuse his behavior," Henry told me.

"Why is he so mean?" I whispered. "He used to be so nice to me. And I loved him so much. And I thought he loved me too," I held back tears.

"I think that's why he's mean, Maybel. He loves you too, but he's dating your sister and doesn't know how to act around you anymore."

I looked at Henry. "I don't understand what you're saying. That doesn't make sense."

"His behavior was bad. I'm not excusing his behavior. I think he is confused about how to act around you now that you're a little older," Henry attempted to explain.

I furrowed my brow and looked at Henry like he spoke nonsense.

Henry breathed deeply, "When you and Bernard met, you were a child. Now, you're still young, but you are no longer a child. You're not quite a woman yet, either. It seems to me, anyway, that Bernard doesn't know how to talk to you or act around you anymore. He can't play with you anymore because you're not a child, but you are not yet a woman. He doesn't know how to be around you anymore."

"He can play with me! But he won't! Because he hates me!" I turned back to my painting with tears welling in my eyes.

"It's a difficult time for you both. It will take time to move through this awkward phase." Henry continued painting.

"He used to be so nice to me and I couldn't wait for him to come to my house!" I cried just a little, but not too much. "What did I do to make him say those mean things?" I couldn't help but begin heaving and crying loudly.

"Maybel, you're beautiful and intelligent. When Bernard met you, you were younger and more childlike. Your body isn't childlike anymore. Maybe you still feel like a child sometimes, and want to play and sit on people's laps, but you don't look like a child anymore. I think that's what's confusing Bernard. He doesn't know how to treat you anymore. He can't really hold you and tickle you and play with you anymore, but you're not an adult yet either. You both just need time to transition between childhood and young adulthood."

"Are you married?" I asked Henry.

"No," he laughed. "I don't have time for a family right now."

"I think you'll be a good father," I said.

He chuckled, "Is that how you see me? As a father figure?"

"You're old," I told him.

Henry laughed, "When I was your age, I thought people my age were old too."

"Aren't you?" I asked.

He smiled, "No, I'm not a whole lot older than you, actually. You think I'm old because you are young. You're in a different stage of life so it seems we are decades apart, but we're merely years apart. When you are my age in several years, you will understand."

"Were you ever a mean boy like Bernard?"

"I sure hope not!" he said.

I continued painting the baseboards. Henry painted the other side of the wall and we were going to meet in the middle.

"Maybel," Henry asked softly, "why wouldn't you talk to me before? You have never spoken to me at birthdays, Christmas, or dinner parties. Why? Did I upset you?"

I paused. I didn't know if I should tell him the truth, but I did. "You're the most handsome man I have ever seen in my life." I couldn't even look at him as I spoke. "And every time I see you, my mouth goes dry and I forget how to speak." I continued painting slowly. "Everyone teases me about that. They tease me because I suddenly turn silent and stare at you with big eyes."

Henry didn't say anything. I felt very embarrassed. I painted a little faster just to be done.

"Thank you, Maybel, for telling me," he said. "I thought I had offended you, but I could never figure out what I had done."

I continued painting in silence for a few minutes.

"You didn't upset me. I am not comfortable at parties. Catherine knows how to act. She's amazing. She goes into every situation confident. She knows how to talk to people." I filled my brush with paint. "She knows what to say." I brushed the baseboard left and right. "I don't know what to say or do." I filled my paintbrush again.

"You don't realize your worth yet, Maybel," he spoke softly. "You will. Just be sure to choose a husband who values you. You're smart and special. Don't settle for just any man."

"I don't know if I want to marry. Boys seem like a lot of work. Ms. Ethel at the post office is ninety-two. She gets around better than her grandson who is fifty-one. One day, she stopped me and said, 'Maybel, my husband dropped dead when I was twenty-five. That's why I'm ninety-two!'"

Henry laughed.

"I might become a spinster lady. People pity them because they can't find a husband, but they seem really happy."

Henry looked at me as I spoke and laughed. "Maybe I won't marry either." He brushed excess paint from the bristles of his paintbrush.

"Have you ever dated anyone?" I asked him.

He glanced at me. "Yes, many women. I haven't been as lucky as Bernard and Catherine. They found each other as children. Most people are not as fortunate and spend many years trying to find someone with whom they are compatible."

"Why didn't you want to be with those women? Or did they not want to be with you?"

Henry continued painting. He was trying to find his words, I could tell. "A little of both. I wasn't looking for a long-term relationship when I was young. I broke some hearts. And then I thought perhaps I could settle down with a woman, but she broke my heart."

"Which one broke your heart? The lady from the last Christmas party, Bernard's birthday party, the spring festival, that one party that I think was in the fall one year but I can't remember, or was it at the Charleston's wedding anniversary party two years ago?"

Henry looked embarrassed. "I didn't realize I showed up with so many different women."

"Catherine says she's never seen you with the same woman twice. I don't think I have either."

Henry continued painting in silence.

"I'm sorry, Henry. I think I implied you're a slut, but I didn't mean to. This is why I keep quiet. I don't know how to behave. I'm sorry."

Henry sighed and shook his head. "No, Maybel, you weren't mean. I should be more discriminating in my choices of women. I do want a family. I don't feel I'm worthy of a good woman though."

Henry shoved his paintbrush in the paint can and stood up. "Why am I telling you this? I'm sorry, Maybel."

"It's ok," I said. "Has your penis ever fallen off?"

"What?" Henry spun around to face me.

"At one of the Charleston's parties, I was watching you talking to a pretty woman and Catherine said, 'I can't believe his penis hasn't fallen off yet.' And I asked her if she meant that you used your penis so much that you wore it down to a stub, or that you caught a disease from a prostitute, and Catherine laughed and said, 'Either one.'"

Henry's mouth was agape. He stared at me for a full thirty seconds, just staring, wide-eyed and unmoving. "I've never been with a prostitute. I've never had any diseases. My penis hasn't been worn down to a stub, nor has it fallen off."

I continued painting this gray color along the baseboards. Gray was my least favorite color because it was indecisive. Gray couldn't decide if it wanted to be black or white, and that annoyed me.

"Maybel, I won't ever be able to find a good wife. No good woman will want me. I've been with too many women. Why am I telling you this?"

"How many women have you pleasured?" I asked.

'I don't know! A dozen? I'm not sure."

"Would you marry a woman who has been with a dozen men?"

"No, I would probably not," he sighed.

"Oh, well, you're a hypocrite then, and you'll live a lonely life. You've been with a lot of women, but you desire to marry a virgin."

"She doesn't have to be a virgin."

"Ok then, how many men is too many men? Is she allowed to have had sex with two men, five men, or exactly how many men do you feel is too many?"

"God, Maybel! I don't know!" He paced around the barbershop. "This is insane. Why am I talking to you about this?"

"I don't know. I'll go back to being mute. You seemed happier then. Actually, most people seem happier when I don't talk. I think it's because I'm honest, and people don't like honesty. Once Catherine cut her hair short and asked me if I liked it. That was a very bad day for us."

He sat back down and we finished painting in silence. When we were all done, I stood and spun around. I liked the light gray and medium gray a little more. The barbershop looked good.

Henry drove me home. He looked good driving and we passed the candy store and I pretended not to notice Elsie and Effie staring at me with their mouths wide open. I liked being in an automobile. I liked my classmates being jealous. And most of all, I liked sitting next to Henry.

Bernard was on the front porch with Catherine when Henry stopped in front of my house. "Drive away!" I hissed.

"What? Why?" Henry looked confused.

"I don't want to see Bernard!"

"I can't stop in front of your house then drive away with you. Just walk inside without talking to him."

"Will you come with me?" I pleaded.

Henry turned off his automobile and sighed. "Alright, Maybel. Let's go."

We stepped out of his car. "You know, Maybel, this doesn't have to be a dramatic moment. It's only as dramatic as you let it be."

"Says the man who thinks he'll die alone and childless!"

Henry paused, "Die alone and childless? Well, that's putting it bluntly. I didn't really think of it that way. I would like to think...."

"Can you please just come with me? We'll talk about your poor choices later," I said.

Again, Henry paused, "I don't think I've made a lot of poor choices, some maybe. I supposed I could make improvements...."

"Ok, I take back everything! Can you kiss me in front of Bernard?"

"Absolutely not!" Henry said firmly.

"Fine, just walk me to my door," I huffed. "But pretend we've been having the most wonderful conversation."

Henry walked with me up our walkway and as we got closer to Catherine and Bernard, Henry pretended to be in the closing stages of a conversation. "And once the praying mantises mate, the female mantis rips the males head off just for fun because she enjoys watching the male die alone and childless."

I turned back and gave Henry an expression that I'd hoped communicate my confusion and dislike for his absolutely stupid choice of conversation topic to make Bernard jealous of my time spent with this gorgeous man.

"What wonderful conversations we've had, Henry! Thank you! See you tomorrow!" I smiled, hoping Bernard felt bad that I had a new friend who was more handsome than any picture of any Greek God I'd ever seen.

I went inside and closed the door behind me.

Two weekends later, I awaited the opening of the barbershop salon. Henry suggested the name Family Hair Care and Mr. Charleston and Bernard liked the name.

There was to be a ribbon cutting at noon on Saturday. Mommy, daddy, Catherine, and I dressed nicely and went to show our support for Mr. Charleston.

Catherine wore a dark purple dress with a matching dark purple ribbon. I wore the plainest dress mommy would let me wear. If it were up to me, I wouldn't go, but I had to go, so I wore a light purple dress and matching hair ribbon. I hated it. I felt like I wore a costume.

"Yes, Maybel, it is a costume!" Catherine had exclaimed while helping me braid my hair. "You're on stage. You're an actress. You are not Maybel. You are Myrtle, or Mavis, or whomever you want to be. Pick a persona!"

"Princess Lala Dolly," I said.

Catherine looked at me like I was ridiculous. "Ok, Maybel, when you dress up and are in public, you are no longer Maybel. Maybel doesn't like dressing up. Maybel doesn't like socializing. But you aren't Maybel. You are Princess Dolly."

"Princess Lala Dolly," I corrected her.

"Yes, that's the one! And Princess Lala Dolly loves people, she loves attention, and she performs beautifully at social functions."

"She sounds horrible," I said.

"Maybel, do you like Mr. Charleston?" Catherine asked me.

"Yes," I smiled.

"Then go be Lala Dolly for Mr. Charleston."

"Princess," I said. "Princess Lala Dolly."

Catherine smiled with thin lips. She looked irritated. The more irritated she became, the thinner her lips became. "Great," she smiled, "Now let's go, shall we?"

"Maybel, sweetheart, you look lovely," mommy said as we walked to our horse carriage.

"Thank you, mommy! I look like you!"

Mommy smiled.

When we arrived at the barbershop salon, a crowd had already gathered. Members of the city council and other business owners were standing around congratulating Mr. Charleston.

Bernard and Henry stood behind Mr. Charleston. Unfortunately, Bernard looked really good in a suit and my eyes swept up and down his body.

Henry wore a tailored dark blue suit with a striped tie, a white handkerchief neatly folded in his suit pocket, and he pulled a shiny gold pocket watch out of his pocket. His shoes were shined and his black hair neatly groomed. His face was so perfect and sun-kissed.

Catherine nudged me. "Stop staring at Henry like that. You look at Henry the same way you look at cake at a birthday party; you stare at it until it's time to finally eat it."

"I would love to put his lips in my mouth," I whispered, and Catherine's eyes shot open.

"Maybel!" She first admonished me, then she giggled.

Her cheeks flushed, "I would too," she quietly laughed.

There was a ribbon cutting and speeches. They were all boring. I stood politely with a pleasant facial expression mommy had taught Catherine and me how to do in situations such as this. "Relax your face. Don't smile, but don't frown. Have a relaxed expression that makes it appear you are paying attention, but not necessarily agreeing or disagreeing with what the speaker is saying, in case your mind wanders, and you have no idea what is being said anymore."

Bernard was professional and didn't look at us longer than a quick glance. Henry nodded at Catherine and me. I was wearing my Princess Lala Dolly mask and apparently both Henry and Bernard had their own masks. I liked this serious mask Bernard wore. He looked like a professor and I found him more attractive.

The mayor's wife watched Henry. The reverend's wife, baker's wife, commissioner's wife, and every other wife, girlfriend, mother, and daughter were watching Henry. I would have to congratulate him later on only having sex with a dozen women. There were at least a dozen women here who would strip naked for him right now. How he only had sex with a dozen women in his lifetime showed great willpower.

After all the ceremonial pomp and circumstance we had to endure, it was finally over. I was hungry and wanted to go home and get out of this obtrusive Lala dress.

Bernard came and sweetly kissed Catherine's cheek and I walked away. I went up the steps and wandered around the building inspecting all the finishing touches. They really did an excellent job renovating this building. There was excellent attention to detail. That had to have been the work of mommy, Catherine, or Mrs. Charleston, because men would never think to add flower pots, to paint the basement bricks, or lay down decorative rugs at all the entryways.

"Does it meet your approval?"

I turned to see Henry approaching.

"Mmmm!" I nodded my head.

"Please don't tell me you've gone mute again," he smiled.

"A mute person couldn't tell you they'd gone mute," I giggled.

Henry laughed, "True enough, Maybel."

"I have to congratulate you on one other thing," I told him. "I thought a dozen women was a lot, but after seeing a dozen women here undress you with their eyes, I realized you having been with only a dozen women shows great restraint on your part."

"Thank you?" Henry asked.

"It's indeed a compliment. I've never once had to turn away a boy. I've never had a boy want me. So, for me to be in a crowd and have every single man want me, I can't even imagine how that would feel. Catherine would though. She probably has to turn down a dozen men daily."

"Catherine is quite beautiful," he said.

I picked up an interesting rock at my feet. It had a seashell fossil, which I thought was interesting.

"You are too, Maybel," he said softly.

I looked up at Henry. He suddenly put his professional mask on again. "Thank you for coming to show your support," he smiled politely, then turned and left.

I took my rock back around to the front of the building. Mr. Charleston greeted me. "Hello there, Maybel. Do you like the decor?"

"Yes. Can I keep this rock? It has a seashell fossil."

Mr. Charleston chuckled, "Yes, dear, it's all yours." He continued past me to shake the hand of another man in attendance.

"Thank you for coming, Maybel." I looked up to see Bernard.

"You're welcome, though I didn't come willingly. I found this rock though, so there's a silver lining," I said.

"We're having a late lunch at my home. You're welcome to come," Bernard was neither friendly nor unfriendly. He was still wearing his professional mask.

"I'm hungry but my desire to get out of this dress far outweighs my desire for food right now," I told him.

I took my rock and waited for mommy and daddy by our carriage. I had had enough socializing for the day. I wanted to go home and go swimming in my pond alone, and away from all these masks.

To my great disappointment, our carriage went to the Charleston's home for lunch and more socializing. Mommy, daddy, and Catherine went inside and I walked home. As soon as my feet hit our floor, I began undressing all the way upstairs to my room, where I stripped down to my underclothes.

My family would be at the Charleston's a couple hours socializing, so I took a piece of bread and jam and ate it on my way to my pond. I was weary of geese, but none were around, thankfully.

I walked into the cool water and swam to my peaceful island where I sat on a large rock under the shade of an oak tree. There were little butterflies and moths flitting about my feet. I heard fish and frogs splash and swirl the water. The breeze smelled like pine trees. I sat in my peaceful place and thought about what to write about next.

I imagined a beautiful bird. It was large, like a peacock, with beautiful long feathers that cascaded like a waterfall from its head, wings, and tail. The feather waterfalls were of purples, blues, reds, and pinks, with scattered gold and silver plumes. Its call sounded like flute music. It flew over lands near and far, and every time it landed, an admirer took a feather. It's only one feather, each thief reasoned. When the beautiful bird was down to one last golden plume, it landed in the field of a poor peasant girl. She came to it and gave the bird a drink of water from her cupped hand. She gently stroked the now bare and featherless skin of the bird. The bird waited for her to pluck its last feather but she did not. She returned to her little house where she lived with her little brother, her frail mother, and her injured father.

The little bird saw the family sit together on their dirt floor and enjoy each other's company, though they did not eat that night. The bird laid down next to the little girl and died. The bird's body turned solid gold, its eyes into emeralds, its beak into a diamond, and its clawed feet into rubies. The peasant family took the golden bird to the market and traded it for bread.

I can think of a better ending later, I thought. I was hungry again and decided to swim home. I waded into the now warmer water, because it was late afternoon, and swam across the pond. I walked up the little hill to my house, and suddenly Bernard wrapped me in something and yelled at me to go put clothes on.

"What are you doing, Bernard?" I screamed.

Bernard held my shoulders. "You're only wearing your underclothes!" he yelled at me. He began buttoning his shirt that he had wrapped around me.

Henry was shirtless standing next to Catherine, who was wearing a short-sleeved shirt and short, lightweight pants we wore for swimming.

"You're not wearing a shirt either!" I said to Bernard.

"I don't have breasts," he replied angrily.

I looked down. "I don't either, compared to Catherine!"

Catherine blushed.

"You can't walk around wearing only your underclothing!" Bernard lectured me.

"It's my house, my pond, and you're supposed to be at your house socializing!" I reminded him.

"It's a warm day. We decided to show Henry the island," Catherine said.

I couldn't even look at Henry. His beautiful body had no shirt. I really wanted him to take off his pants too. I kept my head down low.

"Shy again, Maybel?" Catherine giggled.

"No!" I said, still looking down.

Bernard held my arm tightly. "Come, Maybel."

"Your fingernails need trimmed," I complained. "They're digging into my skin!"

Bernard pulled me toward my house.

"Did you file your nails into points? They're like little needles!"

Bernard loosened his grip as we neared my house. "You need to be more careful, Maybel! You're not a child anymore!"

"You just called me a baby not long ago!" I reminded him.

"Well, you're not! And I was teasing you!" Bernard said.

"I'm going to go upstairs to put on my shirt and shorts I use for swimming, Bernard. You don't have to stay here with me and monitor my every movement!"

"Put on the swimwear with long sleeves and long pants," he ordered.

"Do you want to come upstairs and pick my clothing out, daddy?" I said sarcastically.

"No, Maybel, I just don't want Henry to keep staring at you like he was!" Bernard said, angrily.

My eyes widened. "Henry was looking at me?" I smiled big. "What did he say?"

"He said you're a child," Bernard said dryly.

My smile turned into a frown.

"Well, Catherine doesn't look like a child, and Henry is irresistible, so you better get back out there before he steals your girlfriend!" I bounded upstairs leaving Bernard in the kitchen.

I changed into my short-sleeved shirt and shorts because I couldn't fathom Handsome Henry caring what I wore. When I stood next to Catherine, nobody would notice if I were naked and juggling knives.

Instead of joining them outside, I made myself a sandwich and sat at the kitchen table writing down my bird story.

Catherine came inside. "Why didn't you come back out?"

"Eating," I replied without looking up from my paper.

"We're going swimming now," she said.

"Ok," I said. I stayed seated, writing my story.

"Are you not coming because you're still mad at Bernard?" Catherine asked, annoyed.

"Bernard made it clear he doesn't want me around and he wants to be alone with you so he can kiss you, and I'm guessing to see if you'll have sex with him if you already haven't."

"We haven't had sex!" Catherine said.

"Because I'm always around. I'm not going to be a tag-along anymore, so you two go enjoy each other's bodies."

"God Maybel! Maybe it's better you stay here! You are rude, insinuating I am one of those kinds of girls who have sex before marriage!" Catherine railed at me.

"I bet Bernard has had sex. Boys like that reputation. Girls are shamed for doing the same thing," I said.

"Bernard hasn't had sex!" Catherine became more irritated.

"Ok," I said.

"Why do you think he's had sex? Has he said something?" Catherine asked. She looked suddenly distrusting and skeptical of Bernard.

"No, I just assumed all boys try to have sex with whomever lets them. Henry has been with many women. If you had as many men as he had women, you wouldn't tell anyone about it."

"No, I would not," Catherine said firmly.

"Nor would you tell me if you had sex with Bernard," I told Catherine.

"I've never had sex and neither has Bernard!" Catherine was now very angry at me.

"You're not telling me you had sex because, like you said, you're trying to shelter and protect me, but you know what, Catherine, if I had sex with Henry, I would announce it to everyone that I had sex with Handsome Henry! People would say, 'Hello Maybel, nice weather, isn't it?' And I would say, 'I had sex with the most handsome man in the world, and yes, the weather is nice.'"

Catherine suddenly giggled, despite her anger at me.

"The reverend would ask me if I have anything to confess and I'd say, 'No, but I have something to brag about!'"

Catherine laughed harder, "Maybel, you're funny!"

"Did you see his beautiful chest, Catherine? It looked like a washboard! I could wash my unmentionables on his chiseled stomach muscles...."

Catherine laughed again.

"...With me still wearing them!"

Catherine squealed with laughter, "Goodness, Maybel! You're making me blush!"

"We're sitting outside, Maybel!" Bernard stuck his head in the kitchen window. He looked angry.

Catherine and I froze. "How much did you hear?" I managed to squeak out.

"Enough to make even Henry blush!" Bernard snapped.

My eyes widened. I was mortified, but Catherine laughed so hard tears slid down her cheeks.

"You should see your face," Catherine could barely speak, she laughed so hard at my frozen and mortified expression.

My feet were glued to the floor. I couldn't decide if I should run upstairs or to the train station and never return.

Bernard came in through the kitchen door followed by Henry. "Are we going swimming or not?" Bernard asked angrily.

I stood in the kitchen, my feet still stuck to the floor, and stared at Henry with big eyes and no voice to speak.

Henry was indeed blushing. It was the first time he'd ever looked not in control of his emotions or body. His cheeks were red and he looked away from me, embarrassed and awkward. "You have quite the way with words, Maybel," he glanced at me, then looked away again.

"I broke you!" I whispered, stunned.

"What?" Henry looked back at me.

"I made you blush and awkward, just like me!" I squeaked, my voice returning.

"I'm not broken, Maybel, just shocked to hear a woman speak like a bawdy sailor," Henry told me.

"He called you a bawdy sailor!" Catherine still had deep belly laughs.

"He called me a woman! Bernard, did you hear Henry? He called me a woman, not a child!" I smiled widely.

"He was being polite," Bernard said dryly.

"No, I was being truthful. You are a woman, a young woman, but definitely not a child anymore," Henry said.

"See! Not a child!" I stuck my tongue out at Bernard.

"You just proved my point, Maybel, by sticking your tongue out at me!" Bernard said.

"Hush, boy!" I held up my hand to Bernard. "You're speaking to a woman; use good manners!"

I sat back down at the table and began writing again. My face felt hot from embarrassment because the most handsome man in the world called me a woman.

"Catherine, Henry, let's go swimming," Bernard motioned for them to come. "We'll just go without Maybel."

"I'll stay and keep Maybel company," Henry said.

I looked up at him, my big eyes returned.

"Fine, we will all stay here," Bernard said, annoyed.

"You didn't want me to tag along, Bernard, so I've stopped tagging along. You are free to go kiss Catherine alone," I said.

"Come on, Bernard!" Catherine smiled. "Let's go!" She pulled Bernard outside.

I offered Henry a piece of candy from the bowl on the table. He took a cherry lollipop. "Those are my favorite too!" I said, also taking one.

I ignored Henry while I sucked on my lollipop and finished writing my story. I wanted to get it all out of my head and onto paper so I could begin a new story tomorrow.

"Maybel, Bernard always tells me how much he loves your stories," Henry spoke gently.

"Bernard has poor taste. Why are you being rude to me?"

"What? No, I didn't mean.... Oh," he laughed, "You're joking. I see. Alright then, Maybel, Bernard tells me you are an amazing writer, and although Bernard sometimes makes bad choices and acts like a spoiled brat, perhaps he is right when he says your stories are captivating. May I read a story?" Henry asked me.

I smiled very big and giggled, "Sure, there are some in the bookcase and some in my bedroom. There are probably several in Bernard's bedroom that I wrote while there. May I kiss you?"

"What?"

"You are so beautiful," I told him.

"Ok, Maybel. I'll sit here and you walk around the table and bend down and kiss me," Henry said.

I froze.

Henry laughed, "You see, you're too young."

"If I come around the table to kiss you, you'll let me?" My eyes were the size of teacup saucers.

"Yes," he said.

I felt like I was about to faint so I dropped my head and continued writing.

Henry laughed.

"I'm not a child," I tried to say, but it came out garbled.

"It's ok, Maybel, just relax. You're fun to tease and your sense of humor is very good," Henry smiled sweetly at me. I wanted to lick the dimple in his cheek.

I wrote another minute then looked up at Henry. "How are you so in control of your emotions and body all the time? Catherine is too, and I've always marveled at how composed she is. You're even more composed. You don't get angry, sad, happy, I've never heard you burst out laughing, and I had never seen you blush before today. When you walked to the podium today, you walked confidently and with purpose. Your voice is always steady and your movements steady and deliberate. How do you do that? I have never been able to do any of that, ever."

Henry paused and considered my words. "I don't know, Maybel. It's not something I was aware of. How do you see such detail in ordinary things?"

"You are most decidedly not ordinary, Henry," I whispered.

Henry blushed.

"You blushed again," I smiled.

"I suppose I have never met someone like you before, and just maybe, you are the only woman to ever make me lose control." Henry's blush darkened.

I blushed too, then looked down at my paper nervously.

Mommy and daddy were gone to a play one evening, and Catherine was at whatever party she was attending. I took a bath and changed into my nightgown even though it wasn't anywhere near bedtime. I laid on the sofa writing. My back was stiff so I slid over the arm of the sofa like an eel over rocks, trying to work out the stiffness.

"Maybel, are you ok?"

"Bernard? What are you doing here? Did you forget to knock? I've been told it's very important to knock so you won't accidentally see your father naked."

"What?"

"Why are you here?" I asked Bernard.

"I'm sorry I hurt your feelings. I do like having you around. I like being with you. I just, sometimes, I don't know how to be around you."

"What do you mean?" Bernard made no sense.

"I'm dating Catherine, but I like playing with you and being silly with you. You make me happy and I look forward to being with you. It really confuses me because you're perfect and beautiful and smart but you still like to play tag and you sleep with a toy bear. I don't know what to do."

I sighed and sat on the sofa properly. "I'm sorry I called out your hypocrisy."

"You did?" Bernard looked confused.

"You kissed my neck, then said you expected me to not kiss anyone like that until marriage. And then I said you were a mean hypocrite and I never wanted to see you again."

"You didn't say that." Bernard still looked confused.

"Didn't I? I must have said that inside my head then. Sometimes I say things inside my head, thankfully, instead of saying them out loud. And other times, my thoughts come spilling out of my mouth like verbal lava. Just spewing hot, angry words everywhere."

"Catherine kissed my best friend tonight."

"You kissed me. We're a very loving family."

"I know I don't have any right to be mad, but I am."

"Do you want to kiss me again?" I asked.

"Don't you feel guilty we kissed? Catherine's your sister."

"Yes, but deep inside me, I'm still very mad at her right now. She lied about not knowing how babies are made. I've been completely ignorant of everything, and she did nothing to help me understand. And Edith's older sister told Edith about sex, and Edith told Catherine, but Catherine wouldn't tell me!"

"Kissing me will not make you feel better about Catherine lying. It will only make you feel worse," Bernard told me.

"That's likely. Your breath smelled bad."

"I meant you'll feel worse about kissing your sister's boyfriend!" Bernard cupped his hand to his mouth and exhaled then breathed his own breath. "My breath doesn't smell bad!"

"Why are you here?" I asked.

Bernard sat next to me on the sofa. He wrapped his arm around my shoulder. "I'm sorry I said you're annoying sometimes."

"You hurt my feelings," I said.

Bernard squeezed his arm around me, hugging me. "The truth is I lock my door to keep you away. Sometimes when you play around with me, that thing that happened when you licked ice cream off my neck happens, and Catherine has noticed."

"See, you and Catherine do more than kiss. How would Catherine know you're hard unless she sees you naked?"

"Because my pants stick straight out! Because when she leans over to kiss me, I'm already as hard as granite!"

I thought for a minute. "Your penis gets hard when you and I play together?"

"Not every time," Bernard said quickly. "It's just, you roll around on me trying to get me to play with you, and you play with my hair, and hold my hands, and sometimes I can't control my body. I don't mean for it to happen. Men can't always control that part of their body."

"My nipples got hard when you kissed my neck. I couldn't control that either," I said.

"Maybel," Bernard shifted his position, "this is what I meant by being too blunt."

"How is me being honest about my nipples any more blunt than you telling me I make your penis hard?" I looked at Bernard. "Wait," my eyes widened, "Is your penis hard now?"

"Yes, Maybel, you said your nipples got hard when I kissed you! Of course I'm hard right now!"

I glanced down at his waist then back up at his eyes.

Bernard covered his waist with a pillow.

The front door opened and slammed shut. "I'm sorry, Bernard!" Catherine came inside crying. "I lost control of my sensibilities!"

Bernard stared at the floor with his jaw clenched.

"Bernard, it was an accident! Haven't you ever lost your senses and done something stupid?" Catherine tried to reason with Bernard.

"I've kissed someone else too, Catherine." Bernard looked up at Catherine solemnly.

"You have?" Catherine looked heartbroken.

"Yes, Catherine, I have. And you weren't my first kiss either. I lied about that. I'm sorry I lied."

I tensed up.

"When did you cheat on me?" she asked, tears forming in her eyes. "Was it one of my friends? Was it Edith?"

"No," Bernard said. "It doesn't matter. You kissed Samuel, some other boy whose name I don't even know, and now my best friend."

Catherine stood with her arms crossed looking down at the floor. She looked angry and sad.

"Maybe we just need some time apart again, Catherine." Bernard stood up and walked to the door.

"I'm not going to see you again?" I felt tears welling. After Bernard and I went out west, he broke up with Catherine, and I was very sad to not see him again for months. I didn't want to be without Bernard. He teased me sometimes, and I wanted to hit him for being rude, but I still loved him.

"I'll take you fishing tomorrow, Maybel. I'll still see you."

Bernard turned to Catherine. "But you and I need some time apart to figure out what we want."

As it turned out, I didn't go fishing with Bernard. I felt that would maybe hurt Catherine's feelings, as though I would be choosing Bernard over my sister. I wanted Catherine to love me again, and play with me like she used to, so I stayed away from Bernard.

The rest of the summer passed with Bernard spending time in traveling to San Francisco with his parents. His father had some business to attend to and wanted Bernard to learn how to be a businessman and handle their family affairs.

Catherine and I spent time together and I was able to, on occasion, get her to play with me like she used to. She was actually still quite good at throwing baseballs and hitting them. I was faster than her at climbing trees, but she was still the faster swimmer.

I felt guilty for not wanting Bernard to return. I finally had my sister back and I never wanted to lose her again.

"Maybel, I have bruises and I'm still picking twigs out of my hair!" Catherine complained.

"You look beautiful, darling," daddy said. "Can you please pass me the butter?"

Catherine handed daddy the butter. "My fingernails are worn and dirty every evening after we play together," Catherine said, annoyed.

"I rather like having my two, little girls back," daddy winked at us.

Mommy smiled, "I do too! You're playing together again and enjoying each other." Mommy beamed and patted Catherine's hand.

"I guess it's fun," Catherine admitted, "but I can't go to Edith's birthday party like this. They'll think I'm an unkempt child."

"Then don't go!" I said excitedly. "Stay here with me!"

"I love you, Maybel, but I do want to attend a party from time to time with boys and girls my own age," she said.

I frowned.

Catherine sighed, "You're welcome to come with me, Maybel."

"Why? What did I do to anger you for you to punish me thusly," I lamented in my most theatrical voice.

"Why don't you go with Catherine, dear," mommy suggested.

"Ok," I said.

"Really?" Catherine asked.

I couldn't tell if she was happy or regretting asking me.

Daddy sighed, "I like it better when you both climb trees and get dirty."

"Oh, honey, it's just a birthday party," mommy patted daddy's hand.

"You're both growing up too fast," daddy looked sad. "I miss the days when you both ran to me when I came home and sat in my lap while I read stories."

"You read to us last night," Catherine giggled.

"I know, and I loved it," daddy winked.

"When is the birthday party?" I asked.

"Tomorrow," Catherine said, "early afternoon."

"Oh, tomorrow afternoon? Are you going to start getting ready now?" I teased.

"Yes, Maybel! I have so much to do! My nails, hair, and choosing accessories always takes time."

I rolled my eyes. I had been joking about getting ready for tomorrow's party now, but Catherine wasn't.

We washed dishes and tidied the kitchen. I followed Catherine upstairs to her bedroom and laid on her bed. "What do you want me to wear?" I asked.

"My old, purple dress." She grabbed it from the closet and tossed it on my stomach.

"Catherine, when is Bernard returning?"

"How would I know?" she asked sharply, "I'm not dating Bernard anymore."

"When are you getting back together?" I asked.

"We broke up, Maybel. We're not getting back together."

"Oh," I said. "I feel guilty for feeling happy that you're not going to date Bernard because you spend more time with me now."

"I've enjoyed this summer, Maybel." Catherine smiled at me.

"If you date another boy, will you save a couple days a week for climbing trees with me?" I asked hopefully.

"Yes, Maybel," Catherine laughed.

Catherine looked thoughtful. "I've been thinking about your friend Danny and the problems he's faced. I want to do something to help people who face those issues. I've been thinking about how to get shop owners to agree to sell to everyone equally, regardless of what color they are or where they came from."

I sat up. "Really, Catherine?" I smiled.

"I wrote to our mayor and asked for a law to be put into place. It's not much, but I wanted to at least try."

I smiled and jumped up and hugged her. "Oh Catherine! I'm so proud of you!" I kissed her cheek. "You have to tell Bernard! He'll be so happy!"

"I think maybe it doesn't matter now," she said. "Life without Bernard isn't as bad as I once feared. You know, Maybel, I'm learning from you how to be independent. I want to thank you."

"Oh Catherine! That means so much to me!"

"You're fearless, Maybel, and I'm proud of you."

I felt my eyes sting from budding tears and I hugged Catherine. "Thank you," I whispered as I held her tightly. My big siter was proud of me.

"Maybel, are you almost ready for the party?" Catherine peaked her head in my door.

"Catherine, why did you invite me? You never invite me to parties," I said, wondering why she wanted me to come. I embarrassed her with my lack of etiquette.

"I don't invite you because you never want to go to parties. I'd like you to come to this one."

"Why?"

She hesitated, "I don't have a date."

"You go alone to lots of parties. Why can't you go alone to this party?"

"Maybel, I don't want to be there alone. Can't you please come with me? I feel lonely without Bernard."

"Tell Bernard you are sorry and want to date him again."

"I can't."

"Why?"

"I don't know if I want to date him. I like the security of dating him, but I am enjoying being free."

"Then go to the party alone. You'll immediately attract the attention of every boy in the room, because you always attract the attention of everyone, including all the girls. Everyone wants to be near you, boys and girls alike."

"Maybel, I'm scared."

I looked at her skeptically.

"I am scared! Just because I look confident doesn't mean I am confident!"

"Ok, I'll go. I'll stay long enough for you to attract a horde of admirers, which should take about fifteen minutes, then I'll return home."

"Thank you, Maybel! I was worried you'd find a way to wiggle your way out of going."

"Catherine, I don't do well at parties."

"I really need you!" Catherine looked scared. I couldn't say no.

Catherine dressed me up like one of her little dolls. It wasn't too bad. I enjoyed talking to Catherine and I'd been missing her since she became interested in boys.

We arrived at Edith's house and Catherine held my hand tightly.

"Why are you shaking?" I asked Catherine.

"I'm nervous."

"Your hand is sweaty."

"I am extremely nervous," she said.

"I have never seen you nervous before. It's making me nervous," I told her.

"I'm often nervous Maybel, I'm just good at hiding my emotions."

"I've never been good at hiding my emotions," I said.

"No!" Catherine exclaimed, her expression dripping with sarcasm. "You hide your passion so well!"

Catherine and I giggled hard. It was a family joke that I had never hidden my excitement or anger well.

"Hello, Catherine, Maybel."

It was Bernard with a blonde on his arm.

I felt suddenly strange. Catherine squeezed my hand. I looked over, and she looked odd. I'd never seen her expression before. I had no idea what this new look on her face meant, and that worried me.

I'd never been comfortable around gatherings, even ones with people I knew and liked, but I was especially nervous when it was a room full of people I didn't know. I looked down. I knew I looked strange standing there with my head down staring at the floor, but I felt lightheaded. Normally, I'd look to Catherine for guidance, but she offered none. I had never in my life seen her at a loss for words at a party.

Catherine stood and stared at Bernard and his date. Catherine's grip loosened and her hand felt weak. I looked over at her and she looked like at any second she would burst out in tears. It scared me, her behavior. She always guided me, made excuses for my lack of social graces, and helped me through social situations. Now though, her hand laid limply in my hand, and that both terrified and saddened me.

I looked back up at Bernard. He was looking at me, not Catherine. His date watched Catherine.

I looked over at Catherine again. I did not want to see her look weak. I wanted her to be strong. I felt strong when she was strong. I felt that whatever strength Catherine had lost, I had gained. I was Catherine's protector now.

"Congratulations on your new baby, Bernard. Your mother told my mother the good news. This must be the baby's mother. Nice to meet you, I smiled at the blonde. Bernard, we're looking forward to meeting your new, precious, little cherub. Have a lovely evening."

I held my head high and led Catherine toward the dance floor. I could hear angry whispering behind me. "You have a baby! You got a woman pregnant?"

The angry whispering continued as I led Catherine away.

"You know that bicycle Bernard bought me, and how jealous you were?" she asked me.

"Yes."

"It's yours."

The autumn festival drew people from far and wide. Many of our neighbors rented rooms to visitors as the hotels quickly filled.

This year, as an added attraction, there was a dunking contraption. The sign above it read, "Dunk The Dowdy Dirty Rascal."

All the boys and young men lined up, and for a nickel, you received three balls and could dunk the boy sitting on the dunker by hitting the wooden sign labeled, "Dummy Dunker!" The boy sitting on the ledge would then fall into a vat of ice-filled water.

Of course, a game of sorts quickly began to form. Girls paid to have a chance to either not dunk the boy if she liked him, and to dunk him if she didn't like him.

The first boy was Arnold and the crowd heckled him, of course. "Edith, dunk him!" Edith didn't hit the dunker and the girls around us all cooed, "Edith loves Arnold!"

Amanda didn't dunk Billy, Elsa didn't dunk her younger brother Fritz, and Eliza didn't dunk her fiancée Andrew. This was quite boring as far as I was concerned, but everyone else was absolutely enthralled seeing which girls paid for balls, and for which boys they intended to not dunk.

Suddenly, boys found out with certainty which girls liked them, and some boys even had three or four girls buy their turns to not to dunk him. This was the point where it got interesting. Clearly some rivalries were being formed, and some allegiances were being forged between friends.

Now it became a web of who liked whom, and who was not dunking a boy to retaliate against a girl who refused to dunk a boy the girl liked, or her friend liked. More and more people crowded around as more and more boys were either getting dunked out of spite between girls, or not getting dunked because a girl liked him. It had become quite a spectacle and the jeers and laughter had become almost deafening.

At last Bernard took his turn. I knew Catherine wasn't going to dunk him, but to my surprise, three other girls didn't dunk him either. Catherine's face flushed red and she shot each of them looks that scared even me. There were whispers amongst the crowd. A fourth girl bought her three balls and barely tossed them as she smirked at Catherine. There were more than whispers now. All eyes were on Catherine. Bernard's face tried to convey confusion to Catherine and he kept shrugging his shoulders as though he had no idea those girls fancied him.

Behind Catherine's obvious rage, I began to see hurt, confusion, and the possibility that Bernard had betrayed her while they had dated, spreading across her face.

"Don't you cry one tear, Catherine," I whispered. "Don't let them see you cry."

Catherine didn't answer me, because if she opened her mouth, she would cry. I knew this, because when we saw grandpa have a heart attack and die in front of us when we were young, Catherine clenched her teeth and refused to speak until after the funeral, when I found her sobbing on the ground in the garden one night. I held her that night, and now I was about to comfort her again, because unfortunately for Bernard, I couldn't tuck my feelings away to be released at a later date in private.

I bought a dollar's worth of balls. I looked back at Catherine and smiled. She weakly smiled back, no doubt waiting for night time to fall so she could sneak out and cry in the garden in privacy.

I turned back to Bernard without a smile. He looked scared. "Catherine! I swear I don't know why those girls didn't dunk me!" The girls giggled amongst themselves like they had secrets and enjoyed Catherine's sudden distrust of her loyal Bernard.

Bang! I dunked Bernard. Bang! Bang! Bang! Bang! Dunk after dunk I hit the center of the dunker's trigger each and every time without hesitation.

The crowd began chanting my name! I had four balls left and I threw the next one and simultaneously screamed, "Oops!" as it hit one of those troublemaking girls right on her nose. Blood spurted forth. "Sorry!" I called out. "The sweat on my hand made my ball slip." I held up my remaining three balls yelling, "I'll be more careful, I promise!"

The three other troublemaking girls scrambled like cockroaches to escape. One tripped over the other and landed face down in the grass but immediately popped up and looked at me quickly before she skittered away with her three other little cockroach friends. The crowd, instead of being aghast, actually roared with laughter.

Bernard could not leave with his honor, so he remained seated, awaiting his fate, which I was about to seal.

I was angry at Bernard, because he was at that party with that blonde girl, and now I was mad because it appeared Bernard had a lot of admirers. I held my last ball and looked Bernard straight in his eyes and threw the ball at his stupid nose. With my final ball, I cracked his nose open, and blood poured down liberally, turning the water red.

Again, the crowd roared with jeers and raucous laughter. I took Catherine's arm and led her away. "Let's go home," I said quietly.

Catherine remained silent. We walked home and Catherine went to her room.

I followed her up the stairs, but she stopped me from entering. "I need to be alone," she began crying. She shut her door and I sat on floor in front of her door listening to her sob.

Several hours must have passed. I awoke to the house being darker, and Catherine had opened her door and was now looking down at me. "Thank you Maybel, for staying," she said through tears.

I got up and hugged Catherine. We went and laid down in her bed and I didn't say anything. I waited for her to be ready to talk, if she wanted to talk.

Several days passed and Catherine seemed happier. She and I helped daddy make a new potato bin in daddy's workshop for mommy. We signed the bottom, 'To mommy: Love, Daddy, Catherine, and The Great Maybel.'"

Catherine went to town to see her friend Earlene at Charlie's candy shop. I stayed home and helped mommy bake bread. When it was time to cool the bread loaves on racks, I took a bag of old, stale nuts we couldn't eat anymore, out to our garden to feed the squirrels and chipmunks.

I saw Catherine and Bernard coming up the path to our house. They were holding hands. They were walking and pleasantly talking to each other. They didn't notice me as they approached, lost in each other's eyes.

Suddenly Catherine noticed me. I was sitting with a bag of old nuts, waiting for my legion of squirrels and chipmunks to draw near.

"Maybel! Bernard and I have reconciled," Catherine said happily.

I stared at Catherine and threw out a nut.

A chipmunk dashed from right to left in front of where I sat.

"Oh Maybel, I promise I'll still climb trees and play baseball with you from time to time."

I threw out another nut. Two squirrels became bloodthirsty and one nipped the other in the neck, then took the nut.

"Maybel, I thought you'd be happy to have your big brother back in your life!"

"Uh huh," I mumbled, tossing out another nut.

This time, a chipmunk took the nut, then a gray squirrel lunged at the chipmunk and stole the loot.

Catherine continued speaking giddily, "Bernard had heard from our mutual friend that I wrote our mayor about a law requiring shop owners to sell food to Indians and black people at a fair price. Bernard came to thank me, and, well, we're going to dinner tonight!" Catherine beamed happily.

Bernard looked at me pleasantly, with neither happiness nor sadness. He only looked at me, and I looked back into his eyes, searching, wondering why he chose to return to Catherine.

"That's nice." I threw a nut at Bernard's feet and a squirrel skittered by and snatched it up.

"And who was the blonde at that party, Bernard?" I asked with a level and firm voice.

The next nut I threw at Catherine's feet and two squirrels fought over it, causing Catherine to squeal and jump.

"She was just a girl one of my friend's suggested I take to the party," Bernard said.

"Did you kiss her?" I asked, throwing out an acorn at Bernard's pants leg. A squirrel scampered by.

"No, Maybel," Bernard said.

"And all those girls at the festival who fancied you?" I asked. I threw two acorns at Bernard's shins, and three squirrels descended from the tree tops to vie for them.

"No, Maybel, I haven't kissed anyone," Bernard answered.

Catherine looked up at Bernard and smiled and Bernard bent down and kissed her.

I threw the entire bag of nuts at Bernard's head, and from every tree and bush, appeared a squirrel and chipmunk running to Bernard, vying to be the victor in this nut war. The squirrels ran to Bernard and Catherine, and several even scurried up Bernard's pants, thinking he was a tree. They scratched Catherine's legs, and when Bernard smacked one off his chest, it latched onto his thumb and bit hard.

Catherine and Bernard screamed and ran away into our house. I continued sitting on the bench watching the squirrels try to cannibalize each other over nuts. I still felt sad though. I missed Bernard but I was angry at him.

Catherine and Bernard apologized for their transgressions and forgave one another. I enjoyed Bernard in my life, but I had been enjoying Catherine's attention more. I was saddened when Catherine resumed passing her afternoons and evenings with Bernard.

One afternoon, shortly after Catherine and Bernard began dating again, Bernard came looking for Catherine and I answered our door.

"Catherine is in the ballroom with her piano teacher," I said.

"Maybel, I've missed you," he smiled brightly at me.

"I missed you too," I said. I had missed him, but he represented my sister's absence from my life, and so I had not missed him a great amount.

Although I wanted Catherine to be happy, I was alone again, as they often slipped away to hold hands and kiss while I stayed home and wrote about the adventures I wished I were having.

"I know Catherine and I were apart, but I thought we were friends. Why didn't you come to me and ask me to play?" Bernard seemed hurt. He looked a little like a boy when he said that, not like the man he was growing to be.

"You don't like playing with me," I frowned. "You act like playing with me is a bother," I said.

"It's not," he said. "I really missed you."

"Well, you act like I'm an annoyance."

"Maybel," Bernard's voice was soft, "I like being with you. I've missed you so much. You never came to see me when Catherine and I were not dating."

I didn't believe Bernard missed me. "You and Catherine have always spent most of your time trying to escape me so you could be alone with each other." I was still hurt by all the times they tried to get rid of me.

"I know, Maybel, but I really do like being with you." Bernard offered a small smile, but I didn't care if he had smiled really big. There had not been big enough bandages placed around my heart to heal my pain. I had felt unwanted and rejected by Bernard for too long.

"You think I will come running into your outstretched arms whenever you are bored. As soon as Catherine is ready to kiss you and hold your hand, you'll again try to get rid of me."

I told Bernard to wait for Catherine to finish her piano lesson by himself because I had plans.

"With whom?" Bernard grew curious.

I ignored him. I walked around him and out my front door.

"Where are you going, Maybel?"

"I'll be back later. Go wait for your girlfriend to finish her piano lesson," I huffed.

I walked to the Charleston's mansion to see Mrs. Charleston. We were to brush the horses and have tea together. I liked Mrs. Charleston a lot.

I walked past the carriage entrance and up the path to the stables. I saw Mrs. Charleston in the distance brushing Big Ben. I waved.

"Good afternoon, Maybel," she smiled at me. "So good to see you. Bernard, can you bring Daisy Mae around? Her mane needs to be brushed, too."

I flung my head around so fast I heard a vertebrae crack in my neck. "Bernard? What are you doing here?"

"I followed you. You're easy to track, Maybel. You would be a horrible hunter. I could hear you and see you a mile away."

"What do you want?" I asked angrily.

"To play with you," he smiled.

I hated when he smiled at me like that because it made my heart beat faster and my stomach flutter. "I'm here to help your mother," I said dismissively. I didn't want Bernard to know I still liked him a lot and had missed him too.

"It's alright, dear, you and Bernard go play," Mrs. Charleston winked at me.

The few times when Bernard indulged me in playtime, were the highlights of my days. Those times had become more rare, so I cherished them when they did happen.

Bernard chased me through the corn stalks. I ran fast, weaving in and out of rows of tall corn. The leaves on the corn stalks sliced my cheeks, neck, arms, and legs as I ran. They felt like tiny paper cuts and my dripping sweat made them sting. I didn't slow down though because I was winning. I ran through a spider web and felt it crawling on my neck. I wiped it off and continued.

I ran up the ramp to the hay bales and jumped from the highest hay bale into the pile of hay below. Bernard came tumbling after me and narrowly missed landing on top of me.

"Race you to that tree," I yelled. I still enjoyed playing, even though I was older now. I felt like I was supposed to be poised like Catherine, but I wasn't. My body might be changing, but my heart still yearned for the freedom of the outdoors.

Bernard sprinted after me. He was taller and stronger now. His muscles were more defined and I felt something inside me whenever he was near. I was embarrassed by this feeling, but also confused, because I didn't understand why I felt different inside whenever Bernard was close.

"Ha, ha, Maybel! You finally won a race!" He tousled my hair and I pushed him away.

He rubbed my hair again until it was even more messy than it was when we started playing.

"Stop it, Bernard!" I licked my fingers and was almost close enough to his ears when he grabbed my arms and threw me down onto the grass, landing on top of me.

"Ow! Bernard! Get off!"

"Stop hitting yourself, Maybel!" He used my own arm to slap myself in my own face. I felt my cheeks flush red with anger and I threw him off me but he still had hold of my hands and I rolled on top of him. I became intensely aware of his hard muscles beneath me, so I rolled off him and stood up quickly. I didn't know how to react to my enjoyment of Bernard's body underneath mine.

"Stop messing up my hair, Bernard!" I yelled.

"It's already messed up, Maybel! It never looks neat and tidy!" he laughed.

I ran back to the hay pile and when Bernard followed me, I quickly turned around and threw a wad of hay right at his stupid face. He spat out all the little pieces with annoyance. "I don't know why I play with you! You're such a child!" He stormed off out of the hay pile and back toward his stables.

"Are you leaving because you're embarrassed about your hard penis that I felt when I was on top of you?" I yelled angrily.

"Shut up!" he yelled back.

I sat in the pile of hay wondering if my hair really was always messy. My hair was thick and wavy. It never wanted to be tamed, but neither did I.

I stood up and walked to the stables. "Maybel, would you like to help me braid Ben's and Daisy's manes now?" Bernard's mother called.

"Yes," I called back.

"You should brush Maybel's mane, mother, she needs it more than Big Ben and Daisy Mae!" Bernard laughed.

I shot Bernard an angry look but I felt embarrassed that he was probably right. I dragged my feet, kicking clods of dirt as I approached.

Bernard left, I presumed to return to Catherine. Her piano lesson was likely finished by now.

"Maybel, would you like to weave in blue ribbons into their braids?" Mrs. Charleston asked.

"Yes, Mrs. Charleston."

"Maybel, you can call me Anna," she reminded me.

"My mother says I have to call you Mrs. Charleston out of respect."

Mrs. Charleston smiled at me and handed me a brush and a long, blue ribbon.

"Do you remember what I taught you before about brushing a horse?" Mrs. Charleston asked.

"Yes, Mrs. Charleston," I answered.

I brushed Big Ben while Mrs. Charleston brushed Daisy Mae. Big Ben was my favorite. His tail was a glossy black color and we sometimes braided and weaved ribbons through his tail, too.

"Maybel, why do you look sad?"

"Bernard said my hair is always messy," I pouted.

"You know, Maybel, I always had messy hair too," she smiled at me.

"Your hair is beautiful, Mrs. Charleston." And it was. She had the most gorgeous, long, black hair that she wore in braids or sometimes swept up and pinned. The shorter hairs around her face that weren't tied back, curled in little ringlets, adding to her beauty and charm. Her eyes were emeralds, like Bernard's.

"When I was your age, my hair was as wild and free as the mustangs out west," she smiled kindly at me.

I continued brushing Big Ben and feeling like an ugly child nobody wanted to play with because they look or act different.

"Maybel, there was a boy who used to make fun of my hair, but you know what, I didn't care. I was wild and free like those mustangs. Do you know who else is wild and free like those mustangs?"

"Who?" I asked, still feeling sorry for myself and brushing Big Ben's beautiful mane.

"You, Maybel."

I looked up at her. She smiled at me.

"Mrs. Charleston, did you kick that boy who made fun of your hair?"

She chuckled as she helped brush Big Ben's mane. "Yes, Maybel, and later I married him," she winked at me.

I continued brushing Big Ben and wondering why she would ever want to marry a stupid boy who made fun of her hair.

I arrived home and Catherine stood with a man at our piano. Bernard sat on a chair and looked bored. Catherine smiled as I entered the ballroom. "Maybel, this is Matthew. He's filling in for Mrs. Billings. He spent a summer in Germany studying and playing piano under the best composers in Europe," Catherine beamed.

"Charmed," I said. I was not impressed. He looked like knew a lot about smelly cheeses and French wines.

Matthew was blonde and beautiful, but he wore tight pants, which Catherine explained was fashionable right now in Europe. I went to shake Matthew's hand to give me a reason to accidentally push Catherine's sheet music off the piano and onto the floor. I wondered if he could bend over without splitting his pants at the seam.

"I'm so sorry!" I lied. Catherine's papers scattered about the floor.

"Maybel has no social graces," Catherine furrowed her brows at me.

"Matthew, I'm so sorry! Would you be a dear and hand me Catherine's sheet music? My lower back has been hurting today. I'm so sorry Catherine!" I pretended to exude great sorrow about my lack of social graces.

Matthew bent down in a way I had never seen anyone else bend over before. He didn't bend at his waist, like a normal person. He bent his knees out, kind of like the way a frog kicks in water, or the way a ballerina squats down with her knees going outward.

My eyes popped open wide and Bernard tried hard to stifle his extreme amusement. Catherine glared at me.

"Here you are, miss," Matthew jovially popped back up and handed Catherine her sheet music.

"Lovely meeting you." I tried to speak without giggling, but all I could think about was whether or not I could get away with ribbiting or croaking at Matthew without Catherine turning into a feral beast and punching me. I decided not to tempt Catherine's ire.

"Good say, sir," I turned and left, and Bernard followed me. His face was red from holding in laughter.

Once in the kitchen, I whispered, "His legs looked like frog legs when he bent down, didn't they? You saw that too, didn't you?"

"Yes!" Bernard laughed. "You are so naughty, Maybel! And I love being with you!"

I often wandered into Mr. Charleston's bedroom when Catherine told me she wanted some time alone with Bernard. Mr. Charleston liked to take naps, and I enjoyed cuddling up next to him and reading his newspaper while he snoozed, and when he awoke, we did the puzzle section of the paper together. Sometimes we did crossword puzzles, and other times we did word search puzzles. He held me in his arm. He felt safe like daddy.

"Maybel, whenever you come here and spend time with me, I can't help but wish you were my daughter. I wish I had had a daughter just like you."

"Why didn't you have more children? Was is because Bernard was too much to handle and you decided one of him was enough?" I said dryly.

Mr. Charleston chuckled, "No honey, we wanted more children. We wanted a houseful of children, but we couldn't have any more babies." Mr. Charleston seemed saddened by his revelation.

"If I were your daughter, tell me truthfully," I whispered, "I'd be your favorite child, wouldn't I?" I smiled.

Mr. Charleston laughed loudly, "Oh Maybel, sweetheart, mommies and daddies don't have favorites."

Bernard came into his father's bedroom. "Maybel! Come back to my room!"

"No!" I yelled. "You told me to go away!"

"Stop pestering my father!"

"It's quite alright, Bernard. Maybel and I have come to enjoy each other's company while doing crossword puzzles."

Bernard came to me and took my arm. "Come on, Maybel! Catherine and I are done studying. She went home. We thought you'd gone home too."

"Oh, done already? What were you studying, my sister's mouth, her tongue, or her body?"

"Don't be crass, Maybel! We did not do anything more than a peck on the cheek."

I laughed.

"Come on, stop bothering father. I'll make you hot cocoa downstairs," Bernard persisted.

"It's alright Bernard, Maybel and I enjoy our nap time. Maybel, what is a seven-letter word for annoying?" Mr. Charleston read the next hint in our crossword puzzle.

"Bernard!" I laughed.

Bernard looked angry but Mr. Charleston laughed.

"Ok, Maybel, let's go." Bernard scooped me up in his arms but I held onto Mr. Charleston's arm tightly.

Mr. Charleston pulled me into him. "Bernard, I don't mind spending time with Maybel. She can stay."

Bernard became angrier. "You used to make me leave you when I was younger!" Bernard yelled and slammed the door as he left.

I looked up at Mr. Charleston, not knowing what to do.

Mr. Charleston sighed, "I'm sorry, Maybel. When Bernard was young, he always wanted to play, but I was busier with my businesses and wanted to either work or sleep. Bernard was hurt, and rightfully so."

"Do you still have those businesses?"

"Yes, but I became wealthy enough to hire people to do more of the work. I moved here so I could have more time with Bernard and his mother, but the damage has been done."

"I'll be right back," I told him.

I went to Bernard's room where he was still sulking. "Bernard, your father wants to see you."

"I don't want to see him," Bernard said.

"We're having problems finding an eleven-letter word for letting go."

"Forgiveness," Bernard said.

"I know," I said gently, "Will you come? Please, Bernard?"

Bernard stood up from his desk and followed me into his father's bedroom. "Yes?" Bernard asked.

"We want to do a crossword puzzle with you, Bernard." I took his hand and pulled him to his father. "Lay beside your father and we'll all finish the puzzle together."

"I'm too old to lay beside my father," Bernard grumbled.

"Oh, come on, Bernard, just one puzzle," Mr. Charleston patted the bed.

Bernard sighed but I felt that he was secretly happy to get his father's attention.

I laid beside Bernard. Bernard was in the middle, and I put my head on his chest while Mr. Charleston called out puzzle hints. Bernard and I called out answers and Mr. Charleston wrote them down. We lost track of time and did many more than one puzzle. Bernard laid on his back and wrapped his arm around me. I held his hand and happily melted into his embrace. I missed Bernard. I wanted him to be nice to me again like when we were younger.

Bernard pulled me over his body and put me between him and his father. He wrapped both arms around me tightly and pulled me into him. Mr. Charleston smiled at us and kissed Bernard's forehead, which surprised both me and Bernard. "I'm sorry I spent more time working than being with you," he spoke softly to Bernard. "I don't know how to make it up to you. Maybe you can help me learn, Bernard. I love you. I never realized how a father was supposed to show love until I saw Maybel and Catherine with their father. I just want you to know, Bernard, that I love you and I'm sorry I've never known how to be the father you deserve."

There was silence and I watched the pain in Mr. Charleston's face. I turned my head to look at Bernard behind me. He cried silent tears. I turned my body around to face Bernard and I hugged him with all my strength. "Thank you," Bernard whispered to his father, and to me.

I felt Mr. Charleston behind me wrap his arms around me and Bernard, hugging us both. Mr. Charleston then asked if he could make us a sandwich. "I don't know how to cook, Bernard, but I'll do my best."

Bernard smiled, "Thank you."

We went downstairs and Bernard and I sat next to each other at the kitchen table while Mr. Charleston tried to figure out where the bread and knives were kept. He opened drawer after drawer looking.

Mrs. Charleston came into the kitchen looking amused as she watched Bernard and me sitting at the table while her husband looked completely lost in the kitchen.

She smiled and opened a drawer and handed a knife to Mr. Charleston. "Yes, there it is! Thank you, sweetheart!" he kissed her cheek and she giggled.

"May I watch the show, too?" She sat next to Bernard at the table.

"Alright then, bread. Where are you, bread?" Mr. Charleston wondered aloud.

We giggled at Mr. Charleston. "Try the upper left cabinet," Mrs. Charleston laughed and squeezed Bernard's hand.

"Ah! Found you, bread!" he exclaimed, then pulled the bread out and showed us like he had just won a prize.

We laughed and watched Mr. Charleston try very hard to do his best making sandwiches for all of us. Bernard's smile looked like a little boy's smile.

"Bernard how is school going?" Mr. Charleston asked after he sat down to join us at the kitchen table.

"It's going well," he answered. Bernard happily bit into his sandwich like it was the most amazing sandwich that had ever been made.

"And how are you and Catherine doing?"

"We are fine," Bernard answered.

"Marriage and grandchild soon?" Mr. Charleston winked at Mrs. Charleston.

"No," Bernard laughed, "I want to have my medical practice established first so I can spend more time with my family."

Mr. Charleston looked suddenly sad. "I should have done the same," he said quietly.

"I like what we're doing now, father." Bernard quickly said. "I like this. Can we have sandwiches together every afternoon, or even once a week?"

"Yes," Mr. Charleston smiled. "I didn't know you liked sandwiches that much," he chuckled.

"I don't care what we eat. All I've ever wanted was to eat a meal together every night like Maybel does with her family," Bernard said.

"I want that too, Bernard," Mr. Charleston smiled, and took Mrs. Charleston's hand. "What do you think, honey? New beginnings?"

"Yes," she smiled. "I would very much like to eat with you every day."

"If I cut back on my business dealings, Bernard, we won't be doing as much traveling, we'll wear less expensive clothing, have less parties, and we'll be making a lot of cutbacks," Mr. Charleston warned.

"Nothing would make me happier, father."

"Alright then," Mr. Charleston smiled. He held Mrs. Charleston's hand to his mouth and kissed it. Mrs. Charleston smiled and looked very happy. No one was happier than Bernard though.

"What shall we do together this evening?" Mr. Charleston pulled his wife onto his lap and she giggled and kissed him.

"I honestly don't care as long as we're together," Bernard said.

I picked up my sandwich and stood up. "I'm happy for you, Bernard. Enjoy your parents," I smiled.

"Where are you going?" Bernard looked confused.

"You finally get to spend time with your parents. I am letting you have them both to yourself," I told him.

"Stay, Maybel. I don't want you to go." Bernard took my arm and pulled me back into my chair.

"Are you sure?" I asked. "You can finally spend time with your parents and I'm leaving you alone and not pestering you," I said.

"Stay, Maybel." Bernard said firmly.

"What's for dessert?" I asked.

"What do you want?" Bernard asked.

"That's a good answer. You'll make a fine husband," I said.

Bernard smiled, "Cake, cookies, or custard?"

My eyes widened, "That's the perfect name for a dessert store! Three C's! Cakes, cookies, and custard!"

"I'm taking a break from business," Mr. Charleston said, "but if you ever want to start another business together like the barbershop, Bernard, that would be a great name."

"It would," Bernard agreed. "What color would the building be, Maybel?"

"Pink of course," I said.

"Men don't want to dine in a pink store," Bernard disagreed.

"Oh, they will. It will be designed for young women as a safe and affordable place to meet their boyfriends after school. You may not want to go to a girly pink store, but you would, because it will be marketed toward young ladies who will be spending time there. You will go wherever the girls go, Bernard, and the girls want pink."

Mr. Charleston laughed, "You see, this is why I love how your mind works, Maybel!"

"I suppose you make a good point, Maybel," Bernard conceded. "I don't want to do business with you right now though, father. I want to spend time with you fishing and shooting bows and arrows, and not doing business."

"You know how to shoot bows and arrows too?" I asked Bernard.

"Yes. Who else do you know that can shoot bows and arrows?" Bernard asked me, surprised.

"Henry. He taught me," I answered.

Bernard frowned, "You've been spending time with Henry?"

"Yes, he's nice, and he doesn't yell at me to go away like you do," I said to Bernard.

"Does your father know you've been spending time with Henry? I cannot believe he would allow you and Henry to spend time together."

"Yes, he knows."

"Unbelievable," Bernard said.

"Henry's nice," I said. "He comes over almost every evening to help daddy in his workshop."

"Ok, Maybel, after lunch, let's go shoot bows and arrows. You're coming right, father?"

"Yes, Bernard, I'm all yours, son."

Bernard smiled, "I like this, father. Thank you."

"I like this too, son."

"Are you sure you want me to tag along, Bernard?" I asked him as we walked out back with bows and arrows.

"Yes, Maybel," Bernard said.

"That fence post is our target," Bernard pointed. "You can walk closer when it's your turn, Maybel."

"No need," I said.

Bernard laughed, "Ok, Maybel," he said smugly.

Bernard shot first and hit the fence post easily. His father and mother both hit it too.

"Your turn, Maybel," Bernard tickled my ribs. "Let's see how well you do."

"Ok, Bernard!" I chirped happily and easily hit the post.

The look on Bernard's face made me happy. He was more than a little surprised.

"Looks like we have ourselves a worthy opponent," Mrs. Charleston wrapped her arm around my waist and smiled at me.

"We could make a bet?" I winked at Mr. Charleston.

"You don't have any money to bet!" Bernard laughed.

"Neither do you now that your father has given up working constantly!" I laughed.

"Fine, Maybel, loser makes dinner tonight," Bernard said smugly.

"I don't know how to make dinner," Mr. Charleston said.

"Well then, you should be on the winning team, father. Who is your partner?" Bernard asked with a sly smile.

"Me!" Mrs. Charleston smiled at Bernard. "Mommy and daddy want steak, potatoes, green beans, and cake tonight."

Bernard smiled, "Ok, mommy, it's a bet!"

"You haven't called me mommy in years," she smiled.

Bernard suddenly blushed. "Maybel has perhaps influenced me," Bernard squeezed my arm playfully.

"Maybel has been a very good influence on our family," Mrs. Charleston patted my arm. "Now let's see if you are still a good aim, Bernard." She playfully winked at her son.

"I like my steak medium-well," he smiled and winked back at his mother.

"Well, you'll be cooking it, honey," Mrs. Charleston laughed, "so you cook your steak however you want it."

Mr. Charleston laughed, "Either way, I get steak, so I'm happy!"

Bernard stood behind me. "Hold here instead. This will give you better accuracy."

"Put your legs apart a little more," Bernard held my thigh and pulled it a little to the side and back. "You'll have better balance."

I shot my arrow and it did go farther with more accuracy.

Mr. Charleston chuckled and stood in front of his wife. "Can you adjust my legs, honey? I don't think I'm standing correctly."

Mrs. Charleston giggled and playfully slapped her husband's arm.

"Don't be afraid to grab hold firmly and pull my leg wherever it needs to go to help me maintain my balance." Mr. and Mrs. Charleston laughed and playfully touched each other. Their playful banter was catching and I saw Bernard smiling happily at his parents.

"You're actually pretty good with a bow and arrow," Bernard told me.

"I'm better than Catherine, but not as good as you."

"Catherine knows how to shoot a bow and arrow?" Bernard asked, surprised.

"Yes, she does ok, but mommy's better than her, and I'm better than them both. Daddy's pretty good."

"All of you know how to use a bow and arrow? How?" Bernard looked confused.

"Henry," I said.

"How much time does Henry spend with you?" Bernard looked concerned.

"He often picks me up at school and eats dinner with us, then helps me with math. Mommy likes when he comes over because Henry helps with dishes and daddy likes when Henry helps build furniture for rich people."

Bernard looked really sad. "Father, I'm not going to boarding school anymore. I'm staying home, and I'm eating dinner every night with you and mother."

"Bernard, your boarding school gives you the education you will need for college," Mr. Charleston protested.

"I'm not going back to boarding school. I'll get a tutor if need be," Bernard said.

"Tutors cost money, and I won't be working as much," Mr. Charleston countered.

"Then I won't go to college. I'll either learn how to be a businessman from you, or how to make expensive furniture for rich people from Maybel's father."

"You've always dreamed of being a doctor," Mr. Charleston said.

"I've always dreamed of having a family. I want a family. I don't care about anything else," Bernard replied.

Bernard was resolute. Mr. Charleston didn't argue with him either, which completely shocked me.

"We'll try it your way, Bernard, and if it doesn't suit, we'll figure something else out," Mr. Charleston held Bernard's shoulder.

Bernard seemed shocked too.

"Thank you," he whispered, stunned at how easily his father gave in to Bernard's desire to quit everything they'd been working toward to build a wealthy empire and social status.

"Your mother and I won our bow and arrow bet, but I'd like to help you make dinner, Bernard. What do you think, honey?" He squeezed Mrs. Charleston's waist.

"I think I've never been happier to cook," Mrs. Charleston smiled so sweetly up at her husband.

Bernard reluctantly returned to boarding school after his parents promised to have Saturday dinners with him at school, and some Fridays, when Mr. Charleston did not have to work. Mommy said Mrs. Charleston said that Bernard hated being away from home and sometimes became withdrawn and sullen. Consequently, Mrs. Charleston asked mommy for a favor. Mr. and Mrs. Charleston wanted to take Catherine and me to visit Bernard to cheer him up and out of his sadness.

Saturday arrived, and I bounced into Catherine's bedroom. "Wakey, wakey! Rise and shakey!" I jumped on her bed and stuck my face in her barely awake face.

"I'm awake," Catherine mumbled.

"I'm taking you somewhere today! Remember you promised to spend the day with me?" I excitedly hugged her.

"Where are we going?" Catherine asked as she wiped drool from her lips.

"Mr. and Mrs. Charleston are taking us!" I said.

"Where?" Catherine opened her eyes wide enough to clearly focus on me.

"It's a surprise!" I giggled.

"No, thank you." Catherine closed her eyes again.

"We're going to spend the night at the house Mr. Charleston bought for Bernard!" I couldn't contain my giddiness any longer.

"Does Bernard know we're coming?" Catherine yawned.

"No. It was supposed to be a surprise for you both but I can't keep surprises!"

"I'll get dressed," Catherine said sleepily. I expected her to be more enthusiastic.

Catherine came downstairs polished to perfection in pink. I wore a plain blue dress because there was no point trying to compete with Catherine when it came to looking like a calendar model.

Mr. and Mrs. Charleston came to our house and we took their automobile because it was faster. Mrs. Charleston greeted us warmly. She wore a beautiful pale green and white dress and a matching green hat. Emeralds dangled from her ears. Daddy's eyes took too long admiring her beauty, I thought. He averted his eyes the moment he heard mommy open the front door.

Mommy kissed Mrs. Charleston's cheek and gave her a basket of bread and jam. Mr. Charleston politely kissed mommy's cheek. Daddy did not kiss Mrs. Charleston's cheek. He seemed awkward and only politely nodded at the Charleston's.

The automobile allowed us to reach Bernard faster, thus allowing us more time to spend with him. Mr. Charleston found a place for his automobile amongst the bushes of the school's campus. We walked inside and down a long corridor. Boys milled about and became very interested in us as we passed, more specifically, they were interested in Catherine, and maybe a little bit in me.

Mr. Charleston knocked on Bernard's door and Catherine and I hid on either side in the hallway. He opened his door and smiled at his parents then Catherine and I jumped out and hugged Bernard. We giggled and laughed and Bernard looked surprised and very happy to see us.

Boys had come out of their dormitory rooms and stood watching. There were whispers and chuckles as the boys watched Catherine kiss Bernard. Catherine liked the attention because she held onto Bernard's waist and kissed him again to louder jeers and laughter.

Bernard grabbed a small bag he had ready by the door and we left back down the hallway. Catherine held Bernard's hand and enjoyed looking straight ahead pretending to ignore and be unaware of all the boys' eyes watching her hips sway as she walked.

We walked to Bernard's house. Mr. Charleston bought Bernard a house where they could spend their Friday nights and Saturdays together. I could not fathom being rich enough to buy a house simply to have a place to dine once or twice a week. It was very near to Bernard's boarding school, and we easily arrived in only several minutes. A white, picket fence surrounded a small and beautiful, wooden home. The house was painted white and the trim was a dark blue. The large oak tree had a swing hanging from its branch. I immediately loved this small and perfect home.

Inside the kitchen, there were clean, white countertops, and the cabinets were new. "Daddy made these cabinets!" I smiled. "I helped him!"

"Yes, Maybel, he does great work!" Mr. Charleston smiled. "And so do you, sweetheart! Your father drove my company's truck and installed them with my lovely wife's help." Mr. Charleston kissed Mrs. Charleston's cheek.

"Why didn't you come too?" I asked.

"I was in the city with Henry that day looking for new business prospects," Mr. Charleston said.

"Maybel, would you like to go to the market with me?" Mrs. Charleston asked. "Bernard and Catherine can catch up while we purchase our food. I have a new recipe for fish I want to try."

"Mother has been learning to cook more." Bernard hugged his mother tightly and kissed her cheek.

"And father and I talk about his childhood and my future as a doctor." Bernard hugged his father and I realized I either had never seen them hug, or I couldn't remember seeing them hug before now.

Bernard and Catherine sat in the family room with Mr. Charleston while Mrs. Charleston and I walked to the market. The quaint little grocer's store was in the town square.

"Every man we passed stared at you," I told Mrs. Charleston. "You're really pretty."

Mrs. Charleston smiled, "Thank you, dear. You are quite beautiful, too."

"Nobody stared at me."

"Oh, but they do, honey," she winked at me.

Inside the store, a short, jovial man greeted us. "Ah, Mrs. Charleston, good to see you again. How may I help you?"

"Good day, Mr. Sutterly, have you any fish? I'm trying a new recipe."

"Certainly, Mrs. Charleston, cod or salmon?"

"Cod, please. Lettuce and potatoes too, Mr. Sutterly, and carrots and tomatoes, thank you."

Mrs. Charleston paid with a hundred-dollar bill and Mr. Sutterly had to run across the town square to the bank to make change.

Mr. Sutterly returned with Mrs. Charleston's change and we walked back to Bernard's house.

"I'm afraid I have never cooked much," Mrs. Charleston smiled shyly at me. "Bernard wants us to have family meals every Friday and Saturday night, so I am really trying to learn."

"I've never seen Bernard happier," I said. "I don't even remember seeing him hug his father before today."

"Yes, we're getting closer as a family," Mrs. Charleston smiled. "We are grateful to you, Maybel, and your family, for showing us how a family is supposed to be. I suppose Mr. Charleston's parents were busy making money, and Mr. Charleston never knew a family was supposed to hug and cuddle on the sofa and read together at night. And then he watched your father with you and Catherine, and I think he realized how much he had missed as a boy, and how much Bernard had missed."

"Did your family hug and read together at night?" I asked her.

"Maybe sometimes, but father was often hunting and farming and mother worked quite hard helping him. We were close, but perhaps we could have been closer."

"Well, you're closer to Bernard now, and Bernard seems the happiest I've ever seen him. I watched Bernard sit next to his father on the sofa and they laughed as they talked."

"Yes," Mrs. Charleston smiled. "I'm the happiest I've ever been too," she hugged me.

We sat down to dinner and ate Mrs. Charleston's new recipe of fish in a creamy sauce. It tasted like I missed my mother's cooking.

After dinner I washed dishes with Catherine then Catherine brewed coffee. "Maybel, will you take this cup to Mrs. Charleston and I'll find sugar for Mr. Charleston and be in shortly?"

I took Mrs. Charleston her coffee. "Catherine is getting sugar for yours," I told Mr. Charleston.

I sat beside Mr. Charleston and Bernard sat with his mother. Mr. Charleston put his arm around my shoulder. "What do you think, Maybel? Do you like this house?"

"Yes," I replied. "I love it. It has a swing in the yard, too!"

"Ah, I just knew that would be your favorite thing about this place!" he squeezed my shoulder.

Catherine came in with Mr. Charleston's coffee, then sat in a chair beside Bernard. She reached over and rested her hand on his. Bernard smiled at Catherine.

"May I go swing now?" I asked Mr. Charleston. "It's a pretty swing in a pretty oak tree."

"Of course, sweetheart," Mr. Charleston said.

Outside, the evening breeze felt good and I swung high. A girl's head peeked over the fence. She had strawberry blond hair and freckles.

"Do you live here now?" She called to me.

"No, just visiting a friend," I replied.

"The handsome boy that comes on the weekend?" she giggled.

"Yes," I giggled back. "He's my sister's boyfriend."

"Do you want to go do something together?" she asked me.

"Sure, let me ask his parents. Wait, what's your name? Mine's Maybel."

"Mine's Sally. I live next door."

"Ok, I'll be right back." I jumped off the swing and ran inside.

Catherine sat with Bernard's parents and they were conversing about Catherine's desire to become a school teacher. Bernard was in the bathroom.

I asked the Charlestons, and they allowed me to go as long as I didn't walk too far away and returned by dusk.

I went to Sally's house next door and met her parents and brother. They were plainly dressed like my parents, but they talked funny.

Sally asked me to walk around town and I was excited to do something other than sit amongst the proper and polished Charlestons and prim Catherine.

"Why do your parents sound different?" I asked Sally as we walked along the perimeter of Bernard's boarding school.

"They were born in England," she answered.

"Oh," I said. "Have they met any kings or queens?" I asked.

"Yes," she said. "I haven't though. I was born here. I've never met my English grandparents either. Mum says they're dead but they aren't. That's just what she says. She says 'dead' and 'dead to me' have vastly different meanings."

"Oh," I said. I wasn't sure what to say next.

"That's the rich boys' school," Sally pointed to Bernard's boarding school. "Sometimes the boys sneak out at night. My brother and I have seen them around town sometimes. They're not supposed to leave their school grounds but they do."

"What do they do when they escape?" I asked curiously.

"They come to our poor kids' school dances," she giggled. "We're not really poor, but compared to them we are. That boy next door, the one your sister is dating, I've seen him around too. He came to my school's dance last year and danced with my friend Jessica."

"Oh? Do tell!" I said.

"Wait, how long has your sister been dating that boy? I don't want to start a fight," she said.

"Oh not long," I lied. "You can tell me. I won't tell my sister," I lied again.

"Ok, well Jessica said he was a really good dancer and had a smooth voice and the most beautiful eyes she'd ever seen."

"He's ok, I guess," I said, trying not to sound too interested in Sally's extremely interesting gossip.

"What did he say to her?" I asked.

"She asked him if he would like to kiss her but he said no. She asked if he had a girlfriend and he said no, so Jessica got mad that he didn't want to kiss her. She thought he probably only wanted to kiss rich girls. Are you rich?"

"No, definitely not," I laughed.

"Your sister looked rich," Sally said.

"My sister likes to play dress up and pretend she has money," I laughed.

"Well anyway, that's all I know about your friend. He's handsome, dances well, and was not attracted to my friend Jessica."

"Have you ever seen him kiss anyone?" I asked.

"You want to know if he cheats?" Sally smiled slyly.

"Yes," I said.

"I haven't seen him kiss anyone," Sally said. "The boys he comes to dances with like to kiss girls around town, and girls want to kiss them too because they think they'll be the next Mrs. Rich. But they never are. The boys eventually graduate and leave and never return as they promised. That's why I don't dance with them. They lie and promise castles for sex, then disappear with notches on their belts marking all the virginities they've taken."

My eyes widened.

"Look, there are some of the rich boys now," Sally pointed to boys walking toward town.

"I don't want to talk to them! They sound horrible!" I said. "Let's go somewhere else."

"So you don't want to sneak into their dormitory?" Sally again smiled slyly.

"We can do that?" I asked, intrigued.

"Yes, the older boys are supposed to watch over the younger ones, but they don't care if rules are broken so long as fun is had. They let girls inside. And the teachers don't tell the parents because then the parents won't pay their expensive tuitions."

"Ok, maybe just walk in and out real quick," I said. "But I don't want to do anything too naughty, and I have to be back by dusk."

"Ok," Sally smiled like a sly fox.

We entered the side door and walked down the hallway. "Hello, Sally, who's your friend?" a boy passing by asked.

"I know who she is," another boy said, peaking his head out of his room. "You were here visiting Bernard, weren't you?"

"Yes," I said, my voice a hair above a whisper.

"Are you his girlfriend?"

"No," I said.

"Well then, would you like some special drinks?" he winked at Sally.

Sally smiled at me.

"No," I said. "I have to go back now. Nice meeting you. Goodbye." I turned and walked quickly back toward the side door.

Sally ran to catch up to me. "Wait," she tugged my arm, "it's just one drink. We have plenty of time before dusk."

"I'll walk you home," a voice said. A nice-looking boy came out of his room and put his hand on my shoulder and pushed me gently toward the door.

Sally stayed behind. I walked faster so the boy wouldn't touch my shoulder. Outside, he told me to stay away from the boarding school. "Not everyone is bad, but you did meet some bad students just now," the boy said. "It's best you stay with Bernard."

I kept my head down and walked fast enough that he was a safe distance behind me. I ran inside the Charleston's house and sat on the sofa next to Bernard where I felt safe.

"Are you ok?" Bernard looked concerned.

"Yes," I said.

There was a knock on the door and Mr. Charleston answered. It was the boy who saved me from that strange situation in the boarding school. "I was making sure your friend arrived safely," the boy told Bernard.

"Where were you?" Bernard asked.

"Sally took me to your dormitory but I left almost immediately because it felt strange being there with all those boys," I said.

Bernard looked angry. He looked at the boy standing at the front door expectantly.

"Everything is fine," the boy said. "Your friend here wanted to leave and I made sure she arrived here safely."

"Thank you, Tom," Bernard said.

Tom left and Bernard looked angrily at me. "Don't ever do that again!"

"We walked in, I felt like all the boys were staring at me, I wanted to leave, and that boy Tom followed me home. He said he was your friend."

"He is. Did anyone touch you, hurt you, or make any untoward comments?" Bernard asked me.

"No," I said. "I walked in, didn't like being surrounded by boys, then left."

"How do you always find trouble?" Bernard asked me.

"I don't! Trouble finds me! I was swinging in the yard and that girl wanted to walk around town with me."

"Stay right here beside me, Maybel." Bernard's brow was furrowed.

"Yes, father," I said sarcastically, then folded my arms.

"I don't know how your father has maintained his sanity," Bernard looked at me.

"I told you already, he drinks special cider!" I replied.

Mr. and Mrs. Charleston laughed but Bernard did not.

That night, Catherine and I shared a bed. We laid together talking. "What was the dormitory like," Catherine whispered.

"Too many boys staring at me. I felt uncomfortable. One boy asked if Sally and I wanted special drinks. That's when I turned and left."

"I want to see what it's like inside the dormitory when parents are not around. I'm curious," Catherine said.

"Don't be. It was strange," I told her.

"They let you walk inside? Nobody tried to stop you?" Catherine looked curious.

"Nobody was at the side door. Sally said the boys are not well-monitored."

"I wonder how many local girls walk in and flirt with Bernard?" Catherine mused.

"Sally said Bernard doesn't kiss any girls. He doesn't cheat, Catherine," I assured her.

Catherine turned on her side and adjusted her pillow.

"Catherine," I whispered, "I won't tell mommy or daddy if you want to go lay in bed with Bernard and do some flirting of your own," I giggled. I nudged her foot under the covers with my foot.

"No, Maybel, I don't do those things," Catherine whispered back.

I started to drift off to sleep when Catherine said, "Maybel, will you come with me?"

"Where?" I mumbled.

"To Bernard's bed. If we get caught kissing, and you're there, we can just say we were telling ghost stories or something."

"I don't want to lay next to you while you make noises!" I protested.

"I only kiss Bernard! We don't do other things!" Catherine said.

"Can I narrate you kissing Bernard?" I asked.

"What?" Catherine's voice sounded confused.

"Like the narrator in a play." I changed my voice to sound theatrical. "And here we see young Bernard kiss Catherine hard on her pretty, rose petal lips and that's not all that's hard," I giggled loudly.

"Shh! The Charlestons will hear you!" Catherine giggled softly.

"I doubt that. I saw Mr. Charleston cup Mrs. Charleston's bottom on their way to bed and she giggled. They're probably in bed now trying to make Bernard a big brother!" I giggled into Catherine's ear and she smacked me away with her pillow.

"Shh!" Catherine giggled, "You are so naughty, Maybel!"

"I learned from my mentor." I leaned into her ear again and whispered, "You Catherine! You are my mentor!"

Catherine giggled

"My professor of all things naughty," I laughed. "I am your clay and you are my sculptor! Make me as good at lying to daddy as you!" I giggled into her ear.

"Well first of all, Maybel, you need to learn how to do The Face. The Face will get you anything you want. You hold daddy's hand like this," Catherine intertwined her fingers in mine, "and then pout your lips just a little."

I pouted.

"No, that's too much," she directed me. "It has to be subtle. And then make your eyes look sad, but hopeful. Think about how a fawn's eyes look."

I tried my best.

"Oh, no, no, no, Maybel!" Catherine laughed hard. "You look like you just pooped in your underwear!" She laughed so hard she cried.

The door opened. "What's so funny?" Bernard asked. He closed the door and sat on the bed.

"Nothing!" we giggled.

"Maybel? Are you ok?" Bernard looked concerned at me.

Catherine turned to look at me and saw me attempting The Face again and started laughing hysterically.

"If I looked at you like this, Bernard, would you give me whatever I wanted?" I batted my lashes.

"As long as what you wanted was toilet paper, then yes," he said.

Tears streamed down Catherine's face, she laughed so hard.

"Can I stay here tonight?" Bernard asked. "I'm lonely in my room listening to you two having fun."

"Your parents would be so mad at all of us!" I said.

"I'll sleep on the floor." Bernard laid next to the bed.

"I'll sleep beside you," Catherine smiled.

"I get the whole bed to myself?" I smiled widely.

Bernard and Catherine laid next to each other on the floor whispering and giggling.

"Now I feel lonely," I whined. "What are you two talking about?"

"Actually, we were talking about dinner," Bernard whispered. "We didn't care much for it, but don't tell my parents. I really appreciate that my mother and father are trying so hard to ensure we dine together at least once a week."

I laid on the floor next to Bernard. "I want to be in the conversation too," I pouted.

"Alright, Maybel," Bernard sighed, annoyed at me. He laid on his back and Catherine and I curled up on either side of his chest.

"Tell us a scary story, Maybel," Catherine whispered.

"I have the perfect story," I began. "It's about a captivating witch at a school dance named Jessica."

Bernard pinched my arm.

"Yes, Bernard? Do you have something you would like to add?" I asked playfully.

"No, Maybel, I do not." Bernard poked my ribs as if to beg me not to say anything too detailed that could be incriminating.

I continued my story. "The witch kissed a boy named Bertram," I said.

"She most certainly did not!" Bernard poked my ribs again.

"Have you told this story before, Maybel?" Catherine asked.

"Hmm? No. I just thought of it tonight."

"This witch Jessica said that Bertram had a small penis and was dreadful in bed."

Catherine laughed.

"Bertram would never touch that witch or any other witches, and Bertram is quite well-endowed, Maybel, get your story straight!" Bernard began tickling my ribs.

"Stop, I'm going to pee!" I laughed.

Bernard continued tickling me. "I'm going to pee!" I whined.

"Go pee, Maybel!" Bernard stopped tickling me.

"Haha, I lied, I don't have to pee," I giggled.

Bernard reached down and playfully spanked my bottom.

"Ow!" I laughed.

Bernard rolled over to face Catherine. "Storytime is over," he held Catherine and kissed her.

"I can hear your lips smacking," I complained.

They continued kissing and laughing softly. "I'm sleeping in Bernard's room!" I said and left.

I laid down on Bernard's bed and picked up the book he had been reading. It was handwritten. I was surprised to see it was Bernard's handwriting in a journal he was writing. I read his latest entry.

"Maybel and Catherine came today, along with mother and father. I wanted to kiss Maybel. Catherine kissed me instead. I watched Maybel swinging outside and her dress fluttered up her thighs. I got hard and had to go to the bathroom to relieve myself. I know I shouldn't have such thoughts about her, but I do. I get hard whenever she sits or lays beside me. I turn away from Maybel, and kiss Catherine, and pretend Catherine was the one who made me hard. I want to kiss Maybel, but she only thinks of me as a brother. Every time I see Maybel though, I want to lay on top of her naked body and watch her come underneath me."

I slammed the book shut and put it exactly as I had found it on his bed. If I stay here, Bernard will know I had to touch the book in order to set it on his nightstand and he'll wonder if I read his journal. I reasoned that if I went back to bed with Catherine, I could say I walked into Bernard's bedroom and suddenly turned around and went back to bed with Catherine because I was lonely. I'd been in here too long to have immediately turned around and left, though, I realized. That will sound suspicious. I paced the floor trying to think of a way to make it look like I didn't see his journal there. I'll say I sat on the end of the bed, realized I needed more blankets, then got up and left before getting in bed. That's plausible.

I went to the door and was about to open it when Bernard opened it and looked nervously at me then glanced at his journal on his bed.

"Oh, I was just giving you some time to kiss Catherine, and then I was going to get back into bed with Catherine, and you can sleep in your bed rather than on the floor."

I started past Bernard but he grabbed my waist firmly and pushed me back in front of him so that we faced each other. "Maybel, everything ok?"

"Yes, why?" I spoke quickly, probably too quickly.

"Are you upset about something?" he watched me closely.

"No, why would I be upset? I've had a good day here." Again, I spoke fast and high-pitched.

Bernard scanned my face. "Goodnight, Maybel," he said and let go of my waist.

"Goodnight, Bernard," I looked down. I knew my eyes would betray me so I kept my eyes averted.

Bernard then cupped my chin and slowly leaned down to kiss my cheek, but I turned my face a little and kissed his lips. Bernard then held my face with both hands and kissed me. We stared at each other for a moment. I continued past him and returned to bed with Catherine.

"Why did Bernard leave?" I asked her.

"He suddenly got up and said he needed to check on you to make sure you had enough blankets," Catherine said, annoyed.

"Sorry, Catherine. You can go to his bed and I'll stay here."

"No, I'm tired," she said with annoyance. "Let's go to sleep."

I rolled over and stared at the wall a long time before I could fall asleep.

Catherine and her friends were at our house studying one evening. Handsome Henry was in the workshop with daddy, and mommy was buzzing around the house like a hummingbird serving drinks and cookies.

Bernard was sitting beside Catherine, and Edith and Arnold were sitting together. Several other boys and girls were at Catherine's study group.

I felt really young next to everyone. They ignored me because I was Catherine's little sister. I sat with them anyway because they fascinated me. A couple of the boys were handsome and I stared at them. Bernard threw a wad of paper at my head. He made a motion for me to unwrap it.

"Stop staring at boys!" it read.

I wrote back, "They're more handsome than you!" then threw it and hit his head with my crumpled wad of paper.

"Maybel, your sweater is on inside out," Catherine said to me.

I looked down. I wore Catherine's old cream-colored sweater. Mommy made me put on one of Catherine's old bras earlier because she said my breasts were getting too big to not wear bras. I hated bras. They were tight and itchy.

I started to take off my sweater to turn it right side in but Catherine yelled at me. "Not here! Go upstairs!"

"I have a shirt on underneath!" I yelled back.

"Go upstairs!" Catherine yelled again.

"Fine!" I yelled and stomped toward the stairs.

"Brush your hair and put something on your chapped lips!" Catherine yelled after me.

Her friends laughed and I blushed from embarrassment and anger.

I went upstairs to fix my sweater and looked at myself in the bathroom mirror. My lips were dry and chapped. I put a dab of lip softener on my lips and brushed my hair up and into a pretty hair clip.

Instead of returning to Catherine, I went to see daddy. He and Henry were sitting and talking, rather than working.

"Hello, sweetheart," daddy said. "Are Catherine's friends still here?"

"Yes."

"What brings you out here to see me?" daddy smiled.

I leaned against a pile of wood. "Catherine embarrassed me in front of her friends by saying I needed to go brush my hair and put something on my chapped lips."

"Well, you look beautiful honey," daddy said.

"Thank you, daddy."

"Hello, Maybel," Henry said.

"Hello," I said.

"Why don't you sit here with us?" daddy offered.

"What's the topic of conversation tonight?" I asked.

"Oak or walnut." Daddy rubbed his palms together looking happy.

I sighed, "I'll go back to Catherine."

"You're a cat, Maybel," daddy laughed. "You come out here to see what I'm doing, then you go back inside, never staying long enough for me to pet you."

"I'll let you scratch behind my ears later, daddy."

Daddy chuckled, "Very well."

I returned to the dining room table. Bernard watched me enter the room. He put his arm around Catherine's shoulder.

I sat down next to one of the handsome boys. The conversation about history was boring but at least the view was nice. The boy next to me had black hair and brown eyes. He wore a red shirt and brown pants. I was mostly fascinated by how his hair was perfectly combed. Not a hair was out of place. People with perfect hair fascinated me because my hair was unruly.

He smiled at me. My heartbeat skipped.

"Would you like a cookie?" He offered me one of mommy's cookies.

I accepted it and smiled back.

"I've seen you around school," he winked at me.

I giggled like an idiot.

"I'll save you a seat at lunch," he smiled.

I giggled again. I couldn't speak because I was so awkward.

All the boys and girls were talking more than studying.

"Would you like to go for a walk after studying?" he whispered to me.

I smiled, "Yes."

He smiled back, "I'm Tommy," he said.

"Maybel," I said.

"I know who you are," he winked. "You're the reason I came here tonight."

I blushed.

"Maybel," Henry called from the dining room doorway. "Your father needs your help in his workshop."

I groaned. I stood up and followed Henry. When we were outside, I whined, "Henry you interrupted my flirting. That boy likes me."

"I know. That's why I interrupted," Henry said.

"What? Why?" I stopped walking.

Henry turned to face me, "I saw him flirting with you and I didn't like it."

"I already have someone who acts like my big brother. His name is Bernard, and he is annoying."

"You'll thank me later," Henry said.

"I will not!"

I turned around on my heel but Henry caught my arm. "I recognize a boy who wants to take advantage of you. I know that's what he would do."

"Henry! Why are you acting like Bernard? You're supposed to be fun! Please don't turn into an annoying, big brother like Bernard!"

"Maybel, I do not like that boy. Do not talk to him anymore or I'll involve your father."

I could not believe Henry's audacity. I shook my arm free and spun around to leave but Henry again grabbed me. He pulled me close. "Maybel, you don't realize how much you've changed recently. Boys are noticing you more every day. Your body has changed. I used to be one of those boys like that boy inside flirting with you. He's no good."

"You're good, Henry."

Henry sighed, "No I'm not, Maybel, believe me, I'm not. Can you please just stay out here with your father and me tonight?"

"Bernard is inside. Bernard doesn't care that I'm talking to that boy and usually Bernard is the one acting like you are now."

"Stay here with your father and me, please?"

"Fine!" I stomped my foot and growled.

I stayed in daddy's workshop. I sat on a stool with my arms folded.

"Why is my kitten extra hissy tonight?" daddy asked as he inspected a jar of screws.

"Henry didn't like the boy who was talking to me inside."

Daddy smiled, "I like you more and more each day, Henry."

"It's not fair," I pouted. "Catherine can have a boyfriend, why can't I?"

"Well, if it were up to me, neither of you would have boyfriends, but mommy says I have to let you two grow up."

"He's a nice boy," I said.

"I trust Henry's judgement. If Henry sensed something about this boy, I trust the boy isn't a good match for you." Daddy picked out a screw that was to his liking from the jar.

"I should be allowed to decide," I said. I felt anger at Henry and daddy.

"Very well, then, Maybel, go back and sit with this boy. I'll let you decide." Daddy plucked another screw from his glass jar.

I stood up quickly before daddy could change his mind, and before Henry could change daddy's mind.

I returned to my seat next to Tommy. Everyone was now studying math. I sat back in my seat hoping the math part of this study session would be over quickly.

Tommy passed me a note. "Have you ever been kissed?" it read.

I wrote back that I had.

Tommy smiled. He wrote a note saying he was looking forward to our walk together.

I thought to myself that just because I'd kissed a boy didn't mean I'd kiss him, and his forwardness made him less attractive.

I wrote back that I had to finish helping my daddy cut and sand a cabinet and then I returned to daddy's workshop.

"Hello kitty cat, you seem less hissy," daddy smiled at me.

"I wanted to hear more about the oak versus walnut debate," I said with a furrowed brow and my arms crossed. I did not like that Henry had been right.

Daddy smiled, "I'm glad."

I angrily plopped down onto the apple crate sitting next to daddy and Henry. My brows were still squinched together and my arms still folded angrily. Daddy took two boards from a stack and put them side by side. "Oak is the strongest. I'm partial to walnut for decorative purposes."

I sighed and slunk down on the apple crate where I sat. I stayed with daddy and Henry until Bernard came into daddy's workshop looking for me.

"Catherine wanted to know where you'd gone," Bernard said.

"Henry didn't like that boy, so I stayed here," I muttered.

"They've all gone home," Bernard said.

"Daddy, how many more stories about oak and walnut are there?" I asked.

"You may go inside if you wish," daddy chuckled.

Bernard walked back to my house with me. He put his hand gently on my shoulder and stopped walking. "Henry was jealous of that boy, Maybel. I could tell."

"Henry's old and doesn't care who flirts with me. He has a hundred girls around him at every party your parents host."

"That may be, but he likes you."

"Do you like me, Bernard?"

"Yes, Maybel. I like you very much."

"Are you going to kiss me?"

Bernard looked surprised at my candor.

"Neither will Henry kiss me," I said, and walked inside.

"Maybel, who have you been kissing?" Catherine asked the instant I opened the kitchen door.

"What? Nobody," I told her.

"Tommy told Samuel that you said you'd been kissed, and Samuel told Rebecca, who told me."

"Who have you been kissing?" Bernard asked. He looked upset.

"No one. I lied about being kissed," I said. The truth was, I'd kissed Bernard when I was young, and before I understood the implications of kissing someone. And I kissed Paul, whom I missed very much because he had been nice to me.

"I figured as much," Catherine snorted. "You're too young."

"You kissed boys when you were about my age!" I furrowed my brow. "And I could have kissed Tommy tonight if I'd wanted!"

"Tommy walked back to town holding Samantha's hand, so no you couldn't," Catherine laughed.

"Well, he asked me to walk with him after studying," I countered.

"Well, he's not with you, is he? He went with a girl his own age. You're too young for him," Catherine said. I didn't like her tone.

"He's Bernard's age, he's not old like Henry."

"I'm not that old," Henry walked into the kitchen.

Catherine rolled her eyes at me. She turned to Bernard, "Let's go for a walk," she said.

Bernard didn't seem thrilled about taking a walk but he left with Catherine.

Henry leaned against the kitchen counter watching them leave then turned to me. "Would you like to take a walk too, Maybel?"

"Why?"

"It's a lovely evening."

"Alright," I said.

We walked to the front door. Catherine and Bernard had just left. I found a shawl to wear in case it got colder. It was lightweight and knitted by my grandmother.

"That's a nice shade of lilac." Henry admired my shawl.

"Granny knitted it for me for my birthday," I told him.

"Your family has quite the talented seamstresses and clothing designers. I've been telling your father that opening a clothing store with such a talented wife would prove most profitable."

"You smell good," I told him.

"It's probably wood stain," he laughed.

"You smell like a forest."

"Interesting way of describing my smell," he chuckled.

We walked along the street and into town.

"Would you like to sit by the pond and toss bread to the ducks?"

"Sure," I said. "I don't have any bread, though."

"I'll buy us a slice from that vendor," Henry said.

We sat at one of the benches surrounding the pond. There were young men and women holding hands and gazing lovingly into each other's eyes.

The three ducks closest to us spied the bread in my hand and charged. I squealed and landed in Henry's lap for safety, then tossed the entire slice before they bit me. They nipped each other's wings, arguing over who got the prize. A smaller duck waddled innocently nearby, pretending to be uninterested, until he suddenly dove into the midst of the commotion and stole the entire slice.

I slid off Henry's lap. "There's Catherine," I said, nodding in the direction of where Catherine stood with Bernard and Tommy and Samantha.

"Looks like the only boy who has ever flirted with me found someone else," I sighed.

"That boy is not the only boy to flirt with you," Henry said.

"I'm not Catherine," I replied, "I don't have perfect hair and I don't dress well. This afternoon, I had my sweater on inside out, and Catherine told me to go fix my sweater and put something on my chapped lips. I was so embarrassed and everyone laughed." I felt hurt remembering.

"I'm sorry, Maybel. You look very pretty no matter what Catherine or anyone else says."

"Do you want to kiss?" I asked Henry.

Henry looked surprised. "No," he said quickly. "You're lovely, Maybel, I just don't think that's a good idea."

"I understand," I said.

"I like you, Maybel, it's just,"

"It's ok, Henry. I don't really care either way. I just wanted to know if you liked me. Bernard said you were jealous of that boy flirting with me."

"I was, I mean, I just didn't think he was right for you. I could tell he was going to be too forward with you."

"I just asked if you wanted to kiss me, so apparently I'm too forward. I'm the girl version of Tommy," I snorted.

"I wouldn't say that. You're lovely, Maybel."

"Can we go home now? I'm cold."

Henry took off his coat and wrapped it around my shoulders.

"Thank you," I said.

We walked away from the pond and toward home. "Henry, I think you are a nice man. You said earlier that you were bad, like that boy Tommy, but you are good."

"Thank you, Maybel. I like you, too."

Henry took me to my door and I returned his coat. "Thank you for the stroll," I said.

"It was my pleasure. Goodnight, Maybel."

Henry left and I sat on my sofa thinking about how beautiful my children with Henry would look. I began writing several random stories, quickly jotting down the scenes that formed in my mind.

Catherine returned with Bernard. I was in the middle of writing a story about a French monk who could turn water into gold, but the French people killed him because they preferred Jesus' ability to turn water into wine. "Those lushes," I giggled to myself as Catherine walked in with Bernard. They both looked angry.

"See! She's right here writing! She's fine!" Catherine screeched.

I looked up at them, confused.

Catherine looked angrily at Bernard. She turned to me, "Where's Henry?"

"I don't know, he left," I answered.

"Bernard is upset that Henry took you for a walk to the pond," Catherine folded her arms angrily.

I considered Catherine's statement. I wasn't the best at deciphering exactly why someone was angry.

"Are you angry about me walking with Henry, or being at the pond? If was walking, Henry and I walked because it was a lovely evening. If was about the pond, we sat on a bench and fed angry ducks until I got cold. I'm not sure why you'd be upset at either activity, Bernard."

Catherine looked at me like I was stupid. "Honestly, Maybel!" She stormed upstairs. I heard her door slam.

"Maybel, may I sit with you?" Bernard looked tired.

I held my papers with one hand and patted the cushion beside me.

Bernard sat next to me. "Catherine is mad because I told Tommy not to ever talk to you again, and then I became angry when I saw you sitting with Henry. I'm sorry I upset Catherine. I guess I'm just really protective over you."

"I'm very confused right now. Henry says boys are noticing me more."

"They are." Bernard leaned back and looked even more tired.

"When you come over tomorrow, can we go somewhere together? How about the art show at the library, or the pond to feed ducks, the nice ducks, not the demon ducks? I've been bored and Catherine doesn't want to do anything with me."

"I won't be over tomorrow. You're welcome to come visit me at my house though," Bernard turned his head to look at me.

"Why can't you come here?"

"Catherine is really mad at me right now," Bernard said.

"Oh. I guess I'll see you after a couple weeks when she likes you again," I said.

"We'll see," Bernard kissed my cheek. "Come see me anytime," he said, then left.

A couple weeks passed, but I had not gone to see Bernard, and anyway, he had returned to boarding school.

I did see Henry often, though. He and daddy had coffee in daddy's workshop several times a week, and I saw Henry when Catherine and I went to the hardware store with daddy. Catherine liked to flirt with Henry when daddy wasn't paying attention. Henry didn't return her flirtation, but was polite.

And then, finally, Bernard returned from school for a short break. I saw him on his front porch talking to his father. They were drinking tea with cinnamon sticks.

I ran from the street and across the lawn to greet them.

"Bernard! You're back!" I yelled as I hurled myself up the steps and into Bernard's arms.

I then gave Mr. Charleston a big hug. "Maybel," he said, "you know you can visit Mrs. Charleston and me when Bernard isn't here. We miss you."

"Aren't you busy running an empire? Daddy says you're really busy."

"We are never too busy for you," Mr. Charleston smiled at me. I sat beside him on his stone, porch wall. The stone was thick and white with little sparkly quartz stones.

I leaned against Mr. Charleston. He felt stronger than the stone.

"Bernard why haven't you come over?" I asked.

"I only just arrived home," Bernard smiled at me. I liked Bernard's smile.

"Is Catherine still mad at you?" I asked.

"I don't know yet. I suppose I'll find out sooner rather than later." Bernard nodded to the street where Catherine walked toward our home with friends. She waved at Bernard as they continued walking.

"Maybel," Mr. Charleston whispered and smiled cheekily, "why was Catherine mad at Bernard? I know nothing of this gossip."

Bernard sighed and sipped his cinnamon tea.

"Henry didn't like a boy who flirted with me, and Bernard told the boy to never speak to me again. Catherine got mad because Bernard was being overprotective, like usual. And Catherine got mad that Bernard got mad that Henry and I sat on a bench at the pond feeding insane ducks that had been bred to eventually usurp humankind."

"Oh!" Mr. Charleston chuckled loudly. "I like this gossip and will have to tell Mrs. Charleston everything once she arrives home from riding Big Ben!"

"If Big Ben sired a boy horse, let's name the baby Bigger Ben," I looked up at Mr. Charleston and we laughed together. I loved Mr. Charleston's humor and playfulness.

"I suppose I should go talk to Catherine," Bernard sighed. "She's with friends so she won't yell as much."

"Ha! You underestimate Catherine's school teacher voice!" I giggled.

"Good luck, son," Mr. Charleston snorted.

Bernard and I walked to my house. "If Catherine is still mad, will I ever see you again? I can't come to your house because I'd be betraying Catherine. And I can't go somewhere with you because that would be a date, and while you don't have to live with Angry Catherine, I do. If you and Catherine no longer spend time together, I'll never see you again, and I've really grown to like you, Bernard. I even miss you when you return to boarding school."

Bernard took my hand and squeezed it as we walked. "I miss you too, sweetheart. I love when we're together playing or reading, and of course when we eat custard."

I hugged Bernard there in the street.

"Has Catherine been seeing any boys?" Bernard asked. He didn't look angry or sad.

"I don't think so. She goes to study groups sometimes," I replied.

"Have you been seeing any boys?" Bernard asked hesitantly.

"No."

Bernard smiled, "Good. No boys are good enough for you," he said.

"Have you been seeing any girls?" I asked him.

"No, Maybel. I have not seen anyone. I've been quite busy with my studies to even leave my dormitory room."

"That sounds horrible." I stuck out my tongue.

"It will pay off when I'm a doctor. I've been thinking about business ventures, too. Father and Henry seem to do quite well, and I'd like to learn about business, too."

"Can I learn too?" I asked

"I don't see why not. I'll talk to father," Bernard scratched my back playfully.

"Bernard," Catherine called from our porch.

Bernard immediately dropped my hand.

"Hello, Catherine," he said.

"Bernard, I'm so sorry, but my friends Edith, Lucy, and I are going to the library shortly."

"I understand, Catherine. My studies have increased as well," he replied.

"May I talk to you inside?" Catherine asked softly.

"Yes, of course," Bernard answered.

Catherine's friends, Edith and Lucy, and I followed them inside. Mommy seemed happy to provide cookies and tea. Catherine took Bernard to daddy's office.

I chatted with mommy in the kitchen while Edith and Lucy stayed in the family room.

After several minutes, Catherine came to our kitchen. "Mommy, I'm going to the library now with Edith and Lucy."

"Where's Bernard?" I asked.

"He went home," Catherine said nonchalantly, then left.

I finished telling mommy about Greece. I'd read a book about mythology. I asked mommy if the Greeks, when they read our Bible, called our stories myths.

"When you meet a Greek person, ask your question," mommy said.

"Where are the Greeks?" I asked.

"In Greece, honey, hand me that towel." Mommy pointed to the towel near me.

I handed mommy the towel so she could take a pot from the oven.

"Are there any Greek people around here?" I asked.

"I haven't met any. Ask the Charlestons the next time we have dinner. They've been to Greece." Mommy stirred the pot of stew.

"I'll go ask now. May I take them cookies?"

"Of course, dear. Please send my regards. Oh, and ask Mrs. Charleston to drop by for Saturday's quilting bee."

"I will mommy," I said, and dashed out the door.

I walked into the kitchen without knocking. I felt comfortable enough with the Charlestons to do so. I walked up the steps to Bernard's bedroom.

I opened his door. "Bernard, do Greek people call the Bible mythology?"

Bernard looked up from his book. He laid on his bed reading.

"You have the strangest thoughts in your brain, Maybel."

"Well do they?"

"I don't know. Maybe?" Bernard closed his book and stretched.

"Why did you come back here?" I asked Bernard.

"Catherine said she needed time to think. She thinks I fancy another girl. And she said something about needing time apart to see what our hearts desire." Bernard sighed, "I have no idea what she wants. I don't understand girls."

"Did she say if we were allowed to spend time together?"

"She didn't say," Bernard said. "It upsets me that you won't spend time with me unless Catherine and I are dating, Maybel. You and I can be friends even if Catherine and I aren't dating."

I suddenly had one of my naughty streaks. "Are you dating Catherine or not?"

"I honestly have no idea. I'm completely confused about what is going on," Bernard shrugged.

I ran and jumped onto Bernard. I kissed him and giggled. "It's not cheating then!"

I giggled and ran home.

Later in the summer, Bernard and I had decided to go exploring to look for lightning bugs. We were standing under an old, oak tree when a lightning bug landed on my chest, just under my chin.

"Hold still, Maybel," Bernard whispered.

He ever so gently lowered his finger down just below my chin and touched just below my neck, at my collar, right beside the lightning bug. We held our breaths as it crawled onto Bernard's finger. He lifted his finger up in front of my eyes. The lightening bug lifted its wings and glowed bright, but didn't fly. My eyes were wide and my breath shallow. My mouth was slightly open as I watched the little lightning bug glow on and off with its wings raised, but it didn't fly. It sat on Bernard's fingertip, poised for flight, but it didn't fly. Bernard ever so gently lifted his thumb and touched the lightning bug's glowing bottom and it took flight! It soared upwards. I watched it fly up to the top of the oak tree, glowing intermittently. When I looked back at Bernard, he wasn't watching the lightning bug. He had been watching me. When our eyes met, he slowly leaned toward me and paused, just before his lips touched mine. He looked into my eyes and gently pressed his lips onto mine. I didn't turn away. His kiss felt good. He moved back and watched me for my reaction. I wasn't upset. I wanted his kisses. He gently touched my cheek and kissed me again. I let him, and I liked it. He parted his lips slightly and I felt his tongue ever so gently touch my tongue. I returned his kiss and then another kiss.

Bernard reached around the back of my neck and pulled me toward him. His other hand pressed against the small of my back. He kissed me and then kissed my neck, and then my shoulder. His breath was hot and I felt his hands caress my back and arm slowly and gently. I wrapped my arms around his neck and felt myself float away, up into the swarm of lightning bugs overhead.

Bernard's hand slid slowly up under my shirt and just below my breast. He paused. His thumb lingered underneath the lining of my bra and my nipple hardened.

I wanted to know what Bernard felt like under his shirt, so I pushed my hand up under his shirt and over his hardened stomach muscles. He breathed in and pushed his tongue further inside my mouth. His thumb moved along the bottom of my bra but he did not push further.

I moved my thumb just underneath the edge of his pants and he breathed in sharply.

Bernard pulled back. He held my chin under the old, oak tree and looked deeply into my eyes, then he turned and left. I remained there staring up at the stars that were just beginning to peak through. The lightning bugs still glittered and twinkled above me.

I had been noticing my growing breasts and I felt like I wore a new body. Snakes shed their skins, and their new skins looked the same as their old skins, but were longer and thicker. My body felt different. It felt as though I had shed my childhood skin, and it had been replaced with bigger breasts, hips, and thighs.

I still wanted to play in the cornfields, but a part of me felt like I was supposed to be too old for such things. I didn't want to primp and take time to do my hair every morning like Catherine, but I also wasn't sure if I was too old to continue climbing trees and playing tag. So far, I was not enjoying my teenage years much. I could not stop my changing body or the way boys now looked at me. I didn't feel old. I felt like I deserved more simplicity, for at least a little while longer, but the breasts growing on my chest and the hair growing under my armpits and between my legs told me my days of running through fields and throwing baseballs were limited.

I didn't see Bernard for several weeks after he kissed me. He had returned to boarding school. I wasn't sure what to do or say around him now, so for the first time since meeting Bernard, I was relieved he had left.

Fall came, and with it, the Autumn Festival, Bernard's break from boarding school, and Catherine's and my break from school. I liked school, but not enough to be sad for time away from math.

I was nervous about seeing Bernard, but fortunately our time apart reset our friendship, and he was not awkward around me when he came to visit Catherine. Catherine was at her piano lesson, so I asked Bernard if he'd like to go play in the cornfields and orchard.

"You cheated, Maybel!" Bernard yelled.

I ran ahead of him through our apple orchard.

"You have long arms and legs!" I yelled back at him. "Daddy calls this leveling the playing field!"

"You can't get a head start and call that fair!" Bernard yelled at me.

"Well, you can't have arms and legs twice the length of mine and call that fair!" I laughed as I touched the tree at the far end of our field.

Bernard finally caught up to me. "That's not fair, Maybel, and you know it!" He crossed his arms.

"Stop whining, Bernard!" I laughed as I held onto the trunk of the apple tree with one hand and swung myself around.

Bernard caught me mid swing. "Maybel, you're infuriating!"

I giggled at him, which only seemed to further annoy him. He held my waist as I giggled and tried to escape his hold.

"I'll race you back home, and this time I'll let you win!" I enjoyed teasing him, watching him huff.

I was a tomboy at heart. I loved the outdoors. And I loved playing with Bernard, even though we weren't young children anymore.

"I'm not going to play with you if you cheat, Maybel!"

"Ok, Bernard, I'm sorry I beat you on a level playing field." I laughed. "We can go back to you having an advantage in height and strength." I smiled up at him with a cheeky grin.

Bernard still held my waist as I flailed my arms mocking him.

He moved one arm behind my shoulders and pulled me into a deep embrace and kissed me. I looked up at him surprised. He seemed equally surprised. He pulled me into another kiss and I felt his tongue slip inside my mouth. I didn't resist. I liked the feel of Bernard's body against me.

Bernard caught his breath. He gently pushed me back a little. "I'm sorry. I didn't mean for that to happen again," he said.

We stared at each other for a moment then Bernard suggested we return to my house.

I didn't say anything. I didn't know what to say. We walked in silence back to my house and Bernard left with Catherine to the candy store.

I stayed home and wrote a story about a very confused girl named Amelia and her twin sister, Agatha, who stole Amelia's identity, and then stole Amelia's boyfriend, and then got run over by a carriage fleeing from Amelia. The living twin, Amelia, did not tell anyone she was alive, nor did she explain that her twin, Agatha, who pretended to be Amelia, was dead. Amelia moved away because she didn't want to continue life with her ex-boyfriend, who thought she was now trampled and dead. I reread my story three times and was just as confused about what I'd written as I was about why Bernard kept kissing me. I figured my story was as confusing as my feelings for Bernard and for Catherine. Perhaps if I sorted my feelings for Bernard, I could then write a less-confusing story.

The next week passed slowly as Catherine spent most of her time away from home with her friends. I stayed home dancing by myself, helping mommy sew, and helping daddy gather apples for cider. "This jug is for you," daddy said, as he poured cider into a large ceramic jug. "Now this jug," daddy winked at me, "has a little autumn cheer inside, so don't drink from this one," he chuckled. "I'll be taking another jug of autumn cheer to Mr. Charleston," he winked again.

"Can I come," I asked.

"I don't see why not," daddy said. "Let's go then."

We arrived at the Charleston's house and Mr. Charleston smiled widely when he opened the door to find daddy holding a large jug. "Come in, good sir!" Mr. Charleston happily welcomed us, and even more happily took and poured the cider jug into cups for himself and daddy.

"Maybel, dear, Bernard is around here somewhere. Why don't you go find him while your father and I catch up?"

"Yes, Mr. Charleston," I said. I felt as though Bernard had been ignoring me since he kissed me in the orchard. I was bored, though, so I went to find Bernard.

I walked into the kitchen, then the study, and finally into the family room where I found Bernard reading.

"Why are you here?" he looked up surprised.

"Daddy delivered autumn cheer to your father," I answered.

"I'm busy, Maybel," he returned to his book.

I sat on the sofa next to him. He looked over at me annoyed. "I said I'm busy."

"Your father told me to come find you so they could catch up," I said.

"I'm not a babysitter," he went back to reading.

"I'm not a baby!" I said angrily. "Clearly you realized that several times now!"

"Shut up, Maybel!" he stood up and walked out of the room.

I found some paper in the study and passed my time waiting for daddy by writing down a story. It became a long story because daddy and Mr. Charleston were quite enthusiastically enjoying their cheery drinks.

I went to the kitchen for water. "Why are you still here?" Bernard's voice came from behind me.

"Our fathers are still catching up," I replied.

Bernard looked annoyed.

"I'm bored. Do you want to go do something?" I asked.

"No." Bernard turned around and started up the stairs. I stubbornly followed.

"I'm busy, Maybel!" Bernard yelled back at me.

I continued following him up the stairs. At the top, he turned around angrily, "I don't want to play, or read, or paint with you, Maybel, I'm trying to be polite, but go away!"

I watched him stomp angrily down the hallway. I begrudgingly went back downstairs and into the study to write down more of the story I'd started.

After some time passed, my hand became tired from all the writing. I sat back and breathed deeply. I suddenly realized Bernard had been watching me through the glass doors. He looked startled when I looked at him and he turned and walked quickly away.

"Bernard!" I yelled. He did not answer me, and when I went to the door and looked for him, he was nowhere to be found.

I went to the kitchen and the drawing room, but he was not there. I walked back to the study and sat down at the desk to continue my story. I couldn't understand why Bernard was ignoring me. I wanted to talk with him, or do anything other than sit here alone. I spent enough time alone at my home.

"Maybel? Ah! There you are!" Daddy entered the study. "Let's go home, shall we?"

As we were leaving, Mr. Charleston opened the door for us. "I trust Bernard was a good host, Maybel?"

"He was busy," I said, disappointed.

Daddy and I walked home. He was quite chatty from drinking his cheer. "Maybel, how was your visit with Bernard?"

"He didn't want to do anything. He said he was busy."

"I see. What did you do then?" he asked.

"I wrote a story. Oh no! I forgot it in the study!" I was worried someone would throw it away.

"You'll retrieve it next time, dear, not to worry," daddy comforted me. Then with a sudden realization he added, "Let's return Wednesday afternoon! It will be a grand excuse to deliver more autumn cheer, and perhaps I'll even bring Mr. Charleston one of my finest cigars!"

Daddy was happy with his plans to catch up again with Mr. Charleston. I was not as happy.

On Wednesday afternoon, daddy and I set off to the Charleston's home. Daddy carried a large jug of cheery cider and I carried a box of cigars.

Mr. Charleston again answered the door, and again he was brimming with joy as he and daddy went to Mr. Charleston's den where he kept his guns, tobacco, and whiskey.

I went to the study to collect my story. It wasn't on the desk. I searched underneath the desk, the trash cans, and behind the cabinets.

"Maybel what are you doing?" Bernard asked as he entered the study.

"I'm looking for the story I wrote," I answered. "Can you help me?"

"It's not here," he said.

"Well, where is it?" I asked.

"Mother found it and read it. She said it was really good. I read it too, as did father and grandmother."

"I just came here for my story, so as soon as you give me it, I'll leave!" I snapped.

"It's in my room. Stay here and I'll go get it." He walked down the hallway and I heard his footsteps going up the stairs.

When Bernard returned, he handed me my story. "Mother and grandmother wanted me to tell you to pursue writing."

"Why?" I asked.

"You have a gift," Bernard said. He wasn't smiling or friendly, just making a statement, relaying a message.

"Do you want to go do something?" I asked.

"I'm busy," he answered, and turned to leave.

"Why don't you like me anymore, Bernard?" I asked bluntly.

"I'm busy, Maybel. Have a good day." He left me standing in the study.

I went to the den to tell daddy I would walk home alone. "Maybel! Mr. Charleston here tells me he read your story and he thinks you're quite the writer! Well done, sweetheart!"

"Thank you," I said quietly. "I'll be heading home."

"See you at home, Maybel dear," daddy called after me.

At the autumn festival, I sat opposite Catherine and Bernard on a hayride. Catherine chatted enthusiastically with several of her friends, leaving me to braid straw and create stories in my mind to pass time.

I was thinking about maybe creating a story of a little girl and boy who were born bound together at her left wrist and his right wrist, making their childhood awkward because they had to go everywhere together. They only had to buy one pair of gloves though, because only her right hand and his left hand could fit into gloves, as there were no gloves that were big enough to be put on their bound hands. Every other year, she picked which pair of gloves they would wear that winter, and she always picked pink. On alternating years, he picked black.

I braided three cords of straw and then braided those cords together. I was about to start another set of braids, and reached for the longest straws I could find, and two of them happened to be nestled between Bernard's ankles. When I reached for them, I glanced at Bernard while deep in thought about what I could make from these braids.

Bernard had been watching me. He had a curious expression on his face. When he realized I looked up suddenly and caught his gaze, he quickly looked away, embarrassed.

"Bernard do you want to braid with me?" I asked.

"No, I'm not a child, Maybel," he said sarcastically.

"You used to braid with me," I pressed.

"I used to be younger," he watched me, looking annoyed at me, but for what reason I could not understand.

"Fine, sit there staring at me," I muttered, annoyed.

"You have straw in your hair, Maybel. You're a mess. You're too old to be playing around in straw looking like you've never brushed your hair," Bernard growled at me.

I looked up hurt. "Shut up, Bernard!"

I went back to braiding. The story about a little boy and girl in my head took a sudden dark turn. I decided the little boy was tired of being made fun of every other winter for wearing pink gloves on his one unbound hand, so while the girl was asleep, he sliced their wrists apart, and the girl woke up with blood spurting out of their now unbound wrists. She screamed as the boy looked at her then slunk down in their bed, dying. He'd severed the artery they shared.

Oddly, I felt better after killing off the boy in my story and looked up at Bernard with a wicked sneer on my face. Bernard had been watching me again. He looked at me with disgust and threw a wad of straw at my face. I spit out some straw and had had enough of Bernard's bad attitude lately, so I jumped at him and shoved two fistfuls of straw into his face. He grabbed me in a head lock and pushed me down beside him.

"Sit down and stop being annoying, Maybel!" he hissed at me.

Still in a headlock, I tilted my head up as best I could to look at him in his eyes and snarled, "Just so you know, I wrote a story in my head where the boy died, and guess what? I've decided to name him Bernard!"

Bernard pushed my face into his armpit, "Shut up, Maybel!"

"What is going on with you two?" Catherine asked, finally noticing us.

I looked up from Bernard's armpit, "Your stupid boyfriend needs a bath!"

Bernard released me and pushed me away. "Nothing Catherine, everything is fine."

Catherine rolled her eyes at Bernard and me and turned back to her friends.

"Why have you been so mean to me lately?" I whispered to Bernard.

"I don't know, just leave me alone," he whispered back.

I was sitting beside Bernard now where he'd pushed me down next to him. I crossed my arms and pouted. After several minutes of silence, Bernard sighed and wrapped his arm around my shoulder. "I'm sorry, Maybel," he whispered. "I don't know why I've been mean to you. I don't know how to act around you anymore."

"Well you can be a whole lot nicer," I whispered into his ear.

I felt him breathe out deeply and his shoulders sunk down. "I know, Maybel. I'm sorry."

I looked up at him beside me. He finally looked back at me. His eyes looked especially green this afternoon. I rested my head lightly on his shoulder and gave me a small hug with his arm still around me. He slowly kissed my head and I heard him whisper, "I love you."

Aunt Mary came to visit the next weekend. My older cousin, Shanna, did not accompany her mother. Catherine confessed to me she was relieved because Shanna was beautiful and played piano and danced well, and Catherine said didn't need any more competition for Bernard's attention.

Bernard was out in daddy's workshop helping him paint, while Catherine talked to mommy and Aunt Mary in the family room.

Our baby cousin, Wally, came to visit with Aunt Mary, and I loved tossing him up in the air and catching him. He giggled and giggled when I did that.

I played with Wally while Catherine, mommy, and Aunt Mary talked about family, fashion, and new recipes.

Aunt Mary didn't think she could have any more children and then came along Wally. He was a roly-poly, little baby, who liked playing peek-a-boo. His giggles were contagious.

Wally crawled away and into the kitchen. I crawled after him, which delighted him beyond measure. I snuck him a tiny dollop of pie filling. His eyes got wide when I put the spoon to his lips and he tasted the sweet filling. I suddenly noticed Bernard smiling at me while leaning against the kitchen door. When he saw me looking at him, he swallowed hard and looked embarrassed.

"Bernard, wait, don't leave. Tell me why you have been grumpy toward me. I haven't done anything to warrant your bad manners."

"I know," he said. He didn't say any more so we stared at each other.

I held Wally and he tugged my hair and sucked on it.

"You'll be a great mother," Bernard said softly as he watched me and Wally.

Catherine came into the kitchen and reached for Bernard's hand. "Mommy wants me to pick up her stationary order at the store."

I followed them into the family room and put Wally into Aunt Mary's lap. I quickly ran to catch up to them outside.

"Can I come?" I ran to catch up to Catherine and Bernard.

"No," Bernard said.

"Why not?" I whined.

Catherine looked puzzled. "Why not, Bernard? It's just to the store and back for mommy."

"Fine, you can come." Bernard reluctantly agreed.

I hadn't told Catherine about Bernard kissing me because I didn't want her to be mad at me, or refuse to take me places with her.

Catherine went into the store to purchase stationary for mommy.

I remained outside with Bernard. "Why don't you want me around Bernard? I haven't told Catherine because I don't want her mad at me."

"Stop talking, Maybel."

"My kiss must have been off-putting. Did my breath smell bad?"

"Just shut up, please, Maybel!"

"I want to go to the art exhibit at the town hall with you and Catherine," I said.

"No. Why can't you leave us alone, Maybel? Go make friends so you don't have to be with Catherine and me constantly."

"You're really cruel, Bernard." I looked away because I felt tears forming.

Catherine finished mommy's shopping and returned. We walked home together, the three of us. Bernard was silent and seemed annoyed at my presence.

Catherine took the stationary inside to mommy. "I'll be right back and we'll head to the art exhibit."

"Why must you insist on tagging along?" Bernard said with annoyance, as soon as Catherine had gone into our house.

"It's never bothered you before. Why do you suddenly hate me now? What did I do?" I asked.

"Maybel, you didn't do anything." He sighed and wiped his face with his hands exasperatedly. "I kissed you and I'm sorry. I feel very guilty about that. I'm trying to spend less time with you, because if I don't, I'm worried I'm going to kiss you again."

I was surprised by his candidness.

"I like you a lot, Maybel, but you have made it clear you only like me as a brother. You aren't attracted to me the same way I'm attracted to you. I'm trying to respect your wishes to remain only friends, but it's painful for me to be near you and not kiss you."

I was about to tell Bernard that I was attracted to him too, but Catherine returned from giving mommy the package of stationary. She smiled up at Bernard and took his hand, and Bernard leaned down to kiss her. Catherine looked happy and Bernard smiled at her and kissed her again. They left to the art exhibit, holding hands and kissing again at our front gate.

There weren't many girls my age living nearby. Really, Catherine was my only friend. Bernard was my friend too, but he and I were going through difficulties in our friendship now.

I decided to stay home with mommy while Catherine and Bernard went to town to see the art exhibit.

"Oh, Maybel! You're here!" Mommy smiled at me. "Why aren't you with Catherine and Bernard?"

"I don't want to be a tag-along anymore," I said. "I wish Hannah and Nora lived close by."

"Why don't we spend time together then? Your Aunt Mary left with Wally, so it seems we are both feeling a bit lonely. Let's keep each other company then, shall we?" She kissed the top of my head.

"Mommy, did you ever feel lost when you were my age?"

"Oh goodness, yes! I'm a little sister too, remember. Your Aunt Mary often went about doing her own thing, so I had to figure out what my own thing was. Turns out, I really enjoy designing dresses. You'll find your own passion too, dear."

"You and Aunt Mary are best friends though," I said, confused.

"Yes, we are now, but you know, growing up is hard sometimes. I'm certain you and Catherine are best friends too, and will continue to be best friends forever."

I sighed, "I'd like that."

Mommy kissed my forehead and we drank tea together on our sofa. I'd never thought of her and Aunt Mary when they were young, but I supposed there were a lot of things I'd not yet considered.

That evening, I sat on my back porch composing stories in my head. I was not in a particularly cheery mood, so it was about a boy who ate so much candy he slowly exploded.

Bernard came out and sat beside me. I didn't acknowledge his presence.

"Maybel, I know you are mad at me and confused. I'm sorry. I do enjoy having you around. I'm just feeling very guilty about what happened."

"You mean when you kissed me?" I was deliberately direct.

Bernard looked down at his hands that were wrapped around his knees. "Yes, Maybel," he said quietly. Bernard looked sad, and honestly as confused as I was about his actions.

"You are sorry about kissing me?" I continued my directness.

"Yes," he said. His voice was quiet because he was embarrassed of kissing me, which caused a flame of anger to widen inside me.

"I'm not an ugly troll under a bridge or a wicked witch living in the forest! You don't have to be so embarrassed of kissing someone as horrible as me!" I angrily confronted him.

"That's not it at all! Why do women find such odd ways of interpreting what I say? I'll assume from now on that we're speaking different languages and I'll tread more carefully!" Bernard looked positively exasperated.

"Bernard, I don't want Catherine to be mad at me, so I haven't told her what happened. Then you got mad at me. I don't even know why you are mad at me. No matter what I do, or don't do, one of you is going to get mad at me, and then I'll be all alone like I was today."

"I wasn't mad at you. I was mad at myself," Bernard said. "I don't know how to be around you anymore without kissing you. I'm confused about everything."

A couple days later, I was outside chasing one of our chickens around trying to catch her, and put her back in her pen, when I almost ran into Bernard.

"Catherine's not here," I breathed heavily.

That damn chicken was either getting faster, or I had not been keeping as active as usual. I was winded.

"Here, Maybel," Bernard thrust a pretty bag into my arms.

"Do you not see I'm busy?" I grumbled. "Fanny is going to taste good tonight after all this running she's made me do!"

"You named your chicken Fanny?"

"She has a big behind," I smacked my lips. "You're going to taste good with roasted potatoes!" I yelled at Fanny as she gleefully ran under our fence and out of sight.

I opened the pretty bag Bernard had brought. It was a box of special candies from some expensive store in Germany. I knew it was expensive because it looked like I should bow to it before opening it. I thought it had likely passed through a queen's hands on its way over the ocean to me.

"My grandparents sent this to me," Bernard said.

"You don't like them?" I was amazed he didn't want fancy European chocolate.

I opened the box to smell the chocolates. There was a handwritten note:

"Dear Bernard, here are the candies you requested for your lovely girlfriend. We look forward to your wedding."

"Oh, Catherine didn't want them? Good, more for me!"

"They aren't for Catherine. I knew you'd love these so I wrote my grandparents a couple weeks ago and asked them to send me some to give to you."

"The note says they are for your girlfriend. And I didn't know you were planning on asking Catherine to marry you soon."

Bernard grabbed the note and read it. "These chocolates are for you, Maybel. They must have assumed you were my girlfriend, and no, I'm not planning on asking Catherine to marry me."

Bernard looked frustrated. "Maybel, I tried to do something nice for you. I'm really sorry about making fun of you and being cold toward you."

"Are you also sorry for being rude and ill-mannered, and because you have treated your discarded tissues with better consideration than me?"

"Yes," Bernard said.

"And you think chocolate makes up for all the years of your spoiled, bratty, petty, and mean behavior? You think chocolate makes up for years of teasing me?"

"No, I know it doesn't," Bernard said.

My wrath was only building momentum. "I learned a new word at the hardware store."

Bernard sighed and put his head in his hands.

"Fuck. It means to have sex, but the expression I learned that applies to you is fucker, and more specifically dumb fucker."

Bernard didn't argue with me.

"I don't want your fucking peace offering. See how versatile this new word is?"

"I went insane for a while, Maybel! I went completely insane from jealousy! Boys are noticing you more, and sometimes, I think Henry likes you. I miss you though, and I'm sad when we fight. I am still jealous, I still don't know how to be around you and not want to kiss you, but I love you more than my jealousy and confusion."

I shoved the bag of beautifully-wrapped chocolates into Bernard's chest. I loved sweets, though, so I grabbed them back from him and angrily stomped inside my house.

It was time for this month's quilting bee. I walked with Catherine to Bernard's house because mommy was hosting this month's quilting bee, and she didn't want us there. She said some of the ladies could get a bit rambunctious. Catherine and I glanced at each other smiling when mommy said that, because mommy was the most rambunctious of them all. Mommy liked to drink wine more than quilt at their monthly quilting bees.

"Have you finished that blue quilt?" I asked mommy.

"No, dear, it's a difficult pattern."

Catherine stifled a giggle. "You started that quilt when I was five, mommy."

"Very intricate stitchwork," mommy said.

Catherine and I giggled as we walked to Bernard's house. "The stitching really is intricate though, and even harder to do when you're drunk," Catherine laughed.

I laughed, too. "I don't think it's meant to be intricate stitching," I giggled. "I think it was meant to be a straight line but 'intricate' stitchwork sounds better than 'drunken' stitchwork." Catherine and I laughed harder.

The upstairs of the Charleston's mansion had more than a dozen bedrooms, a billiard room, lounge, bar, and a smaller library than the one downstairs. I stopped outside the billiard room. I didn't want to be pushed out of Bernard's bedroom and feel rejection yet again. "You go on, Catherine," I said. "I know you two want to be alone. I'll go play in the billiard room."

After Catherine walked far enough away down the long hallway, I went to Henry's bedroom. The door of the guest bedroom Henry used was open. I wandered inside. The bed was made and nothing looked cluttered or messy, like someone was occupying the room.

I heard the tap in the bathroom run. I walked to the bathroom door. Henry was standing at the sink shaving his face.

"Hi, Henry," I said shyly. I hid halfway behind the doorframe.

"Oh, hello, Maybel. What are you doing in my bedroom?"

"Your door was open. Can I stay with you?" I was so nervous I could feel my heartbeat in my toes. My hands felt cold and clammy. I was lonely though, and Bernard had said he and Catherine sometimes didn't want me around because I was annoying.

"Bernard and Catherine are in Bernard's bedroom." I watched Henry with big, pleading eyes. I hoped he'd let me stay.

Henry chuckled, "Are they now?"

"Yes. I'm lonely. Can I stay and watch you?" I still hid halfway behind the doorframe. My face was squashed against the frame as I fidgeted with the hand towel by the sink. I was terribly nervous to be speaking to Henry, much less be in Henry's bedroom.

"I suppose," Henry hesitated. His cheeks and chin and neck were lathered with shaving cream.

"Daddy lets me help him shave," I told him. "Can I help you?"

Henry paused thoughtfully. "Have you ever cut your father while shaving?"

"No, not on purpose."

Henry chuckled, "I think I might like to shave myself."

I took a tiny step closer to Henry and looked up at him. He carefully shaved his face slowly in front of the mirror, above the beautiful, ceramic sink embossed with roses.

I suddenly realized he had stopped shaving and was watching me.

My eyes widened, like a doe when she sips water from the stream, then hears you step on a twig, and looks up in terror. I watched him back.

Henry sighed. He sat down on the toilet. "Alright, Maybel, you can make one, slow sweep down my cheek, very, very carefully."

I smiled happily.

Henry sat with a straight back and tilted his head upward toward me.

I stood between his legs and very carefully and smoothly shaved one, long stroke.

"Can I do another?" I whispered hopefully.

Henry smiled, "Yes," he said.

I continued shaving Henry's face until he was clean-shaven all over. I took a towel from the hanger over the sink and returned to Henry and gently wiped the remaining shaving cream from his face and neck.

Henry smiled sweetly at me. "You did great, sweetheart."

I leaned down and very lightly kissed Henry's lips.

Henry was not mad, but he didn't look like he wanted to continue kissing me either. "Maybel, sweetheart, I love you, and that's why I can't kiss you the way I want to kiss you."

I was thoroughly confused by Henry's remark. "Why doesn't any boy like me?" I felt my eyes getting glassy with tears.

"They do, Maybel," he said softly. "I like you a lot." Henry sighed, "You're young and you deserve a better man than me."

"I'm older than Catherine was when she kissed Bernard."

"You're more innocent than Catherine, and that's the difference," Henry argued. "I may be a tomcat, as you've joked, but even I have enough morals and a sense of what is right and wrong to know that I do not want to be the man who takes your innocence."

"I've already been kissed by other boys," I crossed my arms. "And I know what a penis looks like."

Henry looked taken aback. "Who?" Henry paused, "Never mind, don't tell me. I'm sure I know, and to be honest, I don't want to bloody my knuckles today as I have a business meeting."

Henry stood up and looked at himself in the mirror to make sure he didn't have any stray hairs. He turned back to me. "I have to leave, honey. Stay away from boys," he said, and grabbed his coat from the doorknob and left.

I threw myself, belly down, onto Henry's bed. I rolled over onto my back and looked up at the ceiling. I was bored, and Catherine and Bernard didn't want me, so I took the paper and pencil from Henry's nightstand and began writing a story about a snapping turtle that snapped the penises off swimmers who teased girls and made them cry.

"I'll only play hide-and-seek with you if you promise not to suddenly quit and go eat cake like you did last time when you left me in a closet," I told Archie.

"Ok, Maybel," Archie began, "I won't quit to eat cake, but to be clear, if I am offered cake, I'll want cake, so if someone offers me cake, I'm going to yell out 'cake' then go downstairs for cake."

I rolled my eyes. "Fine."

"And Maybel, it's almost time for tea and cake, so don't be surprised if we have to stop and get cake soon."

"Why don't you just go downstairs and wait for your cake now then?" I began to lose patience with Archie.

"Because I like playing with you, Maybel. You're smart and pretty and you hide really well."

"Oh alright, I'll count and you hide," I sighed.

We were upstairs playing. Archie ran toward the game room.

"I haven't started counting yet, and now I know in which room you're hiding!" I yelled after Archie.

"It's ok, you'll never find me!" Archie yelled back at me.

I didn't even bother to close my eyes when I started counting. "One, two, three...."

"Can I play?" I jumped, startled by the voice behind me.

I turned, and there was Michael! "Hello, Michael!"

Michael quickly kissed my cheek. "I wanted to kiss your cheek last time we played together, but Bernard wouldn't let me, so I decided the next party we attended together, I would kiss your cheek before he starts following us around."

"Oh, he's off kissing my sister somewhere, I'm sure. He won't be bothering us," I assured Michael.

"In which room did Archie go?" Michael asked.

"The game room," I answered.

Michael hopped off, still as fast as a jackrabbit.

I began counting loudly again. "Four, five, six, seven, ok ten, ready or not, here I come!"

I ran into the game room and immediately saw Archie's feet protruding from underneath the billiard table. I pretended he was good at hiding and walked around the table calling his name. "Archie, where are you? Michael, where are you?"

As I rounded the billiard table, Archie giggled.

"Did I hear giggles?" I asked.

Archie stopped giggling.

"Oh, it must have been my imagination," I said.

I continued walking around the room and heard Archie's high-pitched giggles behind me as I walked toward the large, leather chairs with the globe on the stand between them.

"Michael, I bet you're over here!" I jumped behind the chairs thinking he'd be there, but he was not.

"Got you, Maybel!" Michael picked me up from behind and spun me around laughing.

"Where were you?" I laughed.

"I'll never tell!" he laughed.

"You haven't found me yet!" Archie giggled.

"Maybe Archie is in a different room?" Michael loudly suggested.

"Oh yes, let's go look," I yelled.

"No, I'm in the game room," Archie squealed.

"Oh, Maybel, I think I see a foot!" Michael said.

Archie pulled his feet further under the billiard table.

"Are you sure? I don't see any feet," I said.

Archie stifled a laugh.

Michael suddenly dropped to his belly and pulled Archie out by his ankle. "Found you!"

Archie stood up and dusted off his pants. "That was a really good hiding place wasn't it, Maybel!"

"The best, Archie!" I congratulated him.

"I'm going to count now, and you two hide," Michael smiled mischievously.

"Ok!" I yelled, and scrambled out the door.

I ran quickly into a bedroom and hid behind thick, heavy, brocade drapes. They were velvet and fancy and fell all the way to the floor.

I heard Michael outside calling for me and Archie. His footsteps passed the room where I hid.

What felt like a long time standing behind drapes passed, and I began to think Archie left me for cake again. I sat down on the floor. I heard footsteps pass the doorway again. It was very quiet and I figured the musicians downstairs had stopped because it was time for tea and cake.

I shifted around and started to stand when I again heard footsteps out in the hallway. The music began playing downstairs, and I heard a man's and woman's voices inside the room where I hid. I peeked through the heavy drapes and saw Henry, the most handsome man in the world, holding a woman. He held her in his arms and kissed her neck as he pulled her dress down off her shoulders.

The woman giggled and reached for Henry's belt buckle.

Henry pushed her hands away and pushed her shoulders back onto the bed. Henry undid his belt buckle himself and unbuttoned and unzipped his pants.

The woman sat up on the edge of the bed smiling up at Henry. "I can help you with that," she said seductively, and reached for the waist of his pants.

Henry again pushed her hands away. He let his pants fall to the floor and began unbuttoning his shirt. His penis was long and thick. His bottom was round and firm. And his legs were muscular. I watched Henry, admiring his every taught muscle.

The woman stood up and kissed Henry as he unbuttoned his shirt. Henry didn't open his mouth or touch her tongue with his tongue. She tried to help him unbutton his shirt but he whispered, "I can do this myself."

She smiled and giggled again.

Henry took off his shirt and let it fall to the floor. His back muscles were well-defined and his stomach was hard. I wanted to be that woman as she playfully touched his chest and stomach muscles. I wanted to feel his arms. They were thick and defined as well.

Henry unzipped her dress as he sucked on her neck. Her dress fell to the floor and Henry, with one swift and skillful move, pushed her onto her back, pulled apart her thighs, and pushed his penis all the way into her. She began moaning and Henry wasted no time enjoying her body. He thrusted hard and fast and groaned as he pulled himself out and orgasmed onto her stomach. He took his clothing and hers from the floor and put them onto the bed then reached into his bathroom for the hand towel over his sink. He handed her the towel and she wiped her stomach.

He quickly pulled up his pants and buttoned his shirt. The woman stepped into her dress and pulled it up. "Will you zip my dress?" she asked.

Without answering, Henry zipped her dress.

They stepped into their shoes. "Let's get back to the party before anyone notices our absence," Henry said.

Henry walked to the door and opened it for the woman to walk through, and then he closed the door behind them.

I quickly threw the drapes to the side and bolted to the door and listened for movement. I cracked open the door and peeked through. The hallway was empty.

I tiptoed down the hallway and downstairs, reasoning Archie and Michael had given up, and were already downstairs getting cake.

"Maybel, where have you been?" Bernard found me just as I took my last step off the stairs.

"What? I'm fine." I shuffled away before he could grab me, and walked quickly toward the dining room.

"Maybel, have you seen Michael?" Bernard caught up to me and grabbed my elbow.

"I haven't found him yet," I said as I shook myself free.

I started walking quickly again, weaving my way through beautiful gowns and glinting shirt cuffs.

"Maybel, stop walking!" Bernard grabbed my arm and pulled me to the side, out of the paths of partygoers. "Sit beside me at dessert. I don't want Michael to flirt with you."

"Aren't you supposed to be off somewhere shoving your tongue down my sister's throat?" I snapped at Bernard.

"Don't be crass, Maybel. It's my job to make sure nobody takes advantage of you."

"You shove your tongue down my sister's throat. Who watches Catherine to make sure you don't take advantage of her?"

I turned sharply on my heel and nearly ran into Michael. "Where have you been? Did you forget about our game?" Michael asked.

"I got sidetracked, I'm sorry. I came downstairs figuring you and Archie got tired of trying to find me," I told Michael.

"Michael, stop holding Maybel's hand," Bernard pulled me toward him and pried Michael's hand from mine. "Maybel, come sit beside me."

"I want to be with Michael! You aren't my boss, Bernard!" I squirmed free from Bernard and grabbed Michael's hand and we bolted around the corner.

It felt good to be naughty and run from Bernard. Michael and I ran to an empty alcove, giggling the whole way.

Michael held both my hands and smiled at me. He leaned toward me and kissed me. I smiled back and let him kiss me again.

"We should get back to the party, I suppose," I told Michael.

"Let's stay here and kiss." Michael pulled me close and kissed my lips and his hand brushed lightly over my breast.

"Michael, I pulled away from him. I don't want to do that."

"Fine," Michael seemed annoyed and walked past me and left.

I stood there thinking about what had just happened. I shook my head and told myself to forget about Michael. I returned to the main area and smelled cake. People were sitting in the dining room eating cake and chatting. I saw Michael talking to Bernard and Michael pointed toward me.

Bernard came to me. "Stop running away from me, Maybel, I'm only looking out for you. You're coming with me and sitting next to me."

Bernard took my hand and I followed him.

"This was easier than I thought," he said to me. "You're not even putting up a fight."

I just stared ahead and let Bernard lead me.

Bernard found Catherine at the long dining room table. She was sitting with a friend. Bernard pulled out my chair and I sat down. Bernard sat between me and Catherine.

Michael came and sat directly across from me with a girl whose hand he was holding. Michael smiled at the girl and held her hand. He glanced at me then continued flirting with the girl, telling her how pretty she was. They giggled and whispered, then got up and left before touching their cake.

244 - E. D. JUMPER

I poked my cake with my fork. I wasn't hungry anymore.

I started to get up, but Bernard put his arm around my shoulders. "Maybel, why must you go wandering off? Why can't you just sit here with me and your sister?"

"No one here thinks I'm pretty," I hissed, "so don't worry Bernard, no one is going to take advantage of me."

I went to the study where there were boxes of puzzles. Michael and I played together with these same puzzles during the first Christmas party I attended here at the Charleston's mansion. I had insisted on putting together all the pink and purple pieces while we chatted and giggled all night. I dumped out a box on the table and held a pink puzzle piece in my hand, staring at it while remembering how much fun Michael and I had that night. I looked up and saw Michael and that girl walking slowly past the study doors holding hands. Michael noticed me and kissed the girl's lips.

I sighed and threw the puzzle piece on the table. I didn't want to walk home alone, so I decided to go up to Bernard's room to wait out this party alone in peace.

I walked slowly up the stairs, leaving the smell of cake behind.

Henry ran into me as he came quickly out of the game room. "Oh, I'm sorry Maybel, are you alright, sweetheart?"

I stared up at Henry as his naked, thrusting body suddenly filled all the places in my mind.

"Are you ok, honey? I ran into you rather hard."

I was frozen. Henry's huge penis pushing in and pulling out of that woman's vagina and her moans had taken over my sight and hearing.

"Maybel, come sit. I'm afraid I hit your head."

Henry took my hand and I looked down at his hand with wide eyes, watching, in my mind, the hand that now held my hand rub that woman's nipple. One of his hands touched her vagina, I remembered, and I kept staring at his hand holding mine as he pulled me toward the sitting area.

Henry sat on the leather sofa and pulled me down next to him. He brushed my hair back and looked into my eyes.

"Your pupils look alright. I don't think I hit your head hard enough for you to need medical assistance. How are you feeling? Where does it hurt?"

"I'm ok," I barely whispered.

"You're talking to me," he smiled. "I was afraid you'd gone mute, yet again."

"I have to get past your beauty before I can speak," I attempted a joke.

I looked down at my hands on my lap. I felt sad that Michael kissed me then quickly found another girl.

Henry brought me back from my thoughts. He wiped my eye. "Why are you crying? I'm sorry I wasn't looking when I came out of this room and into the hallway. Did I bump your nose?"

I hadn't realized I was crying. "You didn't bump me," I said. "Nothing hurts."

Henry put his finger under my chin and lifted up my face. "Then why are you crying, sweetheart?"

"Michael was my friend I met at my first Christmas party here at the Charleston's, and today he kissed me, but now he's kissing another girl because I told him to stop touching my breast."

Henry's lips pressed together and his jaw muscle stiffened and became pronounced. "Someone touched you?"

"I told him to stop and he did. He looked mad though and started kissing another girl in front of me to make me jealous and it really hurt my feelings." Tears fell down my face as I told Henry what happened.

Henry pulled me into his embrace. "I'm sorry honey," he whispered. "Some boys and girls are bad and hurt people. I'm so sorry he did that to you."

"I'm ok. I'm just sad." I tried to talk between deep breaths and sad, little sobs.

Henry rubbed my back and kissed the top of my head. He held me a long time and a snot bubble in my nostril popped against his perfectly pressed shirt.

"Maybel, there will be boys who want more. They will try to get more. Some of them may try to take more. Now look at me," Henry made me look into his eyes. "I'm going to start teaching you how to defend yourself. I'll make sure that if you ever meet a boy who tries to take more than what you want to give, you'll know how to hurt him."

"Bernard already taught me some things. My daddy did too. And Mr. Charleston taught me how to punch. Please don't tell daddy about Michael. I don't want Michael to die. He didn't touch me again after I told him to stop."

"I won't tell your father since Michael left you alone. I will speak to Michael myself though, Maybel."

"He'll hate me for sure then," I said.

"Then he's stupid. He needs to learn how to behave though, and I'll be sure to explain to him what he did wrong after I've gotten his attention with a left hook." Henry winked at me.

"Maybel, I'm sorry some boys are like Michael. He tried to make you feel bad for not letting him touch you. He tried to make you jealous. Maybe he'll grow out of this bad behavior and become a good man, or maybe he won't. You did the right thing though, Maybel. You told him no, and then you told me."

Henry hugged me again. He kissed my forehead.

"Henry, were you bad and then grew up to be good?" I asked.

"I have never touched a woman the way Michael so boldly touched you."

"That's because girls always wanted you to touch them, I'll bet," I said. "You never had to want them. They always wanted you first."

Henry winced. He looked upset, even troubled, and a sudden look of fear passed across his eyes making him look like a little boy.

"Why do men like breasts?" I asked him.

"I don't know, Maybel. Men like women's bodies. When you get older, you'll begin to think boys look handsome."

"I already do," I smiled. "You're handsome."

"Thank you, but I meant you'll begin to like boys your own age eventually."

"How old are you, Henry?"

"How old do you think I am?"

"My daddy is thirty something, so you are probably about thirty something."

"Maybel! I'm not old enough to be your father! I'm only about five years older than you!"

"Really? Are you sure?"

"Maybe five and a half years older than you. I'm certainly not in my thirties though!" Henry seemed offended about looking old, which amused me.

"Then why do you look and act so old?"

"How do I look and act old?"

"You act like an adult, not a child. You dress like perfection. You have confidence and you act like you don't have questions about dating, school, sex, or growing up. You already know everything and you're not afraid of anything."

Henry laughed, "If only I were the man you described, honey." He kissed my forehead chuckling.

Henry put his arm around my shoulder. "I had to grow up fast to survive in some ways. I don't know much, and a lot of things scare me. I'm glad to know I look like the man you described, but I'm only a normal person. I have my own problems and burdens to bear. But thank you, Maybel, for seeing me as better than I am."

"You're welcome, Henry. You're nice to me and I like you."

"I like you too, sweetheart. I smelled cake baking earlier. Would you like a piece?"

"Yes, I do now," I smiled.

Henry stood and took my hand. "Let's go."

We went downstairs and sat together at the dining room table. Henry smiled at me. "See, this is turning into a nice afternoon now, isn't it?"

"Yes," I agreed.

Bernard came to us. "Maybel, where have you been? You weren't in the ballroom, the study, or the drawing room."

"I was upstairs and ran into Henry and now we're eating cake. Why aren't you off somewhere kissing your girlfriend?"

"She's talking about fashion," Bernard sighed. "Do you want to go outside and swing or play ball?"

"What? You, Bernard, want to spend time with me? Usually you tell me to go away so you can be with Catherine."

"I'm bored. I thought I'd play with you until Catherine is done talking about fashion," Bernard said.

"You only want me around when you're bored, but when I'm bored, you tell me to go away if you have a better option."

Henry snorted, "That is what you do, Bernard. Looks like Maybel here wants to be treated with more respect."

Bernard gave Henry an angry glare then left.

"I'm surprised Michael was able to get a moment alone with you given that Bernard hovers over you like a jealous boyfriend," Henry said, then took another bite of cake.

"Bernard is always bossy and tells me to go away, then makes me sit next to him so boys don't bother me, then tells me to go away so he can go off and kiss Catherine without me pestering them while they kiss with their tongues."

Michael stood in an alcove near the dining room and kissed that girl.

My shoulders slunk. "He's kissing her in front of me on purpose," I whispered to Henry. "I don't like him anymore." I poked my cake with my fork and slumped my shoulders even further.

"He's young and stupid, Maybel. Ignore him," Henry advised.

"It's hard to when he purposely sees me and kisses her right in front of me. You know, the first time we met he was really nice. We played hide-and-seek and put puzzles together."

"That was before he started liking girls. When a boy starts to like girls, he starts acting strangely because he suddenly doesn't know how to talk to girls anymore. Everything becomes awkward," Henry explained.

"You're not awkward. You don't even have to try to kiss a girl, they take one look at you and beg you to touch their breasts."

Henry again looked sad, which I thought was odd. "I wish they didn't want me so much sometimes," he said.

"Why?" I asked, confused.

"Sometimes I want to be invisible, I suppose."

"I don't have to try to be invisible," I said.

"Maybel, would you like to dance with me?" Henry asked me suddenly.

"No." I continued shoveling cake into my mouth.

"May I ask why?" Henry looked surprised. I may have been the first girl to tell him no.

"Bernard always laughs at me when we dance. He says I step on his toes, and my hair is always messy, and my feet are always dirty from playing outside barefoot."

"Bernard is apparently still stuck in that awkward phase when boys act stupid around girls they secretly think are pretty," Henry said.

"I respectfully disagree, Henry."

Henry chuckled, "Come dance with me, please? I promise I won't make fun of you."

"Well, maybe. It might be fun to dance with you."

"I'll make sure to spin you in front of Michael," Henry winked at me.

"Oh, that sounds fun! Let's go!" I stood up.

"Wait, sweetheart, sit back down for just one second," Henry motioned for me to sit.

I sat down and Henry took his napkin and wiped my cheek and chin while he smiled sweetly. "A little cake escaped your mouth."

I blushed, "See, I am messy." I was embarrassed.

"Don't feel bad, honey; it's actually very endearing. You're so innocent in all things, and I wish we'd met when we were both young children and closer in age."

"I don't mind that you're thirty, Henry." I smiled cheekily at him because it amused me that Henry didn't want to be labeled an old man.

"Maybel," he chuckled, "I'm not much older than you, it's just that a couple years seems like a big difference at your age."

"What does a couple years feel like when you're thirty?" I asked him.

"If I really were a big brother to you, I'd turn you over my knee and swat your bottom," Henry laughed and pinched my cheek gently. "Let's go dance, shall we?"

Henry stood and pulled me up. He clasped my hand in his and led me to the ballroom, making sure to pass in front of Michael.

I tried to ignore Michael and not look at him, but curiosity got the better of me, and I glanced quickly at Michael. He was watching Henry hold my hand and he looked angry. I couldn't suppress a little smile, and my heart felt fluttery and happy.

Henry danced with me and I was surprised at how well he moved his hips and legs. In the bedroom he moved like his body was stiff, and he did not appear gentle or loving. I had never seen anyone have sex before, but I had always imagined it would be more relaxed and there would be kissing and touching and gentleness. Now, in Henry's arms, he moved with a gentleness and his eyes looked kind and loving. His hips were against me and he moved them gracefully.

"Bernard was wrong," Henry smiled, "You dance well."

"I don't think a thirty-year-old man should be flirting with me," I teased Henry.

"I'm not flirting," Henry replied. "I'm being polite. You dance horribly."

I looked up at him and was about to cry.

"Oh God, Maybel, I was joking! I'm so sorry, I thought it was your strange sense of humor to say something untrue with a straight face."

"Well, I don't like it when people do it to me." I buried my face in his chest to wipe the tear that had formed.

"Maybel, sweetheart, I am so sorry! I will never joke like that again. You are breaking my heart right now."

I finished rubbing my face on his shirt and looked up at him. "You can joke like that but maybe next time can you wink very obviously?"

"Yes, honey, I promise." Henry held my head tightly against his chest and we continued dancing.

"You really are a good dancer, sweetheart." Henry kissed my hair as he held me.

I looked up at him again. "Henry, will you go outside and play with me? I don't want to dance anymore."

"Yes, sweetheart, I would love to play with you."

We walked past Michael again on our way outside. It was a nice afternoon.

"Do you want me to show you the slate waterfalls?" I asked Henry.

"Yes, Maybel, that sounds fun."

"You've not seen them before?" I asked, surprised.

"I have, but not with you," he smiled. "Your playfulness and childlike innocence makes everything better."

"I'm not a child, Henry. I told you already, I know how to make a baby."

"Yes, well, don't make any babies until you're old and married."

"But you can do it without making babies," I said.

"You don't know if you're going to get pregnant or not, so don't do it unless you're married."

"How many babies do you have?"

"None," Henry said.

"That you are aware of," I smirked.

"I have not made any babies," Henry said.

"Oh really, you're a virgin?" I asked.

Henry looked terribly uncomfortable. "Well, no, but I have not gotten anyone pregnant."

"You can have sex without putting your penis in a woman's vagina, did you know that? You should start doing that instead. But you still have to be careful, Henry," I cautioned, "because you can still get diseases."

"I have never once gotten a disease."

"That's good. I heard on the playground that your penis will fall off," I told him.

"That's not true," he said.

"Well, I hope not for the sake of your penis," I said.

"Maybel, how do you know so much about sex?"

"Bernard told me so that I could be aware of what boys might want me to do with them, and that way, boys cannot take advantage of my naivety."

"I suppose that was a wise decision on his part," Henry admitted.

"What does it feel like?" I asked.

"Sex? Maybel, I can't talk to you about this."

"Why? I want to know if it feels just a little bit good, or really good. After you have sex, do you want more?"

"Maybel, I know Bernard told you how a baby is made, but you don't need to know more than that. It would be bad for me to discuss specifics with you. And don't ask Bernard for specifics either. He should not be discussing how good it feels with you either. It's not right for a man to discuss such things with you. You're still young and innocent. Take it from me, innocence is precious; treasure it for as long as you can. Innocence is taken from us far too early in life as it is."

"Bernard doesn't know how it feels. He's a virgin."

Henry snorted, "Oh, I'm sure."

I look up at him confused.

"Did Bernard tell you he was a virgin?" Henry looked surprised.

"Yes," I said.

Henry looked skeptical.

"You think Bernard and Catherine have had sex?" I asked Henry.

Henry looked like he was carefully construing his answer. "I'm really not one to know about how long the average person keeps their virginity, Maybel. I lost mine when I was far too young."

"How old were you? Were you younger than me?"

"I don't like talking about it. Maybe one day I'll explain. I can't now. I don't like thinking about it."

"You look sad," I remarked.

"I am."

"I'm sorry." I took his hand.

"Me too." Henry squeezed my hand.

"Today, Maybel, will you help me remember how to be a child?"

"Of course!" I delighted in teaching Henry. "First, we have to take off our shoes. Next, you have to roll up your pants to your knees. And you should probably roll your shirt sleeves up too."

"I like your enthusiasm, Maybel."

"I have a shirt and shorts under my dress. Do you mind if I take off my dress so mommy doesn't get mad at me for getting my dress dirty?"

Henry paused, "Does Bernard let you?"

"Yes, he takes off his clothes too, except his undershorts."

"You're getting a little older, Maybel, maybe you shouldn't do that."

"Why? I'm still wearing clothes. I'm not going to be naked."

"Don't your parents get mad?" Henry asked.

"We're not naked, Henry. Can I take off my dress or will that make you uncomfortable?"

"I suppose you can," he said reluctantly.

"Will you help me?" I turned around so Henry could undo the back of my dress.

Henry didn't touch me.

I turned back around. "I can't undo my party dress. Can you do it?"

"Maybel, it feels wrong to undress you," Henry looked flustered.

"Why? I have on a shirt and shorts. I'm not showing you any of my private parts."

"Ok," Henry said reluctantly.

I turned back around and I felt Henry's touch on the back of my neck. He slowly unzipped my dress.

I turned to face him again. "Thank you." I pulled down my dress. "See, everything is completely covered."

I walked to a bush and draped my dress over a branch. "Are you coming? You can keep your clothes on if you want. Your mother isn't here to yell at you."

Henry unbuttoned his shirt slowly. I stood in front of him. "You are really slow undressing."

"I'm nervous. You're watching me."

"Shall I turn around?" I asked Henry.

"I don't know. This feels awkward."

"Then keep your clothes on," I told him.

"I don't want to get dirty," Henry said.

"You're such a princess. Catherine is a princess, too. She doesn't like to get dirty either anymore. She used to be a tomboy like me, you know. Then she started liking boys. I suppose if I weren't such a tomboy, boys would look at me differently. Daddy says he likes that boys aren't interested in me. Can you go slower, Henry? You're moving so fast you're just a blur."

"I'm going as fast as I feel like going, Maybel. Have some patience." Henry took his shirt from his body and tossed it on a large rock.

"I'm not good at being patient," I said.

"Clearly," Henry said dryly.

Henry undid his belt and eventually took his pants off. He tossed them on the rock as well.

"You look nice, Henry," I said.

Henry looked uncomfortable. "Thank you. You as well."

"Thank you, now let's go be children," I giggled.

I took Henry's hand. "Let's run!"

I ran fast but Henry ran faster. "Henry! You're supposed to make it seem like you're not a whole lot faster than me! Bernard pretends to be only a little bit faster than me!"

"I'll try to deceive you better next time," he laughed.

"Ok, first, we walk out to the middle of the creek and kick splash each other, then we rinse the mud off in the waterfalls."

I kick splashed Henry first, then he barely splashed me at all.

"Are your legs not as strong as they look?" I asked him.

"You said to pretend to be weak."

"Not that weak, Henry!"

Henry splashed me so hard my entire body was drenched. I laughed and ran to him, kicking water at him the whole way.

"Maybel, I'm all muddy."

"That means we're playing like children really well," I giggled.

Henry held my arm. "Am I allowed to trip you and make you fall into that deep puddle beside you?"

I looked down and to my side and Henry pushed me into it.

I popped back up ready for battle.

"Oh no, I have awakened the angry part of Maybel's personality," he teased.

I put my hands on his chest and pushed with all my might but he didn't budge at all.

"Can I push you down again or are you going to pout?" he laughed at me.

"I'm going to push you first!" I used a rock to set my foot against, and I pushed with all my might again, but Henry still wouldn't budge.

He picked me up and wrapped me behind his neck over his shoulders.

"No!" I screamed, "Don't toss me! The water's not deep enough and I'll hit a rock!"

I shifted my weight and managed to wrap my legs around his waist and climbed down a little. I clung to his chest with my legs wrapped around him.

"I'm not going to drop you in the water, Maybel! I promise! I was just teasing you!"

I breathed deeply. "You promise?"

"Yes!"

"Ok." I loosened my legs and Henry lowered me safely down.

"I'm not allowed to play koala like that anymore, you know, with my legs wrapped around your waist. Bernard says it looks like we're having sex so he doesn't let me do that anymore."

"Well, Bernard is right."

"Let's go to the waterfalls now," I took Henry's hand.

The waterfalls fell from slate protruding from a large hill. There were many waterfalls, some big and some small. I took Henry to my favorite waterfall.

"This one is my favorite because it's not too big and not too small, and the water isn't too fast or hard, but it's not weak either."

I walked under the pouring water and let it wash over me from my forehead, down my long locks of hair, to my toes. I felt little pebbles run down my scalp, back, and down my legs where they hit the water, swirling and pooling at my feet.

I opened my eyes and Henry was watching me with a shy smile. "You're beautiful, Maybel."

I smiled back. "You are, too."

Henry came and stood by me and I watched the mud and little pebbles and silt run down his shiny black hair, down his eyebrows, and perfect nose and lips, and all the way down his legs where they settled on the slate beneath our feet.

I looked back up at Henry. He looked happy. "See, I told you playing with me will make you all better again."

"I do feel better. Thank you. I feel different, lighter, with less burdens to bear. Can we do this again next week? I never really got to play like a child when I was young." Henry relaxed under the water.

"We can do this whenever you want. I'm always begging Catherine and Bernard to play with me."

"This is more fun than I've had in a long time. You don't understand how I've been feeling, Maybel. I haven't been well. I actually feel better now." Henry smiled and held my hands. "Thank you, sweetheart, you saved me."

"I'm happy you're happy, Henry."

"I am happy. I haven't been happy in I don't know how long. This feels amazing, Maybel!"

I smiled up at Henry.

"Maybel, I love you."

"I love you too, Henry. You've always been nice to me."

"Maybel, may I kiss you?" Henry asked softly, as though he were scared I'd say no.

"Yes," I giggled. I felt bees buzzing in my tummy. "I'll always be happy the most handsome man in the world wants to kiss me."

Henry stood watching me for a moment. The water fell from his hair onto my forehead. He leaned down and kissed me sweetly. His skin was warm against me. I looked up into his eyes and he smiled so sweetly.

Henry stood looking down at me for a moment. He pulled me against him and held me under the waterfall. I rested my head on his chest and hugged him back.

"Maybel," he whispered, "let's climb that tree you told me about."

I looked up at him smiling. "Ok!"

We walked through several more waterfalls and climbed up the hill. "This is my favorite tree here by the falls to climb," I told Henry. "I climb faster than I run, so you don't have to hold back."

"Alright," Henry smiled, "I won't."

I started climbing and was quite proud of myself for how fast and steady I went until Henry effortlessly passed me.

Henry was sitting on a branch at the top admiring the view when I finally made my appearance through the branches.

"This is breathtaking," Henry looked around with a happiness I'd never seen in his eyes before.

My jealousy immediately disappeared. My pride had been hurt, but now, watching Henry, I felt his happiness and it made me smile.

"You look really happy, Henry," I smiled.

"I am, Maybel. I am happy." Henry held out his hand and I took it. He pulled me onto a branch next to him. "Sit here with me for a little while, Maybel."

We held hands and looked around at the treetops beneath us. The breeze was gentle and warm. I watched the squirrels in the adjacent tree playing and giggled softly as they chased each other.

I felt Henry pull my hand lightly. When I looked over, he was smiling at me. "I like watching you. The way you look at everything is so full of curiosity and amazement."

I smiled back at Henry.

Henry continued watching me curiously. His smile was so sweet and I could see what he looked like as a boy when he smiled.

I felt myself blushing under his gaze. His eyes were sparkling all the colors.

"I should return to the party before mommy and daddy notice my absence," I whispered, not really wanting to leave though.

"Don't forget Bernard," Henry said dryly. "I'm sure he's banded together a search party."

We climbed down and Henry jumped off a lower branch and held his arms up for me.

"I can jump too, Henry. I'm still a tomboy."

"Yes, but just this once, may I catch you?"

I giggled and let myself fall into his arms. He caught me and set me lightly on my feet.

"Let's go get our clothing, shall we?" Henry held my hand.

"I hope a racoon didn't steal our clothes. A racoon stole my clothes the last time I was here," I told Henry.

Henry looked at me, puzzlement all across his face.

"Sometimes I see him running through the woods still wearing my best dress," I solemnly sighed.

Henry started laughing. "You're really good at keeping a straight face!"

I laughed, "I like watching you smile."

Henry squeezed my hand.

We walked down the hill. "My underwear is dry now," I said. "Is yours?"

"Yes," he answered.

I pulled my dress over my head. I turned around and asked Henry to zip my dress. I felt him slowly tug on my zipper and pull it up to the back of my neck.

I turned around. "Would you like me to help you?"

"I can reach my zipper," Henry chuckled as he held his pants and zipped up his zipper. "You can help me with my shirt cuffs though."

Henry put on his shirt and I took his top button and pulled his shirt in front of him and fastened his collar. I fastened the button below that. I continued fastening his buttons until I reached just above his belly button. I felt his body tighten. I looked up into his eyes.

He now looked like a little boy, but scared. "I can finish buttoning my shirt," he whispered.

"I'm sorry, Henry. Did I hurt you?"

"No." Henry pulled me to him and wrapped his arms around me. You've never hurt me. You're perfect, Maybel, and I love you.

"I love you, too." I reached my arms around his neck and stood on my tip toes as I pulled him down and I kissed his cheek.

I felt Henry relax a little. "Thank you," he kissed my forehead.

Henry finished buttoning his shirt and we put our shoes on. Henry moved slowly, like all the weight he'd shed playing with me, poured down onto his back, again rendering him troubled and sad as he watched memories play in his mind.

"I cannot let a woman unbutton my shirt or pants," Henry suddenly blurted out. "It's because of what happened." Henry swallowed hard. "I have to initiate everything. I have to be on top. I have to be in control. I won't let a woman touch my penis or satisfy me with her mouth," Henry breathed deeply and his breaths were shaky. "I feel embarrassed telling you this. I've never told anyone this ever. You're easy to talk to, Maybel. Please don't tell anyone anything I've said."

"I won't," I promised. I didn't understand what Henry said, but it felt like it was important to him and he looked scared when he spoke.

I very gently reached for Henry's hand. "I'll protect you, Henry. I promise."

Henry swallowed hard and squeezed my hand. "Thank you," he whispered. "I love you, and you are the first woman I've ever felt comfortable talking to."

"I love you, too," I said.

We slowly walked back toward the Charleston's party. I felt Henry begin to relax a little once again.

Bernard came out his back door and walked to us. He looked upset when he noticed us holding hands.

"Where have you been, Maybel?"

"Just out losing my virginity. I think I pulled a leg muscle and my back is sore. What have you been doing, Bernard?"

"We weren't doing that," Henry quickly said.

"Of course not, Maybel is a child," Bernard looked at me.

"Where's Catherine?" I asked. "She probably wants you to dance with her."

"Let's go find Catherine then," Bernard put his hand firmly on my shoulder.

"I meant you should go dance with your girlfriend. I'm staying with Henry."

"We're having a wonderful time together," Henry said. "I've already asked Maybel if we can play together next week," Henry smiled at Bernard.

I knocked Bernard's hand off my shoulder and took Henry's hand. "What do you want to do now, Henry?"

"I want to bathe, actually. I have creek bed pebbles in my underwear, I do believe. I'll go upstairs now, Maybel, and return soon."

Henry went inside and Bernard took my hand. "You can bathe in my bathroom, Maybel."

"I don't want a bath," I said, annoyed at Bernard's attention.

"Your hair has tree bark in it," he argued.

"It's fashionable in Paris, ask Catherine!" I snapped.

"Maybel, I'm trying to be helpful so no one makes fun of you for looking disheveled."

"You make fun of my appearance all the time," I reminded him.

"I'm allowed, we have a special bond and can be honest," Bernard said.

"You look horrible," I told him.

"What? Why?" Bernard looked taken aback.

"Special bond, remember? I can be mean and you'll just have to forgive me no matter what, isn't that the way it works?"

"Ok, I'm sorry," Bernard said.

I turned around and walked back into Bernard's house. Bernard followed. I started up the stairs.

"Where are you going now?" he asked me.

"To get a bath! Stop following me and go away!"

I ran the rest of the way up the stairs. I heard Bernard's footsteps behind me.

Michael walked angrily out of the game room. Henry stood in the doorway of the game room rubbing his left hand.

"I'm never talking to you again!" Michael yelled at me.

I slugged Michael. He stumbled backward and into the wall behind him. He clenched his teeth and held his jaw and stared at me with anger. He then turned and went downstairs.

"What the hell was that about, Maybel?" Bernard asked.

I looked at Henry who was now standing in the hallway angrily watching Michael go downstairs. He was still rubbing his left hand. "I got Michael's attention and enlightened him." Henry winked at me, then went down the hall to his bedroom.

I went to Bernard's bedroom and into his bathroom.

"Maybel, what happened?"

"Henry took care of everything. I'm fine now."

"Maybel, I'm supposed to watch over you and protect you, not Henry!"

"I'm fine, everything is fine. Can you go find Catherine and let me bathe in peace?"

"I'll wait here." Bernard laid on his bed and took a book from his nightstand.

"You're waiting for me in bed? I've already had sex once today, Bernard, I can't possibly have more."

"Please don't joke about that. It makes me upset," Bernard said, looking up from his book.

"Why?"

"Because I don't want to think about you with anyone like that!"

"Why? You have sex with Catherine."

"No, I don't."

"I told Henry you were a virgin but he didn't believe me."

"Don't tell Henry I'm a virgin!" Bernard snapped angrily.

"Why?"

"It's different for men. We want people to think we have lots of sex all the time. Men don't want to be virgins."

"Why don't you want to be a virgin? Have you told Catherine? Maybe she doesn't want to be a virgin either."

"I don't mind being a virgin, I just don't want Henry or my friends to know I'm a virgin."

"So, you're saying your friends think Catherine is a slut who has lots of sex all the time with you? Does Catherine know about this?"

"No, and please don't tell her."

"Maybe Catherine wants people to know a handsome, rich boy chose her to have quick and unsatisfying sex."

"Girls tell people they're virgins even when they aren't. Boys and girls are different that way," Bernard explained.

"Henry had sex today," I blurted out.

"Today? With whom? How do you know?"

"I was playing hide and seek with Archie, and while I was hiding, Henry brought a woman into the room where I was waiting to be found, and I saw them have sex."

Bernard stared at me.

"Henry doesn't know I saw, so don't tell him."

"What was it like?" Bernard looked fascinated.

"It looked like what you told me it would look like," I replied.

"How long does sex last?" Bernard asked.

"How long can you masturbate?" I asked.

"A while, but I imagine sex would feel so much better than my hand that I would come really fast."

"That's disappointing," I said. "Maybe you should lie about your inability to satisfy a woman."

"Oh, what do you know about it? How would you know what is a sufficient amount of time to spend having sex?"

"Well, when I touch myself, it takes longer than five minutes for me to scream," I pointed out.

"You scream?" Bernard looked at me with wide eyes.

"Don't you?" I asked.

"Don't your parents hear you?" Bernard asked.

"No, I don't pleasure myself when they are in the same room as me. I have boundaries, Bernard."

"Maybel," Bernard sounded exasperated, "how long do I have to go to satisfy a woman?"

"It's not a race. Take as long as you can," I answered.

"So, ten minutes?"

I rolled my eyes and sighed, "Poor Catherine."

"Well, you said Henry only lasted five minutes," Bernard huffed.

"Yes, and I will not be thinking about him when I masturbate anymore."

"You think about Henry?" Bernard looked upset.

"Well, not anymore," I said.

"Have you ever thought about me?" Bernard asked.

"Have you ever thought about me?" I asked Bernard.

"No, you're a child," Bernard huffed.

"I've never thought about you, either. You're too young. I like older men," I smiled wryly at Bernard.

"I saw you and Henry holding hands," Bernard looked irritated.

"That's not all I held," I snorted and giggled.

Bernard's eyes flashed anger.

"I'm joking, Bernard."

"Stop joking about you being with boys in that way."

"Henry is not a boy, he's a man," I corrected Bernard.

"Stop, Maybel, it makes me mad, even if you are joking."

"I see you kissing my sister every day."

"Does it make you jealous?" Bernard asked me.

"No, I'm used to watching you kiss her. When I have a boyfriend, you'll get used to watching me kiss someone."

"No, I won't."

"Why do you care? I'm not your girlfriend and I'm not really your little sister. I can have sex with anyone I want right now if I desired," I said bluntly.

"Shut up, Maybel. And Michael found another girl to kiss so I don't have to worry about him anymore."

I became angry and went inside his bathroom and slammed his door.

"Oh, it looks like I hit a sore spot," Bernard yelled.

I opened the bathroom door. "I didn't want Michael anymore. That's why he found someone else."

"Right," Bernard said sarcastically. "You probably annoyed him to the point he discarded you like a three of clubs in a poker game."

"I discarded him for grabbing my breast, and Henry took care of Michael for me, so go be with Catherine, I don't need you, I have Henry!"

I slammed the bathroom door again and ran bath water while I undressed.

I took a nice, long, hot bath so I could have some peace and quiet away from Bernard acting strangely and annoying lately.

When I finished, I wrapped a towel around myself and opened the bathroom door. Bernard was laying on his bed reading.

I went to Bernard's closet to find a shirt. I chose a soft green shirt and a pair of cotton shorts. I took them to his bathroom to dress. After I finished dressing, I jumped into bed beside Bernard and knocked his book out of his hands to annoy him.

"Why aren't you with Catherine?" I asked.

"She's mad at me for worrying about you all day. Also, she saw me punch Michael and accused me of acting like your jealous boyfriend. I told her Michael grabbed your breast, and Catherine then bloodied Michael's nose and lip, but she was still mad at me because she still thinks I was acting like I'm your boyfriend."

"Catherine hit Michael for me?"

"She made Michael bleed. It was great. Catherine is quite the boxer," Bernard laughed.

I smiled. I was happy I had people who cared about me and protected me.

"I'm sorry I said you were annoying and I made a rude comment about Michael not wanting you." Bernard held his arms out for a hug and I put my head on Bernard's chest while he hugged me.

"I love you, Maybel. Sometimes I don't know how be around you anymore. I got really jealous because you were with Michael. I was angry that you and Henry got along so well, and sometimes, I think Henry is attracted to you, and that just makes me madder." Bernard breathed in deeply. "And Catherine got mad at me because she said I'm in love with you."

I didn't reply. I laid on Bernard's chest listening to his heartbeat.

I took a deep breath. I continued laying with Bernard. We joked about Catherine's possible secret life as a professional boxer and giggled.

I changed into my dress and Bernard walked me home and kissed my cheek.

"See you tomorrow, Maybel."

"Yes, Bernard."

Catherine apologized to Bernard for being mad at him over the incident with Michael. She told Bernard she agreed I needed protecting because I somehow always found trouble. I told Catherine that trouble found me. I had no idea Michael would do what he did. Catherine reminded me that after church one Sunday, Eddie Prescott asked me to taste his lip balm to judge whether or not it was too sweet, and I was about to lick his lips, when Catherine punched Eddie's stomach so hard he vomited on her shoes.

"I was nine, Catherine! I didn't know!"

"Well, you should have more common sense than what you have!" Catherine railed at me.

Bernard would be leaving soon for boarding school, and Catherine asked if I wanted to join them for a small picnic in Bernard's orchard.

Catherine and I took cookies and cider and met Bernard at his house. We then had a little picnic in his apple orchard. His family had many apple trees that daddy said produced good cider. Of course, daddy mixed the cider with alcohol, so I assumed that extra kick was what he liked most about the cider produced from the Charleston's apples.

Lately, I had been keeping my arms in a folded position across my chest. My breasts had begun growing much bigger, and I was embarrassed. I didn't know what to do with them, so I'd been crossing my arms a lot lately.

"Maybel, race you to the top!" Bernard laughed as he darted up the apple tree.

"That's not much of a challenge, Bernard," I said. "It's a very short tree," I laughed.

"Oh, come now, Maybel, where is the girl that always accepted any challenge?" Bernard taunted.

I wanted to climb trees again, and run through the orchard like we used to do, but I felt embarrassed of my body. I didn't know how to hide this change in my chest other than to cross my arms and hope nobody asked me to do anything that required two hands.

"Maybel! Catch me!" Bernard jumped down. I thought he was going to land on top of me so I instinctively reached upward. He landed beside me laughing. "The look on your face, Maybel!" he laughed.

I playfully swiped at him with one hand while my other arm laid across my burgeoning breasts. "Stop it, Bernard!" I laughed.

"Maybel, what do you say to a challenge?" he grinned. "Run to that tree," he pointed to the largest apple tree at the edge of the orchard, "Then over to that tree, then climb to the top of this tree!" His eyes beamed.

"Go ahead, Maybel, you've been begging me to run, climb, and swim all summer long," Catherine laughed, "and you always win! Let's see how you fare against a more formidable opponent!" she winked at Bernard.

My competitive nature was greater than the apprehension I had about my breasts suddenly being in the way. I agreed to Bernard's challenge and we ran to the first tree, but my heavy skirt was catching on weeds. I stopped to examine my skirt. "I'll just give you the first-place badge of honor," I said while picking little weeds from my hemline.

"Maybel, just take it off! You have on the shorts your mother sewed, don't you?" Bernard said irritably.

"Yes," I replied "But,"

Bernard interrupted me before I could finish. "Honestly, Maybel, you have been acting so strangely!" he said, annoyed.

I wanted to go home. I had always been eager to run and climb with anyone, but all I wanted now, was to go home and hide my chest, and my hips and thighs, which were beginning to thicken into something other than the skinny bean poles I was used to having. Mommy was in the midst of sewing a new skirt for me because she'd noticed how tightly this one pinched, and that made me even more embarrassed. I couldn't stop my body from changing, and I couldn't stop anyone from noticing.

"Bernard, I am tired," I lied, "I want to go home."

"Maybel's upset her breasts got big," Catherine giggled. "She can't reach up and take a glass from the kitchen shelf without knocking over the bread basket on the counter. She isn't used to her breasts sticking out so far."

"Catherine!" I shouted, "Don't say!"

"You look beautiful, Maybel, and you'll get used to your bigger breasts soon," Catherine said with a much kinder tone. "I went through that phase too, and you'll feel more comfortable soon, I promise," Catherine said. She could at times be very comforting and soothing, but I nevertheless wished she would not have mentioned my changing body to Bernard.

"I just want to be invisible for a while," I muttered.

Catherine and I walked home together. I told Catherine I felt like I wore a new body and I very much disliked this new body. Catherine was sympathetic, much more sympathetic than when I got my first period and had questions about intercourse. I was grateful to have her to talk to about these kinds of things, and it was nice to be alone with her for a while and have my big sister's undivided attention.

After dinner, I took my papers and two pencils, in case one pencil broke, and put everything I needed into a bag and set off for the woods behind my garden.

I came to a clearing and sat on a rock.

I began writing about a fox named Franny who made herself invisible by never talking. She stood still and never spoke. One by one, everyone who ever knew her began to ask where she was.

"I'm here!" Franny called.

But it was too late, and her family and friends could no longer see Franny. And then, Franny noticed her family and friends began fading away from her eyesight, too. They became shadows, and then outlines, and then wisps of air, and finally they became nothing.

Franny the fox grew lonely. She begged to be seen again but to no avail. She perished when lightning struck her tail and severed her spinal cord. Also, a piano fell on her. I erased those last parts; they felt out of place.

"This is stupid," I muttered to myself. "I'll finish this story later."

I came from our pond to our house wearing white linen shorts and a sleeveless top. There was a short, heat wave passing through. It would likely turn cold again in the next day or two. I wanted to enjoy the brief warmth before another cold spell.

"Maybel!" Catherine yelled at me, "Go get dressed! You know we aren't allowed wearing our underclothes when we have guests!"

Catherine was sitting with Bernard in our garden. Bernard stared at me wide-eyed.

"Who's here?" I looked around the garden.

"Bernard is here!" Catherine yelled. She looked at me like I should recognize Bernard as being a guest. "Go get dressed!"

"Bernard's not a guest. He's like family by now," I said.

"Maybel, go get dressed right now! Your clothes are wet and clinging to your body!" Catherine continued unnecessarily yelling at me and I continued ignoring her as I walked at a leisurely pace toward home.

"Cover your breasts!" Catherine yelled in her schoolteacher voice.

"Fine, Catherine, I'll go get dressed, but Bernard doesn't look like he cares. He thinks of me as an annoying, little sister! Isn't that what you always tell me, Bernard? That I'm an annoying tag-along and you wish I'd leave you alone?" I stuck my tongue out at Bernard for added emphasis.

Bernard sat on the bench bent over, his elbows resting on his lap and his arms propping up his head. He immediately looked down at his shoes when we looked at him.

He didn't answer me. He continued sitting bent over.

"Bernard, tell Catherine you don't care if I wear these clothes so I don't have to go put on a heavy and hot dress in this heat."

Bernard mumbled something that sounded like he didn't care what I did.

"Just go, Maybel!" Catherine screeched at me.

"Why are you so upset, Catherine?" I asked her.

Catherine huffed loudly, "Come on Bernard! Let's go!" She pulled on Bernard's arm but he shook himself free from her grasp.

"I need to sit for a while. My stomach hurts." Bernard sat doubled over.

Catherine became irate. "Go away Maybel! Leave us alone!"

"What did I do, Catherine? I just came home from swimming and you're angry at me and yelling for me to leave. I haven't done anything bad!"

Catherine sat down beside Bernard on the bench with her arms crossed and her face was red with anger.

"Fine, I'm leaving!" I yelled at Catherine.

I went into the kitchen and poured a glass of water and took some crackers on a plate to Bernard. I opened the kitchen door and Bernard was still bent over, while Catherine was hissing about something that angered her.

"I can't control it, Catherine! It just happens sometimes! I'm sorry, alright!" Bernard said with exasperation.

"Here, Bernard," I said as I approached.

"What do you want, Maybel?" Catherine said angrily.

"I have crackers for Bernard."

"Why?" Catherine asked angrily.

"Because his stomach hurts, Catherine," I said, handing Catherine the glass and plate. "Why are you mad at me for bringing him crackers?"

"Oh, honestly, Maybel! You are so naive you seem stupid sometimes!" Catherine spat at me.

I stopped and stared at Catherine.

"I'm sorry, Maybel! I didn't mean that!" Catherine quickly apologized. She looked surprised at herself for having not been composed for once.

I turned and ran back inside crying. I tore off my wet clothes and bathed quickly, then put on a summer dress. My hair was tangled from swimming so I sat brushing it at my dressing table.

"Maybel," Catherine knocked on my door.

I didn't answer.

"Maybel, I'm sorry. You aren't stupid. I was angry when I said that, but I didn't mean it, and I'm sorry."

I continued brushing my hair.

"Maybel, would you like to come to Bernard's house for ice cream and cake? They're having a small party and Mrs. Charleston is playing violin."

I hated parties. And my hair was wet. And Catherine was really mean.

"Please, Maybel?"

I opened my bedroom door. Catherine looked remorseful. "I'm sorry, Maybel," she said. "I was mad because Bernard seemed to enjoy your bathing suit too much. I suppose I was jealous," she said shyly.

I had no idea why Catherine thought that. I hadn't been wearing a bathing suit. I wore my usual outdoor clothes that I wore while gardening. "What are you talking about Catherine? I wore gardening clothes and Bernard has seen me wear my gardening clothes mother sews for us hundreds of times."

"Yes, but not recently, and you're older now," she raised her eyebrows at me expectantly.

I stared back at her confused.

"Your breasts have grown large now, Maybel!" Catherine said exasperatedly. "This is why I said you were naive! You don't seem to pick up on things like you should!"

"Because I'm stupid?" I snapped.

"No, Maybel! I just can't understand how you can write stories about human interaction so well, but not understand situations and people's reactions when they're right in front of your face!"

"Bernard treats me like a child! He says my hair is messy and he makes fun of me. He acts like I'm a child and sometimes he says and does things that make me either cry or get angry. He didn't notice my breasts, Catherine! He only notices you!"

Catherine sighed, "Maybel, he notices your body, and I know you don't mean to get his attention, but can you please wear more clothing when he's around?"

"Fine, Catherine! Is this dress I'm wearing ok? You can still see my elbows though. How very scandalous! I should probably cover my ankles too, lest they bring about salacious remarks from our neighbors!"

Catherine looked annoyed. "This dress is fine, Maybel. Are you coming to the Charleston's with us?"

"Do you want me to come? What if Bernard notices my wrists and cannot stop staring at them?"

"Yes, I would like you to come with us, but lose your sarcasm." Catherine tried to suppress a snarl.

"My sarcasm follows me everywhere I go, like my shadow," I replied.

"Pretend it's a cloudy day, then," Catherine growled through clenched teeth.

"No promises. I do want to watch Mrs. Charleston play violin though. You say they have cake and ice cream?"

"Yes," Catherine rolled her eyes. "Let's go."

Bernard was downstairs sitting on the sofa. He stood up but didn't look at us. Catherine went to his side and leaned up for a kiss. Bernard quickly pecked her lips.

"You want some birdseed to go with that pathetic peck, Bernard?" I asked dryly.

"Maybel is coming with us, Bernard," she said as she took his hand.

Bernard still didn't look at me. He only nodded and led Catherine out the door.

"Nice day," Catherine attempted small talk.

"Yes," Bernard and I replied in unison.

Bernard and I spent the afternoon watching his mother play violin and not talking to each other. Catherine clung to Bernard as she whisked him about the ballroom, enjoying the attention dating a Charleston brought.

I ate cake with Archie. I burped, Archie burped, and we didn't care if the other had cake stains on our faces.

Bernard came by to drop off a bottle of whiskey his father had bought daddy in Ireland while on business.

"Good day, Maybel, is your father in?" I opened the front door to accept the pretty, green bottle full of Irish cheer.

"He's in his workshop. Would you like me to give this to him, or would you like to take it to him yourself?"

"I'll leave it here for him," he answered. "My father would like me to tell your father to drop by anytime for a cigar, and also, to bring this whiskey with him when he comes," Bernard chuckled.

"I'll tell him. Thank you."

Bernard paused expectantly.

"Oh, I'm sorry, Bernard. Won't you come in?"

I didn't want Bernard to come into my house though. I had begun having feelings inside me, desires to kiss Bernard and feel his body against mine. It was almost too much for me to handle when I was near him. I wanted him to touch me, so I stayed as far away from him as possible when he came to visit Catherine. I stopped going with Catherine to Bernard's house because we always somehow ended up playing or wrestling or laying in front of the fireplace reading together. Sometimes the smell of his skin made me tingley between my legs, and these new feelings confused me.

I began pretending to be busy, or pretending to have schoolwork that demanded all my time on weekends and school breaks. Unfortunately, I needed help with math.

Bernard followed me into the family room. "Maybel, I've been wondering what happens in the story you last told me? Have you finished it?"

"I haven't written an ending for that story yet, but I have an idea. I haven't sat down and thought about it much lately. I've been preoccupied with math and other studies, but especially math." I frowned. I hated math.

I felt awkward around Bernard; I couldn't be near him and not become flustered.

Bernard smiled warmly, "Let me help you with math, and then perhaps you could finish the story?"

"I suppose that would be fine. Catherine is in town helping mommy with her dresses right now, and they don't need my assistance at the moment. Thank you, Bernard, for your help."

We sat down at the table in our family room. I didn't know how much time had passed when I finally laid my head onto the table, effectively giving up.

"Just concentrate, Maybel!"

"It doesn't make any sense, Bernard! There are numbers and letters!" I looked up, exasperated.

Bernard took a deep breath. "Ok, I'll show you again. You put equations together like this." He scribbled a bunch of numbers and letters down that looked unreasonable to me. I stared at him like he had just spoken to me in Egyptian hieroglyphics, as though he said, "cat, falcon, triangle, squiggly sword, three horizontal lines" to me.

"I don't understand math, Bernard. It doesn't make any sense." I felt really unintelligent next to Bernard.

"Look, if you just pay attention, you'll understand."

I put my forehead down on my math book and spread my palms out on the family room table. "It doesn't make any sense. I can't visualize how these numbers are supposed to fit together. It's a puzzle with half the pieces missing," I whined.

"Maybel, you think up stories, right?" Bernard, I could tell, was trying very hard to exercise patience with me, but it was waning.

"Yes," I answered.

"Well, I don't understand how you do that. And I know I'll never be able to describe people and places like you do in your stories. You see the tiniest details most other people never see, but I can appreciate your ability. Open your mind just a little, and at least try to understand math."

"Bernard, write a story right now."

"Maybel, do math right now."

"See, we're at a standstill," I said.

"Maybel, you are the most stubborn and exhausting person!"

"Bernard, I can no more understand math than you can imagine a fanciful story. I cannot understand why you cannot write a story with intricate details about emotions and descriptions about the scenery. You cannot understand why numbers, and especially numbers with letters attached, make no sense to me."

Bernard sighed, "You make a fair point. My brain understands all the things your brain does not. I suppose if we put our brains together, we could then create something magical," he sighed, tired of trying to make my circle of a mind fit into his square mind.

I smiled, "You do my math homework, and I'll do your literature homework."

Bernard returned my smile, "I suppose we are each very good at things the other lacks."

I pushed my math book away, smiling. I hoped Bernard would see me pushing my math book away and take my hint. Math time was over.

"Will you finish your story for me now, Maybel?" Bernard grinned. "It's just, you left it at such a crucial point, and I've been waiting on you for what feels like forever to finish."

"Oh, no thank you," I said. "I don't think it has an ending."

"What?" Bernard looked surprised I wasn't agreeable to finishing my story.

"I don't feel like finishing it," I said. "Maybe one day I will, but I'm not motivated now."

"Are you serious?" Bernard asked, incredulously.

"Anyway, I'm done with math, too. I'm unmotivated to study math anymore today, and that story you want me to finish is boring."

"I have never, in my life, met someone as exhausting and frustrating as you," Bernard said calmly, although he bit his lower lip and clenched his hands on the arms of the chair where he sat.

"I feel like boating. Do you want to come with me, or are you needed back at your home?"

"I fed and brushed the horses already. Father and I discussed a business acquisition, and mother and I made lunch. I'm free. Finish the story, Maybel. The boy was just about to be speared by Polynesian dancers and the girl was walking on hot coals to show her good favor to the Polynesian Gods. Finish the story!"

"I might. I'm bored of that story now though. Maybe later my interest will be reignited." I stood up and walked toward the back door.

Bernard followed. "I know you aren't finishing the story just to irritate me!"

"That's not it," I said. "I've moved on to another story about an English schoolteacher from hundreds of years ago who inadvertently fell into a bog and woke up in present-day England. She saw a woman mathematician and tried to strangle her because she thought the mathematician was a witch. Did you know people back then thought smart women were evil? I think that's fascinating."

"I'll buy you custard every day for a year if you finish that damned story!"

"Oh, I don't know, we'll see."

"You know exactly how to irk me, and I swear you enjoy irritating me!"

We walked through the garden toward the pond. I was having some problems concentrating because Bernard was wearing a light, cotton shirt that showed his muscular chest. It was cold out-side, but I enjoyed icy swims sometimes in early spring. Winter kept me inside and I did not enjoy being caged. I yearned for spring, and even though it was cold, the pond was not frozen, and I wanted a taste of what summer had in store for me. We had decided to row to the island and back. I wore my pale blue, cotton shirt and linen pants I wore around the house when I cleaned and got hot. Mommy just finished sewing these because my breasts became too big for the summer clothes she had sewn last year. I hoped these clothes would last through summer, because I didn't want my body to change anymore.

We walked along the bank of the pond. The water was calm.

"You create the end to your story while I row," Bernard smiled at me as he held the boat for me to step inside.

I agreed and we sat opposite each other in the little row boat.

"Maybel, tell me more about the boy and girl in the story," Bernard asked. He paused, then said, "And their pet squirrel. Why must you always put squirrels somewhere in your stories? And cows, why are there always donkeys too?"

"Because I like squirrels, and I like cows, donkeys, and oxen, Bernard. If you don't like squirrels, cows, donkeys, and oxen, I suggest you write your own story," I grinned.

"Ok, fine, Maybel, keep your squirrels. Why not add a spider from time to time?"

"Because I don't care much for spiders, or praying mantises either, for that matter," I said.

"Really? I assumed you liked spiders," Bernard watched me quizzically.

"And why would you assume that?" I asked incredulously.

"Well, I guess because you haven't minded the one that's been crawling on you the last five minutes."

"What?" I stood up, rocking the boat with my sudden jolt.

"Just kidding, Maybel." Bernard laughed deeply.

"I'm not finishing the story now, Bernard!" I yelled, annoyed.

"You will. And then, if I like the ending, I won't tip the boat," he winked.

"You're impossible!" I yelled.

Bernard laughed harder, and with my unsteady weight, and his absolute uproarious laughter, the boat tipped and we fell overboard.

"Bernard!" I screamed.

Bernard had the audacity to continue laughing at me. "You look like a kitten who's been trotting through a sudden downpour," he continued laughing at my expense.

"Ok, fine, Bernard, you want to know what happens to the little boy and girl in the story? She hits the boy so hard his nose falls off and then bakes pies every day for the rest of their lives knowing full well he can't smell his favorite pie wafting in the window sill. And that, Bernard, makes her so happy!" I emphasized the last sentence to convey how angry I was.

For some reason my ending caused Bernard even greater fits of laughter. "Oh Maybel! I'm going to cry from laughing so hard! That's the stupidest ending I've ever heard!" His face was red with pure amusement and laughter.

"I'm leaving!" I screamed, and began swimming toward the island.

"Oh, come now, Maybel! That story was unbelievably silly!" he laughed.

I swam ashore my little island and Bernard followed, dragging the boat.

"Maybel, where are you? I was only teasing! Remember when we used to tease each other? Just because you're older now doesn't mean you have to lose your sense of humor!"

"Who says I've lost my sense of humor?" I threw a pine cone from high above and hit him hard, right on the side of his head.

"Ow! Maybel!"

I didn't stop with one. I had amassed quite a few pine cones while he was bringing the boat ashore and I gleefully hurled them as hard as I could, hitting his chest and arms.

"Maybel! Stop it right now!"

"Or what?" My pine cone banged into his knee and splattered apart.

"That's it, Maybel!" he growled.

In an instant he was inside the tree and shot up toward me as fast as one of the squirrels in my stories.

He barreled up the last couple branches and was about to yell at me to quit throwing pine cones at him when he suddenly stopped right in front of me, his hands around my arms, preventing me from throwing another pine cone. He stopped and stared at me.

"Maybel!" He sucked in his breath hard and stared at my breasts.

"What? If you pretend there's another spider on me again, I'll finish you off with the rest of my pine cones, Bernard!" I yelled at him.

Bernard stammered unintelligibly.

"What?" I suddenly became worried. Bernard's face was blank with shock.

"Bernard are you ok?" I held his shoulders, afraid he'd lose his balance and fall.

"Your clothes are wet, Maybel," his voice was low and strained as his eyes took in my now very large breasts.

Bernard was frozen. He was looking at me with a look I'd never seen before.

I noticed his body and how it looked in wet clothing too. His clothing clung to every muscle.

He looked up at the sky and took a deep breath. He breathed deeply until he composed himself enough to descend.

I followed. We reached the last branches, then jumped down and landed on soft ground, cushioned by pine needles.

Bernard turned to me. Again, he stared at my body. The wet clothes didn't leave much to his imagination I was sure, because there was not much guessing as to what was underneath his clothing either.

"Let's go home, the sun has set," Bernard said as he held the boat steady for me to enter.

Bernard began rowing us back home. He watched me as he rowed. I watched him too, because his arms and chest were strong and I wanted to touch them. I wanted Bernard to hold me in those strong arms.

I took a deep breath and looked up. I wanted a distraction. "Bernard, look, there's Orion."

"You remember," he smiled sweetly at me.

"I had a good teacher," I smiled back.

We pulled the little rowboat up the bank and secured it, then walked home. We did not speak to each other, and I was relieved to go upstairs to my bedroom and be alone.

Months passed and Bernard was away at boarding school. I didn't visit his house on the weekends with his parents. I preferred staying home and helping daddy and Henry in daddy's workshop. Henry taught me a couple wrestling moves, which made Catherine jealous. Catherine asked to be taught how to defend herself, too. Henry obliged, but looked terribly scared to teach Catherine, as daddy leaned against the doorframe sharpening his hunting knives while congratulating Catherine and me on how well we were learning to kick and punch.

When Bernard returned home during a break from school, he taught Catherine and me some ways to thwart a bad man, if the need arose. Really, I thought Bernard was jealous watching Henry's body so closely against Catherine's as he taught us how to defend ourselves against someone who grabbed us from behind.

"Bernard will you help me?" I asked. We were alone in his stables and he was teaching me how to throw a man off me, if the man were on top of me. He worried I was too naive to know when a boy wanted more than friendship. My classmate, Vincent, walked me home one day, and Bernard said Vincent was no good. I disagreed, so Bernard took it upon himself to convince daddy I needed to learn how to defend myself more due to my naivety.

Bernard held my wrists. "I can help you, but I won't," he smiled and winked.

"I don't like you anymore," I said flatly.

"That's fine, Maybel, but you're going to finish this lesson anyway."

Bernard took me down with one push and was on top of me in an instant.

"That's not fair!" I shouted.

"Maybel! Pay attention!" Bernard shouted back. He was on top of me and I hated that he could so easily pin me down.

"Nobody is going to sneak up on me like that!" I protested.

"You don't know that, Maybel! You must be ready!" Bernard used his knees to push my knees out and was quickly atop me in a very awkward position.

"Did you teach Catherine these things?" I asked, as I tried to roll from side to side, but to no avail.

"Yes."

"And how did she do?"

"Well, if you must know," Bernard smirked, "her lessons ended with us kissing."

"You're disgusting, Bernard!"

"Oh, Maybel, maybe one of these days you'll fall in love and kiss someone."

I was angered that Bernard assumed no boy had yet wanted to kiss me. "Maybe I already have, Bernard!"

He looked taken aback. "Who?" he demanded.

"No one that you know!" I taunted.

"Who's been kissing you, Maybel? I'll break his face!"

"Oh, so you can go around kissing my sister, but no one's allowed to kiss me?" I said with a sneaky smile.

"Maybel, who's been kissing you?" he became agitated.

I enjoyed seeing the vein in Bernard's neck protrude in anger. "Maybe no one. Maybe someone. I'll never tell!" I laughed.

"Maybel, stay away from boys!" He grabbed my waist and in a split second, pushed himself on top of me harder. "Do you see this? Some men are bad, and you must stay away from them, and you must practice learning how to defend yourself!"

"The only person I need to learn how to defend myself from is you!" I punched his chest.

"Your punches feel like a fly kicking me," Bernard laughed. He looked like he enjoyed my frustration.

"Well, how about this?" I punched his jaw with my other fist.

"Did you just hit me? I think a gnat just flew into my jaw," Bernard picked up a wad of hay and dusted it over my face.

I became irate. "Bernard! Get off me!"

"Make me, Maybel!" he teased.

"You're going to regret this, Bernard!"

"You keep saying that, but I've yet to regret anything!" Bernard let go of one of my wrists and tickled my ribs.

I punched him repeatedly with my free fist, but to no avail. I finally began crying in frustration. "Why are you meaner to me than Catherine?"

"Because Catherine lets me kiss her, and you're just an annoying, little child," he smiled down at me.

I felt my lips turn down into a pout, but I didn't want them to. I wanted to look tough.

"Oh Maybel, I'm teasing you. You're such a baby!" Bernard got off me and laughed. He stood up and held his hand down, offering to pull me up, but I rolled over onto my side, away from him, and crossed my arms.

"Maybel, stop pouting, you big baby!" His voice was trying to conceal his laughter.

Bernard grabbed my hands and pulled me up. "Maybel, I'm sorry. You used to not be so sensitive," he said, with a little kindness in his voice.

"Well, you used to be a lot nicer to me!"

"That's probably true, but you were younger. You're older now and you need to be tougher when boys try to kiss you."

"You kissed me," I said. I pushed Bernard away hard. "Maybe there's a boy that likes me, Bernard. And maybe I like him, too. Is that so hard to believe? As you said, my hair is always wild, my knees scraped from climbing and playing, and I'm not proper, like Catherine, but not every man cares about such things."

"Maybel, listen to me, you are beautiful and completely naive. Stay away from boys."

"Bernard, you are the only boy to ever hurt me. You kissed me, pushed me away, and told me my hair was messy and that I was bad kisser. No other person in this world has ever hurt me or made me cry as much as you have!"

"I did. I'm sorry, Maybel. I know I caused you pain and I'm sorry. I don't know how to make things right, but I will."

I didn't see Bernard the remaining weeks before he returned to boarding school.

Catherine spent a lot of time at the library, in study groups, or at lectures in the city. "Look, Maybel! Look at how beautiful the autumn colors are!" Catherine gestured toward the maple trees in our front yard and along the street.

"Yes, they're beautiful," I replied. I was very sad. Bernard was gone, and Catherine preferred being with friends than with me. I sometimes walked far into the forest, beyond the orchards, and screamed as loudly as I could until my throat hurt. I had never dealt with change well.

"Catherine, I don't want you to leave me," I pleaded.

"We're just going to the library, Maybel. We'll be back soon." Catherine left down the street with Edith and Arnold.

Mommy was working in our front garden. "Maybel, where would be a good place to plant this lilac bush?" She motioned to two places, one by the walkway and the other closer to the white, wooden gate.

"Mommy, Catherine doesn't want me around, Bernard has already left for boarding school, and I'm so lonely!" I cried like a little child.

"Oh, come here, dear." Mommy held me and kissed my cheek. She stroked my hair, which always relaxed me. "Catherine has been really enjoying her study groups and Bernard will return from boarding school in only a couple weeks for break, and besides, you've made new friends in school with whom to pass time on the weekends."

"Nobody my age lives near me mommy! Catherine has many friends living nearby! All the girls my age live miles away!"

"Then make friends with the older girls, or perhaps even the girls several years younger than you, like Mrs. Matthews' daughter. She's only a couple years younger than you. They moved here not long ago, and I'm sure Susan would be thrilled to have a friend show her around town."

"Susan likes to play tea party with her father's taxidermied animals mommy! I don't want to have pretend tea with a dead fox!" I cried.

"Maybel, dear, Catherine is two and a half years older than you, and had to adjust her pastimes accordingly, as did Bernard. They played games with you that they had already outgrown. That's what big sisters and brothers do."

"Fine, I'll have pretend tea with Susan, but I hate her creepy stuffed animals! They are quite literally real, stuffed animals!" I huffed as I stomped inside.

The next afternoon I was to meet with Susan at her home. Mommy had so kindly arranged the meeting, despite my hesitance.

"Ok, I need to make more friends," I thought, as I arrived at Susan's house. I hesitated, then walked up Susan's steps to her front porch.

"Hello, Mrs. Matthews. Is Susan available?"

"Oh! It's so good to see you, Maybel," she hugged me warmly. "Susan has been waiting all morning!"

"Hi, Maybel!" Susan ran to greet me. "I'm so happy you're here!" She grabbed my hand and led me to their family room where her taxidermied fox, chipmunk, and opossum sat in little wooden chairs around a little wooden table.

I swallowed hard. I wanted to go home already.

"Maybel! Look! My father stuffed this mouse for me!" She shoved a small, furry, taxidermied mouse into my palm. I screamed and flung it into the wall where it bounced off and back to hit my eyeball.

"It's ok Maybel, you didn't hurt Banjo."

"Banjo?" I tried to regain my composure.

"Yes, that's her name."

"It's a dead, girl mouse?" I asked, confused.

"Yes, daddy accidentally stepped on her children out in our garden and he then broke her neck so she wouldn't have to bear life without her babies."

I stared at Susan, having no idea how to respond.

Susan retrieved Banjo from behind the sofa and put her in a tiny little wooden rocking chair next to the fox.

"Are you sure you want to put Banjo next to a fox?" I asked. And then I remembered they were all dead, and I wondered how long I had to stay until I could run home.

After a painful hour of playing tea party with Susan, Banjo, and her army comprised of a dead rodent, a marsupial, and a fox, I had finally stayed a polite amount of time, and excused myself, saying I needed to finish my history homework.

I returned home, and mommy asked how my afternoon had been with Susan. "She has a dead mouse named Banjo," I yelled.

Mommy chuckled, "But did it bite you?"

"It was dead, mommy!"

"Exactly," replied mommy, "Nothing to worry about, dear." Mommy licked her finger and turned the page of the newspaper.

I went upstairs to bathe the day away.

"Catherine," I entered her room. She was brushing her hair at her dressing table.

"Did you ever not want to play with me?" I asked.

"What?"

"When we were growing up, were you annoyed to play with me?" I felt insecure asking her so bluntly, and anticipating her response.

"Maybel, why are you asking such questions?" She continued brushing her hair in her mirror.

"Catherine, I spent an afternoon with Susan Matthews."

"Ah, yes," Catherine chuckled, "mommy told me."

"I didn't want to play tea party with Susan. Were you annoyed to play with me when we were younger? Mommy says older sisters have to adjust and play with their little sisters accordingly. Did you ever not want to play with me?"

"Ah, yes. I see. It's called compromise. I didn't always love playing tag or climbing trees, Maybel, but I loved you, so I sometimes did things like that to make you happy."

"So you were pretending to like playing with me?" I asked, feeling betrayed.

"Maybel, stop with your dramatic inclinations. I sometimes enjoyed those things, but not every time."

"Then why did you pretend to have fun?" I was angry now. "I thought we were best friends, Catherine!"

"Maybel, calm down! I enjoyed being with you. That was not a lie. Sometimes I would have preferred spending time doing other things, but I still enjoyed being with you." Catherine went back to brushing her hair.

"Do you think my hair looks better up like this, or down like this?" Catherine asked as she held her hair in different positions.

I sat on Catherine's bed staring at her. I could not believe she was dismissing my feelings like they were unimportant.

"I think you should cut your hair short, since that's the style now in Paris," I said.

"Really?" She held her hands over her shoulders to see how her face would be framed with short hair.

"I like it," I said cheerily.

Catherine moved her head to the left and right, still covering her shoulders to see how short hair would frame her face.

I walked out of Catherine's room and back into mine.

I sat on my bed contemplating whether or not my cherished memories with Catherine were all a lie. Did she utterly detest playing with me the way I detested playing with Susan and her strange animal friends?

I considered Susan for a moment. Mommy said she had few friends. I had told mommy it was because she played with dead animals. I suddenly, and very oddly, felt sad for Susan because I realized we were both alone.

I ran downstairs. Mommy was baking. "Mommy, did you want me to play with Susan because neither of us have friends?"

"Well, sweetheart, you both have friends, it's just that you both seem to spend a little too much time alone." She opened the oven to pull out a tray of cookies.

"I figured maybe, since you're both alone much of the time, who knows, maybe you have more than your solitude in common."

"Mommy, people stay away from Susan because she plays with dead animals. How can you compare us?"

"Well, Maybel honey, you're both a little different. I'm not saying different is bad," she quickly added.

"You both seem to be alone a lot of the time. Can you maybe find something else to do together? You both seem to have such vivid imaginations. What do you think about using your shared creativity as a foundation on which to further your friendship?"

I considered mommy's advice. She made a good point. "Maybe, mommy. I'll think about it."

I yanked a cookie off the tray and started upstairs before mommy could reprimand me, but it was scalding hot, and I tossed it in the air. It landed back on the baking tray.

"That's what happens when you steal," mommy winked at me.

Susan had provided a much-needed distraction, and filled a very sad and lonely void in my life since Catherine was gone most every afternoon.

Her oddities were challenging at times, but I'd grown fond of those peculiarities as she always kept me on my toes, discovering new weirdnesses upon every meeting.

Unfortunately, Susan had been sick lately with respiratory distress. I spent several afternoons a week at her bedside telling her stories. After one such afternoon, as I was leaving, her mother tearfully told me that Susan had never been as happy throughout her childhood as she was now with my friendship. I was surprised and confused because I hadn't done anything to warrant such love and devotion from Susan. I told mommy what Mrs. Matthews had said and mommy's response was simply to tell me that sometimes the greatest gift is your presence, not presents.

"Mommy, I'm home from school. I'll help with dinner, but first I have to wash the bird poop out of my hair. Those little asshol, I mean obnoxious birds, shit, I mean pooped on me, as I walked under the elm tree outside our house!" I huffed up the stairs to get fresh clothes, but halfway up, I heard mommy let out a pitiful cry of pain.

"Mommy, what's wrong?" I ran back downstairs and into the kitchen.

"Maybel, you need to go to Susan's house now. She's dying."

"What?"

"The doctor is there now. Susan won't live through the night."

I stood staring at mommy. Mommy was crying hard at our kitchen table. Daddy's hand was on mommy's shoulder, slowly rubbing it in small circles, trying to comfort her. What hurt me more than mommy's crying, was the single tear that slowly fell down daddy's cheek. I'd never seen daddy look so helpless.

I went upstairs without saying a word. I washed my hair in the bathroom basin and put on a clean dress, and then sat in my bed, covers wrapped around my shoulders, staring out at the setting sun. The sky was purple and wispy clouds were shades of red.

Mommy slowly opened my door and sat down gently beside me.

"Mommy, it's a beautiful sunset."

"It is."

"It will be Susan's last," I whispered.

"Then perhaps you should enjoy it one last time with her."

"I'm so scared, Mommy!" I began crying so hard my body began convulsing with waves of sobs.

"People keep leaving me mommy! I can't take this anymore! I can't lose someone else!" I cried hard into mommy's neck.

Mommy held me tighter, and through gentle sobs, she whispered, "This isn't about your pain, Maybel, this is about being with Susan when she needs your friendship most."

I breathed slowly to calm myself enough to get out of bed. Mommy was right. She and daddy walked with me to Susan's house.

I really did not want to walk up those steps because all I felt was that I was experiencing everything for the last time. The last time knocking on her door. The last time climbing her stairs. The last time opening her bedroom door to greet her.

"Maybel," she turned her head as I stood in her doorway, too scared to take my last step toward her. "You're here," she breathed weakly. Her breath rattled in her chest.

I took my last step toward her and sat beside her on her bed for the last time.

"Don't cry, Maybel," she wheezed.

I hadn't even realized I was crying. But there were tears streaming down my face when I touched my cheeks.

"Please don't leave me, Susan!" I started sobbing and I buckled over crying into my lap. "Please, just don't leave me!"

"I'm sorry, Maybel," she could barely speak and the rattling of built-up fluids in her lungs sounded like with every breath she was further drowning.

I breathed in very slowly with my hands covering the tears and snot on my face. "I'm sorry, Susan, I'm upsetting you and making it harder for you to breath." I breathed in slowly again and wiped my face on my sleeve.

With one final, slow breath, I sat upright next to Susan in bed, finally composing myself as much as I could, given my breaking heart.

"Tell me a story?" Susan reached her hand over to mine, but her grasp was weak, and her hand felt cold and hard, like she was already dead.

"Of course, Susan." I held her hand as I began my story.

"There was a girl who was very lonely who thought she was above playing with a child, but she did anyway, and she really started loving her time spent with the young girl. Then the young girl got sick, and the older girl felt like she was losing her little sister and cried a lot."

"Not your most imaginative story, Maybel," Susan whispered, "But it's my favorite one yet." She tried to smile but she was so weak, and her eyes slowly closed as her head tilted gently into her pillow. Her breathing was so loud. I watched her for several minutes, her parted lips, her strained breathing, her pale complexion.

I still held her small, cold hand in mine. "Thank you, little sister, for your short time with me. I love you." I leaned down and kissed her forehead softly.

And for the last time, I left Susan.

That evening something inside me broke.

"Maybel?" A man approached me as I stepped off the last stair step and onto the wood floor of Susan's family room.

"Yes?" I was tired, not physically tired, but emotionally drained.

"I am to give you this." He placed Banjo in my palm.

I looked down at that ugly, little, dead rodent and for some reason, I felt myself smiling and I didn't even understand why.

I looked back up at the man. He had short, curly blonde hair and his face was solemn. He turned and walked up the staircase. I smelled his cologne as it wafted back downstairs.

I looked back down at that creepy, little mouse in my palm. I closed my hand around it, feeling its little bones shifting under its dead fur. I wondered if I was supposed to keep this thing. I grimaced at the mere idea of opening my trinket box twenty years down the road and finding this thing at the bottom, underneath all my beloved memories, and screaming because I forgot it was there.

I was shaken from my imagination by daddy, who gently put my coat over my shoulders. He kissed the top of my head. His face looked like tears had been shed.

Mr. and Mrs. Matthews both hugged me and thanked me for my friendship with Susan. "It is I who thanks Susan for being my friend," I replied.

Mommy, daddy, and I walked home together in silence, spare a sniffle here and there.

"I need a minute alone," I said when we entered our front door.

I walked out to the old oak tree and threw Banjo as hard as I could into the night air. "Sorry, Banjo," I called after her. "And I'm sorry, Susan," I said quietly.

The next morning, I awoke with utter sadness laying atop my chest with the weight only sorrow can carry. I did not get out of bed. I stared at my ceiling. I was so scared my body felt cold deep inside. It was the kind of fear that envelops you, and pins you down until you can barely breathe, and there's no more feeling in your arms, your legs, or your face.

Mommy opened my bedroom door. I could not turn my head. I continued staring high above, past the ceiling, past the roof, and past the clouds above, wondering if Susan was there thinking about me too.

"Maybel, Susan did not die."

My neck snapped toward mommy.

"What?"

"Susan's unwell, but she's alive. Her brother returned yesterday and brought with him a new medicine from his laboratory in Connecticut."

"What?" I jumped out of bed and stared at mommy.

"Maybel, she's still very sick, sweetheart, but she has not died."

I could not speak though my mouth was agape.

"Mrs. Matthews says you are welcome to come visit Susan," mommy smiled, although she looked tired from a sleepless and sorrowful night, I guessed.

"Yes, I'll go now!" I said excitedly. "Oh shit! Banjo! Damnit!"

"Maybel, do not swear," mommy said, but seemed too tired to truly care or enforce the rule. Mommy looked like she had been up all night imagining herself holding me or Catherine, waiting for us to take our last breaths the way Mrs. Matthews had spent last night with Susan.

I ran downstairs, still in my nightgown and hurriedly donned my coat, then ran out to the old oak tree. "Banjo! I know you can't hear me because you're dead and all that, but where the hell did you land?"

I decided this endeavor would be fruitless and returned to daddy's workshop. I found his gun and went out to the orchard where field mice were plentiful. Unfortunately, it being winter, there weren't any around.

I kicked over some rotting cornstalks with my boot and one scurried out. I aimed and shot it. I had not considered the explosive impact of a shotgun at short range on a field mouse and was now covered in bits and pieces of brown tufts of fur.

"Damnit!" I screamed.

I ran back toward home, but suddenly remembered the river rats Susan and I had seen just below my house, near the stream, close to Bernard's home. I ran with daddy's gun to the stream and kicked the stump near the edge where we'd last seen that big, gray rat not too long ago. To my sheer amazement, my luck had improved and it came wobbling out, fattened by all the mice he'd consumed, do doubt! He was probably a large part of the reason the field mice population had dwindled.

This time I aimed at the head and had moved back far enough to not make the whole thing explode. I shot it dead and only half its face fell off, but it was definitely dead.

I grabbed its long rope-like tail and began running toward Susan's house.

"Maybel?" A familiar voice called.

I turned around and there stood Bernard.

"Oh! Bernard! Why are you home?"

"Why are you carrying a bloody rat, a shotgun, and why is there fur stuck to your nightgown?"

"All good questions, Bernard," I called over my shoulder as I sprinted to Susan's house.

I knocked on Susan's door. The blonde man answered. His eyes shot wide open.

"Can I see Susan, please?"

"Maybel, is that you?" A very weak Susan called from her family room sofa.

"Susan! Please don't be mad at me! I threw Banjo in a field last night and then when mommy said you were alive, I killed a rat for you! Can your father stuff it if half its face is missing?"

There was silence. Suddenly I realized how I must have looked. The rat was dripping blood onto the Matthews' wooden living room floor.

Susan, still weak, began laughing hysterically and with her laughter, color painted her face, the color of life. Susan's face lit up with color and life! She no longer looked as though her blood had already been drained!

"And people think I'm the weird one!" Susan laughed. She coughed, trying to clear her lungs and breathe.

"Susan, relax." The blonde man went to her side.

"Please, you're causing her distress," he said to me, "Please take the rat outside."

"Oh! I'm sorry!"

"No! Theo! Let me laugh!" Susan coughed. "I bet you never thought you would hear my laugh again, so let me laugh!"

"Calm down, please, Susan." He rubbed Susan's back.

"One moment, Susan." I chucked the rat out Susan's front door and it splattered on Bernard's shirt. "Oh! Sorry Bernard! I didn't know you had followed me here."

"Maybel, you're running around in your nightgown carrying a gun and a dead rat."

"Yes, I guess I am," I said, and shut the door in Bernard's face.

I returned to Susan. "Rat's gone."

"Was that Bernard?" Susan asked weakly.

"Yes, I shut the door though, because I accidentally hit him with the dead rat, and I don't even know how to explain that yet."

Susan again began cackling hysterically.

"Shh, calm yourself, Susan," the blonde man whispered.

"But Theo, Maybel just threw a giant, dead, and bloody river rat at her sister's boyfriend!" Susan alternated between laughing and coughing.

"Can you come back later, miss? Susan needs to remain calm," the man told me, more so than asked me.

"Oh! I'm so sorry! Susan, I'm so sorry!"

"No! Theo! Maybel can stay, and I'll laugh until I die, which is what I almost did! It's better than crying until you die!"

"Please Susan, I'm trying to keep you alive. I love you." He kissed Susan's forehead.

"I love you too, Theo."

"Maybel, this is my brother, Theo. He's a chemist. He thinks he's really smart," she smiled at him.

I went to greet Susan's brother and held my hand out, but I saw rat blood still covering my hand, so I quickly pulled it back. Susan giggled.

Theo looked thoroughly disgusted by me. His face looked like he was about to vomit, which only spurred Susan's giggling.

"Susan, perhaps I should go bathe and get dressed. I'll return later. Nice to meet you, Theo."

"Theodore. Likewise."

I walked out and picked the rat up off the steps and chucked him across the road and into a ditch.

I passed Bernard in our kitchen on my way upstairs. I supposed Catherine would be home soon. With all the hubbub lately, I'd completely forgotten Bernard was due home for Christmas break.

It was Christmas Eve. My family planned to attend the Charleston's annual party. I planned to sit with Susan as she recuperated.

"Maybel, can I come to the party with you?" Susan asked. "I've never danced before."

"Susan, I'm staying here with you," I said.

"But Maybel! Why? It's one of the biggest parties ever, I've heard!"

"Then why have you never attended?" I asked.

"We moved here not long ago, and also, I've never had anyone with whom to accompany me," she stated plainly. Then added rather sheepishly, "No one really wanted me."

"You cannot attend a party, Susan," Theodore said. "You need to rest."

"Theo! I almost died!"

"And that's why you need rest!" He kissed the top of her head.

"Theo! I might die tomorrow night and then the end will still be the same! I'll never have been to a grand party, and I'll never have danced with anyone!"

Theodore was about to interject when their mother spoke up. "Theo, Susan is right. She's never been dancing. And what if this new medicine fails? What then, Theo? Susan is right. She'll have died either way and still, either way, she'll never have been to a grand party or danced with a boy."

I felt a pang of fear when Mrs. Matthews said Susan's medicine might fail.

"I'm against this," Theodore began, "but, if you must, I'll accompany you, and I must request we stay no longer than two hours."

Susan squealed with glee and hugged her brother dearly, and then her mother.

"Maybel, what do I wear? How do I arrange my hair?" Susan looked nervous.

I gave her the biggest smile I have ever smiled. "Leave that to Catherine! She loves dressing me up like one of her porcelain dolls!"

Susan giggled.

"We'll be over in about two hours with dresses and I'm sure about three hundred hair accessories!"

"Three hundred?" Susan's eyes were wide with excitement.

"Well, I've never actually counted Catherine's accessories, but let's just say she has amassed a lot over the years!"

Susan smiled up at me like I was some sort of religious savior. Her expression, as well as her total admiration of me, completely baffled me. I'd always been Catherine and Bernard's annoying tag-a-long. I'd never experienced being the admired leader before.

Catherine and I finished dressing and were braiding each other's hair. "She means a lot to you, doesn't she?" Catherine looked at me as we were sitting side-by-side on her bed.

"Susan? Yes, I've grown fond of her company."

"It's nice, right? Having a little sister look up to you as though you were God."

I paused braiding her hair and watched her closely. "Catherine, can you even imagine how lonely and sad I have been? My whole world has been you and Bernard. And then my world was gone. I cried, Catherine, I cried so hard for so long all these years when you left me to be with your friends and Bernard. You don't understand what it's like to be the awkward, little sister living in her gorgeous, intelligent, perfect sister's shadow. I had to find someone else with whom to pass my terrible solitude. I wouldn't have survived without Susan and her interesting ways."

"You would be surprised, Maybel, at how well you will not only survive, but thrive, when you assumed you would die."

I watched Catherine.

"Maybel, I'm learning a lot by going to lectures at the library in the evenings and attending speeches in the city by notable authors.

I continued brushing her hair and clipping small braids up around the knot at the top of her head. I, on occasion, accompanied Catherine to lectures, but I still wanted more of Catherine's attention here at home, singing and dancing, like we did when we were younger.

"I didn't know how independent I was until recently," Catherine looked at me. "You've always been independent, Maybel. You've always been free. I never realized how amazing and strong and independent you've always been and I'm truly proud of you."

I stopped brushing her hair and stared at her. Catherine surprised me with her candor. "Thank you, Catherine." I hugged Catherine tightly. I was so happy that my big sister was proud of me. I reeled from Catherine's compliments.

Catherine then sat more sullenly. "Maybel, of course I don't want there to be another woman, but I think Bernard fancies another."

I froze.

"No woman wants to be in a position where she has to compete with another woman. I love Bernard, I do. I don't want Bernard and me to break up, but if we do, my world will not come crashing down around me like I thought it would."

I was shocked at how different Catherine was now. She had only ever wanted to be the wife of someone rich and socially connected.

Catherine looked pensive in thought. She then turned to me with a newly-formed brightness in her eyes. "There was a time I would have been utterly crushed thinking of Bernard with another woman. I don't wish him to break up with me, Maybel, but if that were to happen, I'm so much stronger now," she said with a happiness and strength I'd never seen within her before. "Maybel, you've always been free, and to be honest, I've always envied your self-reliance. I never thought I was as strong as you, and that made me jealous."

"Really?" I was shocked. "You envied me?"

"Yes, Maybel, why does this surprise you?"

I looked at Catherine and her perfect hair, her perfect dress, her perfect everything. "I've never been popular or had lots of friends or knew how to make my hair look pretty like you. I've always been Catherine's little sister. I've never been Maybel."

Catherine held my shoulders tightly and looked into my eyes, "Maybel, listen closely, we always want what another has. Look at everything you do have, and you won't want."

Catherine, I sensed, like one of my characters in my stories, was experiencing an awakening.

We arrived at Susan's house, Catherine and me. Theodore opened the front door. His face changed from wondering who was at the door, to sweeping us up and down with his gaze, clearly intrigued, and looking with utter amazement at the two women in evening gowns standing before him.

"Yes?" He asked. "How may I help you ladies?"

"We're here to take Miss Susan Matthews to her first ball," Catherine said in her most attractive voice. She held her hand out to be kissed.

Theodore stared at Catherine, who was by everyone's opinion, the most dazzling woman in town. She wore a dark, red, silk dress that clung to her beautiful body.

When he finally composed himself, he gingerly took her hand and lightly kissed it.

"And whom shall I say is calling?" he asked, almost breathlessly.

I felt my eyes and mouth droop into an unamused and annoyed countenance. "It's me, Theo. I'm Maybel. We've met," I said dryly. "Oh, I'm sorry, I meant to say Theodore," I added sarcastically.

"You must call him Theodore," I said to Catherine with my pretentious voice.

"Maybel!" he exclaimed incredulously. "I didn't recognize you without a bloody rat and shotgun in hand!"

Catherine shot me an absolutely curious glance.

"I can, on occasion, clean up nice, Theodore," I said, a little annoyed.

"Please, call me Theo," he smiled.

I rolled my eyes as I pushed past him.

"Susan!" I greeted my newly-appointed little sister, who was now, by association, Catherine's little sister. And Catherine, as she always had done, took her role as big sister very seriously. Catherine had always dressed me up like I was her little doll and shown me off to guests and relatives at all our get-togethers. It was now Susan's turn to be Catherine's doll.

"Hello, Susan," Catherine kissed Susan's cheek. "I've heard the most wonderful things about you."

Susan watched Catherine and her absolute beauty with awe.

"Susan, sweetheart," Catherine continued doting on Susan, "I've heard about your health, and I'm so happy you are improving," she sat beside Susan and smiled sympathetically.

"I'm feeling better, Miss Catherine," Susan said, still in awe at this woman who looked like she leapt from the pages of a fairytale.

"Please, just Catherine," Catherine smiled kindly.

"Susan, mother wants to apologize for not having the time to sew you a proper, new, ball gown. We have, however, brought you our old gowns. We hope you can find one suitable," Catherine smiled sweetly.

I held up our old dresses. "Would you prefer royal blue, light blue, pink, red rose, lilac, dark purple, or dark green?" I smiled as I twirled around, holding the dresses by their padded hangers, and letting them fly out around me as I spun through the family room giggling. The hems of the dresses flew out around me and danced with me.

"You look like a rainbow cotton ball!" Susan squealed, and I laughed as I spun faster.

"Oh, my Heavens!" Mrs. Matthews exclaimed. "Your mother has designed and sewn all these dresses?" Her face was shocked, and shown awe and admiration.

"Why is your mother not dressing all the wealthy people on the east and west coasts? Why has she not presented herself in Paris?"

Mrs. Matthews took her spectacles up from around her neck and inspected mommy's perfect stitches. "Maybel, will your mother allow us to take these dresses back to Connecticut when we next visit our family? These dresses need to be shared with the rest of the world. They're truly exquisite."

"I'm sure that would be fine," I told her. I was curious about this connection to Connecticut.

"May I wear the pink dress?" Susan asked.

"You may wear whatever your heart desires," Catherine told Susan. Catherine made everyone fall in love with her.

We helped Susan dress and she looked utterly magnificent!

Catherine tamed Susan's thick, blonde curls.

"How did you get my hair to look nice, Catherine?"

"I've lived with her all my life and still have no idea how she makes my unruly, wavy hair look nice," I laughed.

Catherine smiled at Susan, "You look amazing, honey."

Susan beamed at Catherine.

As we were leaving, Susan was chatting emphatically with her parents and brother. Her excitement made me excited.

I whispered to Catherine, "You really are an amazing big sister, Catherine. Thank you for this," my eyes teared.

"Thank you for being the most amazing, little sister," she kissed my cheek, but before she could pull away, I pulled her in tightly and whispered, "I love you so much."

"I love you too," she whispered back. "I'm sorry I haven't been around as much. I'll spend more time with you, I promise."

I hugged Catherine tighter.

Susan, her parents, brother, and Catherine and I walked to the Charleston Manor. When we arrived, both doors opened at once.

"May I present Miss Susan Matthews, Theodore Matthews, and the elegant Mr. and Mrs. Matthews!" The butler roared.

Everyone silenced.

Catherine turned to Susan. "Your first ball must be special," she winked. Catherine held her hand to Susan, who accepted. Catherine led Susan down to the ballroom floor and into Bernard's awaiting embrace.

The band began playing a slow and melodic melody. Bernard smiled down at Susan, the way he used to do with me. He led her skillfully around the ballroom and when she stumbled, he smiled kindly, and whispered in her ear. She smiled up at him and they continued. I knew what Bernard whispered. He used to whisper to me when I stumbled.

The rest of the partygoers began slowly moving inward and dancing around Bernard and Susan. Mr. and Mrs. Charleston took Mr. and Mrs. Matthews and Theodore in as their special guests of honor. I went to mommy and daddy, who stood back from the crowd.

Daddy kissed my cheek. "I'm proud of you and Catherine," he kissed me again.

Mommy's eyes were teary. "You know dear, a mother always wonders if she's done well. We question our decisions, and worry that we've done or said the right things." Mommy held my cheeks tightly in her hands. "I see how much compassion toward others you and Catherine show, and I know daddy and I have done well raising you two girls."

Mommy and daddy hugged me. I was a little misty-eyed. They held hands and went to the dance floor while I stood alone.

"She's still creepy!" I heard a voice behind me giggle.

I turned around and two girls maybe a year older than Susan stood watching her dance with Bernard.

"And she can't dance!" the other girl added.

They both laughed and walked toward the study.

I followed close behind.

I had read a book written by an Englishman who lived in Africa. He wrote about the lion prides on the savannah. What I found most interesting was his description, not of the people, not of the flora or fauna, but of the interactions between lions.

One lioness, he described, killed another who batted her cub with her paw. The mother lioness bit the offending female once, in her jugular, and that lioness fell to the dirt and was dead in minutes, without one, small sound coming from her mouth. This image was well within my mind as I followed the two, young ladies to the study. They sat down on the sofa there in front of the fireplace. I was right behind, and even startled them with my stealth.

Without a word, I sat on the edge of the sofa, my shoulders and hips turned to their direction. I slowly leaned toward them and whispered, "Say one more mean thing to Susan, and I'll slap the shit out of you both."

No sneer, nor any smile played across my lips. I did not blink for the entirety of my time sitting beside them. In fact, no emotion played across my face, nor in my heart. Something had broken inside me the night I thought Susan would die. And these two faces looking back at me, as confused and scared as they were, were no more to me than two females swatting my cub. I could not feel empathy for their position in life. To me, they were expendable, collateral damage, in this play called life, in which we were all puppets.

The two girls looked at each other and smirked. "Let's go, Beatrice," the one sitting closest to me told her companion.

They walked out to the dance floor, and as they passed the wood and glass doors, they looked back, only to find me poised, back straight, head held high, with a steely gaze.

They turned and quickly left.

I sat with Susan on New Year's Eve. She was tired from the Christmas Eve party, and another night of glamor and dancing didn't seem optional.

We played cards and told stories. Theo was still home to see Susan through her illness and he wasn't horrible company. I found him a bit arrogant, but after some days passed, he relaxed some and was more tolerable.

"Maybel, please don't stay here with me if there's a party to attend." Susan looked into my eyes and held my hands in her small hands.

"Susan, I don't much care for parties, and I'd rather be here with you anyway."

Susan had the sweetest, little-kid smile.

"Maybel, thank you."

"Susan, this is where I want to be."

I was not lying. I honestly wanted to be here with Susan. I did not care for glamorous parties.

When I saw Susan dying, something truly broke inside me. I was determined to do something good with my life. I wanted to help people, but I didn't know in which direction to begin.

"Theo, what do you do in your lab? You make medicines, correct? What else does your position there entail?" I asked him. He was sitting on a chair across from Susan and me.

"I use my chemistry background to discover new ways to create chemical compounds and reactions to help either cure illnesses or prolong a person's quality of life."

I paused thoughtfully, "I used to want to be a school teacher like Catherine," I said. "I want to help people."

"And what do you want to be now, Maybel?" Theo asked.

"I have been thinking about being a nurse," I hesitated, "but my math skills are not good," I admitted, "so I cannot be a doctor."

"Would you like to be a doctor?" Theo asked. He was not condescending or arrogant. He seemed genuinely curious about my future.

"I don't know, Theo. I want to help people. I am not good at math or chemistry, but I am good at writing and interpreting literary works. What do I do with that?" I asked, feeling worthless at my lack of practical mathematical skills.

"You would be surprised, Maybel. There are many career options out there you have never heard of, and many more career paths that have not yet been invented."

"What do you mean there are jobs that have not been invented?" I asked curiously.

"Before the scientists that preceded me identified elements used in chemistry, my job had not yet been invented."

I considered Theo's words carefully. "I have never thought about that, Theo. Thank you, that is surely something to consider."

I thought about what he had just told me. He made a fascinating point. "Theo, I'll either be a teacher, a nurse, or something not yet discovered."

Theo smiled, "That sounds lovely, Maybel."

"Susan," I asked, "What will you be?"

"A writer, like you."

"I'm not a writer," I giggled.

"Not yet," she said. "You have to write your stories down into a book first."

"That's a fair point," I laughed. "I suppose I'm not diligent at writing down all my stories."

"It's ok, Maybel, I wrote a lot of them down for you." She nodded toward a box of papers on her little tea table surrounded by her stuffed animals.

"You've written them down?" I asked, surprised.

"Well, some of them. I can't remember them all the way you do, Maybel. I wrote them down but I couldn't remember all your visualizations, the way you tell them, but I tried."

I almost cried. "That's so sweet, Susan."

"Don't get too excited, I couldn't do them justice, the way you tell them, but it's a start."

I hugged Susan hard. "Thank you," I said.

"You're welcome, Maybel," she smiled. "Maybel?" Susan asked.

"Yes?"

"Happy New Year!" she grinned.

I looked at their clock. "Oh yes! Happy New Year, Susan!" I hugged her again.

"And Happy New Year, Theodore."

"Happy New Year, Maybel. Happy New Year, Susan," he leaned over and kissed Susan's cheek, then mine.

I blushed. Susan giggled at my blush.

"I'll walk you home, Maybel," Theo said.

"Thank you, Theodore."

"Maybel, please call me Theo," he smiled shyly at me.

"I'll see you tomorrow, Susan," I hugged her yet again, because she was alive.

Susan smiled, then yawned, "Night, Night, Maybel."

Theo walked me home. At my gate we stopped. "Maybel, I have been wanting to thank you for how kindly you have treated my sister."

"I haven't treated her any differently than I treat any of my other friends."

"Yes, I know, and thank you for that," he said. "It's just, you have been good to Susan, and I know she doesn't make friends easily. She's," he paused, "very imaginative and creative. Some people don't understand how imagination and creativity are blessings. They only see the strangeness of it all."

Theo leaned down and kissed my lips. "Thank you, Maybel. See you tomorrow."

He turned around and began walking home.

I opened my gate and walked inside my home.

Catherine was smiling ear to ear. "Well, well, do you have a suitor, Maybel?"

"What? No! He was thanking me for my kindness toward his sister."

"Yes, but of course," Catherine giggled.

Bernard, on the other hand, was not smiling. I walked past Bernard and headed upstairs to bed.

"Maybel," Catherine sat on my bed. "Bernard's been asking about you."

I shrugged.

"Are you ignoring him, or angry at him perhaps?"

"No."

"Then why don't you come to the candy store for old time's sake? Bernard wants to say goodbye before he returns to school." Catherine seemed concerned because I'd been withdrawn lately.

"I'm going to Susan's house," I said.

"You don't even know which day or time we're going to the candy store," she pointed out.

"I'm just busy, Catherine."

Susan and I walked through town later. Theo had told her to walk a little more each day to regain strength and endurance.

"Maybel, don't walk with Susan, you'll catch fleas." Doris taunted.

"Yes, Maybel, from Susan's real, stuffed animals!" Beatrice added.

They giggled. They were the two, obnoxious girls from the Christmas party. Susan looked down but didn't speak.

"Susan, may I see Mr. Montgomery?"

Susan handed me her ugly, stuffed opossum.

I held the tail of the dead opossum like a whip and with one fierce blow, I whipped Doris' left cheek, and on my return, Beatrice's right cheek. The scraggly opossum's ear tore off in Doris's hair clip and its glass eye flew off and landed in Beatrice's hair.

"Maybel Wyndham! You are disgusting! I'm telling my mother!" Doris screamed.

"You will regret this, Maybel!" Beatrice chimed in.

"In that case, I had better make my punishment worthwhile!" I snarled at them.

I slugged Mr. Montgomery into those two shrews so hard its little stuffed head popped off.

"Go ahead and tell your mothers and fathers you were picking on a little girl who almost died, you shriveling, little shrews! Tell them you made a little girl's life miserable with your lies and gossip! And I'll be here waiting when you return!"

"Come along, Susan." I held my head high and led Susan away with an aire of superiority. "Let me know if they bother you again," I said loud enough for Doris and Beatrice to hear.

We continued down the street and as we passed the candy store, Charlie stuck his head out. "Ladies, come in. Have some custard, my treat," he winked.

I was not expecting free custard, but Susan was already happily skipping inside.

"My sister was a lot like you, Maybel," Charlie told me. "She once knocked me off our porch when I made fun of her dress, and the wind left my lungs so fast when I landed, I thought I was going to die. I miss her terribly."

He looked wistfully at a portrait on the wall above me the way old people look when they're seeing ages past play out behind their eyes.

Charlie went back to his work behind the counter while Susan and I enjoyed our delicious dessert.

Susan and I walked around town chatting about school and I told her another story I'd composed in my head. Susan was a strange girl with curly blonde hair and a plain face, but there was a spark about her that made her far prettier than any other girl I'd ever met. She had an imagination that matched mine, and I had begun to thoroughly enjoy our long talks.

I walked Susan to her house and said goodbye. "Maybel, thank you," Susan hugged me tight. "I love you so much."

"I love you too, Susan." I was surprised by her childlike openness and I watched her skip inside her house.

When I returned home, mommy had made my favorite meal and a pie was cooling on the window sill. "Hello, dear," mommy greeted me with a kiss on my cheek.

"It's not my birthday, mommy," I said watching the pie cool.

"I don't tell you enough how special you are," she said.

I sat down beside daddy, and mommy laid our plates in front of us. "Maybel, I heard about what happened in town."

I suddenly felt like a small child about to be punished.

"I'm not saying what you did was right, but what those two mean girls did was not right either." Mommy laid a large piece of pie in front of me.

"I will, however, say this, you may eat your dessert first tonight." Mommy leaned down and kissed the top of my head and lingered a little longer than usual, stroking my hair as she hugged me.

I looked at daddy to gauge his reaction. Daddy simply winked at me and smiled, with what I felt was immense pride.

"How did you hear about me defending Susan?" I asked, genuinely surprised and curious.

"Small town, big whispers," Daddy winked at me again.

The next day I was playing cards with Susan at our family room table when Bernard came by. "Care to go to the candy store, Maybel?"

"No, thank you, we're playing cards," I said curtly.

"Can I come?" Susan asked excitedly.

"Yes, I suppose so," Bernard said rather begrudgingly.

Fortunately, Susan didn't seem to notice. She skipped happily to the coat rack, and then held Bernard's hand as we walked. I had been open and loving when I was younger, like Susan was now. I had not realized how guarded we became as we grew older.

The candy store was empty and not many people were walking around town. We sat down facing the window and watched the few people who did pass by.

"Maybel was a little younger than you when I used to take her and Catherine to this candy store," Bernard smiled kindly at Susan.

"Really?" asked Susan.

"Yes. It wasn't many years ago really, was it Maybel?"

"I suppose not," I said, "but it feels like it was a long time ago."

"That's because time moves more slowly when you're young," Charlie said, as he put down our sweets in front of us. "Time speeds up when you're old like me," he chuckled as he went back behind the candy counter.

Susan and I chatted about our upcoming plans. Susan told Bernard all about the stories I enjoyed making up for her.

"She used to tell me stories too," Bernard said with sadness.

"Why don't you tell Bernard stories anymore, Maybel?" Susan asked me.

"I don't really know, I suppose. Bernard is away at school a lot and Catherine is away most of the time, and I only have you now to listen to my stories," I smiled at Susan.

"We certainly have fun with our imaginations, don't we?" I scruffled her little, curly head.

"Yes, we do," Susan smiled back.

We finished our sweets and Bernard and I walked Susan home. "Maybel, let me walk you home as well," Bernard said.

"Catherine's not here, Bernard. She's helping daddy at the lumber yard," I said as we descended Susan's steps.

"Yes, I know Maybel, I've been trying to talk to you alone all of winter break," he said with frustration.

"Why?"

"You know why, Maybel!"

"Every time we're alone lately, we kiss, Bernard. I like kissing you, but Bernard, I love Catherine. She's not just my sister; she's also my best friend. I've decided not to be around you because clearly neither of us can control ourselves."

"I don't want to lose your friendship, Maybel, and what happens if Catherine and I marry? How are you going to stay away from me if we're family?"

"What do you mean "if" you marry Catherine?" I seized on that one, small word he uttered.

"Nothing, Maybel. You're right. I'll see you in the spring, that is if you're agreeable."

Bernard left and walked home without a goodbye.

Mrs. Charleston asked me to visit Bernard's college to see what I might think about their literature classes. We were repotting plants in her conservatory. Mrs. Charleston grew herbs all year round and delighted in giving them to mommy and Mrs. Matthews.

"I'm thinking about becoming a nurse, Mrs. Charleston, but honestly, I don't know what I want to be."

"You've still got time to decide. Why don't you come with Mr. Charleston and me while we visit Bernard's college? He will not be moving there for quite a while, but we're going to visit beforehand to make sure everything is in order."

"I'll have to ask mommy. She seems sad whenever there's talk of Catherine moving away to college, so I'm not sure she'll even entertain the idea of me leaving anytime soon."

"It's only for one night, dear. Mr. Charleston and I thought you might enjoy seeing the campus and meeting with professors. Let me know what your mother says, honey."

"I will, Mrs. Charleston." I looked at the plants I held in my fingers. The sage smelled good. "Mrs. Charleston?"

"Yes, dear?"

"I don't really know what I want to be, and sometimes that makes me sad."

Mrs. Charleston came to me and rested her hand on my shoulder. "It's going to be ok, sweetheart. Not everybody knows exactly what they want to be. Since you are going back and forth between being a teacher or a nurse, you must want to be someone who helps others."

"Yes, I want to help people."

"There are many ways to help people. Have you ever read a book that makes you feel better?"

"Yes. I like short stories and books about people who discover things."

"And what do they discover?"

"Sometimes they discover a new place or a new idea. Sometimes they just discover something about themselves. And some books are about murder, and there's always a man who thinks he's smart, and he puffs on a pipe, and suddenly he realizes who the perpetrator is. If I became a police officer, I'd definitely smoke a pipe!" I giggled.

Mrs. Charleston laughed, "I love the way your mind works, Maybel."

"I'll ask mommy tonight. What am I supposed to do there?"

"I'd like to show you the college. Perhaps you'll attend college there someday," Mrs. Charleston smiled at me.

"With Bernard?"

"There's an excellent literature program there. I thought perhaps you might be interested. Your stories are very good, Maybel, I want you to know that."

"I'll ask mommy," I sighed deeply. "I don't know what I'll do about college yet. I'm very confused about most things."

"You'll do great, dear."

Mommy and daddy both wanted me to go to Bernard's college and visit with the literature professors, and their incentive to encourage me to go with the Charlestons, was that Mr. and Mrs. Charleston told mommy and daddy there was a scholarship program at Bernard's college that, if I won, would provide me with free tuition, room, and board. I was hesitant to go. Bernard and I were sometimes on good terms, and sometimes he teased me and I wanted to beat his face in with a large rock. Mommy, and especially daddy, convinced me to at least take a look at the college, mainly because daddy didn't want to pay tuition.

Bernard looked out the window on our way to his prestigious college. He was confident, and his posture and facial expression exuded intelligence, wealth, and authority.

I did not exude any of those characteristics. I was just me. Catherine exuded grace, charm, sophistication, and perfection. I could see why they made a good couple.

When I was alone with Catherine, she was normal. When I was alone with Bernard, he seemed normal. In public, however, Bernard and Catherine changed. I didn't recognize them when they had their masks on in public.

I felt like a child next to Bernard and Catherine. They spent so much time looking and acting polished, that they lost themselves in their costumes they wore in public.

I had already decided I would not attend this college. I imagined myself walking to class, and a rich boy or girl made a snide comment about me to his or her friends and Bernard laughed, pretending he didn't know me.

Perhaps my imagination was inaccurate, and I was just scared of the unknown, but it hurt me to think that Bernard would do that. My vivid imagination accompanied very real emotions, and even if those emotions were imagined, it still really hurt.

"Maybel, will you come visit me on weekends if you are able?" Bernard asked me as we strolled through his college campus. Mr. and Mrs. Charleston were speaking to the president of the university, and Bernard and I were walking around, admiring the early spring blooms.

"I will ask mommy and daddy. I think I would not be able to stay long, as it's a night on a train to get to your college, and a night back."

"Yes, I suppose you would spend the whole weekend traveling." He sounded sad. "You know, though, I could drive home to see you on the weekends. The drive would not take nearly as long. Have you thought about what mother said about attending my college?"

I giggled, "I still have to finish high school. I'll be in college soon enough."

"I'm scared I'm going to lose you," Bernard said quietly.

"Why Bernard? We'll still see each other on school breaks, like always."

"Every year it gets harder and harder to leave you when I go away to school. I hate leaving you. And you're so beautiful and intelligent that some boy is going to want to spend all his time with you, and I've been living in fear every time I return home from break that you'll have a boyfriend."

"Boys don't stare at me. They stare at Catherine. And every girl we've ever walked past, stares at you, so you're the one who will find a girlfriend. Boys don't notice me."

"I notice you," Bernard said.

I glanced up at him, "And yet, you've done nothing about it."

There were many other students admiring the lawns, architecture, and exploring their class-rooms. The medical school facilities were advanced and the grandiose stone building had the name Charleston carved in massive letters above the entryway.

Mr. and Mrs. Charleston joined us on the lawn. Mrs. Charleston's arms were full of folders and papers from their meeting with the president.

I nodded toward the medical building, "I had not realized the surname Charleston was so common. Your last name must be quite common in these parts, Bernard. I've seen the name Charleston on many of the buildings."

Bernard appeared uncomfortable and looked away. Mr. Charleston put his hand on Bernard's shoulder, chuckling as we walked.

Mrs. Charleston smiled at me, "Shall we explore the literature halls now?"

"Yes, Mrs. Charleston." I wasn't anxious to attend this college. I wasn't acclimated to high society. Catherine was, and I wondered why she hadn't considered attending college with Bernard.

"Mrs. Charleston, if I decided to become a teacher, does this college offer courses for me to become a schoolteacher?"

"Yes, dear."

"Is Catherine enrolling here? I haven't heard her mention attending Bernard's college."

"I don't know, Maybel, but I think she had talked about possibly applying to several colleges to the north and east, although she still has plenty of time to decide."

We walked along the paths to the literature classrooms.

"Maybel, dear, have you brought your stories?"

"Yes, Mrs. Charleston."

"Good. Let's introduce ourselves."

Mrs. Charleston accompanied me through several classrooms while Mr. Charleston and Bernard followed. "Maybel, this is the dean."

I shook the dean's hand. He stood with excellent posture and his voice sounded like he enjoyed hearing himself talk.

I felt very uncomfortable in this atmosphere. I wanted to go home immediately.

After speaking to the dean, Mrs. Charleston handed him my stories. "For your consideration, Mr. Fellowes."

"Thank you so much Mrs....?"

"Charleston."

The dean raised his brows. "Charleston? Ah, forgive me, please! I had no idea! I'll read these stories right now! Please forgive my ignorance, Mrs. Charleston! Please, may I get you anything to eat or drink? Shall I show you toward the executive dining hall for our most distinguished guests?"

"No, thank you, Mr. Fellowes. We'll be exploring the art department now."

"Yes, of course, Mrs. Charleston. It has been a pleasure to meet you." Mr. Fellowes looked like he wasn't sure if he should bow to Mrs. Charleston or shake her hand.

Mrs. Charleston took me to the art department. It was a large building with columns. Large, wide windows brightened every classroom, and the walls were lined with beautiful paintings that were separated by sculptures.

I walked over to the display case admiring the paintings. The engraving said Francine Charleston. I wondered if she was any relation to Bernard.

A boy a little older than me approached. "Quite the painting, don't you think?"

I smiled and was about to reply that yes, it was quite breathtaking, when he pinched my bottom and said, "I look forward to seeing you around campus," then he walked away.

I turned and walked quickly to Mr. Charleston. Mr. Charleston was tall and muscular and looked like he could wrestle a bear. He lovingly reminded me of my father. I sat next to Mr. Charleston and held his sleeve between my fingers. I was scared.

"Maybel, sweetheart, what's wrong? You look shaken."

I didn't want to tell him what happened because I was scared. "Nothing, I'm fine," I said.

"You're quite unconvincing, Maybel. What's wrong?"

"Nothing, I just wanted to sit by you."

Mr. Charleston wrapped his arm around me. "Maybel, do you like this college?"

"No," I replied quickly.

Mr. Charleston paused, "What did you like best about this college?"

"Bernard is here."

Mr. Charleston chuckled, "Alright dear, and what did you like the least?"

"I don't fit in. Everyone is rich."

I sat very close to Mr. Charleston. His arm wrapped around me, and I was scared, so I rested my head in the crook of his shoulder. That boy who touched my bottom walked by. He looked at me and smiled. I leaned farther into Mr. Charleston. I looked down at the floor.

"Maybel, honey, did someone scare you? I'm not mad. I'm not upset with you. I am only wondering why you seem frightened."

"No, I'm fine." I stayed glued to Mr. Charleston as I watched that boy walk around the room in front of me.

"Maybel," Mr. Charleston spoke gently, "did you know I was a fighter? I fought other men in a boxing ring. Do you know what that is?"

I looked up and shook my head no.

"I trained and punched a bag, building my strength, then I practiced fighting other men, and I was quite good. I beat other men. I knocked them down. They didn't get back up." Mr. Charleston held me tightly. He leaned into my ear, "Is there anyone here you think deserves a beating? Maybe they weren't behaving the way a man ought to behave?"

I shook my head yes.

Mr. Charleston leaned into my ear again. "Who's the scoundrel?" he chuckled. "Don't worry, darling, I won't make a scene." He sat back and winked at me.

I looked at the boy who grabbed my bottom. I felt really scared.

"Oh? And what did he do?" Mr. Charleston leaned back down to my ear, "Don't worry, honey, I promise I won't make a scene. I am only curious as to why you seem a bit nervous. I promise I won't embarrass you, sweetheart."

I hesitated. I was scared of Mr. Charleston's reaction. "I was looking at that pretty painting over there in that display case, and he pinched my bottom, grabbing me, and said he would see me around campus, and I got scared." I watched Mr. Charleston. I was afraid he would be angry at me.

"Oh, I see," Mr. Charleston said softly. "Don't worry my dear, I can promise you he won't bother you around campus."

"Maybel, sweetheart, let's go find Mrs. Charleston, shall we?" He held my hand and I clung to him. Every boy I saw was going to touch me. I was scared. Every boy looked like they were going to reach out and touch my body.

I held Mr. Charleston's hand and walked closely next to him as he took me to Mrs. Charleston. "Dear," he said to his wife, "would you mind taking Maybel to get ice cream and cookies?"

Mr. Charleston looked at Mrs. Charleston. They didn't speak but they seemed to understand each other. Mr. Charleston gave my hand to Mrs. Charleston. He kissed my cheek, "Would you like chocolate, vanilla, or both?" he winked at me.

"Both!" I smiled.

"All right then, I'll meet you at the house in an hour," Mr. Charleston tousled my hair.

Mrs. Charleston held my hand and we walked away. We went to a custard shop near campus. Afterward, we walked to a small house close to campus. Mr. Charleston was on the porch with a bloody bandage around both his hands. He sipped whisky. He winked at me. "You should see the other man!" He roared with laughter.

"Maybel! Why didn't you tell me a boy touched you?" Bernard demanded.

I didn't want to talk about it. I walked slower and behind Mrs. Charleston.

"Maybel, I would have killed him!"

"That's why I intervened, son. You're going to medical school, not prison," he held Bernard's shoulder and squeezed.

Bernard and I stayed the night in the house. It had three bedrooms, a kitchen, two bathrooms, and a large living room. I considered it a fairly large house. It wasn't as large as my house, but it was incredibly smaller than Bernard's mansion.

Mrs. Charleston and I went to the grocer's and bought meat, potatoes, and vegetables. She and I cooked a delicious meal. She showed me herbs in the small garden in the little, fenced-in yard behind the house. The fence was wooden and white, and I really liked the small garden.

There was a swing on the back porch painted white. The house was wooden and painted white, with a dark, blue trim. The shutters were also dark blue. It was really cozy and I felt relaxed here. The feeling around the house was very calm. There weren't many places I felt calm, but I felt calm here.

After dinner, we played croquet in the backyard and drank the freshly squeezed lemonade Mrs. Charleston and I made. After the fiasco with that strange boy in the art's department, I didn't like this college or its campus at all, but I really enjoyed the peace and serenity this little house provided.

I sat beside Mr. Charleston on the swing out back. I liked him. I leaned on his arm. "Thank you for protecting me today," I patted his hand, which was no longer bandaged, but looked raw.

"Maybel, I will kill for you," he winked at me and wrapped his arm around me.

"I will kill for you, too. I'll just need a solid alibi, the best that money can buy."

My Charleston laughed heartily and pulled me tightly against him. He winked at me, "You've got it, sweetheart!"

After we chatted inside in the family room, Mr. and Mrs. Charleston said goodnight and went to bed. Bernard and I had been sitting on opposite ends of the couch, but as soon as his parents went to bed, he smiled at me. "Sit beside me, Maybel?"

"Yes!" I giggled, and jumped onto the couch cushion next to him. He pulled me onto his lap.

"You said not to sit on your lap!"

"I changed my mind!" He kissed my cheek.

"Your bags are in your bedroom already," he said.

"Thank you, Bernard."

"I can move them to my bedroom if you get scared," he smiled cheekily.

"I'm scared," I giggled.

Bernard laughed, "I miss you beside me."

"I missed you, too. I liked when you held me at night when we were younger. It was the only time I slept well."

"Maybel, come." He held my hand and pulled me up. He led me to his bedroom.

"Bernard, my bags are already here."

"I was hoping you would stay here," he blushed. "I missed you, Maybel. I like going to sleep with you and waking up with you."

"Me too," I said.

I undressed in the bathroom and put on my nightgown and brushed my teeth. Bernard came into the bathroom as I was finishing up. "Maybel, will you help me with my tie?"

I reached up and loosened Bernard's tie. He watched me while my fingers fiddled with his tie. I caught his gaze and he blushed.

"Thank you," he said.

"You're welcome." I looked up at him, at his thick wavy hair, his strong jaw, and his full lips.

"Maybel?"

"Yes?"

"I have to undress now," he said.

"Ok." I sat on the edge of the bathtub. "What time are we leaving tomorrow?"

"I'm not sure. Maybel, I have to undress now."

"I'm unsure why you are repeating yourself. You already told me that."

Bernard blushed, "Maybel, go out into the bedroom."

"I've seen you undress before. You're wearing undershorts, aren't you?"

"Well, yes, but I haven't been in a bed with you since we were younger, and so, it's a bit awkward."

"I can go to the other bedroom if you are uncomfortable," I said.

"No, it's just...." He looked at me curiously and his eyes narrowed, "You're very much enjoying this aren't you!"

"Yes," I giggled. "You look very uncomfortable and I find that funny!"

"Maybel, I will swat your bottom!"

"Well, you wouldn't be the first today!" I giggled.

"Damnit, Maybel! I will kill him!"

"Bernard, calm down! I was joking!"

Bernard looked insane. His eyes flashed anger and his fists were clenched.

"Bernard, I'm ok," I reassured him.

"You weren't ok! Father said you clung to him like a scared, little child!"

"I'm not a child, Bernard! Maybe he scared me, but stop calling me a child! Just because I don't want some stranger grabbing my bottom doesn't mean I'm a child!"

"I know you aren't a child, Maybel! I don't want anyone to touch you or hurt you!"

"Catherine is going to college, too! Why aren't you worried about her safety?"

I felt my face flush. "You're only upset about me because you think I'm your little sister, and maybe sometimes, I don't want you to think of me as your little sister, Bernard!"

"Believe me, Maybel, I do not think of you as my little sister!"

"Then why do you act like my angry, protective brother?"

"I don't! I act like your husband!" Bernard froze. He stared at me. "I'm sorry, Maybel. I didn't mean I'm your husband."

Bernard exhaled deeply. "I guess it doesn't matter if I undress in front of you. As you said, I'm wearing an undershirt and shorts."

Bernard began undressing. "Bernard! I can't handle my lust! Stop unbuttoning the cuffs of your shirt! I'm unable to contain myself! I see your bare wrists!"

"Funny, Maybel," Bernard said.

"I'll leave you to your modesty, Bernard." I closed the bathroom door as I left.

Bernard came to bed wearing only his undershorts.

"You look different," I said.

"How?"

"I think you look more like a man now." I admired his strong shoulders and arms, and his taut stomach.

"You look more like a woman, and less like a girl every time I return home from school. I always dread returning to find you've gotten a boyfriend."

"I'd worry more about Catherine. She's the one boys always want."

Bernard slid into bed beside me. "Come here, Maybel." He pulled me into the crook of his arm. "I've really missed laying with you, and talking and joking with you all night. Truthfully, you're my best friend."

I sighed. I was disappointed. "You're my best friend, too," I said, feeling a little sad that he used the word friend to describe me.

Catherine came into my room. She had spent the weekend at her friend Rebecca's house. "Maybel, how was your visit to Bernard's college."

"It was ok, I guess. I don't want to attend that university though."

"Oh, why not?"

"I don't fit in. It's a nice place, but I will look at other colleges when the time comes."

Catherine smiled, "I'm sure you will find the right place for you."

"Catherine?"

"Yes?"

"Are you thinking of attending Bernard's college?"

Catherine suddenly looked past me, out my window. A mist of sadness over her eyes formed. "I guess don't fit in there either, and anyway, the tuition is too expensive. It's one of the most expensive colleges in the country. We don't have that kind of money."

"Maybe you can win a scholarship, too?" I asked hopefully.

Catherine snorted sarcastically, "Sure, Maybel." She rolled her eyes at me then left.

The next day, I came inside from my walk around the garden. I'd made two new friends by our pond, the bluebird couple sitting on a tree branch. Mrs. Charleston was sitting with mommy in the kitchen having tea.

"Maybel, Mrs. Charleston is here! Come say hello!" mommy called happily to me.

"Hello, Mrs. Charleston," I smiled.

"I have been telling your mother about the college we visited. I was also wondering if you'd like to help me plant some herbs? I have a lot of lavender plants and you're more than welcome to take several for your garden here."

"That sounds fun," I smiled.

"I made a chocolate cake too," she winked at me.

"That sounds more fun!" I giggled.

Mrs. Charleston and I planted the tubs of lavender and sage near her kitchen. The little garden was surrounded by slabs of slate arranged decoratively. My knees were dirty and dirt caked my fingernails. I itched my eye and got dirt on my face. I tried to wipe it off and got more dirt on my cheeks.

"Maybel!" I heard Catherine's voice calling me. Of course, Catherine came to me at the exact time I accidentally smeared dirt all over my face.

I was looking down, patting the dirt with my hands around the base of a sage plant. I rolled my eyes as I finished patting the soil. "Hello, Catherine," I sighed. I didn't bother hiding my dirty face.

"What are you doing here?" she smiled. Her arm was around Bernard's waist. Bernard looked surprised to see me.

"I'm auditioning for Mrs. Charleston's puppet show for children," I replied.

Catherine looked confused, then suddenly realized I was being sarcastic.

"Funny, Maybel."

"I thought so too," I said.

Mrs. Charleston chuckled.

Bernard watched me as he held Catherine's waist.

Catherine took Bernard's hand and they went inside. I continued planting sage. As with my trip out west, Bernard had been close to me, but chose Catherine when we returned home. I wanted to be rid of both Catherine and Bernard because I was in a very bad mood suddenly.

"Maybel, would you like to come in for cake now?" Mrs. Charleston asked me.

"Yes!" I exclaimed. I would rid myself of Catherine and Bernard after I ate delicious cake.

We went inside and I went toward the downstairs bathroom to wash my hands and face. "Oh, Maybel," Mrs. Charleston called, "Mr. Charleston is in there. Why don't you use the one upstairs?"

I went upstairs and washed. I was drying my hands when I heard Catherine's voice. I quietly tiptoed down the hall to Bernard's room. The door was slightly ajar. I peeked inside and Bernard was kissing Catherine.

I returned to Mrs. Charleston in the kitchen. I took a cookie from the cookie jar and nibbled its edge.

"What's wrong, dear?" she asked. "You suddenly look so sad."

"I'm fine," I continued nibbling. I stared down at the kitchen table, looking at the little lines in the wood. The grain of the wood was very narrow in some places and wider in others.

"Mrs. Charleston, here where the lines are narrowly spaced means it was a dry couple of years, and here on the table where the lines are widely spaced means there were several years of wetness, right?"

"Yes, Maybel," she smiled. "You paid attention."

"I did. You're interesting. That's why I pay attention to you."

She smiled, "You know Maybel, my father made this table for me and gifted it to me on my wedding day. This center panel here on the tabletop is my life from birth to marriage. You see, it starts here," she pointed to one side of the panel, "and ends here, when I got married and left my father's house." She pointed to the other side of the wooden plank.

"This panel of wood is your life?"

"Yes. My father planted a tree when my mother became pregnant with me. You see here, there were three very wet years during my first three years of life. The lines are wide because the tree grew a lot those years. Then, as you see here, there were four years of hardship for farmers because of draught; the lines are very narrow because the tree didn't grow much. And moving down the lines of my life, this little knick in the wood is where I marked when I first met Bernard's father."

I counted the lines. "You were nine?"

"Yes," she smiled.

"I met Bernard when I was eleven."

"Yes, I know, dear."

"We're not going to get married though," I said bluntly, then took another bite of cookie.

"Maybe not, or maybe you will. I suppose there's a fifty percent chance either way. Has Mr. Charleston taught you about odds during your gambling lessons?" She winked at me.

I giggled and blushed. "No," I replied, "I'm not good at math. I leave the math to him and I identify everyone's tells."

Mrs. Charleston laughed, "You two make a fine team."

I heard Bernard and Catherine laughing as they passed the kitchen. I looked down at the kitchen table. Bernard stuck his head inside the kitchen and told his mother he was taking Catherine on a walk.

I felt Mrs. Charleston gently pat my hand. "What's made you sad, sweetheart?"

I looked up at her. "He is a lot nicer to me when it's just the two of us, but when Catherine is near, he ignores me and wants to be with her, and I don't like that. I know they are dating, or sometimes dating, actually, I'm never sure what their relationship status is, but neither are they. It's confusing to me when Bernard switches back and forth between treating me like a girlfriend, and ignoring me like I'm his sister."

"Yes, that would be difficult, Maybel. Maybe he's confused, too. Relationships and people change constantly. Maybe you can talk to him and you both can decide what to do about your ever-changing feelings?"

I looked down at Mrs. Charleston's life on her kitchen table. "Mrs. Charleston, what do these other planks of wood represent? These two thin planks?"

"My younger brother and sister never made it to adulthood, Maybel. Those are the trees from their short lives. My father added these planks to my table because my brother and sister would never live to have a table of their own."

"I'm so sorry, Mrs. Charleston!"

"Life is short Maybel, too short to let it pass before you get a chance to live. Please talk to Bernard, because I don't want a rift between the two of you to cause you to never want to come visit me. I think of you as my daughter, Maybel, and I know Mr. Charleston does too."

I went to daddy's workshop to sit. Sometimes I just wanted to sit and watch daddy measure, cut, and sand.

Henry was there, and they must have been talking about naughty things, because they stopped laughing like little boys over something crass when I opened the door.

"Oh, hello, Maybel," daddy said.

"Hi, daddy. Can I sit and not help you cut, measure, or sand? I just want to be with you."

"Sure, sweetheart," daddy said, "but first, tell your old dad what's wrong."

"I'm fine, daddy."

"Very well, don't tell me," daddy replied.

Daddy went back to talking with Henry while I sat on the chair on the other side of the workshop. I didn't want to be alone, but I didn't want to be near enough to be a part of the conversation. Daddy said I was like a cat in that respect.

Catherine came into the workshop. "Oh, hello, Henry. I didn't know you were here."

I rolled my eyes from behind the big barrel of scrap wood. I knew she knew Henry was here, and I knew she enjoyed flirting with Henry.

"Have you seen Maybel, Henry? You two have become such good friends." Catherine's voice was higher in pitch. That was her flirty voice.

I rolled my eyes so hard I glimpsed the inside of my brain. I wondered what Catherine was up to because she was clearly either planting seeds of some design, or fishing for information.

"She's sitting over there behind that barrel," Henry said.

I raised my hand and twiddled my fingers.

"Oh, Maybel, good, I don't need you for anything, I just hadn't seen you lately. Anyway, daddy, can I go on an evening stroll with Bernard?"

"I suppose, sweetheart. Don't be gone long."

"Yes, daddy," I heard Catherine kiss daddy's cheek.

"I hope you're still here when I return, Henry," Catherine flirted.

"Goodnight," Henry replied.

Catherine left. I heard daddy joke with Henry. "You're absolutely terrified to flirt back in my presence, aren't you Henry?"

"Yes, sir," Henry chuckled.

"I like that," daddy said.

"Yes, sir," Henry repeated.

"Henry has always been very polite and respectful, daddy," I called from behind the wood.

"Come sit with us, Maybel," daddy called.

"I want to stay here and mope," I called back.

"Very well," daddy said.

They continued talking about things I didn't care about. Someone was selling a tractor and the price of paint went up.

My bottom got numb. I stood up and stretched.

"Oh!" daddy jumped, startled. "I forgot you were back there, Maybel! I'm glad I didn't tell a naughty joke!"

"Can you tell it now?"

"No, honey," daddy smiled and chuckled.

"Daddy were you a tomcat like Henry when you were young?"

"No, honey."

"Why not? You're just as handsome."

"I'm not, but thank you for saying so."

"Why weren't you a tomcat? Is it because you and mommy got married young?"

"That may be part of it, but mostly because I didn't want to be a tomcat."

"Why though? I thought all men lived vicariously through Henry."

"Well, some do, but I am just a one-woman kind of man. Mommy is the only woman for me, always has been, always will be. Men like to joke, and that's fine sometimes, but I wouldn't want my life any other way."

"I wish it were that easy for me. I want just one good boyfriend, but I think if you want grand-children, daddy, you'll have to depend on Catherine to continue our family line. I think I'm going to live here forever with you and mommy."

"That's fine, sweetheart."

"I love you, daddy."

"I love you too, baby."

I hugged daddy. "Daddy, can I hug Henry goodnight or would that make your gun accidentally go off?"

"Accidentally?" Henry asked. "You have a malfunctioning gun?"

"No," daddy and I replied in unison.

"That's just what we'd tell the court," I said.

"You can give Henry a hug goodnight," daddy said.

I hugged Henry and he sat rigid and only patted my back with two fingers only for two seconds while watching daddy the whole time.

"Daddy, Henry has always been polite and respectful," I said.

"I know, honey," daddy smiled.

I left and went inside. I sat writing at the table in the family room with mommy sewing next to me.

"Do you like playing with marbles, Henry?" I asked.

"I did, a long time ago."

"You don't now?"

"No, Maybel," he smiled. "I haven't played in years."

"Will you play with me now?" I was bored and wanted entertainment.

Henry thought for a minute. "Yes, I suppose I could play with you for a few minutes, but why do you want to play marbles? You're not a child anymore."

"Well, what else is there to do around here? I do not like primping and spending hours on my hair, my face, or my dresses. If you take that out of the equation, Bernard has tutored me in math, then what else am I supposed to do?"

Henry thought for a moment. "I suppose there isn't much to do here. We'll play marbles," he said.

I sat down on the marble floor of Mr. Charleston's great, big office. Henry sat in front of me. He looked terribly awkward.

"You don't play with boys and girls my age, do you?" I asked him.

"No, Maybel, I don't."

"It's ok. I can teach you."

I showed Henry how to shoot marbles. The marbles were glassy and pretty. I liked the way the sun from Mr. Charleston's office windows came in and lit up the marbles like stars in a clear night's sky.

"Will you have tea?" one of the kitchen staff asked.

"No, thank you, Mrs. Dewey," Henry answered. He turned to me. "Maybel, you prefer hot chocolate, don't you?"

I smiled, "Yes."

"Mrs Dewey, two hot chocolates, please."

"Yes, Mr. Fox," she replied.

"I like your last name," I said. "I like foxes."

Henry smiled.

"Henry, will you tell me a story?"

Henry looked confused. "A story? What kind of story?"

"Any story. Do you know any stories?" I asked him.

"I'm afraid I don't," he replied.

"Can you make up a story?"

"I don't know how, honey. I'm sorry." Henry shot his marble and did better than I expected.

"It's ok. If I tell you a story, do you think you could learn how to tell stories and then tell me one?"

"I can try, but I make no promises," he smiled softly.

"Alright, have you heard about Ireland, Henry?"

Henry smiled, "Yes, Maybel. I've been there."

"Oh. Well then, I cannot tell you this story. It's a made-up story. If you've been to Ireland, then you will know I have no idea what I'm talking about."

"Go on then," Henry laughed, "Tell your story. I don't care if it's accurate."

"Very well," I said. "It's about a banshee."

Henry raised his eyebrows mischievously. "Sounds like this will be a good story," he smiled.

"One day, in the Emerald Isle, a banshee called Irena lived in a cave in a cliff by the ocean, over-looking the passage between Ireland and God. Irena could see which ships sailing toward Ireland would make a safe landing, and which ones would perish in the ocean, meeting God in their ships, with their wooden planks of the haul ripped out, and pushed asunder, from being impaled onto the jagged, rocky outcrops in the deceivingly, shallow waters."

"Irena could see the faces of the souls aboard each ship as they sunk into the depths of the cold, black water. She was especially sorrowful when she spied young maidens who were destined to perish. Irena screamed at them, and often, they heard her wails just before their ships struck rock and they catapulted with a sudden jolt into the water, their bodies lost forever, but their souls freed and sent roaming along the shores for eternity.

One such voyager was a young woman named Dohna. Dohna was a fiery redhead on her way to work for a rich family in the city. Dohna heard the sharp shrills of the banshee Irena's wails, but not in time to save herself. She plunged headfirst into the protruding, black rock that cut and sliced through the water, stopping only a mere three inches from the surface of the ocean so as to entice, then ensnare each sea captain to his doom."

"Sweetheart, time to come home," daddy called for me. His meeting with Mr. Charleston was finished.

"Ok, daddy. Do you want the rest of my hot chocolate?"

"Thank you, honey," daddy took my mug.

"Wait, what happened to Irena and Dohna?" Henry asked. He stood up with a handful of marbles and put them in my hands. His hands were warm and lovely and smelled like Bernard's rich, spicy soaps.

"I don't know yet," I said.

"How does the story end?" Henry pressed.

"I haven't written it yet."

Henry looked distraught. "How were you able to tell me all that, but you haven't finished writing it?"

"I was writing it in my head as I told it. I have no idea how it ends," I said. I never understood why people wanted endings to my stories. I didn't think the endings mattered as much as other people thought they did. I liked the journey of my characters, not their endings.

"When will you finish it?" Henry asked.

I shrugged. "Daddy, can we have bacon for dinner?"

"That sounds wonderful," daddy smiled at me.

Daddy turned to Henry. "Frustrating, isn't it? She doesn't finish most of her stories," daddy chuckled.

"Maybel," Henry took the leather, marble pouch from the floor and placed it into my hand. "Please finish your story and tell me later."

I smiled.

"Good luck," daddy laughed. "I'm still waiting on the ending of the story about squirrels in your hair you told me when you were five," daddy laughed and tousled my hair.

Daddy led me outside. Mrs. Charleston and Bernard were returning from the stables. Mrs. Charleston's hair was long and thick and flowed beautifully behind her. Bernard towered over his mother. He was now very broad-shouldered and muscular.

"Oh, good, I've been needing to speak with you about carpentry," Mrs. Charleston spoke to daddy.

"Bernard, please take Maybel back to the stables while I talk to her father about carpentry."

I ran and hugged Bernard. "Hi, Bernard!" I wrapped my arms around his chest.

"Hello, Maybel. You've gotten taller since my last school break."

"I'm still a lot shorter than you," I smiled up at him. I took Bernard's hand and twirled around him. "Did you miss me?"

"Always, Maybel," he smiled.

Bernard led me back to the stables. "You look nice," he said softly. He put me on a stool so I could brush Big Ben's mane.

"Big Ben's hair is wild and free like mine," I laughed.

"Would you like me to brush your hair too, Maybel?" Bernard joked. He tugged playfully on my hair.

"I'm still not as tall as you, even standing on this stool." I looked up at Bernard's forehead trying to gauge how much taller he was than me.

I wrapped my arms around his neck and hugged him tightly. "I really miss you when you're gone," I said.

"I miss you, too." Bernard kissed my cheek, close to my neck and earlobe. It felt good when he kissed there, better than when he kissed just the middle of my cheek.

I returned his kiss by kissing the same place on his neck.

And then we stared at each other for a moment.

Bernard cleared his throat. "Shall we ride?"

"Yes," I said.

"Which horse will you take?"

"We aren't riding together? I'm scared to ride alone," I said.

"You can ride with me then," he said.

"Front or back of you?" I asked.

"Either," he said.

I chose the front.

Bernard and I rode out to the far fence line. Whenever Bernard returned from boarding school it was like this, a little quiet and awkward at first. Bernard said it was because he wasn't used to seeing the same people during school breaks. He was used to moving around and living somewhere different during each school break. Every time he returned, he told me I was growing up so fast, and that every time he came home, I was taller and looked older.

"Are you done being quiet?" I asked. "I don't like the first part of meeting you again when you return from school."

"I'm sorry, Maybel. It always takes me some time to get reacquainted with being home again. I've never come home on breaks to the same place with the same people before, and every time I see you, you look so much older. You're changing and growing up so fast."

"You always say that," I said. "Every time you return, you say the same, exact thing."

We looked far out over the fields and streams.

"The sunsets here are beautiful," Bernard murmured. "You can stand along this fence and watch the sky for miles while the colors change and fade."

"Can we?" I asked.

"Watch the sky now?" Bernard looked at the horizon. "I suppose we can. I have nothing planned this evening."

I smiled, "Let's dance!" I took his hands and began dancing to the song I hummed.

"Your dancing has improved," Bernard said. "You must have been practicing a lot since the last time we danced."

"No, I haven't," I said.

"Good," he said. He looked relieved. "You don't have a boyfriend then?"

"No," I said, and continued humming and dancing.

"I'm glad. I don't want to see you dancing with boys. You're growing up too fast as it is."

"I save all my dances for you. You're my favorite of all Catherine's friends."

Bernard smiled but looked sad at the same time. "You're my favorite, too. I'm not just Catherine's friend, though, you can call me your friend too, Maybel." Bernard smiled at me, and his green eyes were lit up by the sunset.

"Spin me, friend," I giggled.

Bernard spun me. I hugged him and looked up at him.

Bernard picked me up and sat me on the fence. He was behind me and wrapped his arms around me. "Look at the pretty colors," he whispered into my ear.

The sunset was dazzling.

We rode Big Ben back to the stables. I sat in front. I was a little cold now and it was nice having Bernard's arms around me.

"Are you coming to my house tonight?" I asked. "Catherine is having friends over for a campfire."

Bernard held my waist and helped me down. Big Ben was quite possibly the tallest horse I'd ever seen.

"No," he said. "I'm staying home tonight."

"Why?" I was sad. I wanted to be with Bernard.

"I've been thinking about you and Catherine lately. I think I need a little time apart from dating Catherine. My classes are getting more difficult. I need to study more, and I can't when Catherine always wants me to go to parties with her."

"I'll never see you anymore," I said.

"Of course you will. We're together now."

My heart sank. "I should go home before it gets later. Maybe I'll see you before you return to school." I hugged Bernard.

"You can come to my house anytime," Bernard said.

"Ok, Bernard."

"I'll see you tomorrow," Bernard called after me.

"Ok," I waved. I knew I wouldn't see him tomorrow.

I walked down Bernard's carriageway. He came running behind me. "Wait, let me walk you home."

"It's ok, I know the way."

"You act like we'll never see each other again," Bernard said.

"I don't think Catherine will want me to spend time with you if you break up with her," I said gently.

I held Bernard's hand while we walked. When we approached my house, the smell of smoke from the campfire wafted toward us. Boys' and girls' laughter and shrieks came to our ears.

Bernard let go of my hand. "I don't want Catherine to think you're the reason for my breaking up with her."

"Why would I be the reason?" I asked him, confused.

Bernard sighed, "Because I like you, but obviously my affection is not returned," Bernard muttered. He seemed annoyed.

"I like you too," I said. I often felt like math wasn't the only thing I couldn't quite grasp. Sometimes conversations and people's reactions confused me too.

When we opened the gate and walked around the corner, Catherine was sitting with a girl and two boys. Several more girls and boys were standing or sitting around the fire.

Daddy stood watching the fire, proud of his handiwork. Henry stood beside daddy. They had their arms crossed across their chests, admiring how high they stacked the brush.

"It's the crisscross pattern," daddy said proudly. "The tighter you weave the branches, the more condensed the fire. That piggy in the middle is going to cook perfectly even on all sides, and that's how you do it, son." Daddy nodded happily toward the fire.

Henry smiled so brightly when daddy called him son.

They stood nodding and grunting like men do when they're happy with the results of their hard work.

"I hope Mr. Clayton down the road sees this fire and smells this pig. He always brags about his brush stacking, but I'm telling you right now Henry, his way is not as good as my crisscross method."

Henry nodded and grunted. Apparently, Henry communicated something to daddy with his nod and grunt, because daddy grunted back an affirmation and nodded. I wondered what they communicated to each other in this form of grunting and nodding.

A boy off to the side put a twig in a girl's hair and the girl took it out and playfully slapped his shoulder. Her friends giggled because she was the object of flirtation. The boy's friends laughed and hit his shoulder because he'd successfully won a girl's attention.

Every few minutes a girl would walk in front of Henry and smile at him. Henry politely nodded, but did not return their attention. Henry didn't seem to ever care about flirting. If Henry wanted sex, he never had to flirt for it.

Catherine smiled and waved at Bernard.

"Hello, Bernard," Catherine came to us. She happily hugged Bernard and kissed him. Bernard didn't back away from her kiss.

I went to stand beside daddy and Henry.

Daddy wrapped his arm around my shoulder. "How was your visit with Bernard?" daddy asked.

"We rode Big Ben and watched the sunset," I said.

"What happens to Irena and Dohna?" Henry asked me.

"Who?" Henry's question to me surprised me. I didn't know what he was talking about.

"Your story," Henry said expectantly.

"Oh, yeah," I said. I thought for a moment. "I don't think it has an ending."

Daddy chuckled, "Frustrating isn't it?" he asked Henry.

"I became vested in your story, Maybel," Henry said. "I really want to know what happens."

"So do I," I snorted. "It was a good story and started out great," I said.

"Yes, Maybel," Henry said impatiently. "When will you finish it?"

"I don't know yet," I said. "But daddy, I just now in my head finished the story about the squirrels in my hair when I was five. I had those squirrels in my hair and I took a hot bath, and out fell the squirrels from my hair and plop, plop, plop into my hot bath water they went. You poured potatoes and carrots over me and we ate squirrel soup together." I laughed at the imagery in my mind.

Daddy laughed, "Wonderful ending, Maybel! I love it!" He shook his head and laughed again. "You have the best imagination."

"Thank you, daddy. I'm going to go sit by the fire," I said.

"Don't talk to any boys that remind you of me," Henry called after me.

I turned around. "Don't be silly, Henry, nobody here is as pretty as you, except daddy of course." I winked at daddy and he winked back.

I sat on a log by the fire. Catherine and Bernard were across the campfire and under a tree leaning against the trunk. They held hands and talked.

I spent the next hour talking to Albert, a boy from Catherine's class. Bernard and Henry kept taking turns pestering us.

"Maybel, come with me please, to the kitchen. I need help." Bernard reached down for my arm.

"What do you need help with?" I asked him.

"Something," Bernard said.

"What thing?" I again asked.

"Come, Maybel." Bernard held his hand closer to mine for me to take.

I begrudgingly took Bernard's hand.

"What do you need help with?" I asked as we walked inside.

"Who is that boy?" Bernard asked. Bernard appeared irritated, but I wasn't sure if he was irritated with me or Albert.

"He is Catherine's friend. His name is Albert, but his parents are from France, so he pronounces it like Al Bear," I laughed. "Like a bear, Bernard!" I laughed again. "Can you believe it? Al Bear," I chuckled to myself.

Bernard was not nearly as amused as I was. "Come sit by Catherine and me," Bernard said.

"Are you and Catherine dating or not?"

Bernard rubbed his forehead. "I don't know. I was thinking about what you said, and maybe you were right, and maybe I will never see you again if Catherine and I break up. I really like you a lot, Maybel. I miss you when I'm away at school."

"I miss you too," I said.

"But you don't miss me the same way I miss you, and that both saddens and frustrates me."

Bernard watched me closely but I had no idea what he was talking about. Bernard took my hands. "I'm frustrated because you don't like me the way I like you," he said.

I was confused by Bernard being upset. "I do like you, Bernard. I've always liked you. I tell you so all the time."

Bernard let out a big, annoyed sigh.

"I'm going back to sit with Al Bear," I said. "Why don't you come sit with us?" I attempted a small smile. I hoped Bernard would stop acting strangely and come sit with me.

"I don't like him. He's pestering you," Bernard said.

"No, he's not. We're talking about catnip."

Bernard looked surprised and confused. "Catnip? Why?"

"Al Bear trains cats."

Bernard blinked slowly. "Are you joking with me right now?"

"Yes," I smiled.

"Maybel, you are difficult to understand," Bernard complained.

"You might understand me better after wine. That's what daddy says."

"Yes, I imagine so," Bernard sighed.

"Come sit with us," I said.

"I'll come sit with you, but if he tries to hold your hand, I'll punch him," Bernard grumbled.

"What if he tries to hold your hand?" I asked Bernard.

"What?"

"You're prettier than I am," I winked at Bernard.

"Maybel," Bernard smiled, "I sometimes want to be mad, but when I look at you, I can't. You always know what bizarre thing to say to make me laugh."

"I like you too, Bernard. You're always my favorite."

"You as well," he said quietly.

We walked back to the campfire and Bernard sat between me and Al Bear. He didn't talk to Al Bear though. Bernard talked to me about catnip, which made me giggle. Al Bear got up and went to another girl on the other side of the campfire.

"Maybel," Bernard whispered, "do you see that star right above your head, the big, bright one? That's my favorite star. I love you, you know."

"I love you, too," I said.

Bernard seemed sad though. He took my hand and we leaned against each other until the fire began to cool. Catherine talked to friends and the fire went out completely. I went to bed and Bernard went home while Catherine continued to enchant her guests with her charm.

I didn't much care for the grandiose parties like Catherine did. She sucked in all the looks and admiration and filled herself with other people's energy. She thrived on the energy a party provided whereas I felt drained and uncomfortable.

I retreated to Bernard's bedroom and sat in his chair under his lamp and read a children's book he must have had as a little boy. It was on his bookshelf and contained colorful depictions of dragons, knights, fairies, and ogres. The drawings fascinated me as much as the stories, which were handwritten on faded parchment paper. The illustrations were done by hand as well in inks, paints, and pencils.

"Maybel, what are you doing here?" Bernard came in and asked.

"Reading. What are you doing here?" I returned his question.

"It's my room," he smiled as he unbuttoned his shirt.

"Bernard, go easy on my virgin eyes!" I exaggeratedly hid my eyes with my hands.

"Funny, Maybel. I spilled cake on my shirt and have to change." He took off his dress shirt and tossed it into his bathroom.

"What are you reading?" he came toward me.

"The most wonderful book I've ever seen in my entire life!" I exclaimed and held the cover up for him to see.

"Ah, yes, my grandmother made that book for me. She's quite talented, isn't she?"

"She's amazing, Bernard! Why hasn't her book been published and copied a million times?"

Bernard laughed, "I'll tell her she has an adoring fan."

He laid on his bed and patted the place next to him. "Come, Maybel, lay beside me. I haven't read this book in ages."

"Read it to me?" I smiled.

"Of course, sweetheart. I loved this book as a child."

I laid beside Bernard and rested my head on his bare chest while he read in an animated voice. His voice changed for each of the characters, which made me giggle. "You will be such a good daddy!" I laughed. "My daddy used to make his voice change too when he read stories."

Bernard chuckled, "I used to read this a lot to my younger cousins."

Bernard continued reading with my head laying on his shoulder and my arm draped across him, lightly hugging him.

He kissed my forehead and stroked my hair as he began another story. "Bernard, this is so fun!" I smiled.

"It is, isn't it!" He kissed my lips then looked surprised that he'd just kissed me. I watched him wide-eyed.

Bernard pushed me back onto his pillow and gently pressed his tongue inside my mouth, kissing me with such passion I moaned softly. He pushed the book away and pulled me tightly against his body and nuzzled my neck and kissed my shoulder. I lost my breath from his sudden and intense affection. His skin was warm and smelled so good as he laid on top of me kissing me with increasing passion.

I let my hands explore and caress his chest and his strong and hard back muscles. He eagerly held me and let his tongue explore my mouth. His hunger and passion made me want more.

"Maybel," he moaned, "if I don't stop now, I won't want to stop later." He kissed me again and breathed deeply, then pulled back. "I'm sorry. I love you so much, Maybel."

He looked down at me. His eyes were pained. He walked to his closet and put on another dress shirt. He watched me as he buttoned his shirt. And then he turned and left.

I didn't want to stay in his bed. I wanted to go home. I was confused.

I went downstairs and winded my way through the mass of perfectly dressed partygoers. Everyone was dressed well and wanted everyone else to notice. I passed nine distinctive perfume scents on my way to the grand entryway. I was certain they were all from Paris.

I had almost reached the front door when Catherine grabbed my arm. "Maybel, it's time for the toasts."

"I'm tired. I'll see you later at home," I mumbled, keeping my head low. I wanted to leave. Everyone confused me.

"No, Maybel, mommy told me to come get you. Mr. Charleston is toasting daddy. It's a surprise. Daddy doesn't know."

I'm sure my face accidentally showed my annoyance at having to stay. "Maybel! Smile and pretend to be happy for daddy!" she snapped.

I followed her to the ballroom and stood by mommy. I searched the room for daddy and amongst all the perfect hair and perfect faces, Bernard stood watching me intently.

I quickly looked away. "Where's daddy?" I whispered to Catherine.

Catherine didn't answer. I turned and looked to both sides but she was gone. "Mommy, where's Catherine?"

"By Bernard, of course," she nodded toward where Bernard stood.

I looked back at Bernard and saw Catherine making her way to Bernard. Bernard was still watching me. When Catherine arrived at his side, I watched her grab his hand and he jumped, startled by her presence, as she woke him from his intense gazing at me. She smiled and pulled him down for a kiss. I saw their mouths open slightly and their tongues touch. And then Bernard straightened up and stood staring at me again, but his eyes looked different. He looked sad.

I turned away and started to leave again but mommy grabbed my wrist. "It's almost time," she smiled.

I kept my head down watching everyone's polished shoes and heels. Mr. Charleston tapped his glass with his fork. "Mr. Wyndham, my good friend, get up here," he boomed loudly and merrily. I saw daddy cross the room blushing as everyone clapped. Mr. Charleston thanked daddy for both his friendship and business partnership. "And who knows, perhaps we'll soon share grandchildren," he winked at Bernard and Catherine.

Catherine beamed at the attention and wrapped her arms around Bernard's neck and they kissed while everyone applauded. Mr. Charleston then directed attention back to daddy and I watched as Bernard's eyes came back to me. We continued staring at each other.

There was another applause and I took that moment to escape. I weaved my way behind the crowd and out the door.

As I walked past Susan's house, I heard laughter. I hesitated because I thought maybe it was too late to visit but I was confused and lonely and wanted to be with Susan. I knocked quietly on the door and Mr. Matthews answered.

"I'm sorry it's late," I said quickly.

"Nonsense, come in Maybel," he smiled.

"Maybel?" Susan ran to greet me. "Do you remember my brother?"

"Yes," I said.

"He's here!" Susan said excitedly.

"Oh, that's nice, Susan." I tried to feign excitement, but really, I just wanted Mr. Matthews to suggest we go outback and shoot things or into his workshop and dissolve into a vat of acid little mud figurines that I'd be glad to make into Bernard's image. I wondered how I could work guns and acid into a conversation with Mr. Matthews.

"Do you want to shoot something or dissolve something in acid?" I blurted out.

"Always, honey. I'll get my coat," Mr. Matthews said.

That was easier than I'd anticipated, I thought.

"Bad day, dear?" Mrs. Matthews asked. She gave me a hug and a peck on my cheek. I liked her sweet, little pecks.

"Yes," I replied.

I looked back at Mr. Matthews. "It's not too late to shoot things?"

He laughed, "You can shoot anything at any time here, sweetheart."

"Father, they're girls. They shouldn't be shooting guns," Theo complained.

"Have you seen your sister shoot? She's better than you!" Mr. Matthews laughed and patted Theo's shoulder.

"She is not! I easily beat her last year!" Theo said, his pride was hurt.

"That was last year, son," Mr. Matthews laughed as he patted his son's shoulder again. "Let's see how you fare this year!"

"Even Maybel's better than you now," Susan giggled.

"She's not," he said annoyed.

Susan laughed. "Actually, she probably is, Theo. Maybel's has a lot of bad days this year, so we've practiced a lot!" she giggled at me.

"Yes, sorry about that," I said as we walked out back carrying pistols and shotguns.

"You're too young to be so troubled Maybel," Theo said. "What has been troubling you?"

"Bernard!" Susan piped up.

"Your sister's boyfriend?" Theo asked, surprised.

"Yes," I mumbled.

"Why?" Theo asked.

"I don't know," I mumbled, not wanting to answer.

"Sometimes he's nice to Maybel and sometimes he's mean," Susan stated as a matter of fact.

I grumbled, "I don't want to talk about it."

"What did he do now, Maybel?" Susan asked with exasperation as we arrived at the edge of the woods.

"He's just annoying," I grumbled.

"Did he kiss you again?" she asked bluntly.

"Susan! I told you not to tell anyone!" Tears began welling in my eyes.

"Oh, yes, sorry, Maybel!" Susan covered her mouth, her eyes wide because she'd told my secret.

"Can I just blow things up now?" I began crying.

"There, there, dear, you can't hit a target with tears in the way." Mrs. Matthews handed me her handkerchief.

"Thank you," I blew my nose, then tucked her handkerchief into my bra in case I needed it later. Then I blew five holes into targets Mr. Matthews had hanging from a clothes line.

Theo's eyebrows raised. "Wouldn't want to be Bernard right now!" he whispered to his father.

Mr. Matthews whispered back, "You should see the vengeance she takes on her little mud figurines in a vat of acid!"

There I stood in my party dress and heels with a pistol in one hand and a shotgun in my other hand. "Let's make this interesting," I said. "Susan and me against the three of you."

Theo laughed hysterically then realized I was serious. "Oh," he said, "you're actually serious? What are you wagering?"

"I have five hundred dollars in my bedroom, cash."

They stared at me. "I'm serious," I said. I had one thousand dollars from my gambling stints with Mr. Charleston, but it was not my style to boast.

"Fine, Maybel, we'll take your bet," Theo said arrogantly. "I need a new suit to wear to the Charleston's extravagant parties we never seem to get invited to," he said with a bit of resentment when he spoke the word 'Charleston.'

"You were invited," I said incredulously. "I know you were invited because I saw your invitation being written by Mr. Charleston."

"Hmm, interesting," Theo said, not at all interested. "Must have gotten lost in the mail," he said sarcastically.

"Or Bernard didn't want you to come because you kissed Maybel after the Christmas Eve party." Susan's eyes widened and she slapped her hand across her mouth. "Sorry, Maybel!" she said in a high-pitched voice.

"Let's just start shooting," I snapped.

Rocks were lined up along logs and tree stumps and lit with lamps that hung well above the tree stumps. Theo, his father, and mother picked off twenty-six rocks set on the stumps and logs, while Susan and I picked off thirty-four. I smiled smugly at Theo, who was by far, unamused.

Mr. and Mrs. Matthews were having a delightful time even though they lost to me and Susan. They were playful with each other and I envied their love. Mommy and daddy loved each other like that, too.

We headed back home. Mr. and Mrs. Matthews excused themselves saying Mr. Matthews accidentally spilled his drink on his shirt and Mrs. Matthews was going to wash it.

I was sad because I would have to continue home. "I guess I'll see you tomorrow Susan," I said.

"You're leaving?" Susan looked sad.

I watched Mr. and Mrs. Matthews giggling upstairs. "I thought you were all done for the night," I said.

"Oh, no, mother and father are going upstairs, but we can still play with acid," Susan said.

"Oh good," I sighed, "I don't want to go home."

"You can stay here tonight then, Maybel!" Susan said happily.

"Ok," I smiled. "Let's go dip Bernard's clay likeness in acid," I smiled, happy to be staying with Susan and her family. I loved her family, even Theo was more tolerable now than when I'd first met him.

"Ladies, you can't play with acid unsupervised," Theo said.

I rolled my eyes. "We know what we're doing, Theodore!"

"Yeah, Theodore!" Susan giggled.

"It's Theo, Susan, except for Maybel, she can call me Theodore," he smirked at me.

"If I give you back the five hundred dollars you owe me, can I call you Theo?" I smirked back.

"No," he smiled.

"Fine, Theodore," I said.

We went to their father's workshop and I got the clay figurines Susan and I had made previously from Mr. Matthews' storage bin.

"I'll make tea," Theo said.

Theo went to their kitchen while Susan and I poured some strawberry juice from a glass jar. It was really sweet and really good.

We giggled as I tossed Bernard's likeness into the acid and it bubbled and foamed, the air bubbles making his figurine push up and appear to be dancing and bobbing, gasping for air, until it finally gave up and sank to the bottom of the vat, disintegrating along the way.

I laughed hysterically as I watched Bernard's last breaths bubbling up to the surface. Susan handed me another glass of strawberry juice and we merrily drank as she tossed in a figurine of a boy who teased her in school.

"Oh look! Maybel!" she gasped. "Anthony's head just popped off and sank!"

I giggled until I gasped for air. "Looks like he's had a bad day!" I laughed and drank more strawberry juice.

I threw in another figure I'd sculpted. It had a stethoscope wrapped around its stupid neck. "Goodbye, Dr. Dumb Bernard!" I giggled as the figure hit the acid and broke into pieces, bubbling and frothing until finally surrendering to defeat and plummeting to the bottom of the acid vat.

Susan laughed loudly, "Bernard looks so broken up about something, Maybel!"

I screeched with laughter.

"What did he do tonight, Maybel?" She gulped more strawberry juice.

"He kissed me really passionately," I giggled. "He's such an ass," I laughed.

"Girls! What are you drinking?" Theo yelled.

"Berrystraw juices," Susan giggled.

I laughed at Susan's slurred speech.

"That's Mr. Wyndham's special juice! Stop drinking it!" He yelled at us.

"No," I said, "daddy makes special cider and we're not allowed to drink it. He doesn't have any strawberries," my lips were becoming numb and I slobbered.

"Dear God! You two get in here immediately!" Theo ordered.

Theo came to Susan and dragged her over to me, then dragged us both inside.

He tossed us onto the couch then went upstairs.

"Susan," I smiled at her.

"What, Maybel?" She smiled back at me.

"I want you to know that I love you and your family. I love being with you and your family. You're my favorite of all the people," I cooed.

"Maybel, I love you too. You're better than Catherine," she said.

I started crying. "Really?"

"Yes, Maybel," Susan said.

"Thank you," I sniffed.

"We should go tell Bernard that," Susan declared.

"You're right, Susan," I said emphatically.

We eventually got to our feet and the next thing I realized, we were stumbling across Bernard's cobblestone drive by his carriage entrance.

"Huh, that was fast. How'd we get here Susan?" I mused.

"Maybel, this horse likes me," she said.

I turned. "Oh! Big Ben! I love you so much Big Ben!" I hugged him and he whinnied.

"Benny loves you too," Susan giggled.

"He has better taste than Bernard," I whinnied back at Big Ben.

"I think you confused him, Maybel," Susan said. "You may have whinnied a bad word at him."

"Oh, I'm sorry Benny," I patted his neck.

"Ladies! Get back home now!" Theo hissed.

I grabbed Susan's hand. "Run!" I shrieked. "Run, I say!"

We ran around the corner and into the kitchen.

"Oh, hello, Maybel," a voice said.

Susan and I hid under the table. I peeked my head out and there was sweet Archie eating cake.

"Hello, Archie," I smiled. "If a man comes in asking for us, would you be a sweetheart and tell him we ran into the crowded ballroom?" I asked him.

"Anything for you, Maybel," he smiled, his mouth full of cake.

The door slammed. "Where did the two girls go?" We heard Theo's voice.

"Well, hello there, would you like some cake?" Archie asked jovially.

"Where did the two girls go?" he asked impatiently.

"Well, let's see, I did see two young ladies head to the ballroom," he told Theo.

We heard Theo's footsteps running away. I patted Archie's leg under the table.

"I love you, Archie," I slurred.

"I love you too, Maybel. Do come visit, won't you?"

"Absolutely!" I smiled as Susan and I crawled out from under the table.

"Oh Maybel?"

"Yes, Archie?"

"Bernard's looking for you," he told me.

My smile vanished.

"What shall I tell him?" Archie asked me.

"That you haven't seen me," I begged.

"Will do, Maybel."

"Thank you, Archie," I said gratefully.

"You're welcome, Maybel, and Maybel's beautiful friend." He smiled shyly at Susan and she smiled back.

We ran toward the study. "Not there, Maybel," Archie called. "Go to the drawing room or solarium."

"Thank you!" both Susan and I called over our shoulders.

I led Susan to the drawing room, which was occupied by a group of men puffing cigars. "This way, Susan," I grabbed her arm and we trampled upstairs stumbling and laughing.

"That's Bernard's bedroom," I whispered, in between giggles. "Let's go to this guest bedroom," I started toward the bedroom decorated in blue.

"No! I want to see what Bernard is like on the inside!" Susan darted like a little, drunken rabbit to Bernard's bedroom.

I followed her, hiccupping along the way. "Susan! Bernard will find us in here! This is where he sleeps!"

I shut Bernard's bedroom door. "Susan! Stop!"

"Maybel, these illustrations are beautiful!" She flipped the pages of Bernard's grandmother's storybook, amazed by the detailed drawings.

"It really is gorgeous, isn't it?" I said.

"Maybel, who made this?" Susan was entranced by the book.

"Bernard's grandmother," I answered.

"She's amazing," Susan whispered.

"Yes, she is," Bernard said.

I spun around. "Bernard!" I gasped.

"Maybel, where did you go?" Bernard asked me.

"To Susan's house. I won five hundred dollars for shootin' shit good," I hiccupped. "Then we dunked you in acid. But I'd like you to focus on the five hundred dollars I won," I hiccupped again.

"Are you two drunk?" Bernard looked between me and Susan, who was hugging the pretty book and dancing with it.

"No," I hiccupped. "We shot guns, dipped you in acid, and drank strawberries," I couldn't stop hiccupping.

Bernard sighed, "You're drunk."

"Why do you kiss Maybel but date Catherine?" Susan asked.

Bernard looked taken aback. "What?" he whispered.

Susan spoke louder, as though Bernard hadn't heard her, even though he clearly had heard her. "Why do you kiss Maybel but keep dating Catherine?" Susan enunciated her words to ensure Bernard could hear and understand her. "Which one do you want? Pick one. It's not buy one and get the other one free you know, Bernard!" Susan smiled, completely unaware of the implications of her words, and completely drunk and happy.

"Yes, Bernard," I finally found my voice. "I love you, and I love kissing you. And I love being with you, but you treat me like horse shit, and I'm madder than an old wet hen about it! I've never been mean to you," I slurred and swayed, the strawberries really setting in. "But you're an ass to me! I am a good person and I deserve respect!"

"Yes, you are right, Maybel," he said quietly.

"Are you embarrassed of Maybel?" Susan asked.

"No, of course not," Bernard continued watching me.

"Then why do you kiss me in secret?" I asked.

Bernard didn't speak. He watched me and he looked sad. "I love you," he whispered. "You always introduce me as your future brother-in-law. Do you love me as a man or as your brother, Maybel?" he asked me.

I swayed a little and put my finger up like I was about to say something important, but suddenly I felt like there was something in my belly that didn't want to be there. I ran to Bernard's toilet and burped the loudest burp I'd ever burped.

"I didn't vomit," I yelled out triumphantly.

"Bernard," I leaned against the bathroom door frame, "I love you, but you kiss me then act like you're embarrassed of me."

"I'm not embarrassed of you!" he said.

"If you weren't doing something bad," Susan slurred, "there would be no reason to hide your love for Maybel. You're hiding your love for Maybel. You're embarrassed because you know damn well you're behaving poorly!"

"And you're dating my sister," I added, "and you need to either stop kissing me, or break up with Catherine, because you're a cheater. Why are you a cheater?"

I held my hand up to shush Bernard. "Wait," I said, "I'm cheating on Catherine, too!" I started crying. "I'm horse shit too! We're both horse shit, Bernard!" I hiccupped.

"I'm sorry, Maybel. I know I've behaved badly. I love Catherine, but somewhere, I don't know when, I fell deeply in love with you, and now I'm confused and I don't know how to keep from hurting Catherine or you."

"Break up with one of us," I burped.

"I don't want to come between you and Catherine. I honestly don't know how to remedy this situation," he said.

"I'm breaking up with you, then!" I said loudly and defiantly.

I turned to Susan, "See! I sure told him!"

"You sure did, Maybel! You're so good!" she applauded.

"Susan, let's go back to your house," I said. "I'm done here."

"Can we get some of Archie's cake for our walk home?" She asked.

"Oh, of course!" I said. "That's just a given, Susan," I hiccupped.

We stumbled past Bernard.

We very slowly made our way downstairs by sitting on the steps and scooting down one step at a time.

"Maybel, dear, are you alright?" Mr. Charleston asked when we scooted safely to the bottom step.

"Yes," I whispered, my finger in front of my lips to indicate he should be quiet. "Daddy's strawberries are special. Shh!" I said.

Mr. Charleston burst out laughing. "Alright dear, off you go," he said, as he stepped over us on his way upstairs as Susan and I sat on the bottom step.

Susan and I grabbed the entire three-tiered cake off the kitchen table and headed to Susan's home.

We shoved cake into our mouths on our walk home. When we arrived to Susan's house, Theo was fast on our tail. "Wait up!" he yelled.

"Oh, hello, Theo," Susan smiled and waved, chocolate cake crumbling off her fingers to the ground.

"Hi Theo," I said. "Door," I added. I giggled. "Theo Door," I laughed.

"I've been looking all over for you two!" he said.

"We got cake," Susan stuck her hand out to Theo.

Theo looked at it disgusted. "I'm not eating smashed cake off your fingers!"

"There're three tiers, Theo," she said with a full mouth. "Odds are, there's a tier here I haven't smashed completely."

Theo sighed, "I am hungry," he grabbed a chunk of untouched cake from the middle tier. "This is really good!" he remarked.

"That's why we stole it," I said.

"You stole it?" Theo looked aghast at us.

"Borrowed," Susan corrected.

"Mmmm, yes, what Susan said. We borrowed a cake," I said.

We went inside and shared our cake with Mr. and Mrs. Matthews, who had returned from upstairs looking disheveled and very happy. They didn't ask where the cake came from or why Susan and I still slurred our speech, and that's why I loved the Matthews. "I love you Mr. and Mrs. Matthews," I smiled like the drunk that I was that night.

"We love you too, dear," they smiled back at me.

"I have to go get my nightgown. I can't sleep in my nice dress. It's uncomfortable." I looked down. "Oh yes, it also has cake on it, doesn't it?" I was still tipsy.

"You can use my nightgown, Maybel," Susan said, while simultaneously licking between her fingers to get all the chocolate.

"I'll go get mine so I can leave a note for mommy and daddy so they don't worry about where I've gone." I stood up a little wobbly.

Theo stood up and put his hands out in case I fell. "Oh, it's ok, Mr. Door," I giggled. "I'm good at walking. I've been doing it for years."

"Mr. Door?" Theo asked, perplexed.

"Yes," I giggled, "Theo Door," I laughed at the way it sounded. "Mr. Door," I giggled at my joke.

Theo rolled his eyes. "I'll come with you to make sure you don't fall down drunk in the middle of the street."

"I'm not drunk," I said.

"Right, let's go then," Theo held my arm as I unsteadily walked to the door.

"Susan, aren't you coming?" I called.

"She's fast asleep," Mr. Matthews chuckled. "I'll carry her to bed."

I held Theo's hand as we made our way to my house. I was still a bit unsteady and Theo was kind enough to make sure I didn't wind up in the ditch.

"Maybel, may I ask you a personal question about Bernard?" he asked.

"Sure, ask," I replied.

"You said he kissed you."

I didn't answer.

"I'm sorry, I have overstepped my boundaries," he apologized.

"No, I'm waiting for your question. You said you had a question. That was a statement."

Theo sighed, "You are exasperating!"

"Ha! That's what Bernard always says!" I laughed.

"Maybel, did Bernard kiss you?"

"Yes."

"Why?" he asked.

"I don't know. He says he loves me. But he's been with Catherine forever so I don't know why he kisses me."

"Kisses? He's kissed you before?" Theo asked, surprised.

"Yes, several times."

"Maybel, he's enjoying having a girlfriend and a mistress."

"Mistress? I'm a mistress?" I stopped on the porch just before entering my house. "I'm the bad person in a play?" I started crying.

"No, Maybel, I didn't mean that. You're young, naive, and being taken advantage of. Bernard is the bad person in your play. You need to stay away from him. He's hurting you and Catherine."

"Catherine kisses other boys," I said.

I opened the door and stumbled in. "I'm a very bad sister."

Theo caught my arm and stood me up.

"I think you have had a skewed view of relationships from observing Catherine and Bernard," Theo said. "Perhaps you truly don't understand that kissing someone other than your boyfriend or girlfriend is bad."

"You kissed me after the Christmas party," I reminded him.

"I wasn't dating anyone when I kissed you. You weren't dating anyone either. I'm trying to explain to you that Catherine shouldn't kiss other boys while dating Bernard. And, Maybel, Bernard shouldn't kiss you while dating Catherine."

I slumped over, shoulders down, and sulked toward the stairs. I started up the stairs but tripped and fell onto the steps. I didn't bother getting up.

"Are you ok?" Theo asked, concerned.

"Just leave me. I'm very confused," I mumbled.

"Maybel, you'll get through this. Just take a deep breath and put one foot in front of the other until you no longer stumble."

"When do the special strawberries go away?" I asked. "I'll be able to put one foot in front of the other better after these special strawberries go away."

"I meant in life; you just keep going. But the strawberries will be gone by morning," he added.

"Ok, I'll keep going. Can you help me?"

"Yes, Maybel." Theo picked my limp body up and stood me upright.

We slowly climbed my stairs and went to my bedroom. "Ah, my bed! I love you bed!" I crashed down into my gloriously comfortable sheets. I wrapped the sheets around my head and nuzzled them. "You're the best sheets ever," I kissed them.

"Right," Theo sighed. "Maybe you should just stay here tonight, Maybel."

"Where else would I stay?"

"With Susan," he reminded me.

"Oh! Susan! I forgot! I came to get my nightgown." I stood up, "Theo, I love you," I said.

"No, you don't. You're drunk."

"No, I'm Maybel," I giggled.

"Perhaps you should just get in bed and go to sleep. Don't go downstairs. You'll fall and get hurt."

"Yes, Mr. Door," I giggled.

"Goodnight, Maybel."

"Oh, Theo," I called to him as he stood in my doorway, "am I a bad person? Are Catherine and Bernard bad?"

He sighed, "No, none of you are bad, I suppose, though you should really create and enforce some boundaries between you and Bernard. As to Catherine and Bernard's relationship, they shouldn't kiss other people."

"Are you in a relationship, Door?"

"No, Maybel." He turned to open my bedroom door.

"Wait, Theo, since you're not in a relationship, can I have a goodnight kiss like last time?"

"No, you're drunk. I don't take advantage of such situations. Goodnight, Maybel."

"Wait!" I yelled, "Can I come home with you?"

"Maybel, you're drunk and falling down. Stay in bed."

I got up and walked to Theo without falling down. "See! I'm cured!"

Theo sighed, "Alright, fine. Get your nightgown, shoes, and coat."

"Aye, aye, Theo!" I smiled, "Door," I added.

Theo started down the stairs before me and reached up to hold my hand. I made it safely downstairs.

"Theodore, would you like something to eat?" I took some crackers from the kitchen counter and jam.

"I suppose that might be nice." We went outside and sat together on my front porch.

"This jam tastes amazing!" he marveled.

"Your mother made it," I said. "She makes the best jams."

"She really does!" he agreed.

"Theodore, what's your favorite color?"

"Blue, I guess. Red. I don't know, why?"

"I don't really know you well. I figured I'd ask." I continued nibbling my cracker.

"What's yours?" Theo asked me.

"All of them, depending on my mood. If I need cheering up, I like pink. If I'm angry, blue is calming. If I'm sick, I like green, because it's the color of a happy forest."

"I never thought of it that way," he mused.

"Where do you live?" I asked.

"Connecticut, on the beach, overlooking the ocean."

"The last story you wrote with Susan, what was it about?" he watched me curiously.

"We wrote a story together about the life of a pinecone," I smiled.

"Tell me," he urged.

"It was supposed to be a short story, but it became long, because the life of a tree spans decades. The tree witnessed a lot." I suddenly felt a little sad. "The tree saw a lot of families pass through and leave."

"The tree likely felt the tiny fingers of little boys and girls climbing its branches too, did it not?" Theo smiled. "I'll wager the tree was quite happy from decades of children enjoying its branches and shade."

I smiled at Theo. "Yes, you are right. I need to remember the happy times more than the bad times."

We continued staring out, asking each other random questions and admiring the night sky and buds forming on the trees.

"You can barely see the new growth," I told him, "but in the moonlight, you can just barely see the outline of little buds taking shape. I like watching blooms. One day they are buds, and then in the evening, you look again, and you see tiny leaves."

"I imagine that's what being a parent is like. One day Susan was in diapers and the next day she was walking and babbling, and a week later she went with mother to the city to buy a bra." Theo stared off, probably reliving Susan's life through flashes of memories somewhere in his mind.

"Do you want children?" I asked.

"Yes. Do you?" he returned my question.

"Yes, I want at least two, but less than twelve," I laughed.

"You'll have your own school with eleven children," he chuckled.

"How many do you want?" I asked him.

"Oh, I don't know, a boy and girl at least. Maybe two boys and two girls, something like that."

"What will you name them?"

"I haven't the slightest idea," he said. "And you?"

"A girl named Isabel, pronounced like my name, Maybel. You can name your son Theodore and call him Teddy," I suggested.

He smiled, "I like that."

"What's your favorite animal?" I asked.

"A dog and cat."

"I like them too," I said, "but I'm fond of squirrels, bluebirds, and ants, as well."

"Ants?"

"Sure, why not?" I replied, "They seem nice. Just not inside my house. They're only nice when they are outside somewhere."

He chuckled, "You're interesting, Maybel."

"You are too, Theodore."

I stretched my legs out and looked around at the garden and the street. The air was fresh, a little crisp, but not too cold. Theo nibbled his cracker. He was a lot more handsome now that he acted less arrogant.

"What do you do in Connecticut?" I asked.

"I work in a laboratory with chemicals, inventing medicines, and creating new uses for compounds. On weekends, I box at the local gym. I don't have time for anything else."

"You don't have time for a girlfriend?" I asked.

"No, I don't." Theo looked down at the porch floor. He looked sad now.

"Your laboratory sounds very mathy," I said.

He laughed, "Yes, it is."

"Did Satan recruit you himself, or did one of his underlings?" I kept a straight face.

"What?" His eyes widened and he looked confused, and also a bit scared of me.

"Satan invented math. Nobody told you that? I'm certain it's true. Who else would put numbers and letters together and expect a person to make sense of it?"

"I think you are joking," Theo squinted at me, "but I'm not sure. Are you joking?"

"Yes, Theo, I am joking about you being recruited by Satan. I firmly keep my stance that Satan invented algebra though. He's forcing you to recite his spells every time you work with chemical equations though, Theo. Algebra is satanic incantations. You saved Susan's life, so I'll let your relationship with the devil slide for now."

"I'm not, I don't worship Satan. Are you joking with me? I can't tell anymore."

I sighed, "I'm sorry, Theo. I am, indeed, joking. I'm not good at math so I blame the devil. Really though, I wish I could understand math. I'm great at writing and understanding literature though, so I suppose we all have things we're good at, and things with which we struggle."

Theo watched me with a soft smile. "You seem sober now," he said.

"Yes, I think I am. Must have been the crackers."

"Then may I give you that goodnight kiss you asked for?"

"Yes," I smiled.

Theo leaned toward me and kissed me. And then we kissed again. We continued kissing and were so completely lost in each other's eyes that we didn't notice Catherine and Bernard on the porch until Catherine cleared her throat loudly.

I looked over at them. "Yes?" I asked, annoyed.

"Hello, Theodore," Catherine smiled.

"Hello," Theo replied.

Bernard only watched me. He wasn't outwardly angry, but he definitely wasn't happy. He maintained composure, but stared at me intently and appeared unhappy watching me kiss Theo, so I kissed Theo again. And we kept kissing. They went inside and the door closed.

"Bernard is jealous," Theo chuckled. "Catherine has to know Bernard is attracted to you. It's obvious."

"I'm moving forward, like you said." I kissed Theo again. "One foot in front of the other until I make it to the other side."

"I should probably get some sleep," I yawned. "I will stay here tonight."

"Will I see you tomorrow?"

"Yes," I smiled. "Maybe you can win your five hundred dollars back," I winked.

Theo kissed me again. "See you soon, Maybel."

"Goodnight, Mr. Door." I went inside and took off my coat.

Bernard was holding Catherine's hands and they spoke in whispers. Catherine looked up with tears in her eyes when I walked past the sofa where they sat.

"What's wrong, Catherine?"

"Bernard wants more time to study," she cried.

Bernard's face was solemn.

"I hate studying too, Catherine, but you don't need to cry about it, unless he's teaching you math."

"Bernard's breaking up with me, Maybel!" Catherine said loudly.

"You know, to be honest, I think I'm still feeling those magical strawberries, because I don't care. You both kiss other people and apparently my view of how relationships work is skewed now because of you two. You should have broken up years ago." And then I burped. It wasn't a normal burp. I felt like air that would have been a fart came up through my intestines, my stomach, and out my mouth, very loudly. I ran to the bathroom downstairs and crackers, cake, and the fermented taste of strawberries came hurling out of me and into the toilet.

I washed with cold water and staggered to the stairs and laid on the bottom step. Bernard stood over me. "I'll put you to bed."

"Wait! Who has Bernard kissed?" Catherine asked angrily.

"Me," I groaned. I wasn't sure if I was about to die tonight, but I figured I might.

Catherine looked livid and betrayed.

"I'm sorry, Catherine," I said.

"When?" Catherine growled.

"Tonight," I said.

"I'm sorry, Catherine," Bernard said. "I love you, but I kissed Maybel, and I know you've kissed several men. I do need to focus on my studies, but we've both kissed other people. We've dated since childhood. Maybe we're both curious about what it would be like to kiss other people."

Catherine didn't look as angry now. "I have wondered too," she admitted.

"May I help Maybel get to bed so she doesn't fall and break her bones?" Bernard asked.

"Yes," Catherine said, and sat down in the kitchen.

"Just so you know, Bernard, there's a highly probable chance that I'm going to vomit again. And I might do it on you, on purpose, because you made my sister cry."

I heard Catherine snort from the kitchen.

"I'm sorry Catherine, and I love you!" I called over Bernard's shoulder as he carried me up the stairs.

Bernard laid me in my bed. "Bernard," I said, "I found out I'm your mistress. I'm not going to be anyone's mistress and I want you to know I'm creating boundaries that you will not overstep. Number one is no more kissing."

"I'm sorry, Maybel. I know I've hurt you and Catherine, but somehow, I'll make it up to you both."

"Bernard? You knew about the other boys Catherine has kissed?"

"Yes, Maybel."

"Why didn't you get mad?"

"Because those other boys weren't kissing you," he answered.

"Oh," I said.

"Goodnight, Maybel."

"Goodnight, Bernard."

"Oh, Bernard?"

"Yes, Maybel?"

"I still love you, but I'm very mad, sad, and confused right now, but I'm told we're supposed to keep walking forward. Maybe one day I will be able to look at you and not want to stab you in your neck with a knife."

"I love you too, Maybel," he closed my door and I heard his footsteps going downstairs. I heard his voice and Catherine's mumbling, then the front door closed.

I wanted to talk to Catherine but I was too tired to stay awake and I drifted off to sleep.

Mrs. Charleston asked my mother to allow me to attend a women's author's convention with her because she thought it would be good for me to see influential women authors.

We did not attend such a gathering. Instead, Mrs. Charleston brought me by train to a large gathering around the statehouse in the city. There were women wearing brightly-colored beads around their necks and their hair was intricately braided and tied in styles I'd never seen before. The men wore feathers that flowed from their crowns to their buttocks. Some men wore no shirts. I was fascinated by the paints on some of the men's and women's faces.

"Why are some people yelling at the Indians?" I asked Mrs. Charleston.

"A lot of people do not understand our ways. They read stories in newspapers and books and think we're wild heathens. We hold gatherings occasionally to show people we're good, and to dispel misinformation."

Mrs. Charleston nodded and smiled at a few people as we walked. "I'm Indian as are all the men and women here gathered to show solidarity in front of lawmakers. We want to be treated the same as all Americans."

I had never noticed Mrs. Charleston or Bernard were not white until Bernard told me. I still could not see anything Indian about them. Bernard pointed out that his skin browned in the summer whereas my skin got red and burnt, but that was the only difference I could see between us. I didn't even know Danny was Indian until he told me and he was half Indian. Bernard thought I was lying when I said I didn't know Danny was Indian until Danny told me. I didn't know though. Danny was nice and I loved meeting him in the park to play. I liked him because he was nice. Bernard smiled when I told him that.

There were men and women yelling at the Indians, in different accents like Irish and German, and different colors, both white and black. They called the Indians heathens and told them to go away. I did not want to stay because I felt the anger inside the people yelling and it made me unable to breathe well.

"Why are people angry?" I asked Mrs. Charleston.

"People get mad when they don't understand," she said.

I did not like the feeling of anger I felt flowing through everyone, but I did like some people. There was a white man who smiled at an Indian boy and a black woman and a white woman talking and smiling at each other.

"That's what you focus on," Mrs. Charleston said to me, "the love."

"There's not much," I said.

"There's enough," she squeezed my hand.

Inside me I felt big ups and big downs as I searched the crowd. There was love, but the hate hurt.

"Just see the love, Maybel," Mrs. Charleston told me.

A man got up to speak. He was engaging. He said a few words in a language I did not understand but he was calming and I found myself able to breathe better. He spoke English too and his presence was both strong and gentle.

I realized Mrs. Charleston was watching me. "He is a good speaker don't you think?"

"Yes. He is calm. I didn't understand some things he said in another language, but I know he said good things."

Mrs. Charleston smiled at me.

Another speaker stood at the podium. His voice was smooth. He spoke some words in English mixed with another language as well.

There were many more men and women speaking. I couldn't understand every word but I understood their intentions. They were humans and wanted to be treated as such.

The stories about Indians I read were violent, but Bernard told me my history books were written by white people. The people in front of me speaking and dancing today were kind.

Mrs. Charleston went off to speak to some of the Indians gathered. I thought maybe they were friends and family. She spoke to two men in particular who had been the first two speakers at the podium. They were both in leather, beads, and feathers.

I wandered around watching and listening. There were some people of what appeared to be varying colors and religions who appeared to be mean, and some who appeared to be nice. I was fascinated with all the different people, but I found their emotions, which were either very happy or very angry, to be draining, and I needed to sit.

I sat with my back against a tree where I felt most peaceful. I closed my eyes and looked up. The wind moving the leaves relaxed me as long as I focused on them entirely and nothing else.

I saw Mrs. Charleston wandering around. I thought she was looking for me. I stood up and was going to let her know I was fine but one of the Indian speakers, the first speaker at the gathering, approached me.

He spoke to me in another language.

"Oh, I'm sorry," I don't speak that language.

"Are you enjoying yourself?" he asked me, and then said something else to me in another language.

"Yes," I smiled politely.

"What did you think?"

"Your speech, as well as the speeches of those who followed you, were very good and moving." I smiled at him and he smiled back.

"You don't know who I am do you?" His smile was soft and charming.

"What is your name?" I asked.

"In my tribe, I am White Wolf."

I stared at him blankly. He wore paints on his face. His chest was bare. He had feathers and beads around his head, and he wore cowhide on his legs.

"Nice to meet you, Mr. Wolf," I smiled.

He winked at me and left.

I continued to Mrs. Charleston. She had indeed been looking for me and had become worried.

"Maybel, are you ok?" She held my shoulders and searched my face.

"Yes," I said. "Would it be rude to ask that Indian over there if he might let me look more closely at his beads?" I nodded toward the man who spoke secondly at the podium.

Mrs. Charleston smiled, "You may, Maybel. I'm sure he will appreciate your interest in our culture."

I went to the man. His back was turned to me. His beads were colorful and I really wanted to touch them, but I didn't want to be too forward.

"Excuse me, sir?"

The man turned around and looked surprised to see me. He smiled shyly.

"Sir, may I look at your beads? I like the pretty colors. Did you weave them together? How do you make these patterns? My mother has an eye for color and patterns. I wish she were here to see your necklaces."

He laughed softly at me and smiled brightly. He took a necklace off and put it around my neck.

"Oh, no, sir, I cannot accept this!" I took his necklace up over my head but he put his hands up.

"I want you to have this." He took it from my hands and put it around my neck again.

"Thank you!" I smiled. I couldn't contain my excitement. I jumped up and down. "Thank you!"

I bounced away to Mrs. Charleston. "Look! He gave me this!" I squealed.

Mrs. Charleston smiled, "He must have appreciated your open mind toward our tribe."

"Come, Maybel." Mrs. Charleston took my hand. She led me around the courthouse lawn. "What do you think?"

"I want to make these necklaces. Do you know how to make beads? Do you know how to weave them?"

Mrs. Charleston squeezed my hand. "I'll teach you how to make them, sweetheart."

"Can you teach me how to braid hair in all these different ways? I've never seen some of these hairstyles before."

"Yes, honey," Mrs. Charleston laughed.

We walked over to the where several Indians stood talking.

"Bernard," Mrs. Charleston called.

The Indian who had first approached me turned. He looked at me then at Mrs. Charleston. He came to us and kissed Mrs. Charleston on the cheek.

"Maybel," he said gently, "it's me, Bernard."

I looked at him and wondered how I had not recognized him. I was embarrassed.

"I didn't recognize you, Bernard. I'm so sorry!"

"Nobody would recognize me," he winked at me.

"I should have," I said. I felt stupid I couldn't see past his face paint and feathers and the beautiful beads he wore.

"You were nice to me, Maybel, even though you didn't know it was me talking to you," Bernard said to me.

"I like you, Bernard, even when I don't know it's you," I replied.

"I know, Maybel. And I love you." Bernard kissed me right there in front of his mother and I felt myself blushing as he pulled away. I glanced nervously at Mrs. Charleston next to me. "I am not embarrassed of kissing you, Maybel," Bernard said.

Mrs. Charleston reached for my hand and squeezed it. "I know you love my son, Maybel, and I know he loves you."

"Maybel, there's someone else here," Mrs. Charleston said. "Henry," she called to the man who gave me his necklace. He sat off to the side, away from everyone, under a tree. He was alone. I suddenly realized I had never seen him alone before, void of the company of lustful women. I saw how lonely he looked, even under his face paint.

Henry stood and walked to us. He watched me as he walked, watching my face change to amazement as I searched his face for some sign of Henry. Henry's beautiful face was hidden behind paint so I had not recognized him.

"Hi, Henry," I said. "I am very embarrassed I didn't recognize you and Bernard!"

"This is how we know who our real friends are," he smiled and kissed my cheek. I giggled nervously because his bare chest was now very close to me and it was as beautiful as his face.

"Where is Paul then?" I asked, trying to distract myself from Henry's bare chest with his beautifully sculpted muscles.

"He was here at this gathering yesterday, Maybel. I'm sorry. Perhaps another time you will meet again," Mrs. Charleston told me.

I really missed Paul. He was my age and had never been mean to me or teased me the way Bernard had. Bernard's teasing sometimes made it hard to like him. He teased me, then was nice to me, then teased me again. I did not enjoy the ups and downs and not knowing which was coming next.

"Why didn't I know who Bernard was?" I mused aloud.

"Honey, we may look different, be in different bodies, but our souls recognize each other," Mrs. Charleston said. "Your soul knew Bernard, even in a body that looked different."

"Well, I knew you were nice and I liked you," I admitted.

"I know, Maybel," Bernard tousled my hair. "I liked you, too."

Several people, some of them Indian, and some who were white and black, came to Mrs. Charleston asking for quotes for their newspapers. Mrs. Charleston and Bernard turned their attention to them.

Henry took my hand. "Maybel, I want to show you something." He led me to the shade of an oak tree. Stand here with me and watch.

We stood and watched. We stood and watched so long I became fidgety. I bent and straightened my legs up and down, scratching my back against the bark.

"You can't sit still for long, can you?" Henry asked me.

"I can," I said indignantly, "but we've been standing and watching for an hour!" I sighed.

"It's been twenty minutes," Henry corrected me.

"Twenty long minutes," I replied.

"What have you observed?" he asked me.

"Just people walking and talking," I answered.

"Watch me." Henry walked all the way over to the far side of the courthouse lawn, turned, then walked back to me.

"What have you observed?"

"Your gait suggests you favor your left foot," I said.

"What? I do?" Henry looked surprised. "No, I meant what have you observed about the people around me as I walked through the crowd and back?"

"People were walking around talking, same as before."

Henry looked at me disappointedly. "Wait here, Maybel."

I sighed and sat down on the grass with my back leaning against the tree trunk. I braided blades of grass. There were discarded acorn caps strewn about the grass underneath the oak tree and the reason for all the acorn shells was now just above my head. A squirrel scurried down the trunk, and we surprised each other as he almost landed on my head.

"You weren't expecting me to be at your doorstep, were you?" I laughed as he shot back up the trunk at lightning speed.

"Maybel, who are you talking to?" Henry asked as he approached.

"A squirrel," I replied.

"Of course, why would you be doing something normal?" he smiled at me.

Henry was dressed sharply in a finely-tailored suit.

"Watch me again," he instructed me.

Henry walked toward the far side of the lawn but did not get more than ten paces away before two beautifully dressed women approached him. He politely excused himself and a man came to shake his hand and smiled at him. I heard the man say something about business and guessed they knew each other. Henry continued to the far edge of the courtyard but before he arrived there, he was stopped by several more women and another man. He turned and came back toward me. It took a long time before he returned to me. Women accidentally on purpose bumped into Henry.

"What have you observed?" Henry reached down and pulled me up by my hands.

"Women want you and men want to be you."

"Why?"

"You're tall, beautiful, and everyone wants you to make love to them," I answered, as though the answer was blatantly obvious.

"Why though? Why do they want my attention?" Henry pressed.

"Those women wanted more than your attention, Henry. I heard their undergarments drop to the ground from all the way over here."

"Maybel, they didn't want me. Nobody wants me. They want the costume I now wear before you. No woman or man has ever approached me when I am Indian. Nobody except you. You've always liked me no matter the costume I wear. Thank you, Maybel." Henry leaned down and kissed my lips and I nearly lost my balance. He steadied me, and his big, strong arms wrapped around me did nothing to strengthen my weak knees. I reached up and pulled Henry's neck toward me and kissed him. He let me kiss him. And he kissed me back passionately, his tongue lightly touched mine, and his hands held my neck and waist close against his beautiful body.

Henry smiled at me.

"I've wanted to kiss you for a long time, a real kiss, not a peck," I said nervously.

"Maybel, I really like you," Henry said, and kissed me again. He held my waist with one hand and my neck with his other hand. I felt his body against me. He felt experienced and confident and so gentle. He had never had to be aggressive because everyone willingly gave themselves to him. And so he kissed me gently and confidently, and I really liked his affection.

We slowly pulled away from each other. "I think I heard my own undergarments drop to the ground," I giggled nervously.

Henry smiled at me. "I want you to know how much it means to me that you like me as an Indian, too. I love you, Maybel. And I've never said that to a woman before."

"I love you, too," I whispered.

Henry took my hand and led me into the crowd. Women smiled at him as he passed and then looked sourly at me when they saw him holding my hand.

Henry led me around Mrs. Charleston and Bernard, who were still answering questions from reporters.

"Maybel, may I drive you home? I would like to speak to your father about business."

"Yes," I answered. I liked the idea of sitting beside Henry in his automobile.

"I also wanted to spend a little more time with you, Maybel," Henry said quietly. "I enjoy talking to you." A very light, red color spread across his upper cheeks when he said that. Henry never looked anything but confident, but now, he looked shy.

I smiled and my heart beat fast. I squealed internally, because the most beautiful person in the world held my hand and wanted to drive me home.

We were at the Charleston's manor, for some party for someone or something, I couldn't remember, and while I normally evaded party invitations, Catherine mentioned Handsome Henry would be there, and I really wanted Susan to see him.

"Susan, the most beautiful man in the world is here. Do you want to see him?"

"Yes!" she said with a big smile.

"He's standing in the study by the fireplace in a dark blue suit," I said.

Susan and I giggled as we walked past the doorway. The two large doors were open and guests went in and out socializing.

I stopped Susan before we walked by. "When we walk past the doorway, glance over at the fireplace, but pretend you are just glancing in, not that you are specifically looking for Henry."

"Ok," Susan smiled really big. "This is exciting! We're spies like in books!"

I smiled back, "Let's go," I whispered.

We walked past the doorway and glanced over at the fireplace. "He's not handsome," Susan was disappointed.

"That wasn't him. I wonder where he went. Let's stroll by slowly pretending to admire the architecture or something," I suggested.

"Ok!" Susan became excited again.

We again went past the doorway, this time more slowly. We pretended to admire our surroundings. "Lovely door, don't you think, Maybel?" Susan said in her best imitation of a lofty art curator.

"I didn't see him! I know he's in there! Ok, we'll stroll in, take a book from the shelf, pretending to be interested in it, and come back out here," I told her our next strategy.

"Good plan, Maybel!" Susan smiled. I enjoyed Susan's excitability.

We walked into the study. There were some adults here and there chatting. We went to the bookshelf and I took a book from the shelf and opened it. I turned around with the book covering Susan's and my face, except for our eyes, so we could look around casually and not be detected.

Unfortunately, we must have looked obvious. Daddy and Mr. Charleston sat at Mr. Charleston's big desk watching us and laughing. "Maybel, honey, what are you reading?" daddy asked me.

He stood up and came over to me smiling. He looked over my shoulder at what Susan and I had supposedly been reading. "Let's tell Mr. Charleston what you've learned about the human digestive system. Is it a fascinating read, Maybel?" Daddy chuckled as he spoke.

"Yes," I shook my head.

"Well do tell, Maybel," Mr. Charleston laughed.

"I'm still learning. I'll finish it later," I said.

"Oh, I see," Mr. Charleston and daddy laughed pretty hard at us.

"Henry left a few minutes ago," daddy winked at me.

"Who?" I feigned innocence.

"Let's go eat something, Maybel, and put our newly-acquired knowledge of the digestive system to use," Susan suggested.

I thought Susan made an excellent addition to our excuse for why we were in the study, but daddy and Mr. Charleston laughed harder.

Susan and I walked quickly out of the study and around the perimeter of the ballroom and then I saw Henry in an alcove talking with a beautiful woman. "That's him!" I told Susan. "He's talking to the woman in the black dress.

"Susan and I stopped and stared. "He's really is the most beautiful man in the world!" Susan's voice sounded dreamy and whispery.

"Let's get a little closer," Susan said.

"Stand behind the pedestal with the big fern. Don't let him see us," I cautioned.

We walked around several people and stood behind the large, decorative pedestal with the fern that looked like it had just woken up and hadn't tamed its mane yet. Green leaves shot out at all angles.

"Where did he go?" I asked Susan.

"I don't see him anymore," Susan answered.

"Walk around the pedestal just a step or two to see if he moved to the side a bit," I said.

We took two steps around the plant but he wasn't there. "Go around another step," I said. We stayed close to each other and peeked a little farther around the plant but he wasn't there.

"Take another step, he's bound to be there somewhere," a voice from behind us said.

We jumped, completely startled to hear a voice so close to the back of our heads. Henry stood behind us laughing.

Susan and I both breathed in and froze, staring at beautiful Henry with big eyes and red cheeks from embarrassment.

"Good evening, Maybel, how have you been?" Henry asked me.

There was silence on my part and on Susan's.

"Who is your friend?" Henry looked at Susan.

"Ssss...." was the only sound to come from Susan.

Henry looked back at me for clarification. "Sally? Sarah? Sadie?"

"Suhhhh...." I mumbled.

Henry stared back at me confused.

Susan and I stared at Henry's gorgeous face.

"I can stand here and return your stare all night," Henry smiled, still staring into my eyes. His beautiful, beautiful eyes made my mouth dry and my tongue tripled in size, rendering me unable to speak. If he would stop looking at me with his beautiful, beautiful eyes I might be able to form a word with my mouth.

"Susan!" Susan suddenly yelled loudly.

I shook my head yes.

Henry turned his gaze to Susan and reached out his hand to her. "Nice to meet you, Susan, I'm Henry."

Susan looked at his hand then turned around and ran out the front door. I watched her running, then I turned back to Henry with my big eyes, then darted after Susan.

I ran out the front door and Susan was darting through the lawn like a cat after a bird. "Susan! Wait!" I screamed. Susan kept after that bird, running at top speed.

"Cake!" I screamed.

I said the magic word that made her stop.

"Chocolate?" she yelled back.

"Yes!" I yelled.

Susan walked back toward me. "Maybel, I thought you were exaggerating, but you weren't. He really is the most handsome man in the world!"

"I know," I laughed. "I didn't run into the pedestal supporting the fern accidentally on my way out, so I really think I'm finally getting less awkward around Henry," I said happily.

We walked around back to the kitchen. The cake was in the dining room. Thankfully Archie was eating cake at the kitchen table. "Archie, can I ask a favor of you?"

"Certainly, Maybel," Archie smiled at me.

"Will you please go to the dining room and get two pieces of cake for us?" I asked Archie.

"Ok, Maybel." Archie paused his cake inhalation and left the kitchen.

Susan immediately swooped down and dipped her finger into Archie's icing. "He'll never notice," she shrugged her shoulders.

Archie came back into the kitchen without cake. "He's coming with the cake, Maybel." Archie told me.

"Who's coming with the…"

Henry smiled as he walked into the kitchen balancing three saucers of cake. "Hello again, ladies."

Henry sat at the table across from Archie and put a piece of cake next to Archie and a piece next to himself. "Now, who wants to sit beside me?" he smiled at me. He placed the third plate of cake next to where he sat.

I pushed Susan.

Susan looked back at me like I'd made her walk the plank.

She walked around the table and sat next to Archie and smiled at him. "I'm Susan."

"You're beautiful is what you are," Archie smiled back at Susan and Susan giggled and blushed.

I had no idea Archie was a flirt. He usually sat in the kitchen eating cake at parties.

Henry looked back at me and patted the seat of the chair. I nervously sat down.

"What have you been doing since we last saw each other?" Henry asked me.

"School, writing," I said.

Henry swallowed his bite of cake. "What else?"

"We don't travel or host parties so just school and writing," I said quietly. I was very nervous inside but I was trying hard to talk.

"What about you?" I asked.

"I'm learning more about business from Uncle Charleston. He's brilliant. I'm amazed by his knowledge and the way he conducts business." Henry smiled at me.

I took a bite of cake.

Archie continued sweet talking Susan. Susan seemed smitten, which surprised me.

"I've read several of your stories you left here. May I read more?" Henry asked.

"Yes," I said.

"Maybel, have you considered starting a newspaper column with your stories?" Henry seemed genuinely interested in my stories and publishing them.

"No. Bernard thinks I should write a book. And he wants me to attend his college," I said.

"You two are getting along better then?" Henry asked me.

"We still argue but we have always loved each other," I told Henry.

"I can see the way you look at each other. I know you care for each other." Henry wiped his mouth with his napkin.

"Come dance with me," Henry stood and held out his hand.

I shook my head no. "I'm not a good dancer and I'll faint if you hold me."

Archie laughed at me then turned to Susan, "Please allow me to be seen dancing with the most beautiful woman here," he took Susan's hand and she went with him, leaving me alone with Henry.

My heart thumped.

Henry reached down very slowly and took my hand in his. "May I have this dance, Maybel?"

I began shivering. "You're too beautiful for me, and I don't move gracefully, and I'm really scared of being in front of people."

Henry gently pulled me up and smiled, "Then let's dance here."

He pulled me a little closer, but not against his body. He was calm and careful and very respectful. His fingertips lightly grazed my waist. My hand was cold, sweaty, and limp in his hand. I didn't look him in his eyes because I would faint. We danced for one song like that, barely touching. I didn't feel uncomfortable or pressured, and I relaxed a little. When the music coming from the ballroom stopped, Henry lightly kissed my hair on the top of my head.

"Thank you for the dance," he smiled sweetly down at me.

I looked up at him shyly, "You're welcome."

Henry took our plates to the sink and then smiled kindly at me as he left the kitchen.

I felt faint so I sat down at the table. After a few minutes my heartbeat slowed and I could feel my body again. I hadn't realized how terribly nervous I'd truly been. I stood up and took a deep breath.

Bernard came into the kitchen. "There you are, Maybel, come play cards with us."

"Ok," I said. I was still floating in the clouds. I followed Bernard out of the kitchen and to the drawing room where he played cards with Catherine, Susan, and Archie.

I sat down beside Bernard on one side of me, and Susan on my other side. I could swear I still felt Henry's fingertips on my waist and my hand Henry held still buzzed with electricity.

"Your turn, Maybel," Bernard nudged me with his elbow.

"Which card game are we playing?" I asked.

"Poker. Maybel, are you ok?" Bernard asked me.

"Yes, I'm fine. Just tired," I said. I was not tired; I was reeling from Henry's hand on my waist. I didn't tell Bernard that.

"It's seven in the evening!" Bernard said.

"It's been a long day," I replied. I could still feel Henry's lips on the top of my head.

Bernard sighed, "Do you want to play or not?"

"Yes," I said. "Aces high, twos wild, winner takes all."

"That's my girl," Bernard smiled and picked up a card.

I had become so engrossed in understanding everyone's body language for my own benefit so I could slaughter my opponents and win, that I hadn't noticed several people had gathered behind where Bernard, Susan, and I sat. Catherine was on Bernard's other side and Archie was on Susan's other side. We sat in a circle around the round table in the drawing room.

I, of course, won.

"May I play?" a voice asked.

"Yes," Bernard said, indicating an empty chair beside Catherine.

After the cards were again dealt, I heard Henry's voice across from me asking the dealer for two cards.

My head shot up instantly. "Henry?"

"You just now realized I was here?" Henry smiled.

"I was concentrating on winning, not on your beautiful face," I said.

Archie laughed, "You should see his baby picture. The nurses all swooned."

I laughed at Archie's comment.

"You've finally met your match, Maybel," Archie cautioned me. "Henry is really good."

"I'm sure a baker's dozen of women out there agree," I smirked.

Henry had the plainest face. "Read my tell, Maybel," Henry dared me.

"Make one and I will," I smiled.

"I don't have tells," he said.

"We'll see," I narrowed my eyes.

"Maybel is finally able to speak to Henry without stuttering; how wonderful," Bernard said sarcastically. There was a hint of irritation in his voice.

"Bernard's tell is he raises his right eyebrow when he lies," I told everyone.

"Thank you, Maybel," Catherine smiled happily.

"Yes, thank you Maybel," Bernard said dryly.

"Did everyone notice his right eyebrow raise? When he said thank you, he was lying," I smiled at Bernard.

Everyone laughed. Bernard looked at me with a smirk and pinched my ribs, tickling me.

I giggled, "Does anyone want to know his other tell?"

Bernard put his cards down and wrapped his arm around my neck and clasped his hand around my mouth. "Maybel, I will put you over my knee right here in front of everyone," he laughed and kissed my cheek, then let me go.

"I won't tell them," I giggled at Bernard.

Later we sat outside at a campfire Bernard and Henry made. I wondered why Henry wanted to play with us. There were three women who came outside with us and they did not seem to enjoy the outdoor bugs. Henry had never played with us before, and I wondered why he wasn't inside with those women, dancing and kissing the winner in a shadowed alcove off the ballroom.

The three women vied to sit next to him on the log. I sat next to Susan and she sat next to Archie. I couldn't understand why Archie was here either. I only ever saw him inside eating or playing indoor games. He sure seemed to like Susan though, and she seemed to enjoy his attention.

Bernard sat beside me and pulled Catherine down beside him. I wondered if that meant they were on friendly terms again, or if they were dating.

Bernard started the conversation by playing a game called favorites. We all went around listing our favorite this or favorite that.

When I was asked my favorite things, Bernard always answered for me, and I hit his arm each time. "Stop telling everyone I like squirrels! My favorite animal is a dog!" I paused, "and cats. I also really like horses."

"But you write about squirrels all the time!" Bernard said.

"I like squirrels too," I said.

Bernard put his arm around my shoulder, "Tell everyone about your trained army of squirrels," he laughed.

"I was mad at Bernard and I had my squirrel army attack him!" Bernard and I leaned into each other laughing.

"I was so mad at you!" he squeezed me against him. "And I was also so terrified of you!" He tickled my side as he pulled me against him laughing.

When Bernard was asked his favorite color, Catherine answered blue but I guessed dark green and I was right. Bernard pushed me playfully.

"How did you know?" Bernard asked me. "I always wear blue."

"Only at formal affairs, because that's what you're told to wear. At home you wear dark green a lot," I said.

"What's my favorite color," Henry asked me.

"A deep shade of red, almost an orangish-red, like the sunset," I said.

"Yes, that's correct," he said, impressed. "I've never worn that color before though."

"I know," I said.

"Then how did you know," he asked, genuinely surprised.

"You come out of parties to admire sunsets and you appear most satisfied with the ones that have deep reds and oranges," I told Henry.

Henry sat back and watched me curiously.

Bernard put his arm around my waist, "Maybel notices things." He pulled my head toward his shoulder and kissed my hair while watching Henry.

Bernard kept his hand on my waist. I didn't mind, but I thought it was strange because he gestured with his other hand, meaning it wasn't around Catherine's waist. I wondered if maybe they were not dating, and were perhaps just friends now.

I didn't care for groups, or talking in front of people, so I excused myself, saying I needed to get a drink of water. Instead of returning, I went upstairs to Bernard's bedroom where I felt safe and calm. It was quiet there.

I read a book on geography. It was boring, but it relaxed me.

After an hour or so, I decided to go back down to the campfire. I wanted a glass of water and some fruit also. I started down the hall and Henry emerged from his bedroom with the woman in the black dress. I stopped immediately and stared wide-eyed.

Henry saw me and pushed the woman away from his lips. He looked at me and I looked at him.

The woman leaned in for another kiss and Henry let her, then grabbed her elbow and led her down the stairs.

I stood in the hallway until I was sure they had descended the stairs and dispersed.

I went downstairs and out to the campfire. I sat beside Archie.

"Where have you been?" Archie asked.

"Reading about China," I answered. "I lost track of time," I said.

"We're talking about secrets, Maybel," Archie said. "What's your biggest secret?"

Everyone stared at me. Henry sat back down at the campfire with the woman in the black dress. The other two women got up and left when they noticed the top three buttons of Henry's shirt undone and the unkempt hair of the woman in the black dress.

"Maybel?" Archie asked.

"I kissed a boy," I said.

Catherine giggled and so did Susan. Bernard didn't laugh and neither did Henry.

"Who was it Maybel?" Archie asked.

I looked down into the fire. I didn't answer.

"Bernard, how many girls have you kissed?" I heard Henry ask.

"A lot less than you!" Bernard joked and everyone laughed.

I continued staring into the fire. I wondered what happened after the first fire. Many, many generations ago, the first people to see fire, what did they think? I wondered.

"Maybel!" Someone yelled my name.

"What?" I looked up startled.

Catherine had been trying to get my attention. "Who was your first crush?"

"Why?" I asked.

"We're playing a campfire game, Maybel, who was your first crush?" Catherine repeated her question.

"Do we have to be honest or are we just making up answers?" I asked her.

"Honest," Catherine said.

"Who did you say was your first crush?" I asked Catherine, anticipating her answer to be Bernard.

"Bernard," she said.

"Ah ha!" I exclaimed, "We're making up answers then! Your first crush was the boy from our church picnics who was forty years old!"

"He was fifteen, Maybel!" Catherine crossed her arms, annoyed.

"But you were eight! He may as well have been forty! If you are eight, a fifteen-year-old looks the same as a forty-year-old!" I laughed.

"He was nice and I liked him," Catherine said, "but my first real crush was Bernard."

"And who was yours, Bernard," I asked.

"Catherine," he said.

Catherine kissed him, and they kissed for what felt like forever. Their kissy noises and lip smacking annoyed me. "Are you two dating or not? I cannot keep up with your relationship status," I said, and several of their friends gathered around the campfire stifled giggles.

"Maybel, who was your first crush?" Henry asked. I felt he was trying to distract me from Catherine and Bernard.

"You," I said.

The woman in the black dress laughed at me.

I looked back into the fire. I should never have come here, I thought. I watched a moth land in the flames and sizzle.

"Does anyone else wonder what the first people to see fire thought?" I asked. "Imagine, you are sitting in a cave somewhere eating the fish you caught but you don't know about fire, so you're eating your raw fish, and suddenly lightning strikes the trees faraway in the distance. You wonder what just happened. The dusky sky begins to brighten and turn red and orange. It's terrifying to you because you have never seen fire before. As the night wears on, the fire spreads and you gather your family and leave. By morning, you are still walking away from where the fire started when the breeze suddenly shifts and blows from behind you. Suddenly, you lift up your nose and smell the most delicious smell you have ever smelled. You grab your children and walk back toward the fire and wild pigs lay roasting in the embers of the fire and you realize the delicious taste fire can make when it burns a pig's carcass."

Everyone stared at me.

"Bacon!" I yelled. "Bacon!"

Everyone stared at me except my dear Susan. "That's a great observation, Maybel! I like it!"

"I do too," Henry said.

The woman in the black dress laughed at me and Catherine stared at me, probably annoyed that I always embarrassed her, even though I never meant to. I embarrassed myself more than I could possibly embarrass anyone else.

I stood and went inside. This was what happened whenever I tried to be normal and socialize. I should have stayed home like I usually did. I stood in the kitchen by the sink pacing and wringing my hands, waiting for mommy and daddy to say it was time to go home. I could hear people talking and laughing around the campfire. I kept telling myself over and over to act more normal.

Henry came into the kitchen. He stopped and looked at me. I didn't want his pity so I turned around.

"Maybel," he walked toward me.

I backed away. I didn't want his disgusting sex hands or sex lips near me. "Don't touch me," I turned away. "You have that woman all over you."

"You and Bernard playing poker and sitting around the campfire," Henry began, "You're in love with each other and that made me jealous. I never get jealous!" Henry appeared agitated and confused.

"I like you a lot, Maybel. The more time I spend with you and your father, the more I like you, and tonight, for the first time ever, I was jealous!" He shook his head and rubbed his forehead. Henry looked at me then left.

I stared, watching him walk through the crowd beyond the kitchen and leave.

I went back outside to ask Susan if she was ready to walk home together. Susan wasn't sitting at the campfire. I walked around the house to the back gardens. Susan and Archie were holding hands and sitting together on a bench. "Hello, Susan. How are you doing?" I wanted to give Susan an excuse to leave if she didn't want to stay.

"Great, Maybel. We were talking about cooking. Archie wants to be a chef."

"Very good, Archie," I said. "Susan, I'm going home. Would you like to come with me?"

"I'd like to stay here a little longer," Susan smiled at Archie.

"And I'd very much like to sit with the prettiest flower in this garden," Archie smiled at Susan.

"Enjoy yourselves," I winked at Susan.

I walked back inside and toward the front door. I saw mommy talking to Mrs. Charleston. "I'm going home," I said. "I'm tired."

"Do you have someone to walk you home?" mommy asked.

"No, it won't take long. I'll be fine," I said.

"Henry will walk with you," Mrs. Charleston said.

"He left. It's ok, I'll be fine," I said quickly.

"He hasn't left yet. Henry," she called.

"Yes?" I heard Henry's voice from somewhere off to my side.

"Oh, I don't want to trouble anyone. I can stay here and wait until you and daddy are ready to leave," I told mommy.

"Nonsense," Mrs. Charleston said. "Henry, sweetheart, will you please walk Maybel home?" Mrs. Charleston asked Henry when he came closer.

I looked down. I just wanted to walk home alone. It wasn't far.

"Yes," Henry said. His hand was on the small of my back guiding me through the crowd. He wasn't as gentle as before when we were dancing in the kitchen.

"Have a good night, Mr. Vincent," I said as Henry led me through the front door.

"Good night, Miss Maybel," he smiled at me. I missed my grandfather every time I saw him.

We stepped down onto the lawn and Henry took my hand.

I really did not want to touch his hand. I would have to wash my hands as soon as I got home. I imagined where he put his hands on that woman, or perhaps inside her, and I shook my hand free.

"Maybel, I'm sorry," Henry apologized.

We continued walking.

"You told me I'm always in control of my voice and my movements. I had not considered that, but you were right. I saw you and Bernard tonight and how much you love each other, and I became very jealous, but I had no right to be jealous. I'm sorry, Maybel," he looked down at me. "I now realize why Bernard is having such a difficult time. I should have behaved better though, Maybel, and I am sorry."

"What does sex feel like?" I asked.

Henry looked taken aback. "Wait until you're married," he said.

"Ok, I will, but what does it feel like? It must feel good to make everyone act so strangely," I said.

"It feels good with someone you love. I cared for a woman once, and she broke my heart," Henry said.

"If it feels bad with women you don't love, then why do you do it?" I asked.

"I wanted to relieve myself. I don't know, Maybel, men aren't that complicated. I needed a release. It feels good, but not like it feels when you are in love. Wait until you are in love."

"Why did you make love to that woman tonight?" I asked.

"I didn't make love to her. I had sex with her. There is a big difference."

I sighed, "Why did you have sex with her?"

"I saw you flirting with Bernard and I became jealous and angry."

"I was not flirting!"

"You both were flirting with each other," Henry said angrily.

"Catherine flirts with boys. We all flirt!" I became angry, and when I became angry, I tended to say things that did not make sense. "That's a part of our charm! We're a loving, flirting family, like dancing donkeys and talking cows!"

Henry looked at me. He looked confused. I often confused myself.

I attempted to gather my thoughts more clearly. "I was recently told that I have a skewed sense of how relationships work because of both Catherine and Bernard. Maybe I do. But you do too, Henry. Bernard and I were laughing and joking with each other. I don't see that as flirting. Maybe you see it as flirting because you have never had a healthy relationship with a woman, and don't know how to be with a woman unless you are spreading apart her legs and satisfying your needs."

We arrived at my house and Henry opened my gate. "Goodnight," he said quietly, and looked down.

I went inside and turned around. Henry glanced at me then left.

The next morning after breakfast, Susan came over to my house. She had the biggest smile.

Catherine smiled at Susan, "I know that smile. You kissed a boy, didn't you?"

"Yes," Susan blushed.

Bernard rolled his eyes.

"Was it Archie?" Catherine smiled.

"Yes," Susan giggled.

"Was he a good kisser?" Catherine asked Susan for more details.

"Yes, and he tasted like cake!" Susan's smile widened and Catherine and I laughed.

"I don't want to think about my little cousin kissing," Bernard's face looked disgusted. "I'm going to the kitchen for water or food or anything to not have to sit here and listen to this conversation."

"What about you, Maybel?" Catherine asked me. "Did Henry kiss you when he walked you home?"

Bernard sat back down on the sofa. "Henry walked you home?"

"Yes," I said.

"Bernard, we're discussing your cousins and how well they kiss," Catherine said sarcastically. "I thought you didn't want to hear about how well Henry kisses?"

"Henry kissed you?" Bernard asked, becoming protective of me.

"No," I said.

Bernard relaxed and sat back in the sofa.

"I thought for sure Henry would have at least given you a polite kiss on your cheek," Catherine continued, glancing at Bernard to see his reaction.

I didn't want to think about Henry because I had seen him coming out of a bedroom with that woman. I just stared down at the patterns in our rug.

"Ah, so he did kiss your cheek!" Catherine teased, watching Bernard. "Maybel doesn't kiss and tell!"

Catherine giggled and that vein in Bernard's neck protruded.

"No, Henry didn't kiss my cheek. He was a perfect gentleman," I assured Catherine.

"If Henry tried to kiss you, would you let him?" Susan asked me. "Or would you freeze up and stare at him making unintelligible noises like we both did last night?"

Catherine and Bernard both laughed.

"I would definitely not have let him kiss me last night," I said.

"Why? He really is the most beautiful man in the world!" Susan cooed.

"Because he had sex with that woman in the black dress and I wouldn't want to kiss a man who tasted like he just finished having sex with some random partygoer." I turned my lips into a disgusted face thinking about where he kissed that woman.

"He had sex with that woman in the black dress?" Catherine looked suddenly distressed and sickened.

"How are you surprised?" I asked Catherine. "You were the one who told me you were surprised his penis hadn't fallen off yet. Oh, by the way, I asked him if it had been worn down to a stub yet either, and he said no."

At that Bernard and Susan laughed loudly. Catherine did not laugh though. She looked disturbed.

"When did Henry have sex with her?" Catherine asked me.

"When I left and went upstairs for some quiet time reading about China in Bernard's room."

"He left the campfire with her, but was only gone fifteen or twenty minutes. I don't think that's enough time. You must be mistaken Maybel," Catherine said.

"They came out of a guest bedroom kissing, Catherine, but you're probably right, they were probably in there reading about geography like I was doing in Bernard's bedroom," I said sarcastically.

Bernard and Susan again laughed.

"If they did have sex, Henry must not be good at it. My parents go on for an hour or longer," Susan told us.

We stared at her with our mouths agape.

Susan continued, "I read a book by a French author about a woman named Madame DuBois, and she called men who were quick between the sheets 'selfish lovers.' It sounds like Henry is a selfish lover."

I blushed and laughed really hard, and Bernard laughed too. Hearing Susan talk about her parents and selfish lovers was funny coming from her mouth.

Catherine still seemed distracted and upset. She excused herself and went upstairs.

"What do you want to do today?" Susan asked me then turned to Bernard and asked if he had any leftover cake.

Bernard smiled at her, "Is it cake you want to put in your mouth, or Archie?"

"Bernard!" I yelled. "Susan is too young for your bad language!"

"Oh, you're allowed to talk like a bawdy sailor but I'm not?" Bernard asked defensively.

"Boys can't talk that way to a girl! Susan is young!" I snapped.

Bernard sighed, "You're right." He turned to Susan, "I'm sorry I made a crass comment, Susan. I will be more appropriate from now on."

"It's ok, Bernard, I've heard both boys and girls say much worse at school," Susan told him. "And, yes, I want to see Archie again today," she smiled. "There being leftover cake would just be a nice bonus."

Bernard and I laughed.

"Alright then, Maybel, will you please go upstairs and get Catherine?" Bernard asked me.

I went upstairs and knocked on Catherine's door. "I have a headache," she said.

"It's me," I called through the door. "Can I come in?"

"Yes," she said.

I opened her door and she was laying on her bed looking sad.

"Do you want me to get you a cold towel for your head?" I asked Catherine.

"No. Is Bernard upstairs with you?" Catherine was looking past me out toward the hallway.

"No," I said.

"Close the door," Catherine said, her voice sounding strange.

I closed her bedroom door.

"Henry kissed me last night," she said.

My eyes opened wide with surprise and curiosity.

"Ok, well, actually, I kissed him, but he returned my kisses. He kissed me passionately, Maybel."

"Did you think he was a good kisser?" I asked.

"Yes, a really good kisser," Catherine said. "We kissed after you went home and Bernard was away talking with his father and their business associates. That was after he had already had sex!"

"Oh," I said, connecting the dots. "You kissed him after he had done things with that woman and you are now afraid you got a disease."

"What? No! I mean I wasn't thinking about diseases, but I am now!"

"Henry says he's never had a disease," I assured Catherine. "I'm certain you are healthy," I told Catherine. I made a mental note to not drink from the same glass as Catherine for several weeks though, just in case.

"I meant I'm upset because Henry was so attentive and sweet. He was gentle. I thought he liked me and he made me feel like the most beautiful woman at the party. But he was lying. He just wanted to see with how many women he could have sex last night!" Catherine looked downcast and troubled.

I paused then whispered, "Did you have sex last night?"

"No, Maybel, but he's so handsome I almost forgot I had a boyfriend!" Catherine said guiltily.

"Maybe you should tell Bernard?" I cautiously suggested.

"No, I am going to forget it happened and never let myself get swept up in anything like that again!" Catherine said definitively.

"If Bernard kissed someone else, would you want to know?" I asked.

Catherine looked up at me, her face void of emotion. "No," she said. "We all make mistakes. Even if Bernard kisses someone else, he always comes back to me. He wants me, Maybel, not whomever he kisses."

"He's been kissing women?" I asked, surprised. I wondered how many.

"I suspect," Catherine said. She turned her gaze from the ceiling to look at me. "He kissed you," she said sourly. "I suspect he's kissed others, too. But," she paused, "I've kissed other men, and Bernard and I always return to each other."

"Well, speaking of kissing, Susan wants to go to Bernard's house to see Archie. That's why I came up here. Are you coming?" I asked. I didn't want to continue talking about Bernard kissing me or anyone else.

"No, I don't want to see Henry," she said.

"Ok, I'll tell Bernard you have a headache if he asks why you're staying here. Do you want me to send him up here?"

"Sure," Catherine sighed. She rolled over and readjusted her head on her pillow.

I returned to the family room. "Catherine has a headache. You can go upstairs, Bernard. I'll go with you to see Archie, Susan."

Susan and I arrived at the Charlestons. "Good morning, Vincent," I said.

"Well, good morning, Miss Maybel!" Vincent said cheerfully.

"Oh, Vincent, I brought you a piece of chocolate," I said, and pulled it from my pocket.

"Why thank you, sweetheart!" Vincent happily took the candy.

"Hello, Mr. Vincent," Susan said. "May we see Archie?"

"Of course, Miss Susan. He's probably in the kitchen eating cake," Vincent winked at us.

Archie was indeed eating cake in the kitchen and Susan happily joined him. "Good morning, Susan!" Archie smiled. "Here I am eating cake and I thought my day wouldn't get any sweeter, but I stand corrected," Archie took Susan's hand and kissed it.

"Oh Archie," Susan giggled and blushed.

"Well, I'll leave you two alone," I smiled at Susan.

I headed upstairs to Bernard's bedroom. I figured I may as well finish reading my chapter about China.

I opened Bernard's door and there sitting at Bernard's desk reading was Henry. "Why are you here?" I asked him.

"I'm reading a story you left here," he said. He didn't look up at me.

"I wrote it on paper, not a heavy stone tablet," I told him.

Henry looked up, confused.

"Paper is portable. You can take it elsewhere," I said.

I laid down on Bernard's bed with his geography book. I wanted to continue reading about China. There was a picture of a winding wall. I wanted to see a picture of the Imperial Palace, not the Great Wall. I already knew what a wall looked like.

"Who is the bird in this story? Does the bird represent someone in particular?" Henry asked.

"I write a lot of stories," I said. "You'll have to be more specific."

"The bird with the long colorful feathers," Henry said.

"Again, be more specific," I told him.

"The bird died and the family traded its golden body for bread. That's stupid. They could have traded all that gold and all those jewels for so much money they would have all the bread they could eat for the rest of their lives. How very short-sighted! It's maddening!"

"Yes, well, maybe that's why they were poor to begin with. They were short-sighted," I said while turning a page of my book.

"What stupidity!" Henry exclaimed.

"Yes, a lot of people make stupid decisions. I hear you kissed Catherine last night." I looked over at Henry.

Henry looked up from reading. "She told you?"

"Yes."

"Did she tell Bernard?"

"No."

"I made a stupid mistake," he said.

"Yes, one might say you traded gold for bread," I said.

"I'm sorry, Maybel, I don't know why I did that."

"You'll again have to be more specific. You don't know why you had sex with that woman in the black dress or why you had sex with Catherine?"

His eyes widened. "I didn't have sex with Catherine!"

"Oh, my mistake, I must have interpreted the situation incorrectly," I said. I had not interpreted it incorrectly; I wanted to gauge Henry's reaction.

"I shouldn't have done anything with either of them," Henry said.

"You hurt my sister's feelings, you know. I told her I had seen you coming out of your bedroom with that woman, and Catherine was disgusted thinking she'd kissed you after you put your mouth all over that woman's body!"

"I didn't kiss that woman anywhere but her mouth!" Henry exclaimed.

"Susan's right, you are a selfish lover."

"What?" Henry looked shocked.

"Catherine said you were only gone from the campfire for fifteen or twenty minutes, so let's say it was twenty minutes. Five minutes to walk upstairs and five minutes to walk downstairs leaves ten minutes to get undressed and have sex. You're a selfish lover."

"I am not!" Henry said, appalled.

"I wouldn't want to have sex with you. You don't kiss between a woman's legs, and from start to finish, you're done in ten minutes. I actually feel sorry for that woman. She had sex with a stranger and all she got was ten minutes of pathetic sex and she didn't even get paid."

"I am not a selfish lover! God, Maybel! I hope you very soon go mute around me again!" Henry looked very upset.

"I can't. I don't see you as perfection anymore."

"I told you," Henry said, "I wanted to relieve myself last night and she was willing. I didn't want a romance. I'm much more thorough when I love someone."

"You should write that down in your apology letter to that poor woman. 'Dear Woman In The Black Dress: I do not remember your name, or even if I asked for your name. I'm usually a better lover, but only with women I care about. Signed, Henry.'"

Henry's face turned red with anger. "I see now why Bernard was so cruel to you! Perhaps I should not have intervened!"

"Well, you and I are both truth seers and we're both quite blunt," I said, aggravated. I rolled over onto my back and put the geography book close to my face so that I couldn't see Henry in my peripheral vision.

I continued reading about China and emperors. I really wanted to try the noodles I saw in the drawing on one of the pages.

"Here's a truth I see," Henry began. His voice was level and he sounded morose. "You whine about Catherine not wanting to spend time with you, but would you want Susan tagging along with you and Bernard if Bernard stared adoringly at Susan all the time? Catherine has to know you two love each other and that's why she has been so distant toward you. She doesn't want you around tempting Bernard, and I don't blame her. Bernard chose Catherine, not you."

Henry spoke with accurate insight. I knew he did, because I felt the truth in his words and in my guts. The truth stung like I imagined Mr. Matthews acid vats stung my ceramic replications of Bernard.

"Maybel?"

I rolled my eyes and pulled the book down.

"I'm sorry," Henry said. "I'm sorry you don't see me as perfection anymore, I'm sorry that I hurt your sister's feelings, and I'm sorry that I hurt your feelings. I like you, Maybel, and I'm not used to caring about a woman. After I got my heart broken, I decided to never fall in love again. I like you a lot though, and I was angry at myself for being jealous of your relationship with Bernard."

I sighed deeply. "You are right, Henry. I know you are right, because whenever I feel a feeling in here," I touched the place under my rib cage and just above my stomach, "I know I'm feeling the truth. I think about everything all the time, but I had never thought about Catherine distancing herself from me because of the way Bernard treats me. I had never considered that before, which surprises me, because I always think about everything."

I laid there in Bernard's bed and stared at his ceiling. I now had a lot to think about, and I was very confused about this sudden revelation.

"Henry," I paused, "I was blunt with you because I was mad at you for having sex with that woman. I was jealous. I have always had a crush on you. I've seen you with women before and never cared, but over the years, I've really begun to like you more, and when I saw you and that woman in the black dress coming out of your bedroom, I was surprised at how jealous I suddenly felt. I was angry, and I took out my anger and jealousy on you by being mean to you. I'm sorry."

Bernard walked in. "Why are you two in my bedroom?"

"I wanted to see what sex felt like and I figured after being with ten-minute man over there, it would be like experiencing sex, but not so much that I would lose my virginity," I told Bernard.

Bernard laughed but Henry did not. "I came here to read Maybel's stories, and she came here because she enjoys watching me suffer under her relentless torment," Henry said dryly.

"You and me both," Bernard sighed to Henry as he laid down beside me.

"Maybel move over, you're laying in the middle of the bed," Bernard nudged me with his elbow.

"No, I was here first," I said, not bothering to look up from my book.

"It's my bed!" Bernard said.

I continued reading. "Have you ever been to China?"

"No," Bernard answered.

"Yes, you have," Henry said. "You were a baby though, so perhaps you don't remember."

"Then yes, Maybel, I have apparently been to China."

Bernard pushed me over to the side of the bed. "Why must you make everything so difficult?"

"When you find something you're good at, you dig in," I answered.

I curled up on Bernard's shoulder with the geography book. "Show me where you've been again."

Bernard wrapped his arm around me and held the other half of the book. He flipped through pages. He sighed, "Oh, I don't know, here, here, here," he pointed to places on the map. "These places don't matter to me. I like being here in this town."

"Are you still going to start your medical practice here?" I asked.

"Yes," he squeezed my waist, "Are you still going to be my nurse?"

"Can I hold stock in your practice?" I looked at Bernard and smiled.

Bernard laughed, "It's not that kind of a business. It's just a medical practice."

"Can I own half?" I asked.

Bernard sighed, "Sure, honey, you can own half."

"Can I name it?" I asked.

"What do you want to name it?"

"Family First Medical Care. I liked Henry's name, Family Hair Care, and you always say you don't want to travel, you just want to stay home and put your family before business, so that's why I chose Family First."

Bernard smiled sweetly at me, "I love it."

"Do you two intend to date?" Henry asked us.

I froze. I felt Bernard stiffen next to me.

I looked over at Bernard. Bernard turned away from me and toward Henry. "No," he said.

I wasn't dating Bernard, but I suddenly felt rejected again. I always felt rejected when I was with Bernard. It made me sad.

"Alright then, now that I know what your intentions are, Bernard, I would like to ask you, Maybel, to come with me to the candy store to discuss your stories before I return home." Henry held out his hand for me.

I felt Bernard's arm around me tighten. I left Bernard anyway. I didn't want to spend time with Henry because I still felt strangely about him having sex with whomever let him. I didn't want to keep being hurt by Bernard though, so I left with Henry.

Henry and I sat at the candy store by the window and ate ice cream cones while we watched passersby. I liked when my schoolmates saw me around town with Henry. I really hoped Elsie and Effie would walk by. I wanted to be seen with Handsome Henry and those two were the biggest gossips.

"Maybel, do you like plays, music, art museums, riding bicycles, boating, or anything such things?"

"I like those things," I said. "I like them sometimes. I mostly enjoy writing and drawing. I play cards and put puzzles together with daddy, and mommy teaches me how to sew and knit. And I love climbing, and running, and swimming. Catherine was a tomboy like me before she started liking dresses and hair bows and boys. I miss Catherine."

Henry looked away from me for a moment, then turned back to me looking a bit sad. "I know I hurt your feelings when I said Catherine doesn't want you around because you are her competition to be the next Mrs. Charleston. I should not have been cruel to you. I am sorry, Maybel."

"You were honest," I shrugged my shoulders. "You were right. What you said made sense. I'm blunt, too," I told him. "And the truth always hurts."

Henry watched me for a moment. He looked ashamed of losing control and saying something hurtful to me. He changed the subject. "Tell me about your school, Maybel." Henry leaned back and watched me.

"I'm not popular like Catherine. I don't have many friends. The friends I do have live out in the country. My teachers are ok, I suppose. My English teachers have never been impressed with my writing, but daddy says it's because those who can, do. And those who can't, teach."

"I like your stories," Henry said. "Your father is right; your teachers are jealous. Talentless people, when they see talent, try to pull talent down. Makes them feel better about themselves."

"What is the first thing you notice about people," I asked Henry. "I notice how they make me feel."

"I don't normally think about those things, Maybel; men rarely do, but I do remember that I noticed your intelligence," Henry said quietly. "I noticed your big imagination when you spoke. I noticed you danced like butterflies too, sometimes you were here, and then just as quickly as you came into the room, you flitted away. That's what I noticed about you, Maybel."

I smiled, "Thank you, Henry, for noticing me."

"Thank you, Maybel, for always searching for the good in me. Maybe there still is some good somewhere inside me."

"Henry, what do you do? I don't know anything about you really."

"What would you like to know?" he asked me.

"Whatever you want to tell me," I said.

"I don't even know where to begin. I don't know how to begin either," he said quietly while staring out the window.

"You don't have to talk," I said. "We can just walk around or ride in your automobile or just sit here."

"Thank you, Maybel."

"You're welcome, Henry."

"May I take you somewhere?" Henry asked me shyly.

I looked at Henry. He looked nervous. Henry was never nervous; he was always perfectly composed.

"I feel embarrassed and awkward asking you to go do something together. I have never asked a woman to go somewhere with me."

"You've never been on a date?" I marveled.

"No. I have never been on a date. Women always come to me and they don't want to date." Henry stared out the window. "They only want a pleasurable evening. There was a woman I cared for deeply, but we never went on dates. We went to parties together, but I never picked her up at her house and took her to a play or to dinner."

"Neither of us have had a real, first date," I mused.

"I was not given a choice to experience many firsts," Henry said quietly as he stared off into the distance. He looked sad.

I didn't want Henry to look sad. I wanted him to look like perfection, like he looked before I realized he was just a normal human.

"I've never been on a date either," I said quietly, more to myself than to Henry. "Sometimes I wish I had a real boyfriend who took me on dates and kissed me openly, not secretively. And after each kiss, Bernard said he was sorry and that he made a mistake. I'm not a mistake, Henry," my eyes stung from developing tears. "I never thought I was a mistake until Bernard treated me as such."

"Maybel," Henry turned to me with a sudden brightness and happiness in his eyes, "will you do me the honor of being my first date?"

I felt myself leave my body for a moment, and then I thought about daddy, and my soul came slamming back down into my body. "I would like to go somewhere with you, but I don't think my parents will let me," I said softly. "They are protective."

"I understand, Maybel. If I were your father, I would be protective too," he said. "I imagine if I had a daughter, I would also keep a gun named Arthur near me at all times to scare away boys."

"Arthur is only for shooting roosters," I said, then licked my ice cream cone. I wasn't licking fast enough and it was running in streams down my fingers and hand.

Henry took his napkin and dabbed my lips. "You're getting ice cream all over yourself."

I suddenly stared straight ahead. I had a revelation. "Oh," I marveled, "Arthur is for killing cocks!" I suddenly realized the joke and laughed so hard dribbles of ice cream came running out of my mouth and down my chin. "Oh daddy!" I giggled, "Daddy has the best sense of humor ever!" I laughed harder.

Henry also laughed. "He does have the best sense of humor, and he passed on that trait to you, Maybel. I respect you both, and I enjoy spending time with you and your father."

"Do you want to go to my island? We never did go there that day you and Bernard came to my house."

"Yes, maybe for just a short time. I have to leave tonight though. Uncle needs my assistance securing a foothold for our company in Missouri."

"That's ok, I don't think I could tolerate you much longer than an hour or two," I winked.

We continued sitting side-by-side chatting and watching people pass by on the sidewalk outside. Henry continued licking his ice cream cone. A little dot of ice cream fell onto his chin and I dabbed it with my napkin. "I've never met anyone as messy as me," I laughed.

"You still haven't," Henry said, as he wiped ice cream off the tip of my nose with his thumb.

Henry and I finished our ice cream. He opened the door for me on our way out and held it for me to pass through. "May I hold your hand now?" he asked shyly.

I smiled and took Henry's hand. Henry interlaced our fingers together and smiled down at me. We walked like that to my house. "We can row to the island and back," I told him. "I won't keep you out late."

Henry chuckled, "Thank you, Maybel."

"You need your beauty sleep," I smiled at him.

"That I do," he said.

I thought he was much too pretty to know how to row, so I instructed him to get into the boat and I would push us off and jump in.

"Maybel, I can do that. Why don't you get in? I know how to row a boat." Henry rolled up his shirt sleeves and pants, then took off his nice shoes.

"I very much want to see my pretty boy get dirty. Go ahead, Henry," I laughed.

Henry got into the water wearing his nice pants pushed up to his knees. He waded into the water halfway up his calf, then got into the boat. I started rowing us but he took my oars. "You know how to row?" I asked.

"Maybel, do you think I am weak, or perhaps stupid?"

"No," I said.

"I know how to do a lot of things outdoors. My grandfather taught me."

"Oh," I said. I wondered if that was the same Indian grandfather that Bernard told me about. I wasn't sure where Henry fit in Bernard's family tree.

"Is your grandfather who taught you how to row the same Indian grandfather Bernard has out west?"

"Yes," Henry smiled warmly.

"Do you know Paul then?"

Henry chuckled, "Yes, Paul is my cousin, too."

"I went out west with Bernard and stayed at Paul's house. Paul and I played together and we practiced kissing with our tongues," I blushed and giggled.

"I know," Henry laughed. "I saw you two. You were sweet together."

"You saw us?" I asked, surprised.

"Yes," Henry said.

"You were there? Where?" I asked him. "I didn't see you." I was going back in my memories trying to find him at Paul's house.

"That's because you were too busy kissing Paul," Henry laughed.

"Where were you though? I didn't see you at dinner or outside," I said.

"I was there one day visiting family and spent most of the time on the porch talking with grandfather and grandmother. You and Paul were stuck to each other and likely didn't notice anyone else."

"I miss Paul. Does he have a girlfriend now?" I asked, hoping he did not.

"I have no idea. I don't ask him those kinds of questions," Henry said.

"Will you tell him I said hello and that I miss him?"

"I will, Maybel," Henry smiled sweetly at me.

"I wonder if Bernard will agree to take me back to visit Paul. I'll have to ask him again. That would be a lovely visit." I smiled thinking about seeing Paul again.

"I doubt Bernard will ever let you see Paul again," Henry snorted. "Bernard was very unhappy with how much you and Paul liked each other."

"Bernard acts like my protective brother when he's not kissing me himself," I angrily remarked.

"He was not, and is not, acting like your protective brother," Henry said. "He acts like your jealous boyfriend."

"Catherine always tells me Bernard only thinks of me as a little sister."

"Well, Catherine is wrong," Henry chuckled.

Henry rowed is to the island and we pulled the boat up ashore.

"You're surprisingly strong," Henry told me.

"You're much stronger than I expected too," I said. "I just thought you were fun to look at. I didn't know you could actually do things."

"I'm not just a pretty face," he laughed.

"No, you're the most-prettiest face," I giggled.

"It's beautiful here," Henry looked around at the trees and the water.

"Henry, sometimes you look like a happy boy," I told him.

Henry turned to look at me. "What do you mean?" he asked.

"Sometimes when you get lost in sunsets, or looking at trees, or the reflections in the pond, your mask goes away. And then I see your real face. When I see your real face, you look so happy and childlike. Your eyes are big and curious and your smile isn't fake anymore. You're really smiling."

Henry looked at me and his eyes were bright and shining. I couldn't tell if green, brown, or blue was the most dominant color. "I suppose I do wear a mask most of the time. As in poker, when conducting business, I don't want to reveal what I am really thinking."

"Then stop resting your right index finger on your right temple when you are annoyed, and stop leaning back in your seat when you're satisfied with your hand."

Henry looked down at me. "Do I really have tells?"

"Yes," I said.

"I'll pay more attention to those two things," Henry winked at me.

"You have more than two," I said, "but I don't want to tell you about the others in case I need to ask you an important question," I winked back.

Henry smiled, "Fair enough, Maybel."

He parted his lips as though he were about to say something but he didn't.

"Can you climb trees well?" he suddenly asked.

"Yes, that's my specialty," I said.

"When I win, you have to buy me whatever I choose at the candy store," Henry said.

"When I win, you have to buy me an entire cake!" I laughed.

Henry got ready to sprint. "One, two, three, go!" he yelled.

Henry shot up the tree faster than I'd ever seen Bernard. I was far behind him. I couldn't believe he could move so fast and I was more than a little jealous.

I climbed to the top maybe five whole seconds after Henry.

"How are you so fast at climbing trees?" I asked him, surprised.

"I've always been good at climbing trees."

I looked down below me angrily. I was a lot slower than Henry.

"Maybel, look at me," Henry said softly.

I did not look at Henry. I was pouting. Henry beat me at climbing trees.

"Maybel, I know you and everyone else think I'm handsome and that handsome people are stupid. I don't sit around looking at myself in the mirror all day. I was born this way. I didn't choose this. I like math, fishing, climbing trees, I'm excellent with a bow and arrow, I'm devastating with a gun, and sometimes I'm sad because people only look at me like I don't have feelings, like I'm just a man who sleeps around."

I lifted my eyebrow and glanced at Henry quickly, then looked away.

"Ok, last night I was bad. I lived up to people's expectations of me. I slept with some woman I'd just met. I'm not going to do that again. I'm going to settle down and I will never cheat on my girlfriend or wife."

"Ok," I said.

"You don't believe me," Henry said.

"I don't think you will cheat. You've already had every kind of woman there is. You already know when you walk into a room what every woman looks like under their dresses. You already know what they will kiss like and what each one will feel like underneath you in bed. You have grown bored with them. Now you are looking for something on a deeper level, like what you said Bernard and I have."

"I do want what you and Bernard feel for each other, but I do not want what you two have. You deserve a man who loves you openly in public, and Bernard has never, nor will he ever give you that. He's with Catherine. Let him go, and hopefully he'll let you go as well."

"I know," I turned away quickly. I didn't want Henry to see my face look pathetic.

"What I have learned, Maybel, is that the love you and Bernard feel for each other is the love I want." Henry pulled my chin toward him, "I would never hide you. I would hold you on my arm in front of everyone. That is the way you deserve to be treated."

I felt exposed so I changed the subject quickly. "I owe you whatever you want at the candy store," I said.

"I have to go home soon. How about another day?"

"Ok," I said, and started climbing down the tree.

When we reached the bottom, I turned and lifted my hand up to Henry. "Do you need help down? I don't want you to scratch your pretty face."

"I can jump down, Maybel." He smiled and leaped off a branch much higher up than I was tall.

We got into the boat and Henry again rowed us home. We didn't speak. Henry looked around at the pond and trees and bugs skimming along the water. I watched Henry. He was still beautiful if you didn't focus on his well-used penis.

Henry walked me to my house. "See you later, Henry," I said.

"Maybel, I want to thank you for a lovely day spent together. You always make me feel light and happy, and for that, I am truly grateful to you." He then kissed my cheek and smiled so sweetly. He watched me for a moment, smiling softly at me, and then he left.

I went inside our kitchen door. Catherine was standing by the window. "Why was Henry here?"

"He beat me at my own favorite pastime. He's like a beautiful tree squirrel," I murmured.

Just after dinner there was a knock on our front door. Bernard had dined with us and he answered the door.

"Henry?" I heard Bernard say.

Henry walked in. "Maybel, I need help delivering a small chair. Are you available to help me?"

I jumped up from the floor where I'd been drawing and ran past Henry, down the walkway, and flung myself through the open window of his automobile. I didn't want Catherine or Bernard to come. I enjoyed my furniture deliveries with Henry. He bought me custard and took me to the stationary store afterward.

Henry came walking down the walkway and opened his automobile door like a normal, boring person. "I see you are able and willing to help me on this delivery," he chuckled.

"Drive! Now, Henry! Before Catherine and Bernard ask to come!"

"Alright, Maybel, calm down. They can't fit in the backseat anyway as there's furniture already there."

"Bernard will find a way to weasel his way into our adventure so drive fast now! Please, Henry!"

Henry laughed as he pulled out quickly into the street. "We're off on our adventure, you can relax now, Bernard and Catherine are not running after us."

I started giggling uncontrollably, "Henry, you pulled out fast! Is that the first time you've pulled out?"

"If I weren't carefully concentrating on driving safely, I'd put you over my knee right now!"

"Oh Henry," I giggled, "Save that kind of talk for later!"

Henry chuckled, "You're fun. I always have a good laugh and feel better when I'm with you."

"I like you, too," I smiled.

We drove south toward farms and fields.

"Henry, I thought you were leaving tonight. Did your plans get cancelled?"

"Yes," he said. "I cancelled them."

Henry drove us to a house and took the chair up to the porch and knocked. An elderly man looked pleased and thanked Henry as he shook Henry's hand.

Henry returned to me and we began our drive back toward town. Henry turned onto a country road. "Care for another adventure?" he winked.

"Yes!" I practically screamed.

Henry took me to a cliff overlooking fields and a stream. The stream sparkled like snow under midday sun because the sun was setting and made the water glow brightly. "This is why my Indian name is Bright Water," Henry smiled. "When I was born, my father said my eyes looked sparkling, like bright water. This place has gorgeous sunsets," he smiled at me. "I do still have to leave for business, and I'll be gone a month or more, but I wanted to share the sunset with you first."

"It's beautiful," I agreed.

Henry sat beside me on a blanket he laid down for us. He watched the sunset quietly. His face changed from man to boy. I watched his eyes and saw flickers of memories playing behind his irises.

"My favorite book when I was a child was about a teacher who was kind and helped her students. I don't remember the name of the book but I can still recite all the words," Henry said quietly.

"Once my brother John got sick and I thought he would die. He'd been bitten by a snake and our grandfather healed him. He's a Medicine Man, Maybel. I know you know our family secret, and I like that I do not have to hide that part of me from you."

Henry watched the setting sun while he spoke. It was almost as though he were talking to himself at times, but when he looked over at me sitting beside him, I could actually feel him looking into me as he spoke. "I can keep a beat on my grandfather's drum during our ceremonies. I had a pet groundhog named Amy when I was seven. Sometimes when I watch operas, I cry, but I never let anyone see me cry. Once in Paris, I fell into a river and almost drowned, and that was one of only two times I've ever seen my father cry. The second time was when my little sister died. My little sister was my best friend. She was one year younger than me and we did everything together, and then one day she got sick and died when I was six and she was five. I've missed her every day of my life."

I felt frozen. I didn't even blink as Henry spoke.

"I'm trying to be a good man, but maybe I won't be. A man can only run from a woman for so long. I can only resist a beautiful woman for so long until she flirts with me at just the right time and I give in to my body's needs."

"I know I'm bad, Maybel. I'm being honest with you and I know you'll think less of me for my honesty, but please listen."

"I don't remember how old I was. I realized very young that girls were attracted to me. An older girl did things to me that felt really good. I didn't realize I'd had sex until years later."

I looked over at Henry, shocked. "She took advantage of you," I said.

"Yes," Henry said.

"She's bad," I whispered to Henry.

"Yes," he agreed.

"I'm sorry, Henry," I said.

"I suppose that's why sex never meant much to me. I never had the innocence to wonder what kissing a girl would be like, or to wonder what sex would feel like. All the innocence of childhood, of wonderment, and excitement to hold someone's hand, to anticipate what their kiss might feel like, was taken away from me before I ever knew what innocence was."

I watched Henry with immense sadness.

"That's why I've never wanted to do sexual things with you, Maybel; I will not take away your innocence."

"I've already kissed," I said. "My first kiss was a long time ago." My voice was barely above a whisper.

"Bernard never should have been kissing you or holding you and cuddling you like he did!" Henry suddenly became angry. His countenance changed and his eyes looked hurt from remembering things.

"Bernard took a lot of innocence from you!" Henry said angrily. "And my innocence was completely taken!"

I winced. I could feel Henry's pain.

"I'm sorry I get so angry sometimes," Henry breathed deeply. "I see something, or someone says something, and suddenly I'm a boy again, and I see my childhood that I thought was ok, through the eyes of an adult that now understands what happened from a broader perspective. I know Bernard wasn't as bad as the older girls were to me. I didn't even know it was bad until I started looking at my childhood through an adult's eyes. Sometimes I get upset and I overreact. I'm sorry, Maybel."

I sat there staring at Henry. I felt sadness when I looked in his eyes, like I was slowly sucking in all his pain and it made me painfully sick.

"You and I both deserved better, Maybel," Henry said softly. "I never asked to look this way. I never asked for the attention my looks bring me."

"I kissed Bernard too, of my own free will. It wasn't all his fault; he and I both made bad choices. I know I'm a bad sister." I stared off into the sunset too as I spoke. It was easier than looking someone in their eyes because if you stared at the sunset, it was like you were talking more to yourself than to judgmental ears.

"Perhaps, Maybel, but he's older and should have been a better influence. As for me, I don't really know how to be better. I didn't have wonderful adults in my life. My mother and father are good parents, it's just other adults in my life, teachers, nannies, neighbors, many of the other people in my life were bad."

"Did you tell your parents?" I asked him gently.

"I told them some things. Nothing was done. It's different because I was a boy. If a man did that to you, your father would kill them. My parents and my brother John didn't take me seriously. I think other boys thought I was lucky and they were jealous of me."

"I'm sorry, Henry. Not everyone is bad."

"I know," Henry said quietly. "It's only sometimes that I have these memories that come up from somewhere deep inside me and I've never known how to quiet them."

"Maybe you shouldn't," I suggested. "Maybe you should yell it, sing it, paint it, and write it. Quelling it hasn't helped, so maybe try the opposite."

Henry smiled weakly, "Thank you." Then he looked pained again. "I don't know why I tell you things. I feel embarrassed and I'm scared you will think poorly of me."

"I like you, Henry. You seem nice. At first, you're just a pretty face, but below that, you're nice," I said.

Henry smiled softly.

"I like to write when I'm really sad or really angry. When I'm happy, I write nice stories, but when I'm really sad or really angry, all my feelings come hurling out onto my papers, and then, into my mind, rushes peace. Do you want me to help you write?"

"Yes, I think that might help me. It works for you then?"

"Yes, it really does," I said.

"Give me some time to think. I want to try, but I need some time."

"You can wait, but it works best when you just sit down and you're crying hard, or you're so mad, you rip the paper with your pencil because you're pressing so hard into the paper. You write whatever first enters your thoughts, and then it's on paper, not in your heart, and you start healing finally."

Henry smiled softly, "Thank you, Maybel, sweetheart."

Henry and I watched the stars appear. We didn't speak, but we held hands. After Henry drove me home, he left for his business trip, and I went upstairs thinking about the men who had chased me and Danny through the woods. The sudden realization of looking at what had happened through older, less-naive eyes, made me shake myself to sleep as I curled up into a ball in bed, with the covers over my head.

It was a very hot, summer night and mommy, daddy, Catherine, and I were in our family room commiserating together in the relentless heat and muggy, moist air. All of us now had very curly hair, even daddy's short hair couldn't escape the humidity, and mommy kept tousling and kissing his hair and giggling. "You look so darling," she cooed and pinched his cheek.

Daddy wore only his undershorts while mommy, Catherine, and I wore lightweight and airy sleeveless shirts and shorts. It was too hot to care about modesty, and anyway, it was just the four of us so it wasn't any concern.

We had been sleeping in the family room lately because the upstairs rooms were even hotter and had barely a breeze.

Daddy and I sat at mommy's sewing table and were engrossed in piecing together a puzzle while Catherine played piano and mommy cut fabric for more summer clothes because the hot days showed no end in sight and our clothing became wet with perspiration easily.

There was a knock on the front door. We looked at each other puzzled because it was late. Daddy looked out the window, then opened the door.

"Everything alright?" daddy asked.

"No," I heard Mr. Charleston's voice.

"Come in," daddy told him.

"Our house caught fire. I'm sorry to trouble you, but may we rest here?" Mr. Charleston sounded tired.

Mrs. Charleston and Bernard were behind Mr. Charleston. They all looked sweaty and exhausted.

Mommy jumped up and ran to Mrs. Charleston. "Come sit! Would you like water, something to eat?"

"Let me get my clothes on," daddy hurried toward the stairs, "I'll go put the fire out."

"No, it's out," Mr. Charleston said as he collapsed into the sofa. "Only the back porch and several rooms there burned. All our employees are staying with friends and family while the fire marshal checks for more fires that might be between the walls still."

I ran to the kitchen with Catherine and returned with water and towels. I handed Bernard a glass. "Thank you," he said quietly.

"You have blood on your forehead!" I said.

"I busted down the door to one of our employee's rooms because she was trapped inside," Bernard said.

"Is she alive?" mommy gasped.

"Yes, I pulled her out and took her to the lawn for fresh air then took her to the hospital," Bernard said.

Bernard sat in a chair next to his parents, who were on the sofa. They were all shaken.

I made them sandwiches and cut slices of pie for them while they took turns bathing. Thankfully, they decided to wear our summer clothes. I didn't want to put on a hot dress. Mrs. Charleston wore mommy's summer top and shorts, and Mr. Charleston and Bernard wore daddy's summer shorts that he wore while working in his workshop during hot days.

Catherine put a cloth bandage on Bernard's forehead and sat in a chair beside him holding his hand.

It felt very strange seeing the Charlestons in normal and immodest clothing. I'd only seen them in proper attire. A couple times we'd gone swimming with them in our pond and their pond, but I'd been younger, and hadn't paid attention to people's bodies back then. I now noticed how muscular Mr. Charleston was and how thin and toned Mrs. Charleston was under her clothing. I wondered why I never noticed that before when I was younger swimming with them.

Perhaps it was my own bias, but I decided daddy and mommy were the most beautiful of everyone. Daddy was muscular and mommy was stunningly gorgeous.

The Charleston's, now bathed and fed, were in much better dispositions. Mr. Charleston sat with me and daddy putting our puzzle together. "The fire only destroyed a small portion," he said. "It was mostly startling getting everyone to safety."

"I'm glad everyone made it out safely," daddy said. "Now that you've rested, would you care for a stiff drink?" he smiled.

"I dare say your father is a mindreader," Mr. Charleston winked at me.

Daddy went to get drinks while Mr. Charleston helped me with our puzzle. "Maybel, have you written more stories?" he asked.

"Yes, and now you've given me the idea to write a story about a mindreader."

"Wonderful, I look forward to reading it if you'll let me."

"Of course, there are stacks of papers over there on the bookshelf." I indicated the beautifully carved bookcase daddy had made. "And more in my bedroom if you're bored."

"May I also read them?" Mrs. Charleston asked. She was sitting beside mommy on our smaller sofa nearer to the piano.

"Of course," I smiled at her.

"Maybel, honey," mommy asked, "would you please get Mrs. Charleston more water?"

"Yes," I said, and skipped into the kitchen. I took some chocolates to the Charlestons too.

"Maybel must really like you," Catherine giggled when I handed Mrs. Charleston a chocolate. "She gave you chocolate!"

Bernard laughed, "Chocolates are only given by Maybel to people she loves dearly."

I threw a chocolate piece at his face. "I like you a little bit, Bernard," I giggled. I then kindly handed Catherine a piece.

"Thank you, Maybel," she giggled at Bernard. "Maybel likes me more."

"So do I," Bernard winked at Catherine.

That irritated me and I turned quickly back to Mr. Charleston and our puzzle.

Daddy came in with drinks for mommy and Mr. and Mrs. Charleston. When daddy sat down beside me, I climbed into his lap.

"Aw, what's wrong, baby?" daddy asked me.

"Nothing, I'm fine," I lied.

"You only let me hold you now when you're sick, sad, or tired so which is it?" daddy rubbed my back.

"I'm fine, daddy, sometimes I just like cuddling with you like I used to."

"Alright then," daddy held me and we worked on our puzzle together.

When I looked up, Mr. Charleston was leaning back in his chair sipping his drink and watching us. "You have no idea how lucky you are having such sweet and loving girls," he told daddy.

"Oh, I know I'm very fortunate. I must have been a saint in a past life," he joked. "I have two good girls and my beautiful bride," he smiled and winked at mommy and she blushed.

I secretly wanted to tell Bernard that I would trade him for a piece of chocolate, that's how much I liked him right now.

Catherine sat beside Bernard at the piano and had begun playing. "Care to dance, miss?" Daddy bounced me on his knee twice. "Just like old times, Maybel."

Daddy picked me up and threw me over his shoulder playfully. He set me down on the floor near the piano and we danced. Daddy's back was moist with sweat but so was mine.

Mommy came to us and asked to cut in. I let go of daddy and daddy was about to hold mommy, but mommy took my hands and spun me around. "I meant I wanted to dance with my little girl!" mommy giggled. "Maybel, spin me!" mommy laughed as I attempted to spin her.

Mr. and Mrs. Charleston were feeling the effects of daddy's special drinks too, and happily danced. I spun mommy again and daddy reached out to catch her. They both giggled as daddy pulled her waist close to his.

Mr. Charleston held Mrs. Charleston and kissed her lips, which surprised me. I really wanted to try daddy's special drinks to see why it made two people who'd just survived a house fire not care about the fire anymore.

We were all dancing and laughing in our summer shorts and having the best time. I loved my pink summer clothes. Mommy designed them to look stylish even though no one outside our family ever saw them. Mrs. Charleston ordered a dozen pink and lilac summer clothes from mommy and said she knew her sister would absolutely adore them. Mr. Charleston told mommy she should open a boutique.

"Then designing and sewing would be work, not my most fun pastime," mommy said. "I'll sew for just my family and friends and that way I'll look forward to sewing, not dread it."

"Ah, but that is why you charge three times more for your stunning gowns and employ seamstresses to make them for you," Mr. Charleston told mommy.

Mommy looked like she was considering Mr. Charleston's suggestion.

After a couple hours, my parents and the Charlestons were red-faced and full of giggles. I danced with both Mr. Charleston and Mrs. Charleston. Mr. Charleston moved as beautifully and smoothly as Bernard. Mrs. Charleston was graceful and elegant. My favorite person to dance with was mommy, because she giggled and whispered little jokes into my ear, and she always made everything so much more fun.

At one point, Mr. Charleston danced with mommy, and daddy took Mrs. Charleston's hand. They weren't quite as relaxed dancing with each other's spouses, but still appeared to enjoy themselves.

Once, for a split second, I saw Mr. Charleston admiring mommy's bottom, and when he spun her back to him, he gazed for an instant at her breasts and they both blushed.

Daddy noticed Mrs. Charleston's body also, when he held her waist a little too low, like he did when he flirted with mommy. He suddenly looked startled, and moved his hand up when he realized he hadn't been paying close enough attention to his hand placement. Mrs. Charleston blushed but didn't look upset. She held daddy's strong arm and her hand slid up to his shoulder, and then around his neck as they danced.

Bernard and Catherine stayed together all night, dancing and sneaking kisses. I sat down to watch everyone because they were paired up and I was alone. I watched the way they moved and their faces. Bernard stared lovingly at Catherine as they danced. I wondered if there was a boy somewhere in this world sitting alone and thinking about a girl sitting alone. I wondered if we'd marry someday.

Daddy woke me from my deep thoughts, "Maybel, come dance with me." He pulled me up. I stood on his toes, like I did when I was a child, and he swayed with me.

"You look lonely," he whispered.

"When is a boy going to want me?" I looked up at him. Daddy's eyes were kind.

"Hopefully never," he bent down and kissed my forehead.

I pouted. Daddy pulled me into a mighty hug. "Just stay happy and innocent as long as you can, my love."

"I'll have no choice. No boy wants me," I said sadly.

"If I knew how seriously God was taking my prayers, I would also have asked Him for a million dollars," daddy chuckled.

I frowned.

"Maybel, I love you," he said. "You will be ok. I promise."

"I love you too, daddy." He hugged me and kissed the top of my head.

Daddy and I danced a little longer, then mommy asked to dance with daddy. I was about to sit down when Mr. Charleston reached for my hand. "Miss?" he smiled at me.

I took his hand and he twirled me.

"Maybel, what do you want to be when you grow up? Still deciding between being a teacher or a nurse?"

"Yes, a school teacher or nurse."

"Why don't you want to be a doctor?" he twirled me again like a prima ballerina. I wasn't a graceful dancer but I enjoyed being twirled.

"I'm not good at math."

"Perhaps Bernard can tutor you?" he suggested.

"I doubt that would work. Word problems and math with letters in it just doesn't make any sense to me no matter who explains it to me."

"Come over sometime, Maybel," Mr. Charleston told me. "Bernard and I will help you. You would make a fantastic doctor."

"Does Mrs. Charleston know how to do math well?" I asked.

"Yes," he said.

"Can she help me too? I will need a lot of help."

"Of course, honey," he chuckled.

"Mr. Charleston?"

"Yes?"

"I still don't know if I want to be a teacher, nurse, doctor, or lion tamer yet," I said.

"Lion tamer?" he laughed.

"Or a cowgirl," I added. "The world is a big place. It's hard to say what I'll end up doing. I'll probably be a nurse though."

"Well, whatever you decide, I'm certain you'll do amazing things," Mr. Charleston patted my back.

"Thank you," I said.

The song ended and mommy again danced with Mr. Charleston while daddy danced with Mrs. Charleston. I sat by the wall and watched them as I began to tire.

Daddy and Mrs. Charleston were laughing and daddy spun her a couple times. He paid more attention to his hand placement. Mrs. Charleston, however, danced with both arms around daddy's neck, though that could have been daddy's special drinks making her stumble a little and needing help steadying herself.

Mommy was also a little off-balance tonight and tripped over her own feet but Mr. Charleston caught her and held her tightly. For a second, I thought he was going to kiss mommy, but he just smiled and they continued dancing.

I went outside for a little peace. Daddy's special drinks had made everyone loud and giggly. Bernard and Catherine were sitting under a tree with their hands between each other's legs. They gasped when they saw me. They both stood up quickly, and they were both still clothed.

"Don't tell mommy or daddy!" Catherine begged.

I turned around and went back inside the kitchen. Mr. Charleston was standing behind mommy at the sink reaching around her and whispering softly into her ear while washing his glass in the sink. They weren't kissing, but he was very closely behind her and she was laughing at whatever he'd whispered. The kitchen was dark because all the lights were off and it was nighttime. I quietly went into the family room.

It was empty. I heard Mrs. Charleston laughing in daddy's office. I peeked in and Mrs. Charleston and daddy were sitting closely together laughing at a photo album. Their faces were so close together their cheeks almost touched.

Daddy looked up, "Oh, Maybel," he separated himself from Mrs. Charleston slightly, "I was showing off your baby pictures."

"Oh," I said, confused.

"You were such a beautiful baby," Mrs. Charleston smiled at me.

"Thank you," I said. "I'm going to sleep. Goodnight."

I walked back through the family room where mommy and Mr. Charleston were laughing and dancing and I went up the stairs to my bedroom.

I wanted to ask someone about what was going on, but I had no one to ask. All the people I went to for advice were downstairs and were the reasons for my confusion.

The next morning I was the first one awake. I heard daddy snoring in his and mommy's bedroom. I peeked in Catherine's room and she was in bed alone. Downstairs, Bernard was asleep on the sofa. I assumed Mr. and Mrs. Charleston were upstairs in the guest bedroom. It was so hot and stuffy upstairs and I wondered why they hadn't slept downstairs.

I grabbed a piece of bread and started out the door.

"Maybel!" Bernard whispered. "We didn't do anything! We thought about touching each other, but we were both afraid and didn't touch each other! We didn't take our clothes off either!"

"I don't care what you do! And you're lying anyway! I saw where your hands were!"

"We didn't touch each other! We both were too nervous, and then you came outside!" Bernard pleaded for me to believe him.

"Shut up! I hate you! Go back to sleep!" I yelled as I slammed the front door.

I walked to Susan's house. She answered her door.

"Oh, thank God you're awake!" I said.

"Hello, Maybel!" Susan said happily. "How are you doing?" she smiled.

"Can I stay with you today? Do you want to go somewhere and play together?" I asked.

"Yes, of course! Let me get my shoes." She happily trotted off to put on shoes.

I loved how agreeable and happy Susan was all the time. I spent the next couple days and nights there with Susan. Mr. Matthews had us making all sorts of scientific contraptions and doing experiments. I taxidermied my first mouse. I named her Samantha and glued six sequins on her chest for her bras and one on her butt because she was a modest, God-fearing mouse.

I returned home one morning to change clothes. Daddy wanted me to help him in his workshop with an order he received for a cabinet. I didn't want to spend time with him or mommy because I was still confused about how they behaved with the Charlestons.

"Maybel," daddy asked, while sanding a side of a cabinet, "Why have you been spending so much time away from home? You're at Susan's all day and have been spending the night there."

"I like Susan," I answered.

"Tell me what's upsetting you, honey. When you're home, you're quiet, and you've never been quiet in your entire life. Did someone hurt you?"

"Yes," I said.

Daddy looked up with anger. "Who?" he asked. He looked really mean.

"You were talking to Mrs. Charleston and mommy was talking to Mr. Charleston and you were all sitting or standing too close to each other, and Billy's father left him and his mother for a younger woman, and I'm scared you're going to leave to be with Mrs. Charleston and mommy will go to Mr. Charleston, and I am very unhappy with how all of you were dancing with each other the night of the fire!" I cried hard as I spoke and daddy watched me with pain in his eyes.

"Maybel, I will never leave mommy. We drank too much special cider that night, and maybe we were too relaxed with the Charlestons, but we never had any transgressions."

"I'm sorry, daddy," I sobbed, "I don't mean to say anything to anger you or mommy, but I saw you and Mrs. Charleston and I saw mommy and Mr. Charleston and I really did not like it!"

Daddy sighed deeply.

"Please don't be mad at me daddy," I cried, "but everyone was behaving so strangely that night and I didn't like it!"

"I suppose we drank too much that night," daddy admitted, "but mommy and daddy never kissed or touched the Charlestons, Maybel. It's important you know that."

"But your faces were different, and you danced differently, and you sat next to one another differently," I cried.

For the very first time, I had seen my parents as people, not mommy and daddy. I did not like seeing them as regular people with urges and faults.

"Maybel, I have never been with any woman but your mother. And she has never been with another man. I'm sorry we behaved so relaxed with the Charlestons. I promise you it won't happen again," daddy said.

I was happy daddy said that, but I'd still seen him as a man, and I'd seen him as someone Mrs. Charleston looked at with something different and special in her eyes.

And I'd seen Mr. Charleston look at mommy as a woman. I'd never noticed how beautiful mommy and daddy were until I saw them through the Charleston's eyes.

I'd never noticed how attractive Mr. Charleston was, and I felt strange and ashamed for noticing his beautifully carved chest and the bulge in his shorts.

While it made me feel a little disgusted to see Mr. Charleston in that way, it disgusted me most to realize how handsome and attractive daddy was, and how beautiful mommy's breasts and hips and her taught bottom were. I felt sick thinking about them as people and I wondered if I could ever go back to seeing them as old and boring.

"Daddy, mommy is prettier than Mrs. Charleston, and she is more fun to be with, and you are more handsome than Mr. Charleston, and you are more fun to be with."

"Maybel, I promise you nothing untoward happened between mommy and me and the Charlestons. Mommy and me will never leave each other."

"If Bernard kissed me instead of Catherine, would you be mad?" I asked him.

"Yes," he said with a hint of irritation.

"If Bernard sat close to me and looked deeply into my eyes, would you be mad at him, and protective of Catherine?"

"You've proven your point, Maybel," daddy said dryly. "Nothing happened."

I sensed daddy had become angry so I left quickly. I wanted to tell him Mr. Charleston was whispering into mommy's ear and they were giggling. I wanted to tell mommy that daddy had accidentally put his hand too low on Mrs. Charleston's waist and touched her bottom. I didn't tell anyone anything. I wondered if daddy's special drinks could make me forget the way mommy and daddy and the Charlestons forgot.

I went up to my bedroom to write and draw. I wrote a short story about secrets and the mindreader I told Mr. Charleston I was going to put into a story. The mindreader was a traveler, never staying in one place for too long, because his mind became inundated with endless chatter, which he found bothersome and necessary to escape. When he passed through my town, he was bombarded with so many secrets weighing on the minds of all our townsfolk, that his mind began to melt from the heat of too many thoughts circulating, like ice cream in the sun, and it oozed out of his ears. The pressure of all my family's and friend's secrets so incessantly pulsated within his brain, that his eyes popped from his sockets. He fell to his knees outside our church doors and died.

"Maybel," mommy called from her bedroom. I went in.

"Yes?"

"Daddy told me you were worried about what happened with the Charlestons the night of the fire," she watched me.

I looked down. I wished I could give mommy and daddy some special cider to make them forget I had said anything.

"Mommy and daddy are not cheating on each other and we're not leaving each other," she said.

I just stared at the floor regretting telling daddy anything.

"I'm changing into summer clothes, I'll be down in a minute," mommy said.

I went downstairs and daddy was now sitting on the sofa reading. I walked quickly past him and went to Susan's.

Susan and I went to her room. I immediately started writing.

"What are you writing about?" she asked.

"If you are dating someone or married to someone, you can kiss other people as long as your boyfriend or girlfriend, or husband or wife don't find out," I told her.

"I didn't know that," Susan said.

"Neither did I," I said.

"Are you sure?" Susan asked skeptically.

My shoulders slunk down as I exhaled. "I'm not sure," I said. "There's a lot I don't understand."

"Me too, Maybel," Susan said.

We returned to our writing.

"Maybel?" Susan began hesitantly.

"Yes?"

"I saw Catherine kissing a boy that wasn't Bernard at the carriage station when I was going to the city with mother," Susan looked fearful of my reaction.

I continued writing.

"You aren't surprised, Maybel?" Susan asked.

"I'm very confused about everything, Susan."

"Don't tell Catherine I told you," she begged.

"I won't."

I finished my rough draft and went home for lunch.

The Charlestons were still staying with us because their kitchen had suffered damages.

I sat at the dining room table staring at my empty plate. "Maybel, come help get the plates ready," Catherine called.

I stood and went to the kitchen and brought pots and bowls out to the dining room table and set them on towels so they wouldn't burn the table.

I helped Catherine dish out the food onto everyone's plates.

Catherine sat next to Bernard and they held hands. Mommy and daddy sat next to each other and Mr. and Mrs. Charleston sat side-by-side.

I sat next to Catherine because I was still angry and confused at the adults.

I watched Bernard and Catherine play with each other's thumbs and giggle. Bernard put his hand on Catherine's knee, and she put her hand on his, and they continued quietly moving their hands up each other's thighs, daring each other to go farther and giggling.

I didn't finish my lunch. I pretended to gag and dry heave and apologized profusely and ran upstairs so I wouldn't have to endure another second with any of those people.

I headed upstairs and went to my room. I sat on my bed writing about a girl who discovered time travel. She went back in time to discover who killed her mother a week after she was born. It had been her stepmother. She then went back in time to kill her stepmother's mother so that her stepmother could suffer a life of growing up without a mother. Before she killed her stepmother's mother, it occurred to the girl that it would just be better to kill them both, so she could grow up with her mother. As soon as she killed them, she was zapped back to her present reality and was arguing with her mother about whether or not she was allowed to go to the town festival with a boy. She had no recollection of time travel or murder, because she no longer needed to go back in time for what she wanted most, a mother. A mother who was currently suppressing her teenage desires, but she was a mother who also loved her enough to shield her from boys. The girl never knew how happy her soul was to be annoyed by her mother about such trivial things.

"Maybel?" Catherine knocked on my door.

I jolted back to my present reality. "Come in," I said to Catherine.

"What are you writing about now?" Catherine came in and sat on the foot of my bed.

"Time travel and murder," I answered, then went back to writing.

"Sounds delightful," Catherine replied.

Catherine laid quietly on my bed and stared out my window.

"What did you do today?" she asked.

"Played poker and shot things," I said, not looking up from my paper.

"Of course, what else would you be doing?" she chuckled.

I could tell she didn't believe me. She didn't know the Matthews well enough to know I was being truthful. I declined to tell her Susan taught me how to pick pockets. Susan learned how to do that when they were very briefly homeless after a house fire. She was really good at picking pockets but Catherine would never believe half the stories of my time spent at the Matthews' house. And then I considered how I could tell Catherine the truth without her believing me.

"We pick pocketed Bernard earlier. He carries a lot of cash in his pocket, as well as a picture of me and you together with Bernard at your birthday party."

Catherine laughed, "I wish I had your imagination, Maybel." Catherine slowly stood up. "Sometimes I miss you," she said, "and want to spend time with you." Catherine smiled softly at me then left.

I was surprised and confused as to why Catherine would miss me. I was always begging for her attention.

I climbed out my window and down the tree. I went back to Susan's house. We went to her backyard and walked along the stream. We traveled the stream farther than we ever had and only turned around when a bird pooped on Susan's dress. She took off her dress and walked back in her undershirt and shorts and carried her poop-stained dress inside out so it wouldn't smear onto her skin.

"Why is bird poop white and people poop is brown?" Susan asked me.

"Because that's the way God wanted it, at least that's what reverend Michols said when I asked him."

"Oh," Susan said. "I'm going to ask my brother when I see him. He reads more than one book."

After my visit with Susan, I went to Bernard's and climbed the tree by his window. I didn't think he'd be there, and I didn't want to go home. His house was quiet and peaceful. I didn't want to see Bernard, but sometimes he made me feel better. Sometimes when he put his arm around my shoulder and looked into my eyes, I felt happier.

I didn't see Bernard in his bedroom when I looked through his window. I sat on the roof outside his bedroom. I listened to the waterfalls in the distance coming from the slate creek. I began crying thinking about Billy's mother and father, and although daddy assured me that wouldn't happen, I still wondered. And I was angry at Bernard because I liked him, and I was angry at myself for wanting him to hold me and make everything better.

Bernard never came into his bedroom. I supposed that was for the best. I didn't want to see him kissing Catherine anyway.

I returned home and climbed the tree by my window. I didn't want to see mommy or daddy downstairs because the Charlestons were still staying with us and I didn't want to see them all together.

Bernard was laying on my bed reading my stories. I opened my window and glared at him laying on my bed. "Why are you here?" I asked.

"I was lonely. Catherine wasn't in her room," he answered.

"What do you want?" I asked, annoyed that I was always second to Catherine, at school, and with Bernard.

"I was reading your stories. I love your stories," he smiled over at me.

Instead of going inside my bedroom window, I turned around and sat on my roof and watched the trees and birds and squirrels.

"Maybel, why are you out there? Why don't you come inside and lay with me and read your stories to me?"

"Go away!" I yelled.

Bernard went to my door then stopped. He instead walked back toward my window and crawled out to sit beside me.

I immediately started crying and he held me.

"Why have you been acting strangely?" he asked me.

I tried to tell him I was confused about love, but it came out as deep sobs onto Bernard's shoulder.

"I'm sorry, Maybel. I know I've been teasing you more than usual lately. I didn't realize you were having such a hard time. What's going on?"

"I'm just confused. Can you just hold me and not talk?"

Bernard held me. After I stopped crying, he pulled me between his legs and leaned me back against his chest, wrapping his arms around me and making me feel safe.

"Catherine, do you fancy boys other than Bernard?" I walked into her room without knocking. She was folding her clothes and neatly arranging them in her closet and inside her dresser drawers.

Catherine became defensive. "Why are you asking me this, Maybel?"

"The postmaster told the baker, who told that woman who's boarding in the house on Main Street, who told a girl I know from school that you kissed a boy at the carriage station." I lied. I figured it would take Catherine a long time to track down so many people to figure out who had seen her.

"Are you going to tell Bernard?" Catherine's eyes narrowed.

"No. I was only wondering if it was true. From your reaction, I gather it is true."

Catherine's eyes became a steely stare. "There is a boy I like. There's another girl in Bernard's life, too, Maybel. He's not perfect either."

"I can assure you, I never thought Bernard was perfect," I returned her glare.

"Look, Maybel, if I'm going to spend my life with someone, I want to be certain I've found the right person."

I hesitated before I asked my next question, but I asked it anyway. "Catherine, since you have been with Bernard and other boys, do you think it's possible mommy or daddy have ever been with other people?"

"Don't ask such questions," Catherine said sharply.

"But do you know if they have?" I pressured her.

"I have a vague memory of daddy hugging that girl who used to watch over us when mommy went to visit Aunt Sadie when she was sick. I don't remember any details, but it's always bothered me," Catherine admitted. "Do not tell anyone I told you, Maybel! I'll deny it!"

"May I ask you one more question, but you have to promise to never tell anyone I asked you?" Catherine watched me and was clearly intrigued.

"Do you think daddy and Mrs. Charleston have been inappropriate with each other, and do you think mommy and Mr. Charleston have been inappropriate with each other?"

"Maybel, I've kissed boys other than Bernard because I want to deduce who is my best match. I don't want to hurt Bernard or anyone else. I only want to find a man I know I will never want to cheat on, and my hopes are that the man I choose is the man who is the least likely to cheat on me. No one is perfect, Maybel. Get that notion out of your head."

"So mommy and daddy have been with other people?" I asked, feeling sad.

"I didn't say that. I'm saying it's important for you to meet as many men as possible to ascertain who is your best match," Catherine said.

"If you already know Bernard is not your best match, why do you still date him?" I questioned Catherine.

"I don't yet know if he is my best match," she answered.

"You said he had another woman. Why would you want to stay with him?" I asked her.

"He's probably deciding who is his best match the same way I am deciding who is my best match," she said.

"Who is she? Why don't you go take a stick and beat her?" I asked Catherine angrily.

Catherine smiled at me, which I thought was strange. "I don't want to beat her."

"Why not? I would."

Catherine laughed at me. "If he chooses her, then I will find someone else."

"How do you even know there's another girl? Maybe you're just scared and imagining things?" I told Catherine.

"Maybel, I'm not imagining things. I've seen the way he talks to her."

"What? You know her? Tell me who it is!"

"It doesn't matter. Time will sort out uncertainties. I'll either marry Bernard or find a better match," Catherine folded her socks and underwear and put them neatly into her dresser drawers.

"If you already know Bernard is someone you will cheat on, why do you keep dating him?"

"Because maybe I'll find that compared to other boys, he really is my best match. I don't know he's not the one yet. If I marry him though, I will never break my marriage vows," she said.

"Catherine, did daddy cheat on mommy?" I raised my voice.

"I don't know!"

"Did mommy cheat on daddy?"

"I don't know, Maybel!"

"Are you lying to protect me?" I asked her.

"No," she said, her voice low and angry.

"Are you lying now when you say 'no?'"

"No," she said, raising her voice slightly.

"What aren't you telling me about mommy and daddy?" I asked angrily.

"Just leave it alone, Maybel. It doesn't matter. Daddy comes home to us every night. Mommy is with us every night. Mommy and daddy choose us. They choose our family. It doesn't matter if they have faults or lapses in judgements. All that matters is we are together every night and mommy and daddy love each other through everything."

"What is 'everything?'" I yelled. "You are speaking in a way you know is secretive and it's frustrating! You're having fun at my expense! Tell me the truth!"

"I am Maybel. The truth is we're together every night. How honest are you, Maybel? What are your secrets? Rather than wonder about everyone else's secrets, worry about your own. You're as perfect as me, mommy, and daddy."

The truth stung and I stormed out of Catherine's bedroom. I stomped to Susan's house.

At Susan's house I told her I was upset with Catherine. Susan said with a blunt and honest child's observation, "If you haven't told Catherine Bernard kisses you occasionally, you are keeping secrets too."

"I know. I'm bad." I looked down at my papers. I felt sad and guilty.

"I'm sorry, Maybel," Susan said. "Please don't be mad at me. Please don't stop spending time with me."

"I won't," I said. "You are right. I haven't told Catherine because I don't want to hurt her. Bernard hasn't told Catherine because he doesn't want to hurt her. We're all liars because we are ashamed of the truth because the truth hurts those we love. Do you want to go shoot rocks or swim in the pond?"

"I have to stay home because my cousins are visiting today and will leave tomorrow. Do you want to meet them?"

"Yes! What are they like?"

"The one my age is Susan, and Christopher is a couple years older than you."

"Your cousin is named Susan?" I asked.

"Yes! That's funny, right? We were born a day apart and our mothers named us both Susan. When they wrote to each other about our births, they were surprised to find out they'd given their daughters the same name!" Susan laughed as she explained.

"How does your family differentiate between you two?"

"I'm Sue One, because I was born the day before Sue Two."

"Oh," I said. "Ok. So, for today and tomorrow I call you Sue One?"

"If you want me to answer," Sue One giggled.

When Sue Two and Christopher arrived, I immediately noticed how handsome Christopher appeared, and Sue Two could have been Sue One's twin.

Sue One, my Susan, wanted me to take everyone to my island so we went to my house. The Charlestons were chatting with mommy and daddy and Bernard and Catherine were reading together.

"These are Susan's cousins," I announced. "We're going to the island. We'll be back soon."

"Wait, Maybel, when you introduce people, you tell us their names," mommy corrected my manners.

I didn't want to spend too much time here in my family room when I could be roaming around outside with Sue One and my two newest adventurers so I quickly explained Sue Two's name, then introduced Christopher.

"See you later," I motioned for my friends to follow me through the house. We went through the kitchen and out the back door, and then I realized I'd gained two more explorers, Catherine and Bernard.

Damnit, I thought to myself. I was now in the position of having tag-alongs instead of being a tag-along. I now understood why Catherine and Bernard tried to cut me loose all those times.

I glared angrily at Bernard. He didn't seem thrilled to be with me either. Catherine was already asking Christopher about his studies and plans for his future, likely assessing whether or not he would be a good match. I watched Catherine with disdain.

The six of us started to sink the boat, so Catherine offered for her and Bernard to swim. "Do you know how to swim too, Christopher?"

"Yes, I'm captain of my swim team," he smiled at Catherine.

I rolled my eyes and rowed the Sues and myself to the island while Catherine had a given a good excuse to wear shorts and get wet.

On the island, Christopher stared at Catherine's body whenever Bernard looked away.

We walked around the island while the Sues caught themselves up on what they'd been doing. They both were artistic and painted. Sometimes they liked writing stories, but mostly they enjoyed painting.

Bernard grabbed my shoulder. "Race me up the tree, Maybel!"

"What does the winner get?" I asked.

"Loser makes the winner dinner tonight," he grinned.

"Go!" I yelled, and bolted up the tree.

I won. Bernard came after me. "I'd like steak tonight," I said when he climbed the top branch.

"Fine, Maybel. I'll make sure you get your steak tonight, but my real reason for the race was to get you up here alone."

"I'm not kissing you," I said.

"Are you attracted to me?" he asked.

"No," I said. "You're a cheater," I replied bluntly, "but I am too," I admitted. "Catherine deserves a better boyfriend and sister."

I shimmied back down and returned to the Sues. They were amiably chattering away about the paintings they'd painted and the boys in their schools. "Where's Catherine?" I asked.

"Showing Christopher the different kinds of wild flowers here," Sue Two said.

I saw Catherine by some evergreen trees pointing out rudbeckia.

Bernard emerged from the tree we'd climbed. He sat down beside me on a log. "Maybel, would you like to show the Susans the crawdads?"

"Oh yes!" Sue One exclaimed.

I trudged behind Bernard and the Susans while I heard Catherine pointing out salvia, daisies, and phlox to Christopher.

We waded in mid-shin deep. Bernard pushed me gently causing me to step on a crawdad. I squealed and jumped toward him for safety.

Bernard laughed, "Don't be so squeamish!"

"Don't push me onto crawdads! They tickle my toes and grab onto me. I think they're trying to eat me!"

Bernard laughed and playfully pushed me again.

The Susans played in the shallow water poking the crawdads with sticks and watching them scurry away.

After an hour or maybe two, we returned home. I rowed the Susans while Catherine, Bernard, and Christopher swam.

My clothes were wet and muddy but somehow no one else had become muddy.

"Why am I the only one muddy?" I asked, amazed.

"Because you're Messy Maybel," Bernard teased.

"Don't call me that!" I yelled at him.

Catherine came ashore, wet again from swimming home, and I caught Christopher admiring her bottom as we walked toward our house.

Mommy took a look at me from the kitchen window when we arrived home and yelled out, "Go wash up please, Maybel! You too, Catherine!"

Christopher went to Susan's house to put on dry clothes and I went upstairs to quickly bathe and dress. Catherine took her turn after me. Bernard waited outside on our porch swing until Catherine and I finished so he could bathe. He took a pair of daddy's freshly-washed shorts upstairs that mommy had given him.

I dressed in a light cotton shirt and shorts because it was still sweltering hot. I figured we had all sweated out our modesty by now.

When I came downstairs, my Susan happily waved at me from the kitchen table where she sat with her cousin Susan. They were eating cookies mommy had just baked.

I sat down and shoved a cookie in my mouth. "Wow! Mommy! These are amazing!"

"Thank you, dear. I made my special cookies."

"You know what would go well with this? Daddy's special cider!" I smiled at mommy.

"Nice try, love. But no," mommy giggled.

"Where are Mr. and Mrs. Charleston?" I asked, my voice muffled by smooshed cookies in my mouth.

"At their house accessing damages and trying to get contractors to finish the repairs," mommy said.

"Oh good, they're leaving soon then?" I asked.

"Don't be rude, Maybel," mommy chastised me. "They are our friends and are welcome to stay here as long as they want. Besides, it's nice chatting with Mrs. Charleston every evening on the porch. I feel like I finally have a sister living near me. I miss your aunts terribly," mommy said wistfully.

"Mommy, what was wrong with Aunt Sadie when Catherine and I were little and you had to go away to care for her?"

"She had a bad respiratory infection and we were afraid we'd lose her," mommy looked sad at her memory.

"Oh," I said. "I'm glad she recovered well."

"I am too, honey," mommy smiled at me.

"Mommy, who took care of us while you were gone?" I asked.

"Your father, of course," mommy laughed.

"I meant, who was the girl that looked after us?" I asked.

Mommy shook her head. "There wasn't a girl taking care of you. I wasn't gone that long. You were so young, you must not be remembering correctly."

"Oh," I said, confused. "I guess you're right," I added, not wanting mommy to discover another secret. Our family apparently had many more secrets than I ever imagined.

My heart sank. I stuffed another cookie in my mouth.

"Susans, want to go somewhere and do something?"

"Yes!" they said in unison.

"Oh, Maybel," mommy asked, "Will you please invite the Matthews to dinner? I don't want Mrs. Matthews to spend time cooking when she could spend that time reconnecting with her sister."

"Yes, mommy. I'll ask the Matthews now."

The Susans and I went to Sue One's house and invited everyone to dinner.

"Oh, my! Your mother is the most thoughtful and caring woman! Yes! We would love to come! I'll bring jams for your mother and Mrs. Charleston," Mrs. Matthews gushed.

"Maybel, this is my sister Irene," she held her sister's waist and proudly introduced her.

"Irene is a nurse, so be sure to ask her any questions you may have," Mrs. Matthews smiled lovingly at Irene.

"Oh, yes, Maybel, you're more than welcome to come visit me at the hospital where I work if you're ever in town."

"Thank you, Ms. Irene," I smiled.

Mrs. Matthews and Irene looked like twins with their curly blonde hair and brown eyes, and the Susans were copies of their mothers.

"Maybel, do you mind if I stay here for a little bit with Sue Two? I want catch up more with her," my Susan asked me.

"Of course, I'll see you tonight," I said.

I walked back to my house alone. I knew Susan wanted to be alone with her cousin because they hadn't seen each other in a long time.

I sat in the family room with Catherine, Bernard, and Christopher. I sat down in a chair and watched them on the sofa. Catherine sat in the middle. I decided this was going to be the best play I'd ever seen and I excitedly awaited the fight scene.

Catherine was engaging and animated as she spoke to Christopher on one side and Bernard on her other side. Both Bernard and Christopher were civilized, which greatly disappointed me.

"Don't you agree, Maybel," Christopher asked me.

"What?" I had been imagining a play unfolding in front of me, and had been completely lost in my daydream. I had been picturing Bernard and Christopher spearing each other with long swords.

"Shakespeare was more intuitive to human interaction than any other writer. Don't you agree? I've read some of your stories. Catherine thinks very highly of you as a writer," Christopher smiled at me.

"Yes, Shakespeare was intuitive," I agreed. I wanted to watch my play, not interact with the players.

"Maybel, would you like to go for a walk with me to discuss our mutual affinity for the written word?" Christopher asked me.

"No, thank you," I said simply.

"Oh," Christopher was surprised by my answer. I got the impression no girl had ever said no to him before; he was quite handsome and intelligent.

"Would you like to discuss writing later?"

"Maybe," I said.

"I'm sorry, have I upset you?" Christopher asked me.

"No, not at all," I said, offering no other explanation.

"Alright then," Christopher turned back to Catherine.

I thought Christopher was offended by my lack of interest in his gorgeous face and attractive body.

Bernard was smirking at Christopher.

"Catherine, you seem to know more about discussing novels than your little sister," he said, clearly taunting me, "Would you like to take a stroll?"

"Shakespeare wrote plays, not novels," I said, clearly taunting him.

"Yes, I know that," he said, annoyed.

"Catherine, Bernard," Christopher stood, "shall we go?"

Catherine stood. Bernard did not.

"Catherine, you go ahead. I'm going to take a nap," Bernard said.

Catherine and Christopher left. They were discussing Shakespeare as they walked out the door.

"You better get started on my steak dinner, Bernard," I reminded him.

"I will, right after I write a comparison of Shakespearean plays."

I huffed.

Bernard laid down on the sofa and tried to get comfortable. "Maybel, can I please nap in your bed?"

"Sure," I said.

I washed vegetables with mommy and prepared pie crusts for our big dinner.

"Maybel, will you help me plant an herb garden?" mommy asked me. "Mrs. Charleston has been telling me wonderful things about herbs."

"Yes, mommy," I said.

"Maybel," daddy called from the kitchen door, "can you help me move some shelves around in my workshop?"

"Yes, daddy," I said and followed him into his workshop.

364 - E. D. JUMPER

Daddy sat down on an overturned bucket and motioned for me to sit on the other bucket. "I need to talk to you about something important, Maybel."

I sat next to daddy and looked down at my bare feet, anticipating a lecture.

"Sweetheart, look at me," daddy said, "This is important."

My head was tilted down toward my feet but my eyes looked at daddy. Daddy reached over and with his finger, gently lifted my chin up to look at him better.

"There was a girl I hired who came here for two nights to prepare dinner for us while mommy was away taking care of Aunt Sadie. I didn't tell mommy because I didn't think it was important, and also because mommy was very distressed about Sadie's health."

"Why did you hug her?" I asked.

Daddy shifted uncomfortably. "How do you remember that? You were so young."

"I don't. Catherine does. She said that memory always bothered her."

Daddy again shifted uncomfortably on his seat. "I hugged her to say thank you for helping us through a difficult time."

"Why did you kiss her?"

Daddy's brow furrowed. "How would Catherine know about that? She wasn't even in the room." Daddy became agitated. "Yes, Maybel, the girl kissed me suddenly and it surprised me. I walked her to our door and never asked her to help care for you and Catherine again."

"Ok," my voice was but a squeak. I sensed daddy was angry.

I waited for daddy to tell me what to do with the shelves he'd asked me to help him with, but he instead told me to go help mommy.

I ran quickly out of daddy's workshop and around the side of the house because I didn't want to see mommy. I went in our front door.

Bernard was walking around the parlor and entryway. "Have you seen my shoes, Maybel?"

"Your shoes are in the broom closet under the sack of potatoes."

"Why are they there? I didn't leave them there."

"I did. I was mad at you," I said.

"Where are my underwear and socks, Maybel?" Bernard asked, clearly unamused at my shenanigans.

"They're probably keeping my steak dinner company."

"Maybel! My penis is chaffing in these shorts!" he whispered angrily. Where are my underwear? I need my underwear!"

"Chaffing? Penises chafe? Show me," I was intrigued.

Bernard sighed heavily, "Maybel, you are the most exasperating human being I have ever met in my life! Where are my underwear?"

"At your house where they, and you, belong!"

"You broke into my house?" he asked surprised.

"It's not breaking into your house if you stupidly leave your window unlocked," I insisted.

"What have you been doing in my bedroom?"

"Reading, writing, taking naps. Sometimes I need a quiet place to go now that everyone is at my house," I said.

"Ok, Maybel, I'm going to get my shoes from the broom closet, then go home to get my underwear." Bernard grabbed his shoes from underneath the potatoes and went out the back door.

"Can I come? I'm bored. Everyone is doing things together and I don't have anyone to be with."

"Sure, Maybel," Bernard sighed. "If I told you no, would you stay here?"

"No."

"I didn't think so. Come on then," Bernard sighed.

We passed by Catherine and Christopher sitting on the far side of the garden talking.

"Doesn't that bother you?" I asked.

"Not a whole lot. I've kissed you several times. I can't be mad at Catherine for doing the same."

"Catherine doesn't kiss me," I said.

Bernard looked back at me as we traipsed through the gardens and lawn. "Oh, you're making a joke. It was so funny I forgot to laugh."

"That's a good retort," I giggled. "I'll have to remember that one!"

"Where's Susan?" Bernard asked.

"Which one?"

"Your Susan. I forget which number she is."

"My Susan is Sue One, and she's catching up with her cousin at her house."

"I'm your last choice for someone to spend time with?" Bernard looked at me.

"I'm always your last choice," I looked back at him, unapologetically.

"That's not true," he said.

"It is," I said, as a matter of fact.

Inside Bernard's bedroom, I laid on his bed pretending to read a thick math book while Bernard looked for his underwear and socks.

"Where are they?" Bernard asked, frustrated.

"In your bathroom cabinet."

"That's not where I keep them," he said, annoyed.

"I know. If you hadn't let me tag along you would have made this trip in vain and returned to my house with an even chaffier penis."

"I don't know how your parents have not gone insane yet living with you."

"They drink daddy's special cider," I said.

Bernard laughed.

"Let's go back to your home," Bernard motioned toward the door.

"You go ahead. I want to stay here awhile longer," I stared at the ceiling.

"Maybel, what's been making you act so strangely since the fire? I didn't touch Catherine."

"Go ahead and touch Catherine. I don't have a right to be jealous. Besides, I'll have a boyfriend someday and you can watch us kiss and cuddle for years, and tickle each other's thighs under the dinner table, and walk in on us touching each other." I was sarcastic and mad. I picked the math book back up and pretended to read it so I wouldn't have to tell Bernard my troubles.

"A big fan of physics, are you?"

"No," I said. "I like these drawings and symbols."

"That's physics."

"Then I love physics," I said dryly.

"Maybel, what's making you so upset lately? Maybe I can help you?" Bernard sat on the edge of his bed.

"I've just been wondering whether or not people cheat, why they cheat, and I'm scared that I'll be married and have children, and find out my husband is cheating on me. I know I kissed you, and I let you kiss me. I'm scared about the consequences. I'm terrified that in ten or fifteen years, suddenly all the anger my future husband and I have that we've squashed down, will come bubbling back up like one of those acid burps after you eat beans, and hours later, you burp a sour bean taste that makes you gag because of how disgusting it tastes due to hours of fermentation inside your stomach...."

"Ok, I understand what you're saying," Bernard interrupted me. "You can skip the rest of the burp description."

"That was it. I don't have any more burp details."

Bernard stared at me.

"Anyway, that's why I've been acting strangely. Sometimes you look at Catherine like you love her, but then you kiss me. I'm scared my husband will cheat on me. He'll throw me away for some young babysitter. We'll have two beautiful children, and I'll get a letter from Catherine's husband saying Catherine is sick. I'll go take care of Catherine while my husband kisses and hugs some woman down the street paid to help care for our two children."

Bernard looked confused. "No. That will never happen."

"I have lost faith in everyone I have ever admired. Their secrets are eating me up inside and I don't know how to handle all their lies." I began crying. "Everyone I have ever looked up to has a life that everyone around town sees, and then they have this other, second life, that only a couple people will ever know about."

I began sobbing and shaking. "Why do people cheat and lie and keep secrets? Don't you ever wonder about people and what they're hiding, what their other hidden life is like? Do our parents kiss other people? When my children are older, are they going to ask me if I had boyfriends before their father? Will I lie to spare them pain and my own embarrassment of discussing my life before their father? If you marry Catherine, will your children ask you if you kissed anyone other than their mother, and will you tell them," I lowered my voice to sound like Bernard, "Well, children, let me tell you about your Aunt Maybel, she was quite the looker back in her day, but she slobbered when we kissed!"

"I don't know, Maybel! I don't think about things as intricately as you! I'm a man; my thoughts usually consist of, what's for dinner, and do I have enough time to masturbate before dinner?"

"I'm so confused all the time, Bernard!" My chest heaved as I cried and I couldn't catch my breath. "Everything I ever thought to be true is a lie!"

"Oh, come here," Bernard sighed. He wrapped his arms around me and kissed my forehead. "I'm confused most of the time too, Maybel, but there's one thing I've never been confused about. I've never once imagined a time when you weren't by my side. I used to think you would live with Catherine and me and work in my medical practice. Somewhere along the way, I started wondering if you would ever become attracted to me. I began to lose hope. I figured Catherine would be a good match for me, but I could never shake my daydreams of being with you for the rest of our lives. I look forward to spending time with you when I am away at school. When I come to your house to take Catherine wherever she wants us to go, I stare at your stairs hoping you'll come bouncing down any minute. When I take Catherine home at night, I hope she invites me in and that you'll be downstairs writing or drawing. I never cared if there was anything sexual between us, although I sometimes couldn't fight my urge to kiss you. It wasn't about sex. I just wanted to be near you. I wanted to talk to you and argue with you. I love your humor, even when your wrath is directed toward me. I love you, Maybel. I always have. I always will. I know I've made so many mistakes in how I've treated both you and Catherine. I know I'll spend a lifetime making it up to you. I love you, Maybel. Please believe that. It's the truth."

I sniffled and blew my nose into one of the pairs of underwear Bernard had gathered to take back to my house.

"Bernard, I've lost hope."

"I know, Maybel, and I'm sorry." Bernard held me while I wiped my eyes and tried to calm myself down. "I will fix this," he said and hugged me.

"Bernard, you and I have secrets. It hurts. Our secrets hurt me. I'm so sorry we kissed behind Catherine's back. I love her, you know. I'm a bad sister."

I let Bernard stroke my hair and rub my back. I began calming down and breathing more steadily.

"Maybel, let's go home," he said softly. He pulled me up and we walked home together. I breathed in and out slowly, trying to make my puffy eyes less puffy.

Mommy, Catherine, and I set the table. Mr. and Mrs. Matthews talked to Mrs. Matthews' sister and her husband. The Charlestons and daddy joined in, telling their own stories and memories. The Susans were happily running around outside near the kitchen window, and I couldn't help but smile at them whenever they passed through the garden. I wanted to be carefree again.

At dinner, Bernard and I sat across from each other. Catherine sat next to Bernard and Christopher sat next to her.

"How do you know a chicken and duck cannot mate?" I asked Bernard.

"Because if they could, we would have see results by now!" I had almost worn Bernard down.

"There was a time when no one imagined ten-foot-tall lizards, but we have found dinosaur bones. You can't argue with that kind of evidence!" I smirked and made my voice sound smarter than I felt.

"That's not the same thing! There are no chicken-duck bones to be found!" Bernard was clearly annoyed.

"Would they be called chucks?" I asked.

"I think dickens," Sue Two said. The Susans had come in for cake and sat beside me while I argued with Bernard.

"Oh, that's good," Sue One agreed.

"There has not, is not, nor will there ever be a dicken!" Bernard was agitated.

"How very close-minded of you, Bernard," I taunted him. "I would think a man of science would be more open-minded."

Bernard glared at me while our parents laughed.

"Alright, as a man of science, there is that possibility that there is an unknown out there. Fair enough, Maybel?"

I snorted, "There's no such thing as a dicken, Bernard. You should hold tight your convictions and not let someone persuade you to believe that which you know is untrue."

The entire table burst out laughing, especially Mr. Charleston.

Bernard's knuckles were white and he exhaled slowly. "Alright, Maybel. I'm done arguing with you."

Bernard went back to his drink and his delicious cake mommy and I prepared.

After a few minutes, I looked back over at Bernard, and he was watching me with a smile. I smiled back.

After dinner, mommy, Catherine, and I washed dishes.

Catherine and I barely spoke. I figured she was mad at me because Bernard and I talked throughout the entire dinner.

I went outside to chase lightning bugs with the Susans. The Susans were fun. They were both energetic and happy. I appreciated their good senses of humor.

"May I join," Christopher asked us.

I was a little farther away from him than the Susans, so I pretended I couldn't hear him.

I observed the lighting bugs from as far away from Christopher as I could be without being overtly rude.

I was lost in thought, staring at the lightning bug on my finger tip and wondering why it glowed, when Christopher was suddenly next to me.

"I'm sorry we didn't immediately take to each other," he said.

His presence startled me. "I'm sorry," I said, "I've had a lot on my mind lately."

"Can we meet again?" he asked me.

"What?" I didn't understand his request.

"Hello, miss, I'm Christopher," he held out his hand.

I hesitated, then shook his hand.

"I read several of your stories. You're quite talented," he said.

I didn't look him in his face. I watched the lightning bugs in front of me and in the distance. "Thank you," I said quietly.

Christopher knelt beside me. "Did you know there are places out west where lightning bugs don't exist?"

"No," I said.

"My uncle came to visit one summer and was completely startled when he stood in a field and watched tiny lights glowing on and off. He thought he was dying," Christopher chuckled at his memory.

I laughed, "I can imagine his amazement the first time he saw lightning bugs. The things to which we're accustomed aren't the things to which others are accustomed. If I had never seen one of these bugs, I would be absolutely amazed!"

"Yes," he smiled kindly at me.

I looked away from him. I felt awkward.

"I'm sorry, Maybel. I'll leave you be. I just wanted to come here and attempt to make things right between us."

Christopher walked away back to my house.

I turned back to my lightning bugs. They were mesmerizing when you stared out into the distance and let your eyes unfocus, and little dots of light shined on and off like candles floating.

After some time, I realized I was alone. The Susans must have gone somewhere together to be alone with each other.

I stood up and walked around in the dusk. Laughter and piano playing drifted to me from my home. My stomach tightened. I didn't want to see my parents after they had drunk daddy's special cider. I feared a repeat of the other night.

I went to Bernard's house and climbed through his window. I wanted to stay here until the birds were asleep, because then it would be safe to return home. Everyone would be asleep by then.

I laid in Bernard's bed and watched the shadows moving across his ceiling. I wondered what time it was now.

I heard someone on the roof outside the window so I hid in Bernard's closet.

Bernard came through his window. He was looking around in the shadows. Then he crawled back through his window.

"Bernard?" I asked softly.

"Maybel? Are you ok?"

"Yes, I came here because everyone was drinking special cider and I don't like how they act when they drink daddy's special cider."

Bernard took my hand and pulled me out of his closet. "I couldn't find you. Christopher said he'd spoken to you. I was worried about you."

I just stared at Bernard.

"Maybel, what is wrong? Tell me. I'll do my best to make everything better."

"It's what I told you before. I don't do well with change. I need time to think about everything and let everything settle in my mind," I told him.

"Maybel, come home. Everyone misses you. Everything will be ok." Bernard took my hand and we went back through his window and walked to my home.

I could hear laughter and piano notes drifting down the road before I could see my house. When we entered, everyone was full of cider and they danced happily.

I hesitated, remembering the other night.

"It's ok, Maybel. Take a deep breath and come dance with me," Bernard said.

Bernard took me to our little ballroom dance floor. It was small enough that mommy and daddy danced in the kitchen and the Susans danced together in our family room.

Catherine and Christopher danced together on the dance floor with Bernard and me. When Bernard and I began dancing, Christopher brought Catherine to Bernard and asked for my hand. I looked at Bernard as Catherine quickly pulled him away. I turned back to Christopher and accepted his hand. He led me in two dances. His movements weren't as relaxed and fluid as Bernard's but he danced better than me.

"You're quite lovely when you aren't covered in mud," he joked.

"I'm rarely lovely then," I quipped. "I somehow manage to get muddy in bath water."

Christopher laughed, "I appreciate a quick wit."

"Me too," I said.

"Would you care for a drink?"

"Of cider? Yes, please," I said.

"Nice try, but I think your parents would be quite upset," Christopher chuckled.

"Only if they found out," I smiled up at him.

"You're going to be quite difficult to tame when you're a little older, I can see that now," he laughed.

We went to the kitchen for drinks. Christopher drank a small glass of cider and poured a glass of water for me.

Bernard came into the kitchen. Catherine followed him and grumbled with annoyance, "Your big brother Bernard wanted to make sure you weren't being kissed."

"Catherine," I said, "we were just about to drink cider. Care for a glass?"

"What?" Catherine exclaimed.

"Maybel's drinking water," Christopher said quickly. "I'm having only a small glass of cider."

"We're allowed to drink cider, aren't we, Catherine?"

Catherine watched me, trying to assess where or not she wanted to be an accessory in my lie.

I helped Catherine decide. "It's only wrong if someone finds out. They won't find out," I smiled at Catherine. I figured I'd try the adults' way. Maybe secrets could work in my favor. No one seemed to care about secrets unless they were discovered.

"We're allowed a small glass," Catherine told Christopher.

Christopher looked skeptical but poured all of us a small glass. He handed a glass to Bernard. "You are allowed special drinks, I'm certain."

"Yes, when I visit Europe, everyone drinks. It does not have the same stigma as it does here," Bernard said.

I tasted the cider and decided it was delicious. I went to use the restroom, and when I returned, Catherine, Bernard, and Christopher were outside sneaking their cider in the garden amongst the pretty flowers, so I poured more cider in my cup. Nobody would care if Bernard or Christopher drank cider, but mommy and daddy would not want me and Catherine to drink it. I now knew why; it made people act strangely. I decided I wanted to be able to do whatever I wanted and blame it all on the cider.

I began feeling good. I didn't care about daddy kissing the girl he paid to care for me and Catherine anymore. I never thought I'd be able to forgive that, but two small ciders into my night, and I didn't care anymore.

"Bernard, this is the best drink ever!" I said. "I don't even care about the other night anymore! Why don't more people drink cider? They really should!"

"Slow down, Maybel! No more cider! This can turn bad quickly and you'll vomit tonight and have a headache tomorrow!" Bernard acted like my annoying big brother.

"Have you ever had that happen?" I asked him.

"Yes, unfortunately," Bernard looked ashamed.

"Moderation is important, Maybel." Christopher lectured me. "Men have to learn to control their urges."

Bernard seemed to take that as an insult. "Yes, Christopher, some men have never learned to control their ability to consume alcohol. Have you never had one drink too many?"

"I'm sorry, Bernard, I didn't mean to upset you. I have, indeed, imbibed." He smiled at Bernard. That seemed to quell Bernard's annoyance and they both laughed and began to speak of their poor behavior under the influence of alcohol.

For two, young men discussing their idiotic actions after drinking alcohol, they did not seem to regret their bad behavior. They tried to top each other with who was the more ridiculous drunk.

I grew bored with their showmanship and walked inside to see what everyone else was doing. Daddy and mommy stopped dancing with the Charlestons when I entered our small ballroom. Daddy spun Mrs. Charleston over to Mr. Charleston and took mommy's hand.

The Susans still danced together. They were very happy and giggled a lot. I vaguely remembered being that happy and giggly.

I returned to Bernard, Catherine, and Christopher. Bernard and Catherine were talking amiably with Christopher about how they first met, me throwing mud at Paul, and all the birthday parties and Christmases they had spent together. The way Bernard and Catherine reminisced seemed to draw them closer to one another. I sat nearby and watched them tell Christopher about their first official date. Bernard smiled at Catherine as he talked about the first time he'd kissed her cheek. Catherine gazed lovingly at Bernard when she told Christopher about kissing Bernard on his lips for the first time. I had accidentally witnessed their first kiss, and I remembered it differently. Catherine told the story like it had been a fairytale, but I remembered her confessing to Bernard she'd been kissed before, and Bernard lying when he claimed to have never been kissed.

I felt sad and jealous. It was like reading a book, but I couldn't close the book. The book spoke its words to me, and I had no way to stop what was unfolding. I didn't want to see Bernard and Catherine fall back in love. I felt guilty for feeling that way.

Bernard must have noticed my jealousy and guilt.

"Aw, Maybel looks like a little, angry kitten. Full of anger, but still looking tiny and cute," he chuckled.

Bernard came to me and wrapped his arm tightly around my shoulders. He smelled like the theater, like thick and spicy cologne, and I angrily pictured this smell being the last thing Catherine would smell just before Bernard pushed his penis deeply inside her for the first time.

I ran inside and up to my bedroom. I could still hear Catherine, Bernard, and Christopher talking in the courtyard below me. And then I heard two more voices. It was mommy and daddy. They sounded angry.

I sat by my door and listened. "Yes, she kissed me, and I walked her to the door and never spoke to her again!" daddy angrily told mommy.

"Our daughters know about this! That's probably why Catherine has boyfriends! She grew up thinking married people cheat without repercussions!"

"Stop it! She kissed me and I made her leave!" daddy said.

"But to Catherine's young mind, her father hugged, then kissed a young girl, and in Catherine's young mind, that was acceptable and had no repercussions! That's probably why Catherine doesn't take relationships seriously!" Mommy's voice was angry at daddy, but she cried as she spoke about Catherine's propensity to seek out other partners.

I heard mommy cry and run to the guest bedroom and slam the door. Her sobs were muffled but she was undoubtedly sobbing.

Daddy slammed their bedroom door and I heard him stomp down the stairs.

I decided the cider was wearing off because I was becoming sad again. I waited a few minutes and went downstairs to the kitchen for more cider. I wanted to not feel what I was feeling.

Daddy was sulking on a chair in the family room. The Charlestons and Matthews were dancing merrily. Ms. Irene was quite the dancer! She danced well and had an amazing smile and giggle. Her husband danced with Mrs. Matthews and she danced with Mr. Matthews. Mr. Matthews was quite bad at dancing, but quite brilliant in his home laboratory. I liked watching him try to keep up with Ms. Irene. I found myself smiling at them.

"Maybel, dance with me," daddy was suddenly beside me pulling me onto the dance floor. "I told mommy that girl kissed me. Mommy is very angry. I wanted you to know I told mommy. I was honest with mommy. I'm sorry, Maybel, for giving you and Catherine reason to doubt me."

I watched daddy. He looked sad and ashamed.

"It's ok, daddy. I make mistakes too."

Daddy kissed my forehead.

"Daddy, I drank your cider."

Daddy looked down at me angrily.

"Daddy, it's important to note that what happened to you was worse, so please don't punish me too hard."

To my amazement, daddy laughed at me. "How much did you drink?"

"I know I drank two small glasses and then I started on another. I don't remember if I finished that one."

Daddy kissed my forehead again. "Oh, sweetheart, I don't have to punish you, tomorrow morning is going to do that for me," daddy chuckled.

Mommy came downstairs. I felt daddy tense up. Mommy came to him and held out her hand. Daddy smiled and I felt him relax his body. Daddy took mommy into a loving embrace and they held each other and kissed.

I felt happier. I went to the back porch in search of Catherine. Bernard and Christopher were talking about their schools and teachers. Catherine was standing close to Bernard, who was leaning against the porch post.

Christopher smiled at me when I approached. He sat on the porch railing with his drink in his hand.

"What is the topic of discussion now?" I asked. "Girls, kissing, or are you still going on about stupid things you've done while drinking rum?"

"I've never done stupid things while drinking rum," Christopher said. "That could be because

I don't remember most of the things I do after drinking rum," he nodded at Bernard and they chuckled.

"Rum makes you not remember what you did?" I asked.

"Sometimes," Christopher winked at me and laughed.

Bernard looked out at the garden, avoiding eye contact with me, probably because I told him I didn't like the way people acted after drinking cider.

"You can kiss someone and not remember?" I asked Christopher.

"Some do a whole lot more than that and not remember," he looked at Bernard and laughed, as though they had shared similar stories involving rum.

Bernard quickly deflected the notion that he'd done something with a girl while drinking alcohol. "I haven't done anything like that, Christopher," he nodded toward me.

Christopher took a sip of cider. "No, no, I wasn't saying that," he quickly became more formal and less relaxed with Bernard.

"I'm sorry, Maybel, I should be more reserved when ladies are present," Christopher acknowledged.

Catherine spoke up, "I'd sure like to hear about your drunken escapades, Bernard." Catherine smiled, but it wasn't a sincere smile. It looked fake and plastered on her face like the way Susan's taxidermied opossum smiled. It was a little scary to look at, quite honestly.

"I once stole a horse outside a saloon," he quickly said. "Nothing involving a girl, Catherine." He glanced at me anxiously.

"Do you play sports?" Christopher changed the subject, noticing the tension between Catherine and Bernard and me.

"Yes," Bernard said, looking relieved in the change of topics. "I swim, box, and play rugby."

"You box?" I asked. "I didn't know that."

"I swim and row on our rowing team the most, but yes, I box. Father boxes and has always encouraged me to learn," Bernard said.

"Are you any good?" I asked him.

"I'm not the worst boxer," Bernard chuckled.

"I swim, too," Christopher said. "I enjoy baseball, but I'm most interested in reading and writing and politics."

"I'll vote for you when you run for president," Bernard lifted his glass to Christopher in a toast and knocked back the rest of his cider.

Catherine stood closer to Bernard as he leaned against the porch railing next to Christopher. Bernard reached his arm around her waist and pulled her closer.

Catherine took his glass and Christopher's and went to refill them. I stood awkwardly with my hands in front of me, not really sure what to do with them. I never felt awkward about where to put my hands before, but now that I wasn't a child anymore, I didn't know how to stand or know where to put my hands without appearing stiff and strange. I stood near Bernard and Christopher with my hands clasped, then folded one over the other, then I put them behind my back.

"Maybel, do you enjoy sports?" Christopher asked.

"Yes," I said, putting my hands in front of me, my right hand holding my left thumb.

Christopher expected me to offer more details but I did not.

Catherine returned with four glasses and I drank my glass straight down.

"Slow down, Maybel, or you might just be the one to steal a horse tonight," Christopher cautioned me.

"I might kiss you and not remember that either," I burped.

"Well, the night is young," Christopher winked at me.

Bernard took a big swig from his glass.

"The night isn't young for Maybel," Bernard said. "She's too young to stay up with us. Aren't you Maybel?" Bernard looked at me and I glared back.

"You're not that young Maybel, you can stay awake a little longer, can't you?" Christopher asked.

"I can stay up as late as you just fine, Bernard! I'm not much younger than you!" I snapped at him.

"You still have a teddy bear," Bernard laughed.

I glared angrily at Bernard.

Catherine attempted to intervene. "Let's go dance," she suggested.

"Yes, let's dance, Maybel, before you're up too late and get cranky." Bernard grabbed my hand and pulled me inside.

"Go to bed Maybel! I'm trying to protect you! You shouldn't be around men when they're drinking," Bernard growled at me.

I shook his hand free and pushed him into the wall of the laundry room. "You're drinking! I'll stay away from you!"

"Is everything ok?" Christopher asked. He looked concerned.

"Everything is fine," Bernard said. "Maybel was just going to bed."

"No, I wasn't," I said. "Would you like to dance, Christopher?"

Christopher paused and looked between me and Bernard. "Bernard, you're dating Catherine, correct? You're not dating Maybel, right? I just want to be clear I'm not stepping on your toes when I dance with Maybel?"

Catherine glared at Bernard, "It can be quite confusing which one of us he's dating. I can understand your confusion, Christopher."

"Bernard and Catherine are dating," I said. "Why, just the other night they were outside with their hands between each other's legs. Let's go dance, Christopher." I bumped my shoulder into Bernard's ribs as I walked by him down the hallway.

I took Christopher's hand and led him to the dance floor. "Don't worry about Bernard," I said. "He thinks he's my protective big brother."

"He thinks you're his girlfriend. He treats you as such," Christopher said bluntly.

"He likes Catherine. They were touching each other the other night but he denies it."

"Maybel, Bernard wants you both. You should find yourself a boyfriend so he leaves you alone and remains faithful to Catherine."

I giggle snorted. "Nobody is faithful."

Christopher watched me for a moment while we danced. He watched me as a real, big brother would watch his little sister. "I'm sorry, Maybel."

"Why?" I asked.

"I truly hope you find a good man. You seem nice, Maybel, but you're naive." Then Christopher pulled me into a hug, not the way a man does, but the way I imagined a real, big brother would. He felt sorrow and pity for me, and that made me sad.

"Can we go out for fresh air?" I asked.

"Sure." He held my hand gently and we went out through the kitchen. We walked along the garden path holding hands.

"When you looked at me on the dance floor, you had pity in your eyes. Why?" I asked Christopher.

"You're naive. You're young and vulnerable. I like you, Maybel. You're a talented writer. I hope you find a good man."

"I suppose I am naive. I have not done anything with a man. Did you know Bernard and Catherine have touched each other and done other things?"

Christopher chuckled, "So I've heard. But you don't have to follow that path, Maybel. You should find a man that is in love with only you, not a man you have to share with your sister."

"I'm surprised Catherine's not pregnant," I said.

"Yes, as much as they've done, I would be too," Christopher said.

"I think Bernard said he lost his virginity when he was fourteen," I told Christopher.

"Fifteen is what he told me," Christopher said.

"Quite young indeed," I said.

I had used the same technique with Christopher that I'd used with daddy. I lied and pretended to know more than I did to see what daddy and Christopher would say. And now I knew.

Christopher and I returned home. Catherine and Bernard were on the back porch arguing. They stopped when we stepped through the trellises. Bernard looked at me.

"See, she's fine, Bernard!" Catherine said. "She's not a child. She's allowed to take walks with men!"

"I'm sorry, have I done something wrong?" Christopher asked.

"No!" Catherine and I said.

Christopher turned to me, "Maybel, good luck. I wish you the very best." He kissed my cheek. "I'm going inside to catch up with my aunt and uncle before I leave tomorrow. I hope you keep in touch. One day your stories will be famous."

Christopher went through the back door and away from us. He seemed uncomfortable and wanted to be rid of us. I couldn't blame him. Bernard acted strangely whenever a boy was near me. His personality was so much nicer when it was just the two of us. I didn't like the Bernard that arose whenever we were in a group and another boy my age was present.

"You two had sex when you were fifteen? That's quite young," I said.

Bernard and Catherine stared in shock at me.

"I have never had sex!" Catherine yelled. "How dare you think I'm that kind of girl, Maybel!"

"Well Bernard lost his virginity at age fifteen. I assumed you were the girl to whom he lost his virginity. It appears you have something new to argue about." I glared at Bernard. If my eyes were bows, I had just shot a thousand arrows into Bernard's stupid eyeballs.

I walked inside and into the ballroom. I felt guilty for using duplicitous tactics to elicit information from Christopher, but I also figured that was the only way to get the truth from these liars. But then I thought, what does the truth matter? We're all liars, me included, and learning the truth didn't change much.

I sat in our family room and watched the Susans laughing and playing cards. Ms. Irene and Mrs. Matthews were sitting beside each other giggling like school girls as they reminisced.

All the men stood around talking. I watched them curiously. When Mr. Charleston and I were together, he was kind and soft. When he stood with men, he was imposing. Daddy lets Catherine and me brush his hair and he sits on the couch while we sit on either side of him and trim his nails. Here, in a group of men, he stood strong, drink in one hand, and his voice deep and stern. Even Mr. Matthews, as quirky as he was, stood tall and spoke with confidence around other men.

I wondered if I acted differently, depending on who I was with. Catherine was daddy's little girl and demanded hugs and attention from him at home, but in public she pretended she was too old to snuggle with daddy. I wondered which people brought out different personalities in me, or did I act the same around everyone?

Catherine suddenly flopped down beside me on our sofa. She looked angry. She crossed her legs and crossed her arms. She stared at the floor as though the floor just called her ugly.

I didn't poke the hornet's nest with a stick. I figured her stinger was already out and ready to sting the next person that said a word to her.

Bernard stood by the men. His arms were crossed and his feet a shoulder's width apart, looking manly and tough. I found the men standing in their circle, each one trying to be more tough and stern than the other, was quite fun to watch. They nodded, grunted, and sighed. Their postures were stern and not to be challenged. When commiserating, they furrowed their brows and grunted in solidarity. I had found a new play to watch and these characters were fascinating.

"Maybel," Catherine elbowed my ribs.

"What?" I asked, still watching the circle of nods when Mr. Charleston said something that everyone apparently agreed with.

"Why did you say Bernard lost his virginity at age fifteen?" she whispered into my ear.

"Christopher mentioned Bernard said he had been fifteen," I whispered back.

"Do you think it's true?" she whispered.

"I don't know. I thought you were the one with whom he had sex."

"I was not Maybel!" she hissed into my ear. That scene in the Bible when the snake spoke to Eve flashed through my mind. Catherine sounded like a hissy snake and her spittle hit my earlobe.

"Catherine," answer me honestly. "The other night, Bernard was touching you, wasn't he?"

"No!" she whispered.

"Everyone lies," I said.

"I'm not lying!" Catherine whispered angrily.

"Did Bernard admit to having sex when he was younger?" I asked Catherine.

"He says he told Christopher he had sex when he was fifteen to sound more like a man to Christopher. He says guys say they have sex to sound more popular or something."

"He's telling the truth then, Catherine, just like you and Bernard are telling the truth when you say you have never touched each other," I said sarcastically.

"We haven't!" Catherine turned into a hissy snake again.

"Fine!" I said, "Then maybe Bernard is telling the truth."

Catherine and I sat next to each other with our arms crossed. I knew I'd been hard on Catherine if she had been telling the truth. I'd been too easy on her though if she'd been lying.

"Catherine, daddy kissed that girl who looked after us when mommy was gone to help Aunt Sadie."

Catherine's eyes widened. "You told daddy what I told you?"

"I asked him why he hugged that girl. He did hug her and she kissed him suddenly. Daddy led her to the door and told her to leave and never had her come care for us again. Daddy confessed to mommy. Everything is fine now."

"That's what daddy said?" Catherine looked sad.

"Yes," I said.

Catherine frowned, "If daddy did something bad now, I'd tell mommy. But the hug and kiss happened a decade or so ago. Does it matter now? It only hurt mommy."

"Does it matter that Bernard lost his virginity but not to you? If he tells you tonight that he had sex with some girl while dating you, would you want to know now? Or would that revelation not matter anymore?"

"Maybel, of course it would matter," Catherine sighed. "I would have to be honest with Bernard then. I've kissed other boys. I don't want to go into detail with him about that."

"I don't believe anyone anymore. I'm sad about that," I said. "I lost trust and hope. And I think that's what happens to everyone when they go from child to adult. That loss of trust and hope is what makes a person go from happy like Susan to hopeless like me. Catherine, do you think we can ever trust anyone again?"

"No, we won't ever have childlike faith again. That's what happens when you get older. I have not been entirely honest with you, nor have you with me. We're supposed to be honest with each other because we're family. I suppose honesty amongst family is a lie though. None of us have been truly honest."

"Mommy has," I said. "She's the only good one in our bunch."

"Mommy liked Mr. Charleston's attention. You had to have seen that the other night," Catherine said to me.

"I saw. It was reciprocated. They both enjoyed each other's attention. And daddy and Mrs. Charleston enjoyed each other's company, too."

"None of us are perfect, Maybel, mommy included," Catherine said dryly.

"What did mommy do? Other than enjoy a man's attention?" I asked.

"She was very close to Mr. Charleston the night of the fire. Mommy saw daddy touch Mrs. Charleston's bottom, and then I think mommy kissed Mr. Charleston in anger," Catherine said. "I am not sure, Maybel, but I thought I saw them kiss in the kitchen. I could be mistaken; the lights were off. I heard them giggling and they were standing very close together. I hope I am wrong. Maybe they did not kiss, but they were too affectionate with each other, of that I am sure."

"I saw daddy accidentally touch Mrs. Charleston's bottom. Daddy looked embarrassed and moved his hand," I explained.

"Maybel, it wasn't an accident. That's how men determine if you are willing to go further," Catherine said.

"You better be joking, Catherine!"

"I'm not, sadly, Maybel."

"Daddy did that on purpose?" My eyes were wide.

"I don't know for sure. But I do know men do things to see how you'll react. I am assuming, by my own observances, that daddy wanted to see Mrs. Charleston's reaction. Mrs. Charleston didn't seem to mind his accidental touch."

"You saw all that?" I asked, amazed. "I didn't think you paid attention to anyone but yourself."

"I'm not that involved in myself, Maybel! I'm not some dumb woman who only cares about fashion!"

"I'm sorry, Catherine!" I said. "I didn't know you thought about things. You're guarded and don't tell people what you're thinking."

"I judiciously tell my opinions and thoughts, Maybel. People don't need to know your every thought. Just because I don't tell people what I think daily like you do doesn't mean I am stupid. I use caution."

"I'm sorry, Catherine. I know you're very smart. I just didn't realize how intuitive you were."

"If you would shut up from time to time and listen, you would learn more," Catherine said bluntly.

I kept my mouth shut.

Catherine laughed, "You look like silence is uncomfortable."

I nodded my head but kept quiet.

"Anyway," Catherine continued, "Mommy must have noticed daddy accidentally, or perhaps on purpose, touching Mrs. Charleston's bottom, and thought it was accidentally on purpose. She kissed Mr. Charleston's cheek outside. I saw them. It wasn't a usual peck on a cheek; it was sexual. And Maybel, Mr. Charleston then kissed mommy's cheek as his hand touched just a little lower on her waist than where daddy touched Mrs. Charleston. I know mommy was mad and kissed Mr. Charleston in anger over what daddy did, but Mr. Charleston responded happily to her advances. And then later, like I told you, I thought they kissed in the kitchen, but I hope I am mistaken."

I stared at Catherine.

"I've wondered over the years if cheating matters. Mommy and daddy still take care of us and they do love each other," she reasoned. "Bernard still kisses me and tells me he loves me. Maybe I should just focus on that."

It was excruciatingly difficult to keep silent, but I did.

"We're women, Maybel. If we marry well, we have food and a home. If we don't, we have to worry about which child gets to drink milk that night and which one goes hungry. Sometimes I wonder if that's why so many women are silent."

I stared at Catherine. Then I turned my head to look at Bernard. He had been watching Catherine and me.

I turned back to Catherine. "So it's not about love? It's about survival?"

"I don't know, Maybel. I don't know anymore."

I held Catherine's hand. "I do love you, Catherine."

"You love me the way you learned to love. Maybe when a person says 'I love you,' it means something different to everyone."

I looked back at Bernard. He was still watching us.

"Catherine, I'm either drunk, or tired, or both. I'm going to bed," I yawned.

"Maybel, wait, stay awake. Sometimes being quiet and observing people is fascinating," Catherine watched Bernard and Christopher.

"I'm going to fall asleep and accidentally fart in my sleep. I'd rather fart in my bedroom where nobody can hear me," I said.

"I can hear you farting in the mornings. That's how I know when you're waking up. You stretch and groan then roll over and fart," Catherine laughed and playfully tapped my arm.

"Do I? You can hear me in my room?" I asked, surprised.

"Yes. I can hear mommy and daddy too," she said.

"Mommy farts? I've never once heard mommy fart," I said surprised.

"I hear a lot more than farting," Catherine made a gagging noise.

"They still have sex?" I whispered. "Old people still have sex?"

"Well, they do, anyway," Catherine made a contorted and disgusted face. "Apparently they're both really good at it from what I hear."

It was my turn to make a gagging noise. "Maybe that's why you started kissing so young, Catherine, you were exposed to that kind of stuff a lot earlier in life than me."

"Maybe. You've always been a lot more naive than other boys and girls," Catherine said.

She watched the dance floor where the men were still gathered in a circle. "See, watch Bernard. You can tell by the way he stands he admires his father. He emulates his father's mannerisms."

"I noticed earlier how differently men act when they are around other men," I said. "It made me wonder if I act differently around different people."

"You act the same around everyone. You're awkward and say whatever you're thinking, no matter how inappropriate. But Maybel, that's how I know you're honest." Catherine told me.

I felt a pang of guilt because I wasn't honest with her about my attraction to Bernard or our kisses.

"Bernard looks a lot like his father," Catherine pointed out.

"I didn't notice how attractive Mr. Charleston was until the other night when he wasn't wearing a shirt," I giggled.

"I know!" Catherine giggled. "His behind is round and hard!"

"Catherine!" I giggled. "He's so old! He's thirty-four or thirty-five?"

"I wouldn't want to be with an old man, but I can admire his body from a distance," she laughed.

"Daddy's more handsome," I said.

"I think so too," Catherine agreed.

"So then, the Charlestons are the same age as mommy and daddy?" I asked Catherine.

"I would imagine, yes," Catherine answered.

"The Charlestons are both thirty something? Are you sure mommy and daddy still have sex?" I asked Catherine.

"Oh, I'm sure," Catherine said. "You come to my bedroom often when you get scared. You have never heard them?"

"No!"

Catherine looked at me, "It truly amazes me how oblivious you are. You write about people with such sensitivity and yet, you don't see what is right in front of you."

"I wouldn't know what sex sounds like. Maybe I have heard them and didn't know what I was hearing. What does it sound like?" I asked Catherine.

Catherine leaned over and made weird breathing noises in my ear which tickled me so much I screeched with laughter.

"Are you two still drinking cider?" daddy called over.

We both stopped instantly and stared at daddy, then looked at each other and laughed hysterically. "No!" we both laughed.

Catherine waited until the men went back to talking then leaned over and again breathed and made low grunting noises into my ear and it sent little, ticklish chills up and down my spine so intensely that I slid off the sofa giggling loudly.

"Girls, no more cider!" daddy called.

"We're not drinking cider, daddy!" I called back to him. "Catherine keeps breathing in my ear!" I cackled. "It tickles!"

Catherine was still laughing at me. "Maybel, let's go steal a horse," Catherine whispered.

I looked up at her from the floor. I knew she was joking. "Ok!" I said excitedly.

"I was joking, Maybel!"

"I wasn't! You just need more cider! Daddy calls it liquid courage," I whispered and giggled into Catherine's ear.

Catherine now giggled loudly and the men stopped to look at us again. "That really does tickle!" Catherine whispered, still laughing.

"Let's go take one of Bernard's horses and bring it here!" I said.

"We'll get in trouble!" Catherine protested.

"Only if we get caught! That's something important I've learned lately," I whispered.

"So you said liquid courage?" Catherine asked.

"Yes!" I laughed.

We snuck into the kitchen and poured two drinks. "Bottoms up!" I said. We drank them straight down then went to the ballroom. "Goodnight mommy and daddy," we said.

"Goodnight dears," mommy said. Daddy was telling a story about when he wrestled a giant at a carnival.

We went upstairs and promptly climbed out my window and down the tree. We snuck around the front of the house and crept below the bushes. Finally out of sight and down the street we started giggling. "I can't believe we're doing this!" Catherine giggled.

"We make a good team!" I said to Catherine.

We walked up Bernard's lane. The house was completely dark since no one lived there right now. We walked to the barn and chose a young, but sturdy mare named Daisy Mae.

Daisy whinnied and was excited to see us. "Ready for a ride?" I asked her.

Daisy trotted in place excitedly.

We mounted Daisy and I sat in front. We trotted down the lane. "Maybel, let's take her around the town square!" Catherine became excited.

"Oh, that sounds fun!" I said, excited for our adventure.

We trotted around the square but no one was awake. "Well, this isn't as fun as I thought it would be! We're parading around without a crowd!" Catherine said, disappointed. "We're riding a stolen horse! We need an audience!"

"We have an audience at our house!" I said. "What do you think mommy and daddy would say?"

"That's not the kind of audience I want!" Catherine laughed.

We trotted around the entire square but it was quiet and uneventful. "This isn't the excitement I'd anticipated. Let's just go home," Catherine said, disappointed.

"With the horse, or without?" I asked.

"With of course! I need a little excitement at least!" Catherine tickled my ribs.

"Alright then!" I squirmed under her tickles. "Let's go home, Daisy," I yelled.

Daisy whinnied loudly and picked up her pace. "Whoa Daisy!" I yelled, but Daisy had heard me tell her to go home and her home was her stable where she was accustomed to receiving carrots after a ride. Daisy began galloping fast.

"How do you make her stop?" Catherine yelled over Daisy's loud clomping.

"I don't remember!" I yelled.

"You don't remember?" Catherine screamed, fear taking hold. She gripped my stomach so tightly I felt like I wore a corset.

Daisy bounded back to her stable and stopped abruptly in front of the treat bucket whinnying loudly.

"Ok, ok, Daisy! Shh!" I pleaded.

Catherine slid off Daisy stiff and terrified. I slid off next and fell in horse poop. "Damnit!" I screamed.

"Aw, Maybel! How do you always find a way to get filthy?" Catherine held her nose.

I tore off my dress. "I'll change into one of Mrs. Charleston's dresses. She has hundreds. She'll never know it's gone and I'll return it tomorrow."

I took a carrot from the wooden vegetable bin and gave Daisy a carrot then led her to her stall. "Now remember, Daisy Mae, you never saw us!" I winked at her and she whinnied quietly.

I wore only my bra and underwear but it was a hot night. The door to Bernard's kitchen was locked. "His bedroom window is open," I said.

Catherine looked at me suspiciously.

"I come here for peace and quiet since our house is crowded," I explained.

Sure enough, Bernard's window was open. We crawled inside. I took my balled up smelly dress and went to his closet and took his remaining underwear.

"What are you doing Maybel?"

"Playing hide-and-seek," I laughed and wrapped his underwear around my horse-poop-stained dress and slid it under his bed. "Ok," I dusted off my hands, "that's done."

Catherine giggled.

We went to Mr. and Mrs. Charleston's bedroom. "Where is the light?" Catherine asked.

I felt along the wall near the door. "Found it!" I exclaimed.

I turned it on. The closet was big and full of clothing, more clothing than in all of Ms. Greta's clothing store in town.

Catherine's eyes were wide and envious, dripping with jealousy and her own aspirations of being the next Mrs. Charleston as Bernard's wife.

I took a dress from the closet. I went toward the door but Catherine hadn't followed me. She went to Mrs. Charleston's dresser and all the jewelry on top. "I wonder what kind of jewelry is inside all these drawers if she leaves all this expensive jewelry out in the open?"

Catherine began opening drawers and gasping. "Maybel! You wouldn't believe how many jewels she owns!"

"Hurry up, Catherine!"

"They're all drunk at our house, Maybel. Don't be a scaredy cat!" she taunted me.

"Fine, what does she have that's so impressive?" I scanned the drawers. "They're just shiny jewels."

"You have no idea how expensive these are! I've seen advertisements in newspapers from New York, and these look even more precious and expensive! I bet they're from Paris!" Catherine's eyes looked like my cat's eyes when I was little and tossed her a fish I'd caught and she held it in her mouth and looked up at me like she couldn't believe her good fortune.

"We should go," I told Catherine, before she became a horse thief and a jewelry thief.

We turned off the bedroom light and the house went back to total darkness.

Catherine's voice was already somewhere out in the hallway. "Wait up!" I called to her in the darkness. "How are you moving so fast? Are you part cat? You can see in the dark?"

"Meow," Catherine giggled.

"Huh, you actually do have a sense of humor," I said. "You should use it more often."

"Go to the doorway. I'm going to turn off the light and don't want you stumbling or breaking anything," Catherine told me.

I went to the doorway and Catherine turned off the lights. Suddenly Catherine was beside me.

I jumped. "How do you move so quickly in the dark?"

Catherine didn't respond. I heard Catherine's footsteps already on the stairs. "Wait for me!" I yelled. "I can't see!"

"Come to my voice," Catherine said, annoyed.

I tripped on the first step. "Found the stairs," I announced.

I descended the stairs on all fours so I'd be less likely to lose balance.

We left the Charleston's mansion and walked down the street, hugging the shrubbery for concealment. "Now be quiet," Catherine ordered in her school marm tone. We're almost to our yard. Duck down, go around, and climb your tree quickly and quietly."

I followed Catherine. As we crept along the front of the house, I heard laughing. The night had not slowed down for anyone. They sounded even more wild.

We climbed my tree and I quickly hid Mrs. Charleston's dress in my closet underneath my old clothes I was going to give Susan.

"Go to the bathroom and wipe yourself off, Maybel, before you change into a clean dress. You still smell like a horse."

I narrowed my eyes. "Fine!" I hissed.

I washed myself off but didn't take a bath because mommy and daddy thought I'd been asleep and would wonder why I woke up and decided to bathe in the middle of the night.

I went to Catherine's bedroom. I wore my clean nightgown. "Do I still smell like a horse?"

"Neigh," Catherine whinnied.

I laughed loudly. "You really need to show off your humorous side, Catherine. Why don't you?"

"Because I try to be prim and proper so I can marry well, but I got drunk, stole a horse, and farted all the way up your tree, so what the hell do manners matter now anyway?"

I laughed, "You're funny! I like this!"

"Goodnight, Maybel," Catherine laid in her bed.

"Don't you want to sit in the garden out front and watch everyone in the ballroom and family room? Maybe we'll discover something new?"

"I don't think I can handle any more hard truths tonight. Goodnight, Maybel." Catherine rolled over away from me.

After several days passed, Catherine still had not gone to any birthday parties or book clubs. Bernard had not come over. I wondered why. I was happy Catherine spent more time with me. We took Susan and went swimming and to a play. I was curious as to why Bernard was absent.

"Catherine, did you break up with Bernard?"

"No," she said.

"Did he break up with you?"

"No," she said as she turned the page of her book. We were in her room. She was reading and I was crocheting a scarf for the next winter because I only knew how to crochet in a straight line. The last mitten I made was just a small scarf that I sewed together into a horribly ugly mitten-like thing.

"Why hasn't Bernard been over? Why haven't you gone to see him? Why haven't you gone to any parties with your friends?"

"Bernard hasn't come to me suggesting we go on a date, and I'm not going to him."

"You're both just being stubborn?" I looked at Catherine like she was being ridiculous.

"Yes," she said. "And, I don't know, things feel different with Bernard." Catherine looked down. "Maybel, I need to tell Bernard I've kissed several boys. When you said that me seeing daddy hug that girl when I was young, and hearing mommy and daddy have sex, made me less of a prude, you may have been right. I don't take relationships as seriously as I should. I've kissed several boys. I need to tell Bernard."

Susan came into the study eating a bowl of grapes and strawberries. "There were oranges and pineapples too, Maybel. They taste a little strange because they're from somewhere in Europe, I think. The sauce they were in was European, I bet."

Susan handed me her bowl and I took some fruit. "These are good! I wonder what's in it to make it taste that way?"

"Probably herbs from Mrs. Charleston's herb garden," Susan reasoned.

"I bet you're right," I told Susan.

Susan and I were sitting in the Charleston's study, waiting for the party to start, and thinking up stories and writing them down together. We wondered what the bottom of the ocean looked like.

"What if it's bright pink?" Susan asked.

"If you could swim all the way down there, it would be completely dark wouldn't it? How would you light it up to see what color it was? Candles would extinguish in a jar because there wouldn't be any fresh air added," I said my thoughts aloud.

"You could take a pail and scoop up the bottom of the ocean and bring it up to the surface to see what color it is," Susan said.

"Well, ok, if you want to do it the easy way," I giggled. I was embarrassed because Susan found a better way than I did. I always felt like everyone around me could find solutions to problems better and faster than me.

"What is our story about the bottom of the ocean going to be about?" Susan asked me.

"About whatever lives there," I replied.

"I bet it's fish. I bet fish live there," Susan smiled with wide and innocent eyes. "Big fish with big teeth!"

"And underwater people with underwater pets," I added. "Let's go get more of this fruit."

We returned to the back room behind the other room that had boxes and jars I suspected were used for canning. The fruit was behind more boxes. "They should really put this fruit out in the dining room," Susan said, "I almost didn't find it."

"How did you find this?" I asked.

"I was looking for a jar to put water in to wet my paintbrush, but then I found this fruit, and now I don't want to paint anymore. I think I want to dance."

"This was the part of the Charleston's house that caught fire," I told Susan as I rummaged through the boxes and canning supplies.

"That must be why is smells strange in here. It smells a lot like my Uncle Bill, actually. Aunt Betsy says it's because Uncle Bill likes to drink moonlight."

"Moonshine?" I asked.

"Yeah, that's it."

"I have to pee," I said. I went to the bathroom around the corner.

"I'm going to use the one upstairs," Susan yelled through the bathroom door.

I waited in the kitchen for Susan after I finished. "Maybel, there you are," Henry said. "Have you saved me a dance?"

"Susan and I are going outside to find an adventure."

"And where is Susan?" Henry asked me.

"What? You can't see her?" I asked with wide eyes and a concerned voice.

Henry looked around. "No, Maybel, I cannot."

I saw Susan peak her head around the corner smiling.

"She's right here, Henry. Do you normally wear glasses?"

"No, I do not. You're playing a joke on me, aren't you?" Henry asked, smiling.

"I'm here, Henry!" Susan said, then ducked behind the door.

Henry turned around but Susan has hidden.

"See, she's standing right there," I said.

"Where?"

"Right behind you," I replied, incredulously. "Are you drunk, Henry?"

"No, Maybel, and I know you're playing a joke on me," Henry laughed.

Susan jumped out and hugged Henry. "Surprise, Henry!"

Henry laughed and kissed the top of her head. "Very funny you two!"

"Let's go, Maybel!" Susan skipped toward the door.

"Swings, garden, pond, or waterfall?" I asked.

"Horses?" Susan looked at me expectantly.

"Ok," I said.

"I don't want to ride horses now," Susan said.

"Then why did you say horses?" I asked.

"I would at least like the option to see the horses," Susan said.

"Now I see why Bernard calls me exasperating," I said.

"I'm hungry, let's get more fruit before we go on an adventure," Susan said.

"Good idea," I replied.

Susan and I returned to the back room. "Hey! Where's our fruit?" Susan exclaimed.

Only the fruit juice remained. I took a canning jar and gave one to Susan. "Fill these up," I instructed. "It's not as good as the fruit, but it still tastes alright."

"I can't believe someone took all the fruit!" Susan huffed, then proceeded to gulp the fruit juice.

"This does taste pretty good though, even without the fruit," Susan said. "The first couple sips are strong, but then it's like your tongue gets numb and you don't taste the herbs anymore, you only taste the fruit juice."

I put my jar down and started jumping on the large ottoman stool in the back room. It was squishy and velvety and matched the chairs and sofas. "Hey Susan, can you do a flip?" I did a somersault in the air and landed on my feet, although it was a bit of a wobbly landing.

"Let's find out!" Susan jumped then fell hard on her face and popped back up, "No!" she giggled. "I cannot do a flip!"

"Let's go back to the party in the ballroom and pester Catherine," I said. "I like annoying her. She gets hissy and that amuses me."

"Ok!" Susan squealed.

I loved how agreeable Susan was. I loved having a tag-along.

Henry was standing to the side of the dance floor with two giggling women fawning over him. I marched over to Henry.

"Get away, Henry's my slut!" I hiccupped.

Henry's eyes shot open wide. He took my arm and pulled me away and Susan happily followed, smiling and hiccupping after us.

"You're drunk!" Henry exclaimed.

"No, we're not!" I had a hard time focusing on Henry's face so I squinted.

Henry held my arm and led us outside. Susan skipped behind me as Henry pulled my arm toward his automobile.

"Where did you find alcohol?" he whispered.

"We haven't drunk any alcohol!" I slurred a little.

"Stay out here until you sober up," Henry told us.

"We're not drunk!" I protested. I felt like I was not pronouncing all the words correctly, but Henry knew what I meant, I was sure.

"I'll drive you two to your house, Maybel, and you need to stay there until you sober up!" Henry said.

"No thank you! Come on, Susan!" I took Susan's hand.

"Ok, Maybel!" Susan smiled. I loved how Susan followed me everywhere smiling. I couldn't fathom why Catherine didn't want me tagging along. Except for that bit about Bernard staring adoringly at me and causing Catherine to want me to stay away from them, I was a fun tag-along, too.

Henry grabbed my arm and pulled me back. "You need to sober up before you go anywhere or do anything! Get inside!" Henry opened the door and I crawled inside and Susan followed. Henry came around the other side and got in the driver's seat.

"Henry stole all our fruit!" I yelled to Susan while pointing to the backseat. "Look!"

The fruit was in the canning jars in Henry's backseat in wooden crates.

"Fruit thief!" Susan yelled.

"You ate the fruit in the canning room?" Henry's eyes were wide and his voice was concerned. "How much did you eat?" he asked.

"A lot. Why? It's party food. We left some for the other guests," I told him.

"It's not meant for guests, Maybel. It's special fruit, like your father's special cider."

"Oh, well then, we're drunk, Susan," I told her.

Susan giggled.

"I'm taking you both to your house. You need to stay there and sober up!" Henry started his car.

"Open the door Susan!" I screamed.

Susan opened the door and we ran past the Charleston's house and into the gardens. "Catherine!" I saw Catherine standing next to a man in a blue dress coat. She giggled and batted her lashes at him. Catherine, who is this man?"

"That's not how introductions are made, Maybel!" Catherine said, sounding aloof, like what I imagined the queen of France would sound like.

Catherine turned to the man, "I'm sorry, Lars, my sister has no social graces."

"Lars?" Susan hiccupped.

"Yes, I'm Dutch," he said.

"You talk funny," I giggled.

"Maybel! You're being rude!" Catherine said angrily.

"I'm from the Netherlands," he explained. "English was not my first language."

"Catherine has a boyfriend," I said. "I think," I hiccupped. "Catherine, are you and Bernard dating this week?"

"Maybel!" Catherine hissed.

And then I belched loudly and more than air erupted. I vomited fruit, copious amounts of fruit. The smell hit Susan and she vomited too. A full grape shot from Susan's mouth like a cannonball and rolled onto Lars' shoe.

"Don't you chew your food?" I asked, amazed she could swallow a grape whole.

"I feel so much better!" Susan said to me.

"Oh, me too!" I agreed.

Susan and I turned to leave and Henry took hold of our arms. "Time to leave," he said. Henry firmly held our arms and walked us back toward his automobile.

Henry opened the passenger side door of his automobile and helped me inside, then helped a stumbling Susan inside next to me. "Let's get you two home and bathed and in clean dresses before your parents become furious."

"Aye, aye captain!" I saluted Henry.

Henry drove us to my house. "Go upstairs and get a bath so you don't smell like vomit."

We stumbled upstairs, laughing the whole way.

Susan took her bath first and then me. While I was in my bathtub, I heard yelling downstairs.

I got out of my bathtub and yelled downstairs like an angry pirate, "Aye who goes there?"

"Bernard!" Bernard yelled up angrily.

"That name doesn't ring a bell. Sorry sir, you have the wrong house," I giggled in a high-pitched voice.

I went back to bathing and singing in my bathtub. When I finished, I walked out of the bathroom wearing my towel and into my bedroom.

"Susan, where are you?"

"I'm in Catherine's room trying on her bras," Susan yelled. "Her breasts are huge!"

"Aren't they though!" I yelled back.

I dressed and put my hair up and Susan wore one of my dresses. I went downstairs while Susan finished brushing her hair at Catherine's dressing table. Henry and Bernard were talking loudly in the family room. Bernard was angry that I had been drunk.

"Henry is my new big brother now, Bernard! Unless he wants to marry me and make beautiful babies with me."

Bernard looked angry. He turned and left. I watched him through the window. He strode down our walkway and opened our gate, then was gone.

I turned back to Henry and I kissed him.

"You shouldn't kiss me. I'm old and used," he said.

I looked down. Henry's hands were at his sides. I took his hand in mine. I looked at his fingers and his nails. They looked calloused, which surprised me. I didn't realize Henry used his hands as much as daddy.

"What do you think?" Henry whispered.

I looked up startled. I had been lost in my thoughts. "I like your hands," I said.

"Are you still drunk?" Henry asked.

"No," I said. "I think I either vomited or peed everything out.

Susan came hopping down the stairs. "I'm all clean and ready for another adventure, Maybel!" She bounded to the kitchen before I had a chance to reply.

Instead of following Susan, I addressed Henry, "Why did Bernard leave?"

"He's mad because he likes you. He's mad because he's young and immature."

"I'm hungry, Henry," I interrupted him. I suddenly really wanted whatever I heard Susan munching on in the kitchen.

"Now that you've sobered up, I'll take you back to the party. I'm hungry too. We can eat there."

"Henry, what color is the ocean bottom?" I asked him.

"Probably brown and sandy, gray rocks, something like that," he said.

"That's incorrect. It's bright pink," I told him.

Henry laughed, "It is not bright pink."

"Well, until you can prove otherwise, it's bright pink," I stated.

"Alright, Maybel," Henry laughed again, "I suppose that's fair."

Susan and I sat on either side of Henry at the kitchen table at the Charleston's house, which really seemed to annoy Bernard when he passed through. "Susan look, there's my former big brother."

"Oh yes, I remember him," Susan said, then shoved peas in her mouth.

"My new big brother is prettier," I said.

"Henry is the prettiest," Susan agreed.

Bernard rolled his eyes and continued through the kitchen and Susan and I giggled.

Bernard leaned his head back inside the kitchen. "Henry's babysitting you two! Do you really think he prefers to be with you two instead of the gorgeous women who flock to him? Father told him to watch over you two babies!" Bernard smirked sarcastically.

"Your previous brother is an ass, Maybel," Susan said as she bit into her steak.

I looked up at Henry beside me. "You were told to babysit us?"

"Yes, Maybel," Henry said quietly.

"You don't want to be with us?"

"I do. I've actually enjoyed spending time with you," Henry said.

"Why were you told to babysit us?" I asked him, confused.

"You're older now, Maybel, and some of the people Uncle does business with are unsavory characters. He wanted me to make sure none of them do or say anything untoward."

"Is that why Bernard doesn't like me? He got tired of babysitting me?" I suddenly wished I was drunk again.

"I don't think so," Henry said softly. "I think he's jealous that you are not giving him your undivided attention anymore."

I finished my dinner in silence, reevaluating my relationships with everyone. Henry was paid to spend time with me. Bernard had only been babysitting me when he played with me.

"Maybel," Henry sighed, "I do enjoy being with you, it just so happens that for this party, I am also staying with you to ensure your safety."

I wondered who else had a role in my life, like they were actors who only showed me whatever they were paid to show me. Henry was paid to show me his role as a kind man who talked to me and said nice things to me. I should have known he didn't choose to spend time with me. He never paid any attention to me before.

And then Bernard, I steamed, grew tired of his role as big brother in my life and began resenting having to care for me.

I wondered if Susan was my real friend or just playing the role of my friend. Susan felt like a real friend, but my faith in truth and what was real was fading.

"I'm going home," I told Henry. "You can stay here and have sex with as many women as you can get tonight, Henry. I'll be safe in my house without you."

I turned to Susan. "Susan you can come with me or stay here. I'm sure there's cake somewhere and wherever there's cake, there will be Archie."

"Archie's here?" Susan asked Henry.

"I don't know, Susan," Henry said. "I have to walk Maybel home and I can't let you out of my sight either."

"I'll be in the dining room eating cake!" Susan yelled as she ran toward the dining room, jumping two ottoman foot rests in the process. She really was like a jack rabbit when motivated, I marveled.

"I'm going straight home," I told Henry. "I will be fine!" I went down the hall and Henry followed. I walked past Bernard talking to one of Catherine's friends, and he stood a little too close to her, so I kicked his shin as I passed by.

"See, there's the door!" I pointed to where Vincent stood greeting the guests who were arriving late. "I'm going straight home! Go find some dumb girl to poke!" I quietly hissed.

I walked to the door and told Vincent he looked good in his red tie and matching handkerchief.

"Why thank you, Miss Maybel, my dear granddaughter gave this to me just last week."

"She has quite the eye for good fabric and color," I smiled at him.

"Yes, indeed," he winked at me.

I walked down the lawn, halfway to the street, then veered left into the gardens and out of sight. I wanted to return to the party to observe people. Catherine had fascinated me with her extremely insightful observations. I wondered if I could come to such astute observations, too. People confused me. I wanted to see how Bernard behaved with Catherine's friends, if he flirted with them, and how Henry behaved when he didn't think I was watching. I tripped on a fallen tree branch on my way around the mansion and fell headfirst into deer poop. I sat up and sighed. I was still a little drunk. I decided to bathe yet again, then observe people.

"Maybel why are you here bathing?" Bernard walked into his bathroom where I was now bathing.

"Why didn't you knock on your own bathroom door?" I asked angrily.

"Because it's my bathroom!"

"This bathroom is occupied! Kindly leave," I said dismissively.

Bernard still stood above me. I looked up at him. Catherine was behind him.

"I got dirty outside," I said.

"Messy Maybel," Bernard said sarcastically.

"I'm naked Bernard, under this soapy water. Can you please leave?" I stared at my toes on the faucet.

"Oh, wait, Catherine, can you find a dress for me?" I asked her. "Maybe one of your maids has a dress I can borrow, Bernard?"

"I'll get one of mother's dresses," Bernard said and left.

Catherine crossed her arms and stared down at me from the bathroom door frame. "Couldn't stay clean for just one night, Maybel?"

I looked back down at my dirty toes and pulled them quickly below water.

Bernard returned with a dress and set it on a dressing table and left.

"Maybel, can you hurry up? I want to talk to Bernard about something," Catherine said.

"You mean have quick sex in his bed before you return to the dance floor?" I asked.

"We don't have sex, Maybel," Catherine said, annoyed.

"I don't believe you or anyone else anymore," I sunk lower under the water when Bernard returned.

"What, Bernard? I can't finish bathing if you two stand here staring at me! Go away!" I snapped.

"Just thought I'd let you know your new big brother is having sex with two women at the same time," Bernard smiled sarcastically.

I stared stonily into his eyes. "And you can't even get Catherine to wrap her legs around your waist. Maybe you should be Henry's apprentice? Study under him for a while and then see how many dirty girls you can get to study under you?"

Bernard's face turned bright red.

I looked back at Catherine and growled, "I'll be done as soon as you two leave!"

Bernard slammed his door shut and I finished scrubbing the smell of deer poop off my arms. I dressed in Mrs. Charleston's dress and put my dirty dress in one of Bernard's bags. As I was leaving, I stood outside Henry's bedroom. I wondered if Bernard told the truth, or if he lied about Henry to upset me.

Suddenly someone came behind me whispering, "There you are, my love." I turned around and in the dim hallway light, Mr. Charleston looked thoroughly disgusted. "Dear God, Maybel! I thought you were my wife!" He left quickly and Henry's door opened.

"Maybel, what are you doing here?" Henry asked. "I thought you were home safely."

Two women were behind him in bed smiling and giggling.

"I thought you were a changed man, a family man now," I told Henry. "You'll have quite the large family with as many women as you are trying to impregnate!"

I left Henry at his door. I walked downstairs and on my way to the kitchen door, I passed daddy. Maybel, are you leaving?" daddy called.

"Yes," I said.

Daddy stood next to a terribly shaken Mr. Charleston.

"You look just like your mother in her dress," daddy smiled.

"Oh, this is Mrs. Charleston's dress," I said. "I got my dress dirty," I held up the cloth bag with my deer-poop-stained dress inside. I felt embarrassed because, like Bernard so often pointed out, I somehow always managed to get messy.

"No, it's mommy's dress," daddy said. "Mommy gave it to Mrs. Charleston to wear to a dinner party next week. You look a lot like her in that dress. I never noticed that before," daddy said. "You're growing up too fast on me, baby."

"Goodnight daddy," I said.

I walked home numbly and went to bed feeling strangely. I really wanted to go to college now and be rid of these people. I wanted to be free.

As I laid in bed, I imagined a black canvas, and as I approached, I wiped in front of me with my hands, and wherever I wiped, a scene unfolded underneath. I wiped faster and faster trying to uncover my path but the faster and harder I wiped, the blurrier the picture underneath me became, and I fell asleep confused and scared.

Daddy came into my bedroom. "Maybel," he whispered, "do you want to come gambling with me? Don't tell mommy though, she's already mad at me for taking a bite of pie she had made for Mrs. Matthews."

"Yes! I love gambling!" I said excitedly.

"Shh! Remember, it's our little secret," daddy winked.

"Ok!" I whispered excitedly.

"Honey," daddy yelled to mommy in the kitchen, "Maybel and I are going to the candy store. Be back in an hour or two. Maybe three." Daddy paused, "We'll be back by dinner, Cupcake. Maybel and I may take a walk in the park afterward to catch up with each other."

"Odds are, we'll take that walk and be back in four hours!" I giggled and daddy gave me a look that said to not push my luck, and not mention any words related to gambling, such as 'odds.'"

Daddy and I walked to the candy store. Daddy sat down at the gambling table downstairs in the basement of Charlie's store and I sat on his lap. I was too old to sit on his lap, really, but Catherine and I still climbed all over daddy in the evenings when he finished work. We still enjoyed being daddy's girls.

I wrapped my arm around daddy's neck and looked at his cards. "Am I allowed to help you daddy?"

Daddy looked at the other players, one of whom was Henry, but I hadn't wanted to talk to him since he was with those two women at the party. The other players nodded, indicating I was allowed to play with daddy, so I tapped two of daddy's cards, letting him know he should trade those in.

"How much did we win last time, daddy?" I asked.

"Enough for your college tuition, baby," daddy squeezed my waist.

"Give it to Catherine," I said, "She'll be a good school teacher."

Daddy looked at me. "That's a lot of money, sweetheart."

"She's really good with children, teaching them and getting them to pay attention. When I don't pay attention to her when she tries to help me with math, she has this stare that puts the fear of God in my soul. She could be a Sunday school teacher too, now that I think about it. The way she would stare at children while teaching them the Ten Commandments, nobody would ever steal or covet thy neighbor ever again!"

Daddy and the men laughed. "Yes, Catherine has your mother's stare, like today, when I ate a bite of the pie that was to go to Mrs. Matthews," daddy chuckled. "She could have frozen me with that stare had I looked her in her eyes any longer. Oh, by the way, Harold, you won't be eating my wife's pie tonight," he said to Mr. Matthews, and then paused, "or any night for that matter!" And the table erupted with laughter.

I was confused as to whether or not they liked mommy's pie or disliked it. I liked mommy's pie.

The card game continued and I could tell the men wanted to make crass jokes but were holding back because of me. One of the men mentioned a two-for-one special at the grocery store on candy bars.

"Henry," another man said slyly, "you like two-for-one specials, don't you?" All the men laughed, even daddy, and the man sitting closest to Henry patted him on his back.

"I saw those candy bars for sale," I said, looking down at daddy's cards. I tapped his two of diamonds, reminding him that card was wild. "They were cheap looking, though," I said with a straight face and steady voice. "And sure to give you cold sores," I glanced over at Henry.

The table again erupted with laughter. Daddy whispered, "Do you know what we're talking about?"

"Candy," I said. "Cheap candy makes you sick," I said innocently.

I continued watching daddy's cards and daddy watched me like he wondered if I was innocent anymore, or if I knew the underlying joke that had been made.

"Maybel, we should get home before dinner," daddy said.

"It's not close to dinnertime yet," I pouted. "I want to take all their money, daddy."

I got the feeling daddy was worried I had picked up on their dirty jokes and didn't want me to learn any more bad behavior. I decided to not make any more comments on lewd jokes, no matter how funny my comments would be, so daddy wouldn't stop bringing me to gamble. Daddy and I stayed for the rest of the afternoon and I kept my mouth shut and my face straight and plain, even when the carefully-worded, lewd jokes were hilarious. A lot of the comments the men made and laughed at didn't make sense to me. A couple of them I understood, but most of them didn't make sense so my confused face wasn't feigned.

I really enjoyed gambling with daddy and I really enjoyed taking all the fellas' money.

I proceeded to lose seven straight hands. Daddy was getting nervous, I could tell. "I'm sorry, daddy," I whispered.

"It's ok, baby, everyone has their good days and bad days," he whispered back softly.

The next hand I took everything and kept my straight face even when daddy hugged me tightly and joked with the other men about their loss.

On the way home, daddy asked me if I lost all those hands on purpose. I smiled up at him and he laughed as he picked me up in his big arms and hugged me.

Daddy took my hand, "Let's get home and eat dinner, honey. Remember, we ate custard and walked around."

"What did we talk about?" I asked, "In case mommy wants to ask us separately. She's smart like that."

Daddy laughed, "Your future, college, and all that."

"Ok, daddy."

"Oh, Maybel, were you serious about using that money for Catherine's college tuition?"

"Yes, daddy."

"And how shall we pay for your education? It would not be fair to you if we did not have enough money for you."

"Do we have enough money for me to go to college?"

"Yes," daddy said, "but what if we didn't? You would still put Catherine before you?"

"I don't know what your plans are, but I plan on taking more people's money in card games."

Daddy laughed and squeezed my hand. "You're a good sister and daughter, baby. I love you."

"I love you too, daddy."

Daddy and I set the table while mommy and Catherine brought the food into our dining room. Bernard was staying for dinner.

"Bernard, don't your parents have dinner at your house?" I asked him.

"Maybel, don't be rude," daddy said, "Bernard is always welcome."

"I didn't mean you aren't welcome, Bernard, I meant, don't your parents cook dinner for you?"

"No," he said. "We have cooks who do that."

"Don't you enjoy eating with your parents at your home?" I asked, genuinely curious as to why he didn't want to be with his parents.

"My parents usually work at home or leave to work elsewhere. Mother is working at home in her office right now, and father is tending to a patient at his medical practice."

"When do they eat?" I asked Bernard.

"Whenever they get home and ask the cooks to make them dinner, or breakfast, depending on when they get home."

"If you weren't here, you'd be alone?" I asked, surprised.

"Yes," Bernard said. He looked sad.

"Sorry, Bernard," I said.

Bernard just stared at his plate.

"Do you want to stay here after dinner and paint or write or something?" I asked him.

Bernard smiled sadly, "Thank you, Maybel, I'd like that."

Henry continued to help daddy in his workshop. He showed me affection by bringing me chocolates and trying to engage me in conversation. I liked his attention, but I didn't let Henry know that. I was mad at Henry for being with those two women after he told me he was trying to be a better man.

Henry ate dinner with us almost every night, and one evening, we took a chair daddy made to the rich person who bought it. I was surprised daddy allowed me to go with Henry at night.

Elsie and Effie were sitting on a bench in town. I wanted them to be jealous of me. I scooted closer to Henry.

"Would you like to hold hands?" Henry asked softly.

"Yes," I smiled.

I held Henry's hand. His hands were rough and that always surprised me. I always anticipated soft hands. I forgot Henry wasn't just a beautiful face. He was actually really good at woodworking with daddy and renovating buildings with Mr. Charleston.

"I don't want to ever look into your eyes and see pain or hatred," Henry blurted out suddenly. He glanced over at me and squeezed my hand.

I sat quietly for a moment. I was not sure what to say next.

"Why did the woman who broke your heart a long time ago no longer want to date you?"

"I'm not the kind of man you should fall in love with," Henry said simply.

"You cheated," I guessed.

"Yes," he said.

"If you loved her so much that she was able to break your heart, then why would you want to be with another woman?"

"I didn't. The other woman pursued me. A man can run away from a beautiful woman only so long. If she persists, and the man is aroused one night and lets things go too far, then he cheats," Henry said, showing no remorse, only offering an explanation.

"Only if he's a bad man," I said.

"I am."

"Not all men cheat," I told him.

"Not all men are pursued." He wasn't arguing, he simply stated the truth he knew and had experienced.

"So you think a man is not able to say no?" I asked.

"Maybe once, maybe twice, but a man who has many options and offers can't say no forever."

"I don't like you anymore." I let go of Henry's hand and scooted farther away.

"I know. I don't like me either," he said.

"You know you are in control. You can be good. It's a choice you make," I told him.

"I know. Next time Bernard kisses you, choose not to kiss him back."

Henry angered me. I didn't want to be confronted with the truth. I crossed my arms.

We arrived at the home of a wealthy man. Henry parked his automobile and we went to the door. The butler said to bring the chair around back.

We drove around back and I reached for the other end of the chair.

"Maybel, it's too heavy for you."

"No, it's not," I said, and took the other end of the chair.

"I knew you were strong, but I had no idea you were this strong," Henry remarked.

We carried the chair inside where a woman stood in a red, silk nightgown.

"I might like this chair in my bedroom. Won't you come upstairs and see if you think it would look good there. Your little sister can wait here. I'll have our maid get her a snack," the woman spoke seductively.

"I'm terribly sorry, Mrs. Chambers, I would need another person to help me carry this chair upstairs. Perhaps another day, the man who built this chair and I can return and move it upstairs." Henry spoke calmly as though he hadn't noticed her obvious invitation.

"Oh, I just need you to come upstairs and see if it would look good in my bedroom. Perhaps it won't and we'll end up leaving it here in the parlor. Shall we?" She started up the stairs then turned back to Henry. "Come dear," she reached out her hand and smiled at Henry.

"I'm sorry, Mrs. Chambers. Unfortunately, I cannot help you with decorating advice. I really wouldn't know if it looked better here in the parlor, or there in your bedroom. We do, however, need to be leaving now." Henry put his arm on my shoulder and started to turn us around.

"I suppose it is a school night," the woman looked sourly at me. "When you return, be sure to bring the man who built this chair. He was quite good at helping me last time," she winked at Henry.

"Did you have sex with him?" I asked bluntly.

Henry took my arm and pulled me toward the door but I resisted.

The woman looked surprised at my candor. "A lady never kisses and tells," she winked again at Henry. "You and he should come tomorrow at this same time."

Henry continued pulling me and took me to his automobile. He opened the driver's side door and pushed me inside then sat beside me.

"Did that woman try to seduce you?" I asked angrily.

"Yes. She's a bored and lonely housewife and no, your father did not have sex with her. That woman was trying to assess whether or not I would have sex with her and keep quiet about having done so."

"What did she mean daddy was good at helping her?" I asked with a high-pitched and squeaky voice filled with incredulousness.

"She was overtly flirting and making it known that she was willing to have sex with me and with your father, but of course, neither of us would ever be interested. She's bored and lonely, and likely trying to make her husband jealous." Henry explained with an even tone, but I could tell he was worried about my reaction to the bad woman.

Henry quickly was on the main road again and driving away fast.

"If I weren't there would you have had sex with her?" I asked.

"No."

"Why not?" I asked, disbelievingly. "You can't run from an offer," I reminded him sarcastically.

"I'm trying to make better choices, Maybel."

I sat watching the trees and fences fly past. Children played in yards and horse pastures went quickly by our windows.

"Would you have cheated on the woman you deeply cared for had you not been touched and hurt when you were a little boy?" I asked Henry.

"I don't know. I don't know exactly how much of what I experienced still affects me. I do think I would value sex more though. To me, sex is just a release your body needs. It's not love. When I was with the woman I cared for though, it felt different, and I realized sex could actually mean something more than a desperately-needed orgasm. Then I cheated on her and she hated me."

"Was that other woman worth your orgasm?"

"No," Henry admitted.

"Would you cheat again on the woman you love?"

"No. I've already had every kind of woman there is. Sex is just an orgasm now, like it was before

I was with the woman I really liked. Now, I want sex to be more, like it was when I was with the woman I really cared about. I just don't really know how to be good. I think you and your family are good, so I hope that I learn from all of you how to be better and how to love."

"When was the last time you had sex?"

"That woman you caught me with in the black dress the night of the campfire," Henry said.

I snorted.

"It's true. I couldn't be with those two women that night at the party. I wanted to be with them, but after I saw you, I couldn't get hard."

My eyes flashed anger and I wanted to bash his pretty face in with my heel. "I make your penis sad and limp?" I seethed.

"I meant that I have started to grow a conscious, and to tell you the truth, having a conscious is quite bothersome! I like you, Maybel, and I didn't want to be with them anymore. I pretended to pass out because I was too drunk to have sex. They laughed about me to each other saying my penis wasn't working and they left."

"Then why did the men at Charlie's last poker party joke about you having sex with those two women?"

"Because my friend saw me go upstairs with them and I didn't tell them what really happened. Men like a bad reputation. Women like clean reputations."

We arrived home and Henry walked me to my door. "Give my best to your family," he said. "Goodnight, Maybel."

Henry left. I was surprised he didn't come inside to chat with daddy. He and daddy seemed to get along well and Henry looked up to daddy as a father.

"Did you deliver the chair, sweetheart?" daddy asked.

"Yes. I don't like Mrs. Chambers. She tried to seduce Henry and wants you to come to her house and move the chair into her bedroom, and she was winking when she said that."

Mommy came out of the kitchen holding a knife. "I'll help you move that chair right now!"

Mommy's face, and the way she held that knife, looked like she knew how to fight. I suddenly realized Catherine and I looked like mommy when we were outraged. I was proud and terrified at that moment, and realized why daddy always joked about the Irish blood flowing strongly within the veins of his girls. I now realized, looking at mommy holding a knife and the glaze covering her eyes, that daddy may have been a tad scared when he joked about our tempers."

Mommy grabbed my hand and yanked me out the door still holding the knife in her other hand.

"Dear, please, you know I would never cheat!" daddy pleaded with mommy.

"After you see what I'm about to do, the thought of cheating on me will never cross your mind!" Mommy roared.

"Honey, it has never crossed my mind, I swear!" daddy continued to plead.

"After I found out that slut babysitter kissed you and you hid that from me, I don't know what to believe!"

Mommy yanked me down our sidewalk and into the street still holding the knife.

"Catherine!" mommy yelled when she saw Catherine coming our way. "Turn around and follow me!"

"What's going on?" Catherine asked, worried.

"Get behind me! Mommy's going to chat with a Mrs. Chambers," mommy said angrily.

"Maybel?" Catherine whispered when she was beside me.

I didn't answer Catherine. I was too scared.

Mommy took us to the Charleston's home. "Mrs. Charleston!" mommy yelled to Vincent.

In no more than thirty seconds Mrs. Charleston was downstairs in the grand entryway. Mrs. Charleston saw mommy's knife and looked terrified.

"I need to borrow your automobile!" Mommy yelled.

Mrs. Charleston apparently did not move fast enough. Mommy screamed, "A Mrs. Chambers requested sex from my husband and I'm about to explain the consequences of such forwardness!"

"Right this way," Mrs. Charleston beckoned. Mrs. Charleston asked Vincent drive us.

Mommy sat up front and screamed for Vincent to drive faster and faster and Catherine and I sat in the back. Catherine held my hand. She seemed terrified.

Mommy turned around and stared holes into our skulls. "Let this be a lesson to the both of you! Do not even entertain the idea of being with a man who already committed himself to a woman!" Mommy turned back around and stared out the front window like a dog waiting for the postman to near.

I gave directions and when we arrived, mommy jumped out of the car. "Get out! The both of you!" Vincent was so scared of mommy he jumped out too.

Mommy walked to the door and didn't knock. She opened it. "Mrs. Chambers!" she screamed.

The butler and maid rushed to us. "Get Mrs. Chambers now!" mommy growled.

The woman in the red, silk dress descended the stairs with calmness. A man bolted from the interior of the house and angrily asked who we were and stated loudly that he would have his butler alert the police.

"Mrs. Chambers, I am the wife of the man who built this chair. You requested his presence tomorrow to have sex with you. Let it be known that he does not want you or your disease ridden and well-worn vagina!"

Mommy picked up the chair, the chair that took both Henry and me to carry, and smashed it to the ground. It splintered and mommy's face was full of rage, though she smiled like she belonged in an insane asylum.

"Keep a closer eye on your slut wife!" mommy snarled at Mr. Chambers. Mr. Chambers had wide eyes and a gaping mouth while Mrs. Chambers was oddly calm and sneered at mommy.

"Oh, you are accustomed to wives showing up at your house unannounced at night? Well then, let me cure your dull boredom and slutty ways!" Mommy threw the knife she wielded and it stuck solidly in the wall by the staircase where Mrs. Chambers stood, and pinned her there, because mommy speared Mrs. Chambers' ear!

Catherine gasped and squeezed my hand but I was happy. "Stay away from my daddy, you dirty slut!" I screamed.

"Should you alert the police regarding the discussion I've just had with your wife," mommy said coolly to Mr. Chambers, "I'll return with reporters from the paper, and I'm certain more wives will come forward, and you'll be quite embarrassed by bad press. And," mommy sneered, "I'm very certain someone, or perhaps some people, will be buried in a pauper's grave, in a shallow hole somewhere where coyotes will be happy to carry away any evidence of a crime."

Mommy turned and stared at Catherine and me. "Don't be like Mrs. Chambers," she said with a steely voice. She then grabbed our arms and dragged us to the car.

When we returned to the Charleston's house, daddy came outside. "Honey, everything ok? I did not cheat, I swear!"

"Oh, I know, dear, and you never will once you see Mrs. Chambers' ear. Come along then. We're going home."

Daddy followed us home. "I love you, honey. I swear I have never, nor will I ever cheat."

"I know," mommy said.

Catherine and I glanced at each other then looked straight ahead. We had never seen mommy like this. I wasn't upset though. I liked watching mommy be a protective, mother grizzly bear.

After mommy told Mrs. Chambers she'd end up a coyote snack, daddy was extra kind to mommy, stepping lightly around her, and promising he had always been faithful.

Mrs. Matthews had her husband taxidermy a badger for mommy, and mommy absolutely loved her gift. She mounted the badger on the wall of daddy's workshop.

I thought the badger was cute, and I designed and sewed a green dress, just like mommy's favorite green dress, and put it on the badger. Mommy loved it and kissed my cheek.

"Lovely," daddy smiled, when he saw mommy and me admiring the dress I sewed for mommy's badger. "No one is as lovely as you though, my beautiful wife."

Mommy smiled at daddy.

When Henry visited next, he treaded lightly around mommy and showed up at our door with a bouquet of flowers and chocolates. "I want to apologize for Mrs. Chambers' dreadful behavior, and please know that neither your husband nor I would ever be with such a woman."

"You may stay for dinner if you like, Henry," mommy told him. She took her flowers and chocolates and went to the kitchen. I felt that Henry was on thin ice because of his reputation with women, and mommy was silently, yet loudly, warning Henry to not be a bad influence on daddy.

Henry looked nervous, and if he had plans to be a bad influence, those plans had been violently dashed when mommy speared Mrs. Chambers' ear.

Henry was now going to be an angel and a righteous influence around daddy, if he wasn't already before.

Henry asked daddy if he needed help with anything in daddy's workshop. Daddy said yes. I followed daddy and Henry into daddy's workshop but I lagged behind trying to comb the tangles in my hair with my fingers because I had not expected Henry to arrive.

Henry's eyes widened and he stared timidly at the dead and preserved badger in the green dress and heels mounted on daddy's wall.

"Are all the women in this family as feisty as your wife?" Henry whispered to daddy.

"Yes," daddy answered.

"So noted," Henry said quietly.

I was standing to the side of the doorway still separating knots and clumps of tangles. I had been running through the forest with Susan earlier and wasn't paying attention to my hair at all.

"They are feisty," daddy said. "It can be a good thing, too."

Henry looked at daddy skeptically.

"My wife is a tigress when she gets feisty. Sometimes I barely recover when she's on top of me demanding more." Daddy and Henry shared a chuckle.

I stepped into daddy's workshop still pushing my hair back, trying to smooth it down. Daddy gasped, "How long have you been here?"

"I've been following you the whole time. I was just trying to comb my hair with my fingers but I'm just not refined. How does Catherine have perfect hair all the time? I sneeze and suddenly my hair is full of snarls!"

"Maybel, will you please help me get this bookcase into Henry's automobile?" Daddy looked nervously at me. "It needs to be delivered by Saturday. Since you are here tonight, Henry, would you mind?" daddy asked Henry.

"I'd be happy to help," Henry smiled at daddy.

I helped daddy and Henry put the bookcase in Henry's automobile. "Can I come with you?" I asked.

"No," both Henry and daddy answered.

I returned to the house and Henry left. Daddy came inside and kissed mommy's cheek.

The next day, Catherine asked me to go to a study group with her. "What are you studying?" I asked.

"English literature," Catherine answered.

"You can already speak English, and you know how to read, so what is the point of this study group?" I thought it sounded boring.

"We discuss the author's intention," Catherine said.

"Author's intentions are obvious, and if they aren't obvious, they're a bad storyteller," I said.

"You are an excellent author, Maybel," Catherine said. "Perhaps you can offer insight?"

"To people who don't understand the obvious? If they're too stupid to understand imagery and intention, there's nothing I can do to magically make them smart."

"Please?" Catherine asked.

"Say you'll spend Saturday with me," I smiled.

"I'll spend Saturday with you," Catherine smiled back.

"Ok, I'll go with you," I said.

"Thank you, Maybel," Catherine smiled.

When we arrived at the study group, a boy told Catherine he appreciated punctuality.

"I'm sorry, Spencer," Catherine apologized.

I already didn't like Spencer. "I'm sorry too, Spencer. We were admiring the setting sun remaining a full twenty minutes in the western sky just to get a glimpse of you before settling down below the horizon for the night."

Spencer stared at me icily. He attempted to make me uncomfortable by staring at me for a prolonged period of time. I enjoyed the challenge and stared back at him while wildly gazing into his gray eyes.

I won. Spencer addressed his flock of admirers, thus breaking our ridiculous staring contest.

"Good evening, ladies," he said with an air of self-importance.

"Good evening, Spencer," everyone except me cooed.

"Let's discuss our most recent book, The Dove of Lilies."

I had read that book. It was stupid. The author was stupid and I was convinced when I read it, that the author had a relative in a high-up position at a publisher's business. There was no way that dumb book was published on the author's own merit.

I waited to see what Spencer and his flock of doves said.

There were comments about religion, the color white, and lilies being an allegory for sex.

Spencer commanded the group. He enjoyed attention. I hated him.

"Maybel," Spencer spoke to me as though I were a peasant and he were king. "Catherine says you are a writer. Perhaps we can hear from an expert?" the little cow turd said sarcastically.

"The dove is you. The lilies are all these stupid girls vying for your attention. Raise your hand if Spencer has declared his love to you." I asked the group.

Six of the nine girls raised their hands, a fight ensued, and Catherine laughed heartily as she took my hand and led me away. "I just knew you would flatten Spencer's ego!" Catherine laughed. "Thank you, Maybel."

"Anytime," I happily replied. "The sad thing is, every one of those girls will continue to vie for Spencer's attention, and he will pretend they are his only one, and each girl will believe him."

"I'm not going back to that study group. I will attend a different study group next week," Catherine said. "I like learning new things from vastly varying personalities. Did you know some women have sex with each other and some men have sex with each other?"

I turned my head and stared at Catherine as we walked. "No, I did not know that."

"I think it's interesting. I had never heard of that before. I like learning new things, Maybel. Everyone, including you, think all I care about is hair and clothing."

I didn't say anything to the contrary because I had never thought Catherine's thoughts went much deeper than which color of dress looked most Parisian that spring.

"Do you want to have sex with a woman?" I asked Catherine.

"No, but I think it's a fascinating facet of human nature. I wonder about things, Maybel. Why do people do what they do? Why do they say what they say? I think we're all complex and fascinating, don't you?"

"Yes," I agreed. I did think that. I didn't ever hear Catherine speak about much. When she did speak, it was not usually intellectual.

"Catherine," I hesitated, "do you talk like this around other people? Does Bernard, daddy, mommy, or Mr. Charleston know you wonder about such things?"

"No," Catherine answered. "You're the smart one, Maybel, everyone knows that."

"You are smart too," I said. "You play piano and dance better than me. Why don't you let people know how smart you really are?"

We continued walking. We didn't speak. I finally told Catherine to speak more. "Tell mommy and daddy that you wonder what goes on in people's minds. Don't be afraid to argue with people. Tell them what you know to be true and if you are wrong, then you've learned something new, and if you are right, then they've learned something new."

Catherine smiled weakly. "Maybe," she said, but I knew she wouldn't. She was too used to not letting people know her thoughts. I wondered why.

"Bernard! Guess what?" Catherine said excitedly as Bernard came through our kitchen door.

"What?" he asked. He wore a blue, buttoned shirt and light brown pants. His hair was a little longer than usual and tousled. He hadn't shaved today and I liked his unkempt look maybe even more than his usual dashing and perfect appearance.

"Maybel has a boyfriend!" Catherine squealed.

Bernard frowned.

"He's not my boyfriend!" I said emphatically.

"They're going to the dance together!" Catherine squealed again.

"Just as friends, Catherine!" I reminded her.

"Oh, Maybel! He likes you!" Catherine looked happy with her matchmaking.

"I don't want to go Catherine! I'm only going because you said I'm boring!"

"Maybel, you're not really boring. You're just very backward at social functions," Catherine replied.

"Thank you, Catherine. I'm staying home," I said, annoyed.

"What I mean is, you need practice. You're amazing, Maybel! People just don't realize how amazing you are because you never go out and socialize."

"I don't know what to do when I'm at a party. How long do I have to be there?" I asked.

"A couple hours. You'll be fine," Catherine answered.

"Two hours? Or do you mean longer, like three or four?"

"You'll have fun, Maybel!" Catherine touched my hair. "Up or down, Bernard?"

"What?" Bernard looked up from the kitchen table. He sat eating a turkey sandwich with pickles.

"Would Maybel's hair look better up or down?"

"Shaved. You should definitely shave your head, Maybel." Bernard said.

"Bernard! Stop it! Be serious!" Catherine said angrily.

"I am being serious," he said with a straight face. "Shave your head, Maybel. It's all the rage in Paris."

Catherine rolled her eyes. "Let's put your hair up, Maybel."

"It's not until Saturday, Catherine," I protested.

"We have to plan now! Let's do your hair to see which hairstyle looks best and we'll pick out a dress."

"Hair up, pink dress. Done. Let's go get custard!" I said, hoping Catherine would not make me her toy dress-up doll.

"No! No custard until after the dance!" Catherine said sternly.

"Why?" I was incredulous.

"No sweets so you don't gain weight, Maybel!"

"I won't, Catherine!" I said, very annoyed she had the audacity to interfere with custard time!

"I'd like custard," Bernard said.

"You just want to fatten up Maybel before the dance so no boys want to dance with her!" Catherine yelled.

"She's scrawny, Catherine! A custard isn't going to hurt!"

"I'm not scrawny!" I glared at Bernard.

Catherine snatched my hand. We're going to see which hairstyle and dress looks best. Catherine pulled me upstairs and Bernard followed.

We settled in Catherine's room. Bernard put his plate with his half-eaten turkey sandwich and pickles on Catherine's dressing table, then fell into her bed and got comfortable. He'd been in this situation before, I gathered. This would take a long time, I guessed.

I sat at Catherine's dresser looking at my reflection. I wondered how Catherine always attained perfect hairstyles. I reached up and smoothed a lock of hair between my fingers but my touch must have scared my hair, for each little strand jumped away from each other in apparent disgust. Bernard said my hair was frizzy and unruly. I then asked him how to make my hair ruly, and he said not to bother because my hair was hopeless. Bernard's taunts hurt my feelings, so I threw his pickle at him. He dodged it, but not the second pickle, which I gleefully sent sailing through the air and it slapped across his face.

I sat on the edge of Catherine's bed and watched her go through her closet.

I turned to look down at Bernard laying there with his eyes closed and feet propped up. He was ready for a long night.

"Catherine, how long is this going to take?"

"Until we're done," she snapped.

Bernard touched my arm. His eyes were still closed as he spoke. "Don't rush her, it will be less painful if you just accept your fate."

Catherine did my hair three times and decided on a red dress.

"Do you like this look or,"

"This one!" I yelled. "I like this one!"

"Me too!" Bernard agreed, even though his eyes were still closed.

"You're both saying you like this dress so I'll stop playing dress-up with Maybel!"

"No!" Bernard and I screamed in unison.

"This is my absolute favorite!" I squealed. "I love it!"

"Me too!" Bernard's fake enthusiasm was unbelievable, but he was trying to help me be done with being Catherine's toy dress-up doll so I was grateful.

"We're ready for Saturday!" Catherine said happily.

"Custard time?" I asked.

"No!" Catherine replied.

"Custard time later after Catherine falls asleep?" I mumbled to Bernard.

"I heard you Maybel, and no! We must watch our figures!"

"Well, I figure I deserve a custard for having sat through this!" I joked.

Bernard laughed at my joke while Catherine glared at him.

"Maybel, this boy likes you! The least you can do is show up presentable!"

"Ok, Catherine," I said defeated.

"Who is this boy?" Bernard asked.

"He's a handsome man from a nice family," Catherine replied. "He's a good match for Maybel."

"Do you like him?" Bernard asked curiously.

"I don't even know his last name," I said.

"Good, then I'm not worried." He leaned back and closed his eyes.

"Maybel, Weston likes you. You both have a lot in common," Catherine told me.

Bernard sat up quickly. "Weston O'Dell?"

"Yes, that's him," Catherine said. "You know him?"

"Maybel, you are not going to a dance with him!" Bernard bellowed.

"Ok, I like not going to dances. That's settled." I said happily.

"Why not, Bernard? Why can't Maybel dance with him?" Catherine asked angrily.

"He is the kind of man Maybel must stay away from!" Bernard answered angrily. "You are absolutely not going to this dance, Maybel," he yelled at me.

"No need to yell, Bernard. I enjoy not going to dances," I smiled.

"Bernard! What is wrong with Weston O'Dell?" Catherine looked angry.

"He will take advantage of Maybel! I won't have it, Catherine!"

"You can't stand any man talking to Maybel!" Catherine screamed at Bernard.

"Anyone but Weston, Catherine!"

"No, Bernard! It doesn't matter who the man is! You don't want any man near Maybel!"

"Catherine, Weston is not good to women! I'm trying to protect Maybel!"

"You're always trying to protect Maybel! Maybel is old enough to choose her date!"

"I have only briefly met this Weston fellow once, but I trust Bernard's judgement," I said. "Also, it means I don't have to dress up and talk to people," I smiled. "Let's do something else Saturday."

"No, we're going to the dance! Bernard, let Maybel decide whether or not she likes Weston!" Catherine was not about to budge.

"He treats women poorly and I will not allow Maybel near him, Catherine!"

Catherine turned to me. "If after meeting Weston, and you don't like him, we'll leave."

"You want me to spend hours getting dressed, go to a party, and leave after five minutes?" I asked.

"No, I want you to go out and do something, Maybel! And if you don't like him, we'll leave."

"It seems like a lot of trouble for only attending this event for five minutes," I said.

"You're absolutely set on not enjoying yourself and coming home after not giving this party a proper chance!" Catherine looked exasperated.

"Ok Catherine! I'll go! Be forewarned that I'll likely not enjoy myself and come straight home," I said.

"Fine, just give it a chance is all I'm asking," she said more calmly.

Bernard laid on Catherine's bed brooding. "Maybel, do you remember the kicking and punching techniques I showed you?"

"Yes, Bernard, but you'll be there so I needn't worry." I jumped on the bed and punched Bernard in his arm. "Take that you lousy bastard!" I laughed.

"Ow! Maybel!"

"Did that really hurt or are you condescending to me?"

"I'm absolutely condescending to you, Maybel," he laughed. "You hit like a butterfly kisses," he laughed harder.

"Maybe I hit the wrong spot!" I swung another punch at his stomach and he grimaced.

"Ok, that one was a little better but you really need more practice," he said, and with a light tap, he pushed me off the bed and I fell to the floor.

I popped back up like a hissing cat someone tried to bathe. "Ahh!" I screamed and jumped onto Bernard, shoving a pillow over his face and sitting on the pillow.

"Maybel!" Bernard growled, "Stop it this instant!"

I kicked my heels into his stomach. "Is this how butterflies kiss?" I dug my heels into his stomach and repeatedly pummeled him.

He reached up and pulled me down beside him and wrapped his arms around me tightly and squeezed.

"Can't breathe!" I gasped.

"Bernard, you're hurting Maybel!" Catherine shouted.

"She's fine! I'm just teaching her a lesson. You think you can defend yourself against these boys, Maybel, but you're overconfident and that will get you hurt!"

"Let go! Maybel's face is turning red!" Catherine screamed louder at Bernard.

I gasped for air.

Catherine suddenly broke her dressing room chair over Bernard's back and Bernard let go of me. "Catherine! I wasn't really hurting Maybel!"

"Not anymore!" Catherine screamed.

"I'm fine, Catherine," I gasped, then farted loudly against Bernard. "You shouldn't have squeezed me so hard!"

"Oh, that's disgusting, Maybel!" Bernard waved his hand in front of his nose. "What did you eat?"

"Serves you right for squeezing me!" I giggled.

I looked over at Catherine, who still held half a chair menacingly with her hands.

"Thank you, Catherine!" I smiled at her.

Then I smiled at Bernard. "See, Bernard, Catherine will protect me from Weston and from you!"

"I wasn't really going to hurt you, Maybel. You are overconfident and think you're stronger than you are, and that overconfidence will get you into situations you cannot get out of."

"That's why I have Catherine," I smiled at Catherine as she set the broken chair down on the floor.

"That's right, Bernard. I may not have your muscles, but I am resourceful!" She held up a jagged and splintered piece of her chair and winked at Bernard.

"Alright, you two, I am proud of you both. Look, I worry about both of you and want to protect you. If we are going to a party where Weston will be present, just please be extra cautious and don't get angry with me for wanting to keep you both safe."

"Thank you, Bernard." Catherine leaned down and kissed Bernard.

"Stop kissing him, Catherine, he's poking me in my back!" I yelled.

"Maybel!" Both Catherine and Bernard yelled in shock. Bernard's face turned bright red from embarrassment.

"I'm just kidding!" I giggled uncontrollably. "You should see your face Bernard!" I laughed.

Bernard pushed me away, annoyed.

"I'll see you Saturday, Catherine." Bernard kissed her cheek and left.

I stood up and stretched. "Thank you for protecting me, Catherine." I hugged her.

"Anytime, Maybel, that's what sisters are for. Also," she placed the broken chair leg in my hand, "I need you to fix this," she kissed my cheek. "Goodnight, Maybel."

"Goodnight, Catherine." I took the chair leg into my room and placed it on my dresser as a symbol of Catherine's love for me.

Saturday arrived and Catherine dressed me up like I was her little doll. She did my hair and applied makeup. It wasn't as horrible as I'd anticipated. It was fun spending time chatting with her.

Pout your lips like this, she squished her lips together lightly and I tried to imitate her. She began laughing, "Not that pouty!" she giggled. "You look like a fish!"

"That's the look I was going for," I laughed.

Catherine dabbed lipstick on my lips.

We took Bernard's carriage and arrived at the party fashionably late. Catherine began her high-society charms.

Bernard was at her side being as polite as possible given his boredom at such events.

I didn't see Weston. I went to stand by Catherine and Bernard because I didn't know anyone else well.

"Catherine, where is Weston?"

"I don't suppose he's arrived yet."

"I've been here five minutes," I whispered.

"The clock starts five minutes after you begin speaking with Weston."

"That wasn't specified in our original agreement," I argued.

"It's called a loophole. See, Bernard, I've been paying attention to your business conversations," she winked at Bernard.

"You have a business?" I asked. "The barbershop salon?"

"Just financial dealings, family investments, those sorts of boring things."

I stood by Catherine and Bernard and quietly daydreamed, only smiling and nodding when Catherine said my name and I figured she was introducing me to someone or wanting me to participate in a story she was regaling.

"Bernard, how long does Catherine make you stay?"

"Until she's finished. Don't fight it. It's futile to try and pull Catherine from a party."

"Maybel," Catherine turned to me, "go mingle. Boys won't talk to you if you're standing here. Bernard is the reason boys aren't talking to you or flirting with me, so get as far away from Bernard as possible, otherwise he will stare seethingly at any boy who approaches you."

"What does your seething face look like?" I asked Bernard.

"It's the same face he makes when you hit him with pinecones, Maybel, now go," Catherine ordered.

I sighed and found a quiet corner and sat down on a sofa.

"No sooner had I sat down, than a young man sat beside me. Hello, how are you this fine day, miss?"

"Very well, thank you, and you?"

"Better, now that I've met you. What's your name?"

"Maybel."

He looked surprised. "Oh, excuse me miss. He left at once."

I went back to Catherine.

"A boy came to talk to me."

"Who," Bernard asked.

"Some young man," I said.

"Where is he?"

"Bernard, leave Maybel alone," Catherine reprimanded him. "She can talk to any man she wants. Was it Weston?"

"No. As soon as I told him my name he left."

Bernard smiled smugly.

"Go sit on that red and gold sofa there by the window," Catherine ordered.

"Fine," I relented. Bernard was right, fighting Catherine was futile. Catherine's obstinance would surely prove useful one day. I imagined as a school teacher, she would easily wear down her students until they gave up and just learned math, rather than resist. As a mother, her children would sigh and go brush their teeth rather than listen to her lecture about bad breath for upwards of four hours. Catherine should pursue law, I decided. The criminal would just tell the judge to lock him away so he wouldn't have to endure more cross-examination.

A half hour later, Bernard made his way to me and sat beside me.

My arms were crossed and I surely looked bored and annoyed. "I saw you inching closer to me twenty minutes ago," I stared out the window as I spoke to Bernard.

"It takes a while to devise a plan to escape," he smiled.

Bernard and I sat together on the sofa waiting for Weston to arrive while Catherine chatted with friends.

"We spend a lot of time together waiting for Catherine at parties," I joked.

"Yes, we do. I'm glad you're here. I have someone to talk to," Bernard smiled at me.

"What do you do when I'm not here?" I asked him.

"Sit on a sofa wishing you were here to talk to," he laughed.

I giggled, "You don't like parties at all then do you?"

"I do not," he said.

"I will guess it's because you spend so much time away from home as it is. You've already seen Paris, London, and every other famous city in Europe so your curiosity was quenched early in your life. Your family has money so you don't need to prance around here in expensive clothing boasting about all the places you've travelled to, because you're secure knowing that you have more money than everyone here combined. You don't need to prove yourself."

"You are correct on all accounts," Bernard winked.

"Well as soon as Weston gets here, I can say hello followed immediately by goodbye."

We watched outside the window. The clouds moving were more fascinating than the nearby people talking. I began to wonder what other kinds of jobs Catherine would be able to do well. War General came to mind. Catherine was quite good at motivating people. She seemed to enjoy watching local ball games, mainly the parts when the two teams got angry and pounced on each other, piling on top of each other, and hitting each other until blood pooled in the grass. Catherine looked dainty, but she could sure get vocal when her team wasn't winning. She got us thrown out of a football game once, but made me swear not to tell her school friends. I told her maybe her school friends were just as blood-thirsty as she was.

"Catherine kisses other men and I don't care. I go out of my mind when a man wants to dance with you though." Bernard spoke to me while staring out the window. I had been daydreaming about Catherine when Bernard brought my mind to the present. His voice startled me.

"Catherine told me she kissed a man last year," I confessed.

"She's kissed several but I never cared."

"Why does she tell you?" I asked.

"To clear her conscience I would imagine," he answered.

"Or maybe she wants to see your reaction to see if you love her," I pointed out. "Don't you think it hurts her when she tells you she kissed someone and you don't care, but when a man simply looks at me you go insane?"

Bernard sighed deeply, "I never thought about it that way. Yes, I suppose it does."

Catherine was suddenly behind us. "Did you tell the boys here to not flirt with Maybel?" Catherine's voice was an angry whisper, like a snake that had been prodded with a stick and was now about to sink its teeth into Bernard's jugular

"I have not said anything to anyone at this party."

Catherine's eyes bored a hole into Bernard's skull.

"I may have said something to some young men at other parties about Maybel being off-limits."

Catherine's eyes were about to pop out of her skull.

"Before you get mad, Catherine, I am protective of Maybel because she's completely ignorant."

It was I who was about to coil up and strike Bernard's jugular now.

"And before you get mad, Maybel, you are completely naïve when it comes to a good man wanting to dance with you, and an arduous scoundrel who wants to take you for a walk in the garden so he can accidentally on purpose brush his hand over your breasts."

"That's true," Catherine took Bernard's side. "I love you, Maybel, but you have no sense of when a boy has ulterior motives."

"Naive and senseless are words to describe insipid people," I growled.

"Naive is a nice way of saying that when a drunken college boy tells you he saw a spider crawl into the collar of your shirt, you should not begin to unbutton your blouse to check for spiders," Bernard said.

Catherine snorted.

"I did not take off my shirt! I unbuttoned the first button to look inside!"

"And that's why I called you naive instead of stupid," Bernard said.

Catherine covered her lips to stifle her amusement.

I gritted my teeth, growled, turned, and stomped away as hard as I could without breaking my heels.

I sat in a corner on a pretty, upholstered bench for twenty minutes. I would have walked home, but I didn't know this part of town, and didn't know how to find my way back home. Bernard found me and sat beside me.

"Nobody wants to dance with me or talk to me."

Bernard put his arm around me. "I'll dance with you."

"I don't actually want to dance, Bernard, I just want someone to ask me."

Bernard chuckled, "You're like a cat, Maybel, you want someone to try to pet you so you can act bothered and walk away."

I frowned, "Why won't any boy talk to me or ask me to dance? I did what Catherine said, and stayed away from you, so that a boy could approach me."

"No one here is worth your time and effort, so don't worry about it."

"Bernard, you used to tease me about my hair. Do you think my appearance is still ugly? I don't know how to look beautiful like Catherine, and I think that's why nobody wants to dance with me."

Bernard sighed and squeezed my shoulder. "You were never ugly, and your hair was always beautiful."

"You were really mean to me and you hurt my feelings very much!"

"I'm sorry, Maybel. I was a young boy, and boys are sometimes not nice when they are young."

"You seem nice again now, so I'll forgive you, but for the record, I hated you then because you were so mean."

"I know. And for the record, I cringe whenever I think about the things I said and did to you back then."

"I hope you have a daughter who is treated by a boy the way you treated me!"

"Maybel, do not wish that. I will go to prison."

"Then you should have been nicer to me."

"I know, Maybel."

"No one here wants me. I guess I'll dance with you."

"Can you phrase it more kindly?"

"No," I said.

"It's like I'm your last choice."

"Well, you can't be my first choice since you're dating Catherine, or not dating, I don't know if you're dating, and neither do either of you!"

Bernard sighed again, "I know."

Bernard held out his hand. I accepted and he led me to the dance floor holding my hand gently. He guided me through the doorframe of the ballroom carefully and watched me, making sure I was ok.

"I feel safe with you, Bernard."

"I'll always protect you, Maybel. Boys do like you. And what Catherine says is true, if you are with Catherine and me, boys will likely not talk to you because I'm with you."

"Then why did you find me and come sit beside me?"

"Because I don't want boys to talk to you," he chuckled.

"Well, maybe I want a boyfriend."

"Well, maybe I'll have to continue paying boys to go work for my father's company instead of coming to a dance."

"You paid Weston to stay away from me?"

"Like you said, I have the money." Bernard did not sound at all remorseful.

"You're the reason I'm sexually frustrated?" I dug my fingernails into his shoulder as we danced.

"I had someone within my father's company reach out to Weston and offer him a lucrative amount of money if he would do some work at the company Saturday afternoon. Weston chose to accept the money rather than you. He made the wrong choice, Maybel."

"I can't believe you!" I hissed. "I got all dressed up and came here for nothing!"

"I got to see you all dressed up and dance with you, so I've had quite a pleasurable day," Bernard smiled smugly. I felt my eye twitch.

"I thought I was too ugly and awkward, and that was why no one wanted to talk to me or dance with me."

"Absolutely not, Maybel. You're stunning. Look, Maybel, Weston is not a good man. If Catherine had arranged a date with someone else, I would not have gone to such great lengths to keep you apart."

"I want to go home now. I want to get out of this dress and put on my new cotton pants mommy just made me. They're soft and warm. And you've made me mad, Bernard. I could have just stayed home."

I half-danced and half-pulled Bernard toward the ballroom door so I could half-politely tell Bernard to go away.

"Go away!" I growled as I walked through the ballroom door and into the parlor where Catherine stood mingling.

"Maybel," Catherine turned away from a group of pretty girls, "You need to work on your manners."

"No, I don't, it was my intention to be only half-polite."

"That wasn't polite at all," Bernard muttered.

"I was going to say, 'Go away, ass.' I took off the ass ending because we're at a formal affair."

I turned back to Catherine, "I'd like to go home now. It's been over an hour. Weston is not here."

"Why don't you talk to another young man? Bernard, introduce Maybel to one of your fellow boarding school classmates."

"Only two are here and they both have girlfriends," Bernard said. He looked happy.

"Catherine, I'm going home."

"Alright fine, Maybel, Bernard can take you home and I'll ride home later with Edith."

"I'm allowed to leave? Is this a trick, Catherine? You're really letting me leave?" Bernard looked thrilled.

"Yes, Bernard. You don't want to be here," she sighed. She looked a little hurt, but quickly perked up when two girls from her book club walked over and began talking to her in rapid and high-pitched squeals.

"See you later, Catherine," I said.

"See you later, Catherine," Bernard echoed.

Catherine waved at us but was far too engrossed with her friends to seem further saddened that Bernard and I were leaving.

In Bernard's carriage, he wrapped his arm around me. "Where would you like to go? It's still early."

"Home," I said dryly.

"Very well," Bernard smiled softly at me.

Susan excitedly awaited Theo's visit. She spoke of how great he was and how she wanted to take him to the candy store, the park, the stream in her backyard, and she wanted to teach him to paint.

When I had first met Theo, Susan was dying, and Theo was in no mood to be neither polite, nor pleasant. He walked past me like I wasn't worth noticing.

Mommy had told me that Theo had been under duress and thought he would have to deliver his little sister's eulogy. "Give Theodore a chance, Maybel. Neither you nor I, nor anyone else, come across as likeable during stressful times. When we are extremely sad and scared, we are not minding our best manners."

When Theo arrived, I saw his automobile on the street in front of Susan's house, but I didn't visit them. I gave Susan time with her brother before I went to her house. I waited a day. On the second day, Susan brought Theo to me.

"Maybel! Why haven't you come to my house?" Susan seemed hurt because I had not visited.

"You had not seen your brother in a long time. I wanted to give you time to reconnect. I'm sorry, Susan."

"It's ok, Maybel. I missed you," she said as she hugged me.

Susan ran over and sat on my sofa next to Henry. "Hello Handsome Henry," Susan smiled.

"Hello, sweetheart, how are you?" Henry smiled kindly at Susan.

"I'm well, thank you. This is my brother, Theo," she said. "He's smart, really smart, and he lives on the beach." Susan was proud of her brother and I was too because Theo saved Susan's life with the medicine he brought.

Henry smiled politely at Theo. "It is nice to meet you," he said.

"Likewise," Theo smiled politely.

They shook hands and I watched their hands squeeze each other's hands hard. I had never tried to break the bones of the person whose hand I shook, but Henry and Theo appeared to be doing just that.

"Good day, Maybel," Theo kissed my cheek. "It's great to see you again. You're looking lovely."

"Maybel, will you come have dinner with us tonight?" Susan jumped in my face smiling.

"I'm sorry, Susan, I have already told mommy I would help prepare dinner tonight. Mommy is making a roast. Catherine is helping, too. You are, of course, welcome to have dinner with us."

"Tomorrow, will you come to my house?" Susan asked me. "I want to play with you and Theo."

"Of course," I said. I remembered begging Catherine to play with me, and I didn't want to be the kind of annoyed, older sister Catherine had often been toward me.

"Why don't you stay here? I asked her. Susan looked disappointed and I didn't want her to look sad. "We can play here and spend the day together. I'll have to help mommy later though, but until then, we can spend time together doing whatever you want."

Susan smiled so big. "Thank you, Maybel, I want to ride a cow."

"What?" I asked, taken aback by her request.

"I'm kidding," Susan laughed. "Will you come over tomorrow though and play?"

I laughed at Susan's cow-riding request. "You remind me so much of myself," I giggled. "Yes, I'll be over after breakfast and we can shoot guns, arrows, or paint."

"If you're shooting arrows, may I come?" Henry asked.

"Yes!" Susan squealed. "Please come!"

I laughed, "Then we'll shoot arrows tomorrow, yes?" I winked at Susan. "Boys against girls?"

"Yes!" Susan winked back.

"There's a five-hundred dollar buy-in," I said in a serious tone to Henry. "Bring cash." I didn't smile.

"Oh," Henry looked surprised. "Ok," he said, a little nervously.

"I've got two fifty now," Theo told Henry. "You bring the other half tomorrow morning. I have a debt with Maybel and I intend on being repaid," Theo smiled at me.

Susan and I laughed. "I like hustling people," Susan giggled.

The next day, I waited for Henry to come, and we set off together to Susan's house. "I brought my own bow and arrows," Henry said confidently.

"Susan and I will win," I replied simply.

"Do you really have five-hundred dollars?" Henry asked.

"Do you really have sex with random women whose name you never know?"

"No," he answered. "The last one was named Violet."

"I do have five-hundred dollars, and I'm a better hunter than you," I said. I stared straight ahead. I knew I was better than Henry. "Susan is better than you, as well," I added.

"You thought you were the best tree-climber, too," Henry smirked. "But you were not. I won."

My brows lowered. "You beat me at my game, I will beat you at yours."

"Very well, miss, let's make a steeper wager," Henry said. He wasn't smiling.

"What is your proposal?" I asked.

"May I take you on a real, first date?" Henry looked shy.

"Very well," I said. "If I win, will you kiss me?"

Henry smiled sweetly, "Always, Maybel."

I knocked on Susan's door. "Hello, Susan," I smiled. "Henry is drunk. He thinks he will win."

Susan laughed, "You're so pretty Henry, but we're going to hang your smug, taught, hard, beautiful ass out to dry." She giggled then hugged Henry.

I really adored Susan.

In Susan's backyard, we set up targets. Some were far away and some were closer. The ones that excited me the most were the ones on ropes and pulleys that Mr. Matthews fashioned with his engineering skills. Mr. Matthews was a brilliant man, and I admired is greatness.

"Susan, sweetheart," Mr. Matthews called, "do be a dear and win us money," Mr. Matthews winked.

"Father," Theo called, "I'll give you the five hundred dollars I'm going to win from Maybel!"

"Yes, of course son, but you know Susan is my sweet, little, kitten, and I really feel that I must

412 ~ E. D. JUMPER

encourage her, because soon enough, she will be the smartest woman in a roomful of condescending men, and I want her to know her daddy is her biggest adorer.

Susan beamed with happiness.

I smiled too. "Don't worry, Mr. Matthews, Susan and I will win," I winked at Susan.

Susan and I did well shooting the still targets, but Theo and Henry did better. For the next round, Mr. and Mrs. Matthews stood on opposite sides of the broad line of trees in their back-yard and began pulling the rope through the pulleys and the targets began moving quickly. Moving targets were worth more points and Susan and I were much better than Theo and Henry. Susan and I won five-hundred dollars!

Theo smiled when he gave Susan two-hundred and fifty dollars. Susan then hugged Theo tightly, giggling and bouncing up and down happily.

Henry smiled sweetly at me as I took his money. I promptly gave it to Susan. "Go buy Theo an ice cream cone," I winked at her. "Henry is going to buy mine," I smiled at Henry.

"That I will, Maybel, you won fair and square. I'll take you home now. I have an order to pick up from your father and deliver across town."

Henry took me home. He opened my front gate for me and held my waist. "Would you like to claim your prize?" he asked.

"Yes," I smiled.

Henry leaned down and kissed me with the most gentleness and gracefulness I had ever felt. I wanted so much more than his kiss. Henry made me feel like I was no longer inside my body. When he slowly pulled back, he had to steady me because I felt like my soul had not yet returned to my body.

"That was amazing, sweetheart," Henry whispered.

I nodded because I could not speak.

"If I had won, I was going to take you to have dinner with my grandfather for our first date. I wanted to show you off on my arm, like a prize I had won, like the way a child paints the rainbow for their parents, and their parents hang it on the wall. You're my rainbow, Maybel. You make me brighter. You won, though, so I had the honor of kissing you. I think I won though, no matter who was the better shot with a bow and arrow."

Henry walked me to my front door and opened it for me. "Good evening, Maybel. I love you."

"I love you too, Henry."

"Maybel, would you like to go on a date?" Henry asked me suddenly.

"Yes, I would love to," I smiled. I tried not to answer too eagerly but I failed. I practically shouted, and then I jumped up and down on my tippy toes smiling big.

Henry chuckled, "You really do make me feel so handsome." He continued smiling at me with such sweetness in his eyes and in his smile.

"Maybel, I want to go about this the honest way. I want to ask your father's permission, too."

My smile faded and was replaced with apprehension. "He probably won't let me. I'm his baby." My shoulders dropped.

Henry took my hand and we walked around the house to daddy's workshop. Henry knocked on the door. I went ahead and opened it.

Daddy put down his measuring tape and came to us. He must have sensed something serious was about to unfold.

"Sir, may I take Maybel on a date?" Henry asked daddy. I was surprised Henry was so formal.

Daddy looked at me then back to Henry. He watched Henry for a minute but it felt like an hour because daddy pierced Henry's soul with his unwavering stare. "Yes," daddy said.

"Really?" My eyes sprung open wide.

"Yes," daddy repeated.

I was surprised and happy. I had a whole argument planned in my head about how Catherine was younger than me when she started dating Bernard. I was a little disappointed because I was all fired up with a solid argument that I now didn't need.

"Thank you, daddy!" I hugged him.

Henry reached out his hand to daddy. "I promise to have her home early and I will make sure Maybel is safe and comfortable."

Daddy shook Henry's hand. "I know," daddy said.

"Maybel, would you like to have dinner with me Friday evening?" Henry politely asked me.

"Yes!" I leaped at Henry and hugged him.

"Daddy! This is my first date!" I hurled myself into daddy's chest and hugged him tightly.

Daddy didn't say anything else. He kept composed, but I felt his sadness as he held me and it was a very, great weight of sadness, and dread, because I was his little girl.

Friday came and my stomach was a ball of butterflies, lightning, and bees bouncing off the walls of my insides and making my heart beat strong in my fingers and toes.

Catherine walked past my room, and then suddenly walked backward back to my doorframe. "Why are you getting dressed up?"

"I have a date!" I wheezed. My breath was fading in and out. I was so excited.

"With whom?" Catherine asked. She looked shocked and disbelieving. "Does daddy know?" she asked me, her eyes narrowing.

"Yes!" I exclaimed.

"And daddy said you could go on a date?"

"Yes!" I said.

"Who is your suitor, Maybel?" Catherine looked very intrigued now.

"Henry!" I squealed. My voice could barely carry itself out of my mouth because my lungs clamped shut suddenly. I closed my eyes and tried to relax. I attempted a deep breath.

When I opened my eyes, Catherine was not in my doorway and I heard footsteps quickly descending the stairs.

I heard Catherine scream, "Bernard! You'll never guess what!"

I sighed. I had not known Bernard was here. My hand tightened around my sharp, metal letter opener. I imagined Bernard intervening and wondered if I should injure or fatally slice him.

In an instant there were multiple footsteps barreling up the stairs. Bernard saw me sitting at my dressing table in a beautiful, pale, rose-colored dress and my hair pinned and curled as best I could without having asked for Catherine's help.

Bernard simply stared at me.

I held up my hand that held my letter opener. "I will cut you if you attempt to intervene, Bernard." I glared at him. My upper lip, on my left side, involuntarily twitched.

Bernard continued staring at me. And then he left. I heard his footsteps descend slowly with loud clomps, as though his weight just fell and made loud, thudding noises that echoed up the stairwell.

I heard a knock at our front door and I took a deep breath. I was scared and thrilled with happiness at the same time. My legs were weak but I forced myself to step carefully downstairs and maintain at least a little decorum.

I hadn't had Catherine style my hair or makeup and I knew she would have dressed me up better. I wanted to do this on my own though, and if Henry didn't like my hair or makeup, he might not ask me for a second date, but at least I'd have gone on my first date with the most handsome man in the world.

Henry stood at my front door. Mommy stood beside Henry and watched me enter the room. Mommy smiled and her eyes became watery. Henry held a dozen red roses for me, and mommy held a box of chocolates Henry had given her. Henry wore a dark blue suit, shiny gold cufflinks, a crisp, white, button-down shirt, and shined, black shoes. His tie was a dark red, as was the hand-kerchief in his breast pocket. I had never, in my life, envisioned Henry could look better than he always looked, but tonight, he exceeded even my own vast, imagination. I could not believe what I beheld.

I slowly walked toward Henry. Mommy began tearing up and held a cloth to her eyes and dabbed. Henry never ceased his penetrating gaze at me. I felt truly special.

Henry took a step forward and held out his hand. I took it, and he kissed my hand but his eyes never once wavered from my eyes.

"You look stunning," Henry said to me. His eyes were gentle and loving. He looked like I felt: twelve-years old, scared, awkward, and extremely excited. Henry exuded happiness, like a little boy, an innocent, little boy on his first date. I felt like a little girl and I could not take my eyes off Henry. I didn't care if we kissed after our first date because something about Henry's soul had touched me more deeply than any kiss could do justice.

Daddy stood, leaning against the doorframe of his office. His arms were crossed and he looked sullen. He looked like the energy had left his body the second he told Henry I could go on my first date.

Daddy walked toward me. He kissed my cheek. "You look beautiful, baby," he managed to say in a soft, yet cracked voice.

Henry led me outside and to his automobile. He opened my door and held my hand as I entered. Henry was attentive and loving. I had never met anyone so sensitive to another's needs.

"Where would you like to eat, sweetheart?" Henry asked me after he settled into the driver's seat.

"I don't really care where we eat. Henry," my voice was fast and breathy, "I'm so excited! This is my first date!" I said, smiling and giggling.

Henry looked over at me and he smiled so kindly. "This is my first date, too."

I rested my head on his shoulder as he drove. "You can't tell, Maybel, but I'm so nervous I'm shaking inside. I really want our first date to be perfect. I really like you."

"I really like you, too," I squeezed his hand.

When we entered the city, there were people, carriages, and automobiles. My eyes were wide with excitement. "Henry! Look at everything!"

Henry smiled at me.

"We can go anywhere and I'll be so happy!" I squealed with delight.

I wondered if Catherine felt this excited when she went on her first date with Bernard. I wondered how many first times they'd had together over the years. I had never thought about that before, but now I realized they must have experienced so many first times together.

I told my brain to shut up. I screamed inside my head telling myself to stop thinking. I always had music and memories playing behind my eyes, even when I begged my brain to stop.

Henry parked his automobile. "Maybel, there is a restaurant I'd like to show you."

"May I kiss you?" The words tumbled from my lips.

"Always, sweetheart," Henry smiled.

I leaned over and lightly pressed my lips onto his. I pulled back. "I don't really have much experience kissing," I said, "and I'm nervous."

Henry kissed me. "Don't be nervous, honey. I really like you," he whispered. "You have no idea how much I like you, and how nervous I am right now."

The restaurant looked ordinary from the street but the inside looked like you needed a membership to attend such a fancy restaurant. The walls were dark red and were peppered with sconces that lit private tables separated by dark walnut alcoves. The waitstaff wore pressed, black pants and white button-up shirts with black ties. Clean white towels draped their forearms. A pianist played slow, melodic music on a small stage on the far side of the restaurant. The bar was adorned with shiny brass accents and crystal shelves stocked with fancy-looking bottles of alcohol. A large, embossed mirror hung behind the bartender.

"Mr. Fox!" A man suddenly stood next to Henry. "We were not expecting you! I apologize! How may we help you tonight?"

The man wore a black dress coat and looked like either the owner or the man who was in charge. He scurried around the restaurant alerting the staff of Henry's presence and in no time, we were seated with drinks and staff members eager to please us.

We ate steak and vegetables. It tasted like the cow had been massaged every day before slaughter. The food and dessert were exquisite. After dinner, we walked hand-in-hand to the town square and watched a band play.

"Would you like to dance?" he asked me.

"Yes!" I practically screamed.

Henry held me close to his body. I felt my stomach get tingly like it did before I had to speak in front of other boys and girls at school when we said aloud our book reports.

"May I kiss you again?" Henry asked.

"Yes," I smiled. I felt nervous.

Henry kissed me softly. I felt like I melted into his embrace. No one had ever kissed me out in public. Henry was not embarrassed of me, and we did not have to hide from anyone our attraction.

I felt free. I never knew I was not free until Henry loved me in front of everyone and didn't hide me away. I liked being free. "Henry, thank you," I said.

"No, thank you, Maybel, for the best first date I could have ever imagined." Henry kissed me so gently and so sweetly that I could see our children's faces behind my eyelids as he pressed his lips onto mine.

Henry brought me home early, as promised. He walked me to my front door. "Maybel," he whispered, "May I have a goodnight kiss?"

"Yes." I became all tingly in my tummy again as Henry kissed my lips.

Henry suddenly looked nervous, which was not a look he ever had. "Would you do me the honor of accompanying me on a second date?" he asked.

"Yes," I said. My voice was but a whisper.

"I'm so scared I'll do or say something too forward, Maybel. I fear I do not know how to be a good man. I've never been with a good woman."

"You're perfect, Henry," I whispered.

Henry kissed me and we opened our mouths just a little and his tongue touched mine. I felt myself leave my body for an instant and meld with Henry's soul just above where we stood. It was only for an instant, but what I felt was real.

Henry said goodnight and I went inside my front door. "Maybel, come sit," mommy patted the cushion of the sofa next to her. "How was your first date?" mommy asked. She was positively brimming with excitement.

"It was very nice," I said.

"I remember my first date." Mommy was as giddy as a schoolgirl. "He lived down the road from me. Your Aunt Mary was so jealous!" mommy gloated.

Later that night, I snuck into mommy's and daddy's bedroom where daddy laid in bed reading. "Daddy, why did you let me go on a date with Henry?" I sat down on his bed next to him.

"Henry is a good person. He has been taking steps to be a better man. He is not the tomcat he once was, and I think he truly loves you. I am certain you are safe with Henry. I know he would never hurt you, nor would he let anyone else hurt you. I felt safe in here," daddy patted his chest, "letting you go with him."

"Henry was a gentleman, daddy." I kissed daddy's cheek. "Goodnight, daddy. I love you."

"I love you too, sweetheart."

Henry soon had to leave for a month to San Francisco on business. Mr. Charleston wanted him to help establish a foothold on the west coast. I was very sad to see him leave. He kissed me goodbye and told me he would be home as soon as he could. I felt crushed inside. I didn't want Henry to leave me. I didn't understand why Henry had to go now, for a month, when Mr. Charleston had dozens of other qualified businessmen ready and willing to travel for long lengths of time.

"Daddy," I began, as I sat in his workshop, "don't be friends with the Charleston's anymore. I'm mad. They sent Henry away."

"I know, baby. Henry is Mr. Charleston's most-trusted advisor. He's a hard worker and Mr. Charleston can trust him because they are family. Henry did not have to accept the position, but he did, and I'm glad. I'm selfish, Maybel. I know you two liked each other. I get my baby back a little while longer now. I'm sorry I'm selfish baby, but I am."

Spring had sprung. Little buds dotted the trees. Susan's health had improved and we set about inventing new games, stories, and painting. Though I was not a great painter, I enjoyed art. Susan was an unbelievably talented painter and poet. She taught me oil painting and I found it to be an enjoyable pastime, although I could not draw people, birds, cats, bowls of fruit, or flowers.

Susan said my drawing of the ocean was acceptable. It was a rectangular canvas painted blue. I'm certain she was being polite.

"Maybel, mother and father want me to spend the summer break from school in Connecticut with Theo."

"Oh," I paused. "You'll be gone all summer? Or maybe just two or three weeks?"

"I'll be gone all summer. I'm sorry Maybel, but Catherine will be home, as well as Bernard."

"Yes," I said sourly.

"You're unhappy, aren't you?" she asked me.

"A little," I answered dryly. Henry was gone, and now Susan was leaving.

"Would you like to come with me?" She smiled slyly. "Mommy, daddy, and Theo said it would be alright," she smiled wider.

I thought about a summer away from mommy, daddy, and Catherine. "I'll miss my family," I said.

And then, I thought about Bernard. "It might be nice to see the east coast," I said.

Susan smiled big. Her eyes widened. "Please?" she clasped her hands, looking so sweet and cute.

"I've never been away from mommy or daddy for more than maybe several days," I told Susan. "Have you been away from your parents?"

"No, but my brother thinks the air might be good for my health. And he has a housekeeper who agreed to help take care of me."

"I might like to go Susan, but I'm not sure I want to stay the entire summer away from mommy. I'll speak to mommy and daddy tonight."

I thought about new scenery. I considered my familiar home life against a new backdrop.

"Susan, what is like there?"

"It's grand, Maybel! We can swim in the ocean whenever we want!"

"The ocean? I've never been!" The idea of spending the summer at the ocean was quite tempting. I would miss Catherine terribly though, and Bernard. I loved Bernard, he'd been such a big part of my life for years now, but I was attracted to him. I loved Catherine more than I wanted to kiss Bernard, so perhaps putting space between us for an entire summer would be good for all of us. And I loved Henry, but so did half the town, and I was not certain of his ability to remain faithful. Spending the summer away from all the questions and uncertainties swirling in my mind was beginning to sound better and better.

"I have to think a little more about it, Susan, but it's quite tempting!"

That evening, I broached the subject with mommy and daddy. "Catherine will be sad, dear," mommy said.

"She spends a lot of time with Bernard and her school friends, mommy. Last summer, I was quite lost and sad, I'll admit."

Mommy looked as though she agreed. Catherine had always been social. "Is this what you want, Maybel?"

"I don't know, mommy, but I do know that I do not want to spend another summer lonely and sad. I love Catherine, but she has a lot of social engagements that do not include me, and I'm tired of being the tag-along. And Henry left." I was hurt and angry that Henry left, and my wounds were raw.

I went to the Charleston's mansion to collect all my stories I had ever written and forgotten there.

The library was a peaceful retreat with bookcases from ceiling to floor built into the walls and several ornate benches built into the walls as well. The wood was a dark and ripened walnut. A large, circular, walnut table was in the center of the library. It always smelled like aged wood and dusty book pages in here, but I liked this room a lot. I sneezed frequently, but aside from that, it was quite peaceful.

I looked on the large round table, the benches, and even found a story tucked into the bookshelf from when I was eleven!

Maybel?" Bernard found me. "I didn't know you were here. Vincent was in the kitchen when I went for a snack and he told me you were in our library.

I didn't acknowledge Bernard. I wanted to find my stories, and I had apparently written massive amounts of stories and stuck them in the most random places over the years.

"Maybel, I've been meaning to come talk to you. Over the years, Henry has become an older brother to me and has pointed out to me that I haven't treated you well. I don't have any brothers or sisters to point out my faults the way brothers and sisters so bluntly do. Henry has been giving me advice. He's been having me look at various situations from your perspective, and I'm really sorry about a lot of things I did and said."

I continued crouching under the desk in the corner, looking underneath the table, and inside the drawers, because apparently, eleven-year-old me thought hiding stories in unexpected places was hilarious. One of my letters was folded and wedged between two drawers and had, "Oh, you found me!" scribbled on the front. I imagined my younger self had laughed when tucking this story away into such an odd hiding spot.

Bernard continued rambling. "I didn't realize how poorly I came across until Henry explained my actions and my words to me. I was, at times, quite rude to you without realizing just how obnoxious I was acting."

Bernard watched me as though he expected me to congratulate him on such realizations. His sudden epiphany came too late to my ears. "You can explain yourself using words to distance yourself from your actions, but actions speak louder than words. You want both Catherine and me to kiss and hold. Catherine is the only one you aren't embarrassed to kiss in public."

"I'm sorry, Maybel. I am not embarrassed of you. I should have been more reserved with my affection toward you, but I am not embarrassed of you." Bernard looked sad but I didn't care.

"People always say they are sorry for their behavior, but they never change their behavior.

I went around the shelves and chairs and end tables then got on my tip toes to look for papers on the fireplace mantle.

I now had amassed a tall stack of stories I had written here during parties when I didn't want to be around boring small talk, and whenever Bernard locked me out of his bedroom when he wanted to kiss Catherine and I was too scared to walk home alone.

Bernard followed me around the library as I stood up on my toes, and bent low, and got on my knees searching. He continued speaking to me, apparently thinking I still cared about his apologies. "I didn't realize I was so mean to you. I didn't realize how much pain you were in. I've been reading some of your stories you left behind years ago, and I know I hurt you with my teasing remarks, and you were lonely because Catherine and I snuck away from you. Henry has been talking to me about you. I'm trying to be better, Maybel."

I ignored Bernard's empty apologies. "I think I've gotten all my stories. If you find more, please give them to Catherine to give to me," I said.

"Are you finally writing a book of short stories?" Bernard asked.

"No, I just want to get all my things out of your house in case I never come see you again."

"Always with the theatrics," Bernard sighed. "I'm sorry, Maybel. And I'll see you here in a couple days when we go fishing."

"Why hasn't Henry returned?" I tried hard to hide my sadness from Bernard.

"He's still in San Francisco on business for father," Bernard explained.

I stepped close to Bernard and looked up at him. I breathed deeply and sank into that feeling when you feel yourself melding with the energy another person emits. I wanted to see every expression in his eyes and lips as I asked my next question. "Did you or your father send Henry away because we started dating?"

"No," Bernard answered.

I scanned his face. I tried to feel his feelings.

"Henry is a good businessman. He'll be staying longer than expected, but he will return as soon as possible."

I continued boring holes in Bernard's eyes. "As you said, regarding Weston, you have the money to make the men who like me go away." I stared into his eyes, watching for any tell.

Bernard stared back at me, his expression entirely blank. "Weston made the wrong choice."

I kept staring at Bernard. I knew he would fold his hand before I would fold mine.

"Bernard, tell me the truth, did you or your father ask Henry to leave on business so he would not be here to take me on dates?"

"No," Bernard returned my steely stare.

Usually I could decipher anyone, but there was an invisible wall between me and Bernard now, and I felt I was not able to tell if he was lying or being truthful, and that both angered and confused me.

Bernard left the library and I carried my papers home. I went to sit under the big oak tree in our yard. I brought paper and pencils, a glass of lemonade, and crackers. My squirrel army eyed me from high atop the trees. "I won't be here for a while," I told them, "but mommy will feed you so you'll be ok," I yelled up to them.

"Maybel?" Bernard called from the back porch. "Who are you talking to?"

"Squirrels," I said.

"Of course," he said, "What else would you be doing?"

420 ~ E. D. JUMPER

"Why are you here? Did you follow me home?" I asked Bernard.

"Catherine was supposed to come get me for a walk, but she instead went to the fabric store with your mother, and your mother told me I could come here and have cookies she just baked."

"We have freshly-baked cookies?" I looked down at the crackers in my hands then threw them all as far as I could. My legion of squirrels shook the tree branches and leaves as they delved downward, their little paws pattering along the bark.

Bernard and I took several cookies and we went to the largest oak tree beyond our apple orchard. "I didn't make Henry leave," he said.

I could not get a read off Bernard so I remained quiet.

"I didn't, Maybel," Bernard said.

I bit into a cookie while staring icily at Bernard.

"Will you tell me a story?" Bernard coaxed. "I enjoy your stories and the way you tell them. What were you writing when I found you talking to your attack squirrels?"

I let out a giggle when Bernard called them my attack squirrels, then pursed my lips, not wanting to let Bernard know he cracked my icy facade.

"Please?" Bernard smiled.

"They're just stories about pirate ghosts and angry kings and queens."

"Maybel?" Bernard offered me another cookie.

"What?" I giggled and swiped the cookie away before he could pull it back and eat it himself.

"I am sorry Henry left. I didn't make him leave. I don't want you to be sad or angry at me, or at Henry."

"It's easier for me to believe you sent Henry away than to believe he left me of his own accord."

"I'm sorry, Maybel," Bernard reached for my hand. "I'll never leave you."

I looked off to the side for a second then back to Bernard. "Do you want to hear my story about the boy who loved a fairy?"

"Always."

"The boy's name was Alastair and he encountered two fairy sisters in the woods behind his house. The fairies lived amongst the toadstools and puddles. The two fairy sisters lived inside a rotting log. The boy fell in love with one sister and they spent their days amongst the cattails by the pond's edge. The fairy king and queen ordered their knights to kill the boy because they disapproved of fairies marrying non-magical creatures. The fairy's sister dove into the pond near the cattails and returned to the surface a mighty, colorful fish who instructed her sister and the boy to ride on her back to safety and they did. She carried them to the other side of the pond. The boy and fairy girl ran from the pond and away from the fish and army of fairy knights. The king and queen were enraged and threw the fish to the bank where she gasped for air until her lungs dried out and her tail ceased flopping and she died.

Bernard looked troubled. "Maybel, might you have any kind and happy stories in your big, giant imagination?"

"Yes."

"Please tell me a happy story," he asked.

"Well, ok, but they're a lot more boring," I sighed.

"Make it interesting. I challenge you. And I know you'll succeed," he smiled. He laid down on the grass under the spring blossoms.

I watched Bernard beside me. I liked being next to him even though sometimes I wanted to hurt him the way I felt I'd been hurt by him.

I sighed. I laid down beside Bernard. When he laid with me for hours and talked to me and played with me, I became confused. I rested my head on Bernard's arm and tried to scour my imagination for a story that would make him love and hate and ultimately confuse him, because that's how I felt.

"A boy named Bradley had a puppy named Mary," I began. "They grew up together and Bradley adored Mary. Mary slept at his feet and followed Bradley around. Mary wagged her tail when she saw Bradley return home from school and he ran to greet her and kissed her and told Mary how much he loved her. When Bradley began having interests in girls, he spent less time with Mary. Mary became sad and confused and wagged her tail less and less until she no longer wagged at all. Mary sometimes acted out in anger because of her confusion. She peed on Bradley's carpet and chewed his shoes. Bradley tied Mary to a dog house in his back yard, further isolating her and causing her more confusion. Bradley often forgot to feed Mary, so Mary began slipping away until one day, Bradley left for school and Mary slowly drifted off to sleep and stopped breathing. Little Timothy from down the street untied Mary and kissed her and brought her to his house. Mary began feeling again and she felt happy. Mary thanked Timothy by staying with him and loving him, and Timothy bestowed love on Mary, even when he began dating and then married. Bradley watched everything unfold through the years and was jealous that Mary had left him, in fact everyone left him, and he died alone and sad."

"That's the saddest story you've ever told!" Bernard said.

"Why? Mary found true love."

"Bradley was so mean to that poor dog he'd had since she was a puppy! He deserves to be sad and lonely the rest of his life!"

"Maybe you are right, Bernard. I choose to be happy for Mary for escaping Bradley and finding love. I think it's a happy story."

Bernard stood up. "I had better see if Catherine is ready for our stroll. Then we're supposed to go to a get-together at her friend's house."

I followed Bernard inside. Catherine was wearing a blue dress and looked as though she was ready to leave. She sat in our family room with Edith and Rebecca.

"Hello, Maybel, we were just talking about you. Do you remember when you used to follow Bernard around while I was at piano practice?" Catherine laughed.

"Yes," I said as I passed by them.

"Maybel, wait, stay and chat," Catherine smiled at me.

Bernard sat down on the sofa beside Catherine. Catherine took his hand in hers. It pained me to see that because I was very confused about the way Bernard treated me and felt extremely guilty that I enjoyed spending time with him.

"Bernard, I was just telling Edith and Rebecca how Maybel used to follow you around like a little puppy. Do you remember that, and how you used to grumble when she kept interrupting us when we kissed?"

I had been Bernard's dumb, little puppy for too long. I turned quickly and went into daddy's office.

"I've decided to go to Connecticut," I told daddy and mommy. They sat next to each other over daddy's bookkeeping.

"Are you alright, sweetheart?" Daddy asked.

"Yes," I answered. "I think this will be good for me, to get away and see new things and meet new people."

"Very well," mommy said. Mommy looked sad.

I left daddy's office, but didn't leave his door. I wanted to hear them talking about me. Catherine told me to wait and listen at the door once you leave to hear the truth.

"I think she's ready to leave our nest, honey," mommy said.

"I want just a few more years with my baby," daddy said softly.

"It will never be enough, honey. It's the same when someone dies. We never get enough time with those we love."

"I know," daddy said quietly.

I felt sad. I saw Catherine out of the corner of my eye. She was still sitting next to Edith and Rebecca and giggling. Bernard saw me. I turned around the corner pretending I wasn't paying them any attention and went upstairs to my bedroom.

Susan and I took a train to Connecticut. I mostly watched out the window the entire trip because the houses, train stations, and varying terrains fascinated me immensely. There were trees, hills, ponds, and when we passed by towns, I loved to see what the women wore. Men almost always wore the same thing: dark pants, white, button-up shirts, hats, suspenders, and boots. Men were boring in their attire. The ladies and girls all wore an array of colors and styles of dresses that ran the gamut from poor to wealthy. I liked the middle-class dresses the best. They weren't too simple, and they weren't heavy and hot like the rich women wore. The rich women looked miserable in their thick, layered clothes, and tall, feathery hats. The poor women looked the happiest in thin cloth that let their arms and legs feel the summer breeze, but I imagined they were too cold in the winters.

When we arrived at the train station in Connecticut, Theo met us. He had an automobile because he was a brilliant scientist and was paid accordingly.

"Theo!" Susan yelled excitedly, and ran to him. He picked her up and kissed her cheek.

"Susan, you look healthy!" Theo smiled, and kissed her other cheek. "You have no idea how happy I am to see you looking so well!"

"Maybel," Theo looked at me, "I'm pleased you could accompany Susan. You look well."

"If I do look well, it's because we drank wine on the way here," I smiled. "I find wine gives my cheeks a healthy glow."

"What?" Theo furrowed his brow.

"Just kidding, we drank water. You look scary when you're mad," I laughed.

Susan laughed too. "Theo, Maybel has the best sense of humor!"

"Yes," Theo unfurrowed his brows and said lowly, "Great sense of humor."

"Lighten up, big stepbrother," I smiled, "This will be a lot more fun if you caught a sense of humor. It will be long and miserable if you remain dull."

Theo held Susan's hand. "Let's go home, sweetheart." He turned to me, "You too, Maybel. My home is your home. Please don't make this long and miserable."

"Well, that's up to you," I giggled and so did Susan.

Theo spent most of his time at work during the week working long hours. His housekeeper, Mrs. Murphy, made sure we had food. She generally didn't talk much except when reading the newspaper. Occasionally Susan and I giggled when she broke her silence by yelling her disapproval of something written in the editorial column, or shouting, "Well it's about time!" when she agreed with its contents. Her thick, Irish, brogue accent made everything she said interesting.

Susan and I spent most days cooling off at the beach. We made sandcastles every day, challenging ourselves to create bigger and better castles before high tide. We'd become quite the local celebrities with our ever-expanding and intricately-designed sandcastles. People regularly sought us out just to see what we'd built that day.

At last, Friday arrived, and I was ready for a change of pace. "Theo, can we go dancing, or to a diner, or a play, or somewhere outside the house?" I asked excitedly.

"Yes, Maybel, I need a shower first, and then we can celebrate my finishing a long week inside a boring laboratory." Theo went to his bathroom and Susan and I anxiously awaited our evening entertainment.

"Where do you think we'll go?" I asked Susan.

"I hope somewhere with fish. The fish here are fresh and tasty," she replied.

"I thought you hated fish?" I asked, surprised.

"Oh, I do," she said, "I'm working on my sarcasm. Your sarcasm is much more honed, Maybel, but I'm getting better, don't you think?"

"No, your timing is terrible," I said.

"Really?" She looked like I had just kicked her.

"No Susan, did you see what I did with my face and how flat my voice was? It's called deadpan delivery." We both laughed. I appreciated Susan's humor, which rivaled my own sort of twisted humor.

"Alright, ladies." Theo walked into the family room wearing a tailored suit. He looked dashing and actually took my breath away for just an instant.

"Wow, Theo, you look terrible." Susan said flatly.

"What?" Theo looked surprised by her candidness.

"It's called deadpan delivery, Theo. Maybel taught me."

"You're a bad influence and absolutely the worst big sister ever, Maybel." he said.

I was truly hurt by his words.

"Well, well, looks like the mistress of sarcasm has been upheaved by her students," Theo winked and gently kissed my cheek.

"I'm sorry, Maybel, I think I was accidentally a little too good at playing deadpan delivery. You're a great big sister to Susan."

"Yes, Maybel, you are!" Susan beamed.

I sighed, relieved that he had only been joking, but then became rather annoyed that I'd fallen for his joke.

"Ladies, shall we?" He held Susan's hand and walked toward the door.

"Where are we going, Theo?" Susan asked excitedly.

"It's a secret, but I trust you have packed guns, knives, and a compass, yes?"

We stared at Theo. "No," Susan said meekly.

"See, Maybel, I most certainly do have a sense of humor," he laughed loudly.

Susan and I enjoyed the beach immensely. I had never seen the beach before coming to Connecticut. Susan showed me rock pools with crabs and starfish. I was impressed by the collection of fish and shells within the rock pools, and even saw jellyfish tentacles once. We spent our days running through sand and our nights bathing it out of our cracks and crevices and scalps.

One night, not long after arriving, I went to Theo's room to ask where he kept his towels because the salty night air had made my skin sweaty and itchy.

He was sitting on the edge of his bed holding a picture and a small wooden box was at his feet. He looked up when I entered. Tears streamed down his cheeks. "Maybel, go away!"

I was shocked to see him look so uncomposed. His usual stern and boring scientific mannerisms were replaced with human emotion.

I stood stunned.

"Please just go away, Maybel!"

I took a step back, but his sobs were gut wrenching, so I went to him instead.

I sat beside him and hugged him tightly. I thought he would yell at me again to leave, but instead he let me hug him.

Without a word, I held him for a long time.

"This was my fiancé." His voice was cracked and hoarse from sadness. "I couldn't save her. And I haven't visited her grave. It hurts too much," he said in between gasps of cries.

"I'm sorry, Theo. I didn't know. I thought you said you lost her to another."

"I did. I lost her to herself." His eyes were teary.

"She killed herself, Maybel. I didn't know she was sick. She left me this note."

He handed me a piece of folded paper, warped with tear stains that had been shed and dried and been cried upon in many cycles. The note read: "It's not your fault. You didn't know. Nobody knows. I'm just so tired of pretending to be well. If I had a wound, you would have given me a tourniquet, but what's wrong with me, you can't see."

Theo buried his head in his hands and cried.

"I'm so sorry, Theo." I put my hand gently on his back while he sobbed.

"Maybel, I didn't know. I didn't know."

I hugged him and rubbed his back.

"She always seemed so happy. And then she gave away some personal things to friends and family and it never occurred to me until later that she was making it easier for me, so that I wouldn't have to sort through her things afterward."

"I'm so sorry, Theo." I began crying with him. "I can't imagine your pain."

"I hope you never have to," he cried.

"I had fun with you today, Maybel, and that made me feel so utterly guilty. I don't know how to make my pain go away, and when it did briefly today, I couldn't handle the intense guilt I felt for forgetting her, even for a short time, while I enjoyed myself with you and Susan."

I didn't know what to say, so I remembered what mommy said, that your biggest present is your presence, just sitting there with someone, so that's what I did. I held Theo while he cried and rubbed his back while he told me things that also made me cry.

Theo laid down on his back in bed and stared at the ceiling, but behind his eyes I could tell there were painful memories playing over and over.

"Why did she do it, Maybel?" he whispered, "Why?"

He continued whispering and staring up as though talking to himself. "She always smiled. She always laughed. She had many friends."

I laid beside him and rested my head on his shoulder. "My sister Catherine smiles all the time too," I whispered back, "but she cries in the garden at night sometimes. She doesn't know I know about that."

"Watch her closely, Maybel. You will never know what is going on behind the smiles."

"Catherine is the happiest person I've ever met."

"So was Victoria."

The next day I awoke, still laying on Theo's shoulder. I yawned and stretched.

"Maybel," he began.

"Oh, you're awake too," I said, surprised.

"I've been awake a little while now, but you were sleeping so peacefully I didn't want to wake you. And also," he paused, "it was nice to have someone to hold again."

I sat up on my arm and looked down at him.

"It's the least I could do since you are kind enough to make me breakfast."

"I wasn't about to make you.... Oh," he smiled, "Yes, I'll be happy to make you breakfast, Maybel."

I started to get out of bed when he caught me with his arm.

"Maybel?"

"Yes?"

He pulled me back into his arms and hugged me tightly. "Thank you Maybel," he kissed my forehead.

"You're welcome, Theodore," I smiled.

"Theo is fine," he smiled.

"Can I have pancakes now?" I asked.

He gave a small chuckle, "Back to thoughts of eating, I see."

I hugged Theo again. "I'm truly sorry, Theo," I began tentatively, "You can talk to me anytime. It will help you feel better."

"I've been using boxing at the gym as a means of escape, but I suppose talking could be beneficial too," he winked.

"Come Maybel," he hugged me, "Let's make pancakes."

"Theo?"

"Yes, Maybel, I have maple syrup."

"Thank you, but I wanted to ask you if we can go to the beach again today?"

"I suppose so. It's Sunday and I don't have anything important today at work. Sure, we can go to the beach."

We went to Theo's kitchen. He stirred the pancake batter.

"I had never been to the beach before you took me," I said. "Do you go often?"

"No," he looked down as he flipped my pancake. "I used to go often, but, after Victoria, well, I've not had the desire."

"Does the beach make you sad now?" I asked.

"Yes, it does Maybel." He poured more batter into the hot skillet.

"We can go somewhere else," I suggested.

"No, I rather enjoy the beach with you and Susan. It's good to be out again."

He looked sad, I thought. I didn't believe his words any more than I suspected he believed them.

"What else is there to do other than the beach?" I asked.

"Oh, there're lots of things to do. The shops are nice. There are two opera houses. I used to take Victoria to dance from time to time. She was a beautiful dancer."

"Will you take Susan and me dancing?"

He paused, "I can, yes." He looked sad though.

"We can stay home and read, too, Theo. I liked that story you read to us last night."

"No, no, Maybel, it will be good for me to get out." He placed my pancakes on a plate in front of me.

"I'll go wake Susan. She loves pancakes too," he left down the hallway toward Susan's room.

Susan and I dressed in our nicest dresses and Theo took us into the small town. It was different from home because there were more people and they were all well-dressed. There weren't many farms or fields, which I missed.

"Theo! Look!" Susan yelled excitedly.

There were people performing on the street corner. A man was juggling and another man walked on very tall sticks of wood. "Those are stilts, Susan," said Theo.

Susan laughed and walked closer for a better look. "How do you not fall, mister?"

He smiled down at Susan. "It's easy, Little Miss, I just tell myself I won't fall," he winked.

Theo handed the performer a coin and we continued down the street.

"Look at these dresses!" I pointed to the shop windows. "Mommy makes better dresses and for less money."

"Yes, she does, Maybel," Theo said. "Your mother could really make quite a lot of money here in Connecticut with her skills."

We continued around the block. Men and women strolled arm in arm with parasols. Everyone seemed so proper. I felt insecure. Catherine would fit in perfectly here though, I mused.

"Ladies, it's quite hot, would you like ice cream?"

"Yes!" We both screamed.

"Alright," he laughed, "Let's cool off with a cold treat."

After our cold snack, we wandered back to Theo's house, taking in all the beautiful and clearly very wealthy people along the way. Several people stopped to chat with Theo and their eyes curiously roved from me to Susan inquisitively.

"You are quite popular, Theo," I said.

"No, not really, I very rarely get out these days."

"Don't you enjoy getting out Theo?" asked Susan? "I've had fun getting out today."

"Yes, I used to enjoy it, but I work a lot these days." His voice trailed off and I suspected he was thinking of better times spent with Victoria. I supposed if Catherine or Bernard died, I would spend a lot of time escaping the pain, too.

"Shall we have a quick lunch and then go dancing in the town square?" Theo asked when we arrived home.

"Yes!" Susan and I shouted excitedly.

"On Sunday afternoons, many townspeople gather there to listen to bands play and dance together. Really, they just want to show off their beautiful, expensive clothing," he winked.

"Theo, this is my nicest dress," I became insecure again. "I don't have any more."

"You'll both be more beautiful than anyone else there," he tousled my hair and then Susan's hair.

After lunch, we went to the town square. A band played delightful and fun music. Theo led Susan to the dance area and I stood and watched. Theo was actually a great dancer and Susan was much more graceful than me.

"Miss, care to dance?" A boy my age stood beside me with his hand out. He was blonde and had a couple freckles dotting his cheeks.

"Yes," I replied. He led me to the dance area near Theo and Susan. He was a decent dancer, but not as good as Theo, and certainly not as good as Bernard.

He spun me around and in mid-spin, I saw Theo's look of disapproval, or jealousy, I wasn't sure.

"What is your name, miss?" The boy asked me.

"Maybel."

"That's a beautiful name," he smiled.

"What is your name?" I asked.

"Andrew," he replied.

The band finished their song and I thanked Andrew for the dance.

I walked over to Susan and Theo, who had retired to the shade of a tree when the band stopped.

"Who was that, Maybel?" Susan teased.

"He said his name was Andrew," I smiled and blushed.

Theo didn't seem too happy. "Maybel, I don't want any trouble from these boys. It might be best if you declined their offers to dance. Some boys have untoward intentions."

"He doesn't let me have any fun either," Susan teased Theo.

"Now Susan," Theo protested, "I am to protect you."

"See, no fun." Susan poked Theo in his stomach jokingly.

"Oh Susan, you know I'm only protecting you," he patted her back.

"If I can't dance with the boys here, then will you dance with me Theo?" I asked him.

"Of course," he smiled as he took my hand.

"I'd love for Maybel to become my sister-in-law," Susan called after us as we walked to the dance floor. Susan laughed heartily when Theo turned and shot her an angry and very much annoyed look.

I laughed too. "You wouldn't know what to do with me anyway; I've been told I'm too wild to tame."

"That you are, Maybel." He smiled down at me.

Theo held me and led me around the floor. "You move your hips and feet as though you dance professionally," I told him.

"My footwork is why I'm so highly rated in the local boxing community," he boasted. "Don't let those little boys flirt with you. I'll have to show them my graceful footwork as I simultaneously show them how to eat my knuckles," he winked at me.

"Theo! Are you jealous?"

"Maybe a little," he blushed.

"You know when I first met you, I thought you didn't like me," I said.

"I didn't," he laughed. "Like the mold in my Petri dishes, you've grown on me," he chuckled.

I laughed too. "I understand, I didn't like your arrogance and I never imagined I'd be dancing with you now on the beach, but you know what, I'm glad I was able to forgive your annoying haughtiness." I grinned widely and giggled.

Theo laughed, "It's your spunk that sets you apart from all the other young ladies." He pulled me closer and I rested my head on his chest as we danced.

"Come ladies," he opened the door for us, "We're going to a play at the opera house."

The opera house was dazzling. It was larger than the one back home. The curtains were of heavy velvet and were the color of dark red wine. The brocade was golden.

Theo sat between us. His arm was around Susan's shoulder and she leaned into him and slowly fell asleep as the play continued past an hour. I was quite enthralled by the costumes, the dancing, and the singing. At one point in the play, the actor was speaking about his wife's passing and I looked over to see a single tear rolling down Theo's cheek. I reached over and squeezed his hand.

"Theo?"

"I'm fine, Maybel," he whispered.

I laid my head down on his chest and he held me tightly. He smelled of a rich cologne and I liked the scent.

After another hour, the play finished and the actors came out for a final bow. Susan woke up and we stood and clapped loudly. She had no idea why she was clapping, but but she smiled and clapped heartily. I had thoroughly enjoyed the play and also clapped loudly.

We were walking home when Theo suggested we stop for dinner at a small diner we'd just passed.

"Oh good, I'm hungry!" Susan said.

"Well, sleeping does make one hungry," Theo grinned.

"It really does, and I slept a lot, so I'm really hungry!" Susan grinned back.

We ate a delicious soup and pasta dish. "Theo! This is amazing," I said.

"Yes, I've missed the food here," he said quietly. I assumed he'd dined here frequently with Victoria, judging by the sorrowful expression on his face.

"Ladies, shall we go home? Perhaps Maybel can tell us a story before bed?" he smiled at me.

"Yes, I am tired now," Susan said.

"You slept through most of the play!" he exclaimed.

"Which was quite tiring in itself," she yawned.

We walked home and Susan went to bed while Theo and I sat on his sofa. I told him a story from the viewpoint of a balloon that flew from the west coast to the east coast and all the things it saw in between.

"You're amazing, Maybel," he smiled.

"I like you too, Theo."

"Theo, remember when you walked me home from Bernard's Christmas Eve party? Why did you kiss me?"

Theo shifted uncomfortably. "I suppose, in the back of my mind, it was always something I'd done after walking Victoria home, so it just came naturally to me to kiss the woman I'd walked home." Theo cleared his throat and seemed a little nervous. "I also really liked you," he paused, "after I got past the dead rat and shotgun you carried, of course." Theo laughed and I giggled, thinking about how I must have looked.

"It felt so natural to kiss you, though. I'm sorry Maybel, I should have asked you for your kiss."

I slowly leaned closer to Theo and held his cheek while I kissed him. I moved back just a bit to see his reaction. He didn't push me away so I slowly kissed him again. He put his hands on my hips and pulled me into his embrace.

He kissed me gently but seemed hesitant. I pulled back and looked into his dark brown eyes. He very gently pulled me back into him and kissed me again. I wrapped my arms around his neck and he kissed me more passionately.

Theo brushed my hair off my neck and kissed me just below my earlobe. He was so gentle it tickled a little and I giggled.

I smiled and returned his light kiss with my own light kiss below his earlobe. A small gasp escaped his lips and I pulled back, afraid I'd upset him. He looked into my eyes and pushed me back onto the sofa and kissed me deeply.

I loved the smell of his cologne. He pressed his body against me and kissed me again and again.

He pulled himself back and breathed deeply. "Are you ok? I didn't mean to go so fast."

"It's ok, Theo. Can you just hold me for a while?"

"Of course, sweetheart." Theo wrapped his strong arms around me and we sat together for a long time listening to the ocean waves in the distance.

The next day we showed Theo how we'd been building sandcastles and he was quite impressed, not only by our sandcastle, but also the notoriety we'd amassed.

With Theo's help, as well as help from other boys and girls, we built the biggest sandcastle anyone had ever seen. It had moats and drawbridges and we even made a tiny sand table with tiny sand chairs and put a tiny sand stuffed mouse, a tiny sand opossum, and a tiny sand fox to sit at the table.

An entire day passed at the beach and I felt so relaxed and happy. The sun and sea were good for me.

That night Mrs. Murphy made us stew and salad. "Did you read the paper yet, Theodore?" Mrs. Murphy asked.

"No, I have not had a chance yet today," he said.

"Well would ye look at the editorial section, Theodore," her Irish accent became stronger when she became angry. "I cannot believe what was written today!" She set the paper in front of Theo with her knobby finger angrily pointing to the part that caused her Irish accent to flare.

"Yes, Mrs. Murphy, I'll read it right after I finish eating."

"Oh! Ye won't want to read this on a full stomach! Ye stomach will surely hurt ye!" She loudly proclaimed.

She said more animated things about the article in what I thought was English, but wasn't entirely sure how to interpret her accent.

"I absolutely agree, Mrs. Murphy! You are most certainly right to be mad!" Theo loudly agreed with her. She was busy clanging pots and pans and mumbling unintelligibly, using Irish expressions I could not decipher.

"You can understand her?" I whispered to Theo when Mrs. Murphy was out of earshot.

"Not at all, but when she's mad, you definitely do not want to question her," he chuckled. "I find it's best to say something rather noncommittal like, 'I absolutely understand your anger, Mrs. Murphy,' then follow up with something like, 'You're always right about these things, Mrs. Murphy.'"

Susan and I laughed. "Very diplomatic, Theo!" I grinned.

We finished eating, then waited for Theo to suggest our evening activities. "Ladies, what shall we do this evening? Stroll along the boardwalk by the beach, get ice cream, listen to the band in the square play while we dance?"

"Yes, that sounds wonderful. You're always right, Theo," I said.

"Yes, Theo, we understand your plans and you're always right when you suggest such fun activities," Susan added.

Theo sighed, "You're mocking me, now aren't you?"

"Does that annoy you, Theo? You have a right to be annoyed with such things," I said.

"We understand your annoyance and you're absolutely right to feel that way," Susan chimed in.

"Right. I can see already that this will be a fun evening with you two. Come along my two little mockingbirds," Theo called after us as he walked to the door.

"Maybel," Theo called, "I've received word that your sister and brother-in-law are coming for the weekend. Do show them around, won't you?"

"What? Why?" I asked, annoyed no one had consulted me on the matter.

"Catherine's coming!" Susan screamed.

"Bernard is not my brother-in-law," I told Theo. My sister hasn't married him."

"Fine, then, please show your sister and her fiancé around town," Theo said.

"They're not engaged," I said flatly.

He took an annoyed breath, "Maybel, see to it they're comfortable, will you?"

"Why won't you be here?" I sulked.

"I'll be working most of the weekend," he replied as he ate his toast and drank his coffee.

"You can't spare one weekend?" I was upset. I didn't want to be alone with Bernard. I still really liked him, and I still really felt so guilty about that.

"Work comes first, Maybel."

"You'll never find a wife if you never come out of your laboratory." I tried to guilt him into taking the weekend off.

"That's enough, Maybel. Behave yourselves," Theo raised his eyebrows and looked over his coffee mug at Susan and me. "They will arrive Friday."

I loathed when Theo alternated between talking to me as an equal and talking down to me as a little sister.

Bernard and Catherine arrived, but I was not ecstatic. I had only been in Connecticut several weeks, but I was enjoying my time here and its simplicity. Bernard would only complicate things.

"Hello, Catherine," I hugged her.

Susan bounded up to Catherine and hugged her like she was a long, lost relative giving out cookies and cocoa. "Catherine!" Susan squealed.

"Susan!" Catherine hugged her back.

Bernard had not taken his eyes off me since Susan and I had opened the door. "Hello, Maybel," he said.

"Hello, Bernard," I replied, unenthusiastically.

Bernard awkwardly hugged me, and I even more awkwardly returned his hug.

"Bernard!" Susan hugged him tightly.

"Hello, sweetheart, how are you?" Bernard kissed Susan's cheek.

"I'm fine. Bernard, this is my brother, Theo," she delighted in introducing her brother. She was so proud of Theo, and rightfully so. Theo was incredibly intelligent and driven.

"Yes, we met Christmas Eve," Bernard said, and shook Theo's hand.

"Thank you for coming Bernard, Catherine," Theo kissed Catherine's cheek politely.

"Thank you so much for having us," Catherine smiled too eagerly. I narrowed my eyes at the back of her head when she kissed Theo's cheek.

"Come in, please," Theo motioned for Bernard and Catherine to come in and sit down.

"I'll be working this evening, and much of the weekend, but please feel free to make yourselves at home," Theo said.

"Thank you so much," Catherine smiled sweetly.

Theo kissed Susan's cheek and left for work.

"I want to see the ocean!" Catherine squealed.

Susan grabbed Catherine's hand, "You're going to love it!"

We sat together in the family room to chat for a short while and become reacquainted. "Catherine, I did not know you were coming until just the other day. I'm happy you're here," I said.

"I'm happy to see you, Maybel. I've been missing you," Catherine squeezed my hand.

I was still very curious as to why Catherine and Bernard were here. "So, tell me, Catherine, what made you want to come here? I am very happy you're here," I quickly added, "I had just assumed you had a lot of social gatherings to attend to back home."

"I haven't spent much time with you, Maybel, and I've been feeling guilty about that. I'm sorry," she said.

I smiled politely at Catherine but I didn't believe her. She had preferred to spend time with her friends over me for quite a while now, and I doubted that had changed. I wondered why she suddenly wanted to spend time with me now.

"Bernard knew I missed you, and offered to pay for our trip," Catherine smiled at Bernard, who was sitting across from us in an armchair.

"How nice of Bernard," I said, hoping I had not conveyed too clearly my annoyance that Bernard had helped orchestrate this trip.

"Yes, he's seen how much I've been missing you, and I know he's missed you, too, Maybel."

I pretended to smile sweetly at Bernard, "How kind of you."

Bernard understood my sarcasm, and I suspected he knew why I had left home for Connecticut. Bernard had kissed me, and I had returned his kisses. I felt immense guilt.

We changed into swimwear and were about to set off for the beach. Susan was chatting excitedly with Catherine in the foyer as she finished packing her bag for the beach. Catherine did seem to have a way with people of all ages. She would be an excellent teacher, I mused.

Bernard and I stood together next to them. "The beach weather has been good for you, hasn't it, Maybel? You seem much more relaxed," Bernard told me.

"It's been a very relaxing time here with Susan and Theo," I smiled at Susan.

The front door opened and Theo entered.

"Theo!" Susan hugged her brother. "You're back!"

"Yes, I had planned to work on a project this afternoon but unfortunately, or perhaps fortunately, that project has been delayed."

Theo suddenly noticed Catherine, or rather Catherine's body in her swimwear. "You're leaving for the beach now?"

"Yes! I've never seen the ocean!" Catherine said excitedly.

"Really?" Theo asked incredulously. "I had not realized that! Come, everyone, let's introduce Catherine to the ocean," Theo beamed.

Theo quickly changed his clothes and we walked outside and down a little hill to the warm sand and salt water. Catherine was so excited she could not contain herself. She was ten years old again eating circus food and seeing elephants and acrobats for the first time. Her enthusiasm was contagious. Everyone was excited for Catherine to enter the ocean for the first time.

Catherine tossed off her flowy beach shirt and ran to the water with Susan right beside her. I watched from the sand. I had not seen Catherine like this in years, since we were small children. I smiled as I watched her wade into the water up to her waist and cup saltwater in her hand, lifting it to her lips and tasting the saltiness for the first time. She looked back at me and smiled the way she smiled at me when she was eight. Her happiness made me happy.

Theo had been watching Catherine too, and had now reached the water's edge. He waded over to where Catherine and Susan stood.

"Maybel," Bernard gently touched my arm. I jumped slightly at his touch because I had been lost in Catherine's joy.

"Yes?"

"I've missed you," he looked sadly at me.

I ignored him. "Come, Bernard, let's swim in the ocean."

I ran to Catherine and splashed into the water's edge with enough force to spray Catherine with saltwater where she stood.

"Maybel!" Catherine cupped water in her hand and tossed it on me.

"Catherine! That's not how you fight with sea water! Watch this!" I twisted my arm back behind me and with great force, I twisted my hips and skimmed the surface of the ocean with my palm and blew a massive wave of saltwater onto Catherine.

"Maybel!" Catherine lunged at me and grabbed my waist and twisted, throwing me into the water. We both laughed hysterically.

"Where did you learn that, Maybel?"

"Theo taught me!" I palmed the water, splashing Theo hard in his face.

"Maybel!" He picked me up and threw me over his shoulder. "Catherine, would you like to see a flying fish?"

"Yes!" She squealed.

"No!" I screamed.

Theo grabbed me and spun around, tossing me out into the ocean.

"Theo!" I half swam and half bounced back.

"My turn, Theo," Susan screamed.

"Ok Susan! You asked for it!" He gently tossed her about two feet away.

"Theo! Toss me like Maybel!" she yelled.

"I can't toss you like that; I like you," he smirked at me.

"Theo!" I screamed, "Boring scientists who don't like me get this!" I spun around in a circle dragging my palm across the water spraying his face.

"That's it Maybel!" He picked me up above his head with his surprisingly strong arms, and tossed me like a rag into the ocean.

"Like that Theo! Toss me like that!" Susan screamed.

"Susan, I don't want to hurt you," he said.

"I'll catch her," I called.

"Yes! Maybel will catch me!"

"Ok, here you go Maybel! Catch this flying fish!" He gently tossed Susan to me and I made sure she wasn't in over her head.

We swam and bounced off the sea floor back up to Theo.

"Where's Catherine?" I asked.

"They're sitting in the sand over there," Theo nodded in their direction.

Catherine and Bernard were sitting in the sand with their feet in the ocean, letting the waves gently roll over their feet and legs. They were kissing and whispering to each other.

"Let's build a sand castle," I said to Susan. "Will you help, Theo?" I asked.

"Of course, ladies," he winked at Susan.

When the sun began to set, the sky lit up like a bonfire. It was truly gorgeous.

Theo took Susan to get food at a small store nearby. I laid on my towel and watched the painting above me change from blue to orange to red and finally purple.

"Maybel? Please talk to me." I was startled by Bernard's presence.

"Where's Catherine?" I asked.

"She went to get food with Susan and Theo."

"Oh," I said, now feeling a little uncomfortable.

Bernard laid down beside me. "Maybel, I have missed you terribly. Please come back home with Catherine and me."

"I'm not going to be your puppy anymore, Bernard."

Bernard's shoulders slunk down suddenly and he put his hands to his face and wiped off the sudden guilt and sadness that spread across his features. "I didn't realize I was Bradley in your story until later, and then I felt tremendous guilt and sadness. You are not my puppy, Maybel. I love you dearly. I'm sorry for the way I treated you growing up. Please forgive me."

I returned my attention to the magical, ever-changing sky above. The clouds were light oranges and deep oranges. The moon was rising, and looked like a glittering Christmas ornament next to the twinkling stars that were beginning to peak through.

"Maybel, Theo is attracted to you, I can see that clearly."

"Well, he's not dating my sister, so we haven't kissed," I said sarcastically.

"Maybel, please!"

"Just kidding, we did kiss," I smiled.

"You and Theo kissed?"

"Why do you care? You were kissing Catherine as you waded in the ocean."

The sunset reflected in Bernard's green eyes making them look ethereal. I wanted to kiss him so I threw sand at his beautiful eyes instead.

Bernard closed his eyes tightly, just before the sand hit. His reflexes had quickened exponentially from having played with me throughout the years. "You should be grateful and thank me for making you better at sports. Your reaction time has improved," I giggled.

"Catherine likes Theo," Bernard said, with neither anger nor jealousy as he wiped sand off his face. There was no sadness in his face or voice either.

"And Maybel, Theo likes Catherine's attention." Bernard paused and watched me. "I just want you to be aware of their mutual affection."

"You're just trying to plant seeds of doubt," I told him.

Bernard touched my cheek and brushed my tangled, saltwater-laden hair from my cheek. "We shall see."

"Theo, my stomach hurts."

I crept into Theo's bedroom and stood over him.

"Theo," I whispered.

Theo was sleeping soundly. "Theo," I gently shook his shoulder.

Theo groggily opened his eyes. "What's wrong, Maybel?"

"My stomach hurts. Can you make that drink for me again?"

Theo rolled onto his back and stretched, trying to wake himself from his deep slumber. He wasn't wearing a shirt and as he stretched, I could see the outline of his taught muscles in the moonlight, no doubt from boxing at the local gym.

"Oh, Maybel, just drink some water. I'm exhausted."

"Please, Theo?" I whined, "My stomach really hurts."

"It's probably because you ate too much saltwater taffy, Maybel. I warned you."

I stood there staring at him.

"Oh, alright, come with me." Theo stood up and all he wore were shorts. It was a hot summer and our bedrooms didn't get much breeze. I wore only a light cotton shirt that reached my knees.

We walked to his kitchen and he mixed something in water and stirred it. He held the glass out for me, yawning. "Here, Maybel, drink this, but not too fast."

I did as he instructed. He rinsed the glass and led me to the sofa in his family room. "Sit upright for a few minutes, Maybel."

He sat beside me on the sofa and gently rubbed my back. I belched louder than I'd ever belched before. "Excuse me!" I gasped, embarrassed.

"It's alright Maybel, the drink was supposed to make you belch," he gently patted my back the way you do for a baby.

I leaned into Theo's chest and he continued rubbing my back while holding me against him.

"Thank you, Theo."

"You're welcome, honey. Why don't you go back to bed now?"

"It's too crowded." I shared Susan's bed with her and Catherine, while Bernard slept in my bed.

"Alright, Maybel, you can take my bed and I'll sleep here."

"I can't take your bed, Theo. I'd be a bad guest."

"It's alright, go ahead."

"Can't we just lay here and you keep rubbing my back until I stop feeling sick?"

"I'm too tired to argue, and you're too skilled at arguing. Just go to sleep," he said as he continued rubbing my back.

Catherine woke us up. "Theo, can I sleep in your bed?"

"What's wrong?" He barely opened his eyes.

"Susan kicks like a donkey and spreads out like a starfish in her sleep."

"Oh yes, that," he chuckled, "Yes you and Maybel may take my bed and I'll sleep here."

I got up and Theo stretched out on his sofa.

Catherine and I walked back to his bedroom and laid in his bed. "The sheets smell like his cologne," Catherine whispered.

"Mmm hmm," I mumbled. "Night, Catherine."

"Maybel, why were you laying on the sofa with Theo?"

"My stomach hurt and he made me a drink that makes the hurt go away," I mumbled.

"He's smart and has quite the excellent body," she giggled.

"Yes, just like Bernard," I mumbled. "Goodnight, Catherine."

Thankfully, Catherine and Bernard left. I told Catherine I would miss her and kissed her cheek, but in my heart, I was happy to be rid of them both. My life in Connecticut with Susan and Theo was peaceful. We ate breakfast together, Susan and I played on the sand and shore, then Theo read us stories before bedtime. Sometimes I made up stories and Susan comically acted them out in front of Theo. I welcomed the peace that came when Catherine and Bernard left.

Theo, Susan, and I sat on Theo's wide chaise chair, the three of us, with Theo in the middle. Susan and I were sucking on candy sticks Theo had bought us from a vendor by the beach.

Theo enjoyed reading to us in the evenings and we enjoyed sitting with him and listening. His voice was deep and smooth. He knew how to inflect his voice to make the story interesting.

I felt safe because Theo wrapped his arms around us and pulled us close while he read. I liked resting my head on his strong chest and hearing his heart beat and smelling his cologne. His strong arms around my shoulders or waist made me feel like I was the safest right there with him.

I looked up at him while he read and watched his lips move as he spoke. He looked down at me and winked. I giggled. He tickled my ribs.

Susan and I often fell asleep listening to him. I'd wake up when he carefully picked up Susan and carried her to bed then I usually fell back asleep. Theo always came back to get me and always joked, "You just want to be carried to bed too, don't you?" I did. I liked being tucked in and kissed on my forehead.

I'd gotten into the habit of waking up in the middle of the night and crawling into bed with Theo. I crawled into the bottom of the bed by his feet. I hadn't meant anything sexual about crawling into bed with him. I was often scared and nervous and Theo always made me feel safe.

Sometimes Theo would wake up and ask me if I wanted to lay beside him and rest my head on a pillow but I declined. He would then put a pillow down by the bottom of the bed for me. I just wanted to be near Theo because he helped me relax.

One night I came to lay at the bottom of his bed and he was awake when I crawled in. "Maybel, it feels awkward when you sleep at my feet."

"I don't want to sleep in my room, Theo." I began to get scared he was going to make me return to my room. "I won't get in your way, and I won't take up much space, and I won't keep you awake." I hoped he would continue letting me sleep in his bed.

"Relax Maybel, I just meant that you're not my dog, you don't have to sleep at my feet."

"I don't want you think I'm trying to have sex with you," I stated bluntly.

Theo laughed, "I am not going to have sex with you, Maybel."

"I don't want Susan to come in and think I'm one of those bad women who give themselves to men," I said.

Theo again laughed, "She won't think that. She doesn't even know what sex is."

I was pretty certain Susan did know what sex was, but I didn't say my suspicions to Theo. He still saw Susan as a small child in his mind.

Theo sighed, "Maybel, why do you come in here at night and lay at my feet?"

"I get scared."

"What makes you scared sweetheart? I won't let anyone hurt you."

"I just feel scared but I don't know why." I tried to explain, but even I didn't know why I often felt scared.

Theo sat up. He reached down and gently rubbed my back. I crawled up and hugged him. He pulled me against him and laid me down beside him. I drifted off to sleep with his strong, safe arms wrapped around me.

The next night I crawled into bed beside Theo, not at his feet. He wrapped his arms around me and kissed my neck. "I was wondering when you'd get here," he whispered into my ear.

"I woke up and had to pee. And I wanted you to hold me," I confessed.

"I have been looking forward to your visits. I'm glad they aren't at my feet anymore."

"Do you think Susan will think I'm one of those bad girls who are with boys when they shouldn't be?"

"No," he chuckled. "She comes in sometimes too when she's scared.

"Theo," I hesitated, "Have you ever had sex?"

I felt Theo's shoulders slump underneath my head. "Yes," he sighed. "I was engaged to Victoria."

"When you want sex now, what do you do? Some men have sex with women they meet at parties. Do you?"

"No," Theo said. "I do not."

"Have you ever been to one of those houses where women live and men pay them for sex?"

"Yes, once," he looked guilty and torn.

"Oh," I said, surprised.

"I went there after Victoria left. My intention was to move forward and forget Victoria. I chose a girl that reminded me of Victoria though. She seemed nice and I wanted to continue, and I asked her if she was ok, and although she said yes, her eyes said no. We talked a little and she said she had been orphaned when her parents contracted an illness. Her uncle sold her. I took her to the train station and paid for her to go to her cousin's house in Wyoming. I hope she is ok."

"You didn't have sex with her?"

"No. She was forced into that lifestyle. I looked at her and I imagined Susan if our parents and I died. I've never been to a place like that since. I feel horrible I went in the first place. I went there to escape my torments, but became more tormented after having met that poor girl."

"I've never been to one of those houses," I said. "I figure I should answer such a question if I am to ask such a bold question."

Theo chuckled, "I never thought you had been to one, but thank you for your honesty."

"Thank you for yours," I said.

"It hurts to be honest, but I will always be honest with you, sweetheart," Theo kissed my head as I laid my head on his shoulder.

"I don't want to leave you at summer's end," I told him. "I like living with you."

"I'm going to miss reading to you two, and I'll miss you crawling into my bed. I didn't realize how lonely I'd become until you two came to visit. I think I must have closed off my heart when Victoria left, and didn't even realize I'd done so until you two arrived on my doorstep and brought sand and sunshine into my life once again."

I turned around to face him in the dark. It was difficult to see him but the moonlight provided enough light to see his eyes and nose and a little of his lips. "Theo, thank you for letting me stay here."

"Of course, Maybel."

"I'm going to miss laying with you and Susan while you read to us. I like the sound of your voice." I could barely see his lips smiling in the dark.

"And I like when I lay my head on your chest and smell your cologne."

Theo leaned in and very gently kissed the tip of my nose. I drifted off to sleep in Theo's embrace.

Mrs. Murphy set our soup bowls in front of us then answered the knock at our door. There was Catherine. My soup remained in my spoon and my spoon remained poised in front of my parted lips while I watched her enter my boring, quiet, east coast beach house.

"Why are you here?" I finally found my voice.

"Maybel," Theo said with a highly annoyed tone, "do be kinder to your sister."

"Catherine!" Susan ran and hugged Catherine. "Do you want to play with me?"

"Of course, sweetheart!" Catherine hugged Susan.

"I'm glad you're here, Catherine," I stood and went to her and hugged her. "I was just surprised. I'm sorry I came across unwelcoming."

Catherine ignored my behavior like the perfect high-society housewife and mother I knew she was meant to be, always poised, and always polite. "Bernard and I loved our time here so much that we decided to come for one more weekend before the summer's end."

"Bernard is here, too?" I asked. I was not happy and I knew my annoyance played strongly across my face.

"Didn't you get our telegram, Maybel?"

"No, I did not," I turned and stared coldly at Theo.

"I just received it this evening, Maybel," Theo said. "I was waiting for after dinner to tell you. You seem much more agreeable after your belly is full."

Catherine laughed, "I can confirm. You are grumpy when you're hungry."

By now, I knew my face looked like I'd eaten a lemon. I didn't even bother to hide my irritation.

Bernard entered my summer home with their luggage. "Hello, Maybel," he smiled softly at me. I stared back at him.

Bernard turned to Theo, "I'm sorry for such short notice. I will be happy to pay for a hotel for Catherine and me if this is an inconvenient time."

"Ok, bye," I waved at them both.

"Maybel, your manners are atrocious!" Theo looked angrily at me, which made me angrier. He treated me like a little sister whenever Catherine was near. I hated when Bernard transitioned between treating me like a girlfriend and treating me like an annoying, little sister, but when Theo transitioned between holding me in his bed at night and scolding me like a child, I wanted to rip out his entrails and watch buzzards scatter his remains along the coast.

"You both are of course more than welcome." Theo went to Bernard and took their luggage pieces. I wondered how many buzzards it would take to carry Theo away.

"Follow me to your guest rooms," Theo called over his shoulder, smiling at a giggling and bouncing Catherine who followed closely behind him. Probably nine buzzards, I guessed.

Theo seemed happy that Catherine was here. Susan clung to Catherine because Catherine had a gravitational force that she was born with, and that she used whenever she desired, to make people fall in love with her. Bernard walked behind them and did not seem as happy to be here.

"I would have batted her!" Mrs. Murphy whispered to me in her thick, Irish accent. "You say the word, lass, and I'll dose her with a little laxative. Theo won't find her as attractive, yeah?"

I laughed. I didn't say no, though. I was mad enough to keep that option open, although I knew I wouldn't use it. It was nice to have that possibility available at my will, and it made me happy that Mrs. Murphy saw Catherine's flirty nature and took my side.

Catherine took to east coast life like the socialite I knew she had always been.

I was not pleased that she took to Theo so easily, and was even more disappointed that Theo responded to her charms as much as he did.

I went to Theo's office. "Theo, will you take Susan and me to get ice cream?" Theo was behind his desk in his office." There was a poster of the periodic table of elements behind him on his wall.

"Yes, that does sound fun, I'll go tell Catherine," he said.

"No, Catherine, and her boyfriend Bernard, must be tired from travelling. Let's let them rest. We won't be gone long anyway." I added the part about Catherine not being single to remind Theo to ignore Catherine's flirting.

"You're so cute when you're jealous," he stood up and pinched my cheek, grinning broadly.

"I am not jealous!"

"You are! And it's adorable!" he chuckled.

"I am not!" I stomped my foot, which only made Theo laugh more.

"Catherine is with Bernard, Maybel, so you don't have to worry about her taking up all my attention," he continued smiling because he could see by my face how angry I was becoming.

"Bernard confided to me that he senses Catherine likes you," I said.

"She's a nice, young lady," Theo grinned. "No need to get flushed though. I do not entertain ideas of kissing women who have boyfriends." Theo continued seeing how much further he could push me.

"I'm not flushed!"

"I quite enjoy when you're angry, dear," he sat back down in his office chair with an amused smile.

I crossed my arms and stood before him. "Catherine always gets all the attention, men's attention, other women's attention, kids' attention. Susan thinks Catherine is amazing."

"Well, Catherine is amazing," Theo continued pushing the button that made me most angry.

I started to tear up, but I didn't want him to see me cry, so I quickly turned away and walked to the door. In an instant, he bolted after me and grabbed my arm, turning me around. "I'm sorry, Maybel, I went too far. Yes, Catherine is amazing, but you are too." He held me in his arms.

"I don't want to go back home yet. I want to stay here. I'm not Catherine's little sister here. And I'm not Bernard's little, annoying tag-a-long. I'm just Maybel here, and I like that. For the first time, I have my own identity."

"Relax, Maybel, you can stay here the rest of the summer." He stroked my hair and held me close while I calmed down. His cologne was all over my hair and face now, and it made me feel peaceful.

"Catherine and Bernard are leaving tomorrow morning, so what do you say we treat our guests to ice cream and dancing in the square? I promise not to return Catherine's flirty nature," he winked.

"Ok," I sniffed. "And if that boy is there again, and wants me to dance with him, I will, and I will smile at you when he spins me around."

"Very funny, Maybel, but don't do that; I don't feel like going to jail tonight." He pulled me into a hug, and was about to kiss my forehead when I looked up at him, and his kiss instead landed on my lips. He didn't pull away though, his lips lingered on mine and I welcomed them.

"Oh, excuse us!" Catherine said, surprised. She had opened the door without knocking and Bernard was right behind her.

"Catherine!" I yelled, surprised and embarrassed.

Bernard's face turned red in what I guessed was anger, not embarrassment.

Catherine quickly closed the door.

I looked up at Theo to see his reaction. To my delight, he was not embarrassed to be caught kissing me. "Well, then, perhaps Catherine won't be so overtly flirtatious today," he chuckled.

"You're not embarrassed of kissing me?" I asked, surprised.

Theo looked confused. "No, of course not. Why would I be embarrassed? You're gorgeous, intelligent, and at least you think you're funny."

"Everyone thinks I'm funny," I corrected him. "My humor is well-known throughout the land," I added.

Theo chuckled then kissed me again.

"Theo?"

"Yes?"

"I love you," I whispered.

I was afraid he wouldn't return my affection but he did. "I love you too, Maybel."

I exhaled and my shoulders relaxed. Theo smiled and kissed me gently as he held my waist. "I do love you, Maybel. I'm scared to love again, but I have fallen in love with you, and it feels good to love again."

Theo looped his arm with Susan's then smiled at me as he took my arm too. "Catherine, Bernard, I'd love to show you the town.

"I'd love to see the town!" Catherine said excitedly.

Bernard said nothing. Catherine held his hand while we walked to the town square.

"Maybel! That boy who asked you to dance is here!" Susan said teasingly.

"Maybel! Connecticut suits you!" Catherine giggled. "You have your pick of all the handsome men!" She winked at Theo, but did so with her face turned away from Bernard, so that he had not seen her flirting.

Theo smiled politely while I changed the subject. "I won't be dancing with him tonight, I've been scolded and told not to play with the local boys," I looked at Theo and laughed.

"Just being a protective, big brother," Theo laughed. "A lot like the way you act like Mabel's protective, big brother, eh Bernard?"

Susan and I laughed. Bernard did not. Theo openly mocked how Bernard called himself my protective, big brother while kissing me secretly, and there was nothing Bernard could say without admitting to Catherine he cheated on her as much as she cheated on him. I found Theo's remark funny and comforting, because Theo was defending me and protecting me from Bernard by shining a light on his behavior.

"You've never kissed me the way Catherine said you kissed Maybel earlier in the study though, right big brother?" Susan giggled up at Theo.

Catherine broke the tension by pointing out all the beautiful dresses the ladies wore.

"Mommy makes better dresses," I said proudly.

"She certainly does," Catherine agreed. "Wouldn't it be lovely if she opened her own dress shop!"

"Yes, it would," I agreed.

"Catherine would you like to dance?" Bernard asked when we arrived at the town square.

"I'd love to!" Catherine happily took his hand.

I watched them dancing for a moment. They were a beautiful couple and caught the eyes of the townspeople. Catherine wore a pale pink dress that mother had sewn. She was truly stunning.

I looked over to see Theo watching Catherine as she twirled around effortlessly.

"Catherine is so pretty," Susan murmured.

Theo nodded, probably attempting to avoid saying anything that would upset me.

"Theo, will you dance with me?" Susan asked her brother.

"Yes, sweetheart." He led Susan to the dance floor.

A different boy than last week asked me to dance but I declined. I wasn't sure if Theo would actually hit someone who flirted with me, but I didn't want to find out tonight.

Theo and Susan returned after a song and Theo reached for my hand, "I don't want you to be lonely, Maybel. Let's dance."

Susan made kissing noises as we walked to the dance floor. Theo looked over his shoulder and gave her a look that meant 'Stop right now!' I knew what that look meant because it was the same look Catherine always gave me when I teased her in public. It's the look that older siblings all automatically inherit the day their younger sibling is born.

Theo held me close and whispered in my ear, "I think both Bernard and Catherine are jealous of the attention you have been getting from the local boys."

"Only one boy asked me to dance," I said, "but I declined."

"And more than a dozen boys would have asked you had I not spread the word at my boxing gym that you are off limits," he chuckled.

"You didn't!" I gasped.

"Oh, but I did! I gave your parents my word that I would take care of you."

"By eliminating the competition?" I asked incredulously.

"Well, the end result is the same. You are protected, and as an added benefit, I have you all to myself!" He smiled down at me then spun me around.

Catherine approached along with Bernard. "Maybel, may I cut in? I'd like to thank Theo for his hospitality this weekend and Bernard would like to dance with you."

I looked at Theo and then turned to Catherine, "Yes, that will be fine."

Catherine went to Theo and pressed herself against him while they danced.

I turned to Bernard and he slowly reached his hand out. I slowly took his hand and looked up at him. "I've missed you, Maybel," he said.

"I've missed you too, Bernard."

I let him pull me close. His strong arms and body holding me felt like home. I exhaled deeply and let my head rest on his chest. I really did miss Bernard and I really did miss Catherine.

When the song ended, Theo asked me to join him in another dance. I felt my heart pull away from Bernard more than I felt my body leaving Bernard.

I danced away with Theo while Catherine pulled Bernard close to her for the next song.

"Are you ok, Maybel?" Theo asked.

"Yes," I said.

We finished the song in silence. I was confused. I feared both Theo and Catherine could sense the love between Bernard and me was more than just childhood friendship, and much more than a silly crush. I wanted Bernard to leave because whenever he held me, I fell in love with him a little more, and I wanted our love for each other to go away. I wanted to be alone on the beach with Susan and Theo and let the sun and saltwater bathe away all my thoughts.

The band finished and went for a break. Theo and I went over to where Susan stood under a tree. Catherine and Bernard followed.

"What's wrong Susan?" Theo asked, "You look a little down."

"Nobody asked me to dance," she looked sad.

"Oh, don't feel bad, that's not your fault Susan," I said, "Your brother here let it be known in town that no one is to ask you or me to dance because," I added sarcastically, "Theo is our mighty protector."

"Theo! I want to have fun!" she whined.

"Not on my watch," he winked.

"Well at least it's not because the boys think I'm ugly," Susan pouted.

"Of course not!" I said. "You are beautiful Susan!"

"I agree, that's why I had to threaten all the boys in town," he chuckled.

Catherine was holding Bernard's hand. "Bernard, let's walk around the square and look in the shop windows while the band is on break," she suggested.

"Let's all go," Susan said, "I want you to try the ice cream at the stand on the corner and the taffy at that store," she pointed to the places with the best treats.

I still felt torn between my love for Catherine, my love for Bernard, and this entirely new love I felt for Theo. Of course, I also loved Susan and didn't want her to be mad at me because I kissed her brother, even though I didn't know if I wanted a future with Theo. I considered how angry Susan might be if I hurt Theo's feelings if I decided I didn't want a future with him. I began to feel sick and panicked.

Susan skipped ahead and excitedly yelled back to Catherine, "Catherine! The ice cream here has real strawberries in it! You'll love it!"

Catherine giggled, "I can't wait to try everything, Susan!"

Susan ordered five small ice cream cups for each of us. "Now, you don't want to fill up on one thing!" Susan lectured, "The chocolate ice cream has chocolate pieces and the vanilla ice cream, well, actually, it doesn't have anything in it but it's still so good!" Susan spoke fast and with such gusto that Catherine and Bernard both began laughing.

"You're quite the tour guide, Susan," Bernard smiled at her.

"Wait until you see the different kinds of taffy, and there are chocolates in that store over there," she pointed across the square, "that have chocolate candies from Switzerland! Can you believe that! All the way from Switzerland!"

Catherine looked at Bernard and smiled. "Bernard, you've been to Switzerland, haven't you?" Catherine seemed proud of Bernard's family's travels.

"Yes," was all Bernard said. Bernard never flaunted his family's wealth or political connections, and I liked that about him.

"You've been to Switzerland? And you've eaten chocolate there?" Susan marveled.

"Yes," he replied.

"Then we have to taste all the chocolate there and you can confirm whether or not their claims of authenticity are true!" Susan was brimming with excitement.

I laughed. I still felt my stomach twisting with panic, but Susan's complete and utter excitement showing and sharing with Catherine and Bernard the treasures we'd discovered here in Connecticut made my panic calm a little. I could see this town yet again for the first time through Susan's eyes, and I realized, Susan saw things in ways she'd never shared with me.

Susan held Catherine's hand and spoke of the people around us, but she had never shared with me her thoughts of the townspeople before. It was interesting learning her thoughts.

"That's the old man who owns an orange cat. One time, I didn't have enough money to buy a mint and he gave the shop owner enough money to cover the rest of the expense."

"I didn't know that, Susan. Where was I?"

"I think you were still making our sandcastle, Maybel."

"And there's Myrtle, she is one hundred and one years old." She pointed to a woman sitting with three other women and a baby at a table. "That's her daughter, granddaughter, great granddaughter, and great, great granddaughter with her. They're really nice."

I wondered where I'd been when she met those ladies.

"Ok, Catherine, that's the woman that always flirts with Theo when he buys me lemonade." She pointed to a pretty blond girl at a lemonade stand.

"Oh, really?" Catherine giggled.

"Yes, but Theo is too dense to notice," Susan giggled.

"I do not think she has ever flirted with me, Susan," Theo protested.

"See, dense," Susan said.

"She is very friendly because she wants a tip," Theo countered.

"I'll bet!" Catherine stifled giggles and accidentally snorted.

Bernard tried to hide his grin and Theo blushed deep red.

I didn't think Catherine's joke warranted such laughter.

"Is that an inside joke?" I questioned, not understanding the hilarity.

"Oh, just a little.... tip.... inside.... of humor," Catherine laughed hysterically, as did Bernard and Theo.

I will have to ask Catherine in private why this is funny, I thought.

Our small strawberry ice cream cones were ready and they tasted magnificent!

"Wow! Susan! This is amazing!" Catherine exclaimed.

"Quite right!" Bernard agreed.

Susan was proud of being the one to bring such happiness to our guests.

"Bernard," Susan grabbed his hand, "We must taste the Swiss chocolates now!" She jumped up and down with excitement, and probably a rush of sugar.

Inside the chocolate shop, Susan asked for a sample platter. "Ok," she whispered, "Don't tell anyone you know what real Swiss chocolate tastes like. Let's let them give us their regular candies, and you can judge whether or not the general public gets the real Swiss chocolate."

I giggled. Susan was cheering me up and making everyone else laugh as well.

Bernard took his first bite and deliberately made a series of faces ranging from surprised, to disgusted, to intensely in awe.

"Well?" Susan asked excitedly.

"It's real Swiss chocolate!" Bernard declared.

"Ok, let me try," Susan took the other half of Bernard's candy and popped it into her mouth. "Mmmm it's delicious! You try some Catherine," she held out the platter for Catherine.

Catherine tried a piece and her eyes widened. "These are magnificent, Susan! Thank you for suggesting we come here!"

"You're welcome," Susan was proud of her guidance to the best places in town.

We all took turns tasting the varied chocolates and they were quite delicious. I could feel myself relaxing more and more. I wished I knew why I became so panicked at times so I could not do whatever I did to cause myself such sudden nervousness.

"Let's go back to dancing," Susan suggested, "If we add taffy to what we've just eaten, we'll get sick. If you do get sick, my big brother has a drink that will make your stomach feel better." Susan proudly hugged Theo.

Catherine smiled sweetly, "That's really nice Susan. I hope I don't ever have to drink that medicine, but it's comforting to know it's there if any of us need it." Catherine smiled at both Susan and Theo. Catherine seemed genuinely happy of Theo's accomplishments.

Bernard was interested, too. "May I ask about your medicine? I am studying to be a doctor. I'd love to speak with you about your advancements in medicine someday if you have time?"

"Certainly, Bernard! I love talking about medicine and how I can help people!" Theo's countenance brightened considerably.

"Theodore," Bernard continued, "I heard you saved Susan's life around Christmas time and I've been wanting to ask you about what this new medicine is you've invented, but I didn't want to intrude on our vacation time. When or if you ever have time, I would love to discuss with you how you invented such a medicine." Bernard was animated when discussing the advancement of medicine.

It appeared that Theo returned his animation. "Please, call me Theo," he smiled, "Let's discuss our mutual endeavors over brandy tonight, shall we?" his eyes twinkled.

This was turning out to be quite nice, I reflected. I felt at ease now.

We headed out toward the town square for more dancing. This time, I felt more relaxed when Catherine asked to dance with Theo and Bernard asked to dance with me.

Susan asked to dance with a boy standing near her, but he quickly looked in Theo's direction, and even more quickly declined to dance.

Theo made his way over to the frightened boy and whispered in his ear. The boy then asked Susan for a dance, but did so with much nervousness and stammering.

Theo then politely reached for Catherine's hand and they began dancing.

Bernard held his hand out to me but looked afraid I might say no. I'd never seen him with anything but the most confidence of anyone in the room.

I accepted his invitation to dance and he smiled weakly. "I only seek your friendship, Maybel, nothing more. I just want us to be comfortable with each other, the way we were."

"Me too, Bernard."

We danced together for several songs and it felt like old times in my house, on our little ballroom floor, when I was young and carefree.

The next morning, Catherine and Bernard left for the train station and Theo left for work. I breathed in deeply, ready to return to simplicity. "Susan, can we go make sandcastles today?"

"I thought you'd never ask, Maybel!" Susan giggled and went to her room to retrieve her small pail.

I took another deep breath. Back to boring and quiet and peaceful, I breathed in again deeply.

I returned to the beach daily with Susan, and on the weekends, Theo joined. I enjoyed my summer in Connecticut. I didn't want to return home, but I knew I had to, and after all, I missed my parents.

My last day in Connecticut with Susan and Theo was spent at the beach. "Theo, when will you next visit?" asked Susan.

"As soon as work allows, Susan," Theo smiled kindly at his sister. "You know I'll visit as soon as I can." Theo finished placing a tower on our sandcastle.

"The autumn festival isn't far away, and then Christmas and New Year's, and then the spring festival," Susan suggested.

"I know sweetheart," I will visit as soon as I can. He continued building towers, perhaps to distract himself from Susan's sadness.

"Can we come back next summer?" Susan pleaded.

"Of course. You know you are welcome anytime," he patted her head.

"Then can we return for autumn break, and Christmas, and New Year's?" She asked with such a desperate face that I felt sad for her longing for her brother's attention.

"Yes, Susan, but the weather will be cold and we'll all be confined to the indoors, unfortunately." he said while patting the tower he'd just placed.

"What do you do during the winter months?" Susan asked.

"Mostly I read, study new periodicals, and experiment in my laboratory," he smiled weakly. I guessed he was embarrassed by his lack of social interaction and friendships.

"Theo, instead of us coming here, can you come visit us?" Susan asked, "It sounds as though Connecticut is only fun in summer."

Theo laughed, "Yes, that's probably true."

Later, after Theo read to us poetry, we retired to bed. I dreamed of Catherine and her crying in the gardens late at night. In my dream she was sad and desperate, and I feared she would kill herself like Victoria did, and I awoke shaking.

I ran to Theo's room and curled up at the bottom of his bed shaking uncontrollably. I didn't want Catherine to be mad that I liked Bernard, and I didn't want her to find out that Bernard liked me. I was scared that perhaps she already suspected such things. I didn't want her to kill herself.

Theo touched my shoulder. "Maybel?" he sounded concerned.

"I had a bad dream," I cried.

"Come here Maybel," he lifted me up with his strong arms and pulled me next to him.

"I don't want to go back. I'm scared," I cried.

"Maybel, you'll be fine, and before you know it, you'll return to the beach here with me, or I'll come home to you, Susan, and my parents."

I shook uncontrollably.

"Maybel breathe! Please!"

"I'm so scared Theo. I don't even know why."

"Maybel, look at me," he commanded sternly.

He turned my head to face his and looked deeply into my eyes. "You do not have to be with me or Bernard. Either way, I'll always treasure this summer, and Bernard can only have control over you if you let him."

"How do you even know what I'm worried about?" I cried. "I don't even understand why I'm scared."

"Maybel," he asked, "What was your dream?"

I hesitated, "I dreamed Catherine was crying in our gardens and contemplated killing herself because I like Bernard and Bernard likes me," I quickly blurted.

Theo let out a deep breath. He looked anguished.

"I'm scared that Susan's mad at me because we kissed," I told Theo, "and maybe she thinks we'll be sisters, but how do I know if you and I will get married, and if we don't, she'll probably hate me and I'll never be able to spend holidays with her because you and your new girlfriend will be there."

"Maybel! Calm down! You have traveled so far ahead of yourself you have made the future much worse than it could possibly ever be!"

I shook terribly with anxiety and panic.

Theo held me and whispered to me to calm down and that everything would be ok.

"Maybel," he lifted my chin and looked kindly into my eyes. "Look, I do love you, and I know you love me and Susan. You love Bernard, and also Catherine. It's ok to love people. And it's ok if that love never progresses into marriage. You don't yet know who Bernard will marry, and you don't yet know who I will marry, but what you do know is that you and Catherine have an unbreakable bond, and you and Susan, because of your loving devotion to her during her illness, have an unbreakable bond. You might be upset with each other from time to time, but you'll always be family."

I cried uncontrollably at his kind and soothing words.

"Maybel, look at me," he whispered, "I will always treasure this summer because I have grown to love you, and because, quite frankly, you saved my life this summer."

I looked up, confused.

"I had not been living since Victoria's death. You and Susan helped me learn to live again. Thank you, Maybel."

Theo kissed me passionately. "I'm going to miss you so much."

He wrapped me tightly in his arms and I fell asleep, finally feeling safe.

The next day Theo drove us to the train station and kissed our cheeks goodbye. We boarded the train but I couldn't see him waiting on the platform with all the other loved ones waving goodbye.

"He's really sad," Susan said, a tear escaping her eye.

Susan and I arrived home and spent our evenings as we always had, telling stories, helping mommy with her dresses, helping daddy make his special apple cider, and I even learned how to stuff a opossum. Mrs. Matthews taught us how to can everything for winter. We canned everything from green beans to sauerkraut. I did not care for sauerkraut. We also canned a variety of jams and Mrs. Matthews swore me to secrecy because her jams were the best in the county. The day we made the most jars of jam, though, Susan and I tasted more of that strawberry rum juice in her father's workshop, so I didn't remember the recipe Mrs. Matthews used for canning her famous jams anyway. I wasn't lying when I told her I wouldn't tell anyone her secret recipe. I did, however, hiccup a lot.

When Susan's father taught me how to stuff a opossum, I proudly named him Sir Isaac, because when I shot him, he dangled from a tree branch then gravity got him.

Mr. Matthews was quirky, but highly brilliant. It was a though he were playing violin in an orchestra, but instead of playing the music everyone else played, he played another song. You could hear that someone wasn't following along, and at first it sounded annoying and out of place, but then you realized that song was far more complicated to play, far more beautiful, and his music began to drown out all the other less-talented musicians. You sat there in the audience and only heard his violin playing and you wondered why the other musicians didn't play his song. And then, you realized they couldn't. You might not know how he composed and executed such complicated songs, but you knew when you heard it, that it was on a whole other level of genius.

That's what Susan's father was, a quirky genius. You just had to get past his disheveled appearance, his incredible attention to details that bordered on insanity, and of course, his weird taxidermized animals. Other than those oddities, he was a normal father and fun to be around.

Susan's mother and my mother were typical, loving, encouraging mothers who were always ready for hugs, and to wipe the corners of our mouths with their aprons. The older I became, though, the more I began seeing my mother as a person, not just a mother. I realized had we been born at the same time, we would have been best friends.

The new boy from school kept following me home. He was nice. He carried my books. His name was William. Henry didn't like William. I was not very fond of Henry at the moment for leaving me for several months.

"I'm sorry, Maybel," Henry apologized when he returned, "but I had to leave. I had work to do."

Henry was always over helping daddy, and mommy always made Henry stay for dinner. I was certain Henry liked when mommy fussed over him, and made sure he ate well, and took home food, and she even made him sleep in the guest bedroom when he and daddy had too much cheer. Mommy turned down his bed covers and placed a clean towel for his morning bath on the guest bed for him. Henry looked so happy to have a mother dote on him.

Henry was the best teacher I ever had and continued helping me with homework, especially math, after dinner every evening.

"Are you ready for our second date yet?" Henry asked one evening. He smiled at me and I blushed.

"You know, Henry, we're already an old, married couple. We eat dinner together every night and sit by the fireplace reading together as we snuggle under blankets. I think we skipped the dating part and went straight to our twentieth wedding anniversary." I giggled and Henry smiled happily.

"I hadn't considered that before, Maybel, we do act like husband and wife." Henry smiled sweetly at me, then kissed my lips tenderly. "I like being married to you," he smiled shyly and blushed.

I often felt overwhelmed with college ever nearing and I still was not able to choose a career. I liked helping people, so teaching and nursing seemed a decent fit, but I only really enjoyed writing. I didn't know in which direction to go, and that overwhelmed me.

Catherine always knew she would be a teacher. Bernard always knew he would be a doctor. I still considered ventriloquism, even though I didn't have a doll, and didn't know how to talk with my mouth closed. I wondered why I had to choose now what I wanted to be for the next sixty or seventy years.

Theo was now dancing around in my thoughts, along with Bernard and Henry, and I truly felt overcome with emotions and questions, and that made me exhausted.

Bernard kept coming home on Fridays now that he had his own automobile. I figured he was jealous that Henry was always at our house. Henry never flirted with Catherine, but Bernard still showed up nearly every weekend. I thought it was strange that Bernard was displaying such jealousy now, because he had never been worried about Catherine straying before, although, Henry was the most handsome man in the world, so I could understand Bernard's concern.

Catherine delighted in dragging Bernard to get-togethers, until Bernard began pretending to be interested in woodworking all of a sudden to get out of going to parties with Catherine. Every Friday evening, when I went to daddy's workshop to tell him dinner was ready, there was Bernard sitting beside Henry and daddy. I overheard mommy telling Aunt Mary one weekend, when Aunt Mary stayed over, that daddy was disappointed he could no longer joke with Henry about sex, because if Bernard chimed in with a joke about sex, daddy would assume it was about Catherine, and would have to shoot him, and that would leave a lot of blood. Mommy said daddy didn't want to buy a new mop for Bernard's blood because Mr. Fulton raised mop prices at the supply store after the river flooded.

It was Friday again, and William found me after school. "May I take your books and walk you home?" he smiled shyly.

"You don't have to, William. I don't want you to trouble yourself."

"It's no trouble, Maybel."

I smiled politely, "Thank you."

I wondered when William would realize I was not popular. I wondered if he walked me home to catch a glimpse of Catherine.

"Nice afternoon, isn't it?" William smiled as he took my books. His brown hair was shiny in the bright afternoon sunlight. He wore simple clothes, like me. I liked his simplicity. He wasn't trying to be ostentatious. And then I realized I used the word ostentatious, instead of a simpler word, which was ostentatious of me, and I giggled out loud.

"Oh sorry," I apologized to William for my sudden giggles. "I was thinking of something and laughed out loud. Yes, today is very nice. It's sunny and not too windy."

"Did you struggle with the history test today?" he asked.

"No," I said. "I didn't."

"Me neither," he said.

I did not care for inane chatter, but William was very polite and kind to me.

"Maybel, maybe tomorrow I could take you to the candy store, or the opera house? Would you like that?"

"I'll have to ask my parents, William. Daddy usually asks me to help in his workshop measuring boards, which I dislike, because it's math, and the worst kind of math at that, fractions."

William laughed.

"Do you like math?" I asked him.

"I do, yes."

"Well, I do not. I won't fault you for liking math though, William, we can't all be perfect. Some of us are criminals, some sinners, and some enjoy math."

"I'm in the same category as a criminal because I like math?"

"Well, no. I have a very strange sense of humor, William. I've been told I can be odd and often rude when I'm really just funny, and other people are too dense to understand my special kind of wit."

"Are you trying to be funny now?"

"No, I'm not trying to be funny. I am funny. There's no trying involved," I laughed.

We approached my house. "There's your brother. I should say hi. I don't think he likes me though," William remarked.

I laughed. "That's not my brother. That's Henry. He helps my dad deliver cabinets."

"Oh, you're not related?"

"Do I look like I share the same perfect facial features with that gorgeous man? No," I laughed, "we are not related. I'm fairly certain one or both of his parents are Greek Gods."

"Oh? He doesn't look Greek. Italian or maybe Spanish, ah, I bet it's French. His skin has a brown undertone, not much, but it's there. You know, he has to have some Scottish or Welsh somewhere in his ancestry too."

"I'll ask," I said dryly. I wished William had a better sense of humor.

"Is the other young man your brother then?"

"Who?"

"The young man who drives that expensive automobile."

I huffed, "Oh, right, him. His name is Bernard," I said, annoyed at the mere mention of his name. "No, he's not my brother either. He dated, or maybe still dates my sister. I really don't know what they are to each other anymore. Boyfriend and girlfriend, ex-boyfriend and ex-girlfriend, just friends, wanting to be more than friends, I don't know if they even know their relationship status. Bernard and I used to be close, well, we still are close, but sometimes he annoys me. I think he's jealous that Henry comes to dinner."

"Because Henry likes you?"

I gave him the most confused look. "You just said you thought Henry and I were brother and sister. Why would you think Henry likes me?"

"I thought you were brother and sister because that Henry fellow seems very protective of you. He looks like he doesn't want his little sister to have a boy walk her home. If you're not related, then he's protective of you because he likes you."

I laughed, "Oh, William, you do have a sense of humor! I thought Henry liked me, but then he left on a business trip for quite a while, and when he came back, well, I honestly am not sure what kind of relationship we have now. Bernard comes to our house more now than before. He's jealous that Henry is always here. Bernard returns every weekend nowadays to make sure Henry isn't flirting with Catherine. I am guessing that means Bernard wants a relationship with Catherine."

"Or you. Maybe they both want you. I don't have a chance, do I?" William chuckled nervously.

"I keep thinking one day soon you'll realize I'm not one of the popular students at school, and stop wanting to be around me," I told William. "Trust me, Catherine is the one with whom every boy wants a date, and with whom every girl wants to be friends."

"I don't care about popularity. I like you because I don't understand half the things you say, and that fascinates me. Your humor is either way too intelligent for me to comprehend, or you have some sort of intellectual disability causing me to not be able to understand the unintelligence with which you speak."

I stopped right there and slugged his arm. Our books dropped to the sidewalk.

"Ow! I was being funny like you!" William looked shocked that I hit him.

"You called me stupid!"

"No, I was making a joke that you're stupid, but you're quite intelligent, and that's what makes my observation humorous. Please don't hit me. You should carry my books with arms as strong as yours."

"What's going on?" Henry ran toward us looking like an angry hornet.

I began laughing hysterically. "Oh! I understand now! You were making a joke like the kind I make! I had no idea I came across as such an asshole!" I giggled. "I really need to reel in my delivery!

Perhaps make it more obvious that I'm indeed joking. You know William, that was actually really good!"

"Is this boy bothering you?" Henry got between William and me and stared angrily at William. Henry was already uncuffing and rolling up his shirt sleeves.

"Henry!" I yelled, "William made a joke. I didn't understand it at first and got angry, but I now realize it was actually really funny!" I laughed again, retelling myself William's joke in my mind.

"Hello, I'm William," William held out his hand to Henry.

Henry took it reluctantly and William winced. "Quite the strong grip," William said in a pained voice.

Henry turned and nodded at me and walked back to his automobile. "I'm right here if you need me, Maybel," he yelled over his shoulder.

William bent down to get our books.

"I'm sorry about hitting you, and I'm sorry Henry seemed a little too protective." I bent down beside William to help gather our books.

William had pretty brown eyes. He smiled at me. "Thank you, Maybel, I would still like to carry your books for you though."

"Thank you," I said as we stood up.

"I like that you are strong," he told me.

"Me too," I smiled. "William, would you like to stay for dinner? I know mommy always makes extra food on Friday and Saturdays now that Henry and Bernard are always here. I'm sure there will be enough for all of us."

"Yes! I would love to eat dinner with you and your family, and even the two boys vying for your sister's attention. Do you think dinner will be tense though? Does it get tense with those two fighting for Catherine's attention?"

"Not usually," I said.

"You sound disappointed," William remarked.

"Sometimes I crave excitement," I smiled at William.

"After dinner, would you like to come to my house and see my turtles?" William seemed excited to have a friend.

"Oh, you have pet turtles?"

"Yes, I've been interested in animals, especially animals living in or near water, since I was young."

"Have you collected a lot?" I asked.

"Not really, just twenty-eight turtles, but I have eighty-seven frogs."

"What the hell do you need eighty-seven frogs for?"

William looked at me surprised.

"Oh, sorry," I apologized. "I'm working on being better at being fake. Catherine's teaching me. What I meant to say with respect, was that I was a bit surprised with how many turtles and frogs you have living with you at your home. Where in your home do you keep such a large number of turtles and frogs? Did that sound more polished? Did I sound fake, like I think having that many turtles and frogs is ridiculous?"

"I'm not sure. Do you think I'm ridiculous?" William watched me. I thought maybe I had hurt his feelings.

"No, you seem fine, your obsession with turtles and frogs seems strange and unhealthy though."

"Oh," William definitely looked hurt now.

"People say I have an unhealthy obsession with squirrels. I write about them a lot." I felt bad for hurting William's feelings. I hoped I could repair what my words had broken.

"Squirrels are great," he smiled. "I enjoy watching them play and chase each other during mating season. They're very squeaky when they finally consummate their courtship."

"I'll bet!" I laughed.

"Hello Maybel," Catherine greeted us. "Who's your friend?"

"Catherine, this is William. He has twenty-eight turtles and eighty-seven frogs."

"Well, you win this round, William, I haven't got a single turtle or frog," Catherine smiled sweetly at William.

I was jealous of Catherine because she had the perfect retort to someone claiming to have twenty-eight turtles and eighty-seven frogs. She was neither rude nor accepting of his bizarre collection; she was witty, flirty, and fun with her response. Catherine exuded effortless grace.

Catherine gave William her best and brightest smile and giggled. William blushed and watched her with growing adoration. He sputtered his answers to her questions like an idiot who hoped for a kiss at the end of a date.

"William, let's go see your turtles and frogs now," I said. I wanted to separate William from my sister in hopes that he had not already completely fallen in love with her.

"How about later, Maybel? Catherine is telling me about her rose-colored lip color. I'd love to hear more about how hard it was for you to obtain this particular lip color, Catherine."

I rolled my eyes. "Catherine's boyfriend, Bernard, got it for her a long time ago and she's almost out of that lip color, and can't get more, because she and Bernard are no longer dating. Or are you two dating, Catherine? I'm never sure if you two are in good favor or not these days."

"We're always in good favor, Maybel," Catherine smiled, a bit too forced.

"How wonderful, I can't wait for your wedding. Let's go, William." I grabbed his elbow and spun him around.

"Are you sure we can't go after dinner?" he asked.

"I'm sure," I said.

I quickly steered the subject away from Catherine as we walked to William's house. "So, tell me William, where were you living before you moved here?"

"About an hour south here. My father works for a company that installs telephones."

"That sounds nice," I said.

"Yes, he enjoys his work. I want to study animals and their habitats when I attend college."

"I will either be a teacher or nurse," I said.

"If you could be anything that you could possibly imagine, what would it be?" he smiled inquisitively.

"I don't know, I'll have to think about it. I've never pondered that before, surprisingly."

"Well, we're here," he smiled. We arrived at a modest, but well cared for house. It was white and there were rocking chairs on the porch.

"William, what would you be if reality did not confine your desires?"

"Loved."

"Oh," I suddenly felt very uncomfortable.

"My mother died when I was young. We've moved around every year since."

"I'm sorry," I winced. I felt so bad for William.

"Me too. Let's go around back where I have managed to put tags on all the turtles and frogs I have identified and weighed."

"Oh, they're in your pond?" I was happy to hear William didn't sleep with dozens of turtles and frogs.

"Yes, Maybel. I don't keep them all in my bedroom," William laughed.

"Well, that's a relief," I laughed.

His pond was quite extensive and the far shore could barely be seen, it was so far away.

"You have quite the laboratory here, don't you?"

"My father indulges me since my mother died," he said.

"You remind me of another eccentric scientist I know. My friend Susan's father is odd but very brilliant like you."

"Perhaps one day we'll meet," William smiled.

"Perhaps tonight? After dinner?" I smiled back.

"That sounds nice, Maybel. I'm glad I followed you home every day until you took pity on my lonesome self."

I smiled, "We're all lonely, William. It's been nice getting to know you."

We walked the bank of William's pond for several minutes.

"Is your father home?"

"No, he works long hours," William said sadly.

"Who makes you dinner?"

"I make my own breakfast, lunch, and dinner," William said. He seemed a little sad, but not overly sad like I would be if mommy died and I were alone. I supposed he had accepted his situation by now.

"I think I've taken my mother for granted my whole life," I said, rather guiltily.

"Most people do. I did, as a small child. No matter how sad and lonely I get, it doesn't change anything. My mother is gone. My father says we have to make the best of our situation." William didn't seem angry. He seemed to accept his new and lonely life.

We walked along the bank of his large pond a little longer. With every step, frogs a little way ahead of us jumped from the bank to the safety of the pond water. The constant leaps and splashes made me giggle. The turtles were slower and tucked their heads and feet inside their shells as we passed by them. I stooped down and rolled a turtle back onto her feet. I could have sworn she slowly craned her head upward and smiled at me. I smiled back.

"Shall we return to my home?" I asked William.

"Yes," he smiled softly. "I like watching you."

When we passed Susan's house, I pointed out her house to William.

"She's quite the artist," William remarked.

"How'd you know?" I asked, surprised.

"The birdbath there," he pointed to the birdbath Susan had sculpted and dried. "The mud Susan used comes from soil with a heavy clay content."

"Oh, I never noticed. Wait, how do you know it was my friend Susan who sculpted it?"

"The roses on the column supporting the bath very subtly spell out Susan," William pointed out.

"They do?" I walked closer. I bent down. "Oh! They do! That's very subtle! You are more astute than any detective in any book!"

William laughed.

"Hello Maybel!" Susan called down from her bedroom window.

"Susan! The roses you sculpted spell Susan!"

"I know," Susan giggled. "I made them."

"What other secrets do you hide in plain sight?" I laughed.

"That's it, Maybel, sorry to disappoint you," she giggled.

"This is William," I yelled up to Susan. "He's going to be a scientist who studies animals and his father works for the telephone company."

"Do you have a telephone William?" Susan grew interested.

"Yes," William replied.

"What's it like?" Susan asked with wide eyes.

"Boring when you're the only person who has one," William laughed.

"The Charlestons have one too," Susan yelled down.

"Yes, but they only use it for important business," I told William.

"Who are the Charlestons?"

"You know the biggest house in town?" Susan asked. "That's them."

"That's Bernard's family," I said sourly.

"The boy who is coming to dinner?"

"Yes," I said.

"Maybel, come here when you're done eating. My father loves people who love science," Susan smiled.

"See you soon then, Susan," I called up to her, and then left with William to my house.

"Her brother is a scientist too," I mentioned.

"I'm really looking forward to meeting them," William said.

We entered through my front door. Bernard and Catherine were on the sofa. Bernard looked annoyed when his gaze saw who was behind me.

"Hello again," William said to Catherine.

"Hello there, William," Catherine smiled in her flirty way.

"Let's say hello to my mommy." I quickly led William past Catherine and Bernard.

We entered the kitchen and I hugged mommy tighter than I had ever hugged her before.

"Goodness, sweetheart, are you ok?"

"William's mother died and I've been taking you for granted."

"I'm so sorry!" Mommy went to William and pulled him to a chair to sit down.

"Oh, it wasn't recently," William said. "It was many years ago."

"I just found out about it today," I went to hug mommy again.

"Since you're in such a loving mood, dear, will you be a sweetheart and go get daddy and Henry for dinner?"

"Am I intruding on your family dinner?" William started to stand up.

"Good Heavens no, you sit down! I'll make an extra-large basket to take back to the rest of your family, dear."

William watched mommy scurrying around the kitchen and he was suddenly a little boy wishing my mommy was his mommy.

"Let's go get daddy, William," I said quickly. His pain was still raw, no matter how many years had passed.

I opened the door to daddy's workshop and they suddenly straightened up and wiped their smiles off their faces. I figured Henry had been telling about his latest conquest and daddy was living vicariously through Henry's penis.

"Hi, daddy, this is William. He is new at my school. Mommy says dinner is ready."

"Hello, Sir," William smiled at daddy.

"How are your grades in school?" Daddy asked. Daddy skipped pleasantries when a boy was around and mommy was not within earshot, and unable to give daddy her look with her pursed lips, the one that told him to act better.

"I have all good grades, Sir."

"Best subject?"

"I do well in all of them, but I love science."

"Will you attend college?"

"Yes, Sir."

"Are you planning to kiss my little girl tonight?"

"Daddy!" I stomped my foot.

"No, Sir," William said, "I was taught to be a gentleman."

"Very good, you may leave, initial inspection has passed."

Henry sat beside daddy smiling as though thoroughly entertained.

I glared at daddy then turned and led William inside.

"Daddy gave William an inspection," I complained to mommy.

"He passed," mommy stated.

"He did, but how did you know?"

"I wouldn't have let you take William to your father if he hadn't first passed my inspection," mommy winked at me.

"You weren't rude at all though," I told her.

"Oh, honey, I don't have to be loud and obtuse like your father. I can look at someone and make my inspection without causing ill will. Your father knows that if you bring a boy over and I let him get past me, guns won't be necessary."

I looked at mommy as if to silently tell her she needn't scare my friend.

"Oh, William, please don't concern yourself. Our family has a bit of an odd sense of humor. Actually, my husband does, and Maybel, but after so many years, I suppose have come to partake in such odd humor as well."

"I find it delightful," William smiled.

Daddy and Henry came through the kitchen door. Daddy kissed mommy's cheek. I again noticed William watching them from behind memories of his own mother and father together.

Catherine and Bernard came to the kitchen and we all carried bowls and plates into the dining room.

"After dinner, we're going to Susan's house because William wants to be a scientist, and Mr. Matthews is a brilliant scientist." I told everyone at dinner.

"That sounds lovely, dear. Theodore is there visiting," mommy said.

"Oh good! You'll like him, William, he works in a big laboratory," I said excitedly.

I suddenly noticed daddy smiling wildly while watching Bernard and Henry. He couldn't contain his excitement and laughed, then looked down when mommy gave him her icy stare to be still.

"Why is Theo here again?" Bernard grumbled.

"What's the matter cousin?" Henry grinned.

"Oh, haven't you heard? Theo wants his dear, little sisters to come to his beautiful, beach house all summer long again," Bernard said, each word he uttered was increasingly more coated in annoyance.

"You're not going are you, Maybel?" Henry turned to daddy. "You're not letting her go are you?" Henry looked upset, maybe angry and worried, but I wasn't sure.

"Maybe I'll go, and maybe I won't. Why would either of you care?" I asked, annoyed.

Daddy couldn't suppress laughter, even when mommy kicked him under the table. I knew mommy kicked him because daddy looked surprised then looked at mommy confused.

"I think you should go, Maybel. What a wonderful opportunity," Catherine smiled at me.

"Catherine, how was school today?" I changed the subject.

"Good. We discussed Connecticut in one of my classes. Actually, we discussed all of New England, but I paid particular attention to Connecticut, since that's where you'll stay this summer. Would you like me to tell you all about the geography of Connecticut, Maybel? You can then verify the information with Theo tonight when you go visit the Matthews."

I wasn't sure if Catherine was deliberately trying to irritate me or not. She was so good at being fake that sometimes even I had trouble telling when she was sincere.

Bernard looked irritated with Catherine. "Why don't we all go to visit Theo? I'd like to hear about Connecticut too."

"You've traveled through parts of Africa but never Connecticut?" Catherine asked sarcastically.

"I've been to Connecticut, but I'd like to hear about it from Theo's perspective," Bernard said, crossing his arms.

"Hang on cousin," Henry spoke up, "We need your help lifting some heavy pieces in the workshop after dinner."

"No, it can wait until tomorrow." The gleam in daddy's eyes returned. "Why don't you both go talk with Mr. Matthews and Theo?" daddy suggested to Bernard and Henry.

"Daniel!" Mommy hissed. "Take the boys to the workshop!"

"But dear," daddy pleaded, "Mr. Matthews loves talking about science and things I don't at all understand. If he gets all his talking done tonight, he'll shut up about chemicals and other annoying sciency-type things tomorrow at the hardware store."

"I'm sure William will talk to Mr. Matthews, and Mr. Matthews will be all done talking about chemicals by tomorrow," mommy said.

"Also, sweetheart," daddy patted mommy's hand, "I would like to go with the boys. I enjoy watching Henry and Bernard together while in the presence of my dear daughters, and now adding another young buck to the mix is really just so much better than watching an opera. I have to run and get Mr. Charleston before the first act begins. He enjoys watching the bucks act stupid around the does as well."

Henry furrowed his brow, "I'm not in any competition, especially not with Bernard. He's never mounted anyone in his entire life!"

"He better not have!" daddy stared menacingly at Bernard.

"Are you talking about sex?" I bluntly asked everyone at the dinner table.

"No," mommy spoke up loudly, and with a shrill voice, then asked us how we enjoyed today's weather.

"It was very nice," William said. "I showed Maybel my pond. I'm studying the animals living in and around my pond. I'm going to put the information I've gathered into a journal and submit it as my thesis when I enter college."

"That sounds fantastic," mommy smiled.

"You really would like Mr. Matthews and Theo," Catherine agreed. "They are quite brilliant like you."

William blushed, "Why thank you, Catherine," he said nervously.

Boys became nervous around Catherine. Boys considered me their little sister and never looked at me as someone they were attracted to, but daddy said that's why he wasn't full of gray hair. He said when Catherine started maturing, he started graying, and he would be completely gray now if it weren't for me being so level-headed. Sometimes I wished daddy were all gray, maybe even bald. Sometimes I wondered what it would be like to be sought after and adored by both boys and girls. Boys wanted Catherine and girls wanted to be Catherine.

"Maybel, the potatoes," Bernard woke me from my daydream.

I passed Bernard the large serving bowl. His hands covered mine when he grabbed the bowl from me. I felt a jolt of electricity, but I always felt electricity when Bernard touched me. For that fraction of a second when the electricity surged through my hands and part way up my arms, our eyes locked and I knew he felt our electricity too.

I smiled ever so faintly and he returned my smile.

"Daddy, when you go get Mr. Charleston, will you take the cake I baked to Mrs. Charleston?" Catherine asked.

"Of course, dear. It won't arrive untouched, but I'll certainly deliver the remnants," daddy chuckled.

"Daddy!" Catherine whined, "I want her to like me."

"She loves you, Catherine," Bernard smiled and patted Catherine's hand.

"Are you two dating or not?" I asked them. "I can't ever tell if you are dating, or just really good friends."

"Just friends," they both said in unison.

"Then why do you act like you're dating?" I asked.

"I, too, thought you were dating," Henry confessed. "You can see how confusing it is for us on the outside looking in at you both holding hands and kissing even though you claim only friendship."

"Oh really?" I raised my eyebrows.

Daddy looked excitedly between Henry, Bernard, and Catherine.

"It was a peck on her cheek," Bernard told Henry through a clenched jaw.

Daddy's head snapped back to Bernard, then Henry, then surprisingly to me. I returned daddy's interested look with a look of confusion.

Catherine seemed a little hurt that Bernard downplayed their kiss. "Well don't be embarrassed, will you?"

"Catherine, I didn't mean it like that! I was getting the facts set straight." Bernard glanced quickly at me to see my reaction before continuing. "It was a lovely kiss on your cheek. You know I've always enjoyed our walks and conversations, Catherine."

"You don't want dessert, right?" I asked William. "I'm sure Mrs. Matthews will offer you pie or jam."

"I've made chocolate cake, William," mommy interrupted. "You'll have to eat a slice. Don't be in such a rush, Maybel," mommy scolded me.

"Yes, Maybel," daddy smirked, "do stay and make more entertainment for your old and bored daddy. Say, Bernard, how was your school dance last weekend? Your father told me you took a lovely young lady by the name of Lucy as your date."

Bernard's face turned beet red. Catherine's head snapped toward Bernard's direction. And Henry grew interested, too.

"I took Lucy to the dance because my father asked me to take her as a favor to him. Father has done business with Lucy's father and thought it might be helpful to kindly take Lucy to the dance and perhaps Lucy's father will buy several of father's properties without much haggling over prices."

"Ah, uncle used you to ease his business transaction. I've also been asked similar favors from uncle."

"Not anymore," Bernard said tersely. "You end up making women angry and father had headaches dealing with the fathers of the women to whom you were supposed to be nice."

"Oh, he was nice to them, I'll bet," daddy chuckled loudly.

Mommy must have kicked daddy under the table again because daddy turned slightly away from mommy in order to get his feet further away from hers.

"Yes, Mrs. Wyndham, that sounds lovely," William said to mommy.

Mommy looked up, "What sounds lovely, dear?"

"The chocolate cake you offered."

"Oh, yes, right," mommy laughed. "I forgot where this latest conversation started. It started with cake," mommy laughed again.

Mommy turned to Bernard, "Bernard, dear, how often does your father have you date young ladies to assist him with business negotiations?"

"Rarely," Bernard said.

"And how many business negotiations did you attend while we dated?" Catherine asked tartly.

"None, Catherine. My father wouldn't ask me to take a girl to a dance if I were dating anyone."

"Do you really want cake?" I asked William. "I can bake an entire cake just for you some other day if you'd like to leave right now," I whispered.

"Oh, it's quite alright, Maybel. I'm in no hurry. My father works late, and, well, my house is lonely."

Bernard must have been listening closely although he was not sitting right beside either of us. "My parents work a lot too," he said. There was sympathy in Bernard's voice.

"It can be quite lonely," William said.

"That it can," Bernard agreed.

"Well perhaps you two can find solace and a sense of camaraderie in your shared loneliness," mommy said as she stood. "Catherine, Maybel, let's get dessert."

Catherine cut the cake while I handed her plates to set the slices on. We weren't gone but eight or nine minutes, yet upon returning to the dining room, the dishes had been shoved to the side, clearing a place for Bernard and Henry, who were now arm wrestling.

"This is what having sons would have been like," mommy shook her head. "Thank God I have daughters!" Mommy kissed our cheeks.

"Is this a usual dinner time routine?" William asked me as I sat his plate of chocolate cake next to him and sat down beside with my arms crossed, scowling at Bernard and Henry.

"No," I answered. "Feel encouraged to eat your cake as quickly as possible, William, never mind manners, we haven't had any all evening."

"Oh, this is quite delightful," William said.

"Great," Bernard sneered, "you can arm wrestle the winner."

Bernard quickly put down Henry's arm. "Your turn William," Bernard smiled menacingly.

"No, thank you," William replied jovially while stuffing cake in his mouth.

"What do you mean, 'no, thank you?'" Bernard asked incredulously. "If someone challenges you, you have to accept."

"I'll lose," William replied without fear or embarrassment. "I don't play sports and have no big muscles. I prefer reading about our world, habitats, and the effect steel mills have on the quality of our water sources."

William was neither embarrassed of his lack of muscles, nor did he seem to care the least bit about boys looking down on him for his lack of physical strength.

Bernard and Henry stared at William as though he couldn't possibly be serious. "You get teased a lot don't you?" Bernard asked William.

"Shut up, Bernard! I get teased too, for not being as pretty or perfect as Catherine, and I will not have you make fun of my guest. You better lock your bedroom windows tonight if you say one more rude thing to my friend!"

"Calm down, Maybel!" Bernard attempted to douse water on the fire growing inside me. "I was just surprised. I've never seen anyone be so honest about their lack of strength."

"It's quite alright, Maybel," William assured me. "My father's employment has us moving around constantly. If I'm considered unpopular at one school, it doesn't matter, I'll be moving soon enough and might be the most popular student at my next school. I've learned to not care about perceptions of me. Shall we talk about science with your friends now?"

"Yes!" I said excitedly. I was ready to go to the Matthews' house. I knew Mr. Matthews and Theo would relate well to William and there would not be this tension between boys there.

We went to Susan's house where I was proven wrong. Theo was argumentative with William at every turn the conversation took.

"Oh, Theo, may I speak to you in the kitchen about Connecticut?" I asked.

"Certainly Maybel," Theo smiled and took my hand, which I thought was odd, since we were only going a short couple of steps into the kitchen.

"Why are you arguing with William?" I asked Theo. "He's new at school and I want him to feel welcome."

Theo looked confused. "I'm not arguing with William. In fact, I really enjoy talking with him."

"You seem like you don't care for him at all," I said.

Actually, Theo was haughty and condescending, but I didn't want to be too bold. I was trying hard to reign in my bluntness.

"He's intelligent and argues his point well. I really do like him. I'm sorry I've come across as hostile. I'll pay more attention to the tone of my voice."

We returned to William who was now in a very involved conversation with Susan. Susan's face was animated. William's face, as well, looked happy.

"William," Theo began, "I have enjoyed our conversation."

"Oh, I have as well!" William beamed.

"I may have perhaps come across a little too eager defending my stance, and perhaps a bit too engaged when finding holes in your argument."

"I had no holes. My stance is firm. And you are challenging when you debate; I like your approach very much. We cannot grow if we don't face harsh criticism of our proposals," William spoke with gentle fluidity and enjoyment.

"Exactly right, William. See, Maybel, this is how intellectuals purport themselves," Theo told me.

"Ah, I see, you were worried about me, weren't you Maybel? No worries, men are blunt. Women get offended by directness. Us men thrive on competition, don't we, Theodore?"

"Yes, this is true," Theo chuckled.

"Scientists argue with each other in order to help one another. If Theodore said, 'Nice work, William,' I would never question my theory. Theodore has certainly made me question myself, and I have thoroughly enjoyed our back-and-forth arguments." William smiled at me and Theo. He seemed really happy.

"I didn't realize men showed affection like this," I said, sitting down next to William and Susan on the sofa.

"Thank you though, Maybel, for your concern," William smiled kindly. "If I can survive your father, Henry, and Bernard, I can survive anything," William laughed.

"Those two are at your house again, Maybel?" Theo grumbled and peered out the large bay window facing the road. "Why?"

"Henry is helping daddy deliver cabinets, and Bernard was talking to Catherine," I answered.

"William, you've only just met them, so tell me, as an outsider, why were Henry and Bernard there tonight?"

"Clearly to be in the presence of Maybel and Catherine," William said.

"Exactly!" Theo slapped his knee.

"I think Bernard still cares for Catherine and doesn't want Henry to take her on a date and kiss her," I explained.

"Catherine and Henry don't have to leave the house to kiss," Susan pointed out.

Just when I thought Susan wasn't paying attention, she made astute observations.

"I don't think they're kissing at home because Bernard is always nearby," I said.

William was candid like me. "I think both Henry and Bernard like you, Maybel, but they like Catherine too, so that makes for awkward dinners, I'm sure."

"I usually daydream, so I don't know if it's awkward," I replied.

"Well, you won't have to worry about Bernard or Henry this summer. I'll take good care of you, Maybel," Theo returned to his seat across from me.

"Yes," Susan smiled, "Theo is a good big brother."

I let out a long, annoyed sigh. "I have enough big brothers already. I don't want any more brothers."

"I won't be your big brother, Maybel," Theo winked at me.

"Maybel, I've got to be going," William said. "I've had a lovely evening. Thank you."

"Oh, so soon? I'll walk you out."

I walked William outside and down Susan's steps. "I thought your father would be working late."

"Yes, he will, it's just that I don't know how long I'll be able to live here in this town, and you have enough suitors as is. I'll probably leave before a year is over, and I'm so tired of leaving. I really like you, Maybel. And I'm scared to like people anymore because after I lost my mother, it's been town after town of liking people then losing them."

"I'm sorry, William."

"Look, if it's alright with you, I'd still like to walk you home from school, but just know that I might have to leave next month, or maybe next week, and maybe I won't be able to say goodbye before I'm off to another town."

I pulled William's neck down and kissed him there on the sidewalk in front of Susan's home. I kissed him passionately because I liked him, and something about never knowing what I will lose tomorrow made me want to kiss him today.

The next day, William came to my house and surprised me with theater tickets.

"I didn't expect you," I told him. "I thought perhaps you were trying to politely tell me you did not want to get close."

"I don't want to lose you, but I really like you, Maybel. I'm certain whenever I have to move away it will hurt, but I really want to spend time with you."

"I like you too, William," I blushed.

Daddy peeked his head in from the kitchen. "Ready, baby?"

"Yes, daddy. Just one minute, please."

Daddy looked at William and muttered something under his breath as he returned to the kitchen.

"I'm sorry, William. I have to help daddy today with his work. I was wondering if maybe you would like to ask my friend Susan? She's only a couple years younger than us. What do you think? And later after I'm finished, you and I can do something together."

"Oh, ok." William sounded disappointed. "I don't really know Susan well enough to go ask her on a date."

"I'll go with you," Catherine smiled as she came toward us putting on her coat.

"Oh, well, I guess that will be fine," William said hesitantly.

"I'm on my way to town, and I'll stop off at Susan's with you so you won't feel awkward."

"Ok, thank you," William said. He looked like he wasn't sure about taking Susan.

"You don't have to go with Susan," I said. "I can meet you later."

"No, it might be nice to get out and be social. I'm sure it's better than sitting alone at home."

"It will be fun," Catherine flashed William a dazzling smile. "Come, William, I'll explain the situation to the Matthews."

Catherine bounced down the sidewalk and William followed.

I sulked through the kitchen and out to daddy's workshop. I usually enjoyed my trip to the hardware store, where I learned a new swear word or naughty expression every week, but today I wanted to be with William in case he moved away tomorrow.

Daddy sat on his overturned bucket next to Henry.

"Hello, Maybel, where is your little friend? I heard he came calling for you." Henry's voice was sarcastic and mocking.

"He left." I sat down beside daddy on another overturned bucket.

"Where is the woman you were with last night?" I countered.

"What woman?" Henry looked puzzled.

"Your lady of the evening."

"I went to bed early," Henry said.

"Yes, I'll bet. You got in bed early, and then fell asleep around five minutes later, ten if she was lucky."

Daddy laughed.

"No, Maybel, I wasn't with anyone last night."

"Why? Has this small town run out of women already?"

Daddy again laughed.

"Actually, Maybel, I have come to realize that I want a family at some point in time and I won't find a good woman if I'm not a good man."

"Very insightful," I said dryly.

"It's true. I'm really trying to better myself."

"It really is true, honey," daddy said. "I'm just as surprised as you. Henry is taking steps to better himself and not be a tomcat."

"Why?" I asked.

"What do you mean 'why?'" Henry looked confused.

"I mean, you do whatever you want, whenever you want. You're the only person I know who is truly free," I told him.

"I want a family like your father has. I'll gladly give up alcohol and women for a wife and children like your mother and you and Catherine."

"Who is the lucky lady?" I asked.

"I just want to live a better life, and who knows, maybe everything will fall into place sooner than later," Henry blushed.

"He won't tell me who she is either," daddy winked at me.

"I'm glad to see you happy, Henry," I said. I really was genuinely happy for him.

"Thank you," Henry smiled.

"You'll have the prettiest children," I added.

"Only if they look like their mother," Henry said softly.

"Wow, you really are in love," I said, astonished Handsome Henry wanted to give up every woman ever for just one woman.

"Yes, I am," he again blushed.

"Well, what are we doing today?" I asked daddy.

"We are delivering this to a local buyer," daddy nodded over his shoulder at an intricately carved jewelry box.

"That's gorgeous!" I exclaimed. "May I open it?"

"That's up to Henry. He made it."

"Who's it for?" I asked excitedly. "Can I open it?"

"Of course," Henry said. "It's for my future wife. I'm keeping it until I propose."

"She's has no idea how you will spoil her does she!" I giggled as I opened the lid. It was a puzzle box too, with secret compartments and I had to open them in a certain order.

"I'm glad you like it," Henry smiled softly.

"This won't take three people to deliver it to Henry's bedroom at the Charleston's," I said. "What else are we delivering?"

"A quilt stand for Mrs. Charleston," daddy said, "and Mr. Charleston requested I help him install some doors in the back room."

"To the stills?"

"Maybel! How do you know about the stills?" daddy asked with both shock and anger.

I froze. "How do you know about them daddy?" I asked slowly, hoping daddy wouldn't be too upset.

"I helped install them. Your turn. How do you know about them?"

"Susan and I accidentally stumbled upon some jars of fruit soaked in rum once that made us feel really good, then really bad. We didn't realize we'd drunk alcohol until later."

To my surprise, daddy laughed, "Did you learn your lesson then?"

"Backroom fruit should not be eaten," I said, and daddy laughed again.

"Well come on then, let's load up the quilt stand and jewelry box." Daddy stood up and I followed him outside.

When we arrived at the Charleston's, daddy and Henry took the quilt stand and Henry asked me to take his jewelry box upstairs to his bedroom.

I ever so carefully took it upstairs and into Henry's room. I set it on Henry's dresser. I was so intrigued by the secret compartments and trying to figure out how to open the puzzles that I hadn't realized Henry leaning against the doorway watching me. He was smiling.

"Oh! You startled me!" I turned to face Henry.

"Your father wanted me to tell you he won't be needing your help with the doors in the back room." Henry watched me with a soft smile on his lips.

"What else does he need help with?"

"Nothing, you are free to return home."

"Oh. Ok," I sighed.

"You seem disappointed."

"I'm ok," I assured Henry.

Henry turned to leave.

"Henry?"

"Yes?"

"I'm jealous of the special lady in your life, but I'm also very happy for you. I wanted to date you again. I went to Connecticut while you were in San Francisco. I suppose you met your future wife there in San Francisco. I really am happy for you, but I'm also really jealous. I'm more happy than jealous though."

Henry came to me and looked down at me sweetly. "Don't be jealous," he said softly, then kissed my lips tenderly. "I love you."

I smiled up at Henry. "I love you too, Handsome Henry."

Henry left back down the stairs to help daddy.

I was disappointed though. William, Susan, and Catherine were busy. I considered asking Theo to do something, but figured he was in town to visit his parents. I didn't want to intrude.

I walked down the hallway to Bernard's room. I opened the door and saw Bernard laying on his bed reading.

"You should knock, Maybel."

"You should lock your door, Bernard." I jumped and landed halfway on top of Bernard.

Bernard ignored me and continued reading.

"You know when you ignore me, I want your attention even more."

"I have a chemistry test to study for. I should have stayed at school."

"Theo is a chemistry genius, why don't you ask him for help."

"Theo is still at his parents?"

"Yes."

"Of course he is. This weekend keeps getting better."

"Why are you grumpy?" I blew in his ear.

"I'm not. I'm studying."

I blew in his ear again.

"You are annoying."

"Why?" I blew again.

Bernard turned his head to the side and stared at me.

"Ooooh we haven't had a staring contest in a long time." I inched my nose closer until the tip of my nose touched the tip of his nose.

Bernard swept my hair back while still staring at me.

"I love you," he said quietly.

I wasn't sure if he was trying to distract me so he could win. "I love you too," I said. I continued staring.

"Where's your stupid boyfriend I saw you kissing last night?" Bernard asked. He turned his gaze back to his chemistry book.

"He's at home with a sore back from the wild ride I gave him."

Bernard slammed shut his book hard and stared at me.

"I'm joking, Bernard, why are you in such a bad mood?"

"I saw you kissing William," Bernard said.

"Oh, I'm sorry, I forgot to tell him he has to be dating my sister if he wants to kiss me," I snapped at Bernard.

Bernard's face turned red with anger.

"I've seen you kiss Catherine hundreds of times and one of these days, I'll be married, and you'll see me kiss someone hundreds of times."

"I don't like that Henry, Theo, and now this William boy are all vying for your attention."

"William will likely leave sooner rather than later because of his father's employment. Henry only dates a girl for an evening. And Theo and I do enjoy each other's company, but why do you care? You come to dinner to spend time with Catherine more than ever lately. You drive home almost every weekend now to see Catherine."

"I come to see you. I miss you."

"No, you're jealous of Henry. You come to dinner to keep an eye on Catherine and Henry," I said.

"No, I come because I'm jealous Henry gets to spend every night with you and I can't," Bernard said. He seemed a little shy and hesitant.

"Henry is at my house every night because daddy requests his help delivering furniture. You drive home every Friday nowadays because you love Catherine, and you're jealous because Henry is at our house every night. Henry doesn't flirt with Catherine. He barely acknowledges her presence because he's scared of daddy."

"Henry is at your house every night because he has fallen in love with you," Bernard said.

"Honestly, Bernard!" I stood up. "You are being ridiculous!" I left Bernard there to be in a grumpy mood by himself. I didn't want Bernard's sour disposition to ruin my day.

I went to the Charleston's backroom where daddy, Henry, and Mr. Charleston were putting heavy doors with bolts over the entryway to their secret stills that Susan and I already knew about.

"Daddy, are you sure you don't need my help?"

"You can go back home, sweetheart, thank you for your help," daddy grunted as he hoisted the door alongside Mr. Charleston and Henry.

I wasted no time in leaving the Charleston's in case daddy changed his mind. I wanted to see if Theo was still home and wait for Susan to return from the theater with William. I hoped Susan enjoyed herself. William was a lot like Theo and Mr. Matthews. I thought they would very much enjoy each other's company.

Theo answered the door and invited me in. "Did Susan go to the theater with William, or did she decide to stay home?"

"She left with William. William seems to be a good person. I told him I'd kill him if he kissed Susan so I'm not worried."

I chuckled, "I'm actually surprised you let Susan go with a boy."

"I helped father clean our shotguns while William waited in the workshop with us for Susan to get dressed. William got our not-so-subtle message," Theo winked.

"Daddy wanted me to help him deliver a quilt stand to the Charleston's house, that's why I could not attend the theater with William. Actually, I was surprised he came to my house today. I had thought he was politely telling me he would be leaving town soon as a way to sort of distance himself from me and my eccentric family."

"Maybe he likes eccentric. I've never once been bored in your presence," Theo laughed.

When William brought Susan home, he stayed for dinner, as did I. Mrs. Matthews and I made roast. It was fun cooking with her. She buzzed around the kitchen like mommy did.

"Did you have fun?" I asked Susan.

"Yes! They fought with swords!" Susan's eyes lit up as she talked about the play.

William also spoke animatedly about the play. "I'm really glad I went," he said. "Sometimes I hesitate to make friends since I never know when I'll leave, but I'm really glad I've met you two," William smiled at me and Susan.

After dinner, William politely said goodbye to Susan and me, then went home. I stayed a few more minutes, then returned to my home, where Bernard and Henry sat in our family room playing chess and arguing about some toy Bernard supposedly stole from Henry when they were children.

Daddy and mommy sat on the sofa holding hands and Catherine sat in a chair watching Bernard and Henry while intermittently rolling her eyes at their argument.

I sat on the sofa next to mommy and began nodding off while resting my head on her shoulder.

The Charleston's had invited several friends over for lunch. One of the attendees was a very handsome older boy who immediately got my attention. To my great delight, he noticed me too and smiled. I felt an unfamiliar giddiness. He was tall, with dark brown hair, and bluish-green eyes.

My breath caught and I couldn't reply when he walked toward us smiling and greeting Bernard and Catherine. He looked expectantly at Catherine to introduce me to him.

"Edmonde, this is my sister, Maybel. Maybel, this is Edmonde." He smiled and took my hand, but I could do no more than stare at him.

"Nice to finally meet you, Maybel," he said. "Catherine has told me about your beautiful stories, but said nothing of your incredible beauty."

I blushed and swallowed hard. I couldn't speak. I politely smiled. That was the best I could offer. I inwardly chastised myself because he must have thought horribly of me for not being able to speak eloquently like other girls.

Fortunately, Catherine intervened. "Maybel let's go to the study for just a moment, shall we?"

I nodded, still unable to find my voice.

"We'll only be a moment," she said to Bernard and Edmonde.

Catherine led me to the sofa in the study. "Well, what do you think?"

"He's gorgeous!" I gushed.

"I know! He's the real reason I invited you here!"

"I'll keep Bernard occupied so you two can get to know each other better," Catherine said.

"No," I quickly hissed. "I couldn't talk when I met him! I was too nervous! You have to stay with me!"

"Oh, Maybel! You're doing great! Couldn't you tell how interested he was?"

I shook my head no.

"Maybel, he couldn't stop staring at you! Trust me, he is very interested in you."

"Come, Maybel," Catherine stood and reached for my hand. "Take a deep breath. It's just very light small talk, nothing complicated, so relax."

"You're going to stay with me, right?"

"Yes, Maybel," she sighed. "I'll stay with you for a little while and when you get comfortable, Bernard and I will leave you two alone."

We returned to Bernard and Edmonde, who were sitting in the ballroom while Mrs. Charleston played violin.

Thankfully our attention was on Mrs. Charleston, so I did not have to attempt small talk.

Mrs. Charleston played beautifully. I watched her facial expressions while her bow moved across the strings. She was fully immersed in her music. Her fingers moved gracefully across the strings. Her long dark hair bounced as her head bobbed with her music.

I looked over at Mr. Charleston as he watched his wife, a gentle smile played along his lips and adoration filled his eyes.

I turned my gaze slightly to see Bernard sitting nearby watching me. He also had a gentle smile. When I looked at him, though, he quickly turned away and watched his mother play.

Everyone stood and clapped when Mrs. Charleston finished. She took a polite bow and set her violin down. I watched Mr. Charleston go to her and kiss her cheek and whisper something in her ear that made her giggle and blush.

"Shall we get drinks," Catherine asked.

"Scotch on the rocks," I said. And those were the first words Edmonde heard me utter.

"I'm joking!" I quickly added. "I'll get water."

"I appreciate a good sense of humor, Maybel," Edmonde smiled.

"Well, you'll sure appreciate the hell out of me," I replied.

Damnit, I thought to myself, why could I not act normal for just one evening?

We eventually began dancing and I only stepped on Edmonde's foot once. He had a light touch and didn't try to control me when he led, and I liked that.

Bernard and Catherine kept glancing at us. Catherine smiled at me while Bernard looked unhappy.

Later when Bernard was deep in conversation with friends, I took Edmonde's hand and smiled at him as I gently pulled him to the side of the ballroom. "Let's go for a stroll in the garden, shall we?" I whispered.

Edmonde smiled back at me nodded. We quietly slipped out through the kitchen and into the winding gardens. He held my hand as we walked. "I thought I'd never get a chance to talk to you alone," he smiled.

"Well, here we are," I giggled. "How do you know Catherine?"

"From a study group at the library. We're preparing ourselves for more challenging courses. She's quite smart, you're sister. Catherine speaks highly of you and has told me a lot about you. You two must be quite close."

"Yes, we are."

"Maybel, may I ask if you have a boyfriend?"

"I do not have a boyfriend," I smiled nervously.

"Catherine said as much, but I wanted to ask you anyway." He hesitated, "I hope I am not being presumptuous, but If I didn't know Catherine was dating Bernard, I have to say, I'd wonder if his intentions were to date you."

I looked up at him surprised at his candidness.

"I'm sorry Maybel, I'm sure that is not the case. I want to ask you on a date, but I wanted to be sure you were single first."

"I am not dating my sister's boyfriend," I said defensively, but truthfully, I was ashamed that a stranger could so quickly notice a bond between Bernard and me.

"I'm sorry, Maybel," Edmonde apologized. "I shouldn't have been presumptuous. Would you like to go to dinner with me tomorrow?" he smiled shyly.

"Yes, that would be lovely," I said.

"Wonderful!" he smiled.

He held my hand and we walked back inside the Charleston's house. Inside the ballroom, Bernard was sitting in a chair beside Catherine brooding. He looked up when Edmonde and I returned. Catherine whispered something to Bernard then came toward me.

"Everything going well?" she asked us.

"Yes," I smiled.

"Great," Catherine beamed.

The next day Edmonde did not pick me up for dinner. "I got dressed up for nothing!" I whined to Catherine. Catherine had spent all afternoon dressing me up like one of her dolls again.

Bernard sat in a chair watching us with both boredom and brooding. "I didn't like him anyway," Bernard said with a low, angry voice.

I began tearing the hair accessories out of my hair.

"No!" Catherine held my wrists. "We can still go out! I have another friend with a handsome brother. I know they'll be at the country club tonight. Maybel, you're beautiful," Catherine said. She looked at me admiringly. "You'll come, won't you?"

"Why do you keep insisting Maybel have a boyfriend, Catherine?" Bernard grumbled.

"Why do you keep insisting Maybel not date anyone, Bernard?" Catherine snapped back.

"I just want to go to bed. I'm sorry, Catherine."

I didn't like the way Bernard looked happy that Edmonde did not come to take me to dinner. Bernard looked smug and happy at my misery.

"Did you say something to Edmonde?" I asked Bernard just before I went upstairs to my bedroom.

"No," Bernard said.

"You raised your right eyebrow," I stared icily at him.

"And so I did," Bernard replied with a steady voice. He looked deeply into my eyes without remorse.

Upstairs in the bathroom mirror, I unbraided my hair. I heard Catherine downstairs arguing with Bernard. "I'm trying to find a boyfriend for Maybel so you'll stop being so overprotective of her!"

"I just don't understand why you keep setting Maybel up on dates!" Bernard said angrily.

"Are you jealous of Maybel's dates?" Catherine asked bluntly.

"What? No!"

"Do you want Maybel all for yourself? Is that why you keep chasing away any man that comes near her?"

"Maybel is so utterly naive to men's ulterior motives, Catherine! You know that! Remember when we took her to the circus with us and that boy told her all the chairs by the ice cream stand were trick chairs, props used in comedy routines, and that they collapsed as soon as you sat on them to make the audience laugh?"

I heard Catherine let out a giggle.

"He told Maybel the only chair that wasn't used in the comedy act was the one he was sitting on, and that he'd be kind enough to let her sit on his lap so she wouldn't fall over in one of the trick chairs."

Catherine giggled harder. "You ran over and tackled Maybel before she sat on his lap and then you slugged that boy with his mouth still full of ice cream!" Catherine laughed loudly.

"I'm just looking out for Maybel," Bernard said. "She's a lovely girl, but extremely naïve."

"I suppose you're right, Bernard," Catherine relented. "I know you care for both of us."

It was Bernard's birthday party and we were at the Charleston's mansion. His school friends attended. Catherine basked in the attention of being Bernard's girlfriend, in his mansion, with his wealthy friends watching her with wide eyes and lustful glances.

I wandered upstairs because it was late and I didn't want to be around the partygoers anymore. Henry was laying on his bed reading the newspaper. He was alone.

"Why is your bedroom door open, Henry? Aren't you worried someone will come pester you?" I giggled as I skipped over to him and jumped onto his bed. I laid on the opposite side of his bed because he was too beautiful to lay against and I told him so.

"Maybel!" Henry laughed, I am not a Greek God, stop joking about that.

"I'm not joking," I giggled. "You are all the Greek Gods put together, minus all the weird and disturbing things they do in their tales."

Henry laughed. He patted his bed, right beside where he laid. "You're not pestering me, honey. Come give me a hug. I'm old and can't come to you," he chuckled. "How was your evening, sweetheart?"

I scooted over and gave Henry a big hug. I loved Henry. "It was ok. I didn't dance with anyone, but there were cookies."

Henry smiled, "I'm glad you enjoyed the cookies at least, and I'm surprised no one asked you to dance."

"I wasn't fond of anyone tonight, and even if I were, Bernard chases boys away," I furrowed my brow and sulked.

"I'm sure that pleases your father," he sighed.

"Can I lay with you for a while? We can play cards."

"I don't have any cards, sweetheart."

"They're in your nightstand drawer," I said. "The last party here was boring so I stayed here in your bedroom and played solitaire by myself."

Henry reached over and opened his nightstand. The deck of cards I left were still there.

"What shall we play?" Henry winked at me.

"Rummy? Or poker with just two people?"

"Sure, Maybel," Henry smiled. "Whichever you want."

"Henry why are you up here? There are beautiful ladies downstairs."

"I'm tired. I don't want them like I used to," Henry said.

"Why?"

"I don't know," he sighed again as he shuffled the deck. "I suppose I want something more. I wanted you," Henry looked at me and he looked very sad, "but I messed up and left."

Bernard came into the room. His tie was askew and the top two buttons of his white dress shirt were unbuttoned. "Maybel, why are you in here? You said you were going to my bedroom to write stories."

"I saw Henry's door open. I wanted to be with Henry."

Bernard threw his jacket onto the chair by the bed and laid down on Henry's bed behind me. He wrapped his arm around my waist and pulled me against him. "What are we playing and what are the stakes?"

"Why are the top two buttons of your shirt undone, dear cousin?" Henry smirked.

"I was about to change into my pajamas, Henry. Not everyone has three coat room trysts a night."

"Three? I'm not sixteen anymore, Bernard, I've slowed down." Henry winked at me and I laughed.

I turned my head and kissed Bernard's cheek. "Happy birthday," I smiled.

Bernard relaxed against me. He rested his head against mine. "Thank you. I'm glad you came. I know you don't like large gatherings of people, and neither do I, but thank you for coming."

I kissed Bernard's cheek again. "You're welcome. And when it's my birthday, I want a diamond necklace, an automobile, and a pony."

Bernard smiled, "Be careful what you wish for. You might just get a pony, and then where would she stay? You don't have a barn."

"Florence will stay with you," I giggled. "The diamond necklace and automobile will stay with me."

Bernard laughed at kissed my forehead then leaned his head onto mine as we laid together.

We played two rounds of cards then Catherine came. "Bernard, you disappeared."

"I'm sorry Catherine, I was so bored with Arnold's accounting stories."

Catherine sat on the edge of the bed beside Henry. "You're looking handsome as ever," Catherine winked at Henry."

"Thank you, sweetheart," Henry said.

Henry was more reserved with Catherine than he was with me. Henry's sense of humor opened like a morning glory with me, but only when we were alone. When we were in a group, he remained more stoic.

Catherine flirted with Henry, but Bernard was completely unaffected.

"You didn't save me a dance, Henry," Catherine said. "I was looking forward to at least one dance."

"I'm sorry, honey, I was tired and didn't want to make small talk with strangers."

I laughed, "No woman down there wanted to talk to you. They want you to hold them and press your hips into theirs." I made kissing noises at Henry.

"I'm too tired for that, also," Henry said.

After another hand, I went to Henry's bathroom. When I came back, Catherine had taken my place laying next to Bernard on Henry's bed.

I leaped onto the bed and into Henry's lap. "I get to cuddle with Henry now," I giggled.

Henry chuckled and wrapped his arms around me and held our cards. "Let's win this round, shall we?"

"Hang on, let's make this a little more interesting," Catherine smiled slyly. "Losers have to take off one piece of clothing."

"Catherine!" I was surprised. She was usually so modest and conservative in the way she spoke and purported herself.

Catherine rolled her eyes, scoffing. "Fine, Maybel, it's a game for older boys and girls anyway."

"You've played this before?" Bernard questioned.

"No, but I just thought I'd see what it was like. We can play something else."

"How did you even know about this game?" Bernard seemed alarmed.

"Edith's older sister played it in college in her sorority," Catherine said nonchalantly.

"Edith's older sister is a bad influence," Henry said. "Guard your innocence as long as possible."

"Have you had sex with Edith's older sister?" I asked bluntly.

"No," Henry replied.

"Why not?" I was curious as to why he chose some women over others to share his bed.

"She's your friend. I keep friends and family separate from my bedroom affairs," Henry said, like it was a matter of fact and obvious.

"Oh really?" Bernard laughed. "I'm certain Stella and Norma would say differently."

I felt Henry tense up under me, and Catherine's head snapped around to look at Bernard, and then just as quickly, back to stare wide-eyed at Henry. "You had sex with our older cousins?"

"I did not have sex with your older cousins," Henry said flatly.

"Wait," I gasped, "was that what you were doing with them when I thought you were playing koala?"

Bernard suppressed a chuckle but his eyes were dancing wildly.

"I kissed them both, that's as far as we went, no intercourse," Henry said. He seemed uncomfortable and he felt rigid underneath me.

I turned my head around to look at Henry. "I remember seeing them on you, and they were making noises." I breathed deeply and moaned breathlessly while Catherine blushed and giggled.

"They both wanted more, and while we kissed passionately, I stopped it from going further out of respect for your father and mother. I didn't want your parents mad at me. And also, your cousins were both really aggressive and I didn't like that."

Henry hugged me and pulled me back into his chest. He kissed my cheek. "We're going to win this hand," Henry tickled my forearm.

"Your poker face is really lacking," I said dryly.

"We fold," Catherine said.

"I bet anything Maybel is doing her poker face right now," Bernard said.

"Do you bet your shirt?" I asked.

"Yes. Do you bet yours?" Bernard stared unflinchingly at me.

"Yes," I said. I maintained constant eye contact.

"Show them our hand," Bernard told Catherine.

"To be clear, this is your bet," Catherine told Bernard. "I'm keeping my shirt on no matter what."

"Ah, there's the prude I know and love," I joked to Catherine. Catherine was not amused.

Catherine showed their hand. They had nothing, ace high.

I threw down our hand. Henry and I had nothing, jack high. I started unbuttoning my shirt.

"Maybel!" Catherine looked astonished.

"What? This game was your idea," I said, "Besides, I have three layers on: a shirt, an undershirt, a camisole, and my bra. I guess that's four layers."

I took off my outer layer. Henry pulled off his shirt to expose his bare chest. I looked down and back up at Henry's beautiful, bare chest and shoulders, and butterflies danced in my belly. I realized my mouth was agape staring at Henry's beautiful body, the beautiful body that was pressed against me.

"Maybel, stop acting like one of those annoying girls who drool all over the men playing rugby," Bernard threw a card at me.

"Uhh.... Mmm," was all that came out of my wide-open mouth.

I turned around and took the cards Catherine had just dealt us and smiled like a cat with a mouse when I leaned back into Henry's now-bare chest.

I turned my head upward, "Be a shame if you accidentally kissed my lips right now, you beautiful, gorgeous man." I couldn't help but giggle at myself.

Henry pecked my cheek and I put the back of my hand against my forehead and pretended to faint.

"Maybel, you're ridiculous," Catherine laughed. "Now come on, let's play."

I folded my cards. "We lost again, Henry," I looked back at him. "Take off your pants, my love."

Henry laughed and tickled my ribs. "No, Maybel, but I appreciate your enthusiasm."

"And I appreciate your beautiful body," I pretended to swoon.

Bernard groaned, "Maybel, don't be one of those girls who flirt and act annoying around boys. It's unbecoming and you are much too smart to act like that."

"But Bernard, relax, I'm only a drooling slut for Henry, nobody else, I promise."

I leaned back and sighed as I turned my head and looked up at Henry.

"I love you too, Maybel, and thank you for making me feel handsome," he laughed and playfully kissed my neck.

"I think you two should marry each other," Catherine said. "We could all live together and our children could play together."

"I accept," I smiled at Henry.

"I don't think I'll marry or have children, but if I ever change my mind, and if you're available, I'll happily marry you." Henry smiled sweetly at me.

"I do. I mean, I will. I accept your proposal. Maybel Fox. I like it." I turned and hugged Henry. "I thought you had a special lady in your life that you wanted to marry though, Henry."

"You do?" Catherine and Bernard both asked. They were surprised.

"I do, or rather, I did, but I feel that perhaps her love is for another." Henry looked so sad my heart broke for him.

"She's stupid then," I said.

Henry smiled sweetly at me and brushed my hair back from my temple. "She's not," he said softly. "She seems to adore another, and that's ok. I still love her, and I always will."

"Bernard, let's go to your bedroom so these two can plan their wedding," Catherine laughed.

"I want to play cards," Bernard said. He was suddenly sullen and downright grumpy.

"Bernard just wants to make you lose so he can see you naked, if he already hasn't," I teased Catherine.

"Maybel!" Catherine playfully slapped my arm.

"Maybel, do not take off any more clothing," Bernard warned.

"Bernard! You're interrupting my courtship with Handsome Henry!" I giggled.

Catherine giggled too. "I am serious though. Another ten years and you'll both find yourselves single and wanting to settle down and you'll marry each other."

I held out my hand to Henry. "Ten years. Is it a deal?" I giggled.

"You're the only woman I'd ever marry, Maybel." Henry shook my hand, then very lightly kissed my lips, and I felt myself melting in his arms.

Bernard was in daddy's workshop when I went to collect daddy's coffee and tea mugs to wash. Daddy had a habit of forgetting to bring them inside in the evenings, then opened every cabinet in the mornings trying to find his favorite coffee mug. It was a big, red mug Susan helped me sculpt, dry, and paint. Susan made sure the handle was safely secured before drying, because I had shown her the bird I made with Paul, and I was clearly not good at securing wings, much less mug handles.

"Bernard, what are you doing here alone in daddy's workshop?" I asked him.

"Your father went to the hardware store to pick up more knives for whittling. I think he enjoys having lots of sharp things around to show Henry and me how good he is at carving."

"And you're just sitting here quietly, waiting for daddy to bring home more knives?" I wondered why Bernard was sitting in daddy's workshop instead of being inside with Catherine.

"I was thinking about when my father sat us down and talked about when he was mean to mother growing up. Do you remember?"

"Yes," I said dryly. "That was after you told Henry I was annoying and dirty and I overheard."

"I'm sorry, Maybel. I've thought about what father said more, and I've also thought more about that story you told me about the boy and his puppy. You told me the boy took his puppy for granted. He did not appreciate his puppy. That was right before you left for Connecticut. Do you remember that, Maybel?"

I sighed very annoyedly, "Yes, Bernard, I remember."

"I think my father was trying to tell me to be nicer to you."

"Remarkable perception you have, Bernard," I said sarcastically. "I have daddy's big, red mug and I'm going inside to wash it. Have a lovely evening watching daddy whittle arrows."

"Wait, Maybel, I figured out what my father was trying to tell me with his story. I told him I would be more patient with Catherine, because I thought he was talking about Catherine, and my mother sighed loudly, then hit my father with her rolled-up newspaper saying I got my lack of intuition from him. Father then clarified to me that he had tried to tell me to stop being mean to you. You were right when you correctly interpreted father's story."

I looked around daddy's workshop for more mugs and cookie plates, but did not find any more. "See you later," I told Bernard.

"You know, I am not good at woodworking, Maybel, but I'm getting better."

"Why are you suddenly interested in woodworking? Henry does not flirt with Catherine. You don't need to keep an eye on them," I said with annoyance.

"I like seeing you, Maybel. And I'm jealous that Henry is more a part of your family than I am. Did you see how direct and honest I was just now? I'm getting better at expressing my feelings, too."

I smiled politely then walked toward the door.

"You know, Maybel, when I am here, I sit and listen to your father and Henry making crass jokes as your father stares at me, just waiting for me to smirk, or God forbid, laugh at one of their jokes. I'm certain your father would then ask me what I knew about sex, just before he speared me repeatedly to my death. I know he's been whittling that long pole over there into a point whenever I come over just to taunt me. He sits in front of me making the point of the spear ever sharper.

Then he asks me to touch the tip to see if it's sharp. I know he's doing that on purpose. He would kill me three times over before he stopped to check for my heartbeat.

"Bernard!" I snapped my fingers in front of his face to bring him out of his rambling.

"Maybel, I didn't want to love you because I knew you didn't love me as more than a brother."

"You treated me horribly and made me cry often!" I yelled. "That's why I didn't want to be near you!"

"I know. Mother says I'm like my father when it comes to expressing my feelings. Father got better and so will I."

"I want you know, Bernard, I'm still angry. I have a lot of pent-up anger. And do you know what else I have? A good portion of your inheritance I've won from gambling. I have a lot of money I've won gambling, Bernard, and because I've gambled so often, and for so many years, I know the kind of people who will accept my large, money bag in exchange for slicing your throat. Like the noble Romans always said, 'He who is mean to Maybel will surely get their ass beaten and throat slit.'"

"Maybel,"

"It's a real quote! Are you going to argue it's veracity?"

"I will never again say anything mean to you. I've learned my lesson," Bernard said. "I am really trying to be better and I'm sorry I was cruel to you."

Susan and I ran to town. We visited the pond and candy store, and then we were to head to my house, where we planned to make cookies with mommy. After that, we were to go to Susan's house to make pumpkin bread with Susan's mother. I was excited to be with my mommy and Mrs. Matthews. I liked the snowflakes that sparsely fell as the weather became colder, and I enjoyed the tinsel hung from storefronts. Charlie always had candy canes at his candy store, and the pond in town had geese. The geese liked bread but hated people. I told Susan that when we each had our own homes, we should attract geese to stay with us, and consider our houses their homes, so they would protect our homes from strangers.

"Maybel, how is a goose going to protect you?" Susan asked me.

We were sitting at the pond, and I threw a piece of my sandwich to Mrs. McNalley's gigantic sheep dog while Mrs. McNalley was preoccupied chatting with her sister. One of the geese who had been eying my sandwich, squawked and honked and flapped his wings, making such a commotion that Mrs. McNalley's gigantic sheep dog tucked his tail and hid behind Mrs. McNalley, letting the goose have the piece of my sandwich.

"And that is why you need a guard goose, Susan."

"You're right, Maybel, geese are mean. I'll get a dozen for my yard."

Susan and I drank hot chocolate at Charlie's candy store then started to walk home toward my house to make cookies. It was a brisk afternoon and our noses were red. Henry's automobile approached us in front of the candy store, where all the popular girls stood flirting with all the popular boys. I liked when Henry sometimes picked me up after school, too. I enjoyed seeing Henry's automobile on the street in front of my school because all the popular girls stood with their mouths agape as Henry took my books, my coat, and opened his passenger's side door for me to get in. On this afternoon, Henry opened his passenger's door for both me and Susan. We slid in and I sat close to Henry and pretended I didn't see all the girls and boys staring.

"Maybel, will you please help me deliver a bookcase?" Henry asked, after we drove away from the popular girls and boys. They stared at us as we drove away and that made me happy.

"I'm sorry, Henry, Susan and I are making cookies and pumpkin bread this evening. Can we deliver it tomorrow?"

"You can go with Henry, Maybel," Susan said. "Come get me when you are done. It won't take long will it, Henry?" Susan sat beside me in Henry's automobile with her bag on her lap. She was so sweet and innocent, and I was so happy we had found each other.

"It won't take long," Henry smiled at Susan. "How about I pick you up at your house after we deliver the bookcase and drive around the town square before I take you to Maybel's house to make cookies?" Henry winked at Susan. Henry had a way with people like Catherine did. They were both so good at winning people over.

"Ok, Henry!" Susan smiled back at him.

Henry took Susan to her house and walked her up to her door like the gentleman he was, and then he drove me into the countryside to deliver one of daddy's beautifully carved bookcases.

"You have no idea how differently you are treated than people like me. I have to work for attention. You do not, Henry. People flock to you. People want to be around Catherine. Neither you nor Catherine have ever eaten alone, nor have you ever attended a school dance alone. You do not understand how people react to your beauty."

I was a little annoyed that no boy had asked me to the school dance, and I was most certain that neither Catherine nor Henry had ever had any problems getting a date. I did not want a romantic date; I only wanted a boy to accompany me to the dance so I wouldn't have to hear my friends talk about what an amazing time they had the following Monday at lunch, and then grow silent when they realized I could not contribute to the conversation.

"Don't assume I have a perfect life, Maybel. When I'm speaking about equality on behalf of Indians, I have rotten food thrown at me. Imagine being pelted with smelly, rotting food. Those same people have seen me in expensive tailored suits from Europe and fell over each other trying to please me because they did not know I was the same Indian at whom they had just thrown rotted meat!"

I suddenly felt humbled. Henry did know what it was like to not be popular when he attended Indian rallies.

"I know people think I'm handsome if they think I'm white. I know most of those people are hypocrites. Do you remember the woman I told you I really cared for, and then she broke up with me because I cheated on her with another woman?"

"Yes," I said. "I don't like to think about you being anything less than perfect though."

"She threw rotten meats and moldy vegetables at me at an Indian rally. She didn't recognize me! It hurt me, Maybel. My heart shattered!"

Henry looked like he might cry. I tensed up. I didn't know what to do.

You don't care if I am Indian or white, and I like that about you, Maybel."

"I do like you," I told Henry.

"I know. And I love you, Maybel. I should have simply broken up with her that evening, but I was young, and I was immature. I had sex with her sister and made sure she would walk into her bedroom and find me pleasuring her sister in her bed. I was wrong. I was bad. I should not have done that. I should have broken up with her and left immediately, but my pride wanted vengeance. I'm not proud of what I have done. I'm telling you because I have always been honest with you, and I always will be honest with you, Maybel. I truly love you."

I smiled weakly. I did not know what to say to such a confession. It hurt to imagine Bernard wooing me into bed to get back at Catherine for not liking Indians. I could not imagine the pain Catherine would feel, nor could I imagine how I would feel, falling for Bernard's advances, only to discover he had intercourse with me to get back at Catherine. I sat numbly next to Henry thinking about him as a fallible human.

Henry continued, "I like that you tell me things honestly, Maybel. You are blunt and honest, and you are fiercely loyal. If I had met you when I was younger, I would have asked you to marry me. I can't ask that of you now. I have been with a lot of women, but you are pure, Maybel. Maybe one day I'll be a better man; I really am trying."

"You seem to have matured a lot in recent years," I told him. "I may not have liked you if I had met you when you were young and prideful. Then again, I was much more prideful when I was a child," I reflected. "I think you are good, Henry, and have overcome more obstacles than anyone else I have ever known. I wish you realized how amazing you are. You really need to appreciate all the steps forward you have taken; I do." I reached over and took Henry's hand in mine.

Henry smiled softly, "I like that you always see me as better than I am."

"Did Mr. Charleston or Bernard ask you to go to San Francisco after our first date?" I blurted out my question quickly because I didn't want Henry to have time to think up a calculated response.

"No, Maybel, they didn't make me go. I chose to go. I made the wrong choice and I'm sorry," Henry said. He was remorseful. I believed Henry.

I breathed in a sigh of relief. I had not wanted to think Bernard was behind Henry's absence in my life right after the most amazing first date I could have ever dreamed.

"Auntie Anna asked me to go as a personal favor to her, because she needed someone she trusted to gain a foothold out west. This will be quite lucrative for all involved, Maybel. I'm sorry I left you after our first date. I hope you forgive me and give me another chance one day."

We delivered the bookcase to an old woman then drove to Susan's house. "I'm always amazed by your strength," Henry smiled at me. "You can lift heavy bookcases and cabinets better than most men."

I flexed my arm muscles and then kissed my muscles the way I'd seen the muscular men do at carnivals when they lifted anvils. Henry laughed and tousled my hair. "I love you so much," he smiled at me.

Henry took me to Susan's house and we drove around the town square as he promised. I waved at Bernard and Catherine as they stood in front of the candy store with the popular, older boys and girls. Bernard glared at Henry and Henry tooted the horn on his automobile and winked at Bernard.

"Why are you in such a bad mood, Maybel? You have chocolate, a new dress, and Catherine has given you a stack of stationary to write your stories." Bernard sat on our sofa beside Catherine while I paced by the fireplace.

"She's mad because a boy didn't want to take her to her school dance," Catherine explained.

"Catherine! Don't say!" I said.

"Oh Maybel, Bernard doesn't care about your boyfriends," Catherine said.

"Boyfriends? You have boyfriends? More than one boy?" Bernard asked curiously.

"Yes!" Catherine giggled. "She's attracted quite a lot of attention since she's grown breasts!"

"Catherine!" I screamed.

"Oh Maybel, everyone has noticed. It's not a secret!" Catherine giggled.

I began crying. I didn't want anyone to notice my breasts. They kept growing and wouldn't stop. My clothing didn't fit anymore.

"Catherine, don't tell Bernard!" I yelled.

"Bernard isn't blind," Catherine kept giggling.

Bernard blushed and looked embarrassed. He looked away from me.

"I hate my new body!" I cried.

"You're beautiful, Maybel, everyone says so." Catherine stood and came toward me. She played with my hair. "You really are, Maybel. Bernard, don't you think Maybel's beautiful?"

"You look nice," Bernard said. He still looked away.

"Maybel, don't worry about that boy. You can go by yourself to the dance."

"No! I hate school, I hate boys! I hate everything!" I cried.

Catherine hugged me. "Maybel, boys are stupid. It's for the best that he didn't take you to the dance. You're better than any idiot boy at school. Those boys are too young and immature to realize how great you are."

I cried so hard snot got in my hair.

"Maybel, no boy is worth snotty hair," Catherine said. "Look, Bernard and I are to meet friends tonight but maybe, if Bernard agrees," she looked pleadingly at Bernard, "he could take you to your dance?"

"I will," Bernard immediately agreed. "The boy who didn't show up to take you is an idiot. Fortunately, you have Catherine to help you navigate through all the stupidity of adolescence." Bernard smiled at Catherine and she smiled back.

"Dry your eyes, Maybel, you're going to show those boys what they've missed out on," Catherine said.

Bernard and I arrived at my school but I was scared.

"What's wrong, Maybel? They are boys, and they are immature and stupid boys at that."

"Were you ever immature and stupid?" I asked.

"I still am," Bernard laughed.

"What if he asked a prettier and more popular girl to go and they're in there now?" I looked up at Bernard, worried.

"Then he's stupid and it's for the best you found out before marriage and four children."

"Bernard, I know you're trying to cheer me up. I know you're trying make me feel better, but I'm not popular like Catherine. You don't attend school here so you don't know this, but I'm not popular and I eat lunch alone sometimes. You are handsome, rich, and popular. I'm embarrassed for you to see how my classmates treat me. They don't think I'm Catherine, that's for sure."

"Maybel, come here." Bernard held my hands. "I'm not popular either, sweetheart."

"Yes, you are! You and Catherine are the most popular!"

"I might be seen as being popular when I'm with Catherine, but truthfully, at my boarding school, I've never been popular. Catherine would never have given me a chance if she had met me at school."

"Catherine wouldn't have ever been at your school because you go to an all-boys school."

He laughed, "Well, if she had ever visited my school for more than that one night you both visited me, she would have seen that I, too, eat lunch alone some days. I'll tell you a secret, Maybel. I've never asked Catherine to visit my school for more than a weekend because I'm not popular like she is. I like that in her eyes I'm popular. She doesn't know that I'm not popular like she is at school."

"How are you not popular? You're handsome, you have the best clothes, and you vacation in Europe." I thought Bernard was lying to make me feel better.

"At my school, every boy there is rich and vacations in Europe," he chuckled. "I'm not special or different."

"And rich people have problems, too, Maybel." Bernard's eyes suddenly looked a little sad. "Everyone always feels like they need to bring me down a peg or two, because they think I'm so privileged, that my life is so perfect, and that I have no problems or sadness because of my wealth. They say and do things that are mean because they think that because I'm rich, that my life is perfect, and they want to knock me off the imaginary throne on which they imagine I sit."

I stared up at Bernard. "Oh," I stammered. I had not expected Bernard to be so open and honest with his feelings.

"I didn't know," I said softly. "I'm sorry."

"Maybel, one of the things I like most about you is that you have never cared about my wealth."

"Oh, that's true. I don't care if you are rich or poor. Sometimes you are so nice to me, and sometimes you are an ass, but I've always loved you."

Bernard smiled at me.

"If Catherine visited, she would find the popular boys and ignore you?" I asked.

"Probably," Bernard laughed. "We didn't stay at my school long enough for her to see that I am unpopular that weekend you and Catherine visited, but I'd like to think that if she visited for more than a weekend, and actually walked around campus with me, she would still love me when she discovered my unpopularity."

"Then invite her to your school," I teased.

Bernard laughed, "Maybe I'm not willing to test her loyalty."

Bernard held my hand and walked me into the gymnasium where music played and everyone danced.

"Bernard, I'm scared. Do you want to go do something else?"

"No," he said simply. "I'm here with you and I'm having a good time, Maybel. I don't care about anyone else here. I only see you."

"Come, Maybel," Bernard led me into the gymnasium.

"They think I'm pathetic because my date is my sister's boyfriend." I walked slowly and Bernard was almost pulling me to get me inside.

"Tonight, I'm not Catherine's boyfriend. I'm your date, and I don't care what they think." Bernard kissed me and it felt different. He kissed me like I'd seen him kiss Catherine.

"Come, Maybel. We'll have fun together. We always have fun together. You're better than you think."

I took a look around the crowded gymnasium. The lights were dim and a row of tables along the side had a large crystal bowl of juice and there were plates with cookies piled atop. Under other circumstances, I would have been delighted by the sheer volume and selection of sweets but the boy who was supposed to pick me up at my house was dancing with Betty, and Betty had already had sex with a boy.

I must not have hidden my sadness well when I saw Harry with Betty. "Maybel, what's wrong?" Bernard reached for my hand and turned me to face him.

"My date is here. He didn't come to my house to get me because he brought another girl instead."

"I'm sorry, sweetheart," Bernard held my hand and pulled me into a hug.

"The girl he's with has had sex," I whispered. "Boys always want those girls. They never want me."

"Not all boys want those kinds of girls, Maybel."

"Yes they do," I whispered and looked down. I knew Bernard was trying to make me feel better, but he kissed Catherine all the time because she let him. Bernard liked those girls.

"Bernard, have you ever kissed anyone other than Catherine?"

"You," Bernard said.

"I meant, have you kissed anyone other than me and Catherine?" I asked Bernard.

"No."

"What would you do, then, if Catherine kissed another boy?"

"She has. I don't care," Bernard said plainly.

"See, you date Catherine because she lets you kiss her, not because you love her."

"I do love Catherine," Bernard said.

"If you loved her, you would care who she kissed," I countered.

"I'd be angry if you kissed a boy," he said.

"Only because Catherine says you see me as your little sister," I sighed.

"I don't. My date tonight is a beautiful, young lady who is confident and fearless," Bernard held my face tenderly.

"Where is she?" I asked sadly. "I never see her anymore."

"She's right here," Bernard held my face and looked down at me with the sweetest smile.

"Bernard, I'm not confident or fearless anymore. I'm not popular, I eat lunch alone sometimes, boys don't want me, and I feel awkward in my new body. Can we go, please!" Tears welled in my eyes as I tried hard to not let them fall down my cheeks.

I watched Harry kiss Betty. "You like those girls, Bernard. Catherine lets you kiss her. She kissed another boy and you don't even care because she lets you kiss her and touch her and that's all that matters to boys."

"No, Maybel. I adore you. I wouldn't care if you never had sex with me as long as you are by my side forever."

Bernard pulled me close and danced with me for another song, then he went to the restroom, and upon his return to the gymnasium, several girls stopped him. To my dismay he chatted with them politely. He wasn't flirtatious, but I was sad and felt oddly fragile, which was a new sensation for me.

A boy in my class named Garrett asked me to dance. "Hello, Maybel," I was wondering since your date is busy, if you would like to dance?"

I looked back at Bernard and he was nodding his head and smiling at the girls. It didn't feel like he was flirting, but it nonetheless angered me in my state of fragility.

"Yes," I accepted his hand.

He was awkward but nice. I figured that described me, too.

Garrett came from a farming family and he was kind. I knew him from childhood. I liked him.

The song ended and Garrett and I politely smiled at each other and parted. I looked for Bernard and found him still lost in conversation with the flirting girls. He hadn't even noticed my absence.

I sat on a chair along the wall with other sad boys and girls. I hated this dance.

"Maybel, there you are!" Bernard said.

"You were busy. I decided to sit here," I said, annoyed.

"I was being polite to those girls but I was waiting for you to rescue me from their incessant nonsense," Bernard said, and reached for my hand.

He led me to the table with drinks and he poured me a cup of water.

"Hello, Maybel," a girl smirked at me. She was with her two friends who batted their eyelashes at Bernard. "What are you doing here with such a handsome man?" The two friends giggled.

I didn't know what to say or do anymore so I just stood there.

"Care to dance?" She asked Bernard as she smirked at me.

"No," Bernard replied and led me away.

"Maybel, I fully expected you to punch them."

"I don't know what is happening to me, Bernard. I cry a lot. I'm scared. I get angry. I don't understand what is happening to me."

Bernard began dancing with me. "You're growing up, sweetheart. Your moods are changing as fast as your body. It will get better." Bernard held me.

The song ended and I went to the restroom and while I sat down to pee, I heard several girls come into the restroom giggling. "She's here with a boy. It's not Harry," they giggled. "Harry didn't want Maybel and didn't pick her up at her house." "Harry's with Betty," another girl giggled. "He probably only asked Maybel to the dance as a joke anyway." They all cackled like witches. "Here, let me help you with your hair," one said. "Dab some color on your lips," another girl was talking now. "I can't believe Maybel is Catherine's sister. Catherine is beautiful and smart." "She's Catherine's sister?" a voice exclaimed, "I had no idea! Maybel sure doesn't dress like Catherine!" They giggled and finished primping their hair while I sat on the toilet crying. I'd never cared about those stupid girls before but lately I felt sad and scared and very awkward all the time and I didn't know how to handle all these changes in my body.

I let the puffiness in my eyes subside then returned to Bernard. Five girls were standing around him flirting, while five boys stood off to the side glaring at him. I couldn't handle anymore rejection, especially not from Bernard. I couldn't bear Bernard's rejection, so I turned to leave.

"Maybel," he called, "let's dance."

I turned back around and he had stepped through the circle of girls and came to me with his hand out.

I hesitated. The girls were giggling at me and whispering.

Bernard took my hand and led me toward the dance floor. "You're the most beautiful young lady I've ever seen," he kissed my lips in front of those girls, and in front of Harry.

"Thank you, Bernard."

Susan suddenly appeared. "Hi, Maybel! Theo brought me because I didn't have a date. Bernard will you dance with me?"

"I'd love to sweetheart," Bernard smiled and took her hand.

"May I have this dance, miss?" Theo smiled.

I accepted Theo's outstretched hand.

"Maybel, why do you look so sad?" Theo asked.

"My date is here with another girl. He never came to my house to take me so Catherine asked Bernard to take me."

"I'm sorry, Maybel," Theo held my waist and pulled me closer.

I didn't say anything. I let Theo lead me in a dance. He was gentle.

"Theo, do boys only want to be with girls who have sex?"

"Most do," he answered honestly.

"Did you when you were my age?" I looked up at Theo as he held my waist firmly.

"Yes. Fortunately, none of those girls wanted me," he said.

"Why do you consider yourself fortunate?"

"I don't have syphilis or children by several different mothers," he chuckled.

"If they had let you have sex with them, would you have had sex with them?" I knew I was being invasive but I had so many questions.

"Probably. I'm ashamed to tell you the truth, Maybel. Men are driven by their desire to have sexual intercourse."

"At least you are honest with me," I sighed.

"It's painful to be honest, but I will always tell you the truth even though I know you will think less of me." Theo's eyes were honest. I felt honesty inside me when he spoke.

"Why did you want to have sex?" I asked him.

"I thought it would feel good."

"Why would you think it would feel good if you never had it before?"

"I assumed it would feel good because it felt good when I touched myself, so I thought if a woman touched it, it would feel better," he chuckled.

"Did it?" I asked.

"Yes," he said.

"Did the woman like it?" I asked.

"She seemed to," he chuckled.

"How do you know when someone likes it?" I was not good at judging people's feelings some-times and wondered how other people could understand.

"They moan," Theo answered.

"Like they're sick with a bellyache?" I asked, confused.

"No, a different kind of moan," he chuckled.

"Bernard teased me a lot growing up. Were you mean when you were younger?"

"I sure hope not!" Theo said.

Maybe Theo was mean when he was fourteen or sixteen. I didn't know him then, so I don't know if he was callous and insensitive. He probably was, but the difference was that I didn't get hurt by his mean words and actions. I still felt angry sometimes at Bernard because I knew Bernard while he was going through his 'growing up and moody' phase.

"I think you were right to put space and time between you and Bernard. He shouldn't have kissed you while dating Catherine, Maybel."

"You're honest with me, Theo, so I'll be honest with you. I liked his attention but I know I shouldn't have. I love Catherine and don't want to lose her."

"I understand, Maybel. I think you are confused. You don't understand it's wrong for Bernard to kiss you because he's kissed you so many times it's become natural for both of you. I think Bernard enjoys your attention too, and he enjoys Catherine's attention as well. But it's not right. He needs to choose one of you then remain faithful to the woman he has chosen. Or, even better, you choose, Maybel. You have the power. You choose. Either pursue Bernard or leave him alone to be with Catherine."

The girls I overheard in the bathroom were watching me and whispering to each other and giggling.

"It's really hard being Catherine's sister," I quietly muttered.

"You are so much prettier than Catherine. You have no idea, Maybel. You are the reason Catherine strives so hard. Writing, humor, beauty, you have everything except confidence. I don't know what happened to you, Maybel, but somewhere along your life, you lost confidence." Theo spoke directly and with intention.

I considered Theo's words. "How do I make it all better?" I whispered.

"Only you can know. You'll be ok though. You're smart and resourceful."

I leaned into Theo's hug. I secretly wondered what he felt like naked. I wondered what he did to the girl he had sex with to make her like it. I wanted to know what he knew.

"Were you popular in school?" I asked Theo.

Theo laughed. "No, we were poor and I had tattered clothes. It taught me that some people are only friendly when you have good clothes and a pretty house. I found out early in my life that just because someone is nice to you, it doesn't mean that person is nice."

"I don't think Catherine realizes the girls she calls her friends wouldn't be her friends if she didn't dress so perfectly all the time," I said.

"Maybe she does realize that, and that's why she always tries to impress with her hair and clothing," Theo said.

"Why would she want such horrible and fake friends?"

"Some people have never had real friendships so they don't realize how good a friend is supposed to be, Maybel."

"I hadn't considered that. That's an interesting way to look at it," I mused.

"Bernard grew up wealthy. He might not know the people who compliment him and want to be around him are only doing so because they enjoy his status in high society. But Maybel, you and I know who those people are behind their facade. The people who are nice to Bernard and Catherine aren't nice to us. We can see them for who they are. Some people think being poor is a weakness, but you can turn that weakness into your strength, Maybel. You won't be taken advantage of by those people."

"You're smart, Theo. You understand people."

Theo continued holding me and dancing.

"Theo, if I were older or you were younger, would you date me?"

"Yes, Maybel."

"Is it my age?"

"We're not far apart in age. We are far apart in life experiences. And, you are in a relationship with Bernard, even if neither of you realize it," Theo said bluntly.

"I'm not in a relationship with Bernard!" I became angry and my eyes betrayed me; I started crying when I wanted to be mad.

"Don't cry, Maybel. I don't mean for you to become angry or sad. Bernard has chosen Catherine, not you."

I quickly wiped away tears.

"Maybel," Theo sighed, "I think you are intelligent and beautiful and I certainly don't mean to hurt you. Bernard chose Catherine. He's had opportunities to choose you. He has not chosen you. Find a man who loves you and wants to be with you."

I felt my lower lip quiver.

Theo held my cheek. "You will find someone, Maybel. It's not Bernard. He chose Catherine. You deserve better."

"Why don't you want me?" I asked Theo.

"You're young and I've been engaged and I've had sex. You have done none of those things. I don't want to take those first times from you. You're too special and should have those first times with someone else who is also experiencing those first times. It will be special for you both if it's the first time for both of you. I can't give you that, Maybel. And neither can Bernard."

I stood there looking up at Theo. I knew I looked as pathetic as I felt.

"I do want you, Maybel," Theo sighed. "You have no idea how much I want you. I am scared though. I died inside when Victoria left me. You brought me back to life. I don't want to die again."

Bernard and Susan came looking for us.

"It's late, I need to get you home, Maybel," Bernard said.

"We'll walk with you," Theo said. He held my hand as we walked home.

"I'll take Maybel to her door," Bernard said. "I'm sure Catherine is home by now."

"See you tomorrow, Maybel," Susan waved, blissfully ignorant of Bernard's irritation at Theo.

"May I kiss you goodnight, Maybel?" Theo asked me.

"Yes," I smiled.

Theo leaned down and kissed me sweetly. "Goodnight, Maybel."

"Goodnight, Theo."

Bernard was staring at me when I turned back around. He looked unhappy.

We walked to my home in silence.

Catherine greeted us at our front door. "How was it?" she smiled excitedly.

"Theo was there and we danced," I smiled back. "And Bernard helped me get through the night." I turned to Bernard. "Thank you, Bernard, for everything. You being there for me really means a lot. You have no idea how much it truly meant to me. Thank you. I love you."

Bernard looked sad, "It was my pleasure." He smiled weakly, then took my hand and kissed the back of it gently.

"Goodnight," I said to both Catherine and Bernard and went upstairs to bed.

My math teacher told me that, while I was not failing math, I was getting alarmingly close to failing. I asked Henry to help me after dinner and before we delivered items for daddy. My geometry grades improved, as well as my algebra grades, because Henry was the best teacher I had ever had. He was patient and kind and never made me feel stupid, even though he had to explain everything several times and in different ways.

I received my first A on a math test. I danced around Henry waving my test around. "Henry, you are the best teacher ever and I love you!"

Henry smiled, "I love teaching. I wanted to be a teacher, you know. I wanted to help children."

"Why didn't you pursue teaching?"

"Money," he chuckled. "I saw that money brought power, and with power, I could influence and change education for the better. I donate new educational materials to schools in the poor parts of towns."

I smiled, "That's really nice of you."

"I want children to have better childhoods than I did."

Henry's face always looked like a cloud passed over the sun when he spoke of his childhood. His face was bright and happy, and in the next instant, a shadow crossed across his countenance and his eyes were no longer focused on what was in front of him, but inward, on whatever terrors played there over and over, again and again.

Henry had to go to San Francisco on business for Mr. Charleston again so I was left without a math tutor. I considered asking Bernard for help because he had been driving home every weekend these days to see Catherine. When I asked Catherine if she would mind if Bernard helped me for one hour on Saturday and Sunday afternoons, she began crying.

"We broke up because he has another girlfriend, I'm sure of it, but he denies having another girlfriend. There's a girls' boarding school not far from his school and I think he sees other girls."

"He's here every weekend," I assured her.

Catherine continued sniffling and talking as though she had not heard a word I said.

"And then he said I flirted too much with the boys at the candy shop but that's never bothered him before, and anyway, I'm not flirting! I'm polite, and I smile at whatever stupid thing the boys say because that's what a polite person does."

Catherine seemed to be talking more to herself than to me. She was even arguing with herself.

"Do I smile at boys? Yes. Is that wrong? No. Why is it considered flirting? I think that just because I smile and am polite, does not mean I want to kiss him. Why do boys think that just because you smile at them it means you want to kiss them? They're stupid and think too highly of themselves if they think every girl who smiles at them wants a kiss! Idiots! All of them!"

I was about to tell Catherine that I would just wait for Henry to return to resume my math tutoring, but she was still having a conversation with herself and wasn't paying attention to me.

"And then, do you know what Bernard said?"

Before I could answer, Catherine continued.

"Bernard said I wanted an excuse to break up with him for a while so I could feel guiltless about dating other boys. Ok, yes, there's a boy I am curious about, but that's not why I wanted to pause my relationship with Bernard. I truly think there's another girl in his life."

"I'll just wait for Henry to return," I said.

"What?" Catherine suddenly looked surprised I was sitting on her bed, as though she just now realized that someone else was in her bedroom.

"I'll wait for Henry to tutor me in math instead of asking Bernard for help."

"Oh, you can ask Bernard for help," Catherine said as she turned around and began brushing her hair and muttering to herself about relationships.

I waited a week for Catherine to cool down. I figured I would ask mommy, then again broach the subject with Catherine, once Catherine had time to calm down and cease muttering to herself about how dumb boys were."

Mommy was making breakfast and daddy was admiring her bottom as she moved back and forth between the oven and the sink.

Mommy," I paused, "I've never been good at math and, well, do you think it would be ok if Bernard tutors me...." I trailed off, hesitant of her reaction.

Mommy raised her eyebrows at me, surprised. She didn't say anything. She didn't look upset but she wasn't smiling.

"Henry won't return for a while so do you think Catherine would be mad if Bernard helped me?"

"She won't be excited about that, Maybel." Mommy paused, "Talk to Catherine and be honest with her."

"I did, and she said Bernard could help me, but I don't know if she was telling me the truth. Sometimes I can't tell if Catherine is just being polite," I said, and looked down at the floral pattern of our kitchen tablecloth.

"Cheer up Maybel," mommy patted my head, "It will never be as bad as your imagination will tell you."

I traced the flowers on the tablecloth with my fingernail until Catherine came downstairs. "Catherine, can Bernard tutor me in math or will that make you angry at me?" I blurted out before she even sat down.

Catherine, looked surprised at my outburst. "I already told you, it's fine, Maybel." Catherine, as always, remained prim, proper, and poised.

"You won't be mad at me?"

"No, Maybel."

"Daddy, is Catherine telling the truth or just being polite?"

Daddy sat at the table anxiously awaiting breakfast. Mommy made blueberry muffins and daddy watched intently as mommy took them from the oven to cool on a rack.

"Daddy," I said again. Daddy was far too engrossed in those blueberry muffins.

"Yes, Muffin? Maybel? I meant Maybel." daddy kept staring at breakfast cooling near the kitchen window.

"Catherine says it's ok if Bernard tutors me, but I can't tell if she's being polite, or if she really doesn't care if Bernard helps me in math."

"It's fine, Maybel," Catherine sighed and rolled her eyes.

Daddy finally focused on Catherine and me. He sighed a great, deep breath. "Catherine, Maybel, sweethearts, I have sisters. I grew up with sisters. I have been surrounded by women my entire life, and I have yet to understand the subtleties of their nature."

Catherine and I giggled.

"Catherine, pumpkin, if Bernard tutors Maybel, will that upset you?"

"No, daddy," Catherine said.

"Catherine, my sweet, little, perfect pumpkin, in twelve years, at our dinner table, when you and Maybel have husbands and children of your own, will you suddenly, out of nowhere, without warning, yell out," daddy raised his fist into the air and shouted, "Maybel, remember twelve years ago when Bernard came to tutor you in math? I'm still angry about that!" Daddy then slammed his fist down onto the table for added emphasis.

Catherine and I burst out in giggles.

"No, daddy, I will not do that."

Daddy turned to me. "You may ask Bernard to tutor you then."

Catherine and I kept giggling at daddy. Mommy set our blueberry muffins on our plates and kissed daddy. "You're such a good daddy," she kissed him again.

When I asked Bernard to tutor me in math, he excitedly agreed.

"You seem to really love math, Bernard," I laughed. "In fact, I have never met anyone who loves math as much as you."

"I get to spend time with you, that's why I'm excited," Bernard smiled.

"You can spend time with me not studying math, too," I assured him.

"Catherine and I are friends, but we are not dating, and when we are not dating, you don't come to my house. Now you can come to my house and not feel like you are betraying Catherine." Bernard smiled and seemed really happy as he spoke.

My math grades stayed decent under Bernard's tutelage, but not as good as when Henry taught me. Henry was an amazing teacher. Bernard tried to explain things, but he was naturally inclined toward understanding math with ease, so he didn't know how to explain math to someone who didn't immediately understand.

It didn't help my math grades either that Bernard and I spent more time talking and walking in his gardens than doing math. For as much time as I'd been spending at Bernard's house, I was sure my parents were expecting me to get high marks in my algebra class. I was certain they would be disappointed, because math just wasn't my forte, and also, I usually spent more time persuading Bernard to wade in the stream, read to me, dance, and do absolutely anything else but tutor me in math.

"Ok, a little math now, Maybel."

"Did you see the deer near your front door?" I asked wide-eyed.

"No, I did not. Now time for a math problem."

"There were also puppies!" I exclaimed excitedly.

"Focus, Maybel!" Bernard sounded like a teacher.

"One of the puppies asked me to come outside!" I said enthusiastically.

Bernard sighed, "Do one math problem."

I groaned. "Fine," I crossed my arms.

Bernard said something about numbers and letters and finding 'X.'

"X is a playful little flirt. Always hiding and wanting you to come find her," I told Bernard.

Bernard chuckled, "Ok, Maybel, what is the answer?"

"X doesn't want to be found. She is aloof and flirtatious. She enjoys making me cry. I really dislike this Miss X. Perhaps someday she'll stop playing games and settle down somewhere where she can be easily found."

"Maybel, I swear if you don't try to find X, your parents will know we haven't been studying as much as we say we have and they won't let you come over every weekend!"

"X equals 2 Bernard."

Bernard looked taken aback. "That's actually correct, Maybel! I'm proud of you!"

"See, I have learned a little. I've learned that you really, really love math and can be quite demanding that everyone else around you learn and love math too!"

Bernard laughed, "I've learned a little from you, too. You've helped me see the world a bit differently, more artistically I suppose."

Bernard walked me home. Catherine was sitting with mommy and they were sewing in the family room. "Hello Catherine, Mrs. Wyndham," Bernard said politely.

"Hello Bernard," both mother and Catherine returned pleasantries.

"I got a math question right!" I danced around. "Can Bernard stay for dinner?"

"Oh, I'm sure my mother is expecting me back soon for dinner," Bernard quickly said.

"You're welcome to stay, Bernard," Catherine smiled politely, but didn't seem overly enthusiastic about having her former boyfriend come to dinner.

"Thank you, Catherine, but I must return home now. It was nice seeing you. Goodbye Mrs. Wyndham. Maybel, practice algebra and I'll see you tomorrow."

"I'll see you tomorrow," I giggled.

"You'll practice algebra and see me tomorrow," Bernard said.

"I'll see you tomorrow," I giggled again.

Bernard sighed, "Practice math, Maybel."

"Don't go looking for X without me!" I giggled as he closed the front door.

I turned to mommy, "Mommy, I really did get an algebra question correct! Can you believe it!"

"That's wonderful, dear," mommy smiled at me.

"Catherine what have you been doing today?" I asked.

"I saw some friends earlier for tea. Now I'm sewing with mommy," she said.

"Are you mad that Bernard is tutoring me?"

"No," she replied without looking up from her sewing.

I looked at mommy to see if she offered any reaction. Mommy shrugged her shoulders and continued sewing.

"Maybel, I asked Bernard to accompany me to Betty's house and he agreed. Did he tell you?"

"No," I said.

"I'm sure one afternoon without math won't cause your grades to drop," Catherine said as she sewed. She seemed neither happy nor sad. It irritated me that I often could not read Catherine's expressions.

"Bernard, hold my hand," I asked as I walked from rock to rock, from one end of the stream to the other.

Bernard held my hand. He was strong. His hands felt like I could go anywhere and he'd be there to catch me if I wavered.

We crossed the stream and stepped onto the opposite bank. My cotton, outdoor clothes mommy sewed were getting wetter and muddier with every outrageous act I undertook.

I next dared Bernard to climb the tall tree in front of us.

"You first, Maybel," he gently pushed my shoulder forward and I stepped on a pine cone.

"Ouch! Bernard!"

"Sorry Maybel," he laughed.

"You aren't a bit sorry, Bernard!"

"Maybe not," he laughed.

"Whoever reaches the top first wins, and the loser has to make the other one dinner!"

"Fine, Maybel, you better know how to cook steak!"

"Well you better know how to cook octopus!"

"What? That's disgusting!" Bernard grimaced.

Having distracted Bernard, I shot up the tree.

"Maybel! You cheated!" Bernard ran after me. He jumped up to the third branch, which I considered unfair because his legs were so long.

"I have to make up for your long arms and legs somehow, Bernard! If we had the same arm and leg length, you would have no chance whatsoever beating me!"

I was at the top of the tree a full three seconds before Bernard! "You're getting weaker, Bernard!" I taunted.

"You cheated, Maybel!"

"If we had the same arm and leg lengths you know I would have won by a full minute!"

"Maybe you're right Maybel, but I'll never admit that to anyone else!"

"That's fine, as long as you know," I gloated.

"Maybel, I have to make you octopus now. I don't even know where to get octopus."

"I'll settle for a campfire and hot chocolate."

"It's a deal." Bernard reached out his hand and I shook it. I liked touching him. I liked his hand in mine.

"Maybel, do you see in the distance the outline of the moon vaguely peeking through?"

"Yes."

"At this time of year that means north is there," he pointed to the tree behind us.

I watched Bernard's beautiful, green eyes as he pointed things out to me.

"Maybel, are you paying attention?"

"Yes," I murmured.

"Then what did I say?"

"There's north," I pointed. "Moon's over there," I again pointed.

Bernard stared at me.

"Bernard, I want to show you something. Do you see up into the sky far above us? And do you see down below? Don't you ever wonder what everything feels like?"

Bernard looked at me with questions in his eyes, like he wanted to understand, but he thought I was off on one of my odd daydreamy ways of looking at things.

"When I see the sky, if it's blue, I feel invigorated. When it's white with a sheet of clouds, or gray with no definition, just one board of pale gray slate, I can feel the sky pushing down on me. And the trees are life. The trees have such life and energy. The grass, when it's soft and green and fluffy makes me happy, especially the clovers I step on. When you touch a rock or dirt or tree bark, don't you feel like your grandparents touched the same place when they were your age?"

Bernard watched me, but what made me really happy was that he didn't laugh at me or make fun of me. Instead, he asked me to tell him more.

"Well, everything has an energy, can't you feel it?"

"No."

"Well, it does."

"I believe you, Maybel. There are things in science we can't see, but we know they're there."

"Sometimes when I touch the brick cornerstones of a building, I wonder who laid the foundation, and if he was happy, and when I touched the really old, worn quilt in your mother's room, I wondered what your grandmother, or great grandmother, or great-great grandmother felt while she sewed those particular stitches. And trees, they have been here for hundreds of years. I wonder if a certain tree saw my great grandparents kiss underneath its branches. And I wonder if the tree remembers them when I walk by. I never met my great grandparents, but the tree did. I often wonder if the tree absorbed their energies and memories and if my memories and energies will be in its trunk a hundred years or more from now when my great grandchildren play in its branches as I have done, and as my great grandparents may have done.

Bernard watched me with a soft smile and his eyes were kind and thoughtful while listening to me. He looked fascinated, and not at all disbelieving or condescending, which made my shoulders relax. "Thank you for not making fun of my silly ideas."

"They're not silly," he brushed my hair back.

"Most everyone else makes fun of me," I said.

"Most everyone else isn't as smart as you," Bernard's fingertips lightly brushed my cheek.

"Time for tea with Billy and Betty," Catherine came over and kissed Bernard's cheek.

I thought it was strange that Catherine kissed Bernard's cheek and I wondered if they had begun dating again. Bernard had not mentioned tea with Catherine at Betty's house, and I began to wonder what other things he had not told me.

"You're leaving? But I'm just about to win finally!" I whined. "Can't Bernard stay a few more minutes so I can finally beat him in chess?"

"You're never going to beat me, sweetheart." Bernard smiled smugly.

"Checkmate!" I screamed.

Bernard looked stunned. "I can't believe you won! I mostly can't believe I lost to you, Maybel! You're a terrible chess player!"

"You're rude!" I folded my arms and glared at Bernard.

Bernard chuckled and kissed my cheek. "We'll play again soon."

"No, we won't! I'm going to tell everyone that I beat you in chess and that you've never beaten me since!"

"Oh but I will beat you again!" Bernard laughed.

"No, you will not, because I'll never play you again!"

"Oh come on, Maybel!" he tousled my hair.

I glared at Bernard. I hated when he kissed my cheek then tousled my hair because it confused me. In one gesture he recognized me as a woman, and in the other, he treated me as a child.

He turned to Catherine. "Catherine, where are we going again?"

"Tea at Bettys house."

"She has that cat that hates me," Bernard groaned.

"Just one more game, Maybel?" Bernard sat back down at the table and began arranging the chess pieces.

"No! I beat you that one time and you've never been able to beat me since!" I laughed maniacally.

"That was only five minutes ago!" Bernard said incredulously.

"And you've never been able to beat me since!" I yelled happily.

Mommy knocked on my door telling me Susan was downstairs. I was excited to see her because I enjoyed our adventures. I happily ran to our family room and to my surprise Theo was with Susan.

"Theo!" I squealed, and ran into his outstretched arms.

"Theo came to visit again, Maybel!" Susan yelled. "We're going to have so much fun this weekend!"

I held Theo excitedly. "What do you want to do? Where do you want to go?" I peppered questions in between hugs.

"May we tag along?" Catherine asked.

I turned to see Catherine and Bernard sitting on the sofa. "I didn't even notice you two were here!" I giggled then turned my attention back to Theo.

"Did you bring your car? Is that how you got here so fast? Can we go to the city? Will you take me and Susan to a play?" I excitedly asked Theo questions while holding his hands and dancing around him and hugging him.

Theo laughed, "I've missed your exuberance, Maybel. We can do whatever you and Susan want."

"Are you coming again next weekend, Theo?" Susan asked. "You've been coming to visit me a lot! I love when you visit! You always bring me presents!"

"What did he bring you this time?" I asked. "Did you bring me anything?" I smiled widely and batted my eyes in a joking manner.

"Yes, Maybel, I brought you taffy," Theo laughed.

"I got chocolate!" Susan said. "Do you want to give each other half of each so we both have taffy and chocolate?" Susan asked excitedly.

"Of course!" I giggled.

"Let's go, Theo!" I held one of his hands and Susan held his other and we pulled him toward the door.

"Maybel, Catherine asked to come," Theo tried to pull us back.

"Oh yes! Sorry, Catherine, I was so excited I didn't think to answer you. Yes, come!"

Catherine smiled, "Where are we going?" She held Bernard's hand. Bernard looked annoyed.

"Anywhere!" I said.

Susan and I pulled Theo toward the door while Bernard lagged behind.

"Where are we going ladies?" Theo asked as we piled in his car.

"The city! I want to see a play!" Susan announced.

"Can I sit in the middle by Theo?" I asked Susan. "You got to sit by him last time when he drove."

"Ok, Maybel, but I get to sit beside him at the theater!"

"I'll sit on one side and you sit on his other side," I said.

"Ok," Susan agreed.

Theo laughed, "I feel appreciated. I've never had girls fight over me before."

"Bernard has," Catherine said. "All the time," she rolled her eyes at Bernard and he looked up and groaned, annoyed.

"They weren't fighting over me," Bernard said.

"They were trying to get your attention all evening," Catherine glared at Bernard.

"Maybe they thought I was single because you spent the evening dancing and chatting, but not with me. You see, that's why I like staying home with Maybel. I get bored at parties because you go off and leave me all alone."

"Oh, so you two are dating again," I said. I felt strangely jealous. Bernard and I had been having so much fun during the times he was supposed to be tutoring me in math. I had enjoyed thinking up new ways to procrastinate and not learn math.

"Catherine and I are not dating," Bernard said quickly.

I turned my head around to look at them. Catherine sat with her arms crossed and looked a mixture of angry and sad.

"You're right, Bernard, we are not dating. Sometimes I forget we aren't dating when we kiss goodbye at my front gate after having spent the evening together with our friends."

I raised my eyebrows and watched Bernard.

Bernard sighed. He had a hint of guilt playing across his face when he looked at me.

He quietly turned his attention back to Catherine. "We agreed to attend social events as friends, Catherine, but you are right, we should, perhaps, not let our friendship lapse into something more. I'll be more careful about not letting the parameters of our relationship become blurry."

Bernard spoke carefully and sounded professional, as though he were drafting a contract, not discussing feelings. Catherine looked sad.

Fortunately, Susan, with her childlike innocence, broke the tension. "Can we go camping tonight, Theo? Our backyard has a stream, but Maybel has an entire island."

"Oh really?" Theo seemed surprised. "I would love to see it."

"Then that's where we're sleeping tonight!" I said. "I know how to make a campfire!"

"Can I come?" Bernard asked.

"Bernard, we're having tea with Edith and Arnold tonight," Catherine reminded him.

"They can come camping too," Bernard said.

"Bernard!" Catherine whined.

"Is there any way we can all have tea then camp on the island," Theo asked, trying to be the peacemaker.

"I don't enjoy tea time, unless it's at my house with my opossum and badger," Susan whined. "Have you met Reginald the badger yet, Maybel?"

"No, bring him to tea time with Edith," I smirked, waiting to hear Catherine's shrieking protest. Bernard laughed loudly.

"What? No!" Catherine yelled.

"Do you not want to meet Reginald, Catherine?" I asked. "Well, that's not very polite." I knew I was poking a bear with a stick, but this was too funny to resist.

Bernard laughed even louder.

"I'm sorry, Susan," Catherine attempted to hide her disgust. "Maybe we can meet Reginald another time."

"You'll like him, Catherine," Susan said. "You're both grumpy when you're hungry."

At that, both Bernard and I laughed hysterically.

"Ok ladies, we're almost here," Theo again intervened as the peacemaker.

Theo paid for all of us, which seemed to annoy Bernard and I wondered why. Inside the opera house, there were dazzling lights and the fixtures along the walls and railings around the balconies were sparkling. Our seats were comfortable and Susan and I flanked Theo. I rested my head on his shoulder and held his hand while Susan did the same on his other side.

Bernard was about to sit on my other side but Catherine intervened. "I'd like to sit next to Maybel," she told Bernard.

Bernard stepped aside and let Catherine sit next to me. "Now I have people fighting over who gets to sit next to me!" I told Theo.

Catherine reached for Bernard's hand, and Bernard took her hand, but he looked at me. I looked back at him and wondered why he looked upset. I couldn't tell if he was sad or angry. He looked strange though.

I smiled at Bernard. He didn't smile back. He only watched me as I leaned against Theo.

Catherine saw me looking at Bernard. She leaned over and whispered in my ear. "He's just jealous because for the first time ever, another man has captured your attention. Don't worry about it, Maybel, he had to have known this day would come eventually. Just enjoy the play."

I thought that was such an odd thing to say, and I was going to ask Catherine to explain what she'd said better, but the lights dimmed and the show began.

I quickly got lost in the characters and the singing and dancing in the play. The woman who played the main character was engaging. She was beautiful and moved gracefully around the stage as though wind carried her. And the man who was her lover in the play slept with another woman. The star I fell in love with cried real tears. Her hollowed cries made me cry because I felt her pain in my stomach. The lights went off and then back on and my star was hanging by a rope in the middle of the stage. The entirety of the auditorium was silent. It felt like there was no air left, and everyone suffocated from their breaths being held, watching this beautiful woman dangling down in her sparkling dress adorned with crystals. She looked like a twinkling Christmas ornament hanging from a tree branch. Beside me I felt Theo's chest heaving. His hand was limp in mine and when I looked up at him, tears flowed steadily down and splashed into my eyes.

I knew Victoria occupied his mind. I squeezed his hand. The play finished and Theo wiped his face and composed himself. The opera house was eerily silent with so many people quietly exiting. Muffled cries from both men and women echoed intermittently.

We quietly got into Theo's car. I sat beside Theo and hugged his stomach while I rested my head on his shoulder. Finally, Susan, still somewhat of a child, said as only an innocent child would, "Well that was the worst play ever! I would have shot the cheating bastard!"

I couldn't suppress my giggle and fortunately, even Theo was able to crack a smile. "Susan, I love your spunk," he said.

The tense mood having been broken, we chatted about light subjects such as what kinds of stories to tell around our campfire. I, of course, wanted to tell ghost stories, and Susan wanted to tell stories about a land inhabited by cats who had developed the ability to talk and had humanlike interactions and thoughts.

"Are the mice also able to talk?" I asked. "If so, they can then reason with the cats. Or tell them jokes and make the cats like the mice so much they no longer want to have mice soup."

"That's a good point, Maybel. I think I'll let the mice talk."

"Are there humans in this world too?" I asked Susan.

"Hmm, yes, I think so," Susan answered.

"Are the cats as big as humans, or are they still cat size?"

"Also a good question, Maybel," Susan said. "I think they are bigger than our cats, but not as big as humans."

"Are they the size of lions then?"

"Oh, that's smart, Maybel, let's just make it a world of talking lions."

"But they're still cats, so when they sit and drink wine with humans, and they have a disagreement, they just swat the human off their stool as I imagine a talking lion would do, don't you think?" I giggled.

Susan laughed, "That's funny, Maybel, I'll draw a picture of a drunk lion sitting on a stool swatting a human off his stool, and the human looks terrified as he falls to the ground where the talking mice are enduring themselves to the lion by telling jokes." Susan laughed again, "What kind of jokes do you suppose a mouse would tell to a lion?" she asked me.

"The lion says, 'I like broccoli.' And the human says, 'Nah, you're lion!'" I laughed at my joke.

"And then the lion roars, 'I'm not lying!' and knocks the man off his stool. Then the mice say, 'You really weren't lion when you said you like broccoli!'" I laughed hard at my stupid joke and the ridiculous situation. Fortunately, Susan understood my humor and laughed hard along with me.

"We're home, ladies! I'm not lion!" Theo said.

Susan and I looked at each other and I winked at Susan. We then turned back to Theo with straight faces. "That was a really stupid joke, Theo," I said in a level voice.

"Yes, a horrible joke. Not funny at all," Susan said dryly.

"Oh, come on!" Theo rolled his eyes. "I know you two are doing that weird, deadpan humor thing!"

"You're not lion!" Susan squealed with laughter.

We led Theo inside my kitchen and I made sandwiches to take to our campfire later.

I heard the door slam. Bernard came into the kitchen looking upset. "I'm staying here. Catherine's going to tea time."

Bernard sat at the kitchen table. "It's ok, Bernard," Susan playfully slapped his arm. "We'll have fun."

"I know, thank you, Susan," Bernard said. "I just wish Catherine enjoyed staying home more."

"Bernard, come play," Susan tugged on his hand. "You'll get into a good mood."

Bernard smiled, "Maybel, you used to beg me to play with you all the time."

"I got tired of you saying no," I threw a towel at his face.

"I'm sorry, Maybel."

"Well, Bernard, will you play with me tonight?" I asked.

"No, I'm sorry, Catherine wants me to go have tea with her friends."

I scowled at Bernard.

"What? I can't do that weird, deadpan humor either?" Bernard winked at me.

I threw another towel at him and laughed.

"Will Catherine be home soon? Is she going to sleep on the island with us?" I asked Bernard.

"She said she wouldn't be long. She likes to socialize though, so I don't know," Bernard sighed.

"Well, I'll make her a sandwich in case she joins us," I said.

I handed Susan a basket of food to take and I gave Theo a loaf of mommy's freshly baked bread and a jar of jam. "Your mother made this jam," I told Theo, "I remember how much you liked it."

"Thank you, Maybel," Theo took it from me.

"Are we really sleeping outdoors? Do we have a tent, pillows, and a blanket?" Bernard asked.

"You've slept on the island with me before, Bernard," I said. "We'll take a blanket and pillow so you don't get cold. I'll protect you," I said sarcastically.

"I can sleep outdoors just fine, Maybel. I've slept under the stars plenty of times with my grandfather. We once travelled the forest for two weeks without anything except the clothes on our backs. We caught rabbits and fish for our meals."

"Can I come with you next time you go?" I asked Bernard.

"Sure, Maybel. He will like you. He has a good sense of humor, too."

"He must," I said, "He was able to tolerate you for two weeks."

Bernard threw the towel back at me.

I noticed Theo watching Bernard and me with a quizzical but amused expression. "You two are like a brother and sister," he said. "You argue like Susan and me, and you clearly have a long history together."

"Yes, we do, dear brother," I threw the towel back at Bernard.

"You're not my sister, Maybel, you're a lot less annoying than you used to be, so I now consider you a tolerable tag-along." Bernard threw the towel back at me.

"Well, you're the tag along today," I smirked. "And I don't think of you as my brother anymore; you're way too ugly to be related to me." I wadded the towel up and threw it hard at his face.

Bernard laughed, "This is why I prefer spending time with you than going to parties; you're such a joy to be around, Maybel."

"I told Maybel last summer that she's like the mold in my Petri dish; she grew on me," Theo laughed.

"That's funny, Theo!" Bernard laughed. "You do grow on people, Maybel. And you stay with me like a cold I can't get rid of."

"Ok, you two are going to get my wrath if you keep joining forces against me!" I said.

"I'll be on your side," Susan said, while sneaking goodies from the picnic basket.

"Thank you, Susan," I said.

"Susan! I'm your brother!" Theo said.

"Yes, but Maybel is my sister," Susan stuck her tongue out at Theo.

"That's true, Theo, Susan and I stick together," I smiled at Susan.

"Then I guess it's boys against girls," Theo nodded at Bernard.

"Yes, we'll let them row us to the island. Come Theo, let's go." Bernard motioned for Theo to follow.

Theo and Susan sat next to each other while I sat next to Bernard. Bernard handed me the oars. I handed them back to Bernard.

"Fine, Maybel," Bernard nudged me with his elbow. I nudged him back.

Bernard and Theo both began rowing us to the island. "Wow! With two strong men, we're gliding through the water like ducks!" Susan marveled. "This is fun!"

I was certain Bernard and Theo were in some kind of competition between males by the way they rowed. They didn't say they were competing, but they looked at each other while they rowed like they were competing.

"I have never gotten to the island so fast," I said, amazed at how fast we traveled.

We got out the boat and went to the fire pit we always used. Bernard and Theo went off to gather sticks.

"Maybel, do you think it's ok if I take off my dress and just wear my undershirt and shorts?" Susan asked me. "It's really hot right now."

"I think it's ok," I said. "It's just your brother and Bernard here."

"Are you going to take yours off?" she asked me.

I looked over at Theo and Bernard, who abandoned their sticks and were now hauling logs to the fire pit.

"I don't know," I hesitated, "It will cool off this evening."

"Please? I don't want to be the only one wearing shorts," Susan begged me.

I looked back at Bernard and Theo, who had already taken their shirts off and were now hauling an entire fallen tree to the fire pit.

"Ok, it is pretty hot right now," I agreed. I could feel sweat running down my back and into my butt crack. The miserable dresses we wore were heavy and hot.

Susan and I took off our dresses and wore the simple shirts and shorts underneath that we were only allowed to wear amongst close friends and family, as they weren't modest.

We walked over to the fire pit. "Why is there a tree trunk here?" I asked.

"For the fire," Bernard said.

"I was thinking of just a simple campfire, not an entire tree. We're keeping warm tonight, not smoking an entire cow." I looked at them, puzzled.

"I think we need more wood, Theo. If you need a rest, I can get it myself," Bernard said over his shoulder as he walked back to the trees.

"I'm not at all tired," Theo said. "I'll grab that fallen tree over there."

"It's a bit small, don't you think? Why don't we get that larger one over there?" Bernard pointed to a mighty fallen tree.

"You go ahead, I can carry this tree by myself," Theo called to Bernard.

"I don't think we need more trees," I called after them both.

"Shh," Susan said, "This is fun!"

Theo hauled the tree himself while Bernard watched with a scowl.

Theo placed the tree over the fire pit. "Say, Bernard, do you need help with that larger tree?"

"Yes," Bernard gritted his teeth, "you know there's no way either of us can drag this tree by ourselves."

"Ah, let me help you then," Theo called happily.

Bernard took one end and Theo took the other and they grunted and groaned as they pulled and rolled the massive fallen tree to the fire pit.

"I can't believe they managed to move that tree," Susan whispered.

"I can't believe Bernard agreed to let Theo help him," I whispered back.

"Why are there three trees piled up on the fire pit?" Catherine called from behind us. She was dripping wet in her sleeveless shirt and shorts.

"Catherine? You swam here?" I asked

"Well, I had to, you took our only boat."

"You're done with your tea party?" Susan asked.

"I didn't stay long. It was just an informal get-together," she said.

We walked back to the fire pit where both Theo and Bernard sat on tree stumps staring at Catherine's glistening body.

"Watch this," Catherine whispered to me. She picked up a stick and threw it at Bernard's head. Bernard didn't move out of the way or bat the stick away.

"Bernard! You're supposed to catch the stick!" Catherine giggled. "Play with me! Toss it back."

"Maybe later, Catherine," Bernard still sat on the stump, his arms over his waist.

"Theo, stand up, come with me! I want to show you something on the other side of the island," she reached down to pull Theo up by his hands but he refused to stand. "Maybe later, Catherine." Theo was also bent over as he sat on a tree stump.

Catherine turned back to me and smirked and giggled.

"What's wrong? Are you both tired, or did you pull your leg muscles?" Susan asked, concerned.

"Yes!" They both said in unison.

"That's what happened," Bernard said. "We pulled our leg muscles." He looked angrily at Theo.

Theo nodded, "Yes, leg muscles," then looked at Bernard and sheepishly shrugged his shoulders.

I made a note in my mind to ask Catherine about this. I knew something was going on but I wasn't sure what.

"Do you want to go swimming Maybel?" Susan asked me.

"Sure," I said. Susan and I left and started into the water.

Susan shrieked, "A fish just nibbled on me!"

"Come on, boys," Catherine called as she stepped into the pond. "The fish are nibbling, bring your rods!" Catherine yelled to Bernard and Theo.

"They don't have fishing rods," Susan said.

"Oh, but they do," Catherine giggled.

I looked back at Bernard and Theo, then back to Catherine, and suddenly realized she was talking about their penises. "Oh," I laughed, "you are making a joke about their penises because penises dangle like worms," I giggled and blushed.

"Shh! Maybel!" Catherine nodded toward Susan.

"I already know what a penis looks like. That's a good joke, Catherine!" Susan giggled.

"How do you know what they look like?" I asked, shocked.

"My art books. There're lots of naked people in art."

"Oh," I mused, wondering why I hadn't taken more of an interest in art.

"Shh! They're coming this way, so be quiet," Catherine giggled.

Bernard and Theo came down to the water's edge. "Do you know how to swim?" Bernard asked Theo.

"Yes, of course!"

"Let's go then," Bernard said. "To the other side and back."

"Are you two racing?" Catherine asked.

"Just a fun and friendly swim," Theo winked at Catherine, which Bernard did not seem to like.

Catherine giggled at Theo and Bernard furrowed his brow, causing the crease in his forehead to deepen.

"Let's go," Bernard said, irritated.

Bernard and Theo shot forth swimming quickly to the other side. Theo arrived first and touched the tree on the other side. Bernard picked up his pace and took the lead on the way back, but Theo ultimately won.

"Yay, Theo!" Susan hugged him.

Bernard was a very close second place, only losing by maybe two seconds.

"Congratulations, Theo," Bernard held out his hand and when Theo shook it, their knuckles became white as they smiled not-so-friendly at each other.

"What is the prize?" Catherine asked. "What does Theo win?"

"A hug!" Susan hugged Theo again.

"I'll take it!" Theo picked her up and hugged her. I gave Theo a congratulatory hug as well.

I wasn't sure if Catherine was going to hug Theo, but I didn't want her to, so I suggested we all go eat the sandwiches I packed.

Catherine took Bernard's hand and we walked back to the three trees covering the tiny fire pit.

I handed everyone a sandwich. "Aw, Maybel, you thought of me!" Catherine kissed my cheek.

"I was hoping you'd come," I smiled.

"Sometimes I forget how much I enjoy playing outside with you, Maybel. I'm sorry I go to so many parties. I do enjoy your company."

"I know," I said. "If I were less awkward at parties, I'd join you."

After eating we decided there was no way we could light three trees on fire and not burn the entire island, so we decided to go home.

This time Susan and I sat on either side of Theo while Catherine sat by Bernard.

"Watch this, Catherine!" Susan said. "Watch how fast they row!"

We quickly arrived back home, thanks to Bernard's and Theo's friendly competition.

"It's been a lovely day," Catherine said.

"Yes," Theo agreed. "Ladies, let's tell your ghost stories and other tales at home," Theo put his hands on Susan's and my back and led us toward home. When we arrived at Catherine's and my house, Theo continued leading us around front.

"Where are you going?" Catherine asked. "I thought we were going to tell stories?"

"Oh, I'm sorry, I meant Susan, Maybel, and I will go to back to Susan's and my home so you and Bernard can have a night without your little tag-along." Theo playfully squeezed my arm and pushed on my back to follow him.

"Oh, that does sound lovely, Bernard!" Catherine smiled.

"I wanted to hear your stories, Maybel, and yours too, Susan. Can't we come along?" Bernard asked.

"Certainly," Theo, said politely. "Why don't you and Catherine put on dry clothes and meet us at my house," Theo said.

"Bernard, I want to go to your house and spend time together," Catherine smiled and winked.

"Ah, I understand," Theo winked at Bernard. "Have fun, Bernard," Theo chuckled.

"Let's leave the two love birds alone, shall we?" Theo pushed lightly on my back, urging me to go.

"I need to change my clothes," I said.

"Wear Susan's clothing," Theo said.

"They don't fit," I said.

"Maybel's breasts got a lot bigger this year," Susan said.

I blushed. "Susan!" I whispered, "Don't say!"

"He's not blind," Susan laughed.

"Alright, Maybel," Theo sighed, "why don't you get your clothes and we'll wait here for you. You can bathe at our home."

"Our soap smells like strawberries," Susan said. "You'll like it."

"I do like strawberries!" I said.

"Great, let's go," Theo urged us.

I went to get my clothing and I heard Catherine in her bedroom. I put my clothing in a bag and started to go downstairs.

"Maybel?" Catherine called.

I went into her bedroom. "Yes?"

"Bernard is jealous of Theo," Catherine said.

"Why? Because Theo pulled a bigger tree and won the swimming race?"

"Bernard is jealous because Theo gets to spend the night with you," Catherine said.

"We're just telling stories," I reminded Catherine.

"Theo wants you for himself without Bernard. And Bernard wants to be with you tonight so Theo doesn't get the opportunity to kiss you," Catherine explained.

"Well, Theo wasn't staring at my wet body," I said. "He seems to like you," I admitted with a frown. "Bernard chose you. Every boy chooses you. I'm only going to tell ghost stories anyway. I'm not going to kiss anyone."

I turned and went down the stairs. I wasn't as excited as before though.

I walked outside where Theo and Bernard were arm wrestling on a patio table. I rolled my eyes.

Bernard slammed Theo's arm down, winning the competition.

"I'm ready," I said. "Let's go."

"Well done, Bernard," Theo said.

"Thank you, Theo."

"Have a good evening. Although, I'm sure you will," Theo chuckled. "I suppose that means you win the final round, for I surely won't be doing such things tonight."

Theo reached for my hand then he looked back at Bernard, "Although....." his voice trailed off and he winked at Bernard.

Bernard's face flushed a bright red and the vein in his neck popped out. He looked infuriated as Theo held my hand and led me away.

That evening we sat in Susan's and Theo's backyard and told stories around a modest campfire. It certainly wasn't burning high and bright with three large tree trunks.

Mrs. Matthews opened the back door. "You have visitors," she called to Susan and Theo.

Catherine and Bernard came through the door. Catherine looked annoyed. "Hello again, everyone. Bernard just had to hear your stories," she muttered sarcastically.

"Bernard, I'm not going to take advantage of Maybel," Theo said. "I know you are Maybel's big brother and I would never make any untoward advancements toward your little sister." Theo emphasized Bernard's relationship to me as brother and sister, which seemed to anger Bernard even more.

"Maybel is not my sister!" Bernard scowled. "I enjoy Maybel's and Susan's stories!"

"Very well, Bernard," Theo sighed. "You sit by your little sister, and I'll sit by Catherine. Fair enough?"

"I don't think of Maybel as my sister! But yes, I do feel protective of her," Bernard snapped.

"Catherine, would you care for an evening stroll while Bernard listens to his beloved ghost stories?" Theo asked Catherine.

Catherine looked at me and Bernard. I stared back unhappily.

"Maybe a short stroll, just to get to know you better since Maybel seems to like you so much," Catherine shrugged her shoulders at me.

"Be back soon," Theo took Catherine's hand and led her back through the house and out the front door.

"Maybel, I don't understand what is going on," Susan said. "I'm very confused."

"I am too," I began crying. "Why does Catherine take all the boys and why doesn't any boy want me?" I began sobbing.

"I let this go too far, Maybel. I'm sorry," Bernard sighed. "Theo and I were trying to anger each other all day. It's a male dominance game that I let go too far and I'm sorry, Maybel. Theo doesn't really like Catherine. He's only trying to anger me."

"Well, he's certainly angered me!" I cried. "And so have you!"

"I know. I'll make this right, Maybel. I'll go apologize to Theo." Bernard stood and reached for my hand.

We went through the house and out the front door to catch up to Catherine and Theo.

We didn't have to go far. Catherine and Theo were on the front porch swing kissing.

Catherine looked up surprised. "Bernard, I'm sorry! I shouldn't have!"

"Catherine!" I cried.

"I kissed Theo," Catherine said. "He didn't kiss me! I'm sorry, Maybel, it was my fault!"

"You weren't pulling away from the kiss!" I yelled at Theo.

Susan stood beside me looking disappointed. For the first time ever, she saw Theo as a person, and not her perfect brother. It was crushing to see the way she looked now at Theo.

"You're just like every boy at my school," Susan whispered to Theo. "I thought you were better, but you're not. You'll kiss any girl who lets you kiss her, no matter how your kiss hurts other people." Susan took my hand. "I always wanted to marry a man just like you, but now I don't," Susan pulled me inside her house and away from Theo.

Mr. Matthews was in the family room. I felt like drinking strawberry juice and throwing things in acid tonight.

I heard Bernard and Theo arguing on the porch and Catherine's voice begging forgiveness.

"What's going on?" Mr. Matthews looked up from his evening newspaper.

Susan held my hand and stood next to me looking sad.

"What's wrong Kitten?" Mr. Matthews asked Susan.

Susan looked pathetic and broken. "Theo isn't perfect. He and Catherine were kissing," Susan said with sadness.

"I hate everyone and I want to dunk something in acid," I said to Susan's father.

Mr. Matthews mumbled something about his sisters when they were teenagers and how he was getting too old for this shit.

"Are we also going to shoot, because I'll need my slippers for that bit," Mr. Matthews grumbled.

"Get your slippers, please, Mr. Matthews. I'm having a very bad evening," I started sobbing.

Mr. Matthews sighed, "Oh come here honey, I'm sorry. You'll be ok," he hugged me.

"Muffin!" he called to his wife, "Will you please bring me my slippers? Maybel's having boy troubles again, and our little kitten is very upset at her big brother!"

"Acid or guns?" She called from the kitchen.

"Both!" he yelled back.

"I'll make tea!" she yelled.

"Thank you, Muffin!" he yelled back to her.

"I feel like you are my daughter, too, Maybel, so when Susan goes through boy troubles in a couple years, no matter where you are in this world, can you please come here and help us? I'm getting too old, and I really don't know what to do about boys."

"I promise, Mr. Matthews."

"Thank you, Maybel. And Susan, boys are stupid. I feel like I need to tell you this now. All boys are idiots. And the next couple years will be harder on me than you, honey," he hugged Susan. "Now let's go blow shit up, I have gun powder."

My eyes widened and Susan grew excited. "I love you, daddy!" Susan squealed.

"Me too!" I hugged Susan, who hugged her father.

I still heard Theo, Bernard, and Catherine outside arguing when Susan and I retreated to the comfort of Mr. Matthews acid vats and boxes of gun powder.

"Maybel!" Susan rushed over to me, "Daddy has the volcano set up! Watch this experiment!"

Mr. Matthews aligned various beakers, and from one beaker poured frothy bubbles. "Wow!" I gasped, "That's amazing!"

"Theo used to love this chemical reaction! I dare say he became a chemist because of my demonstrations such as this!" Mr. Matthews beamed with pride as he resumed setting up more beakers and other contraptions. "Do you want to see what a volcano eruption looks like Maybel, on a much smaller scale though," he chuckled.

"Yes!" I excitedly exclaimed.

Mr. Matthews handed us each a little block of sculpting clay. "Make your little village people, girls," he said.

"Susan, Maybel," Mrs. Matthews peaked her head into Mr. Matthews' workshop, "Would you also like a snack?"

"Yes!" We yelled back.

"Wonderful! The bread has finished cooling. I'll slice it and spread jam."

"Freshly baked bread!" I was excited. "Your bread is so delicious, Mrs. Matthews!"

"Why, thank you, Maybel," she smiled at me.

"Volcano time!" Mr. Matthews yelled. "Gather 'round, girls." He bent over his model town. He had a volcano made out of dried mud and little houses and people made of dried clay that he had dried in his fireplace. "Imagine! You are minding your own business, going about your day, when suddenly, the ground begins to rumble," Mr. Matthews voice was animated. "You look up and see smoke arising from the mountain behind your home. He poured something into his mud-dried volcano sculpture and streams of smoke billowed up.

"Girls, do you have your sculptures ready?"

"Yes!" we squealed. I fashioned three, one for Catherine, Bernard, and Theo, but I told Susan they were representative of three girls at school who weren't nice so she wouldn't know she was watching her brother's clay figure slowly dissolve in acid.

"And then, suddenly," Mr. Matthews spoke like a circus showman, "fire, rocks, and lava spewed forth, covering the trees, your home, and maybe even you!" He poured something into the volcano's center and foamy liquid burst forth and down the volcano's sides, covering the miniature, make-believe town.

"Now see girls," he pointed to the little ceramic people we'd sculpted for his make-believe town. "If that had been you, you'd be dead now."

I watched Theo's little clay head pop off and roll down the side of the volcano until it cracked open and fizzled. I smiled.

"Good thing we don't live near a volcano," he chuckled. "Well, that's enough fun with science for today," he said cheerfully. "What fun! We'll clean this mess later. Let's go eat mother's bread and jam!" He pulled off his gloves and we went inside.

Susan and I sat at her kitchen table and ate Mrs. Matthew's delicious strawberry jam slathered over warm bread. I sipped the tea she brewed. "Mrs. Matthews, Mr. Matthews, I love you both."

"We love you too, sweetheart," Mrs. Matthews smiled and her dimple made her look like a happy, and likely precocious, child.

"Girls, are you ready for guns now?" Mr. Matthews' eyes danced and he winked at Mrs. Matthews and she giggled. I loved how in love they were.

I wore Mr. Matthews' old boots out back. I wobbled a bit because they were big boots.

"Ok, this is a delicate process, and you have to be extremely careful," Mr. Matthews warned.

"Ok," Susan and I said excitedly.

Mr. Matthews got his supplies ready and Mrs. Matthews came outside with a tray filled with mugs of tea.

"Can we mix our tea with our strawberry juice?" I asked her.

"I don't see why not," Mrs. Matthews said. "But don't drink too much strawberry juice," she cautioned. "Three glasses maximum, girls."

"Yes, mother," Susan said as she dashed back inside for strawberry rum. She returned with a large ceramic jug.

"Mrs. Matthews, Theo and Catherine kissed, but Theo and I had grown fond of each other over the summer, and now I'm angry and jealous. What should I do?" I asked.

Mrs. Matthews took a deep breath and exhaled slowly. "Blow some things up, I guess. You'll feel better tomorrow. Oh," she paused, "only if you adhere to the three-glass maximum rule. If you don't, tomorrow will be worse."

"Ok," I said, and finished my first glass of strawberry juice.

We blew up some sticks and an old glove that had lost its mate.

I took pleasure in blowing up one of Susan's tattered taxidermized chipmunks. It flew up to the sky and burst apart. Its tiny ear fell on the bridge of my nose and tickled.

"Alright, sweethearts, let's go to bed. It's late," Mr. Matthews said.

"Ok," Susan and I sulked.

We headed inside and washed our tea and juice glasses. Mr. and Mrs. Matthews kissed Susan's cheeks and went upstairs to bed.

I looked outside and no one was on the porch. "I wonder where they went?" I asked Susan.

"Who cares. Let's go to bed, Maybel."

We went upstairs and brushed our teeth and crawled into Susan's bed.

I awoke to Susan's donkey kicks. I went downstairs to sleep on the sofa.

Again, I awoke, this time to Theo's voice. "Maybel, I'm sorry. Catherine kissed me, but I didn't pull away. I'm sorry."

I closed my eyes and rolled away facing the back of the couch. I fell asleep again. When I awoke, Mr. and Mrs. Matthews were sitting beside each other discussing the mating rituals of black bears.

"Oh, you're awake!" Mrs. Matthews said. "Would you like pancakes?"

I sat up and looked around trying to figure out where I was and what happened.

I closed my eyes and fell back asleep.

"Maybel," Susan tapped my arm, "time for pancakes."

I sat up again, still confused. "I think I only drank two glasses of strawberry juice, but I'm very confused about why I'm here," I told Susan.

"Catherine and Theo kissed," she said.

"Oh, right, that happened," I frowned.

We walked into the kitchen and sat down. Theo was eating breakfast.

Susan and I stared at him.

"I'm sorry," he said. "I should have pulled away from Catherine."

I ate my pancakes in silence, as did Susan.

I washed dishes with Susan, then went home. I was very confused and unhappy. I'd lost my summer beach house because I never wanted to see Theo again. I couldn't be too mad at Catherine though, as I had kept it a secret that Bernard and I had kissed.

Henry smiled at me, "How have you been, Maybel?"

Some weeks had passed and Henry had returned. Henry was sitting at my kitchen table. He'd made two sandwiches, one for him, and one for me. He pulled out the chair next to him and scooted the plate he'd prepared toward me.

"I'm fine. Shall we kiss passionately now?"

Henry blushed.

"You blushed!" I giggled and smiled big.

"No woman can make me blush, except you," Henry said quietly, with a shy smile.

I leaned over and very lightly kissed Henry's cheek. "Blush for me, again," I smiled.

Henry blushed deeper. "Maybel," he looked down, blushing more, "I don't want you to know what power you have over me."

"I want to know," I gently pecked his cheek again.

Henry smiled at me. His eyes glowed in the stream of sunlight through the kitchen window.

"Henry, what's the first thing you notice about a woman?" I asked.

Henry sighed, "I don't really think about such things, Maybel. Remember when I told you I was broken and bad? I am. I don't have such romantic notions. I want sex, so I have sex. I don't really notice or care about a woman's eyes, or smile, or whatever it is men are supposed to notice to be considered romantic."

"I notice eyes," I said, ignoring Henry's soliloquy of self-doubt and tragic despair.

"I think that's why your other name, you know the other one you told me about, is Bright Water. It's because your eyes are not one color. It's like looking over water when the sun shines down brightly, and you see all the reflections in the ripples, and just as quickly as they came, they flit away like dancing butterflies."

"I noticed your intelligence," Henry said quietly, "your big imagination when you spoke. I noticed you danced like butterflies too; sometimes you were here, and then just as quickly as you came into the room, you flitted away. That's what I noticed about you, Maybel."

I smiled, "Thank you Henry, for noticing me."

"Thank you, Maybel, for always searching for the good in me. Maybe there still is some good somewhere inside me."

"May I kiss you, Henry?" I asked.

"I'll break your heart. I do not want to make you cry."

"Maybe I'll be the one to break your heart."

"Maybe you already have. I'll never be good enough for someone as pure as you, and that breaks my heart."

"Henry, if you won't let me kiss you, will you resume teaching me math?" I asked. "Bernard has been teaching me, but you explain everything better."

"Of course, sweetheart," Henry smiled.

"What are you reading?" I asked. Henry had a newspaper clipping in front of him.

Henry picked it up and smiled. "These students won a grant from the government for their contributions to science," Henry beamed. "They have won enough money from a federal grant to continue their research."

"That's great, Henry, are they from your hometown?"

Henry kept smiling at the newspaper article. "I wanted to be a teacher. Do you remember me telling you that?

"Yes," I smiled.

"I wanted to give my students what I didn't have. I wanted to teach them about the world, about literature, politics, and business. I didn't though. I went into business so I could make money, because money is power, and I can use power to influence and change things for the better. I gave a large portion of my earnings to my friend from college who became a science teacher. I sent an anonymous and large sum of money to buy microscopes for his students."

I smiled, "That was good of you."

"I can't do much now, but I will. I was thinking of providing guidance to children about what is good behavior and bad behavior from adults, but I don't know how to do that without talking about sex. I think children should know what is good behavior and what is bad behavior. I can't teach that without explaining why it's bad behavior, and parents don't want their children to learn about sex. I have been in touch with a professor of ethics at a university. Perhaps we can figure out how to go about this."

Henry's countenance suddenly looked sad, like a shadow fell upon his face. "I just want to protect children so they know when they're being hurt and can find someone to help them."

I rested my hand on Henry's forearm as he stared at the smiling faces in the photograph. Henry sometimes looked like I imagined Theo's Victoria looked. Henry looked like pain. Victoria wrote him saying if people had seen her pain, they would have given her a torniquet. I wondered if Henry needed a torniquet.

"Henry," I began gently, "some people have such sadness they do desperate things. Have you ever thought about doing desperate things, like killing yourself?" I very quickly added, "Please don't be mad at me for asking; I only want to help you!"

"Yes, Maybel, I came close once, but you took me to the waterfalls behind Uncle's house and taught me how to be a child. We splashed in water and climbed a tree."

"I remember that day," I whispered.

"When I bolted out of the billiard room and accidentally ran into you, I was leaving, because I didn't want to live anymore. You saved me. Thank you, Maybel."

I stared with an open mouth at Henry.

"I don't know if I would have killed myself, but I know I came close. Sometimes I remember things and I can no longer think rationally."

I could only stare at Henry. His admittance jolted me and I felt numb.

"Don't ever let your mind get that bad again, Henry," I finally whispered. "I will always splash water at you and beat you in tree climbing, I promise you with all my heart."

Henry looked confused, "I beat you up the tree."

"Henry, I don't want you to kill yourself, but I will slap you up one side and down the other if you tell anyone you beat me at tree climbing."

Henry suddenly burst out laughing and hugged me. I laughed too, and returned Henry's hug and kissed his cheek. "I love you, Henry," I said. "Please don't leave us. We all love you."

"I know, sweetheart," Henry's voice sounded shaky. "And thank you."

When Henry pulled back, his eyes were teary and red. "Maybel, I knew you were special the day I met you."

"When did we meet? I can't remember. Was it at a party?"

"No, it was the day Auntie, Uncle, and Bernard moved into their mansion here."

"You didn't know me as a child."

"I did. To me, you're still that cute, little girl I took one look at and knew you'd grow up to be stunning and brilliant," Henry smiled at me.

"I don't remember when I first met you," I said, scouring my memories for images of the most handsome man in the world.

"I helped Auntie and Uncle move furniture in and arrange their affairs. You came over with Catherine. I don't think you even noticed me," Henry laughed. "You were too busy chasing a butterfly through the house. You were so sweet and innocent. I remember thinking you would grow up to be beautiful and intelligent. You were talking about what it must be like to live as a fish in a pond and suddenly be yanked up by a fisherman and see a human for the first time. Everyone laughed at you and you became withdrawn at their laughter. I didn't laugh at you Maybel. I knew you were smarter than them."

"Thank you, Henry, you are kind."

"I'm honest, like you, and honesty is not appreciated by dishonest people. You are a good person, Maybel. I thought you wouldn't want someone used like me, and anyway, you seemed so young back then."

"You have a very bad opinion of yourself."

"Others do, too."

"You aren't used or bad, Henry."

"Not in your eyes, and that makes me happy," Henry smiled the most sweet and innocent smile when he looked at me.

"Bernard, did you forget about our get-together with Edith, Arnold, the twins, and Betty and Billy?"

"No," he groaned. "I was hoping you'd forget though." Bernard was lounging on our sofa.

"You're not dressed!" Catherine chided.

"Can't we just stay home, Catherine?" Bernard moaned.

"You always want to stay home!" Catherine said.

"That's because I like being home. I'm always at school, or my grandparents want me to go to Europe, or you want to go to parties. Can't we just stay here?" He curled up on the couch.

"And what will we do here?" Catherine asked.

"Well, we won't have to get dressed up and have small talk with people," he said.

"That sounds horrible," I piped up. "People and small talk! You may as well just kill us Catherine!"

"Exactly!" Bernard agreed.

"Maybel why don't you come? That boy you like will be there." Catherine said with a soft, teasing lilt in her voice.

"Oh?" Bernard asked. "And who is he?"

"Just some boy. And I never said I liked him," I said, annoyed at Catherine.

"Actions speak louder than words, Maybel," Catherine teased.

"I don't want to get dressed up," I said.

"He asked about you the last time we got together," Catherine said.

"He did?" I became more interested.

Catherine giggled. "Yes, he did."

"I guess I could go for maybe a little while," I said.

"Bernard, you can stay home. Maybel is coming with me," she winked at me.

"Ok, Catherine, I'll come too," Bernard said.

"Oh, no, you stay home and rest, Bernard. We won't be gone long," Catherine said.

"I'll come," Bernard said sternly.

"Oh, now you want to come?" Catherine teased. "What changed?"

"I don't want to stay home alone," he said dryly.

"I'll stay home with you," Catherine continued slyly. "And just Maybel can go. We can have some time alone."

"I don't want to go alone," I pouted.

"You'll be fine, Maybel." Catherine gave me a look that pleaded not to argue.

"This was an elaborate plan to get me to go away so you two can be alone together without me?" I yelled. My eyes started to well with tears. "Fine, Catherine! I won't ever tag along again! You two can go have your time alone to kiss and touch each other's bodies!" I ran upstairs to my room. I couldn't believe they had devised such an elaborate plan to get me to leave them alone!

Catherine quickly ran into my room behind me. "Maybel, that's not what I was trying to do!"

"Go away, and go kiss Bernard, Catherine!" I yelled at her. "I won't be a tag-along anymore!" I cried.

"No, you don't understand," she whispered. "I wanted to see if Bernard wanted to stay home to be with you, or if he truly wanted to stay home because he doesn't enjoy socializing."

"What?" I looked at her as though she'd lost her mind.

"Bernard only wants to go wherever you go, Maybel," she whispered.

"That's because I don't enjoy parties and neither does he, Catherine! Wait, so that boy never asked about me, did he Catherine?" I was hurt.

"Yes, he did, Maybel!"

"Really?"

"Yes! Why is it so hard for you to believe a boy might like you?"

"Because they never do! They only ever like you, Catherine!"

"No, they like you too, but you and Bernard are always together wherever we go, so boys never approach you!"

"Bernard and I aren't always together," I protested.

"Maybel, the last time we went to visit with Edith and Arnold and the others, and Bernard wasn't there, what happened? A boy approached you and began flirting."

"I wouldn't call that flirting. He asked if I wanted a glass of juice."

"That's what flirting is, Maybel! You are so blind to things sometimes, yet so able to express feelings in your writings! Open your eyes! Look around!"

"Catherine, what exactly do you want me to do?"

"Come with me. Bernard will make sure all the boys leave you alone. I'm going to flirt with someone and see how Bernard reacts."

"He'll punch the boy you flirt with and our day will be ruined." I paused, "Or entertaining. It could definitely be entertaining," I couldn't suppress a giggle.

"Maybel, I think Bernard won't pay much attention to me flirting with someone. He's only going to care about who you flirt with."

"You want me to flirt with a boy, while you flirt with a boy, to see with whom Bernard gets more angry?"

"Yes!" Catherine exclaimed.

"Catherine, maybe he trusts you so much that he knows you will never cheat on him, and that is why he does not get angry at you."

"I never thought about it like that," she looked as though she were in deep thought.

"This is ridiculous, Catherine. Bernard knows you won't cheat and that is why he lets you flirt."

"Maybe, Maybel. But can you do this one thing for me? I really want to know if Bernard even cares in the slightest bit if another boy likes me.

I relented. I thought Catherine was being ridiculous, but it seemed to mean a lot to her if I went, so I agreed to go.

Catherine did my hair and applied makeup.

When we went downstairs, Bernard was dosing on the couch. "Bernard?" Catherine lightly touched his cheek. "Wake up."

Bernard groggily opened his eyes then his eyes shot open wide as he focused his gaze on me. I rarely got dolled up, so when I did, and walked past a mirror, I often jumped, startled, as I focused on the person in the mirror, which was me, but frilly and lacy.

"Are we going to a party or a wedding?" he asked.

"Just a party," Catherine said. "Let's go get you changed."

"When is the party?" I asked.

"Soon," Catherine replied.

"We'll be late. We should just stay home then," I said, hoping Catherine would agree.

"It will only take Bernard five quick minutes to put on a suit. We'll be there early," Catherine smiled at me as if to tell me we're going no matter what.

We arrived at the Charleston Manor and Bernard went upstairs to change. No more than five minutes passed and he came down looking dashing and well-groomed.

"Isn't it absolutely maddening that men can look so good so quickly?" Catherine looked at him annoyed.

"Yes," I said jealously.

We took Bernard's carriage to the twins' large stone house. Ellie and Nellie were Catherine's friends through her piano teacher. They were a couple years older than Catherine and were both petite blondes with pretty, blue eyes. They looked like porcelain dolls. I had to restrain myself often from poking their cheeks to see if they were indeed real, live girls.

Catherine introduced Bernard and me. "Ellie, Nellie, you remember Bernard and Maybel?" Catherine's high-society voice was out in full force.

"Charmed," they said in unison, and kissed my cheeks the way people do in books from Europe.

We went inside to their large ballroom where a beautiful and well-polished piano sat.

Edith and Arnold had arrived already and were sitting in the parlor. Soon after, Betty, Billy, and several people I had never met arrived. The boy I'd met here before had not arrived. I tried to remember his name but it had escaped my memory.

Catherine held Bernard's arm and led him away. He glanced back at me as he followed Catherine.

I wandered over to a seat by the window and watched outside. I didn't feel much like pretending to be high society and I was really bad at pretending to have proper etiquette anyway.

I felt alone, and like an outcast that nobody wanted to stand near. Catherine said I need to walk over to people and strike up a conversation, or sit next to someone and begin chatting. Whenever I did that, though, the person always looked at me like I was unworthy of their presence and excused themselves to go stand by someone better.

I figured I may as well try to fit in. I stood up and scanned the room. I looked for someone alone, like me, had a gentle and warm smile, and a pleasant disposition. I continued scanning the room and finally decided to enter a different room. Perhaps I would have better luck there.

The drawing room contained couples seated together laughing and flirting. The study had men discussing politics and their terribly bored girlfriends who looked at me with snobbish disdain when I peeked my head in.

I went to the family room where I saw a woman seated by the fireplace. I thought she looked kind, so I sat beside her. "Hello, how are you? My name is Maybel."

"Charmed," she politely smiled at me, but there was no warmth.

"Do you live nearby?" I asked, trying to think of a way to talk to someone without being considered odd or strange.

"No," she said.

"I know the twins through my sister. They have the same piano teacher."

"How nice." She stood up. "It was nice chatting with you." She left.

I'd had worse conversations, I decided. At least I could tell Catherine I tried.

I walked into the ballroom. Catherine stood with Bernard near the piano. There were seven people around her hanging onto her every word. Catherine never had to try to talk to people. People naturally gravitated to her. Catherine never had to think of ways to approach people. People always wanted to approach her first. Catherine never had to try. Everything was always so easy for her.

I went back to the parlor and sat back down on the seat by the window. A young woman came toward me and I looked up happily at her. "Hello, my name is,"

"Excuse me, miss, may I take this chair, or are you waiting for someone?"

"You can take it," I sighed, feeling dejected and like the ugly puppy who never gets picked by any boy or girl, and so goes away sadly, head down, tail tucked between its legs, and dies of starvation, starved of love and food. That was me, I concluded.

"Maybel?"

I looked up. That boy was here.

"Oh, hello," I smiled and stood up.

"I was hoping you'd be here," he said.

"I almost didn't come. I am not one to socialize much," I confessed.

"I'm glad you decided to come." He took my hand and kissed it.

I blushed.

"Would you like a drink, to sit and chat, or perhaps dance?"

"Yes, maybe a drink would be nice. You know, I was just sitting here thinking about you," I smiled at him.

"Oh really?" he smiled.

"Yes, I was thinking you had a lovely name. How do you spell your name, as I know there are several variations?"

"J-o-h-n. What other variations are there? Oh," he paused, "You forgot my name."

I felt my face blush hot red.

"Here's your drink, John," Nellie came by with a glass of wine for him.

"I'm so sorry," I said. "I'm even sorrier I didn't wait thirty seconds for Nellie to say your name."

John laughed, "It's quite alright, Maybel. And by the way, you're really cute when you blush," he winked.

I felt my face get hotter.

"Come, let's sit and chat, shall we?"

"Yes, I'd like that," I smiled.

John and I sat and talked about school, our families, and our life's aspirations. He was studying to be a lawyer, had one sister, and a dog named Orangebelle.

I told him I wanted to be a nurse, that I had one sister, and that I could shoot a tin can from really far away.

"I've never met a woman who could do that. You'll have to show me sometime." His dark brown eyes twinkled with amusement. His hair was short and brown and neatly trimmed. He was undeniably handsome.

"Maybel, I hear music coming from the ballroom. Would you care to dance?"

"I would love that, J-o-h-n," I smiled.

John stood up and reached for my hand. He led me toward the ballroom where we passed Bernard, who had apparently been watching us by the doorframe. I hadn't noticed him watching us. He watched me pass by him while he stood there silently brooding.

Maybe Catherine had good reason to be concerned, I thought. I'd never paid any mind to Bernard at parties before, and I so rarely went to parties anyway, but looking back, he had always been protective of me. I always thought it was his brotherly love for me. And maybe that was all it was. Afterall, I decided, if he truly felt more than brotherly love for me, he would have asked me on a date, and yet, he remained with Catherine.

Catherine was inside the ballroom dancing with a handsome man, laughing and resting her hand lightly on his chest while they swayed to the music. She saw me and whispered something to the man and came to me.

"Maybel," she pulled me away out of earshot from John, "Act interested in him."

"I am interested."

"Good. Act more interested. Laugh and smile," she coaxed.

"Ok," I rolled my eyes.

She turned and went back to the handsome man and I heard her laugh and apologize for having taken so long.

I walked nervously toward John.

"Is everything ok?" he asked me.

"Yes, that was my sister, Catherine," I said. "Would you like to dance now?"

He smiled, "I'd love to."

John wasn't a graceful dancer, but neither was I, so every couple steps, we giggled nervously as we stepped on each other.

"Maybel, would you like some wine?"

"Yes, maybe I'll dance better," I laughed.

"Me too!" he chuckled.

He returned with two glasses of wine and we sipped together along the side of the ballroom.

"So that is your sister, you said?" He nodded toward Catherine, who was giggling and twirling around.

"And that is your, I'm guessing, brother-in-law?"

"No. Catherine isn't married."

He looked confused. "Then perhaps her fiancé or boyfriend?"

"No," I replied simply.

"She seems very friendly," he said.

"Oh, she is quite friendly and outgoing," I replied sarcastically.

"Well then, shall we continue dancing? Or shall I amend my statement to reflect the true nature of our dancing and ask, will you please allow me to continue stepping on your toes, Maybel?" We both laughed.

"You are definitely a lawyer! Yes, we'll again amend your statement to reflect that I, too, would love to continue stepping on your toes!" We continued laughing at our silliness.

John led me to the dance floor again and I let myself be pulled closer into his embrace. He kissed my cheek.

"I'm sorry if I'm too forward."

"If you overstep your boundaries, I'll sue. I've recently met a talented and handsome lawyer," I giggled so hard I lightly snorted. We both laughed at my awkward snort.

"Oh Maybel, I quite enjoy your humor! You are a delight!"

We continued dancing, in our own special way. I had not seen Bernard in a while. Catherine must have been wrong, I thought. Bernard didn't care who I danced with or who flirted with me.

When the band took a break, I excused myself. I needed to pee really badly but I didn't want to tell John that. I walked into the foyer and peeked into several rooms trying to find the bathroom. In one small room off to the side, out of the way, Bernard sat next to a gorgeous, dark-haired woman with his arm around her waist.

He looked up when I peeked my head in. "Hello, Maybel. This is Eliza. She's a nurse."

I'm sure my smile was as fake as my pleasantries when I tried to smile. I couldn't fake a polite voice so I left as quickly as I'd come.

I really had to pee but I also needed to find Catherine. My bladder won and I continued searching for a bathroom. I finally found one thankfully, just in time.

Ahh! I sighed as I opened the door. Catherine yanked me out and pulled me to the foyer. I tripped over my heels and landed on the floor.

"Get up!" she hissed at me. "We're going home!"

She snatched my arm and pulled me up as though she suddenly gained the arm strength of a ditch digger.

"Ow! Catherine!" I fell on my face and my wrists hurt from catching myself on the way down!

"We're leaving!" she snarled.

Catherine pulled me out the front door and onto the sidewalk.

"Catherine! Calm down!" I pleaded.

"I saw Bernard with another woman!" she screamed.

"I saw him too, when I was looking for the bathroom."

"Why didn't you come get me?" she raged at me.

"I was just about to come find you after I finished peeing! I really had to pee Catherine! I drank a little wine."

"He had his arm around her!" Catherine continued raging.

"Well, now you know. Bernard has no intention to date me. He didn't interfere once between me and John."

"I can't believe he was with another woman!" Catherine was stuck in an angry loop.

"He was probably angry at you for flirting with that really handsome man you were glued to all evening."

"I was trying to prove that he cared more about who you're with than who I'm with," she said.

"Well, it appears he doesn't care about either of us," I said. "Or, perhaps, Bernard was trying to make you as jealous as you were trying to make him. Maybe this is just a childish game between you two and nothing more."

Truth be told I wanted to scratch Bernard's eyes out because I was jealous. I was also mad that he had hurt Catherine, even though this was all her stupid fault. I was still loyal to Catherine, and decided to exact revenge on Bernard.

"You're right, Maybel," Catherine sighed. Her shoulders sunk and she no longer looked regal. She looked fragile. Catherine looking fragile made me want to see how fragile Bernard's bones were when subjected to a baseball bat.

Catherine leaned against the stone terrace around the twins' house. "I treated Bernard unfairly and shouldn't have been so childish. Maybe he was just flirting with that woman to make me jealous and it was nothing more."

Suddenly we heard Vincent's voice commanding Big Ben to speed up and there was Bernard and the dark-haired woman sitting in Bernard's carriage, completely absorbed in conversation with each other. Bernard's arm was around her waist and she was sitting close to him.

Catherine and I watched them go by. We looked at each other and we were both shocked. Bernard was taking this woman home with him!

Catherine and I slowly began walking home. "Catherine," I whispered, "Are you ok?"

"No."

We walked in silence a little while longer.

"I want to go to Bernard's," I said. "You can find out what's really going on, if he's having sex with that woman, or if this is all a misunderstanding, and then we leave. You'll be free to find your best match for marriage then."

"Sex? You think he's having sex with her?"

"Well, what else would he be doing?"

"Kissing, things of that nature," Catherine said, suddenly looking even more distraught.

"You and Bernard don't have sex?" I asked bluntly.

"No! Maybel!"

"Has Bernard? I mean with someone else?"

"No! I mean he says he hasn't," she answered.

"Really? After all this time?" I said sarcastically.

"Really, Maybel!"

"Let's go to Bernard's and get this over with," she sounded sad and scared.

Catherine began walking up to the main entrance. I grabbed her elbow and spun her around to face me.

"To the front door, Catherine? No! We're going up the tree by his bedroom window!"

"In heels and dresses?"

"Of course not! Take your heels off," I said.

"My dress will rip."

"Will that matter? You won't have anywhere to wear your dress because you'll be stuck in your bedroom crying about Bernard."

Catherine looked pain-stricken.

"Or not. Maybe he's not having sex," I said quickly. "He's probably not having sex and mommy can fix any rips in this dress."

"Alright, fine!" she huffed, "Show me how to get up the tree! I'll go down swinging, Maybel, I swear I will!"

I smiled wildly at Catherine. I really wanted to see her scream at Bernard they way she screamed at our little cousin's opposing baseball team. They were five years old, and weren't playing fairly, and Catherine got us thrown out of the ballpark because she was angry one of the little boys on the opposing team threw a ball at our little cousin's head. After the game, Catherine slugged the boy's mother because the boy's mother called Catherine obnoxious. Catherine told her to teach her son better manners, which I found ironic and hilarious. And that was the Catherine I wanted to see tonight. She can only be prim and proper for so long until mommy's temper flares within her veins and she becomes unreasonable. I was anxiously awaiting her confrontation with that whore at Bernard's side. I was giddy with bloodlust.

We went around the side of his house and lifted up our skirts so our legs could move freely and climbed the oak tree by his window barefoot. "Now pull your skirt up farther and jump onto the roof," I called quietly to Catherine as I leaped onto Bernard's roof.

Catherine timidly followed. "How many bedrooms have you accessed this way? You seem very comfortable with this sort of thing."

I chuckled.

"Ok," I whispered, "This is his window."

We crept close and pressed our faces onto the glass. "It's empty," I said, "Let's go in."

I opened the window carefully and we climbed inside Bernard's bedroom.

"No one's here or in his bathroom," I whispered.

"Ok let's leave. They're not having sex," Catherine said.

"Wait, where would they be?" I asked.

"Who knows, it's a big house. Let's just go!" Catherine sounded nervous.

"Fine. But I'd rather snoop. Do you see any women's clothing anywhere?"

"No, nothing." Catherine was becoming more timid. I wanted to see Baseball Catherine. I wanted her to get us thrown out of Bernard's mansion.

"Is this a mask you wear when you're painting?" I held up a mask with straps to my nose and mouth. "Look at me, I'm Bernard!" I acted silly, flailing my arms and legs out.

Catherine giggled and put on a pair of Bernard's underwear over her head. "Look at me! I'm Bernard! I only think with my penis!"

We began laughing hysterically at each other.

Bernard suddenly threw open the door. "What is going on in here? Why are you two wearing my jock strap and underwear?"

"Oh no, Catherine! This isn't our house!" I squealed.

"You're right, Maybel! We climbed into the wrong house!"

"Well, goodbye, Bernard!" I yelled as I bolted toward the window.

"Have a lovely evening," Catherine added as she followed quickly behind me.

Bernard grabbed both of us around our waists and held us tightly.

"What the hell is going on? Why did you two leave me at the party?"

"Because you were with another woman!" I screamed and kicked Bernard in his shin and pulled Catherine toward me.

I grabbed the chair from his desk and threw it at his chest and pulled Catherine toward the window.

Bernard threw his chair at his wall and came barreling toward us. He grabbed us again around our waists and all three of us went crashing onto his bed.

I screamed out in my best Mrs. Murphy accent, "Aarrrggghh fight the bloody English bastards!" I had no idea why that came screaming out of my mouth, but I liked Theo's housekeeper's angry Irish accent when she became enraged at politics in the newspaper, so that's what came flying out of my mouth.

I screamed, "Down with ye Limey Bastards!" and kicked Bernard in his stomach. He groaned and I screamed to Catherine, "Git ye to the window, Lassie!"

Catherine looked at me like I was insane, but she did as my angry accent commanded, and we both dived toward the window frame and became stuck.

"Damnit!" I screamed. "It was the bloody custards we ate at the candy store! Our bellies got too fat!"

I felt myself being hoisted back into Bernard's angry grasp.

"Save ye self, Lassie! Long live Ireland!" I screamed.

Catherine bolted out the window, and like a tree squirrel, flung herself onto the trunk of the old oak tree.

Bernard slammed me onto his bed, "What in hell is going on Maybel?" he growled at me.

"You were with another woman!" I screamed in my natural accent.

Catherine burst through the window with a tree branch and hit Bernard over his back, breaking the limb into three pieces. "Get! Off! My! Sister!" she screamed like a banshee!

"Ack! There be the Catherine I been cravin' ta see!" I screamed like Mrs. Murphy.

Bernard tumbled off me and landed on the floor where he stayed. He laid there looking confused and unsure of what had happened.

"Catherine! You came back for me!"

"Of course I did! You're my sister!"

I looked at Bernard and then back at Catherine. "Catherine, I'm about to tell you something, and I need you to focus on that whore at Bernard's side tonight. Focus on the whore, please, Catherine." I took a very long and drawn-out breath. It was so long that Catherine's brows lowered in annoyance and anticipation. "Bernard has kissed me several times over the years and I did not tell you because I was scared you would never play with me ever again. I'm sorry. I should have told you. Please don't be too, terribly mad at me. I love you so much, Catherine!"

I winced, afraid she would charge me and beat me with the wooden shard she still held in her grip.

"Bernard has kissed you several times?" Catherine looked hurt. I didn't want to see Catherine hurt. I would have preferred she drove her wooden shard through my chest.

"Yes," I said. "I'm so sorry. I was so scared you would never play with me again. I was too scared to tell you because I was afraid you wouldn't love me anymore, and I'm terrified to lose you now."

"I'm sorry, Catherine," Bernard moaned from his floor. "I did kiss Maybel. I was attracted to her and I kissed her. Please don't be mad at Maybel. I should have been a better boyfriend to you, and a better friend to Maybel. I am so sorry," Bernard's voice cracked from either physical pain, or maybe he was regretful of his behavior. "You deserve better, Catherine. And you do too, Maybel. I love you both. The woman you saw tonight was my cousin, Eliza. I didn't know she was in town. I think she's still downstairs if you want to confirm that she is indeed my cousin."

Catherine breathed heavily, struggling to regain her composure. "Get up, Bernard!"

Bernard rubbed his back with one hand and his neck with the other. "You broke a tree branch over my back, Catherine."

"Just a medium-sized one," Catherine said.

"Catherine, I'm so sorry I didn't tell you." Tears streamed down my face. I didn't want to lose Catherine. "I should have told you. I waited too long to tell you, and then I didn't know how to tell you. I'm so sorry!"

"Bernard, what are your intentions toward Maybel? Do you intend to kiss her again?" Catherine asked Bernard.

Bernard looked at Catherine, then at me. "No," Bernard said quietly. His eyes were downcast. "Maybel does not seem to be interested in me romantically. I have no intention of kissing her again."

"Bernard is not interested in you, Maybel. Let's go home." Catherine took my elbow and dragged me to Bernard's window.

"You can use the front door," Bernard called from the floor.

"No," Catherine said, "I quite like Maybel's approach."

Catherine flung herself onto the nearest tree and scaled down as though navigating tree branches and defying gravity were her secret talent. I followed her much more slowly. I felt rejected once again. I felt stupid, too, because I kept going back to Bernard for more rejection.

Catherine and I returned home. Catherine did not speak to me the entire way home.

"Do you intend to pursue Bernard?" Catherine asked me at our front gate.

"No," I said quietly. "I don't think he is interested in me romantically. He's never kissed me out in the open where anyone could see us."

Catherine looked at me expressionless for a moment. "That's pathetic. You should have known better, and you deserve better." She turned and passed through our gate and went straight to her bedroom.

My math teacher came to my house one evening after school. He told mommy and daddy that I was not grasping algebra and was failing. I was embarrassed. I had not been able to concentrate lately because all I could think about was how I was a bad sister. Catherine shook my core when she said I was pathetic. I had been rejected by every boy, and I knew Catherine was right; I was pathetic. I knew my grades were suffering from my inability to concentrate. I retreated into my room and wrote stories. They were angry stories. The girl in the stories was always dejected and murderous. After I wrote, I felt better though, and sometimes I bought candies at the candy store after school and left them in Catherine's coat pockets. I hoped she wouldn't be mad at me forever because I imagined her beautiful children in my mind, and I wanted to play with them in the future when she would hopefully forgive me.

One Saturday, I returned from Susan's house and Bernard sat at the table in my family room. I froze.

"Mr. Fulton says you are failing math and I asked Mrs. Charleston to send Bernard here," mommy said. "I know something strange is going on between all you children, but right now, I don't care why you're all acting strangely; you are failing math, Maybel, and you will study until you are not failing math. You are going to college."

Mommy seemed upset. I was embarrassed I was too stupid to grasp math. I was more embarrassed that mommy made Bernard come here to make me less stupid. I sat down at the table and my shoulders sunk. I was embarrassed and uncomfortable and mommy didn't care as long as I passed math.

"I'm not going to college," I told mommy. My voice was quiet because mommy scared me sometimes.

"You will graduate high school," mommy's voice was level and strong. "We'll discuss college later."

Mommy said Bernard would come over and tutor me at our table in our family room while he was on his school break. "Bernard or Henry will tutor you every day until your next math exam, Maybel. Today, Bernard is your teacher, and I expect you to be a good student." She added sourly, "Your father and Henry will likely be at the hardware store all day and come home smelling like whiskey."

"I thought you liked a nip of whiskey once in a while?" I asked her. And then I slunk down in my seat further because mommy was mad at my math grades and I should have remained quiet, lest I bank her ire.

"Yes, well, a nip is fine, but too much means daddy can't pitch a tent in his pants tonight." Mommy continued scouring the skillet in the sink like the skillet had just walked onto her freshly-mopped floor.

"People put up tents in their pants? That doesn't make sense," I said.

"What?" mommy looked startled. "Did I say that out loud? Oh, dear, please pretend I didn't say that!" Mommy's cheeks blushed crimson.

I had to remember that expression so I could ask Catherine what it meant when she returned from Edith's house. I hoped Catherine would talk to me.

"I'm going to the hardware store, be back soon," mommy suddenly took her shawl and left. I wondered if this had anything to do with tents. We didn't have a tent and I hoped she was going to the store to buy one because I enjoyed camping.

"Just look at the shape and the angle, Maybel," Bernard said with frustration.

"I am looking at the shape and angle, Bernard! It looks like a triangle and its angle is pointy!"

Bernard breathed out deeply. I wished Henry were teaching me and not Bernard.

"You're making this more difficult than it is," Bernard sighed.

He leaned back in his chair again and breathed deeply. "It's math. It's not even difficult math. This is the simplest of all math. How do you not grasp such simple concepts?"

I felt stupid when Bernard or Catherine tried to teach me math. I was embarrassed of my lack of intelligence and I hated when people saw how dumb I was.

Bernard must have noticed my frustration with myself. He spoke a little more gently. "You'll understand eventually, Maybel." He rubbed my shoulder. "Let's take a break." Bernard wiped his face with his hands, clearly exasperated with me.

I sat staring at the numbers and letters down on my paper. They had nothing in common with each other. There was no balance on either side of the equal sign even when Bernard said he'd balanced the equation. The little exponents above the numbers waved at me as they sat up there on their number thrones and taunted me.

I drew a little bow and arrow on my paper and shot the exponent off the number four, then drew a crumpled exponent splattered below the number over which it had sat. "Ha ha," I muttered. "You tried to get too big and you were leveled by my arrow. That's what happens when I balance you. You die!" I giggled to myself.

"Why don't we try this again?" Bernard suggested. He looked as unenthused about teaching me as I felt about learning math.

"Can we stop?" I asked.

"Yes," Bernard looked relieved.

"Do you ever wonder what it would be like if we had tails like cats or if our pupils were little vertical slits? What differences do you think a cat can see with vertical pupils? We don't know because cats can't talk, but if they could talk, they would not be able to compare their eyesight with ours because they have never seen what we see through our eyes. It's like trying to describe the color blue to a blind person or the different sounds animals make to a deaf person. You can't understand what you've never seen or heard."

Bernard watched me talk. "I don't understand what you just said, but it sounds like it's probably an intelligent thought."

I sighed, "Do you want to do something?"

"Like what?" Bernard stood up from the table and sat on the sofa. He stretched his legs and relaxed.

"I don't know. I'm bored," I said.

"If you put as much thought into math as you do cats' eyes, you'd be a math professor," he smiled at me.

"Well, you know how to read and write but that doesn't mean you'll ever communicate well," I told him.

"Again, you sound like you said something smart, but I'm not sure," Bernard said. He took off his shoes and laid down on the sofa. He looked up at the ceiling then shoved a pillow under his head. Bernard looked drained from trying to teach me math.

"You aren't Shakespeare, Bernard."

"I know. What is your point?"

"Some people are good at math, and some people are good at communicating," I said.

"Write that on your next math exam," Bernard said dryly.

I furrowed my brows and huffed at him, "I'm only stupid in a world where I'm forced to balance equations. If you lived in my world, you'd be the stupid one." I folded my arms.

"You're not stupid," Bernard sighed. "And you're right about communicating. I don't write as beautifully as you."

"Are you going to Edith's birthday party tonight?" I steered the conversation away from math.

"No, I told Catherine I would attend some social events with her as friends, but we are not dating. We have not been dating either. She makes it sound like we're dating. Sometimes she seems to want to date me again, but really, I think she gets lonely and just wants to have someone to accompany her to parties." Bernard sank further into the sofa grumbling. He disliked parties as much as me. "She enjoys telling people she is attending a party with a Charleston," Bernard said with annoyance. "I like that you don't care about my wealth, Maybel."

Bernard sighed, "It does have its benefits being associated with Catherine, though. My friends don't try to play matchmaker, and when I'm at a party with Catherine, I don't have to deal with chatty girls asking me about my family's wealth and where I've vacationed."

Bernard sighed again and looked at me. "Are you going to Edith's birthday party?"

"No, Edith's older sister always tries to make me feel dumb. She likes to write stories too, and she always peppers into the conversation how the teachers at school chose her stories as the winners of whatever competitions we entered."

"Your stories didn't win?" Bernard asked, surprised.

"No."

Bernard looked lost in trying to remember something. "Did she write that story about the farmer and his wife and children shucking corn?"

"Yes. How did you know?"

"The story was sitting on the coffee table at Edith's house one time when Catherine dragged me there. It was boring and didn't pull me into the story like your stories do."

"The teachers at school liked it better than the one I wrote."

"That's because they're jealous of you, Maybel, and know you're going to far surpass all of them the second you graduate. That's why they're holding you down. They know this will be the only time they get to see you come in second." Bernard smirked, "Your writing will travel to every country while they sit here stewing in their mediocrity."

I was surprised Bernard stuck up for me. "Thank you," I said softly.

"Sometimes I tease you, Maybel, but I get mad when anyone else does. I'm allowed to tease you because I love you."

"I love you, too, Bernard." I said quietly.

"Do you remember when you kissed me a couple different times and said you didn't mean to, and then you got angry at yourself and kept pushing me away?"

Bernard sighed, "Yes, Maybel."

"How did you get rid of your feelings for me?" I asked.

"I didn't. I just got better at controlling myself, sometimes anyway."

"How did you learn to control yourself?" I was genuinely curious.

"Well, I teased you to the point you hated me and didn't want to be around me. I don't recommend that approach. I'm surprised you forgave me."

"You have redeeming qualities, and I missed the chocolates you brought me," I smiled.

"I did bribe you to like me again."

"It worked," I laughed.

"I'm glad. I like teasing you though. You get mad and look like an angry, little kitten, and I want to pet you, but you're scratchy and hissy."

I laughed again.

I really wanted to kiss Bernard. I was angry at myself for still liking him. "I guess I should finish my math homework," I said.

I sighed and opened my textbook. Bernard again sat next to me. He did not look enthused at all about teaching me.

Bernard read the instructions in the next chapter of my math book and rested his head on the palm of his hand, and his elbow on the table, and sighed. He tried hard to teach me math, but it was as though we both held soup cans attached by string on opposite sides of the house, and spoke into them, expecting the other person to understand our words, but we never did.

I couldn't concentrate. Bernard wore an old green shirt with tiny holes around his neckline and waistline. It was his favorite shirt as he wore it often. I loved when he wore this shirt, but Catherine hated it. His eyes glowed, reflecting the green in his shirt. Every time he wore it, I drowned in his gaze. Catherine always frowned when he wore this shirt, saying it had tiny holes and that he was far too wealthy to look poor. I told Bernard that this shirt was my favorite because he was always far more relaxed when he wore this shirt compared to his button-down dress shirts.

I kissed Bernard when he leaned close to write something mathy on my paper. I held his cheek and then his lips. I surprised myself, and him.

Instead of pulling back, he kissed me and pulled me over onto his lap. He kissed me gently, and then more passionately. His breath was hot on my neck as he kissed down to my shoulder.

I breathed harder. His hands were strong and pulled me closer. I put my hand on his hips, at the bottom of his shirt. I wanted to go underneath his shirt and feel his hard stomach and chest.

I tentatively put my fingertips onto his skin. He was hot and his skin was smooth.

Bernard pressed his lips harder against mine and sucked in when I touched his stomach.

"Maybel, I might not be able to stop if you keep going," he breathed heavily.

"I'm sorry," I whispered, and pulled my hand down and out from underneath his shirt.

"You don't have to stop, but if you continue, I won't be able to stop where this is headed very easily. I really want you, Maybel."

I leaned in and kissed Bernard again. I didn't want to stop.

There was talking outside our house. I heard mommy and daddy's voices coming up our walkway. I jumped off Bernard's lap and onto my own chair and stuck my nose in my math book. Bernard hunched over, hiding his huge erection.

"Hello, dears," mommy said to us as she walked in. "Daddy decided to return home from the hardware store early." Mommy winked at daddy and tugged on his hand to follow her. "You can go back to the hardware store after we talk about something upstairs. We'll discuss that thing we were to discuss before you drink more whiskey."

Daddy looked excited.

"Thank you for helping Maybel with math," mommy said as she hung up her coat.

"Yes, thank you, Bernard." Daddy hung up his coat and hat. "I know you are busy with your studies, but we appreciate your help."

"Yes, sir," Bernard said, still hunched over the table.

"Have your father and mother come over some evening, won't you?" daddy asked Bernard.

"Certainly, sir," Bernard replied.

"Lunch will be ready soon, but hopefully not too soon," mommy giggled as she pulled daddy around the corner and up the stairs.

I was nervous. I glanced over at Bernard.

"I should go," Bernard said.

I looked down at my math book. I didn't want him to leave. "Ok," I said quietly.

"Are you coming to my house tonight while Catherine goes to Edith's birthday party?" I asked. I hoped to see Bernard again soon.

"No, but you're welcome to come to my house. You haven't finished your math homework," Bernard said as he scruffled my hair and left.

Kissing me then tousling my hair confused me. I wasn't sure if Bernard thought of me as a woman or a child.

That evening Catherine got ready for Edith's birthday party. She called to me from her bedroom, "Are you coming, Maybel?"

"No," I called back. "I'm still looking over my math book."

"Bernard isn't coming with me to the birthday party. Why don't you ask him for help?"

"He already attempted to help me today."

Catherine peeked her head inside my bedroom. "Go study math, Maybel. You'll need to do better in math if you want to be a nurse."

"I've decided to be a circus performer," I informed Catherine.

"You'll still need math."

"No, I won't," I sung in a sing-song voice.

"Maybel, go to Bernard's and study math," Catherine insisted.

"Why?" I whined, in my most whiny voice. "I studied today."

Catherine came inside and closed my door. "I want to know who Bernard is seeing."

"Bernard's seeing someone?"

Catherine sat on my bed. "He didn't want to kiss me today when I went to his house. I leaned in, and he said if we weren't dating, we shouldn't be kissing."

"Oh," I paused, "I didn't know you wanted to continue a relationship with Bernard since he and I kissed. I'm so sorry about that, Catherine."

Catherine dismissed my apologies. "Bernard and I have had our ups and downs. We always reunite. Today, however, he did not want to kiss me, so I know there's another girl trying to get his attention."

"I'm not studying math to see if some girl comes over to find the area of Bernard's cylinder." I laughed at my silly joke. Catherine did not.

"Maybel, please? I want to know who Bernard is dating."

"I kissed Bernard today," I admitted. "But you're not dating him, so it wasn't cheating," I quickly added.

"Maybel!" Catherine looked either hurt or angry.

Catherine stared at me and she looked pained. I reassessed my interpretation of her emotions and decided she was both hurt and angry.

"Bernard kept trying to make me do math and I didn't want to, so I kissed him. He left." I attempted to explain my reason for kissing Bernard so that Catherine wouldn't be so hurt.

Catherine laughed, "You must have been a terrible kisser for him to immediately leave after your kiss." She snorted and stood up. "I have to finish getting ready for Edith's party." She returned to her room laughing.

Catherine made me mad. I realized Bernard must have thought I had dry lips and that's why he left so quickly. He used to tease me about having dry lips.

I bounded downstairs and quickly over to Bernard's, where I shoved open his window and confronted him.

"Why did you leave so quickly after I kissed you? Catherine said it must have been because I was a terrible kisser."

"You told Catherine?" Bernard asked, surprised.

"She thinks you have been seeing another girl. I said I kissed you because you tried to make me do math, and my kiss stopped your math lesson, and then you suddenly left."

"Oh," Bernard paused. He suddenly looked a little sad. "You kissed me to distract me, so I'd stop teaching you math? I didn't realize that was your intention. I thought you wanted to kiss me."

"Was my kiss that bad? Were my lips dry? Is that why you left so quickly?"

"It was terrible, and I suppose now I should go to that boring birthday party with Catherine since you and I won't be kissing at our next math lesson," Bernard said angrily. He walked around his bedroom in a huff.

I was hurt. "You said you wouldn't tease me again about how badly I kiss."

"It's not teasing if it's true," Bernard snapped.

"I hate you again!" I screamed.

Bernard hit his bedroom door frame with his fist. "Damnit Maybel! You only kissed me to get out of doing math!" He sighed deeply and leaned against his dresser. "You didn't kiss badly. I enjoyed kissing you. I left because I really wanted more than kissing."

My anger softened. "Oh," I said. "Did you like my kiss then?"

"Yes, Maybel!" Bernard angrily huffed and paced. "I like kissing you, and you've always kissed well."

I sat down on Bernard's bed. "I told Catherine that I distracted you with a kiss so she wouldn't be mad at me for kissing you," I admitted. "I hate you again for teasing me though. You promised you wouldn't tease me again but you did."

"Maybel, why did you kiss me?"

"I liked you back then, when you were nice, before you became cold, callous, and mean again."

"It was only this morning!" Bernard said, exasperatedly.

"You've changed, Bernard."

"Are you trying to aggravate me or are you serious?"

I smiled.

"Damnit, Maybel! Come here!" Bernard grabbed me and lifted me up and into his arms, hugging me. "You didn't kiss terribly. I said that because you had just told me you only kissed me to stop doing math! It really upset me."

"I didn't want Catherine to be mad at me. She became all squinty-eyed and seething, and her voice was like a second-grade teacher."

Bernard laughed.

I became serious again. "Bernard, who are you seeing? Catherine said you're seeing someone."

"No one! I didn't want to kiss her again. I wanted you!"

I smiled as I looked up into his green eyes.

I sat down at the kitchen table. Mommy entered the kitchen with a bag of potatoes and meat. "Maybel, why don't you help me prepare dinner?"

"It's lunch time, mommy."

"Yes, I know, but Susan and her parents are coming to dinner this evening.

"Why?"

"Well don't be rude, Maybel. I thought you were friends."

"We are, but I wasn't expecting them."

"Catherine went to see Susan today and invited Susan and Mr. and Mrs. Matthews over for dinner tonight."

I began cutting potatoes. One by one, chunks of potatoes fell into the bowl on the counter. I enjoyed Susan and her parents visiting, but I was surprised I had not known about their visit tonight until just now.

"Why did Catherine visit Susan?" I finally asked.

Mommy was flittering about the kitchen on a mission to make a dinner fit for royalty. "I think since you are studying math with Bernard every afternoon lately, Catherine and Susan have missed you and they've struck up a friendship."

I was surprised. "Oh," I said, "I didn't think I was gone but a couple hours a day."

"I know dear, but Susan has been over frequently asking for you, and I know Catherine is bored now that she is not dating Bernard." Mommy climbed up the small kitchen ladder we had set aside for things on the very top shelves.

"Is Catherine mad at me for seeing Bernard for help with math?"

"No, dear," mommy reassured me, "but she has more time to be bored now. She and Bernard revolved around each other, and now they are not a couple. I think both Catherine and Bernard are trying to figure out what to do now with all their extra time." Mommy climbed back down from the top rung of the ladder carrying jars of food she'd canned previously. She must be where I get my great penchant for climbing and agility, I thought, as I marveled at mommy's tree squirrel-like prowess as she moved the ladder and darted up the steps again.

I thought about what mommy said about Catherine being bored. "Mommy, should I spend less time with Bernard and more time with Catherine?"

"Sweetheart, Catherine is fine. Your math skills, however, could use some help," she giggled and dismounted the ladder, again like a squirrel. She kissed my cheek.

"Am I losing Catherine and Susan?" I felt like I should have realized what had been going on in my absence.

"No, Maybel, things change, situations change. You will always be Catherine's sister and Susan's dear friend. Maybel, dear, things will always be changing though."

Out of curiosity, I climbed the ladder as quickly as I'd seen mommy, but my foot slipped and my lip busted open on a ladder rung. "Maybel, dear, are you ok?"

"No. My pride is hurt. You climb better than me."

Mommy laughed, "Oh you should have seen me when I was young! Daddy called me his little Tree Squirrel!" She laughed heartily at her memory.

"I was just thinking you reminded me of a tree squirrel," I laughed.

Dinner time arrived, and with it, Susan and Mr. and Mrs. Matthews. Mommy and Mrs. Matthews spoke of mommy's dresses and Mrs. Matthews' breads and jams. Catherine and Susan talked about various things they'd been doing together such a riding bicycles and helping Susan's mother make and sell her delicious jam. I had not realized they had been spending so much time together. I didn't think I spent that much time with Bernard or Henry studying math.

After dinner, daddy and Mr. Matthews sipped brandy on the back porch. Catherine, Susan, Mrs. Matthews, and mommy joined their conversation, but I was beginning to tire and really just wanted to sleep. I stayed, though, and tried to look interested. After trying to suppress several yawns, mommy whispered to me that I could sneak out if I'd like.

"I don't want to be rude," I mumbled. I was having trouble keeping my eyes open.

"It's alright dear," she said.

I stood up and politely said goodnight to Susan and Mr. and Mrs. Matthews. I went upstairs and fell into my bed with my dress still on.

The next morning, I woke up and bathed and dressed and went downstairs to breakfast. I was the first one awake. It must have been a late night for everyone, I thought. I made bacon and eggs and eventually the smell of bacon wafting upstairs brought mother and father down.

"Oh, what a delight, Maybel!" Mommy took a small piece of bacon from daddy's plate.

I looked curiously at her and she winked at daddy. "We have an agreement, Maybel. I was in labor with you and Catherine for so long that I am always entitled to a piece of daddy's bacon," she giggled.

"Yes, this is an agreement mommy drafted, signed, and for which I had absolutely no say in the matter," daddy winked back at mommy, "but you and Catherine have been worth the stolen bacon," daddy patted my hand.

"Shall I wake Catherine?" I asked.

"She spent the night at Susan's house," mommy said.

"Oh," I said, feeling left out of their blossoming friendship.

"Why don't you go over and spend the day with them?" mommy suggested.

"I'll go over after my annoying math lesson," I sulked.

I hadn't planned on going to Bernard's house today, but Catherine had stolen my only friend. I kicked rocks all the way to Bernard's house. I wondered if Catherine was mad at me over my math lessons with Bernard, and that was why she stole Susan from me. Catherine had not been interested in playing with me since she began liking boys, and Susan was younger than me, so I wondered why Catherine was suddenly friendly with Susan. Catherine had dozens of friends, yet desired to occupy her time with my only friend.

Mrs. Charleston opened the door. "Hello, Mrs. Charleston. Is Bernard available for my math lesson?"

"Come in, Maybel, I'll go ask him."

I waited in the foyer. Mrs. Charleston returned, "Bernard is available. He's in his bedroom."

"Algebra or geometry?" Bernard held up two books when I entered.

"What's my third option?"

"Physics."

"Ooh, that sounds scary. I'll go with geometry today. At least I can visualize shapes, whereas algebra was invented by Satan."

"Very dramatic, Maybel. Satan invented algebra."

"Ok, Bernard, I'm ready for you to make me cry."

"I have learned my lesson." Bernard spoke softly. He wore a simple white, cotton shirt and brown pants. "I'm not going to push you away, or be mean to you ever again, I promise."

Bernard pulled me into a tight hug. "I really am sorry for teasing you. I cringe whenever I think of the things I said to you and did to you. I'm so sorry. You deserved better and I will spend the rest of my life making things right between us and with Catherine as well."

My face was squished into his chest so speaking was difficult, but I managed to turn my head a little and said, "I meant I'm ready for you to teach me geometry, which will undoubtedly make me cry."

Bernard relaxed his hug so my lips weren't squashed up against his chest and he looked down at me and laughed. "Oh, that's what you meant."

Bernard explained geometry as though he were talking to a child. It annoyed me, but I was also grateful because I apparently only understood math if it were explained to me step-by-step, in very elementary terms.

I laid next to Bernard on his bed as he held his geometry book and explained angles and proofs. My head rested on his shoulder and his arm wrapped around me to hold his geometry book in front of me.

I liked the way I felt resting on his muscular shoulder. It felt sensual. I liked his voice as he explained my math lessons. His voice was much lower than when I'd first met him. His voice sounded like honey tasted, very sweet.

"The angle, Maybel, what is the angle?"

I suddenly realized I had not been paying attention to a single word he spoke. "90 degrees?" I asked.

"Maybel, you haven't been listening at all have you?" He sounded annoyed.

"I'm sorry," I said. I had a hard time understanding math from an old, unattractive teacher, so understanding math from someone as attractive as Bernard proved much more difficult.

I stood up and walked over to the chair near his bathroom. "Ok, please continue, Bernard," I said.

Bernard sighed, "Maybel, you need to take this seriously if you want to graduate high school."

"Please continue, Bernard. I can concentrate better here."

Bernard took a deep breath and explained everything again. I answered his question correctly this time.

"I'm impressed, Maybel!"

"Thank you, Bernard. You're a good teacher."

"You're a good student," Bernard paused, and made sure I was paying attention when he added, "when you want to be."

"Why, thank you," I said. "Give me another problem to solve."

Bernard gave me nine more geometry problems to solve and I got every single one correct.

"Maybel! I'm impressed! You're really good at geometry!"

"I told you, I can visualize shapes. Also, Satan didn't invent geometry. He's more of an algebra and every other math kind of demon."

"Maybel, I'm stunned, really!"

"Thank you, Bernard," I went to sit on the edge of his bed. "Bernard, Catherine spent the night at Susan's house and I'm sad."

Bernard sighed and reached up and cupped my cheek. "This has been hard on her. It's been hard on me. She needs a friend, and Susan's a good friend."

"You two are really not in a relationship anymore? Or are you two simply pausing your relationship for a while like you usually do?"

"We'll always be friends, but I have not kissed Catherine in quite a while. We have been attending social events together as friends. We politely pecked each other's cheeks and held hands. We attend events together because she likes being associated with a Charleston and I like not having annoying girls flirt with me because of my surname."

"Do you feel sad that you are no longer with Catherine? Do you miss her?"

Bernard sighed heavily, "I miss her friendship. I'll always love her but not as a girlfriend or wife. We grew apart. It has been difficult to adjust to having so much time to be alone. I don't want to get back together with Catherine. She doesn't want to be with me. I'm saying it's a difficult time because we were together for so long. She's lost. I'm lost. There is one person I have always wanted in my life though. I've always wanted you right beside me."

"You've never said anything to me like that before," I was impressed by his growing ability to say aloud his feelings.

"I'm trying really hard to express myself better, Maybel. I was thinking that you are getting better at math, so perhaps I should make an effort to express myself better, the way you so eloquently express yourself."

I watched Bernard. "That's kind of you, Bernard."

"Maybel, I'm trying so hard to be more open and honest with you. Please know that I truly love you and when you're not with me, I'm desperate for the time when you will once again be beside me. I'll always love Catherine but our love is different now."

"When will your love for me change?"

"Never," Bernard said.

"You thought your love for Catherine would never change," I countered.

"Maybel, I will try to think of the words to explain it to you but in the meantime, please just know how much I love being with you."

"Bernard, is my math lesson over?"

"Yes," he looked sad. "I suspect you want to leave now?"

"No, I do not. If my math lesson is over, and you think I did well, can we celebrate?"

"Of course, Maybel," he smiled and he seemed truly happy. "We can celebrate any way you want."

"Do you want to maybe make a fire and tell ghost stories?"

"I would love that, Maybel."

"I have to return home and have dinner with my family, and then afterward, we can make the fire by the pond behind my house."

"I look forward to it," he smiled.

I hesitated, "If you come to my house, though, you will see Catherine."

"I'll be happy as long as I'm with you. I look forward to your visits, and the time between the end of your math lesson, and the next day's lesson, is excruciating. I'm happy to see you tonight no matter the location. I will come to your house and if I see Catherine, it will be ok." Bernard gave me a quick peck on my cheek.

I returned home after my math lesson. When I walked past Susan's house, I could hear Theo's laugh come drifting out through the open windows. I thought the smell of his cologne came wafting out too. I missed that smell.

I continued to my house. I felt lost. I wanted to go on an adventure in Susan's woods, just the two of us. I wanted to lay on Catherine's bed while she played with her hair for hours and we giggled about nothing. And I wanted to lay next to Theo on his chaise lounge chair, resting my head on his chest while he read to me. I wanted to sit and talk with Henry in front of my fireplace. And, I wanted to be with Bernard. I was lost and I had never really had a place or a person that made me feel not lost.

I stopped inside my garden gate. I stood there wondering if my life were a story that I were writing, how would I choose to finish the story of Maybel? I had never thought about viewing my life as an unwritten story. If I separated myself from my characters, if I completely detached my emotions, and looked at the people in my life as characters, what would I have them do next?

The rest of the afternoon I was in a complete and utter daze, removed from the people around me, absolutely deaf to their attempted conversations with me.

In my mind, I was trying to see all the conversations and interactions I'd had with people, and all the conversations and interactions I'd seen other people have amongst themselves. I viewed these interactions as an author, not as my own life's experiences.

If this were algebra, I reasoned, I had to take myself out of the equation in order to find the answer. I was X. I had to remove myself in order to find myself.

I wandered out to the pond and sat on the fallen tree near the fire pit. If I were in the sky looking down at everyone, I'd see that I was alone because I never truly felt safe with anyone. I'd see that Susan and I fit so well together because we were both too creative to fit in with a group of normal people. If I were authoring my life's story, I'd see that I had a wonderful family.

Catherine is lost now too; I could see that clearly now. If I were writing Catherine's character, I would write her future with Bernard, since they had been together for so long. I wondered if this was what the real Catherine and Bernard wanted?

If I were the author, with whom would I pair Maybel? Would I write her character to be with Bernard or Theo? And then I considered Henry. Henry made my heart beat fast. Taking all of my own emotions out of this equation, who does Maybel love most as a man, a husband, and a father to her unborn children?

I contemplated having Maybel go to see Theo now. Would this draw her closer to Theo and further from Bernard?

Does the character of Bernard even like Maybel as a girlfriend? Bernard might be with Maybel to stay close to Catherine. Bernard might be with Maybel because he's bored and doesn't want to be alone. Bernard may only think of Maybel as a little sister.

I must take myself out of the equation, I reminded myself. Who does Miss X want to be with? I needed to write this story. I could not allow someone else to write it. My character, Maybel, needs to write her own future. She can't let things play out. Maybel must go and make her own future.

My head began hurting tremendously. My temples were both throbbing.

I laid down on the ground and watched the sun setting above me through the leaves. Maybel needs to stop thinking about things she cannot control. Maybel needs to stop referring to herself in the third person. I giggled at my joke.

"Maybel? Are you ok?" It was Bernard. "We were to celebrate your geometry lesson."

I stared up at the sky again. "I'm lost. I'm lonely."

Bernard sat down next to me.

"Are you here to teach me math?"

"No, Maybel."

"That's a shame. I'm getting better at math. I was thinking today after I left you, that if I were writing a book, and everyone I know, including myself, were characters, how would I finish the story of Maybel? I decided if I were an algebraic equation, I needed to be X, because I'm lost, and I need to remove myself to find myself."

"That's actually brilliant, Maybel. You applied mathematical concepts to real life problems." Bernard looked impressed and watched me with surprise, and I may have been mistaken, but he seemed to bestow upon me a little admiration, or maybe he was congratulating himself for successfully teaching a mathematically unwise person how to do simple math.

Bernard and I sat on the fallen log by the fire pit near the pond.

I still felt like the log beneath my bottom, hollow. "My character Maybel is still lost, Bernard. Maybel loves Bernard but she also loves Theo and Henry."

Bernard broke in front of me. Like crystal, he shattered.

"What will Maybel do?" He looked at me. I could see in his face a small child. When daddy told me my puppy was dead, this is the face I imagined I'd had.

"The author doesn't know what to do with all her characters. Will Bernard return to Catherine? Will Maybel rekindle her attraction to Theo, or will she end up with Henry, the man who has always been sensitive toward and protective of Maybel?" I finally had to stop thinking because my head felt like a lumberjack cracked it open with an axe.

"I need time and space," I told Bernard.

It was finally becoming spring, and I slowly began to feel the energy of the earth waking up from its deep slumber.

I sat down at Susan's tea party next to her stuffed groundhog. Of all her bizarre taxidermized animals, the groundhog was the least offensive.

I poked the groundhog's pink, crocheted booties. "When did you make these?" I asked Susan. "They're cute."

"Theo helped me make them last night."

I laughed, "You have the best sense of humor, Susan."

"He really did help me, Maybel. Look at the bootie on the top, left paw. The stitches are really loose and it looks like a child crocheted it. That's the one Theo made."

"Oh," I said. "Well, he tried."

Susan sat next to me and held her opossum in her lap. "Did you paint your opossum's toe nails?" I asked Susan.

"Yes!" she smiled. "Do you like the color?"

"Yes, red suits her, I think," I told Susan.

"Hello, Maybel," Theo greeted me as he walked into Susan's bedroom where I sat holding a stuffed groundhog wearing little, pink booties. I never would have imagined, years ago, that this would become a normal afternoon in my life.

"Hello, Theo," I replied. "What brings you back into town?" I still felt a little awkward in Theo's company after he and Catherine kissed, but I knew I couldn't remain angry. I kept reminding myself that I had transgressions too, and if I ever wanted forgiveness, I had to forgive.

"I wanted to see my parents and take Susan to a play and dinner," Theo said. He sat down on Susan's bedroom floor next to Susan and me.

"That sounds nice," I told him. "When are you leaving for the play?"

"We'll leave after lunch," he answered.

I sat there staring at the delicate porcelain teacups and saucers. There were roses painted around the mouths of the cups and the rims of the saucers.

"Maybel?" Susan was trying to get my attention.

I looked up. "What?"

"I asked if you wanted to come with us?"

"Yes!" I said. "Sorry, I was admiring the patterns on your tea set."

"I painted them!" Susan smiled.

"You painted them? I thought you bought them with these roses already painted on them! That's really professional-looking, Susan!"

Susan beamed.

Theo had been watching me. I asked him if I'd be interrupting his time with his family. "I was hoping you would come," he smiled sweetly.

"Before we go to the play, can we stop at the stationary store for paints, Theo?" Susan begged. She scooted close to Theo and looked up at him with big, pleading eyes.

Theo snorted, "I cannot say no to you when you do that, and you very well know that!" he laughed.

Susan giggled. "I love you, Theo!"

"I love you too, Susan," he smiled at her.

"Wait, before we go to get paints, do you want to see what Theo brought me, Maybel?"

"Of course, Susan!" I smiled.

Susan took a beautiful marionette from her bookcase. "Theo got it for me from a merchant on the beach!"

"It's really nice, Susan!" I said.

The marionette wore a beautiful blue and green dress and had yellow strings for hair. The shoes came on and off, as did the golden necklace and earrings.

"This is very intricate woodwork," I said, amazed.

"I love it!" Susan exclaimed.

Theo had been watching me marvel over the intricacies of the doll. "Do you know how to play with a marionette, Maybel?"

"No," I said.

"Move the sticks up here to move the dolls hands and legs," he explained.

I tried and the girl marionette flipped upside down and showed her bottom to her audience.

"That's a good first try," Theo said politely.

He then spoke to the marionette, "Miss, this isn't one of those houses," he joked.

"Have you returned to one of those houses?" I asked Theo sarcastically.

"No, I have not. I have, however, named my left hand Gladys."

Theo's joke caught me by surprise and I laughed, snorted, and choked all at the same time.

"What are those houses?" Susan asked innocently.

"There are houses where girls show their bottoms, and the girls live together in those houses," I said frankly.

Susan ignored our hidden innuendo. "Theo, I really love my gift, but can we go to the stationary store to buy more paints now?"

"Yes!" I agreed. "I would like to learn how to paint roses the way you so delicately painted those on your tea set," I said.

"Alright, ladies, let's go," Theo stood up.

I followed Susan and Theo to the family room. "Mr. and Mrs. Matthews were sitting on their sofa looking at a photo album. "Maybel," Mrs. Matthews called, "would you like to see Theo as a baby?"

"Oh, absolutely!" I giggled.

Theo was sitting on a rocking horse crying in the photograph.

"Aw, Theo, you look so happy," I teased.

"The photographer held a doll in front of his camera! I know I was young, but I clearly remember that moment!" Theo said with exasperation, as though he had to explain this photograph often.

"Was the dolly mean to you?" I teased.

"It was a strange looking doll and I didn't care for it!" Theo said indignantly.

"Well, you were a cute baby," I said.

"He was!" Mrs. Matthews said.

"He was, and still is, handsome. Of course, he takes his good looks from me, right dear?" Mr. Matthews combed his hair with his fingers.

"Yes, of course dear," Mrs. Matthews winked at me and I laughed.

"Ok, enough photographs," Theo pleaded. Mr. Matthews wrapped his arm around Theo's shoulder and kissed Theo on his cheek.

I never saw men kiss their grown sons, but the Matthews were a little different than any family I'd ever met. I supposed their affection stemmed from Susan having almost died.

Mr. Matthews hugged Theo, "I love you, son."

"I love you too, father," Theo returned his father's hug.

Theo held Susan's hand and then reached for mine as we walked into town. "I've missed you both terribly," Theo said.

I let Theo hold my hand because I had missed him, and because I liked the way my hand felt in his strong grasp.

"I've missed you, too!" Susan chirped. She giggled and talked about school and her paintings. "What have you been doing as of late, Theo?" Susan asked.

"Working," Theo said. "Boxing. Same as always."

"Will you have time to play with us this summer at our beach house?" Susan asked.

"Of course," Theo pinched her cheek. "I've been looking forward to this summer all year!"

"May I spend this summer with you again, Theo?" I asked.

"Maybel, of course you are welcome!" Theo said.

Theo bought Susan her paints at the stationary store and we were headed back toward her house when Bernard and Catherine stopped us. They had been walking around Bernard's gardens talking. Bernard's hands were in his pockets and he followed beside Catherine nodding his head. His expression was sullen and distant. He looked tired and a little like Susan's marionette, empty and hollow, and as though he were being moved around by someone else, like a doll whose movements were not his own.

"Are they a couple again?" Theo whispered to me as we approached.

"I think they are just friends who attend parties together, but I'm not sure," I whispered back.

"Hi Catherine! Hi Bernard!" Susan yelled.

I winced. "I don't want to talk to them," I whispered.

"Sorry, Maybel," Susan whispered.

"Theo?" Catherine called.

Theo smiled. "Hello," he said politely.

Bernard looked upward sighing, clearly annoyed.

"Theo! We're about to have wine with friends, would you like to join?" Catherine asked.

"I'm sorry Catherine, we're headed back home," he told her.

"Our friends are coming here, Theo," Catherine took Bernard's hand and playfully touched his chest with her other hand. "Why don't you join us, and Maybel and Susan can have cookies and cake?"

"Yes!" Susan squealed then looked sheepishly at me, "Sorry, Maybel," she whispered, "I forgot you didn't want to go, and I really like cake."

"Great!" Catherine said, "Our friends will arrive soon!"

Bernard watched me. I stared back at him as Catherine told Theo about her friends and which young ladies were single. I was annoyed at Catherine because I liked Theo, although we had never publicly proclaimed our attraction to each other.

"I live in Connecticut, Catherine, it's a bit of a walk to meet for a date," he laughed. "Thank you anyway."

Catherine didn't give up. "Enjoy yourself anyway, Theo. There will be lots of fine company," she winked.

I grew more irritated. I wanted to leave for Connecticut now. Catherine had Bernard and now wanted to assign Theo to one of her friends. I was ready for the beach and time away from both Catherine and Bernard.

Catherine knew Susan was the weakest link in our chain of three. "Susan, we have chocolate cake and vanilla ice cream," Catherine smiled. "It's in the kitchen. You remember where the kitchen is, right?"

"Yes!" Susan darted through the garden and the well-kept lawn.

"She's really fast when motivated," Theo noted.

"You should see her when blackberry cobbler is at stake. Do not get between Susan and blackberry cobbler!"

Theo laughed, "So noted, sweetheart."

Bernard's eyes darkened when Theo called me sweetheart. Catherine must have noticed too, because she quickly interjected, "Why don't we all go inside and have cake and ice cream?" she suggested.

"Yes," Bernard quickly agreed.

"Alright then," Catherine held Bernard's hand and walked toward Bernard's house.

Theo and I followed. I felt awkward and wanted to disappear as soon as possible.

Bernard opened his kitchen door and let us in. I felt his eyes on me as I quickly passed by him.

Susan was already at the table eating cake and ice cream with Mrs. Charleston.

"Hello, Mrs. Charleston," I greeted her.

"Hello, dear," she stood and came to me and kissed my cheek. Catherine watched us and I felt Catherine was unhappy with the familiarity between Mrs. Charleston and me. I always assumed it was because I was young when I first met Mrs. Charleston whereas Catherine had been older. I thought that was the reason Mrs. Charleston and I were closer. Younger children are more open and engaging, always wanting to play and always talkative. Susan had been chatting away with Mrs. Charleston like they were old school chums and Mrs. Charleston seemed to sincerely adore Susan.

Mrs. Charleston turned to Theo, "Hello, as I recall we met at the Christmas party," she smiled politely at Theo.

"Yes," Theo smiled and shook her hand.

"I have business to attend to," Mrs. Charleston said. "Have fun and enjoy yourselves," she kissed Bernard's cheek then politely smiled back at us as she left.

"Maybel, cake!" Susan pointed to a plate next to hers. "I got you some already!"

"Where's mine?" Theo joked with Susan.

"I'll get you some." Susan began cutting a huge slice of chocolate cake for Theo. "Catherine, Bernard, do you want some?"

"No thank you," Catherine said.

"Yes!" Bernard smiled. Bernard sat beside me.

"Maybel, you'll be leaving for Connecticut this summer, won't you?" Catherine asked me.

"Yes," I said. I shoved cake into my mouth so I wouldn't have to answer any more of her questions.

"Will you return home before the autumn festival?" Catherine continued asking questions.

I nodded yes.

"Theo?" Catherine asked, "Won't you attend? Bernard and I would love to show you around."

"It will depend on my work schedule, unfortunately. If at all possible, I would love to attend. Thank you for your invitation." Theo was very polite and sophisticated when dealing with people.

He could transition between sweetly talking to Susan, to bantering with me, to sounding like a politician talking to Catherine, and his transitions were seamless.

Thankfully Susan interrupted Catherine's pleasantries. "Can we play in your yard, Bernard? Do you have any baseballs or bicycles, Bernard?" The copious amounts of sugar began hitting Susan's bloodstream.

"Yes, Susan," Bernard laughed. "You may play with anything here you want to play with. There is a tire swing and a couple regular swings tied to tree branches out back on which Maybel has always been partial to playing," Bernard winked at me. "You haven't played here in a while Maybel, the trees and the squirrels scuttling in their branches have greatly missed you."

"I'll remedy that now! Come Susan! To the trees!"

"Theo, stay with Bernard and me. There are some ladies I'd like you to meet," Catherine winked at Theo.

"Do I have to stay, too?" Bernard grinned at Catherine. "You know how much I love parties."

"Yes, of course Bernard, this is your house," Catherine said flatly.

"Oh come, Catherine! We have a little time! Let's show Theo around the grounds," Bernard said.

"I would enjoy seeing your beautiful gardens," Theo said to Bernard.

Catherine sighed, "Alright then, we'll walk around a bit then go inside when our guests arrive."

Susan and I ran to the swings. Bernard ran closely behind me.

"Don't get dirty!" Catherine called to Bernard.

Susan got on the wooden swing and I stuck my head through the tire swing and swung on my belly. Bernard gently pushed me. Theo and Catherine arrived and Theo pushed Susan.

"Do you want a turn, Bernard?" I asked him.

"Yes," he said.

"Oh Bernard, you'll get dirty," Catherine complained.

"That's ok, I can change," he winked at her.

Catherine huffed.

"Catherine, why don't you sit on this other swing and I'll push you too," Theo suggested. Theo was always the peacemaker.

"Alright," Catherine relented.

I pushed Bernard hard. He laughed, "Your arms are much stronger now."

"I'm going to practice boxing in Connecticut, right Theo?"

"Yes, honey, we'll box," Theo laughed.

Bernard hopped off the tire swing and lifted me up on top of the tire.

"Don't make it spin, Bernard!" I yelled at him.

"I won't, Maybel, I'll push you in a straight line."

"You better, because I know some boxing moves now," I joked.

"They've always been like this," Catherine told Theo. "They've always argued like a brother and sister."

Bernard stopped pushing me and slowed me down. "I don't think of Maybel as a sister anymore," he said. "I haven't for a long time."

"Oh? Then how do you think of Maybel?" Catherine asked, her voice seemed direct and antagonistic.

"I think of her as a person," Bernard said carefully.

"Is that a medicinal plant garden?" Theo asked, breaking the tension. "I work with plants to identify which ones can be used for varying ailments. That's how I developed the medicine that saved you, Susan."

"Mrs. Charleston knows all about plants!" I became very excited. "She taught me!" I ran excitedly over to her herb garden.

"This is echinacea, also called coneflower, and this is sage, and over here is lavender." I continued pointing out all the plants and explained their uses.

Theo watched me intently. "Maybel!" he exclaimed, "you know a lot about plants!"

"Mrs. Charleston taught me! She knows everything about every plant, tree, and bush! You really need to talk with her!"

"I will, Maybel," Theo smiled. "I would love to speak with her about incorporating more plants into medicines to heal people."

"Bernard when is your mother returning?" I asked.

"She might be upstairs or maybe in father's office. You're welcome to check."

I was very excited and quickly ran inside. I checked the office first and found her at Mr. Charleston's desk. "Theo uses plants to cure people! Do you want to talk about plants now?" I excitedly asked her.

She smiled at me, "That sounds lovely dear, I'll be out in a few minutes. I'm just finishing up daddy's paperwork."

I looked curiously at her.

"Oh! I'm sorry, Maybel," she blushed, "I think of you as my daughter, you know. I'm sorry, I meant Mr. Charleston's paperwork."

"It's ok," I smiled, "I love you, too," I giggled and ran back to the kitchen for a cookie before returning to the garden. I pocketed five cookies.

"She's coming!" I yelled as I ran out to the garden. I tossed Susan, Theo, and Catherine a cookie.

"Bernard, catch!" I yelled as I threw a cookie at his face.

Bernard caught the cookie just before it would have smashed his nose.

"See, I have indeed made you better at sports!" I giggled.

Bernard chuckled as he bit into his cookie.

Theo was crouched down, still inspecting the herbs. "Theo, wouldn't it be great to work with Mrs. Charleston in your laboratory?" I asked.

"Yes, that would nice," Theo answered politely.

"You can develop new medicines and save more Susans!" I became excited thinking about all the wonderous medicines that could be invented.

"That's my next story! I'm going to write a story about the future where medicines can save people!" I began composing a rough outline in my mind.

Theo stood up and tousled my hair, "I can't wait to read it, sweetheart."

"I'm interested in how you invented a medicine to save Susan," Bernard said. "May I visit you in Connecticut?" I heard Bernard's voice right behind me. I hadn't realized he'd stood so closely behind me.

"What?" I spun around.

"I'd like to learn about new medicines, Theo, if you'll have me?" Bernard asked Theo.

"Yes!" Susan yelled happily. "Catherine, we'll all spend the summer together!"

I stared at Bernard. "Why do you want to come to my beautiful, summer beach house?" I asked, upset.

Theo laughed, "Your summer beach house?" He put his hands in his pockets and chuckled.

I spun back around to Theo. "Our beach house," I corrected myself. "Connecticut is my safe and peaceful place! I just want to build sandcastles with Susan and eat ice cream on the boardwalk with you both in the evenings!" I whined.

"You don't want me to come?" Bernard looked truly hurt.

"I really enjoyed my time in Connecticut last summer because no matter where I went, I was never Catherine's little sister or Bernard's girlfriend's little sister who always tags along. I was just Maybel. And I liked just being Maybel," I said.

"Let's stay here, Bernard," Catherine said. "You did seem very happy there last summer, Maybel, and I understand. Sometimes I enjoy being just Catherine. It can be refreshing to be on your own and away from home. You're not anyone's daughter, sister, or girlfriend. You're just you."

"Thank you, Catherine," I said, relieved. "I love you both; I just want my summer beach house with Susan and Theo for at least a little while. Maybe you can visit for a couple days later in the summer though?"

"Yes, Maybel, that sounds lovely," Catherine smiled politely.

"I'm sorry," I looked at Bernard as I spoke, "I still need time and space." I hoped Bernard would understand what I tried to convey.

"Maybel, come play!" Susan bounced in front of my face. She was still full of sugar, I observed.

Susan and I giggled and ran back to the swings.

Mrs. Charleston entered the garden. I watched Bernard and Theo talk to her about plants while Catherine politely listened.

"Maybel," Susan whispered, "does Catherine like Theo? I mean as a boyfriend?"

"No, why?"

"It always feels like she likes Theo whenever I've seen them together."

"Oh, Catherine flirts with every boy. It's nothing serious," I assured Susan.

"Why has Bernard never cared?" Susan asked.

"He probably knows she's never serious when she flirts. She flirts with everyone. He says they aren't dating anyway. He says they attend social events together as friends, but aren't a couple."

"Oh," Susan said, satisfied with my answer. "Are we allowed to explore?"

"Yes! It's really fun here! I'll show you!" Susan and I ran toward the creek while the others discussed medicines and plants and herbs.

"I'll show you the slate creek and little waterfalls first, then the pond, and then the horses!"

"Wow, Maybel! I love this place!" Susan squealed.

"Me too!" I called over my shoulder as I ran ahead.

Susan and I were covered in dirt, mud, and grass by the time we returned to Bernard's house. "I have trees in my hair," Susan laughed.

"Me too," I said, pulling a twig from my tangled locks.

I stopped quickly. "Oh! The party! Catherine's friends are here!"

I directed Susan around the side of the house toward the back porch. "We're covered in mud and Catherine will complain I'm embarrassing her," I explained. "We'll sneak out and go home and change clothes."

"Ok, Maybel," Susan agreed. I liked being a big sister to Susan. She agreed to everything I said.

There were people milling about in the house and all around the gardens. "I don't think we'll get out of here without being seen," I told Susan. "Let's quickly walk out of here as fast as we can and go home. Oh, and let's go around the kitchen where there're less people, and don't let Catherine see us."

"Ok, Maybel," Susan agreed and followed me.

We went down the hallway and out the kitchen door. Polished guests in glittery gowns stared at us with disdain.

"Maybel!" Catherine screeched. "You're filthy."

"I know, I'm sorry, we're going home to change."

"You're welcome to go upstairs and bathe," Bernard said. "I'm sure you have clothes here from all the other times you've gotten dirty and worn my clothing home," Bernard chuckled.

"Maybel, why must you always do this? Why can't you behave properly?" Catherine whined.

"I'm sorry, Catherine," I sighed.

"Where's Theo?" Susan asked.

"Talking to a young lady out front in the garden," Catherine said.

Catherine turned back to me, "Please go change quickly, Maybel! There is a handsome, young man I want you to meet."

"Susan, I'll show you to the guest bath. Maybel, you can use mine," Bernard said. "Look around my closet for your clothes that have collected over the years from many a day spent getting dirty," Bernard grinned at me. "Messy Maybel," he teased.

"Don't call me that! I don't like it!" I told Bernard.

"Oh, come now, Maybel." He put his hand on my lower back and led me inside. "It's a fitting name."

Bernard showed Susan to the guest bath. "Maybel will find her clothes somewhere in my closet and bring them to you. Soap and towels are already inside."

Bernard followed me to his room. "I know you left clothes in here somewhere," he said while digging around in his closet.

"I'm sorry we embarrassed you in front of your friends, Bernard. I forgot about the party and got lost in fun."

"I wish I had joined you. You look like you had quite a lot of fun!"

"We did!" I giggled. "I love playing here!"

"I love having you here," he smiled at me. "You're always welcome here."

"I know. I've shown up unwelcome too, though," I said, remembering when Bernard went through a stage of being mean to me. "Remember when I followed you around and you got mad and wanted me to leave?"

"I'm sorry, Maybel. I was young and didn't know how to handle being attracted to my girlfriend's little sister."

"What?"

"I've always been attracted to you," Bernard said quietly.

I stared at Bernard and he became flustered. "Let me find your old clothes for Susan."

He rummaged around in his closet and pulled out an old dress.

"When did I leave that here?" I asked. "I looked for that dress many times!"

"I'll put this on the doorknob of the guest bathroom for Susan. I'll be right back." Bernard took the dress and left.

I began looking through his closet for more of my clothing. I found several shorts and dresses and a couple shirts. Bernard returned. "I had no idea how many times I had to change clothes here and wear your clothing home!" I said.

"Messy Maybel," he repeated.

"Stop saying that!"

"Stop being messy," he smiled.

Bernard came to me. "Maybel, you have twigs and," he reached for my hair, "an acorn in your hair! Where did you go?"

"The usual places."

"And what did you do?" he plucked a piece of straw from my hair.

"The usual things."

"Come, Maybel." Bernard led me to his bathroom and sat me on a chair. He began picking debris out of my hair.

"You used to be attracted to me?" I asked softly.

"I still am, Maybel."

"You never said," I told him.

"I thought my attraction was obvious. You never returned my attraction," Bernard said quietly.

"You showed your attraction by yelling at me to not sit next to you in your study while you read on your sofa. How would I be able to return that kind of flirtation? Oh, I know," I reached up and slapped Bernard's face. "Did you feel my love, my passion?"

"I didn't know how to handle my feelings well, Maybel! I was confused and didn't know what to do. I pushed you away and I was mean to you because I didn't want to be in love with my girlfriend's little sister, but Maybel, I've always loved you."

Bernard took a brush from his sink and slowly and gently began brushing my hair.

"You teased me for having messy hair," I said angrily, remembering the hurt I felt. "And I cried often because of you!"

"I know," he whispered. "I'm sorry."

When he finished brushing my hair, he ran bath water for me.

"Are you going to bathe me now?" I asked.

"What?" Bernard looked confused.

"You brushed my hair, ran my bath water, and picked out my clothes for me."

"Oh," he said and looked down, "I didn't realize I was doing that. I guess I'm just going to miss you." Bernard was staring off outside the window to the treetops in the distance.

"I'm not a baby! Stop treating me like a child!"

"I don't! I wasn't thinking clearly. My mind is spinning around about you leaving me and I'm very confused. I'm sorry, Maybel, I don't know what I'm doing! I don't know how to fix everything!" Bernard continued watching me sadly.

I waited for Bernard to leave. He sat on the side of his bathtub instead. "I think Theo likes you."

"Susan thinks Catherine likes Theo," I said.

"She does," Bernard said simply.

"I told Susan that Catherine flirts with everyone, not just Theo."

Bernard just stared into the bath water.

"Is that why you seem not to like Theo? Because Catherine likes him?"

Bernard placed his hands on his temples and rubbed. "I like Theo. I wish I didn't like him but he's a brilliant scientist and a gentleman. That's why I'm worried. He's a good man. I don't like that Theo likes you, Maybel. I don't want you to go to Connecticut because you're going to fall in love with Theo. Maybel," he shook his head, "I've lost you."

"Bernard, I want to bathe, dress, then go home. I'm leaving for Connecticut soon. I'll see you in the fall." I told him.

Bernard seemed lost in his thoughts.

"My clothes are wet and uncomfortable. Go away so I can bathe." I stood up from my chair and walked to the bathroom door and held the knob, indicating I wanted him to leave so I could close the door.

Bernard left and I bathed. I put the dress on Bernard had found for me. It was my favorite dress from last year but I got it wet playing in the rain while Catherine and Bernard held hands and kissed in Bernard's bedroom. I remembered that day now. I had wanted Bernard to dance in the rain with me but he said no.

I put my dress on, but being one year later, I had to squeeze into my dress as my breasts, hips, bottom, and thighs had grown.

I walked into Bernard's bedroom where he laid on his bed with Susan reading a book to her. It was the book his grandmother had written and illustrated. That was Susan's favorite book. It had always been my favorite book, too.

They turned to look at me and Bernard's jaw dropped. "Maybel?"

"Maybel! Your breasts are huge! You look like a model from Paris!" Susan smiled.

"This dress is from last year," I said. "I got it wet in the rainstorm while you and Catherine were in here kissing," I reminded Bernard. "It doesn't fit well, but it will get me out of here and back home where I can change into a larger dress."

"Maybel, you look like fairy princess," Susan said.

I laughed, "Would you like to have this dress? You can take it to Connecticut."

"Yes! I love you Maybel! Thank you!"

I laughed. "You can have any of my things, Susan, you know that."

Bernard continued to stare at me.

"What?" I angrily snapped.

"You are older now," he rolled to his side. "You look like a woman."

He put a pillow to his stomach. "The cake must have disagreed with me. My stomach hurts."

"Let's go Susan, before Catherine screeches at me again to stop embarrassing her in front of her friends."

We went downstairs and through the house to the front door. I became angry because everyone kept staring at me. I knew I didn't fit in, but I didn't understand why they were staring at me so inconspicuously. They could at least pretend to not see me so I could leave with at least a little dignity intact.

"Maybel! What are you wearing and why are you doing this?" Catherine angrily snipped.

"I changed clothing because I was muddy and this was the dress I left here last year. I'm sorry Catherine. I know I embarrass you, but I'm trying to leave so I won't keep upsetting you."

Theo rescued me. "Let's go Maybel," he put his dress coat around me.

"I'm not cold," I said.

"Let's go get you some new clothes, shall we?" Theo led me toward the door and Susan followed.

Theo, Susan, and I left. Theo took Susan to their doorstep. He offered to take me home but I said no. I went home by myself and changed my clothes. I wore my new summer dress mother had sewn for me. It was light purple and lightweight for the hot summer sun in Connecticut.

Susan and Theo knocked on my door. "Maybel, your mother asked us to come for dinner. Mother and father will be here soon," Susan said.

"Oh, I forgot! Catherine said something about dinner here tonight with Bernard. Come in, please."

"I like your dress, Maybel," Susan said, "but that other dress made you look like a princess."

"Thank you," I laughed. "Come in and sit."

Theo and Susan came in and sat in our family room. Mother brought them hot chocolate. Soon Mr. and Mrs. Charleston arrived, as did Mr. and Mrs. Matthews.

"We're celebrating you leaving," daddy tousled my hair.

"Oh, daddy, I love your humor, but be aware, I get to choose your nursing home," I winked at him.

Daddy kissed me, "Oh Maybel, who will I be sarcastic to all summer? I'll just have to save up all my good jokes until fall."

We had a lovely dinner together and good conversation. Mommy and daddy were sad to see me leave. Catherine was looking forward to visiting. And Susan and I listed all the things we wanted to do. Theo laughed, "You two have been planning this all year it sounds like."

"We have!" Susan grinned.

"Theo, I really would like to discuss your laboratory with you after dinner," Bernard said.

"Certainly," Theo replied.

Mr. Charleston grew interested. "A laboratory? Are you a man of science, Theo?"

"Yes, I am," he answered politely.

"Our son saved our daughter's life by inventing a medicine that cured her," Mr. Matthews boasted and Theo blushed.

"I spoke with Theo just today, dear," Mrs. Charleston told her husband.

"You're quite brilliant," Mrs. Charleston told Theo.

"Thank you for your kind words," Theo blushed deeper.

After dinner the men gathered outside on our back porch and talked about science and medicine.

I stood at the door to the back porch and listened. Theo was explaining chemistry and his process for achieving the serum that saved Susan's life. I didn't understand much of what he said. I wished I understood math better.

Mr. Charleston and Bernard were quite fascinated and spoke of the company they'd formed to investigate new ways to approach medicine from a physician's, a scientist's, and even from a botanist's point of view.

"Mr. Charleston, I'm impressed with your open mindedness," Theo said. "I've come against scientists and doctors who have fought me at every step regarding botany and its integration into the medical profession."

"I have no time for narrow-mindedness, Theo," Mr. Charleston sipped his special cider.

"I'm interested in results. You have results. Your proof is walking around inside, no doubt sneaking another cookie," Mr. Charleston chuckled, referring to Susan.

"Theo, I know you are leaving soon," Mr. Charleston continued, "but if you have time, would you be willing to talk more about your findings and your aspirations?"

"Certainly," Theo replied.

I went back to mommy, who was now playing card games with Mrs. Charleston and Mrs. Matthews.

Catherine and Susan were drawing together. Susan was teaching Catherine how to draw a bird. Catherine drew a giraffe.

"It's a bird," Catherine protested.

"Then why does it look like a giraffe?" I giggled.

"Come sit, Maybel. Draw with us," Catherine asked me. "I'll miss you," she added.

I felt Catherine was being sincere. Catherine was at home with me, and her hostess mask was off. Catherine looked at me and she looked sad. I genuinely felt Catherine was sad to see me leave.

"I suppose I could spare a few minutes to draw a giraffe," I said, "They are herd animals, not solitary like tigers, so your giraffe needs a friend."

"It's a bird!" Catherine said, her nostrils flaring at me.

"Maybe if we draw tree tops underneath it, and clouds around it, it will look more birdish," Susan suggested.

We drew trees below the giraffe bird, and clouds around it. "Here, Maybel, I drew this for you," Catherine said. "It represents you leaving the nest and flying high."

"Thank you, Catherine! It means a lot to me." I held her giraffe bird to my chest. "I love it!"

The men came inside and sat in the family room to continue their conversation. Mr. Matthews was lecturing on chemicals. He was quite animated and reminded me of the scientist in a book

I'd read about the future. His genius was far ahead of present day, and ordinary scientists couldn't relate to his high-level and fast-paced thinking. He was often ostracized by the scientific community, Susan said, because they couldn't keep up with him.

I watched Bernard and Theo. They were engrossed in Mr. Matthews' latest findings. I stood up and took my giraffe bird to the table so I wouldn't forget to take it with me.

I went to the kitchen to make hot chocolate and coffee for everyone. While the water got hot on the stove, I finished washing dessert plates.

Bernard came to me as I washed dishes. "Maybel, may I help you?"

"No, it's ok, I'm just finishing."

Bernard stood beside me at the sink anyway. He took the plate I held and rinsed it, then set it to dry.

"Do you remember when you asked me to dance in the rain with you last year? You wore that dress you put on today after your bath."

"Yes," I said. "I asked you to dance in the rain with me but you said no."

Bernard continued rinsing dishes beside me. "I didn't dance in the rain with you because the rain made your dress cling to your body and I thought you were the most beautiful young lady I'd ever seen. You danced in the rain and didn't care what anyone thought. That made you special. It also made me want to kiss you. That's why I told you I didn't want to dance with you."

"Then why did I find you kissing Catherine on your bed if you loved me so much?" I stared at Bernard with anger brewing inside me.

"I have no excuse. Catherine kissed me and I kissed her back. I didn't want to love you. I didn't want to be attracted to you." Bernard continued rinsing the dishes I handed him.

"Why? Because I'm messy Maybel? My hair is always messy and I slobber when I kiss?" I said angrily. "I'm not so much angry as I am hurt. You have been so purposefully mean to me."

"I have. And I'll spend the rest of my life loving you."

"You're still dating Catherine!" I angrily whispered. "She keeps saying 'our friends' and 'we' and making sure everyone knows you two are a couple again! And here you are saying you love me!"

"Catherine and I are not dating. She sometimes acts like we're dating when it's convenient for her to be associated with a Charleston, but we haven't been a couple in a long time."

"You may not think you are dating Catherine, but it's clear she thinks you two are dating. Everyone else thinks you are dating, too. You like having us both, but you only kiss her in public. You say you love me, but you have never acknowledged your love for me publicly."

"You make a good point. I will stop attending events with Catherine. I had not thought about that. You are right. I will talk to Catherine. And Maybel, may I kiss you here and now? I'm not embarrassed of you. I will take your hand and walk into your family room right now and tell everyone I love you and I'll kiss you in front of everyone."

Bernard's calmness angered me. "You can't just say you are sorry and expect all to be forgiven. I don't care that you are rich. You think you can waltz in here and say you are sorry you were mean. You have no idea how many nights I cried myself to sleep because you made fun of me or hurt me out of mean spiritedness. I used to have a crush on you when I was young, but had to watch you kiss and cuddle Catherine every day. How would you feel watching me with another man for years? You can't buy your way out of your bad behavior because I don't care about your stupid bank account!"

"I know," Bernard said simply.

I shoved a wet plate against his chest and left.

I tore off my apron and threw it at his back.

Daddy was admiring Catherine's drawing I'd left on the table in the family room. "I've always admired your imagination, honey," daddy said to me.

"From talking tigers to talking trees and now a flying giraffe. I'm always impressed with your imagination, sweetheart," daddy smiled at me.

"It's a bird, daddy!" Catherine yelled. "I drew it for Maybel! It represents her flying free and leaving the nest!"

"Oh, yes, now I see it!" daddy quickly soothed Catherine's temper. "Ah, there it is! A beautiful bird! Wonderful drawing, pumpkin!" Daddy went to Catherine and kissed the top of her angry, little head.

"I love it Catherine, and I'm taking it with me," I told her.

Bernard brought the hot chocolate from the kitchen. He handed Catherine and me a mug. Susan cleared her throat. "I didn't forget you, Susan, I made yours with extra Chocolate," he winked at her and she giggled.

We chatted awhile about Connecticut then our guests grew sleepy and left. Catherine looked up at Bernard expectantly at the door and Bernard politely kissed her cheek. From her expression I could see she had expected a kiss on her lips.

I hugged Theo and told him I'd see him soon.

Susan was excited. "Maybel, this is going to be the best summer!"

"I think so too!" I said as I hugged her.

Back in the family room Catherine was admiring her giraffe bird and mommy sat on daddy's lap in the big, overstuffed chair. "Goodnight," I kissed mommy's and daddy's cheeks. Catherine handed me her drawing and I smiled and kissed her cheek when I took it from her.

I went upstairs and placed my giraffe bird in my luggage, tucked safely in the side pocket. And then I fell asleep thinking about sand and salty air. My newest adventure awaited me.

Once again Susan and I arrived at Theo's home. This time, Theo drove us. We began talking fast, telling him all the things we wanted to do during summer break.

"My turn!" I yelled. "I want to go to the beach, theater, dance, get ice cream, listen to you read, paint the sunsets because my parents want to see what beach sunsets look like, and I want to try lobster. And can we get saltwater taffy again? Oh, and build sandcastles. Wait, I almost forgot, can you teach me to box?"

Theo laughed, "My, my, you two have given this summer a lot of thought! Yes, we can do all those things!"

"Thank you for letting me come again!" I kissed Theo's cheek as he parked in front of his house. Mrs. Murphy waved from the kitchen window. I waved back. I really wanted to hug her and listen to her talk. I never understood her thick, Irish accent, but she smiled a lot and had an energy that matched the sun's.

"You're quite welcome, both of you, and to be honest, I would have been very sad if I didn't have this summer with you both to look forward to all winter long."

"Can we go to the beach now?" Susan gleefully shouted.

"Yes!" I added, "I've missed the beach all year!"

"Of course, ladies. Go change and we'll be off."

We changed into our swimsuits and met Theo back in the family room.

"Theo, where's your swimsuit? Aren't you coming with us?" Susan asked with a look of disappointment.

"I'm already wearing shorts, Susan, all I need to do is take my shirt off and I'm ready!"

"Oh," she said, "It's so much easier for men to dress."

He laughed, "Yes, I suppose we don't have all the various kinds of clothing and accessories that cause women to take so long to change and get ready for the day."

The beach was full of people, but not terribly crowded. We found a spot and set our bags and towels down.

Susan and I laughed and giggled as we skipped to the ocean. "Theo!" Susan yelled, "Toss me!"

Theo picked up Susan and gently tossed her into the sea. I laughed at Susan when she popped her head up out of the water and a little strip of seaweed fell down her forehead.

"Your turn!" Theo suddenly grabbed me around my waist and wrapped me around his neck like a scarf. I was always surprised at how strong his arms and shoulders were.

I squealed and Susan shouted, "See how far you can toss Maybel!"

"Hey wait a min...." Theo tossed me like a shot put into a wave.

I jumped up out of the water laughing and out for vengeance! "He can't fend us both off successfully! You take one side and I'll take his other side, Susan!"

We circled Theo like lionesses. "I'll toss you both in at the same time!" Theo playfully warned. "It will be a grand sacrifice to the ocean gods! Perhaps with such a sacrifice we'll have good weather all summer long!" he laughed.

"If we toss Theo in, Susan, perhaps the ocean gods will be displeased and spit him back out to the sand and cause catastrophic rains all summer!"

"We had better let him toss us in then!" Susan laughed. "I want good weather this summer!"

"All right you two! You're both going to get it!" Theo grabbed Susan first and hugged her close to his chest as he reached for me. I narrowly escaped and circled behind him and jumped on his back. "You'll never take me alive!"

Theo tossed Susan gently into the ocean then leaned forward until I toppled head first into the surf. I grabbed a hold of his leg and clung to it as Susan climbed onto Theo's back.

"We've almost tamed the beast, Maybel! Stay strong!"

"Ahh!" I screamed as Theo plucked me off his leg and pulled me up into his arms. With me in his arms and Susan on his back, Theo waded chest-high into the ocean and tossed me out. I screamed and swam back to shore with Theo quickly behind me roaring like a beast.

"I've almost got him, Maybel!" Susan yelled. "Run for your life!"

Theo stomped after me and when he got to shallow water he feigned being caught by Susan, who was still clinging to his back.

He laid down in the surf moaning, "Princess Susan has slain this mighty beast!"

"Princess Susan wants ice cream for her troubles!"

Theo and I laughed. "Me too!" I shouted.

"All right ladies, for slaying the beast, you shall both be rewarded."

"What does Theo's laboratory look like?" I asked Susan over breakfast one morning. I was curious where he spent his days.

"I've never seen it," Susan replied. She ate strawberries with her oatmeal and her tongue now made her look like a vampire; it was bright red.

"Let's go there," Susan suggested.

"Excellent idea, Mistress of the Night," I joked.

"Why, because I stare at you while you sleep?" Susan asked.

"You stare at me while I sleep?" I asked her, shocked.

"No, I don't, but why else would you call me Mistress of the Night?"

"You have a red tongue, like I imagine a vampire would have after a night of sucking blood."

Susan laughed, "Oh, right, vampires are a lot less strange than staring at you while you sleep, which I do not do," Susan said. A small smile played across her lips. I was not sure if she was joking or teasing. My humor had indeed been used against me.

We went to Theo's laboratory, Susan and me. He was flirting with a young woman wearing a tailored, dark blue dress and a white scarf around her neck secured by a ruby broach.

Theo looked up surprised, "What are you two doing here?"

The woman looked at me and then Susan. "Oh, that's right, your sisters are in town."

"I'm not his sister," I said.

The young woman looked surprised. "Oh, I see," she said to Theo, then took her pile of folders and left.

"Who was that?" I asked.

"A coworker," he said hastily. "What do you two want? Why are you here? Has something happened?"

"No," Susan said meekly, "we wanted to see where you worked."

Susan looked taken aback by Theo's professionalism at work. I knew from watching Mr. Charleston that there was a husband Mr. Charleston and a work Mr. Charleston. Theo's abrupt work demeanor did not shock me as it did Susan. This was probably the first time Susan saw Theo as someone other than her brother, I figured.

Theo tried to be warmer. "Are you both alright? Do you need my assistance?"

"No," I said plainly. "Why were you flirting with that woman?"

"I wasn't," Theo tried to conceal his irritation with me. "She is the boss' daughter," he whispered, "I'm paid to be nice."

"You didn't have to be that nice, did you?" Susan asked. I liked blunt Susan. We had a lot in common.

"Look, you two should not be here. It's unprofessional for me to have guests," Theo said.

"I don't like her," Susan said.

"What do you two need? I have a meeting in ten minutes."

"We don't need anything. We only wanted to see your laboratory," Susan said. "We'll be leaving, Theodore." Susan turned and walked toward the main entrance.

I looked at Theo, then quickly followed Susan.

Susan and I walked home. It was a nice day, but a bit hot. The men walking down the street near us had sweat stains on their dress shirts, under their armpits, and down the smalls of their backs. A few even had sweaty behinds, pools of sweat under their butt cheeks. I imagined those men smelled bad.

"Why was Theo so mean?" Susan was still steaming about Theo.

I was still curious about why men and women dressed in proper clothing when they could wear more lightweight fabrics. Mommy said the more miserable you feel, the more fashionable you are. Mommy didn't like thick fabrics in the summer, and thankfully didn't force Catherine or me to be fashionable.

"Maybel," Susan elbowed me to get my attention, "why was Theo flirting with that woman and why was he short-tempered?"

"People are different at work. They want to look shrewd and tough and smart and you can't look that way if you are coddling two girls and hugging them and kissing their cheeks."

"He didn't have to flirt with that woman, though. He's supposed to flirt only with you," Susan said. It was a little sad seeing Susan look at her big brother and begin to see cracks in his God-like facade.

"He said he's paid to be nice to that woman because she's his boss' daughter, and anyway, Theo flirted a little with Catherine. I think he enjoys women's attention. Henry likes to flirt too. Some men enjoy when women give them attention. Well, they all probably do. Catherine says boys like it when you smile and giggle and pretend you think they're smart, even if they are dull and dense."

"That sounds tiring," Susan moaned.

"I agree. I'd rather just stay home instead of pretending the boss' daughter or son is an enjoyable person with whom to converse."

"Theo should have been nicer though," Susan said sadly.

"I agree. Mr. Charleston is a tough businessman, but he knows how to be mannerly at the same time," I noted.

"What do you want to do now?" Susan sighed.

"I need to find a florist. Do you know where a florist's shop is located, or do I have to ask one of these men with butt sweat where to find flowers?"

Susan laughed, "Men with butt sweat wouldn't know because they don't have girlfriends or wives with such large pools of butt sweat."

"Good point, Susan," I smiled. "I really admire your deductions. I appreciate smart people."

"Why do we need to find a florist?" Susan asked.

"I'm sending Theo flowers to be delivered at his laboratory, and I'll pay extra to have them accidentally delivered to the woman in the blue dress. The card will say, 'My dearest Theo, Happy anniversary, sweetheart, with love, Leonora.'"

"Who?" Susan asked. "I know you just complimented me on being smart, but I don't understand what is going on."

"The woman in the blue dress needs to know Theo is in a relationship, and if he returns her flirtations, he would not make a good boyfriend, so she'll direct her flirtations elsewhere."

"I have so much to learn from you." Susan gazed up at me admiringly.

Susan and I were eating soup when Theo returned home from his laboratory. We heard him open and close the door and hang his coat in the closet. Susan looked pensively at me. "Do you think he's mad?" she whispered.

I shrugged. I figured the worst he would do would be to send me home.

Theo held mail and fumbled through the letters, as he walked into the kitchen. He sat the mail on the counter beside his other correspondences.

"Good evening, girls," he said as he went to the stove to ladle soup into a bowl Mrs. Murphy had left for him.

Susan and I both quickly spooned soup into our mouths so we wouldn't have to talk.

"I'm sorry I was not overly friendly with you when you came to see me. I was surprised."

Again, Susan and I continued eating so we wouldn't have to talk.

"I should have been less abrasive," he said.

I ate soup as fast as I could without choking. I wanted to go to the beach and watch the moon rise over the ocean. And mostly, I didn't want to talk to Theo.

"I've never seen you at work before," Susan finally addressed Theo. "I don't like the work version of you."

"I have to be severe at work, otherwise other scientists will think I'm weak and question every experiment, every penny I spend, my documentations, my publications, everything. One has to be able to push back if questioned."

"You can be strong and polite at the same time," Susan said meekly.

"Yes, well, not at my laboratory. We are leaders in our field and if there is one miniscule crack in our methods, scientists from around the world will quite enthusiastically degrade us publicly. That is why I have to be perfect at my work."

I finished my soup and stood up from the table and put my bowl in the sink, washed it, rinsed it, dried it, then put it away. Susan soon finished and did the same.

"Shall we go watch the moon?" I asked her as she put away her bowl into the cabinet.

"Yes," she said. She seemed sullen.

"Susan," Theo turned around to address us from where he still sat at the kitchen table. "I'm sorry. I'm sorry to you as well, Maybel."

There was a moment of awkward silence. I didn't know what to say, and walking away right now seemed impolite.

"Please come sit with me," Theo asked us. "I spend nine months alone here. Please come sit with me. I'm sorry. I'll give you both a tour of my laboratory tomorrow if you would like. I'll work on being strong and polite like you said. I don't want to eat alone."

Susan walked toward Theo and sat beside him and he put his arm around her and kissed the top of her head. "Thank you," he said. "I will really try to learn how to be strong in the laboratory and still exude politeness."

I sat on the other side of Theo. He put his arm around my shoulder. I still liked the feel of his large hand on my arm even though he annoyed me today.

Theo paused thoughtfully then turned to me. "How did you know I loved daisies, Leonora?"

Susan giggled.

"I may have been a bit jealous," I admitted.

"I appreciated your jealousy," Theo said. He had tenderness in his eyes while he watched me. "I will be polite without being flirtatious from now on. I never thought I was flirting with the boss' daughter until I saw the look on your face, Maybel. You look really terrifying when you are jealous."

"My actions are worse than my looks," I said with a level voice and unblinking stare.

"In an odd way, I find that strangely appealing, exhilarating, even," Theo smiled at me.

"Would you like to buy us ice cream now?" I asked him.

"Yes, that sounds nice." Theo continued watching me. He finally let out a small and quick exhale as his lips turned upward, like he was amused with me and liked me.

I awoke cold. It was unusually cold. I went to Susan's room but she wasn't there, which startled me. I then ran to Theo's room and there was Susan, snuggled next to Theo. I crawled into bed next to Theo, who was now in the middle.

"Maybel, your toes are freezing," Theo awoke suddenly.

Susan giggled, "You got cold too, Maybel?"

"Yes," I said through chattering teeth. "Why is it so cold tonight, Theo?"

"Probably a storm coming," Theo yawned.

I cuddled up close to Theo and my teeth continued chattering.

"Theo, I'm so cold," I said through shivers.

"Maybel, you'll be ok, here, get in the middle."

Theo lifted me up in his strong arms and I rolled over his stomach and landed between him and Susan.

"Maybel, your toes are tiny, little blocks of ice!" Susan shrieked.

I giggled, "Sorry, I woke up so cold!"

Theo encircled me with his strong arms and pulled me into his chest. "You'll be ok, just relax. You'll warm up soon," he said, half asleep and mumbling.

I felt his hips pressing into my buttocks and I enjoyed him holding me close.

"Maybel, you feel like an ice block against me!" Susan said.

"Sorry, Susan. I'm just so cold."

Theo rubbed my shoulders and arms and pulled me close. "You'll be fine honey, just relax," he mumbled almost incoherently.

Susan and I softly giggled at his mumbling.

I slowly began to warm up and drifted off to sleep. When I awoke, I had to pee really bad. I was lying face-to-face with Theo. His head rested on my cheek. "Theo," I whispered. The wind was howling. "Theo," I said a little louder.

Theo barely opened his eyes, he rubbed my arms, "You'll get warm soon," he mumbled.

"Theo, I need to pee! Can you let me out?"

Theo wasn't awake. He began breathing deeply again.

I crawled over him and my legs were straddling him as I tried to slide off his stomach and touch the floor. My bladder was full and I really needed to pee. My foot touched the floor and I lifted myself up and out from under the covers. I ran to the bathroom and peed.

I ran back to Theo's bed, already shivering again.

I climbed in beside Theo, with Theo now in the middle. I curled around him shivering.

He opened his eyes slightly. "Are you ok, honey?"

"Yes," I said. "I had to go pee and I got cold again."

"Come here," he pulled me closer and kissed me, still half asleep.

He pulled me tightly into him, and I could feel his hard chest muscles against my breasts. Theo began breathing hard again, and I could tell he'd fallen back asleep. My face was pressed against his neck and I smelled his faded cologne. I watched his profile in the moonlight. I wanted to kiss him.

I slowly crawled from under Theo's embrace and went to my room. I slipped under the icy cold covers and though shivering, I slowly moved my hand down my stomach and underneath my nightgown. I touched myself between my legs and a small moan escaped. I moved my fingers around my clitoris in a circular fashion and soon felt myself burning with warmth throughout my body. My breath quickened and I heard my name being called.

I quickly pulled my hand from between my legs and laid on my bed without moving.

"Maybel? Are you ok?"

It was Theo calling me.

"I'm ok, Theo."

He came and sat on the edge of my bed.

"Maybel, what's wrong? Why did you leave? Did you get sick? I told you not to eat so much saltwater taffy." He slipped under the covers beside me. "Do you want me to make you that drink that makes your stomach feel better?" He rubbed my stomach. My nightgown had been shoved up over my breasts while I pleasured myself. Theo pulled his hand back quickly. "Maybel, I'm so sorry!"

"I was, I mean, I just," I began crying from embarrassment.

"Maybel, it's ok sweetheart, it's ok. I'm sorry." He began to climb out of my bed and stood up. My nightgown was still up to my neck and my bare body was exposed.

Theo breathed in deeply. "Maybel," his breath was low and his eyes took in my breasts and the dark curls between my legs.

"Maybel, you're gorgeous," his voice was low and he sounded as though he were in pain.

His penis was now fully erect underneath his pajama bottoms. "I'm sorry," he whispered, then left.

Catherine and Bernard arrived in Connecticut. I was unhappy with their arrival. They invaded my private hideaway from reality.

Catherine was dressed beautifully, as always. She wore a green dress and coat. Bernard wore a dark, tailored suit. They both looked perfect.

I wore a lightweight, purple cotton dress. It was not fancy and I felt awkward next to Catherine, especially since Theo noticed Catherine more than he noticed any other woman in Connecticut.

That night, Bernard took my bed, and Susan, Catherine, and I slept in Susan's bed. I didn't understand why Catherine couldn't sleep with Bernard. They claimed to be only friends, but they always reconciled eventually. I wasn't going to tell mommy or daddy if they slept in the same bed. And Susan kicked like a donkey when she dreamed. I asked her what she dreamed about but she only said she didn't remember, or sometimes she dreamed about playing in her creek, playing with her kitten, or painting. None of that accounted for her donkey kicks, so I didn't know what all that was about. Maybe she needed to stretch her legs before bed, I wondered.

After Susan kicked me in my shin like I'd stolen her purse, I moved out to the family room couch. I wanted to sleep with Theo but I didn't want Catherine or Bernard to find out that I sometimes crawled into bed with Theo when I got scared. I imagined Catherine would accidentally on purpose let it slip to daddy that I shouldn't stay with an older man, then Catherine could have Theo all to herself. I didn't really think Catherine would do that, but that scene kept playing in my head, so I went to Theo's family room instead of his bed.

I laid down on Theo's sofa and tried to get to sleep. It was dark and I could hear the waves of the ocean in the distance. The waves were melodic and I felt myself relaxing.

I must have fallen asleep because suddenly I felt my hips being shaken lightly. I awoke terrified because I didn't know who was touching me or what was going on.

"Maybel, it's me," Theo's reassuring voice made me relax my leg. I'd been about to donkey kick his temple a split second before I heard his voice.

"Why are you out here?" Theo asked.

"I live here in the summers now. Why are you here?"

Theo smiled, "Are you ok, honey?"

"Yes. Susan kicks and Catherine spreads out like a starfish. I came here to the couch so I could sleep."

"Why didn't you come to my bed? I've missed you." Theo sat down beside me.

"I didn't want Catherine or Bernard to know," I said, feeling embarrassed. "I don't think they would tell mommy and daddy, but just in case, I decided to sleep out here on the sofa instead."

"I understand," Theo reassured me. He patted my arm.

"Do you have feelings for Catherine?" I blurted out.

He suddenly looked surprised. "Why do you think that?"

I continued staring at him.

"I don't know her well, so I suppose it's more fitting to say I think she seems nice."

"Do you want to get to know her better? I mean, do you want to court her or do you have intentions of possibly getting to know her more intimately?" My belly tingled from nervousness when I asked that question.

"No, I don't think so. She's with Bernard."

I looked away angrily. "That's the answer you give when you know you would be with someone if that person were single, which, by the way, she is single," I paused, "I think."

"Maybel, the world has an infinite number of alternate endings depending on the choices you make right this instant. I suppose if Catherine were single, then maybe I would allow myself to entertain the idea of a future with her. The timing is wrong. If my family had moved near your house years ago, then maybe I would be the one planning to marry Catherine. And then, maybe

I would have been the one to watch you grow from child to woman before my very eyes, and suddenly wake up one day to realize I'm in love with Catherine's little sister."

I stared at him. "You're talking about Bernard."

"Yes," he said. "I am."

I sighed and thought about what Theo said. He made sense, but I still felt unsettled about Catherine being under the same room as Theo. It was difficult being Catherine's little sister when it came to boys. I was insecure because boys wanted Catherine, and now Theo admitted he felt an attraction toward Catherine, albeit a small one.

Theo exhaled deeply. "In this reality that we are in right now, I've fallen in love with my little sister's friend. And it wasn't something I thought would happen. I can see why Bernard is having such a hard time choosing, Maybel. You and Catherine are both beautiful, intelligent, and have kind hearts. I imagine he's very confused. But Maybel, he can't keep being physically with Catherine and emotionally pining for you. It's not fair to Catherine and he's not being fair to you or himself. Right now, none of you can move forward. The three of you are stuck in time, waiting. And it's not fair to me either, because the longer Bernard has power over you, the longer I have to wait to see if you'll be with Bernard, or if you'll give me a chance."

"I didn't know you considered a future with me," I told Theo. "I thought you liked Catherine because you said I'm quite young and hadn't graduated college yet."

"Every day I fall deeper in love with you. Have you not been able to tell?" Theo held my hand.

"No."

"That is because you're stuck, in time, in space, waiting for Bernard."

I took a deep breath and felt all my insecurities bubbling up and frothing in my lungs, making it hard to breath, but I continued, "Catherine is single. She and Bernard are only friends now. Bernard is not standing in your way anymore."

Theo reached for my hand. "I'm not interested in pursuing a relationship with Catherine. I want you."

I closed my eyes and breathed out. I felt great relief. I opened my eyes and pulled Theo to me and kissed him passionately.

Catherine wanted to stroll through town in one of mommy's gorgeous dresses, so Theo took us into the town square to enjoy music and food. We went to lunch, and afterward, we passed by all the expensive boutiques. Bernard looked bored and so did Susan. I was hot and wanted to dip into the cool ocean. Susan asked Theo to take us to the beach so she could run through the surf, but Catherine didn't want to get dirty.

"I'll play with you, honey," Bernard told Susan.

"Me too!" I jumped up and down excitedly.

Susan and I skipped through the sand and surf with Bernard, our toes squishing into the sand. Every time I glanced inland, Theo was hanging onto Catherine's every word and Catherine clearly loved Theo's attention.

"Theo's just being polite," Susan whispered to me, breaking me from my trance.

"I never meant to flirt with Bernard. We used to play tag and climb trees together. Catherine is clearly flirting with Theo."

"Ow!" I yelled. A squishy ball of sand pounded into my thigh. "Bernard!" I screamed.

"Don't worry, Susan, I won't hit you; I like you!" Bernard laughed and threw dried seaweed at my hair. "Maybel, on the other hand, shall be on the receiving end of all my bad behavior!"

I picked up a very long and thick chunk of driftwood and threw it like a spear at Bernard's chest. "I feel like skewing meat, Susan!"

"Me too!" Susan giggled and hurled a rock at Bernard. "I don't have any driftwood though, just these rocks, so I guess I'll be tenderizing meat!" Susan giggled as she pelted Bernard with small pebbles. Susan was gentle and playful though. I, on the other hand, wanted to know just how fast Bernard's reflexes were. I wondered how fast he could duck if I threw two shards of driftwood at his head in quick succession.

Bernard came barreling toward me laughing menacingly. I swooped into the surf and flung a jellyfish tentacle at Bernard's stupid chest and he screamed like a girl. It was high-pitched and I peed myself I laughed so hard at his girly scream.

Bernard flung the tentacle back into a rock pool and furiously picked me up in an angry bear hug while I continued laughing in hysterics and imitating Bernard's shrilly, little girl squeal over and over again.

"You are going to regret that!" Bernard squeezed tighter.

"Maybel, are you peeing yourself?" Susan asked.

"Uh huh!" I continued laughing.

Bernard suddenly dropped me like a sack of sand. "You peed on me again?" he said, disgusted.

"You screamed like a little girl!" I laid on the sand pointing up at him laughing and peeing all over myself.

After we returned to Theo's house, we took turns bathing. I was becoming more annoyed at Catherine's flirtations. I put on one of Susan's nightgowns. It squeezed my breasts tightly together, making them spill out over the bodice. I walked into the family room where Catherine sat on the sofa next to Theo, smiling and flirtatiously flipping her hair.

Bernard's eyes almost fell from his sockets when I came around the sofa.

"Maybel, why are you wearing my nightgown?" Susan asked.

"Mine got wet. I'm sorry Susan, I can take it off."

"No, it's ok Maybel," she said with innocence, clearly not noticing Bernard putting a throw pillow over his lap and the way Theo stared hypnotically at my breasts.

I sat between Catherine and Theo and held Theo's hand. I kissed Theo slowly, deliberately making sure our kiss lasted a longer time than a usual kiss.

Theo seemed a little embarrassed at my overt affection and he quickly glanced at Catherine, then back to me.

I suddenly wondered if Catherine had kissed Bernard in front of me all those times because deep inside, she sensed Bernard's and my attraction, maybe even before Bernard and I realized our attraction.

Later, after hot cocoa, Susan came into the bedroom where I sat brushing my hair and getting ready for bed.

"Catherine and Theo are attracted to each other," I told Susan. "You can't make your attraction for someone disappear. They'll end up kissing like Bernard kissed me. I can't get mad though, because I never told Catherine that Bernard kissed me that time under the oak tree, or in the apple orchard, or in my backyard," I trailed off trying to remember how many times Bernard and I had kissed.

"Maybe not, Maybel," Susan tried to soothe my suspicions. "But if they do," Susan sat down next to me with a worried expression, "will you still be friends with me even when Theo comes to visit me?"

"Yes, Susan," I said. "Even if they kiss again, I'll still be friends with you."

The next morning, Henry came to pick up Bernard in his automobile. Bernard said they had a meeting that day with Mr. Charleston regarding a new business venture nearby. Bernard promised Catherine he would return the following day. I was a little sad to see Bernard leave, and as Henry's automobile pulled away from Theo's house, I let out a high-pitched scream, imitating Bernard's jellyfish yelp, as I waved to Bernard. Bernard looked annoyed at me at first, then smiled and chuckled as he waved to us.

Theo took us into the center of town for a fun day of sightseeing. There was quite the hubbub going on. As we neared, I heard jeers and shouting. "It's an Indian rally," Theo said. His voice sounded annoyed.

"We should leave," Catherine said. "I've read in the newspapers that Indians can be aggressive."

"They aren't going to hurt anyone, Catherine," I scoffed loudly.

"I've read that too, Maybel," Susan agreed with Catherine. "Maybe we should go."

"I'm not leaving," I said as I pushed my way through. I wondered which tribe this was. The face paints and clothing looked different than those worn by Bernard and Henry when Mrs. Charleston took me to their tribe's gathering.

There was a wealthy looking woman yelling for the Indians to go away. The Indians were standing peacefully in the center of town offering beaded necklaces to passersby. Nobody took their gifts. I approached a young girl who offered me a turquoise necklace. She smiled at me. "Hello," I smiled back.

"Maybel, come back here!" Catherine hissed.

Theo took my elbow and spun me around to leave.

I shook myself free. "Let me go, Theo. She's a girl. She's nice."

I turned back to the girl. "My name is Maybel," I smiled.

"I'm Beatrice," she smiled shyly. She reached the pretty necklace toward me and I happily accepted.

"Thank you," I smiled. "It's beautiful."

"I'm twelve," she said. "And my brother is nine. What's your favorite color?"

"Hmm," I paused thoughtfully, "I like them all. I suppose I'm partial to pink and purple the most, but a nice shade of blue is also pretty. Oh, and green to match my eyes. And amber because there are little flecks of brown in my eyes."

Beatrice giggled. "Wait just a second," she said, then bounced off to a bag behind her. She returned with five necklaces of all the colors I'd mentioned.

"Oh, that's too much," I said. "I don't want to take all your beautiful necklaces."

"Nobody else wants them, and besides, I like you. You're nice," she smiled, and pushed the necklaces into my hands.

I put them around my neck proudly. "I love them, Beatrice. Thank you so much!"

"You're welcome, Maybel," she waved and bounced back to her little brother and several other Indians. I waved at her little brother and he waved back.

Happy with my beautiful beads, I turned back to Theo, Susan, and Catherine, who were standing back, away from the Indians and the crowd of people taunting the Indians.

"Look what she gave me!" I beamed to Theo.

"Let's go back home," he took my arm.

"Why are all of you being so rude?" I asked them.

"We're not," Catherine said, "We just don't want any trouble."

"The Indians are not causing trouble, Catherine," I said.

"No, but their presence has ruffled more than a few feathers," Catherine nodded to the wealthy-looking woman who was now throwing peanuts at several Indians while onlookers laughed.

I lurched forward but Theo yanked me back by my elbow. "Let's go, Maybel, I don't want to be in this crowd when things turn violent."

The rich woman's peanuts hit Beatrice and her brother.

"Oh, they haven't seen violence yet!" I screamed and kicked Theo's shin. He lost his balance and his grasp on my arm loosened.

I bolted forward and ran to that rich woman and grabbed her bag of peanuts and used it to slap her up one side of her cruel face, and back down the other side, until her angry taunts became pleas for mercy.

The crowd laughed at this rich woman in her beautifully-embroidered, silk dress as her knees buckled when I hit her hard with my left hook. These people didn't care who was on the receiving end of violence, as long as they were entertained.

"Anyone else want to throw peanuts at a little girl and boy?" I screamed at them. They laughed at me.

"Are you ok?" I turned to Beatrice and her little brother.

"Yes," Beatrice said, with tears spilling from her innocent, young eyes.

I could see myself in Beatrice in that one instant, and I felt a sudden and all-encompassing sadness envelop me. In her teary eyes, I saw my life flash before me from when I was her age until now.

Standing in front of her, was like looking into a mirror.

Pathetic, was how I felt looking at myself in her. I'll grow up a pathetic, tag-along, and boys will keep choosing my sister while I sit in my room crying and writing. That was what I saw in Beatrice, a mirror.

"Beatrice, you're better than everyone here. Don't settle. You're worth more than you realize. Don't settle, ever. Do you promise?"

Beatrice nodded.

"Maybel, come here," Catherine ordered.

I turned to face Catherine. "Are you embarrassed of me?"

"A little, yes," Catherine hissed.

"And are you embarrassed Susan?"

"A little," Susan said sheepishly.

"And you, Theo?"

"Yes, Maybel, I'm embarrassed by this scene you've created."

I felt wrath bubbling. When I looked at Beatrice and into myself, I kept seeing in my mind all the times Bernard kissed me, yet stayed with Catherine, and all the times this week that Theo welcomed Catherine's flirtatious nature. I saw Theo falling into Catherine's whirlpool of charm.

"When those girls from school laughed at you, Susan, and told me not to touch you because you had fleas, were you embarrassed then? And when I hit them and told them to never again make fun of you, were you embarrassed of me then for standing up for you against your bullies?"

"And you Theo, thanked me for defending your sister. You thanked me for protecting Susan. Would you rather I not have protected Susan? Perhaps I wouldn't be so embarrassing if I were a coward, like you three!" I screamed.

I glared at them as I walked past.

"Miss?" a voice called, "You've got quite the left hook."

I turned to see two Indian men leaning against a tree, smiling at me.

I mouthed the word "Bernard?" at the one who admired my fighting prowess.

He nodded, smiling.

"Henry?" I looked at the other man as I mouthed his name without sound.

He, too, nodded, smiling brightly.

"Maybel, I'm sorry." Catherine caught up to me. "I'm sorry I said you embarrassed me. I was scared of this large and agitated crowd."

"This is White Wolf," I pointed to Bernard. "Say hi, Catherine." I didn't ask Catherine, I told her. I was still seething inside, and I welcomed the opportunity to unleash my wrath on the three cowards in front of me.

Catherine looked terribly uncomfortable. "Hello," she whispered with her gaze averted.

"Hello," Bernard said. "Care to dance, miss?"

"No," Catherine quickly said. "Let's go, Maybel."

Susan caught up to me, followed by Theo.

"You are right, Maybel," Susan said apologetically. "I should have defended that girl. I'm sorry."

"I'm sorry too," Theo said quietly. "I'm glad you protected Susan and that Indian girl."

"How can I make it up to you, Maybel?" Catherine spoke earnestly. "I've never been good at not caring what other people think. You, on the other hand, never care how insane you appear."

"Your apology is terrible," I told Catherine.

"I'm sorry, Maybel. What can I do to make it up to you?"

"Sit with me and White Wolf," I told Catherine.

Catherine looked timidly at Bernard. "Are you a friendly Indian?" she managed to squeak. Catherine watched Bernard nervously.

"Yes," he smiled.

Bernard and Henry turned and sat under the shade of an oak tree just a little way behind them. I eagerly followed. Catherine almost tripped me, she clung so closely behind me.

"Catherine, why are you so scared?"

"Because I have more common sense than you," she whispered. "We're not supposed to leave with strangers, Maybel."

Susan and Theo followed. We sat on the ground in a circle. Catherine practically sat on my lap, she huddled so closely.

"What's your name," Susan asked Henry. Susan seemed more relaxed and open to new friendships than Catherine.

"Bright Water," Henry said.

"I'm Susan," Susan said.

"Nice to meet you," Henry smiled.

Beatrice came skipping over to me. She sat next to me. "Thank you," she said.

"Of course, sweetheart, you are perfect in every way. That woman who was mean dresses nicely to hide her ugliness. Never mind her, or anyone else for that matter."

Beatrice smiled at me and sat closely next to me. I felt friendship with her even though we had just met.

Theo cleared his throat. "Where do you live?" Theo asked Bernard awkwardly, but I appreciated Theo's kind gesture. He was at least trying to be nice.

"A little west of here," Bernard said.

"Us too!" Susan began to relax.

Theo, still attempting polite, small talk, shifted his legs and asked another question. "What is it that you do for a living?"

"I buy real estate and resell my buildings for large profits," Henry smiled. "And this one here," Henry patted Bernard's back, "is beginning medical school."

Theo chuckled, "A man with a sense of humor. Very good, indeed."

"It's true," Bernard said.

Theo looked from Bernard to Henry, then back to Bernard. "Oh," Theo looked surprised. "I thought you were making a joke."

"No, I'm honestly a millionaire," Henry said.

"Oh," Theo said. I didn't think Theo believed Henry or Bernard, but Theo remained politely quiet with his disbelief.

Catherine quietly watched Bernard and Henry. She seemed nervous, but she also seemed to relax a little, and that made me happy.

Susan had been chatting with Beatrice. "Theo, I'm going to go see Beatrice's jewelry," she announced as she stood up. Susan and Beatrice bounded off to a tent with artwork inside.

"Would you like to see our artwork too?" Bernard asked Catherine.

"No, thank you," Catherine quickly replied. I could see Bernard's disappointment even underneath his face paint.

"What kind of musical instruments do I hear playing?" Theo asked.

"Flutes," Henry answered.

"It sounds nice," Theo said.

"Thank you," both Henry and Bernard answered.

"I'm sorry we got off to a bad start," Theo told them.

"Me too," Catherine said. "I've never met an Indian before. I have only heard stories."

"Stories sell newspapers," Henry said. "The truth is boring."

"We're peaceful," Bernard added.

"I can see that," Theo acknowledged. "I'm glad I came to town today. It's been a learning experience, for sure."

"I'm glad you came too," Bernard said, looking at me.

"Now, if you will please excuse me," Henry said as he stood. "I have some business to attend to. It was nice meeting you," Henry reached his hand toward Theo. Theo stood up to shake Henry's hand. Catherine, Bernard, and I stood up as well.

"Miss, it's been a pleasure meeting you," Henry shook Catherine's hand.

Catherine was still quite reserved, but polite.

And then Henry shook my hand and winked at me, then left.

"Thank you for coming," Bernard shook Theo's hand.

He then looked at Catherine. "Thank you," he told her. Underneath his mask, I saw Bernard's apprehension. He looked like a scared, little boy.

Catherine tentatively took Bernard's hand, the hand she had held for years, and limply shook it.

Bernard looked broken, and I felt his sadness from where I stood.

Bernard then turned to me. "Thank you," he whispered, then followed Henry away.

I watched Catherine and Theo to see their reactions.

"This has been pleasant," Theo said.

"It has been nice," Catherine agreed.

I was surprised. "Really?" I asked. "You're both ok?"

"I've never met an Indian," Theo said. "This has been a nice meeting."

"Yes," Catherine said. "I like the flute music, too. The Indians seemed genuinely kind," Catherine added. She seemed surprised and thoughtful by her first meeting with Indians, or rather, what she thought was her first meeting with Indians.

"They are kind," I agreed.

At dinner I sat next to Theo. Catherine and Susan sat across from us. We were at an expensive restaurant. There was a loud crowd in the private banquet room next to our dining area.

"They must be rich people," Catherine nodded to the double oak doors leading to the private dining area.

The doors opened to let that rich, mean woman who threw peanuts at Beatrice inside.

I groaned. "I hope she chokes on a peanut," I sneered.

We continued eating. Catherine kicked me under the table, "Is that Henry?"

Henry came from the private room with the mean woman on his arm. She was flirting heavily with him. They left together through the front of the restaurant.

Not more than five minutes later Henry returned alone and reentered the private room.

"Can we go see who's inside?" Catherine asked. "Who is Henry with inside that banquet hall?" she mused, more to herself than anyone else.

"Let's leave them be. It's probably a business meeting," Theo said.

Catherine suddenly got up and followed Henry. "I thought we weren't supposed to leave with strangers," I yelled sarcastically over my shoulder.

Catherine glared at me then opened one of the double doors, disappearing inside.

"I'll miss Catherine when she leaves," I said. "You have been getting along quite well with Catherine, Theo, I'm sure you'll miss her too."

"Yes," Theo said, annoyed.

"What were you talking about today at the beach?" I asked.

"Her studies," Theo said dryly.

Susan sat and watched. "Theo, do you like Catherine?" she bluntly asked him.

I looked up from my plate.

"Catherine is nice," Theo replied.

"She was flirting with you," I said.

"Can we please have this conversation at home? I've been a part of one public spectacle today, I don't want to be a part of another."

Catherine returned with both Henry and Bernard on her arms. She was between them smiling as she led them to us.

"Great," Theo muttered.

"Bernard! Henry!" Susan squealed.

"Hello, sweetheart," Henry said, and kissed her cheek, followed by Bernard, who also kissed Susan's cheek.

"Hello, Maybel," Henry kissed my cheek. "Thank you for today," he whispered into my ear and kissed my cheek again.

Bernard then greeted me, and he, too, kissed my cheek.

"Would you like to join us in our banquet room?" Henry asked us.

"No, thank you," Theo quickly answered. "I would like a quiet evening, I'm sorry."

"Oh, long day?" Henry asked.

"We met Indians!" Susan boasted.

"Did you now?" Henry pretended to be both surprised and curious. "Were they savages?" he winked at Susan, a twinkle in his eyes.

"No, they were nice," Susan said, then took a bite of her dessert.

"Oh, were they now?" Henry looked at Catherine. "Weren't you scared?"

"Yes, but it was pleasant," she said.

"And you, Theo? How was your experience?" Henry asked.

"To tell the truth, I behaved poorly. Maybel defended a young, Indian girl, and I regret to say none of us here helped Maybel. You are a good person, Maybel. We should have helped you."

I smiled at Theo and he held my hand and squeezed it. "I'm a lucky man," he smiled at me and kissed me on my lips in front of everyone.

"You're dating?" Bernard asked loud enough to draw stares from nearby patrons.

"I suppose we've never made it official," Theo said, smiling at me, "but we've grown fond of each other."

Bernard looked wounded. "Maybel?"

I stared back at Bernard. I didn't know what to say. I thought it was obvious that Theo and I enjoyed each other's company, and most importantly, Theo had never hidden me away like an embarrassment and mistake.

Bernard turned and left the restaurant in a hurry.

Catherine still stood beside Henry and looked lost.

"Have a lovely evening," Henry said farewell to us, then followed Bernard.

Catherine returned to her seat next to Susan. She sat quietly looking down at her plate.

"Why don't we finish eating and retire for the night," Theo suggested. "It's been a long, eventful, and draining day."

Later, I stood outside alone while Theo paid our bill. I enjoyed the salty breeze.

"Maybel," Henry said.

I turned.

"Do you really like Theo?" He asked.

"Yes," I said.

Henry walked toward me. "I always thought either Bernard or I would marry you."

"Neither of you want me," I said dryly.

"That's not true. I have always admired you."

"You just had sex with that evil woman from the Indian gathering," I snapped angrily.

"No, I did not. I was going to satisfy myself without regard to whether or not she enjoyed it, then tell her I was an Indian and leave, but then I thought, no, this woman is so horrible that I do not want any part of my body in any part of hers."

I chuckled.

"I told her to go home and not return, and then I returned to the party," Henry winked at me.

"What were you celebrating?"

"Our new laboratory. Uncle is inside talking to Theo now, I imagine. Uncle was impressed with Theo's intelligence. He'll offer Theo a job."

I was confused. "A job? He already has a job he loves."

Henry continued, "Maybel, I love you. And today at the gathering, I realized that I should have already asked you to marry me long ago. Now Theo has come into your life. And I cannot believe Bernard has not asked you for a date after all this time. To be completely honest with you, I love you, and I've wanted to marry you for a long time, but I have never pursued dating you because you didn't seem interested in me when I flirted with you."

"You flirted with me?" I asked. "When?"

"I've often flirted with you, but I didn't want to be too forward. I respect you and your mother and father. I've never had to flirt with a woman. I've never had to try to get a woman's attention. I honestly don't know what a good man is supposed to do. I was terrified I would be too forward with you and scare you. I constantly wondered if I should put my hand on your knee, or if I should kiss your neck, or if I should press you against me when we danced. I honestly have no idea how good men behave because I've never been with a good woman. I wanted to date you, but I was scared I would be too aggressive with you because I've never known what a good relationship is like."

"I love you, too," I whispered. "I have always loved you."

I paused for a moment and watched Henry's beautiful eyes glimmer in the moonlight.

Henry very gently held my cheek while he leaned in and gently kissed my lips. I felt like my breath left my lungs. He pulled me tightly against him and he kissed me and held my waist, pressing me against his hips. He slowly pulled back and gazed lovingly at me. "I've already told Bernard, that when Theo accepts this new job position, I'm going to ask you to marry me. I gave Bernard a fair warning. And I mean it, Maybel, I truly love you more than anyone. Henry brushed my hair off my shoulder and kissed me again. His lips were so soft and I felt him very much aroused as he pulled my hips against his. "I'll see you back home, sweetheart."

Henry went back inside the restaurant.

I breathed in several deep breaths of ocean air then went inside.

Mr. Charleston was indeed talking to Theo. Catherine was sitting on a bench next to Susan looking bored of their business conversation.

Mr. Charleston shook Theo's hand then nodded to Catherine, Susan, and me, "Good evening, ladies," he said, then left.

Ordinarily he would have picked me up in his giant hands and kissed my cheek, but he was wearing his business mask, and his business mask was serious.

Once we got outside, I pounced. "What was that about? Why are the Charlestons here in Connecticut in my peaceful, beach retreat?"

"They are apparently working with my employers." Theo seemed confused. "They've built a laboratory and asked if I would accept a position."

"What is the position and how much will you earn?" Catherine asked eagerly.

"The position of president," Theo said, awestruck, "and more money in one year than I would earn in ten years working at my present job."

Catherine's eyes bulged.

Theo stopped walking to address us. "It's in England," he said.

"No!" Susan yelled.

"You're leaving me?" I asked.

"I haven't accepted the position," Theo said. He seemed very confused and in a state of shock at whatever Mr. Charleston had said.

"And you won't!" Susan yelled angrily.

"You know we haven't always had money, Susan. You know we made sacrifices to put food on our table years ago. I can't watch my family go through that again."

Susan's eyes teared up and she looked down at the sandy grass as we walked back to Theo's house.

Theo took my hand and I reluctantly let him. I was angry. He kissed me in front of everyone an hour ago and now he considered leaving the country.

We arrived home and Susan immediately went to bed. Catherine went to bathe. I sat with Theo on the sofa.

"I sometimes didn't eat dinner so that Susan could eat. We didn't have much money back then.

Nobody ate lunch with me at school because I only had one shirt and one pair of pants. My shoes had holes and I didn't own socks. Everyone teased me and I usually got beaten by older kids after school because I was poor. I should have stood beside you when you protected that Indian girl. And Maybel, I'm proud of you." Theo squeezed my hand.

I looked over at Theo. "You're leaving, aren't you?"

"Yes," he whispered. "I'm so sorry, Maybel. I cannot relive poverty." "Maybel, you've never had your world crash suddenly and found yourself homeless. You don't understand how much we all take for granted until you suddenly have nothing and you watch your little sister cry herself to sleep because she hasn't eaten in two days. You don't understand because you've never had to live through that Hell. I'm glad you have never been through that, but once you have, you will fight blindly to never have to go through that again."

I sat silently for a moment, thinking. "I'm sorry you and Susan and your parents suffered through that," I whispered softly into his ear as I leaned against his shoulder.

Theo held me like at any moment I would float away into the clouds, a butterfly whose wings he couldn't quite grasp as I slipped between his fingers on my way up high.

Theo kissed me. He kissed me like he was losing me, and that made me cry.

The next morning, I went down to the kitchen. Mrs. Murphy was making breakfast for us and Theo was discussing his new position as president of a company in England with Susan. Susan was quite unhappy.

"Hello, dear," Mrs. Murphy greeted me.

"Good morning, Mrs. Murphy," I said. I felt that everyone was somber this morning. I sat in a chair next to Theo. Susan was on his other side. I hadn't felt like eating, but Mrs. Murphy made fluffy pancakes with butter she'd bought from the countryside, and bacon.

"Good morning, Theo," I said.

"Good morning, Maybel," Theo said. His voice sounded down and trodden.

"Eat, dear," Mrs. Murphy set a plate in front of me. "You have a big day ahead." I loved listening to her thick, Irish drawl.

"What are we doing today?" I asked Theo.

"I'm taking you to see someone at my uncle's publishing company about your stories. We'll be heading to the city soon." Henry said as he sat down next to me.

"What the Hell are you doing here?" I asked, shocked.

"Taking you to Uncle's publishing company to secure your future so no one takes advantage of your contracts," Henry said as he stole a slice of my bacon.

"Good morning, Maybel," Bernard said, as he and Catherine sat down at Theo's breakfast table.

Henry dodged my fork as I tried to spear my bacon away from him.

"You can't just show up and make decisions for me!" I smacked my bacon from Henry's hand before he bit into it.

"There, there, sweetheart," Mrs. Murphy cooed sweetly and placed two more slices of bacon on my plate. "No need to smack the pretty boy," she winked at Henry.

"Maybel, would you like me to help you sign contracts with a publisher, ensuring you will get considerable profits?" Henry asked. "Is that tone to your liking?"

I narrowed my eyes. "Are you condescending to me?"

"What? No!" Henry said.

"You strode into town offering Theo a job in England, and now you want rights to my literary works? Fuck you, Henry, Fuck you too, Bernard!"

"Oh, so you were paying attention to our discussions at the hardware store then, eh, Maybel?" Henry chuckled. "Learned a few new words, have you?"

I took a slice of bacon and smacked his face as hard as you could smack a face with bacon. I wished Mrs. Murphy had made this slice crispier, to give Henry's cheek an extra zing.

"I'm sorry, Maybel," Henry said. "You, of course, don't have to come with me. I am only suggesting this to secure your future, and ensure your contracts are concrete, and that there is no way your future husband can take your money upon divorce."

I whipped my hips around, using them as force to slug Henry square in his jaw. He bled.

"I wouldn't marry a man I'd eventually divorce, and any man I'd marry wouldn't be the kind of man who would request half my bank account!"

Henry held his jaw. "This is why I never asked you on a date. I don't know how to talk to a good woman, and you are a good woman, with a good left hook."

Henry made me chuckle just a little bit.

"I'm sorry, Maybel," Henry said. "I didn't mean anything bad. I thought since I was here, and we aren't terribly far from Uncle's publishing company, I could help you. I'm sorry, and we won't go."

I watched Henry through squinty eyes.

"I'm sorry!" Henry again apologized.

I sighed and tossed a slice of bacon onto the table in front of him. "That's me accepting your pathetic apology," I told Henry.

Henry drove Bernard and Catherine home in his automobile. Susan and I stayed behind with Theo. Susan wanted every second she could possibly have with her brother before he left the country.

"Maybel," Theo approached me as I sat on the bench in his backyard watching the ocean in the distance. "If publishing your stories is something you are considering, I would like to help you finalize a contract with a publisher, instead of letting one of the Charlestons negotiate for you. Will you let me?" Theo spoke softly and was not assuming, as Henry had been. I liked that Theo gave me a choice. He didn't tell me what we were doing, he asked me if he could help.

"Do you think I need a publisher? Do I need a contract? Maybe I just won't publish any of my stories. I prefer writing, not signing contracts."

"You can choose to write, and not publish," Theo said as he sat beside me and wrapped his arm around me. I appreciated Theo's gentle approach.

"Do you not trust the Charlestons?" I asked softly and with reservation.

"I do. I am taking a position of employment under their management, and I wouldn't do that if I didn't trust them." Theo paused and watched the ocean for a minute. "Sometimes, though, Maybel, it might be wise to have an agency with no connection to you or your family represent you. Business and money can be shrewd and without loyalties. I'm not saying the Charlestons do not have your best interests in mind; I'm saying I'm confused at their sudden interest in me, this incredibly new and lucrative position as president of a company, and their sudden interest in your stories. It's probably nothing, but everything right now seems too good to be true. And I wonder, Maybel, what are the motives behind these sudden and rapid changes.

I listened to the ocean as I laid my head on Theo's chest. "You are right, Theo, perhaps it would be better to not have the Charlestons control both of our futures. I would like you to negotiate my contract with your friend in publishing."

The next morning, Susan stayed with Mrs. Murphy while Theo led me inside a magnificent office building. "Theo, look at this place! It's like from a book!"

"It's quite regal, yes." Theo was in his extremely professional and extremely boring and dry persona now that we were officially on business. He didn't smile, joke, or laugh. It reminded me of when we first met, when Susan was sick. I thought Theo was humorless, boring, and a complete snob. His icy exterior made me think he was rude.

How far my perception had changed since then. Once I saw Theo outside of a tense environment, I realized he was one of the most intelligent and compassionate people I'd ever met.

We stood at the reception area and Theo gave our name and appointment time. "Yes, Mr. Matthews, right this way," she smiled warmly at him. "You and your wife are welcome to wait here."

"She is not my wife," Theo said with a calm and even tone.

The woman smiled brighter. "Well, then, please come sit. Would you like any coffee while you wait?"

"No, thank you," Theo answered firmly but politely.

Theo touched my lower back with his finger tips to guide me to the seating area.

"Sit, Maybel. This should not take long."

In an odd way, I found Theo's professional demeanor to be sexy. He was strong, unapproachable, stern, and gave the impression of complete confidence.

Like in dancing, Theo led the conversation and its direction. He was completely and unabashedly brutal when discussing monetary compensation and guaranteeing my financial future should my stories be published.

I wondered why he chose chemistry and being in a laboratory all day instead of becoming a lawyer or the owner of a railroad company.

I didn't understand the terminology used so I remained silent. Theo was aggressive, and for some reason I found myself extremely attracted to this side of him. I hadn't been attracted to him when we first met, so perhaps I was now attracted to his brusque side only because I'd seen his soft side, and knew it was his soft side that would always be with me at night when I became scared and ran to his bed.

Theo stood and shook hands with the publishers. I didn't know what was proper decorum so instead of offering my hand, I just stood there waiting for Theo to tell me what to do.

Theo touched my back with his fingertips and led me out of the meeting. He was silent and although he did not speak, he was controlling and fully in charge of himself and those around him.

I wasn't sure when to expect austere Theo to turn into kind Theo so I remained quiet and let Theo guide me. With that air of superiority I hated when we met, he led me to his automobile. That air of superiority worked for him in this business world we'd just visited. Theo opened my door for me and then walked around the automobile and let himself in. His business persona disappeared as quickly as it had come. He leaned over and kissed me. "That went very well, darling!"

"What happened?" I asked.

"We won," he winked at me.

Susan and I were leaving Connecticut early, because Mr. Charleston said the condition of Theo's employment was for immediate departure to England. Theo would be leaving for England the coming weekend, but Mrs. Murphy would remain in Theo's house as caretaker. Theo said Susan and I could stay, but neither of us wanted to stay in Theo's house without Theo.

My summer in Connecticut had come to an early end. I went to Theo's study to say goodbye.

"Theo," I lightly rapped the large, wooden door. It moved slowly and was heavy as I pushed it open.

Theo was sitting behind his desk, his elbows on his desk and was holding his head in his hands.

"Maybel?" He looked up.

"Theo, it's time for Susan and me to leave."

"I know Maybel." He looked very sad. "Maybel, I'll miss you. I've grown to really enjoy your company and Susan's company. I'm not looking forward to the long winter of solitude."

"I'll miss you too, Theo." I sat on his lap and hugged him. Theo looked at me with absolute pain in his eyes.

"Maybel, you're beautiful and intelligent. I can't imagine you will be single for long. I feel this was our last summer together as you'll likely be in love with some lucky man next summer."

I didn't know what to say to Theo. He looked deeply wounded inside. I kissed him, letting my lips linger on his.

I stood up then leaned down and kissed him again. "I love you, Theo."

"I love you too, Maybel," Theo wiped away a tear from my eye, and then from his eye.

I turned and left, gathering my bags at the door. I couldn't look at Theo sitting there looking so pained, so I waited in the foyer for Susan to say goodbye. She returned, tears streaming down her cheeks, and we left in a carriage to the train station.

I returned home from Connecticut. Theo moved to England, and I was very sad.

I sat in daddy's workshop and traced lines in the sawdust covered table with my finger. I used a long slender piece of scrap wood to push around little chunky blocks of wood. I struck the little blocks with my stick, inventing a game where one block hit another block and whichever little wooden chunk was knocked closest to the wall won that round. So far, the circular chunk of wood I'd named Edgar was the reigning champion. I scooped up the square and triangle shapes, Mavis and Claude, and tossed them in the burn pile. "Don't get cocky," I warned Edgar, "The next round involves a rectangle."

"Maybel, while I love spending time with you, you are sad, lonely, and I can't bear another night of you sitting here gathering sawdust in your hair and mumbling to yourself."

"It must be special cider night. You want me to leave so you can drink with the fellas." I sat hunched over the sawdust bin, twirling the shavings with a wooden rod.

"I want you to be happy," daddy patted my head. "As much as I love your cheerful disposition, I want you to go out and be happy, rather than sitting here all night sad."

"I want to be with you, daddy."

"I want to drink special cider and talk with the fellas," daddy said.

"Can I stay?"

"No, sweetheart. It's just one night a month that we men get to drink and talk about things that you are not allowed to know about."

"Daddy, mommy and her friends would make your discussions with the fellas sound like Bible study. You and your fellas have nothing on mommy and her hens."

Daddy stopped sweeping the dusty floor and looked up at me curiously. "What does mommy say?"

"Can I stay with you tonight?"

"No, men get vulgar when they drink."

"Mommy's friends start with vulgarity and their descriptions blossom into that which vulgarity has no comparison," I said.

"Maybel, what have you heard?" Daddy swept wood shavings into a dust pan.

"Can I stay with you tonight?"

"No."

"Then mommy talks about fabric and patterns," I said.

"That's boring." Daddy emptied the shavings into the bin next to me.

"You want the good gossip, you'll let me stay here with you," I smiled.

"No, Maybel. We'll talk about this more tomorrow, but this afternoon, the fellas will be here and you have to leave. I don't want you around drunken men."

I huffed, "Fine, but when you're old and can't reach your bedpan and you ring your bell for me to come help you, I'll remember this night."

I sulked toward the door and daddy swatted my bottom as I passed by.

"Daddy!" I grumbled.

"Maybel," daddy grabbed my elbow and pulled me into his chest, hugging me tightly. He kissed the top of my head. "I'm sorry Theo left. I liked him, but I'm glad he left because I never would have left mommy, and I'm glad he left now, rather than later in your relationship."

I wrapped my arms around daddy. "I wasn't worth staying for."

"You are. He wasn't worth your love. You're perfect, baby. And now I get to keep you under my roof a little longer and for that, I'm glad he left."

"I can stay here under the roof of your workshop too, since you really don't want me to leave you," I looked up at daddy while he still hugged me tightly.

"Go," daddy pretended to swat at my bottom again as I moved away giggling. He then kissed my forehead. "Go do something fun tonight, and tell me all about it tomorrow. I love you, baby."

"I love you too, daddy."

Henry's brother, John, was visiting, and he and Henry were staying with the Charlestons. I liked John. I only saw him at the Charleston's parties from time to time, but when I did see him, he was always kind to me. He was beautiful like Henry, but Henry was the most handsome man in the world.

"Yes, Bernard used to run behind Henry and me crying for us to wait up," John laughed as he told Catherine and me stories from when they were all young.

Bernard blushed and his eyebrows furrowed.

"Oh, am I embarrassing you?" John laughed.

Bernard didn't say anything. He crossed his arms though.

I giggled, "What was Bernard like when he was young?"

"A spoiled brat," John playfully punched Bernard's shoulder. "It's because you never had brothers or sisters to knock you down a peg or three."

"Yes, and you never properly learned how to share," Henry added.

"Bernard always ran behind us on his little legs crying for us to play with him," John again slapped Bernard's arm playfully.

Henry laughed loudly then mimicked Bernard in a child's voice, "Wait for me Johnny, Henwee, wait for me!" John and Henry made little, pathetic sobbing noises and wiped imaginary tears from their eyes making fun of Bernard.

Catherine and I giggled hysterically.

"Can we please change the subject?" Bernard asked tautly.

"If we don't, are you going to cry?" John laughed.

Bernard huffed.

"Did Bernard have lots of little admirers?" Catherine asked.

John and Henry turned to each other laughing uproariously. "Oh, God no!" John laughed. "Girls avoided Bernard because he was so pathetically awkward."

"Oh, it was a true delight to watch!" Henry slapped his knee while he laughed.

Bernard blushed deeper and clenched his jaw as he spoke. "I did have admirers, but unlike you two, I knew I wanted to get married and have a family, and I would not be able to marry a good woman if I had slept with all her sisters, cousins, and friends. I had the foresight to know that to get a good woman, I would have to be a good man."

"Yes, well, I was shocked when Henry told me that Bernard had somehow managed to get a beautiful girl to date him," John told Catherine.

"And then even more shocked when Henry told me this pretty girl had a beautiful and intelligent little sister that followed Bernard around everywhere he went," John winked at me.

"Well, Catherine and Maybel had not yet met Henry," Bernard said dryly. "Had they met Henry that day at Catherine's birthday party, I likely would never have seen them again. How's Greta doing these days?" Bernard looked at John.

John crossed his arms and huffed.

"Henry took the virginity of the girl John loved most, and also Henry slept with his toy bear until he was fifteen," Bernard announced. "Oh, and John cries at operas," Bernard quickly added.

"Baby Bear was a gift from Granny, Bernard, and I miss Granny," Henry sounded suddenly like a little kid defending his teddy bear and missing his dear granny. "I was her favorite, by the way, Bernard and John," Henry crossed his arms. "And Greta crawled into bed with me. I was young and it felt good. Can you say no to a girl who crawls into your bed and touches you, John?"

"No, probably not," John relented. "Ok, Bernard, we'll stop teasing you."

"Yes, enough teasing," Bernard said, taking pity on his cousins in a way he had not taken with me when we were young.

"You're right, no more teasing," Henry agreed, and John nodded his head in agreement as well.

"Was Henry always handsome?" Catherine asked John.

"Yes, and that is why I learned to never let my girlfriends meet my little brother Henry."

"I didn't usually return their advances," Henry said. "Though just out of curiosity, who are you dating now?" Henry smiled, a gleam twinkled in his eyes.

"You'll not meet her until after we've said our wedding vows, little brother!"

"You're getting married?" Henry asked, surprised.

"Yes, eventually. I do believe my days of sharing my bed with more than one woman are over," John said.

"Who is she? What does she look like? Tell us about her," Henry coaxed John.

"No, absolutely not, Handsome Henry," John sarcastically spoke my nickname for Henry.

"Maybel, why haven't you ever returned to Paul's home out west?" John changed the subject.

"How did you know I visited? I didn't see you there," I asked surprised.

"Likely because your lips were glued to Paul's the entire time," John winked at me.

"Maybel!" Catherine squealed.

"I saw you and Bernard kiss with your tongues and I wanted to see what it felt like," I shrugged my shoulders.

"Maybel!" Catherine's eyes were wide.

"Paul has asked about you often, Maybel. He misses you," John told me.

"He does? Bernard! I have asked you to take me back many times! You told me Paul had likely gotten a girlfriend and had forgotten about me!"

"Oh, no, he most definitely misses you, Maybel," John said.

"Then why hasn't Paul visited Bernard's home?" I asked John.

"Yes, Bernard, why?" John looked expectantly at Bernard.

Bernard shifted uncomfortably. "I've been busy and I am sure Paul has too," Bernard mumbled while not making eye contact.

"Paul isn't busy," Henry smiled.

"He doesn't have a girlfriend," John added, also smiling at Bernard. "He would love to come visit you, Maybel."

Bernard breathed in deeply. "Can we please discuss something else?"

John winked at me. "Maybel, Henry has always spoken fondly of you. I read some of your stories. You have quite the imagination and now you're a beautiful woman, not the girl I first met. I can see why both Henry and Bernard are quite taken with you."

"Yes, well, they don't want to date me," I said bluntly. "and the man with whom I was falling in love likes Catherine, but he left me to live in England, so I had better be a good storyteller, because my own story is quite pathetic."

Everyone stared at me.

"Sorry," I said. "I'm a little bitter right now. Let's pretend I had kept my mouth shut. Let's talk about your newest real estate, Henry. John do you also work in real estate?"

"I do," he said. "I enjoy the accounting part more so than the renovation aspect."

"I love math too," I said with a straight face.

Catherine snorted, "Maybel hates math," Catherine giggled. "It's a joke in our family."

"I prefer writing," I said.

"And what is it you like most about writing?" John asked me.

"Control, I suppose. I can't control how people treat me, but I can control my characters. Sometimes I kill them off in a story if I'm in a bad mood. Other times I let my imagination free to explore the impossible, and I create alternate worlds where anything is possible."

"Fascinating," John said.

"She's killed many a character in her stories because I've angered her," Bernard said.

"Those characters deserved it," I retorted.

Catherine snorted, "I like the story about the boy who froze solid, and his icy prison was shattered by a falling acorn from the squirrel overhead. The boy's icy sculpture shattered into a million pieces, and his little sister either couldn't, or wouldn't, put him back together before spring." Catherine laughed a little too happily at what was fictional Bernard's demise.

"Yes, maybe they deserved a little anger, but how many times has that one character of yours named Mernard been stabbed, trampled by a horse, or eaten by a rogue gang of murderous squirrels?"

"I don't know, Mernard, how many times have you kissed me behind Catherine's back, locked me out of your bedroom so you could kiss Catherine without me being an annoying tag-along, or persuaded your father to offer the man I was going to marry a job across the Atlantic because seeing me kiss Theo made you jealous?"

Again, everyone stared in shock at my outburst.

"I didn't persuade my father to give Theo that job! Theo is actually quite brilliant, and yes, I was jealous! And anyway, you wouldn't have married Theo. Catherine already had Theo under her spell."

"Bernard!" Catherine yelled. "I did not know Maybel had feelings for Theo when I kissed him!"

"Really, Catherine?" Bernard goaded Catherine. "You kissed Henry while you dated me."

John looked at Henry with raised eyebrows.

"Well, you were in love with my little sister the entire time you were kissing me!" Catherine spat.

John breathed out deeply. "This has been better than the theater. Let's have intermission, shall we?"

John proceeded to stand up, and looked expectantly at Henry. Henry reluctantly stood up, too.

"How about a snack?" John asked Henry.

"I suppose," Henry agreed. "I hope the second act is less dramatic."

Catherine and I sat on the sofa together not looking at each other. Bernard was in a chair on the other side of the coffee table not looking at us.

"We'll see how Mernard fares battling chipmunks in his next adventure," I said, and crossed my arms angrily.

Catherine snorted.

"Mernard would not like any rodent to chew his entrails while he was still alive," Bernard replied.

"What about eyeballs?" I wondered.

"Mernard would be displeased," Bernard said.

"Catherine, let's go home," I suggested. "Maybe just a quiet evening at home with mommy and daddy would be nice."

"Yes, I think so," she said.

"I don't want to endure more of John and Henry's teasing. Can I come?" Bernard asked.

"Will you run behind us crying for us to wait for you?" Catherine asked him.

I laughed.

"Don't you want to stay here with John? You haven't seen him in a while," Catherine asked Bernard.

"Yes, Bernard, don't you miss me?" John called in a high-pitched, sing-song voice from the kitchen.

"You two have been eavesdropping?" Bernard called back.

"Of course! We didn't want to miss the show," John yelled. "By the way, Maybel, see if instead of chipmunks, you can work in something more exotic, like fire ants."

I snorted.

Catherine and I walked home together, but Bernard stayed with John and Henry. John promised not to tease Bernard and said he really wanted to go fishing with Bernard and Henry like they had done as children.

"I honestly didn't know you and Theo had grown so close," Catherine said as we walked home. "I am sorry I kissed him."

"Bernard kissed me. I didn't tell you because I was afraid I'd lose my big sister." I was still scared to lose Catherine.

"What other secrets do you have?" Catherine asked me.

"I'm angry and sad because everyone likes you more than me," I told Catherine. "What are your secrets?"

"I've always been jealous of your independence and self-confidence," Catherine confessed. "I was mad and jealous that Bernard loved you. And, I suppose I enjoyed it when Theo seemed to enjoy my attention, because a small part of me wanted you to feel what I'd felt when I watched Bernard watching you."

"Do you think the Charlestons offered Henry and Theo money to leave because Bernard liked me?" I held my breath. "It hurts me less to believe they were sent away, rather than me not being worthy of them staying."

"Money is power, Maybel. Maybe they offered Henry money to take a job in San Francisco. Maybe they offered Theo money to go to England. You and I have never truly suffered. If someone offered you money to go somewhere to invent medicines to save more Susans, would you go? I think you would go, Maybel, because you want the opportunity to help people. And Henry, he didn't grow up with the security of an unlimited bank account. Stop judging so harshly. They were offered opportunities to make money and a better future if they agreed to leave you, and they did, but what I find most interesting, is that Henry returned for you, and so will Theo. Think about that."

We continued walking home together, the breeze gently lifting our hair. The smell of mommy's freshly baked bread wafting to us as we neared home.

I had expected to be in Connecticut throughout my summer break, but now I was home, and

Theo was in England. I didn't know what to do with myself most days. I did not see Bernard for the remaining months of summer. Catherine prepared for college, and I assumed Bernard was preparing to move away as well. Mommy and daddy pressured me to think about college and my future. I didn't want to think about anything anymore. I spent entire days alone on my island, roaming the apple orchards and cornfields beyond my house, and wandering throughout faraway lands in my imagination. Susan and I spent hours writing, painting, and sculpting. We rode bicycles around the town and countryside, and Mr. Matthews taught us how to change a tire, a sparkplug, and how to inspect an engine.

Bernard had broken up with Catherine long ago, but they had attended social events together for a while. After we arrived home from Connecticut, they no longer attended parties together, and neither seemed to have any inclination to reconcile. Catherine seemed content and happy with her book clubs and lectures at the library. She was not dating anyone. She seemed to enjoy being single and carefree. I liked watching Catherine sitting with mommy and daddy on the sofa in the evenings, her hair not perfectly smoothed and formed into ringlets, and her fingernails not perfectly painted. Catherine seemed free and happy, and spent less time trying to appear polished and perfect. I really liked this new Catherine.

I sometimes wondered what Bernard was doing and where he spent his time now that he and Catherine seemed to be completely independent from one another. I didn't go see Bernard though. My heart was still sad that Theo left. Sometimes I did not want to see Susan for fear of hearing that Theo had begun dating. I still spent time with Susan though, because I liked her, and I knew I would have to eventually see Theo, Bernard, and Henry with other women.

The town's summer festival was going strong and people milled about eating fried foods and chocolates. Vendors from far away came to our small town. I enjoyed eating foods I had never tried before.

I wandered around the festival in the park. It was crowded and smelled like meat was being roasted over a fire somewhere until the breeze changed directions, and then it smelled like buttered popcorn and chocolate cakes cooling on racks under the pavilion.

"Oh, hello, Bernard," I stopped walking and stared at Bernard. I had not seen him in a while, and was startled to see him right in front of me now.

I had been thinking about what birds tweet to each other, and wasn't paying attention to anything or anyone in front of me.

Bernard was standing in front of me with his hands in his pockets blocking my path.

"Hello, Maybel. How are you?"

"I'm fine." I stared at him. After an awkward pause I asked, "How are you?"

"I'm well, thank you," he replied.

We stared at each other. I wasn't sure if I should walk around him or keep staring awkwardly at him. I chose the latter. I stood there staring awkwardly at him. He stood equally as awkwardly and stared at me.

For some reason, I asked the question that had just been on my mind. "What do birds say to each other when they tweet?"

Without missing a step, Bernard replied, "They're mating maybe. I think they want to have intercourse and make babies."

"It's summer, Bernard, birds don't mate in the summer."

Again, Bernard did not miss a step. "Maybe the lady bird needs wooing, and the male is asking to take her to dinner until spring, when she may finally agree to nest with him."

"That's an acceptable answer, Bernard."

"Thank you, Maybel."

We continued to stare awkwardly at each other.

"How is Catherine?" he finally asked.

"She's dead."

"What?" Bernard looked shocked.

"Just kidding, she's getting us popcorn," I giggled.

"Maybel!"

"What? Why do you care how Catherine is doing?"

"Because I care about you both still, Maybel. I've known you both a long time and I still care about how you are faring."

I replied, "We fare well. So, farewell!" I said, and stepped around Bernard on my way to find Catherine.

"Maybel, wait, I miss you," Bernard called after me.

I turned around. "I miss you too, Bernard, but Catherine is waiting for me, and I don't know if you should come."

"May I see you again?" he asked.

I took a couple steps toward Bernard. "I don't know," I said softly. "I don't know if that would make Catherine mad at me."

"I understand," Bernard said quietly. "But Maybel, if you ever want to maybe go to the candy store or gamble with my father, you're more than welcome to come over."

"Gambling, you say?" I paused, "I am good at gambling, and I miss your mother and father a lot, to be honest."

Bernard smiled, "They miss you, too."

"I'll have to ask Catherine," I said. "I don't want her to be mad at me."

"I understand," he said softly.

I turned to leave when Bernard caught my elbow. "Maybel?" he asked.

I turned back around and looked at him expectantly.

"I miss you," he said. "I miss our walks in the woods and I miss the stories you tell me."

"I do too, Bernard." I paused, I wasn't sure if I was supposed to say anything else. I tried to think of how to say goodbye, but I've never wanted to say goodbye to Bernard, so I only smiled and turned away and walked toward the vendors selling popcorn.

I found Catherine sitting on a bench near the popcorn stand. She smiled and waved. "Over here, Maybel!"

I went to her and sat beside her. "Thank you, Catherine!" I said, as I nibbled popcorn.

We listened to the band play. Several couples danced. The weather was beautiful.

"I'm sorry Theo left," Catherine said. She did not look at me when she said that. She stared off into the distance watching couples dancing.

"I miss Theo, and I wish I could have stayed longer in Connecticut with him and Susan."

"I'm sorry he moved to England, Maybel. How are you handling that?"

"I'll be ok. I'm happy to see you and Susan. Maybe we three can entertain trouble and mayhem to pass our boredom before you leave." I tried to smile and sound happy, but my inside felt empty.

Catherine nibbled popcorn and watched the band.

"Catherine, are you ok? I mean about Bernard?" I asked.

Catherine watched the band. I wasn't sure if she heard me. And then after a long pause, she replied, "I'm ok, Maybel. We were together for quite a while, but we grew apart slowly, as young love often does."

"Will you get back together?"

"I don't know. I haven't seen him. I imagine we will go separate ways."

"Why did you and Bernard break up?"

"He said he wanted to engage himself more in his studies and prepare for medical school," Catherine said.

I watched Catherine. I wondered what she was really thinking under all her polished answers. I wondered if she wanted to return to Bernard but was too proud to say she missed him.

"I might study nursing, or writing, but," I paused, "just before Theo left, he secured a contract with a publishing company. It is a lucrative deal."

"That's good, Maybel," she responded, while still watching the band.

I was hoping Catherine would say if she was dating anyone. I wondered if she'd moved on.

"Catherine, I passed Bernard while coming to meet you. He said to say hi to you, but I wasn't sure if I should tell you. I wanted to make sure you were ok and doing well first."

"I'm fine, Maybel. Thank you for telling me," she said.

I paused. I wanted to ask her more questions but she remained aloof. I opted to keep my mouth shut, which was not my forte.

"What do you think birds say when they tweet to each other?" I asked Catherine.

"They probably just make noises hoping someone will hear them and return their tweets so they don't feel so alone or scared in this world."

I watched Catherine. Catherine had an amazing intellect that she didn't let most people see, and I never understood why.

Catherine and I watched the band play a while longer. They played well but I could only sit so long before I became restless. Catherine must have noticed me fidgeting and shifting my hips, trying to get comfortable on the wooden bench. "Maybel, let's go walk around," she suggested.

I happily agreed. I was wondering if there were carnival games and if there was an art exhibit again this year.

I followed Catherine through the crowd. We wound our way through families, young couples, and little boys fighting with sticks. I wanted to join in the stick fight, but I resisted my childish urges to beat the little rapscallions.

Catherine led us to carnival games. The carnival workers taunted and enticed onlookers by either teasing them or flattering them. "Oh! Look at this big burly man! I bet he could win a prize for his lady! The big burly man walked by ignoring them. The carnival workers wanted his money so they tried another tactic. "Well look at that! He doesn't want to play because he doesn't have a lady to whom he can give a prize! That's ok, mister, lots of men are too ugly to marry!"

The big burly man picked up a rock and threw it, hitting the carnival worker. The townspeople laughed and called out to the carnival worker, taunting him, and some even taunted the big burly man. "Yeah, Jeff, why aren't you married?" a man chortled.

The man heckling big, burly Jeff was Jeff's cousin, who worked at the hardware store. I knew him from my countless trips to the hardware store with daddy.

Jeff turned and raised his fist at his cousin, then an old woman yelled out, "Jeffrey! Lowell! You two stop this instant!"

The old woman was their grandmother. I knew her from church. I didn't like her.

The townspeople that were gathered around laughed hysterically at the show taking place. It was more entertaining than the band. I didn't like the carnival workers, but I did enjoy throwing baseballs and winning prizes.

Catherine led me past the bawdy carnival workers and into an open area with art and sculptures. "Wow, Catherine, these are amazing!" I awed.

"I thought you'd like them. I saw them earlier and thought you and Susan, with your artistic interests, would enjoy these exhibits."

"I do! I need to bring Susan here!"

"Where is Susan?" Catherine asked.

"I think she's at home right now. We're supposed to meet later," I said.

"Great, bring her here. She'll love this, I'm sure. I mentioned to her yesterday that there would be an art exhibit and she seemed interested."

I saw Bernard nearby and grabbed Catherine's arm. "Catherine!" I hissed, "Bernard is here."

Catherine seemed unfazed. "I'm fine, Maybel. We're all adults."

"I'm not. I'll kick his penis if you need me to. You just let me know!"

Catherine chuckled, "I'm fine Maybel, but thank you," she smiled.

Bernard looked up as we approached and he looked surprised, then awkward. "Hello, Catherine, Maybel."

"Hello, Bernard. How are you?" Catherine asked politely.

"I'm fine, thank you. How are you?" Bernard responded.

"I'm well, thank you," Catherine answered. "I thought Maybel might enjoy this artwork, and perhaps enjoy meeting the artist even more."

Bernard pursed his lips and looked troubled.

"Maybel?" A gorgeous man appeared from behind Bernard.

I looked at him curiously. He looked familiar but I couldn't quite place him. He stood next to a beautiful sculpture and his eyes were a light greenish blue. "Paul?" I screamed.

"Yes, Maybel!" Paul beamed.

I ran to Paul and hugged him. He kissed my cheek and held my waist. "Maybel, I knew I'd see you here!"

"Paul, I have missed you more than you'll ever know!" I hugged him.

"I've missed you too, Maybel! I always knew I'd see you again though!"

Paul took my hand and led me off to the side, away from everyone. "Maybel, I requested to come visit Bernard many times but he always replied you were busy, or that he was away and busy. I wanted to see you so often." Paul then kissed me as he held me. "I've never forgotten you," he said softly.

"I asked Bernard many times to take me to you, but he said no. I wanted to be with you." I then kissed Paul and he smiled. He even smiled while we kissed. I felt his lips smiling as they pressed against mine.

"Would you like to have dinner with me?" Paul asked. He smiled brightly and his eyes were green, like Bernard's, but with more blue on the outside of his irises.

"Yes!" I practically screamed. "Where and when?"

"Tonight at Bernard's house. Maybel! I still have the bowl and bird you made me!" Paul smiled so sweetly at me.

"I have your bowl and bird, too! They've been on my dressing table all these years and I see them every day," I smiled up at him. Paul was tall now, with wide, muscular shoulders, and under his dress pants, I could see the lines of his taught leg muscles.

"Your art is on my dresser where I see it every day, too," he smiled and winked at me. "And I'll see you tonight at seven o'clock?"

"That sounds nice," I said, although I wasn't thrilled about going to Bernard's house right now. It felt awkward because of the break up between Catherine and Bernard. I wasn't sure how to act around Bernard anymore.

"Great! I'm so happy to see you again, Maybel!" Paul held me again and kissed me on my lips. I returned his kiss. Paul kissed me a little more slowly. "You've gotten better," he smiled and chuckled softly.

"Oh, you have definitely gotten better," I giggled.

Paul kissed me again and I felt his tongue caress mine. I lost my breath in the excitement of seeing Paul again after all these years. As our tongues touched, we were suddenly children out west sneaking kisses and giggling as though no time had passed.

"I'll see you tonight," Paul leaned back and took a deep breath. "I've always wanted to see you again, Maybel, and I'm so happy to be with you." Paul again kissed me and held me against him tightly. I felt as though Paul and I had never been apart when he held me and gazed down into my eyes.

I smiled and nodded in an almost trancelike state. His gaze into my eyes was mesmerizing.

I said goodbye to Paul and politely nodded at Bernard. "Oh Paul!" I turned back around to face him, "May I bring a fellow artist to dinner?"

"Of course!" Paul smiled. "I love meeting fellow artists!"

I waved at Paul, and Catherine politely said goodbye to both Paul and Bernard. We wound our way back through the crowd and into a less densely populated area.

"Catherine, are you coming tonight?"

"No, Maybel, I will stay home but you and Susan enjoy yourselves."

I didn't want to go without Catherine but I understood why she would prefer to stay home.

Catherine and I arrived at Susan's home and I asked her if she would like to meet a fellow artist whose exhibit was being displayed in the park.

Susan's eyes shot wide open. "I saw that exhibit this morning, although I didn't get a chance to meet the artist! Yes, I would love to come!" Susan was beyond exhilarated.

"I'll pick you up at a quarter 'til seven then?" I asked.

"Yes!" Susan shrieked. "I will wear your old dress that was Catherine's old dress!" Susan again shrieked.

I giggled, "I'm excited that you're excited," I told Susan.

"Me too," Catherine smiled at Susan. "You'll like the artist. Maybel sure does," Catherine giggled.

Catherine and I went home, and I went upstairs to bathe and dress.

"Catherine," I entered her bedroom, "what do I wear to dine with an artist?"

"Nothing fancy. Something nice, but not something you'd wear to the Christmas Eve ball."

"My pink dress or the red one?" I asked. "Oh wait, or the green one?"

"The green one. It's nice, but not too fancy."

"Thank you, Catherine," I said, and went to my room. I had never been skilled at looking good, so I put on my green dress and just swept my hair up quickly. I dabbed a little color on my lips and just told myself not to worry about looking pretty because no one at the dinner had ever seen me look beautiful like Catherine, so it didn't matter if I just dressed my usual casual way.

I went to Susan's house and she opened the door before I had a chance to knock. "Maybel! You look pretty!"

"You look pretty, too, Susan," I giggled. I loved her exuberance.

"Thank you, Maybel! Susan was bubbly and happy. She still had no cares or worries and I missed being free like Susan.

We walked to the Charleston mansion and as we approached, the house was aglow with candles lighting every window sill. It looked magical.

I had not expected a festive party. I thought it would simply be dinner with Paul, and probably Bernard, too.

I led Susan to the front door because I no longer felt comfortable letting myself in through the kitchen door. I wasn't sure how to go about this transition from being familiar with the Charlestons to being just polite neighbors.

Vincent opened the front door. "Hello, Miss Maybel. It's nice to see you again." Vincent smiled at me.

I'd always loved Vincent. I leapt toward him and hugged him tightly around his belly. He patted my head. "I love you too, sweetheart," Vincent smiled down at me.

Inside there were many people milling about. Vincent led us to the formal dining room. Paul immediately came to me and kissed my cheek. "Maybel," he smiled, "I'm so happy to see you!"

"I'm happy to see you as well. I've missed you so much, Paul." I smiled up at him.

"I've missed you too, Maybel!" He held my waist and smiled down at me.

"Paul, this is my best friend and adopted sister, Susan," I smiled at Susan.

Paul took Susan's hand. "It's wonderful to meet you," he smiled.

"I saw your art this morning and it's beautiful!" Susan bubbled.

"Thank you," Paul smiled. "I hear you are an artist, too."

"I paint, write, and sculpt. Painting is my favorite." Susan's voice was energetic.

"Perhaps I can see your work while I'm here visiting?" Paul asked Susan.

"I would love that!" Susan said excitedly.

"Would you both like to come look at more pieces in the study?" Paul asked. "I'll be taking them to New York next week."

"Yes!" Susan squealed.

Paul led the way to the study. We passed his mother and he introduced us. "Mother, you remember Maybel, and this is Susan."

"Ah yes, Maybel, dear, how are you? And Susan, it's nice to meet you."

Paul's mother kissed my cheek and kindly smiled at Susan as she shook her hand.

"Maybel, dear, have you seen the white wolf again?"

Paul's mother looked so much like her sister, Bernard's mother. "Sometimes she comes to sit on my roof outside my window," I said, "but I think I'm dreaming."

She smiled warmly, "That's wonderful dear. I hope you will again come visit us back home soon."

"Yes, I'd love that. Thank you," I said.

"Mother, I'm off to show them my other pieces in the study. Susan is an artist, too."

"I can tell. I know a sensitive soul when I see her." Paul's mother winked at Susan and Susan happily smiled back.

Paul continued leading us to the study. "I wasn't expecting this many people," I said as we entered the study where, thankfully, it was empty.

"Neither was I," Paul said, "but lots of family came to support me, which is very nice."

"Wow Paul! Are all these your creations? They're amazing!" Susan walked around several sculptures.

"Yes, Susan, I'm happy you like them!"

Bernard came into the study. My stomach tightened. "Bernard!" Susan, blissfully unaware of how uncomfortable this was for me, ran to him and hugged him.

"Hello, Susan," Bernard held her, "how are you?"

"I'm fine. Paul's art is amazing!"

Bernard chuckled and Paul smiled. "I'm happy to meet a fellow lover of art," Paul said.

"Hello, Maybel, nice to see you. How are you?" Bernard asked politely.

"I'm well, thank you, and how are you?"

"I'm well," Bernard said.

"Paul," Susan excitedly pointed to several of Paul's sculptures, "I bet I can guess your favorite sculptors from seeing your works here."

Susan listed several names and Paul's eyes widened with surprise. "You know your art, Susan, and you are exactly correct!"

Susan and Paul began chattering away about different artists and places. My mind began to wander. I tuned them out and began thinking of other random things, like why did Paul sculpt a flower that looked a lot like a vagina?

"Always the dreamer," Bernard woke me from my daydream.

I looked up. Bernard was now standing beside me, and Paul and Susan were still happily chattering away about art and artists.

"Oh, yes, I was just thinking that this sculpture is likely a favorite amongst men," I said.

Bernard chuckled softly and blushed, "Yes, there have been comments made amongst the men in my family."

"Paul has quite the eye for detail," I noted.

Bernard laughed, "Yes, he is quite the artist, indeed."

Bernard watched me and smiled. "Maybel, I'm glad you're here," he said softly.

"Yes, I've yet to see your parents, but I did get to say hello to Paul's mother."

"Perhaps after dinner you can say hello to mother and father."

"Yes, that would be nice," I said.

"We have a little time before dinner is served. Would you like to go for a quick stroll in the garden while they talk about art?"

"Oh, I don't know, I shouldn't leave Susan alone with a man she just met." I looked over at Susan, who was now discussing Paul's paintings in great detail.

Bernard nodded, "You're a good big sister," he said.

"I learned from the best," I said, then immediately regretted saying that.

"How is Catherine?" he asked softly.

"She's well," I said.

There was an awkward silence between us while Paul and Susan were absolutely enamored with each other's passion for art.

Bernard and I stood beside each other in awkward silence. I scoured my mind wondering what was something mundane to talk about. I didn't want to talk about family. "I saw a pretty rock today."

I rolled my eyes at my own self. Why had I said that, I wondered? That was an incredibly random and stupid thing to say.

"I saw it yesterday. It was indeed pretty," Bernard replied.

I looked up at him, puzzled. "How do you know the rock you saw was the same one I saw?"

"How many rocks could there be that are pretty enough to talk about?"

"Good point," I agreed.

There was more silence. And more awkwardness.

"I saw a deer this morning," Bernard said.

"Her name is Frances," I told him.

"How do you know I saw Frances and not a different deer?" Bernard asked.

"Was she brown?"

"Yes," he said.

"Then you saw Frances," I said, as a matter of fact.

Bernard chuckled, "I've missed your humor and imagination."

"I've missed your lack of humor and lack of imagination," I said.

"I haven't missed your sarcasm," Bernard smiled.

"You're being sarcastic when you say that," I smiled back.

"Maybel, would you like some ice cream?" Bernard asked me.

"Are you being sarcastic now? Because I don't joke about ice cream," I said.

"No, Maybel, I'm not joking. We have ice cream."

"Susan, would you like to come to the kitchen for ice cream?" I asked.

"No thank you, you go ahead, we're discussing ceramics," she said, while holding the vagina flower."

I turned back to Bernard. "Ok, well, I guess maybe a little ice cream before dinner would be alright."

The short walk to the kitchen felt like forever. It was awkward being with Bernard now, and the chasm between us made me sad.

In the kitchen, Bernard scooped ice cream into a bowl and put a cherry on top.

"That's a lot of ice cream. I will certainly fill up before dinner," I remarked.

"It's for both of us," he smiled at me. "Is it alright if we share?"

"Do you intend to eat the cherry?"

"You can have the cherry," he laughed.

"Then yes, we can share," I said.

"Thank you Maybel, for your generosity."

"You're welcome, Bernard. If you're nice, I might even give you half."

Bernard smiled, "Maybel, I haven't seen you in a little while. I've missed you."

I paused and took another bite of ice cream. I looked up at him. "Why did you break up with Catherine, and when will you two reconcile?"

"I needed to focus on my studies, Maybel. I needed to spend more time studying and less time at parties and lunches. And," Bernard sighed, "I really don't think either of us wish to reconcile."

"How are your studies now?" I changed the subject.

"I received good marks and I'm at the top of my class," he said proudly.

"That's good," I said. "I never doubted your abilities."

"Thank you, Maybel. How are you faring?"

"Mommy caught me talking to a leaf this morning. I've been better, Bernard."

Bernard chuckled, "I've caught you talking to an assortment of peculiar things."

"It was a curled leaf, and I thought how beautifully it was curled, like a spiral, and so I told it my compliment."

Bernard smiled. One side of his lips curved up just a teeny tiny bit more than the other when he was really amused.

"I've always done well in everything except math, and apparently, math is important in science." I took another bite of ice cream.

"Would you like me to help you?" Bernard asked me.

"No, it's ok. You are busy with your studies. I don't want to distract you and have you break up with me, too."

"I won't, Maybel," he said quietly.

"You look sad," I said.

"I can help you with math," he spoke quietly as he ate ice cream. He twirled his spoon between his thumb and forefinger as he spoke.

"You're sad because I said I don't need you to teach me math? You must really like math the way I like this ice cream."

"I'm sad because I miss you, Maybel. I have enough time to help you with math."

"Your reason for breaking up with Catherine was that you needed to spend more time studying. If I come here for math tutoring, Catherine will wonder why you want to spend time with me but not her. She will feel betrayed if I come here."

"It would be only one or two hours a day," Bernard said. "I'm not that busy with studies," Bernard admitted. "I enjoy being with you."

"Bernard! You ate my cherry!" I yelled.

Bernard looked down into the bowl we shared.

"I'm sorry, Maybel!"

"Now that is betrayal! You stole my cherry like the filthy pirate you are!" I shouted.

"I can get you another cherry, Maybel," Bernard chuckled.

"No, it's ok, I ate the cherry. I just wanted to see your reaction," I giggled.

"Maybel! You sure make things interesting!" Bernard laughed.

"It's my special talent. Anyway, I can ask Catherine if I can come for tutoring for one hour daily. Maybe she won't be mad about just one hour."

"I'd like that, Maybel. Would you like have dinner with me tomorrow night?"

"Instead of tonight, or in addition to tonight?" I asked.

"In addition, Maybel," he grinned.

"See, we're already doing math," I giggled.

"I missed your giggle too," he said softly.

"Dinner tomorrow sounds nice. I'll ask Susan if she's free tomorrow night. How long is your family in town? Are you having these fancy dinner parties every night?"

"I don't know how long exactly they'll be here. I think about a week. And I have no idea if we're having parties every night. They tell me when to come eat and I show up."

"Is there a dinner party tomorrow night? In other words, do I have to dress up?" I asked.

"No, you can wear whatever you like. You look good in anything," Bernard smiled.

"Shall we go get Susan and Paul and head to dinner?" I asked.

"Sure, Maybel. Let's go."

I opened the door to the study and there were Susan and Paul kissing.

"Oh! Sorry!" I closed the door quickly.

"Looks like Paul and Susan enjoyed meeting each other," I said.

"And here I was worried Paul was going to steal your heart again," Bernard said.

"Let's leave them be. We'll knock on the door when dinner starts."

Bernard and I went back to the kitchen.

"Are you upset Paul kissed Susan?" Bernard asked me.

"No," I said.

"Oh," Bernard looked surprised. "Why not? You have asked about Paul for years."

"I know, but I saw the way he and Susan looked at each other and I'm happy for them. They have such a connection. They both love art, and I don't know, it made me happy when I saw the way they adored each other.

Paul and Susan came into the kitchen looking flushed, their lips red from kissing.

"Hello," Susan said, looking embarrassed. Paul didn't make eye contact.

"Shall we go to dinner now?" I giggled.

"Yes," Susan said, still looking embarrassed and shy about being seen.

Susan turned to leave and I saw Bernard grinning from ear to ear at Paul. Paul's face flushed a deeper shade of red, but a tiny smile danced on his lips.

Bernard saw me watching him and wiped the big grin off his face and we headed to dinner.

After dinner, Paul walked Susan home a few minutes before Bernard walked me home. When Bernard and I finally made our way to my house, we saw Paul and Susan at her front door kissing.

Bernard walked me to my front gate but he did not kiss me. "Goodnight, Maybel."

"Goodnight," I said, then closed the gate behind me.

Catherine was inside with mommy and daddy. She smiled and asked how my evening with Paul went. I was confused at first, and then realized she thought I had gone to have dinner with Paul, which I had, but Paul was not with whom I ended the night at our front gate.

"Paul's art is amazing," I said. And it was. Paul had always had a talented eye for the beauty in placement and space.

Catherine winked slyly at me. "I'm glad you had a nice evening reconnecting with Paul," she smiled cheekily.

I didn't know what else to say so I kissed mommy and daddy on their cheeks and headed upstairs to bed.

Catherine headed to college, and I went with her and mommy and daddy to take her to her dormitory. Daddy cried but quickly wiped away his tears and told her we would be there in six days to visit. "I am going to make sure you are safe and happy, baby," he hugged her.

Daddy held Catherine until Catherine finally told him he could let go.

"I'll never let go, baby."

Mommy had to gently take daddy's elbow and ever so slowly pull him toward her.

"I'll be fine, daddy," Catherine said.

"Six days," daddy said.

"Yes, daddy," Catherine smiled. "I love you, daddy and mommy."

Mommy and daddy again hugged Catherine and mommy again had to take daddy's arm and gently tug.

"I love you, Catherine," I said.

"I love you too. You take good care of mommy and daddy."

"I will. I'll be sure to stay out too late with friends and cause them to worry. It'll be just like you never left," I smiled.

Daddy drove us home in Henry's automobile. Henry offered us his automobile to use so we could spend less time traveling and more time with Catherine. Henry had become daddy's son, I noticed. It was nice having Henry around and he genuinely seemed to love mommy and daddy. I loved Henry too. He confided in me his childhood problems sometimes when they got too great for him to handle alone. I was sad along with Henry. It felt good to help him.

The next day was my first day back to school. I took my bag and books and headed downstairs to breakfast. Bernard was eating breakfast with mommy and daddy.

"Why are you here?" I asked. "When does your college start?"

"I'm taking a year off."

"Bernard made us breakfast," mommy's mouth was full of oatmeal and she smiled tightly, like she eagerly wanted to spit out her oatmeal but didn't want to hurt Bernard's feelings.

"Why? Why are you here in my home making my parents breakfast instead of studying to be a doctor?"

"I want to take a year off and work with my father." Bernard stood up and went to the kitchen counter.

Mommy spit into her napkin before Bernard saw what she did. Daddy, however, ate happily.

Bernard took a little box from the counter. "I made you lunch for your first day of school, Maybel," Bernard smiled and handed me the box.

"Why? What's going on?"

"I wanted to make you lunch, Maybel. May I walk you to school?"

I looked at mommy and then at daddy, who was still happily eating oatmeal. Daddy looked up. "As long as I don't have to cook, I'll eat it no matter what it tastes like." And then quickly added, "And it tastes good, thank you Bernard."

"I'll get better, Mr. Wyndham," Bernard said.

"Would be hard for you to make it worse," daddy muttered, but kept eating anyway.

"Would you like more, Mrs. Wyndham?" Bernard asked mommy.

"No," mommy said too quickly, then smoothed it out with, "Have to watch my figure," she smiled. "It tasted good. Thank you, Bernard."

Mommy took my lunchbox and went to the counter. "I'm just going to add a cookie and a mother's love," she smiled at Bernard.

Bernard took my bag and books while I saw mommy quickly add a sandwich she had made to my lunchbox, I guessed in case Bernard's sandwich tasted as good as his oatmeal.

Mommy handed me my lunchbox and kissed my cheek.

"I'll see you tonight, mommy and daddy," I kissed their cheeks.

I was confused as to why Bernard was in my house, but I didn't want to be late for my first day, so I didn't argue with him.

I walked quickly out the door but Bernard followed just as quickly. "You look nice," Bernard said. "Is that a new dress?"

"Yes," I answered.

We continued walking. "Catherine is at college, you know. She'll return in a couple weeks for a short break."

"Catherine and I aren't dating anymore," Bernard said.

"I know, but why are you here? You're not dating me either."

"I know," Bernard said, "but I miss you and want to take you to school."

We continued walking to my school and my school friends waved and greeted me as I approached.

"Ok, goodbye," I said. I was embarrassed my sister's ex-boyfriend was walking me to school like I was some little child.

I walked faster to meet up with my friends from school, leaving Bernard to stand on the street corner watching.

"I didn't know you were dating anyone," a boy I knew said to me.

"I'm not," I said quickly.

The boy smiled, "Good, glad to hear that."

I entered my school building and went to class. At lunch time I opened my lunchbox and found a note from Bernard.

"Have a great first day back at school. Love, Bernard.

I scoffed and crumpled the paper but couldn't bring myself to throw it in the trash. I put it in my bag instead.

I took a bite of the sandwich Bernard made and that quickly made it into the trash without any hesitation from me. I ate mommy's sandwich. Bernard usually made edible sandwiches at least, but this one was just terrible. I couldn't fathom how someone could mess up a sandwich that much.

After school I laughed and chatted with my friends as we left the building. They lived in different directions of the countryside so I rarely saw them outside of school.

"Hello, Maybel, how was your first day back?" Bernard stood by the flagpole waiting for me.

"Did you used to pick Catherine up from school? I don't ever remember you picking her up."

"No, I didn't. I wanted to walk you home. May I?"

I heard my friends giggling behind me.

"I suppose," I hesitated.

When we were away from my classmates, I asked Bernard why he was following me around.

"I treated you badly over the years. I read some of your old stories you wrote when you were younger and I had not realized how much or how often I hurt your feelings. I would like the chance to make it up to you."

"There's no need. I'm fine. You should go to college, Bernard. Aren't your parents angry?"

"No, they practically own my college and I said I wasn't going this year because I wanted to experience the way normal people work and live. I'm learning about business with my father for a year."

I laughed, "The normal person's experience? Your mansion with your waitstaff is not normal."

"I know, but your parents wouldn't let me live in your guest bedroom. I'm living with my parents and I'm making them breakfast, lunch, and dinner every day, and I'm bookkeeping for them as well. And your father is going to teach me how to choose the best boards at the lumberyard tomorrow."

"Bernard, I have a date Friday. Can you please go to college and let me finish high school without you babysitting me?" I was unsure why he was babysitting me, and it angered me that he still considered me a child.

"I'm not babysitting you, Maybel. I enjoy being with you. And what is your date's name?"

"Not you."

"Not You? is that Chinese? He sounds Chinese."

"Bernard, leave me alone."

I walked faster and Bernard followed. I went inside my house and upstairs.

"How was school, honey?" mommy called.

"Fine. Bernard followed me home. Can you feed him and take him back to his house?" I yelled down to her. Bernard's sudden and intense attention to me was odd and irritating.

After I finished my homework, I went downstairs and was happy to see it was only mommy, daddy, and me.

"How was school?" daddy asked.

"Fine. Why did Bernard take me to school and pick me up?"

"I think he's trying to say he's sorry for teasing you when you two were younger," mommy said.

"By not going to college, and by making my lunch?"

"Yes," mommy said.

"That's stupid," I said.

The next morning Bernard made eggs, or rather he attempted making eggs. "May I walk you to school?" he asked.

"It's really not necessary," I said. I took a slice of bread instead of eating the burnt eggs he cooked that were swimming in grease.

Bernard handed me my lunchbox. "I made cookies for my parents last night and put one in your lunch box." Bernard smiled and handed me my lunch.

"Thank you," I said. "Goodbye."

I kissed mommy and daddy's cheeks and walked to the front door. Bernard followed. "I enjoy morning walks. I promise I won't embarrass you in front of your friends."

"Fine," I grumbled.

I closed the front gate behind us. "I don't need a babysitter. Remember when your father made Henry babysit me at one of your parties? I don't need you to babysit me."

"I know. I'm not babysitting you. I know you can take care of yourself. I enjoy being with you," Bernard said simply.

My friends giggled when they saw Bernard and me approaching. "Ok, that's far enough. Goodbye, Bernard."

I walked faster and into my school with my friends, who were still giggling about Bernard.

"He's so handsome," Frannie cooed.

"He's so gorgeous," Rita cooed.

I didn't respond. I didn't want them to ask me why my sister's ex-boyfriend was babysitting me while my sister was away at college. I went to class and at lunch, I opened my lunch box hoping mommy had added a sandwich again. There was another note.

"Dear Maybel, the day we met, the first thing you ever said to me was, 'Who is this strange boy, Catherine?' Love, Bernard."

I rolled my eyes. I thought to myself that Bernard shouldn't remind me of our beginnings because it served to do nothing more than remind me of how he loved Catherine and ignored me, and I wrote that on the back of the note and put it back in my lunch box.

After school Bernard waited for me at the flagpole again. "Hello, Maybel, how was your day?"

"Fine. How was the lumberyard with daddy?"

"I picked out the worst planks of wood."

"Sounds like what I expected," I said dryly.

"I'll get better," Bernard said. He walked me home.

"See you tomorrow," Bernard said to me at my front gate.

I walked into my house and went upstairs to do my homework.

The next morning Bernard made bacon. I didn't think anyone could make bacon taste bad, but Bernard somehow managed to do just that.

Bernard handed me my lunchbox and walked me to school.

At lunch, I opened my lunchbox and Bernard had left me another note.

"Yes, you remember meeting me at Catherine's birthday party, and I often spent time with her while ignoring you. I'm sorry I ignored you. Come to my house after school and you will see I have kept the teacup and saucer you made me that day from the mud with which you hit Paul. It's in my treasure box along with my grandfather's photograph. Love, Bernard."

I ate mommy's sandwich and thought about what to write back.

I wrote, "I cannot go to your house. I have a date with a boy. Go to college."

After school Bernard walked me home. "Goodbye," I said.

"Won't you come to my house?"

I took my note from my lunchbox and thrust it into Bernard's hand. "I have a date. Goodbye."

I left Bernard at my gate and went inside to study. I didn't have a date. I wanted Bernard to go away. It felt strange to be suddenly at the center of Bernard's attention and I didn't know how to feel about his new interest in me. I was very confused.

The next morning Bernard made pancakes that tasted dry and hard.

"Bernard, sweetheart, how many eggs did you use?" mommy asked him.

"Eggs? None," Bernard answered. "How many are you supposed to use?"

"Maybe try two next time," mommy said. "They still taste wonderful, dear."

"Just pour extra syrup," daddy winked at me.

Bernard walked me to school. "How was your date last night?"

"Fine," I said.

At lunch I read Bernard's note.

"I'll go to college with you next year. I have always hated leaving you, and I have always been terrified you'll have a boyfriend upon my return. I like seeing you every day. I love you. Love, Bernard."

I wrote a reply. "I'm attending college far away from your college."

After school Bernard walked me home. "May I come to your house for dinner tonight?"

"It's Friday. I have a date, remember?" I wasn't mean. I reminded Bernard of my date without feeling any guilt though. Bernard was not my boyfriend.

"I'll see you tomorrow then."

"We're going to see Catherine," I said.

"I know, I'm driving you," Bernard smiled.

"Get Catherine flowers. I knew you'd reconcile sooner rather than later."

"Catherine and I are not dating. I'll always love her though, and I want to help your parents by driving them and you."

I turned and went through my gate and closed it behind me.

I went to the library after dinner and met several classmates. It wasn't the date I'd made Bernard believe. I hoped Bernard would be sad knowing his efforts this week had been in vain. He could not erase years of me seeing him kiss Catherine and think I would suddenly be with him simply because he wanted me now. I became angry just thinking about King Bernard suddenly requesting my companionship and summoning me to his court like the king he thought he was. He could get anything he wanted with his wealth, but he could not get me. I figured he would stop pestering me and go to college soon, and I knew he would rekindle his romance with Catherine as they had always done.

After studying history and math, I walked home. Bernard and daddy were on my front porch.

"How was studying with friends?" daddy asked.

"It was a study date," I said, and held up my history and math books. "And there were boys there." I narrowed my eyes at Bernard, "A study date with boys!" I emphasized the word 'date.'

"You know, honey, Catherine always pretended boys weren't with her studying, but you just held up a giant sign saying you were with boys, and that's how I know I can trust you with boys."

"I was with a boy on a date, daddy!"

"If you were doing something sneaky, you would have hidden it better," daddy said.

"I was doing lots of sneaky things, daddy!" I stomped my foot down hard. "It's just that I am not as good a liar as Catherine!"

Daddy smiled.

"I have a lot of homework still. Goodnight, daddy."

I went upstairs thinking I would use studying as my excuse for tomorrow so I could stay home instead of traveling with Bernard. I didn't want to watch him rekindle his relationship with Catherine. They would though, as they had always done.

The next morning, I went downstairs with my textbooks. "I have to write an essay and study geography, so I'd better stay home. Please give my regards to Catherine."

"Alright, honey," mommy said.

That had been easier than I anticipated. I was now free to do anything I wanted all day long.

"Good morning." Henry came into our kitchen. "I'm ready."

I raised my eyebrows, "For what? What are you doing today?"

"Driving you to see Catherine," Henry smiled. "I may even stop for ice cream if you're good," he winked at me.

"Maybel is staying here to study," mommy said as she went to give Henry a hug. "I have some cookies for you, honey," mommy pinched Henry's cheek.

Daddy came downstairs smelling like aftershave. "Let's go scare the boys away from Catherine, shall we!" daddy excitedly smiled. He took mommy's hand.

"Maybel is staying home to study, dear," mommy told daddy.

"Alright honey, see you tonight," daddy kissed my cheek and they left.

I laid on my family room sofa smiling. I had the whole day to dance around singing in my nightgown if I wanted.

"Good morning, Maybel," Bernard walked through my front door.

"Why are you here?" I demanded.

"You didn't need me to drive you to see Catherine so your parents said I could come inside."

"Henry was going to drive us."

"Henry didn't have enough room in his automobile so he was going to take your parents, and I was going to drive you. Your parents said you were staying home to study though."

"I don't have to study; I just didn't want to be with you!"

"I figured as much, but I understand. I deserve your coldness. Have you eaten breakfast? Shall I make us eggs?"

"Oh, please don't," I grimaced.

"Will you play with me today?" Bernard smiled.

I stared at him like he was insane.

"I always took for it granted that you always came to me to ask me to be with you. When you stopped doing that, I realized how much I took you for granted. Would you like to row to your island? We could go to the slate waterfalls behind my house. The candy store is open."

I exhaled in disgust. "Just take me to see Catherine. I may as well go now."

"I'd love to," Bernard smiled. "There's a restaurant nearby your father spoke about fondly. May I take you to dinner there?"

"Just take me to see your ex-girlfriend, the one you dated for years, the one you were going to marry, and the one I know you'll begin dating again."

"We never got quite that far in our relationship, but yes, that's the sister you are talking about. We are not reconciling as we have both discussed our feelings, and decided we will remain friends." Bernard remained polite, which really angered me.

"Why are you suddenly nice? You've never acted this way to me before. It's an act, like a role you play in theater. Stop acting."

"I'm not acting. I genuinely love you," Bernard said.

"This is the way you acted with Catherine. You were polite, and as soon as she turned her head, you told me to go away so you could kiss her without my annoying presence."

"I was mean to you."

"Yes, so go away! I don't want you around! I hate you and I want to be alone! The more you try to push yourself into my life, and the lives of my family, the more I hate you, and the more I want you to go away! You can't possibly think after years of making fun of me and kissing my sister in front of me, that I would suddenly want to date you! If all you want is friendship, then fine, we can be friends, but if what you are wanting is a romantic relationship, know that I do not want to date you after watching you kiss my sister for years!"

"We used to be friends," Bernard said gently. "Do you remember when we played together all day every day?"

"I was eleven and you only played with me to pass your boredom until Catherine returned home! That's exactly what you are doing now! You want someone to play with until Catherine agrees to date you again!"

"I liked being with you. I preferred playing with you than being with Catherine and I should have asked you for a date years ago, but I didn't know how to do that without hurting Catherine. I should have been honest with Catherine and you. I'm sorry, Maybel."

"I had sex with Theo over the summer! And then he left me to go to England! So you can go away! I've had sex! I'm not a virgin!"

"I don't care. I love you and want to marry you."

"Henry and I have touched each other and kissed each other in special places! Go away Bernard! You are not going to want me now! Go!"

"I still want to marry you and I don't care about Theo or Henry."

I screamed in frustration. "Just take me to Catherine! I need to talk to her about a boy at school who likes me and I need her advice."

Really, I wanted to see how Bernard and Catherine behaved around each other.

"Great," Bernard smiled. "I hear the steak at that restaurant tastes wonderful."

Bernard's bizarre indifference after I lied about having sex infuriated me. I expected him to be angry and storm off and never speak to me again.

I suddenly froze at my front door. My hand was on the doorframe and I steadied myself.

"What's wrong?" Bernard asked.

"Nothing," I said quickly. "I forgot something."

I dashed upstairs and into my bedroom. I reasoned that if Bernard wasn't concerned about me losing my virginity and having sex with two men, then he must have had sex too. I thought for a moment. I took several deep breaths. I still wanted to observe what kind of relationship Bernard and Catherine had. I couldn't fathom Catherine would be accepting of Bernard's newfound, open devotion to me, and I expected to see Bernard angry when boys flirted with Catherine. Boys always flirted with Catherine. And then, I figured out how to make Bernard go away. I decided to make boys flirt with me, too. Bernard would be rude to me, like usual when a boy flirted with me and Bernard got jealous, and then I could finally shed his annoying presence. I changed into Catherine's old, lilac dress that made my breasts look plump and clung to my behind.

I walked downstairs. Bernard's eyes popped out of his stupid, handsome skull. "You look beautiful. Is that a new dress?"

"No. It's Catherine's. She wore it that night you massaged her upper thigh under the dinner table," I casually remarked.

"I never went that far. I touched just above her knee maybe, but never farther than that."

"Sure, Bernard," I scoffed.

"I didn't, Maybel," Bernard said as he opened the passenger's door for me.

"I don't care if you did," I said as I stared straight ahead.

Bernard drove us through town, toward the main road out of town, and toward Catherine's college. A boy from school was playing ball with his little brother and stopped to see who had an automobile. He recognized me and smiled and waved. I smiled and waved back.

"He seems nice," Bernard said.

"He's the head of our debate team."

"Oh, so he's the master debater," Bernard smirked.

I made a disgusted noise at Bernard. I secretly wanted to tell Susan that joke later because it was funny.

We drove through fields almost ready for harvest, and past dairy farms and ponds. I loved automobiles so much more than carriages, although I missed watching Big Ben swish his tail.

"I miss you so much," Bernard whispered.

"How many women have you had sex with Bernard?"

"What? None."

"Oh, yes, you're still a virgin," I snorted.

"I am, just don't tell anyone. I don't want people to know."

"Sex feels great," I said.

"I'll let you know after we're married."

"I'm not marrying you. You were mean to me and you cheated on Catherine."

"I know," he replied.

We continued driving in silence for a while. My mind began to forget about being angry as I watched ducks and deer. "Stop!" I screamed.

Bernard stopped so fast the dust in the road churned under us.

"What's wrong?" Bernard looked scared I was hurt.

I opened my door and went to the road in front of us and moved a wee, little turtle to the side of the road. Bernard, from his seat behind the wheel, breathed out heavily, and he rested his head on the steering wheel.

I returned to my seat next to him. "Ok, let's go," I said.

"All that for a turtle?"

"Is something wrong, Bernard? Are you mad at me?"

"No," he said. "I thought something happened to you. I'm glad you are well."

We continued driving and finally arrived at Catherine's college.

"What will you study next year, Bernard? Catherine is taking philosophy, math, English, geography, and chemistry now."

"As a medical student, I will likely take a lot of science, biology, and math classes."

"I'm sure you've already studied anatomy," I said with malice.

"From a book, yes. From a person, no." Bernard did not look annoyed at me. I had not ruffled his feathers as I'd hoped.

"Shall we find Catherine," Bernard smiled at me.

"I'll break you down yet," I said. "I know this calm, and clearly fake demeanor has limitations, and I'll find them."

"I've already thought about all the things you might tell me about: sex and boyfriends, and none of it bothers me. I'm going to marry you. I love you and I don't care who you've had sex with."

"You're not being honest," I said as we walked toward Catherine's dormitory. "You're not acting like yourself. You're acting like a nice person."

"Maybel, look, a flower." Bernard pulled a flower from behind his back.

"Fantastic, you're a magician now instead of a doctor. Thanks," I said dryly as I took the flower.

We went to Catherine's dormitory and I led Bernard to Catherine's room.

"This is where you'll reconcile and have sex with Catherine," I whispered as we approached Catherine's room.

"I'm not having sex with Catherine. I've never had sex with anyone."

"Well, you had sex with someone, otherwise you would not have been so placid with me having sex with two men."

"I have not had sex with anyone, and I don't care that you had sex," Bernard stated calmly.

"Well with Henry it wasn't actual intercourse," I whispered as we stood outside Catherine's room. "It was only his face between my legs. You've at least done that."

"Well yes, everyone has done at least that," Bernard admitted.

I kicked his penis right there in the hallway with onlookers gawking.

"I was joking," Bernard wheezed, "but now I know you're jealous, and that makes me happy," he groaned as he writhed on the wooden floorboards.

"Maybel!" Catherine hissed. "What is going on?"

"There was a fly on Bernard's pants. I killed it," I shrugged.

"Get in here!" she hissed at me. "You're embarrassing me!"

"How was your first week at college?" I asked innocently.

"Fine," Catherine said angrily.

Bernard slowly stood up and hobbled into Catherine's room. "Hello, Catherine," he greeted her.

"Why are you here, Bernard?" Catherine crossed her arms.

"I brought Maybel. She wants to ask your advice about boys."

"Oh?" Catherine raised her eyebrows. "You have a boyfriend?"

"Several boys are interested in me and I need to ask you what to say and do," I watched Bernard smugly.

Catherine smiled, "Let's talk later."

Bernard hobbled over to sit in a chair next to Henry. Mommy and daddy sat on Catherine's bed. Catherine's roommate overtly flirted with Henry.

"Oh, Maybel!" mommy said excitedly, "You came!"

"I missed Catherine," I said. I did miss Catherine, but I wanted to observe the nature of the relationship between Catherine and Bernard.

Henry politely listened to Catherine's roommate flirt. Daddy read a college bulletin about sports. And Catherine looked annoyed at Bernard.

"You look nice, Catherine," Bernard said.

"Thank you, you as well," Catherine replied.

Bernard sat doubled over still.

"And who's this?" Catherine's roommate smiled at Bernard.

"My ex-boyfriend," Catherine said dryly.

"Nice to make your acquaintance," Bernard said.

"I cannot believe you have two such fine, young men with you Catherine," Catherine's roommate said.

Catherine looked annoyed. "Bernard, why don't you take Maybel to the sports arena, or the park, or the candy store around the corner?"

"Ok." Bernard stood up, but still looked uncomfortable standing with his kicked penis. "Maybel? Shall we?"

Bernard and I walked out of Catherine's dormitory. "You wanted Catherine because she is first prize but you settled for me." I felt ugly next to Catherine.

"No, Maybel, I wanted you. I realized I didn't care if other men flirted with Catherine and that seemed to anger her. She flirted with them more to make me jealous and I just didn't care. I know I was wrong. I should have broken up with her a long time ago. I only wanted you, and when boys looked at you, I wanted to punch them. Maybel," Bernard stopped and held my arm. He looked hurt. "I was so angry you didn't return my affection. It hurt me, so I took out my hurt on you by being mean. I'm sorry, and I will eventually prove to you I love you, and I'll prove to Catherine I'm sorry as well."

I walked with Bernard with my arms crossed. I was still steaming mad.

"Maybel, I'm sorry I hurt you and I'm sorry I hurt Catherine."

"You were unforgivable, so stop being nice! I don't want you, and neither does Catherine!"

"I know," Bernard said.

Bernard took me to the candy store instead of the other places Catherine recommended. He still knew my weaknesses.

"Maybel," Bernard said softly, "may I buy you a custard?"

"Yes," I said.

"Chocolate with banana slices and ten cherries?"

"Yes," I said. I acted aloof but really, I wanted those cherries.

Bernard got a dozen cherries.

"I'm not giving you two," I said.

"They're all for you," he smiled.

I ate all twelve even though I started feeling full after five. I was not about to give Bernard any cherries.

"If Catherine came to you and expressed her desire to reunite, what would you do?"

"I do not want to date Catherine. I'll always love her, but I've never loved her the way I've always loved you. I should have expressed my love for you years ago and I am sorry to both you and Catherine."

Bernard's answers seemed too well-thought-out. He sounded poised and polished like Catherine when she spoke like a politician's wife.

"Maybel, may I take you to that restaurant your father mentioned to me?"

"I think I'm going to vomit if I think about food," I said.

"Would you like to take a walk?"

"That might help," I conceded. "I might vomit in a bush though, so it might be better if I go alone. I don't want you to see me vomit."

"I've seen you vomit."

"I don't want you to see me vomit again," I said.

"I understand, Maybel."

I stood up holding my stomach. I suddenly, without warning, burped from the bottom-most part of my gut.

The sorority girls looked at me with disgust.

"Wow! I feel so much better!" I exclaimed.

Bernard smiled and stood next to me, not at all embarrassed.

"If I were at your college and burped like that, you would be mortified to be seen with me, Bernard."

Bernard let out an equally loud burp, maybe even bigger than mine. "I will always be proud of you by my side," he smiled.

I crinkled my nose. "That was disgusting! You're disgusting!"

"I'm sorry, honey," Bernard said.

"Do not call me honey," I said sternly.

"I'm sorry," he said.

"Let's go say goodbye to Catherine," I said.

"Yes, dear," Bernard said.

I turned quickly and Bernard held his penis and bent his waist in anticipation.

"I'm not going to kick you," I said, "but don't call me honey or dear! We're not dating! You have no idea how hurtful you were! That is not something I can forget! Catherine cannot suddenly forget either!" I looked at Bernard with pain in my eyes. "You really hurt me. You hurt my sister."

"I know," Bernard said. "I swear to you I'm sorry. I swear I will make it up to you and Catherine."

"I have another date next Friday, Bernard. I can't forgive you."

"I understand," he said. "I'd like to keep trying though. Maybe you'll see how much I love you one day."

"Love isn't something you suddenly decide you feel. Love is something that prevents you from trying to hurt someone. You didn't love me. You wanted to hurt me. I'm trying to hurt you now. I obviously don't love you."

"I do love you, Maybel. I always have and I always will."

Bernard and I walked back to Catherine's room. Henry was still listening to Catherine's roommate. He looked ready to leave.

"Oh good, you're here. Let's get you home now to finish that essay you said you needed to write." Henry silently begged me to help him leave.

"Ok," I said.

I left with Henry and Bernard looked sad.

On our way home I asked Henry why Bernard was being nice.

"I think he's sorry," Henry told me.

"I told him you and I had oral sex, but not intercourse," I said.

"We've never done anything! Maybel your father will kill me before I hear his gun cock!"

"Bernard won't tell daddy anything. He's afraid of daddy."

"I'm afraid of your father!" Henry looked terrified.

"Daddy's a big teddy bear."

"To you and Catherine!" Henry's voice was high-pitched.

"Bernard didn't care that you and I had oral sex, and he didn't care that I had sex with Theo either!" I said angrily.

"You had sex?" Henry looked jealous and angry, which surprised me.

"Henry, I'm not sure I ever interpret people correctly. Are you jealous?"

"A little," he snapped angrily, "I like you a lot Maybel!"

"I never had sex with anyone. I told Bernard that so he would leave me alone," I confessed.

"You don't want Bernard's attention?"

"No. I used to want his attention, but now I do not. I want someone who respects me."

We arrived at my house. I was stiff from sitting.

"Goodnight, Henry," I said.

"Wait, may I come in?" Henry asked me.

"Oh, yes, of course. I'm sorry," I said. "My mind is elsewhere right now."

We sat together on the sofa. I leaned against Henry and he wrapped his arm around me as he read a funny story. Henry made funny voices for the characters and we laughed.

Henry took his arm off my shoulder when mommy and daddy came home. I didn't understand why boys were scared of daddy, but they were. Bernard came in the front door and sat in a chair across from Henry and me.

Mommy and daddy said goodnight and quickly went upstairs. Daddy patted mommy's behind as they rounded the corner and she giggled and slapped his shoulder.

Bernard sat watching Henry and me from a chair across from us. Henry put his arm back around me and finished the story.

Henry yawned, "Goodnight, sweetheart," Henry kissed my cheek. "I'm tired and going home to bed."

"Goodnight, Henry," I said.

I rested my head on my arm on the sofa and began nodding off to sleep.

Bernard went to the chair by our fireplace and took a blanket and laid it on me.

When I awoke sometime later, the other sofa had been pulled in front of me, and Bernard was asleep on it facing me. We used to sleep together like this when we were younger.

I closed my eyes and fell into a deeper sleep, feeling safe with Bernard nearby.

When I awoke in the morning, Bernard was snoring lightly and drooling. His hair was messy and wavy and I really wanted to run my fingers through it like I used to do. Sometime during the night, he must have gotten too warm and taken off his shirt. He was more muscular than I remembered.

"Good morning!" Daddy farted loudly from behind the sofa where Bernard had slept.

"Daddy!" I grumbled.

"Looks like Bernard spent the night," daddy yelled to mommy. "Where's my spear?"

"In your workshop," mommy yelled back.

"Bernard! Wake up!" daddy yelled, "It's time to hunt Crackadoos for breakfast!"

Bernard halfway opened his eyes. "Yes, Mr. Wyndham. I'm coming."

"Daddy!" I protested.

"Crackadoos are a delicacy, Maybel. Get up Bernard! You'll need to get going soon or they'll go back into hiding!"

Bernard stood and put on his shirt while still half asleep. "Yes, Mr. Wyndham."

"You'll need this," daddy handed Bernard a metal bucket. "Better hurry, son!"

Bernard smiled, "You called me son, sir!"

"Go out back, Bernard!" daddy grumbled, obviously embarrassed of showing Bernard any affection.

Bernard took the bucket and went out our back door.

Daddy turned to me laughing like a giddy school girl. "Every morning he comes back with something different asking if he's found the Crackadoos," daddy giggled. "Every morning I look disappointed and ask him if he needs me to draw a map to his anus too, since he can't find a damn thing with that worthless, rich-boy schooling that taught him nothing of value in this real world outside of luxury." Daddy giggled all the way into the kitchen.

I stood up and went upstairs to brush my teeth and change my dress. I heard huffing and grunting outside my window. Bernard was in our courtyard looking for Crackadoos under rocks with his bucket. I giggled watching him. I sat by my window watching him and I couldn't help but laugh. He was trying so hard to find those Crackadoos.

I heard daddy shouting from the kitchen window, "Do you need me to draw that map yet?"

"No, sir," Bernard answered.

Just before lunch Bernard returned with his bucket full of various dead bugs and beetles. "Are any of these Crackadoos, Mr. Wyndham?"

"No, Bernard, they are not. Go dump that in the burn pile and you can try again tomorrow," daddy grumbled. Daddy sounded annoyed at Bernard's incompetence.

Bernard left out our back door and daddy turned to me giggling like a little boy. "He's so ignorant! Your children will be pretty like you, but dumb like him," daddy continued slapping his knee and laughing heartily.

"I'm not marrying Bernard. He treated me like a dog following him around all the time," I said angrily.

Daddy winked at mommy then looked back at me. "Bernard is ok, honey, but don't tell him I said that. I still have some chores around the house that I don't want to do."

Bernard returned to the kitchen without his bucket. "What shall we do today, Mr. Wyndham?"

"Mrs. Wyndham needs help sizing a dress for one of her very tall clients. You may eat lunch first and then you'll stand on the stool while Mrs. Wyndham covers you in pretty pink fabric and pins it to suit her client's wishes.

"Yes, sir," Bernard said, and sat next to me at the kitchen table.

Daddy smiled at mommy like an excited child awaiting his Christmas morning presents. Bernard looked tired from Crackadoo hunting.

Mommy made us a delicious lunch and daddy ate every bite and then took the rest of Bernard's apple slices. "You weren't eating these were you?" daddy asked him.

"No, sir," Bernard said as he finished the one apple slice daddy didn't take.

"Time for dress making!" daddy rubbed his hands together with great anticipation.

Mommy snorted, "Come on then, Bernard, let's get this over with."

"Yes, Mrs. Wyndham," Bernard said.

I washed the dishes and swept the kitchen floor while daddy kept interrupting my cleaning with reports of what Bernard looked like at every stage of their dress making.

"Baby," daddy whispered, "get in here! Bernard looks great in pink! The neckline really accentuates his cheekbones, mommy says!"

I went into mommy's little sewing room and there stood Bernard on a stool with mommy's client instructing mommy on how many ruffles she wanted around the neckline and how much lace at the bodice.

Bernard looked truly miserable and that made me happy.

"Bernard you look beautiful," I gloated.

"Thank you, Maybel," he said. Bernard looked defeated.

Daddy took my hand and pulled me back into our kitchen. "Maybel, this is so much fun!" daddy chuckled.

I laughed. "It is, isn't it!"

The next morning Bernard made us breakfast. "I made pumpkin bread last night for my parents," he said. "I made extra for you." Bernard looked proud.

Mommy swallowed hard. "How many eggs do you use this time?"

"Pumpkin bread needs eggs, too?" Bernard asked.

"Yes, dear, but your version tastes wonderful. Thank you." Mommy tried to hide her distaste.

Daddy happily ate his pumpkin bread with coffee. "I didn't have to make it, and mommy has extra time to snuggle in bed with me now," daddy smiled big and winked at mommy, who blushed deeply.

Bernard walked me to school. "Did I look pretty in pink?" he asked.

"Yes," I smiled.

"I like when you smile at me," he said.

"Don't get used to it," I wiped away my smile.

"I'll see you this afternoon. Have a great day at school," Bernard said.

"You sound like my daddy walking me to school when I was a child."

Undeterred, Bernard replied, "I bet you were the sweetest and prettiest girl there."

"No, your ex-girlfriend was," I said, and walked into my school building.

My lunch note written by Bernard said, "Remember when we danced at Christmas that first year?"

Attached was a photograph of Bernard and me posing together. He was much taller than me. We were happily smiling at the camera operator. Bernard held my hand while his other hand was wrapped around me. I stared at the photograph longer than I'd realized and suddenly lunch time was over.

After school Bernard waited for me. "Did you like the photograph?" he asked.

"Yes," I said.

I walked a little way with Bernard. And then, I stopped walking. "Everything from our past reminds me of you dating Catherine though. I kept searching the photograph wondering where she was."

"We'll make new memories together, Maybel, just the two of us. I promise."

I still felt awkward with Bernard. "I still feel like I'm cheating on Catherine," I admitted.

"We're not cheating. We're having a lovely afternoon walk," Bernard said.

Bernard took me to my gate. "Goodbye," I said.

"Goodnight," Bernard replied. He knew I had never said goodbye to him until recently and he refused to say goodbye to me now.

"Bernard!" I cried. "I had sex already!" Tears rolled down my cheeks. "Go away!" I pleaded.

"Have you really had sex or are you trying to upset me and see what my reaction would be if you told me you had sex already?" Bernard looked like I kicked his stomach hard, a little like he was about to vomit, and a little like he was going to cry.

"I've already had sex!" I cried. "Go away!"

"Who?" Bernard could barely make the word come from his mouth.

"I told you already! Theo!" I screamed. "So just go away! Please!"

I heaved and cried.

Bernard looked utterly destroyed.

I stood and stared at him as he looked down at the damp ground, and then he slowly turned. He walked with his head down and I watched him leave me, yet again.

I dreaded the next morning without Bernard being downstairs cooking breakfast and packing my lunch. I felt angry at myself for liking his attention. All the years I had yearned for his affection, and now he gave me his full attention publicly. I should have been overjoyed, but I was resentful.

I could not forgive him for all the years of hurting me. It would be best, I decided, to find someone deserving of my love.

The next morning, when I awoke for school, I had my sandwich for lunch already packed and inside my school bag. I had already decided to run downstairs and out the door without looking into the kitchen. I was scared to not see Bernard there holding my lunch.

I sat on my bed and waited until it was five minutes past the time I normally left for school, then ran downstairs. I smelled bacon and heard mommy chattering away to daddy. I bolted to the door yelling to them that I woke up late and that I loved them.

I ran quickly to our gate at the end of our walkway. I felt the stinging sensation in my nose and eyes of tears about to form. I took a deep breath and opened the gate.

"Maybel!"

I turned around and there was Bernard running behind me with a sandwich and an apple. "I don't care about what you did, nor do I care about with whom you did those things. I love you."

"Why? I told you," I whispered, "I've been loved. I'm not a virgin."

"I don't care. I want to spend our lives together."

"I'm late for school. Goodbye, Bernard."

I slammed shut the gate and ran to school. My eyes were bleary though, and I tripped on a slab of uneven sidewalk. I fell hard and my right cheek hurt.

An old woman sweeping her porch saw me and came to me. "Miss, let me take you home. You don't look well."

"I'm fine," I said. "I'm late for school." I felt water on my lips and I smacked them. I tasted salty blood mixed with the toothpaste I'd used earlier.

"Honey, you're not well. I know a good doctor." The old lady came toward me.

"I'm fine," I said. "It's just a small cut."

And then I took three steps and felt my knees burn. I had scrapes all down my knees and shins.

I thanked the old woman for her concern, then hobbled to school. Class had already started and the secretary saw me enter late.

"Maybel Wyndham, what has happened to you?" She looked annoyed at my tardiness at first, and then truly concerned when she eyed me up and down.

"I fell on an uneven sidewalk. I'm fine, really."

"No, you're not! You need to go home now and see a doctor. Your socks are soiled with blood that's trickled down from your knees!"

"Really, I'm fine, Mrs. Trumbull. I just fell and as soon as I wash off my legs, I'll look normal."

"Go home, dear," Mrs. Trumbull ordered.

I reluctantly turned and walked to the front doors. The principal, Mr. Sunders, told me to wait.

"Maybel, I'll drive you to a doctor. I think you may need a doctor. I'll drive you there, and then alert your father."

"It's really not that bad. I'm fine," I said.

"You don't look fine. I'll take you to a doctor. I am certain your parents would insist."

Mr. Sunders drove me toward my home, then turned right. I started to feel my stomach twist. I guessed where we were headed. Mr. Sunders turned onto Cherry Street and I then knew immediately where he was taking me.

"I do not need a doctor," I pleaded.

"I know this doctor. He's a good doctor. Your parents are close by, and I'll go to your house immediately to inform them of your situation."

"I fell! I've had worse scrapes! I promise you I'm fine!"

"Nonsense. Dr. Charleston will look at your bloody gashes along your legs and fix you right up. You have to be careful about these things, Maybel. Infection can lead to amputation and, God forbid, death."

I winced in anticipation. Mr. Sunders took me by my elbow like I was an invalid. "Walk slowly, Maybel. You just never know if something is broken."

Mr. Sunders led me into Mr. Charleston's office. I felt my stomach tighten. My lungs squeezed.

"Maybel!" Mr. Charleston's secretary, Mrs. Appleton, screeched. "What has happened to you?"

"Dr. Charleston! Dr. Charleston!" Mrs. Appleton shouted.

Mr. Charleston came barreling out of his office. "Maybel! What has happened to you?" He swooped down and in an instant, he picked me up in his big, bear arms and carried me into his exam room, not the one for coughs or snotty noses, the one for bad things, like broken hips, and for when a patient's heart stopped.

"I'm fine!" I screamed. "I just fell! Why can't people leave me alone? I'm fine! I've had much worse falls and nobody gave a damn what happened to me! It's just some scratches!"

"Maybel, please," Mr. Charleston blocked my angry swats. "I'm trying to see exactly what needs to be repaired," he pleaded.

"My heart!" I screamed. "My heart needs to be repaired! Your son has broken my heart so many times it's irreparable! I hate Bernard!"

Mrs. Charleston and Henry were suddenly in the exam room. I figured that nosy secretary called them.

"I don't know what to say to a girl," Mr. Charleston pleaded with Mrs. Charleston. He went to her and took her hands.

Mrs. Charleston let go of her husband's hands and approached me. "Maybel," she said softly, "what happened?"

"I fell. Why is everyone worried about me? I only fell!"

Mrs. Charleston patted my hand. "I just wanted to make sure you were ok, sweetheart. You know Mr. Charleston and I love you dearly."

I exhaled loudly. I didn't want to hear her polite talk.

I felt like I had begun a great tirade, but I didn't remember what I'd said, because the next thing I remembered, was waking up with mommy and daddy around a bed in which I laid."

"What happened?" I asked.

"You're fine, baby," daddy patted my hand. "You had cuts on your legs and lips, but you're fine, just some stitches."

I felt groggy.

"You were given some medicine, honey," mommy said. "You were given stitches in your knees and lip. You'll be ok though."

"Mommy, I want to go home."

"We'll leave as soon as you can stand," mommy squeezed my hand.

"Mommy, I'm mad at Bernard. He hasn't treated me well. I don't want to see him ever again."

"I know dear. You were quite angry when you spoke earlier, before the medicine made you sleepy."

"What did I say?"

"Bernard teased you a lot, apparently. You told him to go away and never return," mommy informed me.

I stared out the window. Stupid bluebirds were singing.

"You sounded a bit bawdy, like you had been paying attention at the hardware store," mommy crossed her arms and raised an eyebrow at daddy.

"Maybel, I'm sorry, and I love you!" Bernard called from the hallway.

"Go away!" I screamed.

"Maybel, I don't particularly care for Bernard, or any boy that likes you, and I would rather that any suitors for my little girls," daddy raised his voice, "die in flames if they hurt my baby girls," daddy lowered his voice back to normal level again, "but Bernard isn't the most horrible, obnoxious, piece of horse shit to ever get stuck on the bottom of my boot."

"Thank you, Mr. Wyndham, I think?" Bernard called from the hallway.

"Shut up, Bernard!" daddy yelled back.

"Yes, sir. If I ever have a daughter, I will spend every day apologizing to you."

"I pray to God Almighty you have six daughters, Bernard!" daddy screamed back at Bernard.

"I'll name one Danielle, sir."

"Shut up, number two!"

Daddy paused. There was silence. Daddy returned to speaking to me.

"Maybel, you are smart and you're going to be alright no matter if you marry or not. I'm absolutely, definitively not defending Bernard, but I was an idiot boy once, mommy can attest to that, and I am sorry for things I've said and done when I was young."

"Thank you, sir," Bernard's voice came from the hallway.

"That being said, I will slit his throat with the dull side of a rock if you'd like," daddy watched me, waiting for me to approve his plan.

There was silence from the hallway.

"No thank you, daddy. If a throat needs to be slit with the dull side of a rock, I'll do it myself."

"You're such a good girl," daddy kissed my forehead.

"I love you, daddy."

"I love you too, baby."

Mommy took my hand and whispered into my ear, "I'll do far worse than a cut with a rock. Remember that, sweetheart. I brought you into this world, and I'll take anyone out of it to protect you." Mommy kissed my forehead. "I love you."

I smiled up at mommy. "I love you, too."

"Would you like to hear what Bernard has to say, or would you like to rest before we take you home?" mommy asked me.

"Tell Bernard to go away. I want to finish school and then I'll leave for college. I'm just really tired, mommy."

"As you wish," mommy squeezed my hand.

"Wait," I said. "I want to tell Bernard something. Can you please let us talk alone for a couple minutes?"

Mommy and daddy left and Bernard entered. He looked like he had been listening and was expecting my rejection.

"Maybel, I'm sorry, and I do love you."

"I've never had sex," I whispered. "I'm still a virgin. I said I was with Theo and Henry to hurt you the way you hurt me all these years. I don't think I'll ever be able to hurt you as badly as you have hurt me, and certainly not for so many years, because I'm not cruel. I don't have it in me to be so cruel for so long. I want to be alone. Go to college, or wherever you want to go. I don't want to be with you, Bernard. I'm going to graduate then move away soon. You should move on too."

Bernard looked sad, but also like he expected me to tell him to leave.

"Maybel, I will leave you for now, but not forever. I'm not saying goodbye to you ever."

Bernard looked lonely as he turned and left.

I threw off my bed covers and swung my legs down to the floor. The cold marble floor hurt the soles of my feet and I gasped. I tried to stand but my knees felt like they were ripping apart at seams. I threw my head back and my body followed my head back onto the bed. I laid there for a minute and then Mr. Charleston entered the room.

"How's my favorite patient?" he asked me.

"I think I just broke Bernard's heart the way he broke mine."

"Love is like that," Mr. Charleston said softly.

He inspected the stitches I'd just strained. "You should give your cuts a couple days to heal before walking," he cautioned.

"Ok," I said. I had no intention of laying around for days.

"Maybel, infections lead to amputations. Clean and dress your cuts twice daily, and stay off your legs."

"Ok," I said more willingly this time.

"I'll be around to see you at your house in a couple hours."

I crossed my arms and stared down at my feet.

Mr. Charleston sighed. "Maybel, dear, Bernard gets his stubbornness and prideful behavior from me. I'm sorry. Mrs. Charleston knows all too well how the Charleston men are too full of themselves to know how to be good when we're young. Please know that I changed and Bernard will too. I've always wanted you to be my daughter, honey, and I love Catherine as well, but everyone who has ever seen you and Bernard together knows you two are halves of a whole."

Mr. Charleston left. I moved my legs to hang off the bed again, but I felt a stitch atop my knee bone break apart and I jerked myself back into bed, biting my already swollen lower lip.

By Monday morning, I was healed enough to walk to school. Bernard was in our kitchen and had made eggs. "I have a new recipe. I sautéed squash and zucchini and added them to the scrambled eggs."

Mommy was hungrily eating her breakfast. "It's really good, Maybel!" Her mouth was full as she spoke, and a sliver of zucchini protruded halfway out of her mouth before she hungrily sucked it back in and swallowed it.

I stared at her, gawking. She was usually so mannerly.

"And we had an extra hour to snuggle this morning!" Daddy raised his coffee mug in a celebratory toast and mommy blushed again.

Bernard walked me to school and pulled a flower from under his jacket and gave it to me when we were across the street from school. I heard my friends giggling.

"Bernard, I can't take it into school, I have no place to put it."

"I'll keep it for you until after school," he said.

I sighed and walked into my school building with my friends still giggling.

My lunch note said, "Maybel! I know you're not going to take my flower into school today so it will be with me when I come walk you home. Love, Bernard."

After school Bernard was not waiting for me. I walked home thinking I had rid myself of him. Mommy and daddy were inside holding hands on our sofa.

"How was school, honey?" mommy asked.

"Fine," I answered. I started toward the stairs.

"Maybel," mommy began, "Bernard had to leave today to visit his grandfather. His grandfather is not well."

"Oh," I said. "I'm sorry to hear that." I walked upstairs to do my homework. On my desk was Bernard's flower in a vase with a note.

"I'll be home as soon as I can. I love you, Bernard."

I sat at my desk staring at my flower. I wondered how serious was his grandfather's illness.

The next morning daddy sat grumbling at the kitchen table. "What's wrong daddy?"

"Bernard didn't make breakfast," he said.

"You like Bernard's cooking?" I asked incredulously.

"No, of course not! It tastes horrible!" daddy said, "But it gave mommy and me time to cuddle." Daddy looked disappointed.

I smiled, "Mommy's pancakes and bacon!" I cheered.

"Yes, but I didn't get to snuggle with mommy," daddy pouted.

"Maybel will leave for school soon, sweetheart," mommy winked at daddy.

Daddy suddenly became cheerful. "It's going to be a good day after all!" Daddy began happily eating his breakfast.

The walk to school felt longer and I had no lunch note. After school I was angry with myself for eagerly searching for Bernard at the flagpole even though I knew he wouldn't be there.

When I arrived home, mommy handed me a telegram. It was from Bernard. "Enjoy your lunch today. I didn't make it, so it probably tastes good. Love, Bernard."

"This note was supposed to arrive this morning, sweetheart," mommy said, "but Mr. Williams wasn't feeling well and an interim postman delivered it after you'd left for school."

"He interrupted cuddle time!" daddy bellowed from his office.

Mommy rolled her eyes.

"Thank you, mommy," I said, and went up to my room.

There were two dozen flowers in a vase on my desk. "I don't know how long I'll be here, Maybel. My grandfather is quite ill. Please enjoy a flower every day, and hopefully I'll be home before twenty-four days. Love, Bernard."

The next morning mommy was making oatmeal. She added a spot of butter and a dash of cinnamon.

"How many flowers were in that vase?" daddy grumbled.

"Two dozen."

"Two dozen?" daddy slapped the table. "This is why we should never have accepted Bernard's offer to cook breakfast. I got used to morning cuddle time and now it's gone!"

"Maybel will leave for school soon," mommy winked at daddy.

Daddy smiled, "That's a good point. You don't want to be late, sweetheart." Daddy pushed my books closer to me.

"It's not even close to time for me to leave, daddy!"

"Daniel!" mommy frowned.

Daddy sighed, "Sorry, dear."

Daddy sat back in his chair sipping his coffee. When mommy turned her back, daddy tapped his wristwatch while impatiently staring at me.

"I heard that tapping," mommy said.

Daddy went back to grumpily eating his oatmeal.

At lunch I found myself digging through my food looking for my note, then quickly realizing it wouldn't be there.

When I arrived home, there was a large sign on the front door. "Leave telegrams on porch. Do not knock!"

Mommy greeted me with a kiss and handed me another telegram. "This arrived just after you left for school," mommy said.

"When is Mr. Williams returning to work?" daddy angrily bellowed. "This interim postman interrupted cuddle time again!"

I read Bernard's note. "I miss you, Maybel. Do you remember the first time we kissed? I told you to never kiss me again, but I enjoyed it so much. I was embarrassed because I thought a two-and-a-half-year age difference was too great. I was wrong. I love you, Maybel."

The next morning, I opened the front door to find the postman had left a box with twenty-two individual telegrams, all from Bernard. The first one read, "Dear Maybel, your father sent me a telegram today. Please tell him I'm sorry for interrupting cuddle time. He asked me to either send a month's worth of telegrams now, or cease sending altogether. You should have twenty-two flowers left, so I'm sending twenty-two telegrams, but I hope to return sooner. Love, Bernard."

I took all the telegrams and put them in my bag to read later.

After two weeks passed, it was autumn break, and Catherine returned home. I was happy to see her. We spent the break staying up late in my bedroom while she told me all about college. Susan often joined our late-night conversations. Catherine loved acting worldly and sophisticated, telling us about her philosophy and world culture classes. Susan and I hung onto her every word. Catherine talked about sororities and boys and her professors, while Susan and I ate popcorn and listened intently.

A week passed, and Bernard was still with his grandfather. Henry, John, and Paul were also there. A telegram with a dozen roses arrived. "Dear Maybel, I'm sorry I'm not home yet. Henry and I are taking care of some long-overdue things. John and Paul are helping. Grandfather is improving. I'll return soon. I love you."

A couple days later, Bernard arrived during breakfast. There was a knock on the door and daddy muttered that at least the postman hadn't arrived a half hour later during cuddle time.

Daddy opened the door. I heard daddy say happily, "You can finish up with breakfast, right?"

I thought that was a strange thing to say to the postman. I leaned back in my chair to see who daddy was talking to. "Bernard?" I asked.

"Yes, Maybel," Bernard answered.

Daddy brought Bernard into the kitchen and took mommy's hand and led her upstairs.

"Hello, Maybel, may I kiss your cheek? I've missed you."

"Yes," I hesitated. I didn't want to feel so happy to see Bernard. I felt really happy though.

Bernard leaned down and kissed my cheek and he smelled so good.

Bernard pulled out a chair and sat next to me. "My family's Christmas party is approaching. Will you please be my date?"

"Oh," I paused, "Catherine is returning from college and that was your yearly event together."

"I know, but I want it to be ours now."

"I'll talk to Catherine. She is my sister and I don't want to cause her more pain."

"I understand, Maybel." Bernard smiled at me. "I've missed you," he whispered.

"How is your grandfather?" I changed the subject.

"He wants you to come visit," Bernard said. "He's doing well and seems to be as spry as ever."

"I'm glad," I said.

"Maybel," Bernard's voice caught. "Henry told me about his childhood and that was why I stayed away so long." Bernard's eyes looked troubled and I saw pain in them. "I helped Henry take care of some things." Bernard took my hands in his. "I never knew what had happened to Henry. Thank you for helping Henry through his pain."

I did not speak. I nodded silently.

Bernard walked me to school. "I'll be here to walk you home," Bernard said.

I left him and went inside.

At lunch I opened my lunch box thinking there would be no note since Bernard didn't pack my lunch, but he had apparently snuck one in. It read, "I'm so happy to be home with you. I love you."

Bernard walked me home and told me he had to leave again. Henry was still with grandfather, and Bernard needed to help Henry finish something.

"I'll return this weekend," Bernard told me.

"I'm doing fine without you, Bernard. I don't need you or anyone else."

"I know. You've always been independent and wise," he smiled at me.

I sighed, "Why are you being so nice? No matter what I say, you're nice."

"I'm going to marry you. I love you."

"Goodbye!" I slammed shut my gate in Bernard's face. Bernard was too confident that he could have anything and anyone he wanted and that angered me.

Catherine and I decided to stay home rather than attend the Charleston's Christmas party. I felt awkward about going, and Catherine said there were too many memories there.

"Are you still mad at me for not telling you Bernard kissed me?" I asked Catherine.

"Yes," Catherine said bluntly. "but I love you, Maybel."

"I love you too, Catherine."

"I heard Susan and Paul are a couple," Catherine eyed me. "Are you angry your little sister took the boy you loved?"

"No," I said simply.

"Really?" Catherine asked sarcastically.

"When I saw how they looked at each other, I was happy," I said.

Catherine watched me. She sipped her tea and watched me to see if I told the truth. "Perhaps I should have stepped aside too," Catherine said. "My pride prevented me from being happy for you two."

"You were young, I was young, Bernard is dumb; we all look back and wonder if we could have done better," I said.

"I hear Bernard is trying very hard to date you," Catherine said.

"I'm sorry, Catherine. I'm sorry about Bernard."

There was an awkward pause. Catherine turned to me, "Did Bernard really put on a dress to help mommy?" A smile played on Catherine's lips.

"Yes!" I giggled. "He did!" I giggled harder. "And daddy still makes him hunt for Crackadoos every morning!"

Catherine and I laughed so hard tears streamed down our cheeks. "Daddy said he told Bernard the neckline really brought out Bernard's cheekbones!" Catherine said between long gasps of laughter.

"It really did though!" I laughed. "Mommy's dresses made Bernard look like a princess!"

Catherine laughed harder. "Oh, that's the funniest story I've ever heard!"

Catherine and I continued trading funny stories the other had missed out on.

Bernard came to our house Christmas Eve. "Hello, Maybel. May I spend Christmas Eve with you?"

"I'm staying home with Catherine," I said.

"May I stay a little while?" Bernard asked.

"It's fine," Catherine called from the sofa.

I stepped aside and Bernard followed me into the family room.

"Hello, Catherine. You look lovely," Bernard said.

"I'm wearing an old nightgown," Catherine replied.

"It looks pretty on you," Bernard said.

"Thank you, the neckline really brings out my cheekbones, don't you agree, Bernard?" Catherine suppressed a giggle.

I cupped my hand to my mouth but couldn't manage to stifle my laugh.

"It's not the lovely shade of pink that looks so good on me, but yes, it brings out your cheekbones nicely," Bernard said with neither hesitation nor embarrassment.

Catherine and I squealed with laughter.

Bernard sat in a chair facing Catherine and me on the sofa. "Catherine, you know you are welcome to attend the Christmas party with your parents."

"Too many memories, Bernard," Catherine replied.

"I'm sorry, Catherine. I'm sorry I hurt you," Bernard apologized.

"I'll forgive you when you wear that beautiful, pink dress for me," Catherine smiled cheekily.

I giggled.

"I'll do it, Catherine," Bernard said. He was not smiling. He was serious. "I'm so sorry about everything."

Catherine snorted.

"Bernard, we were just having a girls' night. Susan will be here later. Maybe you should go greet your guests," I suggested.

604 ~ E. D. JUMPER

"I don't enjoy parties, and I only left my bedroom in previous years because you two were there. It's not fun without you both," Bernard said.

"Is Henry there?" Catherine asked.

"Yes, he's there," Bernard answered.

Catherine looked happier.

"He has women all around him as usual," Bernard said.

Catherine sighed and looked disappointed.

Susan showed up wearing a beautiful dress. She looked at us disappointedly, "This is what you meant by 'girls' night?'" she asked sourly.

Catherine stood up, "Susan, I'll go to the Charleston's with you. This will be awkward for me not being Bernard's date, so if anyone asks me where Bernard is, can you pull me away telling me the Duke of Nottingham wishes to speak with me?"

"Of course! I'll add that the Princess of Sweden wants to know who made your gown. Your mother will surely get many more clients. I hope they are all very tall, and that your mother will need a tall model to help, don't you agree, Bernard?"

"Har har har," Bernard said dryly. "The joke is on you, Susan, I have the prettiest cheekbones of all of you."

"I don't know, Bernard, my brother might have you beat. A side-by-side comparison tonight might be necessary."

Catherine and I looked at Susan while Bernard sat frozen in his chair. "Theo is here?" I asked.

"Yes, he returned for Christmas," Susan said.

I had a sudden and frightful anticipation of seeing Theo. I thought he had left forever.

"Theo said this morning he is taking a position at a laboratory in the city. He'll live nearby," Susan added.

"How is that possible?" Bernard suddenly unfroze and sounded angry.

Susan shrugged, "He said he missed us."

Catherine turned to Susan. "Susan, can you help me get dressed, please?"

"Sure, Catherine!" Susan loved Catherine and really looked up to her. She bounced after Catherine and took the stairs two at a time.

I sat on the sofa across from a clearly distraught Bernard. His brows were furrowed and he looked deep in thought.

"Maybel," he finally said, "will you please stay here for just a short while? I need to speak with father. I'll return very soon, just please stay here?"

I didn't reply. Bernard left and I bolted upstairs. "Wait for me!" I yelled all the way upstairs. "Wait! Wait! Wait for me!"

There was no way I was going to stay home if Bernard wanted me to stay home. Bernard should have learned by now that daddy always tells me to be sure to come to the shop after dinner to help him with sanding on days when Henry comes over with bourbon. I used to stay away until I realized daddy was tricking me because he wanted me to stay away. I began listening by the door of daddy's workshop on sanding days, and quickly learned new phrases and crude jokes.

We arrived at the Charleston's. Susan was the only one who looked ready for a ball. Catherine hadn't primped all day usual, but she still looked pretty, and I never cared to play dress up.

"Hello Vincent," I smiled. And then I whispered, "What's on the menu tonight?"

"Well, Miss Maybel, the big potato is in his office talking to the little potato about something important, and your parents are dancing. Miss Susan's parents arrived with a young man. They are sipping wine near the dining room. And of course, the boy you call 'every lady's dildo' is off dancing with some rich man's 'niece.' Vincent exaggerated the word niece because everyone knew which old, rich men had new, and always beautiful, 'nieces' every year.

"Quite the menu!" I giggled and elbowed Vincent jokingly in his ribs.

"Yes, ma'am!" he joked back.

I caught up to Catherine and Susan. They were looking for Theo so I steered them away from where I knew Theo was.

I was bitter that Theo left me. I wanted to observe him from a distance before I accidentally on purpose spilled smelly seafood all over his stupid, smelly head. I hoped there was a whole lot of shrimp sauce in the serving bowl on the dining room table.

I told Susan her brother was probably somewhere around the study, according to Vincent. I didn't say how far around that really was. They wandered off and I circled back to watch Theo.

Theo looked so handsome. I wanted to smell him. I hoped he still used the same cologne. Theo caught my gaze. His eyes widened and he smiled. He approached me.

"Maybel," he kissed my lips. "I've missed you."

"I missed you too," I said quietly. "I was sad you left me."

"I was too. I love you and I should never have left. I'm home now though. I'm going to live and work nearby."

I smiled softly up at Theo. My heart felt sad and broken. "I'll be right back," I said.

I went into the kitchen and right out the door and ran as fast as I could in heels. I went home and upstairs to my bedroom and got in bed and cried. Too much emotion ran through me. My heart broke because of Bernard and Theo, and Henry, too. I cried in bed with my pillow over my head.

At some point I woke up to Bernard banging on my window.

"What time is it?" I asked groggily.

"Nine. May I come in? I'm freezing."

"Nine? I fell asleep last night. It must be two or three in the morning. Why are you here at two or three in the morning?"

I wiped my hair back. There was snot stuck in clumps of my hair and my eyes were still watery from crying. "I guess I haven't been asleep long. My snot isn't dry yet." I wiped my nose with my bed sheet.

My bedroom window was stuck from ice so I had to push hard. Bernard rolled onto my bed quickly, blowing on his fingers and shivering.

"Why are you crying? What's wrong?" Bernard asked.

Bernard sat next to me and rubbed my back.

"I saw Theo at your party. He broke my heart when he left and you broke my heart for years. I don't want either of you." I laid back down facing away from Bernard. "And I thought Henry liked me, but he left, too. Everyone leaves me. You'll leave next."

"Maybel," Bernard rubbed my back. "Let's make a campfire."

"I want to lay here."

"We can tell stories and sip hot cocoa. I brought chocolates in my coat pockets."

"I'm listening," I said. "Go on."

"We can cuddle under a blanket in front of the hot fire and look up at the bright stars while I attempt to tell you a ghost story about a pirate, a king, and a dragon."

I rolled over to face Bernard. "Ok," I whimpered.

Bernard smiled. "This will be fun, I promise."

"Ok," I sniveled, and wiped a lock of snotty hair on my pillow case.

Bernard began gathering twigs and brush. "I've missed our campfires."

"I want to help. Can I gather sticks with you?" I began picking up little branches from around the bases of our trees. I wore cotton pants and a long-sleeved, cotton shirt. Mommy made them for me using green fabric. My coat was long and made of wool.

"Yes, of course. I enjoy doing everything with you. When you were younger and told me you wanted to be a nurse, my first thought was that I wanted you to work with me."

Bernard found several large branches, but a bunny family scattered from a pile of leaves in between two branches. "No, let the bunnies live there, Bernard!"

"I will, Maybel! I'm not going to burn their winter shelter. Now their summer home...."

Bernard stopped when he saw my furrowed brow. "I would most definitely leave their summer home untouched as well," Bernard said.

"How about these branches?" I suggested.

"But Maybel, what if bugs and spiders are underneath? You want me to burn their home, but not bunny homes?"

"Yes," I said.

"As you wish," Bernard picked them up and carried them to our campsite. He started the fire with brush and leaves and soon our faces were aglow with firelight.

"I can hear the screams of spiders, Maybel."

"Stop sweet-talking me, Bernard."

"Maybel, tell me a ghost story," Bernard whispered.

I closed my eyes and took several breaths. I imagined a white canvas. Upon the canvas suddenly appeared two worlds.

The fire had been burning and we sat by its warm amber glow. The light hit Bernard's eyes mixing colors in his irises.

I sat closer to Bernard and pulled the blanket we shared tightly around our shoulders. "This one is about tiny, little wood sprites. They are small, magical creatures who live within and around nature. They're all around us but we cannot pierce their realm with our eyesight. They cannot see us dwelling in our realm either, even though our two realms coexist side by side."

"When we humans cut down a tree, or kill an animal, or put our trash in ponds, they bleed from their eyes. Their blood, which drips and pools in their eye sockets, allows them to suddenly pierce the veil between our two worlds, and for a brief moment, they can interact with humans physically."

"Well, one night, just like tonight, a boy and girl were sitting by a pond, just as we are doing now. The boy took an axe and cut a branch off an oak tree to use as firewood."

"Unbeknownst to the boy and girl, his action had opened a portal between his world and the wood sprites' world, and the little wood sprites' eyes began slowly bleeding."

"The boy lit his camp fire and the wood burned brightly, so brightly that when the boy and girl sat by the fire and warmed their toes, they then saw shadows of small creatures within fire's glow begin to materialize."

"The wood sprites' eyes bled more, and with each drop, the human world became more visible. The tiny sprites became hungry. Their blood loss made them crave the blood of the humans to replenish their own diminished fluids."

"The boy and girl watched with awe as the tiny shadows within the flames became more solid and visible. At first they thought it was smoke from the damp leaves burning, but then a tiny female sprite with ethereal wings and bloodied eyes pierced through the veil, followed by a male sprite, whose tiny fingers grew long, blackened razor-like claws with which he used to spear the human girl's heart. The little male sprite pulled the girl's heart from her chest and feasted on it with his pointy, little blackened teeth."

"The female sprite bit into the human boy's chest with her powerful jaws and pulled from within his liver, which she used to quench her hunger."

"Having replenished their blood loss, their eyes ceased bleeding, thus closing the veil between their two worlds."

Bernard stared at me with wide eyes. He kept staring.

"I'm done, Bernard. My story is done."

Bernard looked shocked at the brutality in my story. "I will never anger you again, Maybel."

I giggled, "I wouldn't ever hurt you, Bernard, but it's nice to know you have a healthy fear of what my mind can dream up, you know, in case you ever do upset me."

"When did you write that story. I've never heard you tell it before," Bernard asked.

"Just now."

"You wrote that story as you were telling it?" Bernard looked amazed.

"Yes."

"How? How can you possibly think up a story like that so quickly?" Bernard asked incredulously.

"I just make my mind quiet and blank like a painter's canvas, and then I see a picture, and then I describe the picture."

"You're amazing Maybel," Bernard whispered.

"Your turn Bernard, tell me a ghost story."

"I can't tell stories like you, Maybel," he looked down shyly. "I will sound unintelligent."

"Bernard, you've seen me attempt math."

Bernard laughed, "Alright then, I'll try." He paused and took a deep breath. "Well, there was a man and woman. They liked each other. They often spent time together. But they grew old and sad. They never knew how to be together or when to be together. They died sad, never having married."

Bernard looked at me and he looked scared of what I would say about his story.

"Your story has the makings of a great story, Bernard. You just need a little help is all."

"It's horrible, Maybel. You can just say it."

"It's not. Tell me more. Why did the man and woman love one another?"

"He loved her because he knew her a long time and he knows all the bad things about her, but he doesn't care. He knows all the good things about her too, and he really likes her."

"See, you know the story in your heart, Bernard. You just need to ask yourself 'why' and 'how' more to figure out the depth of your characters."

"I don't really know any more than that, Maybel." He looked sorry for not being able to express himself further.

"Bernard, when you are with a patient, what is the first question you ask?"

Bernard looked more confident speaking about a topic he knew well and his back straightened and his voice was stronger. "I ask my patient what is wrong."

"And then do you ask your patient to show you where it hurts?"

"Yes."

"In your story, where does the man hurt?"

"His heart and mind."

"Why?"

Bernard's shoulders lowered. "He dies never being with the woman he's always loved." His voice was but a whisper.

"Why does he not tell her?"

"He's afraid."

"You are sitting with you patient, Bernard, and your patient tells you he is afraid. What is your next question?"

"I will ask him why he is afraid. Perhaps if I knew the root of his fear, I could then help him better."

"And why is this man in your story scared? What causes him to be scared?"

"He's scared to tell her he loves her. He's scared she does not love him the same way he loves her." Bernard's eyes looked troubled. "He thinks she may love him differently than he loves her."

"What kinds of ways might you love someone?"

"He loves her as a woman and he wants to marry her. He thinks she only loves him like a brother." Bernard looked sad but he also looked frustrated.

"If a patient came to you and said, I think my heart is hurting, what would you do?"

"I would listen to my patient's heart."

"Listen to the man's heart, the one in the story. What does his heart tell you when you listen?"

"It's breaking, Maybel! It hurts!" Bernard looked down again.

"How do you heal a broken heart?" I asked.

"I don't know, Maybel!" Bernard looked at me and his eyes began to tear up. "Maybel, I can't do this. I just can't."

I watched Bernard sit beside me on the log by the fire, holding his head in his hands. He looked in pain.

"Bernard, finish the story."

"Maybel, the man is in pain and he's sad. He'll die alone. He is alone now. What is more scary than that? There's nothing happy in his life, and he has nothing to look forward to. There's no scarier story."

"When someone is sick, you give them medicine. What is the one thing that will heal the man?" I asked.

"The woman. She will heal him."

"Why?" I pressed. I knew I made Bernard uncomfortable, but I wanted him to think more deeply about his characters' feelings.

"Because he loves her. She always makes everything better."

"Bernard, let me ask you to be the woman in your story. When you use her eyes to look around, what are you seeing? And when you step into her body and use her ears to hear, what are you hearing, Bernard?"

Bernard looked confused. "I have never thought about doing that. I have never considered doing that."

He watched the fire for a long time, so long that I became uncomfortable at what might be tumbling around in his mind. His countenance changed rapidly between confusion, anger, happiness, complete shock, and contemplation. He looked like his soul was in complete introspect.

Then he looked back at me. I became very nervous. His eyes were inside my soul.

"Maybel, I never thought about the woman that way." Bernard looked fascinated, the way he looked when listening to his uncles discuss maladies and treatments of patients. "I know why the woman isn't with the man."

"Bernard, tell your story now." I spoke gently. I was curious as to what was sparking such a glow behind Bernard's eyes.

Bernard sat quietly. He looked into the fire and down at his feet. He then looked at me with a penetrating stare.

"Maybel, the day I met you was Catherine's fourteenth birthday. You were eleven, about to turn twelve. You wore a white cotton dress with a pink ribbon around your waist and a pink ribbon in your hair that you absolutely hated being there. Your hair was partly swept up and pinned on the top of your head and the rest cascaded down in wild and untamable freedom, just like your personality. You hit my cousin Paul with a ball of mud and you cried. I came to help you. You made me a teacup from mud and it's still in my bedroom now. Your eyes were fiery and green with golden speckles and your lips were pink, like rose petals. Your hands were soft when I shook your hand. You cried because you hit Paul, and Catherine and her friends were angry at you for disrupting the party. Your legs were thin and muscular from years of climbing trees. Your arms were slender and toned, again from climbing trees. Your neck was like porcelain, your cheeks were pink like strawberries, and your feet were dirty from playing barefoot. I wanted to kiss you but you were too young. I wanted to always be around you, and so I stayed with Catherine so I could be near you. When you got a little older, I wanted to make love to you every time I saw you, and you have no idea how difficult it was for me to restrain myself. I wanted so much to touch you, kiss you, and hold you that every evening after seeing you, I went home and fantasized about you.

I wondered what it would be like to marry you and have children with you. I wondered what you felt like beneath your dress. And I was mortified for having such thoughts. You were too young for me and I didn't want to hurt you or corrupt you or steal your innocence, but every time I saw you, all I wanted was to feel your lips on mine, your breasts against my chest, and your legs around my waist. I'm so sorry, Maybel. You have no idea how much I've wanted you or how horrible I felt for wanting to take your innocence. I became very angry at myself for not being able to control myself around you, and I took out my anger by teasing you and pushing you away. I know you cried many a day because of me, and I'll never forgive myself for that. I'm sorry I was too scared and weak to just tell Catherine and you the truth. Maybel, I have always loved you since the day I met you, and I will always love you more than I love anything or anyone ever."

I couldn't move. I watched Bernard in the light of the fire and he watched me.

I gained some feeling back into my body and I whispered, "I love you, too."

My body felt heavy and numb and it took several long minutes to be able to move, but then I did move. I wrapped my arms around him and I hugged him. I felt his body release the energy he'd been saving in case I said I didn't love him. I felt him melt into my embrace.

Bernard exhaled years of secrets, and then pulled my face to him and kissed me. "I'm not scared anymore," he whispered.

"I now know why you don't seem to love me sometimes. I know why you are distant sometimes. I know you are sad, scared and lonely too, Maybel. And I'm so sorry. I promise you I love you, and I will spend every day cherishing you. I had never thought to literally go inside you and see and hear and experience everything firsthand through your eyes and ears, and everything makes sense now."

I felt exposed. The sudden exposure of all my thoughts and feelings felt like someone opening a dusty old chest that had been hiding in a basement corner and bringing all its secrets suddenly into the bright light of the morning sun.

With exposure came honesty though, and that honesty brought healing. I kissed Bernard. "I love you," I said.

"Maybel, I love you, too. I always have." He held my hands and then brought me into the most loving and honest embrace and kissed me.

We held each other until the fire died. Bernard took my hand and led me upstairs to my bedroom. He laid behind me in my bed and wrapped his arm around me and kissed the back of my neck. He didn't say anything, for which I was grateful. It was nice to be held, and I fell into a deep sleep in his embrace.

"Good Christmas morning!" Daddy threw open my door and yelled.

"Mirabel! Get my spear! Bernard is in bed with Maybel! Wait, never mind honey, they're both wearing clothing so I don't need my spear."

I heard daddy fart loudly. "Ooh, that one had distance! Bernard!" Daddy banged on my headboard, "Bernard! Wake up! Do you smell smoke?"

Bernard bolted upright and breathed in deeply, then gagged.

"That was my fart, Bernard, get out of my daughter's bed!"

"Wake up Catherine!" Daddy opened Catherine's door. "How's my little pumpkin this fine Christmas morning?"

"Merry Christmas," Catherine mumbled.

"I'm hungry!" daddy shouted. "Bernard! Make pancakes! And use eggs this time!" daddy bellowed.

"Mirabel, can Mr. Charleston come over to play? He said he'd bring a new bourbon the next time he visited and I like bourbon so I was thinking he could come over today?"

I heard mommy groan. "Ten more minutes," she muttered.

"Bernard! Pancakes!" daddy bellowed again.

"Yes, sir," Bernard rolled over and fell to the floor. "I'm used to a much wider bed," he called up to me.

I hung my head off the side of my bed and yelled, "Bernard! Pancakes!"

"And Crackadoos!" Catherine called from her bedroom cackling. I heard mommy and daddy laugh from their bedroom, too.

Bernard climbed slowly up to sitting position. "I shall make thee pancakes," he yawned.

"Use eggs," I giggled.

"Bernard! Take your time making those pancakes!" daddy yelled, then said happily, "It's cuddle time, my sweet cupcake!"

Mommy giggled.

I heard Catherine's feet hit her floor and quickly scuttle out into the hallway. "The walls in this house are too thin!" Catherine yelled.

"Now who's been naughty and who's been nice?" daddy yelled loudly to annoy Catherine and me.

Mommy giggled again.

"Daddy!" Catherine and I grumbled.

"We don't want to hear that!" Catherine groaned.

Mommy and daddy laughed.

Catherine and I ran downstairs fast. Bernard followed.

Bernard made pancakes while Catherine and I supervised. Catherine didn't bother to fuss over her appearance and she burped without embarrassment in front of Bernard.

"What?" she looked at me, "I can do whatever I want now. Bernard and I are not dating." Catherine burped again.

Bernard burped.

"It's disgusting when you do it," Catherine told Bernard. "Mine are dainty."

Catherine's burps were not dainty.

After breakfast, we opened presents. Bernard looked embarrassed, "My presents to all of you are at my house. I'll get them later. I'm sorry I don't have them now."

"And why don't you have them, Bernard? Is it because you stayed the night with my daughter in her bed?"

"Yes, sir," Bernard admitted.

"When you go get our presents, bring your father. Oh, and the bourbon. And my favorite son," daddy said.

Bernard looked confused.

"Henry is my favorite son. You slept in the same bed as my baby girl, so you are in second place."

"I'm your son?" Bernard's face was bright and happy.

"You're in last place; don't get excited," daddy cautioned.

"Yes, sir!" Bernard beamed.

"Here's your present." Daddy tossed Bernard a cookbook.

"Honestly, Daniel," mommy scolded, "you didn't even wrap it!"

"Men don't wrap. Also, I have not murdered you after switching daughters. Consider you not being murdered your Christmas present."

"Yes, sir," Bernard said nervously.

Catherine looked annoyed and I was also a little irritated daddy reminded us of Bernard's relationship with Catherine.

"Daniel! Kitchen!" mommy said angrily.

When daddy returned, he looked irritated at having to address Bernard. "Sorry about the thing about you switching daughters. I'm not really saying sorry to you, Bernard, so much as to my daughters, because I love them, and didn't mean to hurt their feelings by bringing up the past. You're still my least favorite son."

Mommy rolled her eyes and sighed exasperatedly. "My daddy didn't like you at first either," she told daddy.

"What? He loved me! I was his favorite son!" Daddy looked at Bernard when he emphasized "favorite son."

"Only after the girls were born, did he stop referring to you as 'that boy I hope Mirabel isn't serious about.'" Mommy lowered her voice exaggeratedly in a mocking expression of her father's disdain for daddy when mommy and daddy were in the beginning years of their relationship.

Catherine and I giggled.

Daddy sat in his favorite chair. "Bernard, what's for Christmas dinner?" he grumbled.

Mommy smiled at Bernard, "That's his way of saying he's sorry."

Mommy went to the kitchen without seeing daddy shaking his head vehemently 'no' while staring at Bernard behind mommy's back.

Christmas dinner was prepared by mommy, Catherine, Bernard, and me. When the Charleston's arrived, they saw Bernard cooking in the kitchen.

"Oh, dear God," Mr. Charleston muttered under his breath, "he didn't cook everything did he?"

"Oh, no," daddy chuckled, "just the things you and I don't care about, like salad."

Mr. Charleston patted daddy's shoulder. "Good man," he said with relief.

"Where's Henry?" Catherine asked.

"He stayed at our home with his parents, dear," Mrs. Charleston said.

"Invite them over!" mommy yelled from the kitchen.

Catherine bolted upstairs. "I look hideous!" she wailed.

"Good!" daddy said under his breath.

"Must be difficult having daughters," Mr. Charleston handed daddy a bottle of bourbon.

"Very!" daddy said as he graciously took the bottle.

"Bernard, it would be very kind of you to go fetch my favorite son," daddy called to Bernard in the kitchen.

Mommy stuck her head into the family room scowling at daddy. Daddy shrugged his shoulders as he opened the bourbon bottle.

When Henry and his parents arrived, I was very curious to see what they looked like and how they dressed. Mr. Fox was an exquisitely handsome, older version of Henry. Henry's older brother John was beautiful, too. Henry was the most beautiful though. Mrs. Fox was blonde and had beautifully long legs. She had been a ballerina. They were all kind and charming, but Henry would always be my favorite.

After boisterous and lively discussions, we ate cherry pie and Catherine and I were even allowed to have one, small glass of wine. I did not tell daddy that I preferred strawberry juice from Mr. Matthews' special and secret distillery behind his house.

The Charlestons and Foxes left after much welcome and much needed laughs and fun stories.

"Mommy, there's another pie left. May I take it to Mrs. Matthews?" Catherine asked.

"Oh, what a wonderful idea," mommy said.

"Are you coming?" Catherine asked me.

"I can barely move after all that food," I patted my stomach.

Catherine left and I went upstairs to bathe and get ready for bed. I could move around just fine. I didn't want to deal with Theo yet. I was confused about what to do with Bernard, Henry, and Theo in my life.

Christmas break wore on. I loved school breaks, but being cooped up indoors was torture. Mommy said winters with me were like trying to stuff a bolt of lightning into a little, glass ball, or like harnessing all the power of lightning, and telling it to stay indoors for three months and not break anything or wake anyone up early on Saturdays asking for pancakes.

I followed Catherine to a gathering with her friends. Catherine wanted me to come because she heard Bernard would be there. Catherine and Bernard were not dating and Catherine wanted me there for support. The older boys and girls were meeting at a campfire party tonight in the woods. They were playing a game about kissing.

All Catherine's friends were there. They were home from college for Christmas break. I felt out of place. They discussed books, teachers I had not yet met, and they wanted to play a kissing game. The boys and girls who were not in relationships played. The ones in relationships sat on logs around the campfire goading their single friends.

Edith and Arnold were a couple. I sat with them because I felt safer on the side, away from this game. The winners kissed and I didn't want to kiss anyone. I felt that Catherine wanted permission from a game to kiss Alexander. Bernard sat beside me. I was surprised he wasn't going to compete to kiss someone. Every girl wanted Bernard. I felt scared and lonely with these older boys and girls but I was too scared to walk home alone.

I scooted close to Bernard and he put his arm protectively around me. "You don't have to kiss anyone, Maybel." Bernard gave me a squeeze with his arm around me and tickled my ribs lightly. "Just relax, I won't let anyone hurt you."

I leaned against Bernard's shoulder in the firelight.

Catherine won this round and I watched her kiss Alexander on the other side of the campfire flames. Arnold was next to me hooting and hollering at Alexander. Edith laughed. I felt Bernard's arm around me grow tense.

"Sorry Bernard," I whispered.

"We're not dating, she can kiss whomever she wants," he said. His eyes looked angry though.

A girl handed Edith a note and she passed it to Arnold, who then handed it to Bernard. It was from Elinor. She wanted Bernard to play the kissing game. She sat across the campfire with her friends smiling at Bernard. Arnold whispered something in Bernard's ear and slapped his shoulder while they chuckled. I saw Bernard look over at Catherine, who was staring back at him and brooding. Alexander sat beside Catherine and kissed her cheek. It was almost as though Catherine taunted Bernard. I thought the game was short-sighted because relationships can only be repaired so many times before they are irreparable. Like a teacup that has been dropped and glued together, with each drop to the floor, and with each dab of glue, it becomes easier for the handle to fall off again and again until you have to throw away your teacup.

To my dismay, Bernard smiled back at Elinor, then glanced at Catherine again. Elinor took her place on the log in the center of the circle and smiled at Bernard. Everyone began cheering. When the cheers and jeers became deafening, and the laughter and yells were high and loud, I snuck around the older kids standing behind me and ran.

I walked along the dark path back to the main road. I was scared of the quiet and the darkness enveloping me. I heard twigs break and prayed they were from deer, not some boy. My memories kept returning to running through the woods with Danny, escaping the men who wanted to make me their girlfriend. My heart raced when those kinds of memories took over my mind. No matter how hard I pinched my arm, the memories were as vivid as the day Danny saved me.

I finally reached the main road and continued toward home. The pathway was clearer now on the main road, but it was still dark and quiet and the owls stopped hooting and the coyotes stopped yipping. Animal noises meant animals were comfortable. Silence meant something scarier than coyotes was nearby. I walked fast. My breath froze in the night air.

"Maybel!" A hand on my shoulder spun me around.

"Go away!" I screamed and ran. Bernard had grabbed me from behind, sending sudden memories of those men capturing me through my mind and making me lash out with fear. I couldn't breathe and my legs buckled. I couldn't scream and my lungs felt like they were wrapped with a belt. I mustered all my energy and kicked and punched and ran with all my might. I ran home, and Bernard didn't follow.

"Honey! What's wrong?" Henry grabbed my shoulders. He looked as terrified as I felt.

"I got scared," I wheezed. "I can't breathe."

"Did someone hurt you?"

"No," I gasped. My lungs couldn't suck in enough air. I saw spots in front of me. Henry's voice sounded like it got sucked into a train tunnel and echoed off the stone walls.

I felt like I was dying and I let myself die. I didn't fight it. I took a shallow breath then let myself sink into death. I felt myself finally relaxing. My shoulders went from stone to bread dough. I could feel my lips relax into a peaceful expression.

I woke up in Henry's ams in our family room.

I jumped and bolted upright.

"You're safe. You're safe." Henry held me tightly.

"Henry, there were men who tried to hurt me in the woods when I was younger. I was walking home tonight, and everything was fine, and then I looked down at a golden leaf on the dirt path and I suddenly felt that man's breath on the back of my neck. It felt so real in my mind. I ran and I kept running but I was stuck in my mind and it wouldn't go away! It wouldn't go away, Henry!" I slapped my temples with my open hands over and over again until Henry held my wrists at my sides.

"Maybel, look at your sofa. Look at the color. What color is it?" Henry's voice was gentle but firm and commanding.

"What?"

"What color is your sofa?"

I stared at him.

"What color is your sofa?" Henry repeated his question while staring into my eyes unblinkingly. His hands still pinned my wrists at my sides so I wouldn't slap my temples.

"Blue," I wheezed.

"Rub your hand on the arm of the sofa." Henry let go of my wrists.

I looked at Henry but did nothing.

Henry took my hand and guided it to the sofa arm and touched my hand to the upholstery.

"What does it feel like?"

"Soft," I said.

"Do you smell anything?"

"No."

"Can you hear the owls hooting outside?"

"Yes."

"Tap your foot on the floor," Henry gently commanded.

I tapped my foot.

"Where are you now?" he asked me.

"I'm in my family room with you, Henry."

"Good. Nothing is hurting you now. No one else is here. You are safe, Maybel. Squeeze my hand."

I squeezed Henry's hand.

"Take a deep breath." Henry kept his face close to mine so I could not lose focus of his directions.

I took a deep breath.

"You are safe, Maybel. You are right here. It is not then. It is not tomorrow. It is only right now. You are safe," Henry reached up and held my cheeks as he spoke to me softly.

"Henry, I didn't know what those men were going to do to me. I didn't know about sex then." I began breathing faster.

"Maybel, come back to me."

Henry held up his hand. "Touch my hand."

I put my palm on Henry's hand.

"See," Henry said, "you are right here, safe with me. Sometimes I will be doing the most mundane thing and I will smell something, feel a kind of fabric, hear a sound, and in an instant I am five, or seven, or twelve years old, and I'm helpless, and I can't stop someone from hurting me. When your mind isn't here anymore, when it's there, you have to know that right here and right now you are safe. You are remembering something. And then in your mind, you will eventually learn to take control and change what happens."

I began breathing longer and deeper listening to Henry.

"When the older girl sits on top of me, I push her away in my mind. It helps me feel more in control, and that helps me feel better. When you feel like you're being chased, turn around and beat those men to death in your mind. You'll get better at training your thoughts, Maybel. It will get better."

Henry sat beside me and hugged me tightly. I wrapped my arms around him and listened to his heartbeat as he stroked my hair and talked to me about all the things that were right in front of us in the family room. I finally began to feel like I was here, and not there.

"I love you, Henry," I raised my head and looked at him. "I love you so much."

Henry smiled kindly at me, "I love you too, sweetheart."

Bernard came barreling through the front door. "You see, I told you something was wrong, Catherine!"

Catherine's face went from annoyed to concerned. "Your face looks ashen, Maybel. What happened?"

"I'm ok now. Henry helped me feel better," I said. I still clung to Henry for protection from the bad memories that were finally beginning to fade.

Henry continued stroking my hair.

Catherine sat beside me. "What happened, Maybel? Did one of those boys hurt you?" I saw a fire begin to light up in Catherine's pupils. Catherine and mommy looked terrifying when they became protective.

"No, nobody hurt me. I had a sudden memory of those men chasing me through the forest but Henry talked to me and calmed me down."

Catherine relaxed, and dare I say looked a little disappointed she wouldn't get to gut some unruly boy. "You just let me know if anyone touches you," she squeezed my hand.

Bernard sat on a chair beside us. "You looked insane, Maybel, and I honestly thought I'd have to go get father to help you. I didn't know what was wrong with you."

I continued holding Henry tightly, letting him stroke my hair. My lungs began relaxing and I could feel my fingers and toes again. Slowly, my life began returning.

Catherine leaned over and kissed my cheek. "Goodnight, Maybel. You can sleep in my bed if you get scared." She left and went upstairs to bed.

"Maybel, honey, would you like me to stay here with you tonight?" Henry asked me sweetly. "Your parents will be home soon. I was here getting your father's bookkeeping up-to-date. I'll be happy to stay here until they return home from the theater."

"I'll sleep with Catherine," I said. "She looked like she'd be more than a little happy to tear into a gang of rogue, bad men. I feel safe with her."

Henry and Bernard chuckled.

"Yes, I do believe you and Catherine have inherited your mother's fighting spirit," Henry laughed. "Alright then, honey, I'll return home and retire for the night. Remember the calming techniques I taught you."

Henry hugged me tightly and kissed my cheek. "I love you," he smiled sweetly. And then he kissed my lips. It was just a quick peck.

Henry winked at me, "Night, sweetheart."

"Goodnight, Henry," I whispered.

"Goodnight, Bernard," Henry said to Bernard. Henry took his coat from the coat stand by the front door.

"Where's my kiss, cousin?" Bernard asked. There was no smile on his lips, nor playfulness in his eyes.

Henry hesitated. He looked confused. "You're joking, aren't you?"

"Unless you're going to do it," Bernard winked at Henry.

Henry rolled his eyes. He sighed deeply, then walked toward where Bernard sat.

"What? No! I was joking!" Bernard looked taken aback. He slunk down in his chair and leaned away from Henry, who was approaching.

Henry continued walking toward Bernard, then suddenly turned and leaned down toward where I sat. "So was I," he smiled at Bernard, then leaned over and kissed my lips again. "Goodnight, sweetheart," he chuckled.

I laughed at Bernard because he'd been called on his bluff. "You almost used deadpan delivery correctly, Bernard," I joked, "but Henry's joke was better."

Bernard smiled, "Yes, Henry won that round. Night, cousin."

Henry left but Bernard stayed. Bernard continued sitting in the chair next to me. "I'm not leaving," he said. "You worried me tonight, Maybel. I'm staying here and I'm keeping you safe."

"Thank you," I said softly. I was secretly happy Bernard was staying. I was angry that he likely kissed Smellinor, but I was happy to have him here tonight.

"I used to get jealous when I saw you kissing Catherine. I think you were jealous she kissed another man," I said.

Bernard came to sit beside me on the sofa. He wrapped his arm around me. "I was angry she may have been kissing him for the sole purpose of trying to hurt me, or perhaps to make me jealous, but I'm not jealous she kissed someone else, Maybel. And maybe Catherine wasn't trying to make me jealous. Enough time has passed that she and I can be civilized toward each other. I know you probably doubt my veracity, but I don't want to be with Catherine in a romantic way."

Bernard squeezed his arm around me and kissed my hair. I rested my head on Bernard's chest and took a deep breath.

"Are you jealous that Elinor wanted to kiss me?" Bernard playfully squeezed my arm.

"I felt uncomfortable watching you and Catherine try to hurt each other. That's why I left."

Bernard sighed, "I know. I suppose it hurt me a little to see Catherine looking over at me to see if she'd affected me. I wasn't jealous of her kissing that boy though, Maybel. I realized I used to kiss Catherine in front of you to make you jealous, and I suddenly felt like the most horrible person in the world for having done that to you. I saw myself through your eyes, and I cringed. You said you suddenly remembered something tonight, and it all came back to you immediately. Well, I suddenly saw myself through your eyes, and it overwhelmed me. I know I hurt you, and I'm so sorry."

"Did you kiss that bitch?" I snapped.

"What? No! Oh, I should have led with that. I didn't kiss anyone, Maybel. That should have been my first sentence."

"Yes, it should have," I agreed.

"So, you were jealous then?" Bernard playfully poked my ribs.

"I was hurt. I thought you would play that kissing game, and I didn't want to watch you kiss anyone else anymore."

Bernard paused thoughtfully, "You doubt I'll ever be faithful. You spent too much time watching me kiss Catherine. You think I'll hurt you."

"Yes," I said.

"I understand," Bernard said. "Henry has been telling me to see myself through your eyes for several years now. I don't like to see myself through your eyes though. I don't like myself when I look at myself through your eyes. I know I have a lot of repairs to mend. I will make things right, Maybel. I promise."

"Will you stay with me tonight?" I asked Bernard.

"Yes," he laughed, "I've never been shot at before but maybe that's the excitement my soul has been craving," he joked.

I laughed, "I meant we'll sleep on separate sofas here in the family room, like we did as children."

"Can we pull our sofas closer so that we can tell stories and whisper in each other's ears like we did as children too?" Bernard laughed.

"Of course!" I said with a big smile.

"Yes, Maybel, I would love that."

Bernard held my hand and I liked the feeling of his large hand around my tiny hand.

"I still think I'll be shot," Bernard smiled at me, "but it will be worth it just to be near you."

"Daddy won't aim for your waist. I know he wants grandchildren."

"You think about having children with me?" Bernard asked. He smiled and seemed hopeful and happy.

"I am not sure what my future will be, or who I will be with, Bernard, but you seem nice sometimes. Other times, I wonder how easy it would be to hide your remains. All in all, I'm open to giving you a chance to make things right."

"I will never tease you ever again. I will never be unfaithful. I will never give you cause to cry or be angry or feel pain." Bernard kissed my hand.

"Tell me a story?" he squeezed my shoulder.

"I'm exhausted, however, if I must tell you a story, do you want it to be about winged horses or a dog that reanimates to chew apart her master who left her tied to a post to be torn to shreds by wild boars?"

"There is no middle with you, is there, Maybel? Beautiful horses or a vengeful zombie dog. Those are my choices." Bernard continued holding my hand and playing with my fingers, interlacing them with his.

"I never liked the color gray," I said. "It's indecisive. Pick a side. If you pick gray over black or white, the audience will be bored."

"Just this one time, tell me a happy story that will bore me."

"Alright then," I yawned. "Let me think." I had to pause for several minutes, staring up at the ceiling. Sometimes it was hard to quiet my mind enough to let stories form.

I had difficulties quieting my mind when Bernard so tenderly rubbed my hand in his. He stroked and caressed my hand and that both relaxed me and stimulated me.

"'I like being touched,'" the girl told the boy caterpillar when they were young, "'because your attention makes me thrive.'" And then the boy put down her hand onto hot coals and she cried. She took flight then landed on his other side and when he turned around, he was no longer a caterpillar but a butterfly. He flew with her up to the sun and when the heat was too much, he wrapped his wings around her and they fell to the water below. He pulled her down to the depths then released her and she floated. She reached down and pulled him up and he took her to the stars this time and they brightly twinkled. And then he kissed her and she fell to the forest floor and her wings broke. He tore his wings off and laid with her and they watched the stars above until they became the wind, and together they blew away."

"What does it mean?" Bernard whispered.

"I don't know, I'm tired. And when you hold my hand and play with my fingers and rub my palm, I can't concentrate."

Bernard smiled, "I liked it, even if I didn't understand it."

"I didn't understand it either," I laughed, "but they were together until wind, and then they were wind together."

"I want to be with you until wind, Maybel."

"Me too," I smiled.

"Goodnight, beautiful wind," Bernard whispered.

"Goodnight, sweet wind," I smiled.

I woke up to the smell of bacon and Bernard smiling at me as he watched me.

"What did my parents say?" I asked.

"I don't know, I woke up after they began making breakfast. I don't have any bullet wounds though, so I'm hopeful for a positive outcome."

We walked into the kitchen together.

"Good morning," I said.

Mommy smiled, "Good morning."

"Good morning," daddy said. "How was the campfire?"

"We left early and came here. I told Bernard a story then we fell asleep," I said.

"Maybel, will you go wake Catherine for breakfast?" mommy asked me.

"Yes, mommy," I said.

"Bernard, how was the weather this morning when you walked here?" daddy asked.

"I spent the night here, sir."

"I know, I was pointing out that I knew you spent the night, and that you awoke without holes in your abdomen. You should be thanking me."

"Oh, Daniel!" mommy scolded daddy.

"Thank you, sir," Bernard said.

"See, I told you daddy wouldn't shoot your penis off, Bernard; daddy wants grandchildren," I giggled.

"We weren't doing that! Maybel, tell your father we were not doing that!"

"Oh, relax, daddy's a big teddy bear," I kissed daddy's cheek then sprinted up the stairs to wake Catherine.

I knocked on Catherine's door. "Catherine! Breakfast!"

I opened her door and she was sprawled out in bed still. "Catherine?"

"What?" she mumbled.

"Mommy says to come down for breakfast."

"In a minute," Catherine mumbled.

I went back downstairs and sat next to Bernard.

Catherine came downstairs in her nightgown and messy hair. "We're not dating anymore, so this is how I look when we're not dating," she said to Bernard. She plopped down in the chair on daddy's other side.

Bernard watched Catherine and it made me uneasy. Catherine didn't have her prim and proper mask on after years of pretending to be perfect. She ate her bacon like she just woke up and Bernard watched her like he watched someone he was meeting for the first time. I excused myself and went to my bedroom.

Suddenly panic hit me and I felt that familiar belt wrapped tightly around my chest. I laid on my bed unable to move and I could barely take shallow breaths. Bernard had never met Catherine. He met Catherine's representative. I feared Bernard would fall in love with the real Catherine. And I pictured all of us five years from now, entangled in a triangle.

"Maybel?" mommy knocked on my door.

I couldn't breathe deeply enough to answer.

Mommy opened my door and came to me and sat on my bed. "Maybel, are you alright?"

I couldn't move so I laid there.

Mommy came to me and stroked my hair. She talked to me about when she first started dating daddy. "I was engaged to another man. Your father though, oh, he was so handsome. He still is," mommy smiled. "I broke my engagement and fell in love with your father so deeply that I've never looked at another man with even a notion of romance."

Mommy continued, "My father hated your daddy. My father wanted me to marry that other man, but I said simply that your father was like the other side to my everything. Where I felt darkness, he was the light. Where he felt sad, I was his happiness, and so on."

Mommy continued stroking my hair. "Do you love Bernard?"

I nodded yes.

"Bernard loves you. Your father and I know."

"I'm scared he still loves Catherine," I whispered, my voice barely audible.

"Maybe he does and always will. I still love my old fiancé, even though I think nothing romantic about him. I remember the time we spent together fondly, but nothing more. Once I met your father, there were no other men. I've only ever wanted daddy." Mommy smiled so happily whenever she spoke of daddy. I wanted that love with my husband.

"Did daddy love another woman?" I asked.

"No one seriously. He says when he first saw me, he told his parents he met the mother of their grandchildren."

I smiled.

"Maybel, did Bernard tell you he loves you?" mommy asked.

"Yes, but he has always said that. I saw him watching Catherine in the kitchen and I got scared he would fall back in love with her."

"Talk to Bernard," mommy said.

"He'll tell me he loves me, not Catherine."

"You don't believe him?" Mommy still stroked my hair. Her voice was gentle.

"I think he loves me, but in my mind, I keep seeing all of us in five or ten years, and Bernard has an affair with Catherine because he has unresolved feelings."

"Do you think Catherine would do that to you?"

"Yes," I said, "because Bernard and I kissed while they dated."

"Perhaps you should wait then, Maybel. Give them time to truly separate. If he comes to you in a year and says he has not been with any woman and does not desire any woman except you, then he will be yours forever."

"Ok mommy," I nodded my head weakly. My breath was returning but I still felt my lungs were bound by rope.

Mommy kissed my forehead and left.

Several minutes passed and I began to breathe easier. Bernard opened my door. "Maybel, what's wrong?"

Bernard sat beside me on my bed.

"I saw you looking at Catherine. I think you'll have an affair with her to resolve unresolved feelings and I couldn't breathe when I watched you watching her."

"Maybel, no. How can I prove to you that I only want you?" Bernard asked.

"Mommy said if you can go a year without loving another woman then you'll be mine forever."

"Then we'll date for a year," Bernard said.

"No, she meant we have to be apart for a year, and then we meet back up after one year's time, and if you have not been with Catherine or any other woman, then I'll know you will be faithful to me."

"Then that's what I'll do," Bernard said.

"Really?"

"Yes, Maybel. I want you and your parents to trust me. I want you to have faith in my fidelity. I've waited years watching you grow up right in front of me. I can wait another year."

I smiled softly at Bernard.

"Maybel, I only want you. I'll always love Catherine. She'll always have a place in my heart and memories, but I've never loved her the way I have always loved you."

"That's true. You never called her annoying, pulled her hair, or kissed her sister in front of her," I said sourly.

"I will spend the rest of my life making it up to you. I'm sorry, Maybel."

"Bernard, how do you go from loving someone to not loving them?"

"Love changes. We'll love each other, but in a different way," he explained.

"What if your love for me changes?" I asked him.

"What if it doesn't?" Bernard brushed my hair back. "If I cannot see you for a year, may I kiss you goodbye?"

"Yes."

Bernard kissed me and he was so tender. He kissed my cheeks and forehead, too. And then Bernard left. I stayed in bed crying. I didn't want to go a year without Bernard.

I finally sulked downstairs.

"What's wrong, Maybel?" Catherine sat on the sofa reading.

"I'm in love with Bernard."

"I know," she said. "He loves you too."

"Do you still love Bernard?" I asked Catherine, afraid of her answer.

"No, I do not love him as a boyfriend. I love him as a friend."

"I'm staying away from Bernard for a year to see if he still loves you," I told Catherine.

"Well good luck with that. He's in the workshop helping daddy."

My eyes shot wide open. "He's here?"

"No, but did you see how happy you were?" Catherine smiled.

"Catherine!" I whined.

"Oh, go to Bernard, Maybel!" Catherine laughed. "I'm not thrilled about you two kissing while Bernard and I dated, but I've done some regretful things, too. Go be with Bernard."

"Thank you, Catherine. I love you."

"I love you, too, Maybel."

I bolted toward our front door, and then someone outside knocked on it. The knock startled me and I flung myself back onto the sofa beside Catherine.

Daddy went to see who was outside.

"Hello, boys," daddy said.

John came inside with a jug of cider for daddy. Henry and Bernard followed.

"From my uncle," John smiled at daddy.

"Come in, boys." Daddy took the jug and stepped aside for John, Henry, and Bernard to enter.

They were all tall. Bernard looked the most muscular, a little bit like his big, bear of a father, but maybe not quite as intimidating. Bernard was a little more gentle in appearance.

Bernard noticed me watching him and smiled at me. I smiled back, then turned and sat low in the sofa, out of Bernard's view.

I often wanted to break Bernard's nose, but I also often wanted to kiss him.

Daddy told the boys to follow him to his workshop. As Bernard passed by the sofa, he smiled down at me and I quickly held my book over my nose and mouth, as though that hid me and made me disappear.

Suddenly I realized Catherine was watching me and my breath caught and my eyes grew wide.

Catherine rolled her eyes at me. "Oh, come on, Maybel, let's go spy on them. I want to hear what they talk about."

"Ok!" I gasped. I was always ready for an adventure with Catherine and followed her outside.

"We can listen by the door to daddy's workshop and hear most of what they say," I told Catherine, proud of knowing something sneaky that she didn't know.

"Or, we can sit under the window that I left cracked and hear all they have to say," Catherine smiled mischievously.

"How did you know they would all meet in daddy's workshop tonight?" I asked Catherine.

"I didn't. I make it a habit to crack daddy's window when Henry is in town. Henry comes to help daddy with woodworking, but they usually end up talking about far more interesting things," Catherine giggled.

"Like what?"

Catherine blushed. "Just come listen," she said.

We walked outside and crept along the side of daddy's workshop. Underneath the cracked window was a well-worn patch of trampled grass.

"Come here often?" I asked Catherine sarcastically.

"Why yes, I do indeed," Catherine giggled quietly.

Daddy and the boys were talking about carpentry. Daddy suggested they go back to the Charleston's and play cards with Mr. Charleston.

"Well, this was boring," I sighed.

"Sometimes you win, sometimes you lose, Maybel," Catherine shrugged. "You should hear some of the winning conversations though," Catherine chuckled.

"Come on, let's go inside," Catherine sighed. "Maybe mommy is doing something interesting."

We waited until daddy and the boys had gone inside before we returned. I stuck my head inside the kitchen. "It's empty," I told Catherine.

"I bet mommy's in bed reading," Catherine said.

"What do you think John and Henry want to talk to daddy about with Mr. Charleston?" I asked.

"Women, whisky, cigars, and the weekend sale at the hardware store," Catherine replied. "Men are simple."

"I thought you said their conversations were interesting," I said, disappointedly.

"They are sometimes," Catherine said.

"Well, what do you want to do now?" I asked.

Catherine sighed, "I suppose there's nothing interesting going to happen tonight. Let's sit on the sofa and be bored together."

We sat together and put our feet on the coffee table because mommy wasn't around to tell us to get our feet off the table.

"Catherine, I've kissed Henry."

Catherine looked at me with interest, "Did he kiss better or worse than Bernard?"

"You've kissed them both too," I said. "What's your opinion?"

"You first," Catherine giggled.

"Bernard kissed the best," I blushed.

"Really? I thought Henry kissed better. Ok, Bernard or Theo?" Catherine asked.

"Bernard," I said.

"I thought Theo was better," Catherine mused.

Catherine paused and looked tentative. "Maybel, I'm sorry Theo left. He should not have left you." Catherine patted my hand.

"I understand his fear of not wanting to ever experience poverty again," I sighed.

We sat in silence for several minutes staring off, both of us deep inside our own thoughts.

"He might come home tomorrow missing you," Catherine said.

Catherine turned to me with a gleam in her eyes. "Did you two ever," Catherine paused and looked at me expectantly.

I knew what she wanted to ask, but I enjoyed watching her squirm uncomfortably. "Did we share taffy while watching the sunset? Yes, we did," I said.

Catherine did not look amused. She must have known I was being coy. "Did you ever have sex with Theo?" Catherine whispered.

"No," I whispered back giggling. "Did you ever have sex with Bernard?"

"No," Catherine said. "We truly only kissed. Have you ever done more than kiss?"

"No," I said.

"Maybel, be honest, who do you want? Of all the men, who do you want?" Catherine asked me.

"You first," I smiled cheekily.

"Of all of them, I loved Bernard, but we didn't have that special passion between us." Catherine looked a little sour suddenly. "You and Bernard do have that special passion though. I suppose, looking back, you two have always had something special."

I felt really uncomfortable so I remained quiet.

"I suppose I really liked Theo," Catherine continued. "He should not have left you though. And Henry is divine."

I giggled, "Henry is so sweet and pretty."

"There are men at my college who are quite handsome and intelligent, too. I'm not ready to choose," Catherine laughed. "I enjoy my freedom and I have really been enjoying meeting new people at college and learning new things."

"I've always wanted Bernard," I admitted. "He really hurt my feelings though when he pushed me out of his bedroom and locked his door so he could kiss you."

"We sometimes kissed, but they were innocent kisses. We never had that fiery passion for each other that made us want to do more than kiss. And to be honest, I don't understand why Bernard locked his door because we weren't touching each other. Sometimes I suspected he just wanted you to go away because when you were around, he couldn't stop watching you and it broke my heart that he pined for you so."

"I'm sorry, Catherine," I whispered.

"I didn't really want Bernard so much as I was jealous that he looked at you that way and not me. One day, I want a man to love me like Bernard loves you."

"Theo looked at you with love that day on the beach. Although I suppose Henry looks at you that way too sometimes. To be honest, Catherine, every man wants you."

"Well, I want the one that looks at me the way Bernard looks at you, the way daddy looks at mommy, and the way Mr. Charleston turns into a playful puppy around Mrs. Charleston."

I laughed, "He does, doesn't he? And he's such an intimidating man when he's discussing business though!"

"I know, it's quite comical how he goes from being a lion to a kitten at her feet!" Catherine and I giggled.

"Catherine, I love you. I know I should have told you Bernard kissed me."

"And I love you too, Maybel. We will be ok."

"Don't leave me, ok?" I asked Catherine.

"Oh Maybel, I've always loved you more than Bernard. Let's make a pact to always be absolutely truthful to each other about the men we kiss. Let's start right now. Are you going to pursue a relationship with Bernard, Henry, or Theo, or is there anyone else I need to be aware of so that I can steer far away from whoever you are interested in?"

"I love Bernard," I whispered. "I'm sorry."

"Stop apologizing, Maybel.

I said timidly, "I feel really guilty because I love Bernard, but I did love Theo too, and of course I love Henry, and I don't want to hurt anyone."

"And now you know why Bernard led us both on for so long. Don't make the same mistake," Catherine cautioned.

"Oh," I said, surprised. "I had not looked at it that way, from Bernard's perspective."

"What will you do when Theo comes home?" Catherine asked me.

"I honestly don't know, and when I think about all the different outcomes, I can't breathe well." I sat upright trying to slow my breathing.

"Good grief, Maybel," Catherine stood up and grabbed my hand. She pulled me to the door.

"Where are we going, Catherine?"

"To get this over with. You're going to tell Bernard how you feel and then you can breathe better. Bernard and Theo are both good choices, you know. Oh, and don't forget, Henry likes you too."

I had to stop and sit on the sidewalk because I couldn't breathe enough and my head tingled.

"Maybel, let's focus on one thing at a time. You want Bernard. Focus on Bernard. It's nice to know you have options though, right?"

"Mmmm," I breathed.

"Good, get up. We're going. I already know Bernard will say yes so you can just forget about Theo and Henry. There, take a deep breath Maybel, I've got this situation under control. Everything will be fine."

"Catherine, I can't breathe well." I sat down again on the sidewalk.

"We're almost there, don't be a chicken, Maybel." Catherine picked me up and turned around. "Get on my back."

I limply fell into her back and lifted one knee up.

"Put some effort into this, Maybel, and lay off the sweets!" Catherine struggled to get me on her back, and my legs in her arms.

"Thank you, Catherine," I breathed tightly, my lungs still as rigid and frozen as the rest of me.

Catherine managed to get me to Bernard's front door.

"Wait, I don't like ringing the doorbell," I said. "The staff come and announce you, and you walk into the big house, and everyone stares at you, and I'm already unable to breathe well. Can you help me climb Bernard's tree?"

Catherine looked at me and said sarcastically, "You want me to piggyback you up a tree?"

"No, just climb behind me, and if I get scared and don't want to continue, push my bottom up, or spank me, or pinch me to get me going again."

"Like a donkey? You want me to whip you if you become stubborn?"

I paused, "Well maybe not quite...."

"I like this plan," Catherine said as she broke off a thin branch of a shrub.

"You're not actually going to whip me, are you?" I asked, a little nervously.

"Well, I don't know, Maybel, you're not actually going to be stubborn, are you?"

"Catherine!" I pleaded.

Catherine swatted my bottom lightly. "I'll swat as mightily as you are stubborn," Catherine giggled gleefully. She enjoyed this too much.

"You proved your point. I'll talk to Bernard. You don't have to hit me."

Catherine swatted my bottom harder. "Your legs are standing mighty still, miss," she snorted.

"I'm going!" I yelled.

"Atta girl, hyah!" Catherine giggled.

I started climbing Bernard's tree very slowly and I took several deep breaths as I inched forward.

"My arms are trembling, Catherine. I'm scared I'll fall."

"You won't."

"How do you know?" I asked.

"I know you'll climb as well as you know you'll fall. Now climb!" Catherine swatted my bottom.

"You're going to be a hell of a motivational teacher, Catherine!" I snarled.

Catherine swatted me lightly, "Insubordination!" She yelled, giggling.

I reached the roof and climbed onto it. I looked in Bernard's window. "He's not here," I whispered to Catherine.

Catherine pushed open his window and dragged me inside. "Let's plunder until he returns."

"I'm hungry," I whined. "Let's go home."

"Silence!" Catherine held up her swatter smiling at me.

"Follow me," Catherine called over her shoulder.

"Where?"

"The kitchen. You said you were hungry." Catherine opened Bernard's bedroom door.

"I don't think we can just go rambling about the Charleston's mansion," I whispered.

"Fine, you stay here. What do you want to eat?"

"How are you so calm?" I asked. "Catherine, what if Bernard already has a girlfriend?"

"He'll choose you," Catherine said as a matter of fact.

"What if he's already had sex?" I asked nervously.

"Doubtful," Catherine replied.

"How do you know?" I asked.

"He didn't try to have sex with me and I'm more beautiful than any of those girls at his school." Catherine spoke like what she said was obvious.

"Remember how you said you admired my self-confidence? I don't think you were ever lacking any," I told her.

"Sometimes I lack confidence, Maybel, but I am confident Bernard loves you and only you."

"I've seen Bernard's penis," I blurted out.

"What?"

"I wanted to know what a penis looked like so we showed each other what our private parts looked like. I'm sorry, Catherine!"

"When?"

"Some time after he explained how to make a baby," I said.

"What?"

"Well, Edith's sister told Edith how to make a baby, then Edith told you, but nobody would tell me, so I begged Bernard. I'm sorry, Catherine, I really wanted to know what everyone else already knew!"

"What does Bernard's penis look like?" Catherine whispered, her eyes full of curiosity.

"You've never seen it?" I asked, astonished.

"No."

"Like an elephant's trunk," I giggled.

"I've felt it against me when we kissed, but I never saw it," Catherine said.

"You've never seen a penis before?" I asked Catherine. I was a little proud I had done something before she had.

"Oh no, I have, just not Bernard's."

"Who?" My eyes got big.

"There were some boys swimming in the lake one summer, and Edith and I saw them come out of the water naked, though I wouldn't call them elephant trunks," Catherine giggled, "They looked more like little pigeon heads sitting on little pouches."

I laughed, "I'm never going to look at a pigeon the same way again." We continued whispering and giggling down the hallway and stairs.

"Catherine, I know where there's strawberry rum. Do you want some?"

"No, you're trying to delay talking to Bernard," Catherine raised her brush branch menacingly.

"I talk better after rum," I pleaded.

"Everyone talks better after rum. And then you end up talking too much and suddenly all the girls in your sorority know who you've kissed."

"Ok, let's see, where is the bread?" Catherine opened and closed the drawers and cupboards in the kitchen.

"Catherine, I'm scared. Can we go home?"

"No."

"Where is everyone?" I wondered.

"Mr. Charleston's office, the study, drawing room, library, I don't know, it's a big house," Catherine said as she rummaged through more shelves.

"Can we just go home? They're probably drinking and you said not to talk when you're drunk because you'll tell everyone who you kissed."

"If Bernard's drunk, you'll definitely get the truth from him," Catherine said.

"Let's wait until they aren't drinking. We can do this tomorrow. I don't want to open the door to Mr. Charleston's office and a bunch of men turn around and stare at us. What would we say? 'Excuse us, we need to speak to Bernard privately.' And Mr. Charleston would ask how we got inside and we would say, 'We climbed a tree and snuck in a window, like we always do.'"

"You are so whiny when you're nervous," Catherine rolled her eyes. "Fine, drink a very small glass of wine. Where is it?"

"The back room."

"How do you know?" She asked. Catherine looked very intrigued now.

"Susan and I accidentally got drunk on what we thought was fruit juice," I said.

I led Catherine to the back room. "It's in the back room, that's in the back, of the back room."

"Where?" She turned to me, confused.

"Here's the back room." We entered the back room. "And over here is a smaller room in back."

"What is this place? It smells strange," Catherine sniffed.

"There's an illegal alcohol still under the back part of the house," I said.

"What?"

"You didn't know?" I asked, surprised.

"No, Maybel, I didn't know!" Catherine said both incredulously and sarcastically.

"Well, while you were upstairs kissing Bernard behind a locked door, I got bored and explored." I took a jar from the cupboard. "Let's go back to the kitchen to drink this."

I poured a little rum for us both. The kitchen was dark and quiet as there were no staff around.

"No more after this," Catherine cautioned. "A little rum and then we knock on Mr. Charleston's office door and politely ask to speak to Bernard. You tell Bernard you love him and Bernard will say he loves you, and then you can breathe easier."

"Ok," I said, refilling my glass.

"Maybel!"

"You said no more after this," I reminded her. "The limit on refills stops right...." I filled my glass to the top, "now."

"Fine, top off my glass too, then."

"As you wish, madam," I smiled at Catherine.

"What other secrets are in this house?"

"I'm not sure. Let's go find out," I said, walking with my rum toward the ballroom.

I got as far as the kitchen doorway when Catherine snatched my dress and pulled me back. "Finish your drink then we talk to Bernard. No more diversions, Maybel."

"I'm scared, Catherine. If Bernard really wanted me, he would have pursued me long ago, which means he's not serious about a relationship with me."

"I honestly don't know why he didn't, except to say he didn't want to make my relationship with you strained. That's my best guess anyway, but you can ask him yourself now. Bernard!" Catherine screamed.

Bernard, Henry, and John were walking down the hallway to the study. Bernard turned, surprised to hear his name called.

"Did my voice sound louder than usual?" Catherine smacked her lips. "This rum sure hits hard."

"Catherine!" I hissed. "I'm not ready! And mommy said we have to remain apart for a year for me to know if Bernard truly wants to be with me!"

"Bernard, get in here now!" Catherine screamed.

Bernard, followed by Henry and John, entered the kitchen, and I fell to the floor and crawled under the kitchen table.

"Catherine? What's going...."

"Why did you wait so long to tell Maybel you wanted to date her? Is it because you were interested in another girl?"

"Are you drunk?" Bernard asked Catherine.

"No, of course not, I just started drinking. This rum is really strong though and I should've eaten a sandwich first. Why have you not pursued Maybel all these years? Have you been with other women?"

"No, I have not. I'm trying to win over Maybel, but I have a lot of repairs to our relationship I need to mend," Bernard answered. "I'm trying though, I'm really trying." Bernard paused, "Catherine, is everything alright? Why are you standing here alone in my kitchen drinking rum?"

"Tell Maybel the truth. Do you truly love Maybel?" Catherine pressed Bernard.

"Yes," Bernard whispered. "I'm sorry I hurt you though, Catherine."

"Why haven't you fought for Maybel?" Catherine continued.

Bernard sighed, "She never showed much of a romantic interest in me even after all these years. I am really trying to express myself more openly and honestly with Maybel now though, and I hope, in time, I will make up for all those years of teasing her."

"The next time you see Maybel, tell her the truth about how you feel," Catherine said.

"I will," Bernard said. "Catherine, I'm scared I'm too late. I'm scared I've lost her. And I feel very awkward talking to you about this."

"You should have been honest with us both a long time ago," Catherine said.

"I know. I'm sorry, Catherine. I do love you, that was never a lie. I have loved Maybel since the day we met, and I'm so sorry to admit the truth to you, because I love you too, and I do not ever want to hurt you. I ended up hurting you though, and I'm so sorry.

There was such a long pause that I desperately wanted to peek my head out from under the table and see what was going on in silence.

"I knew you loved Maybel. Everyone has always known," Catherine finally spoke. "You should not have been a coward. I was a coward too, and should not have been so utterly terrified to be alone. I'm doing well on my own though, Bernard. I'm ok. Go be with Maybel."

"Thank you, Catherine," Bernard said.

I heard Catherine hiccup. I almost didn't suppress a giggle.

"Catherine," Bernard treaded carefully, "may I ask again why you are here drinking rum at night in my kitchen all alone?"

"Is there a problem? I can't drink rum alone at night in my ex-boyfriend's kitchen?" Catherine defensively asked Bernard.

"I...." Bernard sounded confused as he stammered.

"Do you want me to leave, Bernard? I'm not allowed to be here drinking rum alone in your kitchen at night?"

"You can stay," Bernard said.

"I'll let myself out when I'm done drinking rum alone in your kitchen at night. Goodnight, Bernard."

"Goodnight," Bernard sounded even more confused.

"Always a pleasure, Catherine," I heard John say.

"Yes, always a pleasure, and always entertaining," Henry added.

"Goodnight boys," Catherine said.

"Do you want to come with us?" I heard Henry ask Catherine.

"I can't drink rum alone at night in my ex-boyfriend's kitchen if I come with you, now can I? Goodnight boys!" Catherine said definitively.

I heard them leave. I crawled out from under the big table.

"See, Maybel, Bernard does love you." Catherine helped me to my feet.

"Let's go, Maybel," Catherine took my hand and burped loudly. "I need to eat something. Let's go home and you can fix me a sandwich while I fall asleep on the couch," Catherine hiccupped.

"How are you drunk so fast?" I asked, amazed.

"Oh, excuse me for not having a higher tolerance. If I'd known where they hid their good hooch, I would have built up a higher tolerance by now, I imagine."

The next morning, I thought about what Catherine said as I slowly rolled around in bed stretching and waking up.

I went downstairs to help mommy prepare breakfast. Mommy was already cooking.

"Oh good, mommy's food," I cheered.

"Where's number two?" daddy asked.

I looked at daddy confused.

"Bernard. He's my second favorite son. He didn't arrive to make eggless pancakes and I'm disappointed I did not get cuddle time with mommy."

"He's probably visiting with Henry's parents," I said.

"Ah, yes, I miss number one," daddy sighed.

"I told Bernard we should be apart for a year. Mommy said if we can be apart for a year and still be in love, we will be faithful to each other."

"You look miserable, baby," daddy said as he watched mommy frying bacon.

"Catherine said she is not angry that Bernard and I love each other," I said, as I leaned on my hands and stared down into my empty plate.

Daddy eyed the bacon mommy fried like a cat watching a bird feeder. "A year, you say?" Daddy looked like he was about to drool.

"I don't want to wait a year," I said, "but mommy, you are right. If we can be faithful for a year, we will live happily together forever without straying."

"Yes, dear," mommy said as she turned the bacon over with a fork.

Daddy watched intently. "Are you frying enough bacon, cupcake?" daddy asked mommy. "How many strips are you giving me?"

"Two," mommy called over her shoulder.

"Two?" daddy whined. "Why only two? You usually cook three strips for me."

"Mr. Charleston said with a history of heart failure in your family, I need to cook less bacon and boil more vegetables."

Daddy suddenly looked morose. "I'm not sharing our grandchildren with him! I mean it, Mirabel! Maybel!" daddy looked at me, "I will be the favorite grandpa! They will call me Grammpy and I will be their favorite!"

I looked at daddy confused.

"Oh, you aren't going to wait a year, Maybel, everyone knows you and Bernard have been in love since the day you met! And now, Byron has crossed the line! He is interfering with bacon time! I will be the favorite Grammpy, and when Byron looks sadly at me holding our grandchildren on my lap, I swear to you, I'll look over at him and say, 'You should have kept your nose out of my breakfast bacon and allowed me to have three strips, not two!'" Daddy pounded the table with his fist.

Mommy turned around and rolled her eyes at daddy. "You won't be spending much time with our grandchildren if you keep eating three slices of bacon. We're both going to cut down on bacon slices and we're going to start taking long walks together in the evenings so we'll be alive long enough to enjoy our beautiful grandchildren."

Daddy huffed.

"Daniel! Your father died right in front of Catherine of a heart attack! Do you want your little granddaughter to experience that?"

"No," daddy pouted.

Mommy laid two strips of bacon in front of daddy. Daddy, to my sheer surprise, pushed away his plate. He leaned back and crossed his arms. "Go get number two," he muttered. "I want to see my grandchildren get old." Daddy sulked, but when I got up and walked toward the kitchen door, I glanced at daddy winking and smiling at mommy.

Daddy saw me watching him and continued sulking again, "Bernard isn't horrible, but don't tell him I said that," daddy crossed his arms again, mumbling.

"Daddy doesn't want Bernard to know daddy likes him," mommy explained. "It's a male dominance thing."

I sulked around a bit thinking about everything. I wondered what Bernard might be up to in that big mansion.

The day wore on with Catherine and mommy sewing gowns for the New Year's Eve party at the Charleston's.

"I'm so bored, Catherine." I stretched out on the sofa.

"Go play with Susan until I finish sewing." Catherine threaded a needle carefully as she spoke.

"And then you'll play with me?" I asked her.

"How about we go sledding at the hill for old time's sake?"

"Really?" I became very excited. Catherine hadn't wanted to sled or ice skate in years. Now she burped in front of Bernard, wore her hair unbrushed in front of him, and she finally agreed to go sledding. I was ecstatic.

I began preparing sandwiches for lunch. Bernard still hadn't come over. I guessed he was serious about being apart for an entire year. I was mad at myself for missing him. I finally had time to do something fun like sledding, and Bernard was not here.

Daddy sat at the kitchen table reading. "What do you think about fetching number two for me, Maybel? I need help shoveling snow."

"We're testing our fidelity, daddy," I muttered. "I want to be sure Bernard loves me, and only me, and not Catherine, since they spent years together."

"You spent years together with Bernard too," daddy grumbled, "Everyone knows you and Bernard are going to get married so you may as well go get him." Daddy paused, "Do not, and I cannot be more clear, Maybel, do not tell him I asked him to come over. I don't want him getting a big head thinking I like spending time with him."

"Ok, daddy." I didn't want to appear excited, but I was becoming ever more bored and I wanted to go sledding.

"Go ahead, dear," mommy said. "I'll finish preparing lunch. Tell Bernard I'll have a sandwich ready for him."

I dashed off to Bernard's in my thick coat and boots. My naughty streak came out of dormancy, not that it was ever truly dormant, and I filled my pockets with the snow that settled on Bernard's rooftop just before I pushed open his window.

"Maybel, you're here!" Bernard smiled and I hit him with the snowball from my pocket.

Bernard looked surprised and then even more surprised when another snowball came hurling into his open mouth.

"Maybel!" Bernard picked up the scattered clumps of snow and came after me.

"Whee!" I squealed as I ran around his bed dodging the itty, bitty snowballs Bernard made from my two big snowballs.

"Maybel! I demand another battle!"

"As you wish, but first, I think daddy misses you and Henry. He wants help shoveling snow, but I think he's as bored as I am."

Bernard smiled the whole time I spoke. "You're so beautiful," he said.

I ignored him. "Let's go, number two!"

Bernard kept smiling as he put on a sweater. "I'm so happy you came!"

"Daddy told me to come get you," I said. "I didn't want to come, but daddy asked me to come."

"Maybel, do you like my new scarf? It's not pink, but it'll do."

"It looks nice," I said.

"Guess who made it?"

"Your grandmother?"

"Me! Your mother taught me while you were at school." Bernard handed me a beautifully knitted green scarf. "I made this for you. It's green like your eyes."

"Thank you," I said.

Bernard tied my new scarf around my neck then tugged on it and pulled me close. "May I kiss you?"

"No."

"Very well," he smiled, "I'll ask again another day."

"Where's Henry?"

"With auntie and uncle," Bernard answered.

"Ok, then it's just me and you. Mommy said to tell you she is making a sandwich for you."

"That sounds wonderful," Bernard kept smiling at me.

"Tree or stairs?" I asked.

"Stairs. The tree has ice," Bernard said.

"Boring choice, but I suppose the stairs are safer," I said.

We walked to my house dodging each other's snowballs. Bernard opened my gate for me. Snowballs began pelting us from every direction.

"Number two!" daddy yelled then hit Bernard square in his face with a giant snowball.

Mommy and Catherine hit me and then Catherine hurled another, larger snowball at Bernard.

"Attack!" I screamed.

Bernard and I ducked behind a bush. "Maybel! Did you know about this?"

"No!" I giggled.

"Come out, come out!" daddy yelled.

"Maybel, I have something special for you!" Catherine giggled.

I quickly packed three snowballs and Bernard filled his pockets with snowballs.

"Charge!" I screamed, and Bernard and I threw our snowballs but were pelted with many more.

"I surrender!" I laughed.

"I still have three snowballs left," mommy yelled, and hit both me and Bernard, then used her last one to hit daddy's behind. "Hit your hiney!" mommy giggled.

"Mommy you have a really good arm!" I said.

"Why thank you, sweetheart," mommy tossed snow at me and laughed.

"Hot chocolate time!" Catherine said. "I have peppermint sticks I bought at school if anyone wants some."

Catherine skipped inside. Her hair was peppered with snow but she didn't make a fuss about it. I liked this less-prissy Catherine much better, but I hoped Bernard did not.

"I love this family," Bernard said. "I've never had my parents stockpile snowballs and hit me."

"Invite your father over later, Bernard. We'll make a fort with lots of snowballs beforehand," daddy looked excited.

"Really? We can do that?"

"Sure, why not?" daddy shrugged.

"I've never played with my parents before." Bernard's face was aglow with amazement.

"Understandable," daddy said, "Your parents have been busy building an empire."

"I'd be happier living here and getting pelted with snowballs," Bernard said quietly, more to himself than to us.

We sipped hot chocolate with our peppermint sticks. Mommy dried our socks on the stone in front of our fireplace while Catherine and I played a board game.

Bernard listened to daddy talk about carving. Bernard looked more interested than I was.

"Do you have any boyfriends?" I whispered to Catherine.

"No," she whispered back.

"Why? You're the prettiest girl there."

"I went to dinner a couple of times with some boys from my college, but I don't want a relationship now."

"Is it because you like Henry?" I whispered.

"No. I like Henry, but Henry's a tomcat," Catherine whispered back.

"I hear whispers," daddy announced.

Catherine and I giggled.

"Who's the boy?" daddy asked.

"No boys!" Catherine and I giggled.

"Fine, don't tell me. I'll find out," daddy winked. "I have a spear now, don't I Bernard?"

"Yes, sir," Bernard said.

"It's sharp," daddy smiled and sipped his hot chocolate.

Catherine and I laughed because daddy really seemed to enjoy taunting boys.

"Who's going to help me bake cookies?" Mommy finished drying our socks and walked toward the kitchen calling to us over her shoulder.

"I will," Bernard said quickly.

"You can run to the kitchen, Bernard, but my spear can travel faster than you can run, and farther than the kitchen." Daddy chuckled menacingly as Bernard stood up.

"I'm getting better at cooking, Mr. Wyndham. Cookies taste a lot better with eggs."

"Yes, quite the discovery you've made, Bernard. If only our forefathers knew about eggs," daddy dryly remarked.

Catherine got up and went to the kitchen too.

"Just you and me then, Maybel," daddy smiled at me.

"Daddy, why weren't you mean to Bernard when he dated Catherine?"

"I'm not mean, honey, this is how men communicate. And I never had to threaten Bernard when he dated Catherine because it was obvious they were not in a serious relationship."

"I'm not in a serious relationship with Bernard either."

Daddy sighed, "You and Bernard have always had something special. I knew Catherine and Bernard would likely not marry, but you and Bernard," daddy paused, "I can see that there's something more special between you, whether or not you choose to marry."

I thought about what daddy said. "Daddy, were you mean to mommy when you were young? Did you tease her?"

"No. We met just after high school. We were not children."

"Bernard teased me and treated me like an annoying, little sister. It hurt my feelings."

"I know, baby."

"Why did he do that?"

Daddy sighed, thinking for the right words. "Boys don't think like girls. Girls think things through. Boys are more physical and less intellectual. Mommy says we mature at a slower rate, and that's probably a fair assessment."

"Do you like Bernard, daddy?"

"I think he's been doing a lot of maturing this past year. I think underneath his teasing and whatnot he's always loved you. He should have shown his love in a nicer way, but he never hit you, and I always felt when I let you go places with him, that you were safe and protected. I suppose that's what all parents want most for their children, safety, health, and protection."

I sat for a moment and thought about what daddy said.

"Nobody will be a better husband and father than you, daddy."

Daddy smiled, "Come give your old dad a hug."

I hugged daddy. I considered who hugged the most like daddy: Bernard, Henry, or Theo, or someone I had not yet met.

Daddy and I played cards while mommy and Catherine patiently showed Bernard how to sift flour and roll dough. Lots of laughter came from the kitchen while daddy and I played cards.

"Baby, can you pour me some more hot chocolate?" daddy asked.

"Yes, daddy." I went to the kitchen and Bernard and Catherine were play-fighting with flour.

Bernard patted Catherine's cheek with his flour-covered hand and Catherine giggled and playfully pushed him away. Her hair was sprinkled with flour and Bernard tousled it and they laughed.

"Where's mommy?" I asked.

"Oh, Maybel," Catherine looked startled. "Mommy went to get eggs." Catherine laughed, "Bernard told me he made pancakes and pumpkin bread without eggs."

Catherine playfully slapped Bernard's shoulder and he laughed and sprinkled more flour on her hair.

I poured hot chocolate for daddy and returned to the family room.

"What's wrong, honey?" daddy asked.

"I just realized how Catherine felt watching Bernard and me play."

Daddy sighed, "I swear if he switches sisters again I'll hide his body in a pig pen."

"Do you think Bernard still loves Catherine?"

"Love doesn't die, it might fade like an ember, but embers have grown to burn entire forests," daddy said.

"Oh." My lower lip quivered.

Daddy took a deep breath, "There'll probably always be an ember there. I don't know to what capacity they still love each other, but I'm sure it's nothing, sweetheart. People don't cease feeling overnight, but I really don't think it's anything to worry about."

"Ok, daddy," I said.

Laughter still floated from the kitchen to my ears and it brought nagging seeds of doubt that landed and took root in my brain. I sat with daddy and played cards while I pictured those seeds taking root in my mind and growing fast, like weeds. Thick vines wound out of my ears and nose and pushed out my eyeballs.

"Bernard!" I ran into the kitchen. "Do you still love Catherine?"

Bernard and Catherine stood at the kitchen table sharing a rolling pin while Catherine showed Bernard how to roll out dough. Bernard looked surprised. "No," he said. "Why do you ask?"

"You're standing together sharing a rolling pin while laughing and flirting. I'm sorry, Catherine. I understand now what it must have felt like watching me and Bernard, and I'm so sorry!"

"I'm going on a date with Theo tonight," Catherine said. "I know you two dated, but I told Theo that Bernard was trying to win your love, and that I thought Bernard would succeed. Theo will talk to you today to see how you feel about Bernard, and with whom you want a relationship. I told Theo I knew you'd choose Bernard, and when you do, to pick me up at seven for a date."

Catherine went back to rolling cookie dough like she hadn't said something important.

I stared at Catherine. I felt all the array of emotions. I turned around and left the kitchen.

"Everything ok?" daddy asked me.

"Catherine told Theo I wasn't available to date him, and now Catherine is going to date Theo."

Daddy made a disgusted noise. "Theo's in third place then because he left you." Daddy paused thoughtfully, "He did come back for you though, so maybe I'll bump him up to second place. I'll see how Bernard's cookies taste before I decide whether or not Theo's in second or third place to be my favorite son."

"Daddy, I wanted to decide who to date! I wanted to choose! Catherine made that choice for me and that really angers me!"

"Go down the street right now and take Theo sledding, and afterward, sip hot chocolate together while you watch ice skaters. Go get your coat."

"Daddy, I need a minute to think."

"Go take Theo sledding right now. It's just a fun afternoon out with Theo. I'll tell Bernard you left. Go on and have fun."

"But," I stammered.

"Why are you still here?" daddy asked me. "Go on and have fun."

"I want to go sledding with Bernard," I said quietly.

"Bernard! Get in here!" daddy bellowed.

"I'm already here, sir," Bernard stood around the corner peeking his head into the family room. His smile was bigger than the sun. "You chose me."

"Good, it's settled," daddy said. "You got to choose, Maybel. Catherine didn't choose, you did."

Daddy turned back to Bernard. "Now go get my cookies before they burn, number two! Or are you number three? I'll decide after I taste your cookies."

"Yes, sir," Bernard smiled.

"Daddy?" I whispered.

"Yes, sweetheart?"

"Thank you."

"I love you, baby."

"I love you too, daddy."

Bernard invited me to dinner at his house. "Maybel, Paul will be there."

My eyes brightened.

"I kept you apart from Paul all these years. He could have visited me, and I could have taken you to see him. I was jealous because you liked Paul. I know I should have let you two decide for yourselves what you wanted, but I was so, incredibly jealous of your attraction to him that I never let you entertain the idea of visiting him again."

"Why are you allowing us to dine together tonight, then?"

"If you love each other, I will be happy for you."

"Really?"

"I'll be happy for you," Bernard repeated.

I stared at Bernard. I didn't believe him.

"I will be bitter for a while, I'm sure, but ultimately, I will step back and allow you to choose your own future."

I continued to stare at Bernard disbelievingly. "And your sudden change of heart, letting me dine with my beloved Paul, has nothing to do with Paul and Susan being attracted to one another?"

"Watching Paul and Susan kiss may have made me more willing to entertain the idea of having Paul come visit."

"Susan confessed to me she likes Archie more than Paul, so Paul is free to date me."

Bernard suddenly looked upset and took a deep breath, pausing to choose his words carefully. "I'll probably punch a hole through my bedroom wall and I likely won't attend your wedding, but I'll still try to be at least somewhat decent in my interactions with Paul. I'm trying, Maybel! I'm trying so hard to be better! Please be patient with me!"

"Very well," I smiled smugly, "Susan doesn't like Archie more than Paul. I lied."

Bernard exhaled deeply and his shoulders sunk as he relaxed. "Maybel, I'm so glad. I suddenly felt myself losing you and it hurt."

"I like the way Paul looks at Susan," I said. "And I like the way she returns his adoration. I am happy for them."

Bernard smiled, "You don't want to pursue a relationship with Paul?"

"No, I dol not. I am happy they found each other. Besides, there's another man in whom I am interested."

"Who, Maybel?" Bernard looked crushed. And then, Bernard straightened his back and spoke with resolution. "Whoever it is, doesn't matter. I'm going to win your love and marry you and have lots of beautiful babies with you, providing they all look like you, of course." Bernard watched me for a moment, then very softly brushed a stray lock of hair from my cheek.

I felt his fingertips lingering behind my ear as he brushed my hair back and his gentle smile made me feel happy.

"You are the man in whom I am interested," I grinned cheekily at Bernard.

Bernard suddenly wrapped his arms around me and hugged me tightly. "Stay for dinner, please, Maybel."

"I would like to dine with you tonight," I told Bernard.

"There is nothing I want more than to have you beside me. I will spend the rest of my days loving you the way you deserve to be loved. You can have all the cherries on all my custards and I vow to stomp on all the spiders that come near you."

Mrs. Charleston and her sister, Mrs. Cambridge, Paul's mother, sat next to each other. I could tell they were close. They giggled and whispered jokes about naughty things they did together when they were children. I wished I were sitting next to Catherine.

Mr. Charleston was talking about boats. His conversation was alive with showmanship. Boats weren't interesting, but Mr. Charleston could make any subject interesting. I missed gambling with him.

Paul and Susan spoke quietly. They smiled a lot at each other. Paul shifted in his seat and I could just barely glimpse his hand on Susan's knee.

Bernard and I sat next to each other but I still felt a distance between us, and that made me sad.

"Bernard?"

"Yes, Maybel?"

"After dinner, would you like to take a stroll?" I asked.

Bernard smiled, "Yes, Maybel."

We continued eating our steak in silence. Everyone around us talked loudly and laughed even louder. Bernard and I didn't know how to talk to each other anymore.

I looked down at my peas. I took a deep breath. I wasn't sure what to do next.

I felt Bernard's hand very lightly brush against mine under the table and rest on my chair near my hand, but not touching me.

I looked at Bernard and he looked hesitant. He smiled shyly. I put my hand lightly on his and his smile grew. I felt his fingers intertwine with mine and my pulse quickened.

We finished dinner holding hands under the table. I had held Bernard's hand many times but this time, my heart beat faster. His hands were warm and soft and both our palms were sweaty. I had always fidgeted with Bernard's hands when we were younger, and while he watched me when Catherine was talking with friends. I always had more energy than my body could hold, which resulted in me becoming bored and fidgety. Bernard held my hand to keep me from bouncing around and annoying Catherine and her friends while they chatted about things they thought made them sound intelligent and important. I always held his fingers and climbed all over him and played with his hands and hair and just, absolutely annoyed him tremendously, I was sure. Bernard was always kind to me though, and patient, until that phase he went through when he wasn't nice to me. Fortunately, we seemed to be falling back into our friendship. Bernard continued holding my hand through dessert.

As we ate our ice cream, I did become a little fidgety. Bernard leaned over and whispered, "You held out a lot longer than I expected. You were able to almost get through dessert before you started rubbing and tapping my hand," he laughed quietly into my ear.

"Old habits, I guess," I whispered back.

"It's alright, sweetheart, it's nice to have you back," he smiled.

"You haven't called me sweetheart in a while," I said.

"Would you prefer Maybel?"

"No," I answered.

"As you wish, sweetheart," Bernard smiled and winked.

Suddenly Bernard's face blushed bright red. He was looking across the table. I looked to see what had caused his embarrassment. Mrs. Charleston and her sister, Mrs. Cambridge, were leaning into each other, watching us and giggling. I felt my face blush hot too.

Bernard and I looked down at our dessert but I could still hear little whispered giggles from across the table. Bernard squeezed my hand and I squeezed back.

After dinner I told Susan I was going to walk around the gardens. "Ok, Maybel, I'll probably be in the study talking to Paul about art."

I giggled and left. I knew they would not be talking.

Bernard and I drifted away from the dining room and instead of the gardens, he asked if I'd like to go to the kitchen and talk. He said it was dark outside and he wanted to see my face while we spoke. We sat at the kitchen table where we had eaten soup together since childhood.

"I wanted to ask you if you had reconsidered attending my college?" Bernard asked.

"It's too expensive, Bernard," I said.

"I was really hoping to see you more," Bernard reached for my hands across the table and we held hands.

"We would still see each other on school breaks."

"I'd rather see you for dinner every evening," he said wistfully.

"But then you won't have time to focus on your studies," I winked at him.

"I will always have time for you, Maybel, always." He squeezed my hands and smiled shyly. "Maybel, Catherine and I didn't break up because of my studies. Truthfully, we broke up years ago because we grew apart, but we stayed together because it felt familiar to be with each other."

I looked down at our hands holding each other.

"I told Catherine I loved you when we arrived home from Connecticut, after Theo accepted his position in England. She was not surprised."

My head snapped upward to look Bernard in his eyes with my now very-wide eyes.

"She never said." I wondered why Catherine had never told me that Bernard confessed to loving me.

"I told Catherine I loved her. I said I had always loved you, too, and that I loved being with you. I apologized to her for not having told her sooner and I asked for her forgiveness. She did not immediately forgive me, but she did later. She came to me and said she loved you, and that if you accepted my hand in marriage and I were ever unfaithful, she would tear out my entrails and pour salt and then alcohol into my wounded cavities."

"Catherine said that?" I was so happy I began crying.

"Yes, Maybel, and she absolutely meant it. She brought a knife hidden in her skirt pocket and told me she would first shoot my kneecaps before she gutted me, and then she showed me her gun that she had hidden in her other skirt pocket. I will never be unfaithful to you, Maybel, even without threats to my life, but my God, your family terrifies me!"

"Catherine did that? Catherine loves me and she accepts that you and I love each other," I sniffled. "That makes me so happy," I beamed.

"Did you not hear the part about her bringing a gun and knife? Wait," Bernard stopped and his eyes grew wide, "You just said you love me!"

"Catherine pulled a knife and a gun on you," I shed a few tears. "I love her too," I sniffled. "She is the best big sister ever!"

"Maybel!" Bernard kept staring at me.

"What?"

"You admitted to loving me!"

"Yes, Bernard, I love you, I've always loved you, and I always will love you. Why does this surprise you?"

"Maybel, I was nervous that you were mad at me for hurting Catherine so I tried to give you time, but I decided I had to see you. I accidentally on purpose ran into you at the autumn festival," he admitted. "Then I became terrified that you would run into Paul. Catherine brought you to Paul to watch you two reunite, you know, and I'm sure she wanted to hurt me, and I'm also sure I deserved her ire. I was so scared you would fall in love with Paul before I had a chance to make things right between us. I decided then and there to not attend college. I knew I had to move fast if I wanted you to forgive me and fall in love with me before Paul started visiting more frequently."

"I'm glad you accidentally on purpose ran into me at the autumn festival. I have fond memories of growing up with you and I miss feeling comfortable around you. It's nice to be able to insult you and know that you won't take it personally," I smiled.

"You don't insult me, Maybel, you've always been kind to me."

"No, I haven't, my dry humor goes over your head, dummy," I giggled.

Bernard laughed, "You're absolutely horrible at math."

"Your comedic delivery needs work. That was more rude than funny," I said flatly.

"I'm sorry, Maybel!"

"I was joking, it's called deadpan delivery, idiot," I said dryly.

Bernard looked confused. "You're still doing dry humor, right?"

"See, this is why we can't have children Bernard, I fear they'll be stupid and humorless," I said without a smile.

"Ok, but you're still doing your weird humor thing, aren't you?" Bernard asked, "Because I'm not sure if I should laugh or be offended."

"Be offended. Be very, very offended," I winked. "Did you see me wink just now? Maybe I should start winking more. I think I'll need to wink twice and extra hard for you though, dummy." I winked twice, very obviously indicating that I was indeed joking.

Bernard laughed, "Stop trying to woo me, Maybel, you know I don't want to have sex before marriage."

I laughed, "I'll try to control myself."

"Tomorrow night is the New Year's Eve ball. Will you do me the honor of being my date?" Bernard's eyes were twinkling.

I paused. My stomach began fluttering. "Catherine and Theo will likely attend," I winced. "I don't know if I can handle all this change happening at once."

"May I come to your house and we can play games, drink hot chocolate, and sit in front of the fire together?" Bernard smiled big. He knew my weaknesses. I loved staying home and being boring, and fortunately, so did he.

It was New Year's Eve. Catherine said if I at least came to the New Year's Eve ball for just a few minutes, she would give me a present she had arranged for me. I wondered what it could be and could hardly contain my excitement. I figured Catherine just wanted to dress me up like her doll again, because she came into my bedroom before breakfast with five dresses to choose from and her hair brush.

"The ball is tonight, Catherine, not this morning," I mumbled and farted.

"Why must you always expel gas in the mornings?" Catherine looked disgusted.

"Is there a better time to fart?" I asked sarcastically.

I dressed in Catherine's mint green gown with soft, shimmery fabric and put dangling pearls in my earlobes. Catherine helped me tame my locks. Beautiful, dark, curls cascaded down my shoulders. From our kitchen, I took several cranberries from a jar and lightly pressed them into my lips, moving them carefully back and forth, eliciting trickles of red juice that turned my lips a light shade of red.

We arrived at the Charleston's and were awed, as we were every year, by the beautiful pine wreath decorations and candles that lit the many windows of their beautiful home.

Bernard greeted Catherine at the carriage house and dutifully helped her descend. Bernard held his hand up for me to hold and step down. I stumbled. I was never graceful. Bernard swiftly reached both arms around my waist and steadied me.

"Thank you," I blushed, as I stepped onto the cobblestone path. I was embarrassed, but I was used to being awkward. I took a step forward, regaining my composure, and was going to simply walk to the door of the main house, but Bernard did not let go of my waist. I looked up into his eyes and saw something I'd never seen before. He was staring at me, but not because I'd stumbled and was awkward. He was looking at me differently.

"Your lips are red. Did you bump your lips when you stumbled?"

Mommy and daddy let out a chuckle and Catherine stifled a laugh.

"No," I said, "It's just cranberries."

We continued inside with me tailing our group. I wanted to slip into obscurity. "Can I have my secret present now?" I asked Catherine. "I want to go home where I can stumble without onlookers."

Bernard held the door for Catherine and mommy and daddy. I trailed behind sulking.

"In a few minutes," Catherine called over her shoulder.

"Thank you," I said as Bernard continued holding the door for me."

Bernard touched my shoulder and drew me closer so that I was forced to look him in the eyes. "Maybel, I didn't mean for you to suffer an insult." He continued in earnest, "I was surprised by your lip color. I didn't mean to embarrass you."

I sighed, "It's ok. My family is used to my awkwardness, and fortunately, you are too."

"I love your awkwardness," he smiled cheekily. "It pairs well with your other charms."

I giggled, "Thank you."

The Charleston's mansion was filled with glitter and opulence. Their Christmas Eve and New

Year's Eve parties were grander than anything in my imagination, and my imagination was expansive. There was a band playing and their Christmas tree was at least nine feet tall. I immediately ran to the tree to inspect the ornaments. There were strings of popcorn and cranberries and tinsel from top to bottom. There were at least three dozen small, thin candlesticks on the boughs dripping wax into little tin cups.

"Oh look! There are cranberries in case you want to reapply your lip color, Maybel," daddy joked as he patted my shoulder and tugged my earlobe on his way to drink brandy with Mr. Charleston.

When the band took a rest, Catherine came to me. "Maybel, shall I show you your surprise?"

"Yes!" I said with glee. I could hardly wait.

"Come with me," Catherine said.

We walked past the band, the looming Christmas tree, our parents, and all the chattering guests and onto the back porch. "Where are you taking me?" I whispered.

"Just follow me," she said.

We walked the pathway to the horse stables where Bernard was waiting.

"Bernard will take you for a horseback ride," Catherine smiled and hugged me.

I squealed with delight and wrapped my arms around Catherine. I bounced up and down on my toes with excitement.

"Now listen, Maybel, you know mommy doesn't approve of horseback riding because of her little brother's accident."

Catherine continued, "I will return to the party and if mommy or daddy ask, I will say you are in the garden getting fresh air."

Bernard was waiting beside Big Ben, the tallest and most handsome horse ever. I grinned from ear to ear as I approached him.

"Now listen, Maybel, don't stay gone for too long. Don't dawdle."

I promised Catherine I would be quick.

Catherine turned and walked quickly back toward the party.

I turned to Bernard, who was standing by his horse.

"Maybel," he looked at me with a big smile, "Shall we?"

"Yes!" I exclaimed, with all the enthusiasm of someone about to receive the best Christmas present ever.

Bernard wrapped his hands around my waist and told me to put my leg over the back of the horse as he lifted me up. He hoisted me up with his strong arms, and I did as I was told, and threw my leg over the horse's back. Next, Bernard said to hold steady and carefully lean backward slightly so he could hoist himself in front of me. With his strong arms and legs, he easily managed to pull himself up onto the horse's back in front of me. We rode bareback as he did not have a saddle that would properly hold both of us.

"Are you ready?" he asked.

"Always," I answered.

I was surprised at how high up we sat. The last time I had ridden a horse was with Henry.

"Let's go," Bernard patted Big Ben. Big Ben jerked forward and I grabbed Bernard tightly around his stomach. I pulled close and let out a surprised gasp.

"It's alright, Maybel, I'll go slow."

I relaxed my shoulders but kept hold of his body. The air was chilly and I could see the house alight with candles in the distance. Big Ben sauntered slowly up the path. I held Bernard tightly because the rocking motion was unsettling from this high up.

"Relax Maybel, take a deep breath. You won't fall. Just hold tight and you'll be ok."

I held onto him with trepidation. Being this high up, and Ben walking uphill, I felt as though I might fall backward onto the ground. Ben jerked forward and backward hard with each step. I fell hard into Bernard's back a couple times.

We continued downhill now, causing my body to shove hard against Bernard's back as we slowly and carefully trotted down. I began to relax as we moved across the meadow, along the edge of the pond. The moon was bright and reflected beautifully off the pond water. I became aware of how cold the winter air was on my face and hands yet how hot Bernard's back felt against my stomach.

Big Ben began trotting faster to get up a small hill and I had to hold Bernard tighter because I was again scared I'd fall backward, tumbling perilously to my death.

At the top of the hill, Bernard told me to look down at the pond. The stars were shining onto the glassy surface of the water. I breathed in the night air deeply. We began slowly trotting on level ground along the side of the pond. The slow melodic sound of hoof steps beating the cold, snow-laden ground relaxed me. I felt my shoulders lower and my hips relax and settle into the monotonous rhythm of the horse plodding along the trail. The pine trees were peppered in snow, their lower branches weighed down considerably by fluffy white snowfall. Again, I breathed deeply, and relaxed my shoulders and hips.

I felt more at ease. My breaths became slower and deeper.

Bernard hadn't said much since we departed the stable, but neither had I. The cold night air caused me to shiver.

"Here, let me give you my coat, Maybel," he said.

"No, I'm fine," I replied.

Bernard persisted. He stopped Big Ben and took off his coat and wrapped it tightly around me so that it consumed me, and draped over his shoulders, offering him a little warmth as well. I was grateful to him for the added warmth, but quickly became aware of how close our bodies were now.

We plodded along the trail, passing trees and brush. The slow up and down movements of Big Ben's gait entranced me into a dreamlike state. I held tightly to Bernard, my hands were around his waist, my body pressed into his back.

As we continued our journey, the slow and rhythmic up and down movements began to make my thighs tingle. My body was pressed so tightly against Bernard that I could feel his breathing and the tightness of his muscles against me. My hands had been tightly gripping his stomach but were now more relaxed and wrapped loosely around his hips. I rested my head on his shoulder. I could feel him against me, moving up, down, and back and forth as we moved along the trail. I again became aware of a tingling sensation between my legs. As we continued, I became less aware of the owls hooting and the gentle snowfall, and more aware of the wetness between my legs.

We turned a corner and Big Ben began descending a hill, which caused my body to fall onto Bernard's back, and I could do nothing to increase the space between us. I tried tightening my thighs and leaning backwards but a sudden jerk in Ben's gait slammed me back into Bernard.

We continued down the hill, jerking unsteadily until Ben found a steady pace. Once we were back into a slow and steady descent, I again became aware of the constant, rhythmic movement of the front of my body against Bernard. I couldn't stop the continuous grinding of my thighs and waist against Bernard as we moved slowly down the hill. I felt my face get hot. I swallowed hard. We pressed on in the night, slowly, painfully rhythmically, downward to the valley below.

The horse began a slightly faster pace as we rounded another corner and down a steeper side of the hill. I began breathing more heavily. The tingling in my thighs began to spread down my legs. The downward motion of the steep hill thrust my breasts hard against Bernard's back. I felt my nipples tighten and my thighs were now very wet. The faster gait caused my breathing to quicken as my hips thrusted against Bernard harder.

Big Ben trotted faster down the steep path now, and my clitoris began rubbing against Bernard with such hard and rhythmic pounding that a breathy moan escaped my lips.

"Are you cold, Maybel?" Bernard asked me.

"No," I softly whimpered, not wanting him to guess the real reason for my soft moan.

I felt my nipples pulse with electricity as they rubbed against Bernard. Another moan escaped my lips. I tried to hide my mounting pleasure.

I sucked in air, trying to stifle the pleasure I felt building within my body.

We continued trotting along at a slower pace on more level ground again, but my hips were still pressed hard against Bernard, and I wasn't sure if it was my full bladder or the continuous grinding against Bernard, but I could feel a tiny, electrical pulsing between my thighs getting stronger. I breathed deeply and tried to relax and focus on something else.

All at once, Big Ben began to pick up his pace when he saw the stable in the distance, and I again was thrown forward into Bernard. I moaned from the pleasure. I didn't mean to moan, but I couldn't stop the mounting pleasure the pressure and grinding, and the smell of Bernard's hot skin against my breasts gave me. I felt my body just give in to the rhythmic thrusting of my clitoris against Bernard, and I breathed in deeply as a wave of sheer pleasure pulsated through my body and I moaned loudly as I felt my vagina contract in glorious release. I held Bernard's chest as Big Ben's fast pace thrust me into Bernard over and over. I was still breathing heavily as Ben slowed down and entered the gate near the stable.

"Big Ben gets excited when we round that last corner and can see the stable," Bernard said to me as he slid off the horse."

I remained quiet because I was so embarrassed at what had just happened. I continued staring down, not wanting to look into his eyes.

Bernard held his hand up to me.

I took his hand but did not look at him as I slid down off the horse.

"Maybel, your face is flushed and you're still breathing fast."

"I wasn't scared," I said, my words were hardly audible.

Bernard suddenly looked into my eyes quizzically. "You can wear one of my mother's dresses," he said.

"I don't need to change," I shot back.

"It's ok that you got scared and peed a little. You don't need to be embarrassed."

"I didn't pee and I wasn't scared!"

The cold, wet fabric of my dress clung to my thighs. I gasped in embarrassment. "It's not pee!" I stammered. "I just, I, I didn't pee and I wasn't scared."

"I could hear you behind me whimpering. It's ok that you got scared. Big Ben is a very tall horse. Your face is flushed from fright and...." He stopped. "Oh," he said, and he looked at me as though he wanted to ask me a question, but stopped himself.

We sat together on a hay bale for a minute. I was silent in my embarrassment. Bernard lightly touched my hand. "Let's go inside. I'll find one of mother's dresses for you."

I stood up but my legs were still weak from release and buckled.

Bernard grabbed my waist to steady me but as I stumbled, I reached out to steady myself, and felt something unexpected. My eyes widened when I felt his penis hard against my waist.

Bernard froze. "Maybel, I'm sorry! I didn't mean to, I realized what had happened, and I didn't mean for this to happen."

And with that we headed back toward the party in silence. Bernard walked fast and I could barely keep up. I was embarrassed that he was trying to get rid of me by walking fast, and it reminded me of when I peed on him when we were younger. I followed Bernard upstairs to retrieve his mother's dress from her closet. I took the dress from him without looking at his face; I was mortified. Bernard went toward his bedroom and I followed.

"Hurry up and change, please, Maybel, I need to use the bathroom."

I went in Bernard's bathroom and took my dress off and put Mrs. Charleston's dress on.

Bernard knocked on the door. "Please hurry, Maybel! I really need to use the bathroom!"

"I'm hurrying!" I yelled back.

I looked for a place to hide my wet dress until I could come back and collect it later, at the end of the party. I stuffed it under a towel in the basket sitting in the corner.

"Are you almost done? I really need to use the bathroom!"

I flung open the door. "I'm done!" I said with annoyance.

Bernard pushed me to the side and was about to close his bathroom door when he noticed my dress. He stared at my breasts and hips. His erection was very clearly visible underneath his pants.

"You are stunning," Bernard murmured.

We stared at each other. "You look nice, too," I finally spoke.

Bernard kept watching me. I didn't know if I should go toward him or away.

"Maybel," he whispered. His voice was low. "May I kiss you?"

"Yes," I said.

Bernard came toward me and held my waist and kissed my lips. He felt different. He felt more passionate with me than he ever had before. His breath was deep and he hungrily kissed my neck.

"Remember when we looked at each other without touching each other?" Bernard's voice cracked. He pulled back and watched me. He seemed nervous. "I am about to go insane, Maybel; I need to relieve myself. Can I watch you touch yourself while I touch myself?"

I stared at Bernard. "I don't know. Do other people do that? I mean, is it something we can do?"

"I don't know, Maybel, but I can't go another minute without relieving myself. If you don't want to, you don't have to, but I need to. I really need to." Bernard looked in pain.

I stared at Bernard, unsure if this was something people did. I wondered if this was something he had done with Catherine.

"I've never done anything like that before," I said tentatively. "Have you?"

"No, I have not, but I've also never had a girl orgasm on me before, and I'm willing to try new things with you."

I considered what Bernard propositioned.

"I have to use the bathroom now, Maybel," Bernard turned and practically ran to the bathroom as he unbuckled his belt and flung it to the floor.

"Ok," I said.

Bernard stopped in the doorframe of his bathroom and turned around to me.

"I'll do it," I said.

"You don't have to, Maybel, and if you don't want to, that's ok, but please tell me now so I can use the bathroom, because I'm going insane."

"I want to," I said.

Bernard went to his bed and kicked off his shoes and unbuttoned his pants. He sat on his bed and looked at me. "Are you sure?"

"Yes," I said.

Bernard unbuttoned his shirt as fast as his fingers allowed. He stood up and his pants dropped to his feet.

I stared at his fully erect penis. His body was beautiful.

Bernard laid on his back on his bed and held his penis. He groaned when he wrapped his hand around himself.

I walked toward him and pulled my gown off my shoulders and it fell to my feet. Bernard sucked in air as he took in my now, very-well developed body. He pulled and pushed on his penis as he watched me sit beside him, then lay beside him on my side facing him. Bernard turned on his side and faced me.

I put my finger on my clitoris and rubbed in a small circle. Bernard seemed mesmerized watching my fingers. His body looked rigid and his erection looked longer, thicker, and harder.

I felt awkward, but I slowly pushed my finger inside my vagina. It felt good, but Bernard was staring at me and so I felt a little nervous.

Bernard very lightly moved the palm of his hand around the shaft of his penis. "Will you lay on your back so I can see better?" Bernard whispered, his voice was low and strained.

I laid on my back and spread my legs apart so Bernard could see my finger penetrate my vagina. He grabbed his penis harder and moaned. His moans made me wet and I pushed in and out faster. I used my other hand to rub my clitoris and quickly felt an orgasm building. Bernard breathed faster and suddenly groaned loudly as hot liquid spurt into my eye and down my neck. "Ow! It stings!" I yelled.

Bernard kept holding himself as his body spasmed and shook. "I'm sorry!" he managed to moan. I rubbed my face on his pillow and some cranberry color, along with semen from my eye, smeared onto his pillowcase.

I got up and ran to the bathroom to rinse my eye in the sink.

"I'm sorry!" Bernard moaned again from the bed.

"I'm going to take a bath; this stuff is sticky!" I called over my shoulder.

I ran warm bathwater and slipped in. My clitoris was still stimulated and the warm water swirling between my legs aroused me. I let my hand slip under the water.

Bernard walked into the bathroom and froze. He saw me in his bathtub and became erect again. "May I join you?"

I paused pleasuring myself. "Yes."

Bernard sat in his bathtub facing me. I watched his face and he watched my hardened nipples and my hand moving between my legs. I began breathing harder and moaning softly. Bernard's face flushed. I arched my back as I orgasmed and Bernard lost control and groaned loudly.

I sat staring at Bernard and he watched me too. A small smile played on his lips. I smiled softly back.

Bernard stood up and got out of his bathtub. He held his hand out and pulled me up out of the water and stood me next to him. His penis was against my stomach and was hot on my skin.

He slowly leaned down and kissed my lips. He led me to his bedroom and took his clothes from the floor and handed me my dress. We slowly dressed as we watched each other.

Bernard held out his hand. We returned to the party. Bernard held my hand and stood beside me all evening, which fortunately, was only about an hour longer, and then we gleefully excused ourselves and went to my house to cuddle under a blanket in front of the fire.

"Maybel, come to my college, I miss you."

"I'd love for you to make me dinner every night and clean our house, Bernard, but your college is too expensive."

"I'll pay for your tuition," he said.

"Hmm, I'll think about it," I said.

"Really?" Bernard's eyes were bright and hopeful.

"I don't know, maybe," I laughed.

"Are you being serious or joking? I would love for you to attend my college!"

"I have to consider Catherine's feelings, Bernard. She's my sister."

"Maybel, I understand, but you're such a great writer and the professors at my college can help you further your natural talents. And I really will pay for your tuition."

My stomach tightened with thoughts of change. "Let's slow down. Change makes me feel panic. I'm starting to feel very nervous. Can we not talk about change tonight so I don't go into a full-blown panic?"

"Yes, Maybel, I'm sorry! How can I help you?"

"Let's talk about happy things until I calm down," I said. "Theo taught me how to calm myself when I thought too far ahead into the future. I got terribly nervous at times, and he taught me how to slow my breathing and focus on what is around me until my heartbeat stopped racing."

"Maybel, put your hand up."

I did as he asked. Bernard put his hand up to mine. "What do you feel?"

"You," I said.

"Maybel, you are more wordy than that," he smiled. "What do you feel."

"I feel the lines in your palm and the lines in your fingertips. Your hand is hot. Your fingertips are redder than the back of your hand. Your wrist, when it's pressed against mine, makes little beating pulses against my wrist. Your fingers are long and slender. Your hand is so much bigger than mine."

"How do you feel now, Maybel?" he whispered.

"I feel better," I said, surprised. "Why, I wonder?"

"You are not the only person to get scared and nervous, Maybel. I do, too."

"You don't!"

"I do, and when I do, I think about what is right in front of me. I think about the shape in front of me, its color, and the sound I hear around me. I focus on what the fabric feels like underneath my hands, and what the room smells like. I focus on all that. It helps bring me out of my mind and into the present."

"I didn't know you ever got nervous."

"I used to get nervous when I danced with you," he blushed.

"You were always so composed." I was skeptical.

"I looked composed. And you, Maybel, always looked like you were confident. Were you always confident?"

"No," I whispered.

"Looks are deceiving," he said softly.

"Why were you nervous to dance with me?"

"I didn't want you or Catherine to know how I really felt about you. I loved being near you. I know it wasn't fair to Catherine, but I loved holding you when we danced. I felt I couldn't tell you, because by that time, I had been dating Catherine a while, and didn't want to hurt her. I felt really bad for wanting to hold you because it seemed back then our age difference was much more profound."

"I always danced awkwardly. Catherine has always been as graceful as you. When you danced with me, did you notice my awkwardness?"

"Yes," he laughed. "And I loved it. It meant I could spend more time holding you and teaching you without raising suspicion. All I wanted to do was hold you in my arms, but I felt like a horrible person, because you seemed a lot younger than me back then."

"Why didn't you break up with Catherine sooner, if you wanted to be with me so much?" I thought if Bernard truly loved me, he would have told me a long time ago.

"I was scared. I was scared you saw me only as a brother. I was scared I was being bad because

I wanted someone younger than me who quite possibly only liked me as a brother. I didn't know how to tell you I loved you and not hurt Catherine or come between your love for each other."

"I liked you as a brother at first," I said, "but I also was attracted to you. I wanted to sit in your lap and have you hold me all the time because I felt safe there."

"I should have told you and Catherine sooner how I felt. It feels good to tell you now."

Bernard watched me for a minute. "Are you still feeling scared?"

"A little," I said.

"My mother planted a tree when I was born and it's at my grandparents' house. And when we moved here, she planted another one for me to mark this change in my life. Mother call's it my Life's Tree."

"Yes," I said, "Your mother told me about her kitchen table a long time ago," I smiled. I think having a Life's Tree is a wonderful way to celebrate a person's life."

I planted one over the summer. It's shaped almost like a wishbone, with two main branches coming up from a sturdy trunk."

"It's our tree," he smiled. "I knew we would always be together. It signifies our beginning."

I stared at Bernard. I was surprised. "You've really put a lot of thought into wooing me."

"Do you feel more relaxed now?" he asked me.

"I do. Thank you," I smiled softly up at him.

"Maybel, will you come to dinner again tomorrow?"

"Yes, Bernard."

"Would you like to come earlier and I can begin your math tutoring?"

"Oh, that sounds horrible!" I grimaced.

Bernard looked a little disappointed.

"Can't I just come over to go horseback riding, play ball games, or for any reason other than math?"

Bernard laughed, "Yes, of course, Maybel! I don't have to be tutoring you for you to come here. I only suggested tutoring you as a way to get you to spend time with me," he smiled shyly.

"Custard would have worked, too, you know, for future reference," I smiled back.

"What would you like to do tomorrow? Horseback riding, baseball, or something else?" he asked.

"What are the something elses of which you speak?"

"Anything you want," he smiled and held my hands.

"That's too broad. Can you narrow down my options? I'm not used to options as my family is on a budget.

Bernard chuckled, "I think horseback riding might be fun." He playfully pulled me closer.

"You just want to see if I'll accidentally orgasm again," I laughed.

"Yes, that occurred to me," Bernard smirked.

"I won't accidentally lose control again," I laughed.

"Great, prove it," he said, "Come with me tonight."

"Oh, now Bernard, I just said I wasn't going to come."

Bernard laughed, "Come to the stables with me tomorrow. You can sit in front this time so you won't enjoy it as much," he winked at me.

I laughed, "Ok."

"Maybel," he held his hand out and smiled sweetly at me. "I love you so much."

"I love you too, Bernard."

I left for Susan's house the next morning.

I knocked on Susan's door. I had some time to pass before I was to meet Bernard for dinner and I wanted to ask Susan about Paul. I had not had many chances to bond with Catherine while gossiping about boys, and I certainly couldn't do that now. I looked forward to talking about boys with Susan.

Susan answered her door. "Maybel! Guess what?"

"You kissed Paul," I whispered into her ear giggling.

"Come to my room, Maybel! Let's talk!"

We bounced up the stairs giggling the whole way. We darted into Susan's bedroom and closed her door. Susan whipped around and bounced next to me on her bed and we sat giggling at each other before we even began talking.

"Maybel! I'm in love!"

"You two have so much in common, Susan! It was like watching two souls finally meet after searching for each other after many lifetimes apart!"

"Maybel, I'm going to marry Paul! I know he's the one I will marry!"

"I'm so happy for you, Susan! You're going to dinner tonight, aren't you?"

"Yes! And you're coming with me, aren't you!"

"Yes!" I giggled.

"Maybel, does Catherine know you and Bernard like each other?"

"No, she thinks I went to have dinner with Paul. I haven't told her Bernard and I kissed last night."

"You kissed? I didn't know that!" she squealed.

"That's because you were busy getting to know Paul," I winked and giggled.

"He kissed me and he kisses so well, Maybel!"

"Did you feel like you were floating?" I grinned.

"Yes! Like I wasn't even inside my body anymore!" Susan squealed.

"You two are going to have the most beautiful babies," I giggled.

"Do you think they'll have blonde hair or black hair?" she asked.

"One of each, of course!" I said, and we both giggled so loudly Mr. Matthews knocked on Susan's door and asked if we needed oil for all our squeals.

"No!" we giggled.

"Ok then, how about mouse traps for all the squeaks I hear in there?"

"No!" We giggled and squealed even louder with laughter.

"Maybel," she whispered, "you have to promise not to tell anyone what I'm about to say. Paul and I did just a tiny bit more than kiss!" She smiled the kind of smile that told me exactly what she did.

"Susan, I half giggled and half snorted, I'm going to need that enchanted dress back so I can burn it before either of us has daughters!"

Susan looked quizzically at me and laughed, "Oh Maybel, it couldn't have been the dress, I wasn't wearing it at the time."

My mouth dropped. "Susan!"

"Just kidding, Maybel! We didn't do that!" Susan rolled backward laughing herself into a ball of bouncy giggles. "Oh, your face, Maybel! Oh, your face!" She laughed so hard she panted.

"Susan!" I pinched her arm lightly, "You sure had me! That was sneaky and I truly am proud of how well you've learned deadpan humor from me! I feel I've been a good teacher and you've been an even better student!"

We laughed and giggled until tears rolled down our cheeks. Mr. Matthews knocked on Susan's door. "Susan! A package has been delivered for you!"

Susan looked excited. She opened her door and there sat an oil can and a mouse trap on the floor in front of her room with a card that read, "To my dear, little, squeaky mice, Love, Daddy."

Susan closed her door and we laughed so hard our sides ached. "Oh Susan, I'm so glad I have you to talk to! I love you so much!"

"Maybel, I'm not even wearing that dress as you profess your love to me! I can only imagine how irresistible I am while wearing it!"

"Susan! Don't make me laugh any more, my sides are sore from laughter!"

"Mine too," she giggled, "and I love you too, Maybel!"

I arrived at Bernard's house. Vincent opened the door. "Hello, Miss Maybel," he said jovially.

"Hello, Vincent. Is Bernard available?"

"Go ahead into the family room. He's expecting you."

"Thank you, Vincent. I like your tie."

Vincent looked down. "Oh, why thank you! My granddaughter bought this for me for my birthday."

"She has good taste," I smiled, "And happy birthday!"

"Yes, she does," he smiled back, "And thank you!"

I bounced happily into the family room. "Bernard! I'm here for my dash of math tutoring!" I yelled happily.

Bernard was on the sofa reading. "Hello, Maybel!" he smiled. He stood and came to hug me. "How are you doing?"

"I'm well. Make sure you compliment Vincent's new tie. His granddaughter bought it for him for his birthday."

"I will, Maybel, I'm glad you're here. I always worry you'll decide not to come back to me."

"I'm like allergies, Bernard, you can always expect me to return."

Bernard laughed. "I want to kiss you again. May I?"

"It's May-bel, and no, I cannot kiss someone who cannot remember my name."

"Maybel," he laughed, "I love you." He bent down and kissed me tenderly.

"I like the way you kiss me," I whispered.

Bernard kissed me again. "Bernard, do you remember when you kissed me with your tongue on our way home from visiting Paul?"

"Yes, and I'm sorry. Looking back, I deserved your attack geese."

"I meant, kiss me like that again. You took my breath away that night."

Bernard smiled, "I'll always try to take your breath away with my kisses." He held my neck and kissed me with such passion and gentleness that I felt like I was floating.

"Like that?"

"Yes," I whispered, "exactly like that."

Bernard continued making me breakfast, packing my lunch, and walking me to school. His lunch notes became longer and more expressive as his writing abilities progressed. He greeted me after school with flowers or candies or a little trinket he saw that day that reminded him of me.

Spring soon swept over the land. Bernard's and my Life's Tree began blooming. Paul visited often to see Susan, and Theo and Catherine went on dates sometimes, but they were more reserved in their expressions of affection than Susan and Paul. Susan and Paul were expressive, creative, and their artistic natures allowed for showmanship and the boundaries of what is considered normal to be explored. Paul sculpted five-hundred little, ceramic flowers for Susan and planted them all over her yard one night while she slept. I passed by her house on a Saturday morning and could have sworn there were five-hundred decorative vaginas all along Susan's front yard.

Theo now lived and worked in the city. He came to take Catherine to dinner when Catherine was home on school breaks. Catherine told me she was not entering into another serious relationship until after college because she wanted freedom to date whomever she wanted without feeling trapped in a monogamous relationship. Theo, however, seemed ever-smitten with Catherine. Catherine told me she would likely marry Theo, but was not about to commit until after she graduated college. I supposed I'd want freedom too, after having spent so many formative years being someone's girlfriend.

Bernard held me and looked deeply into my eyes. "Do I get to enjoy you all day today?"

"Yes," I smiled. I sat with Bernard in his family room.

"What shall we do today, sweetheart?" Bernard asked me.

"Swim! It's a very warm day today!" I happily hugged him. It was an exceptionally warm, spring day, and after being cooped up inside during months of winter, I wanted desperately to spend the entire day outside.

"As you wish," Bernard leaned down and kissed me again. "I've wanted to hold you and kiss you for so long." Bernard kissed me again and held me against him. "I will be the happiest man in the world if you let me hold you and kiss you forever."

"I will," I said. "I would kiss you more often if I were taller, but I can't reach your lips. I can easily kiss you all day and every day when you're sitting though."

"I'll remember to sit more often," he pulled me onto his lap as he sat on the sofa and I kissed him. Bernard's lips were soft. I imagined what they'd feel like on other areas of my body.

I looked at Bernard's beautiful eyes and I wanted to kiss him again, but sometimes I was nervous. "Bernard," I whispered, "do you like the way I kiss?"

"Yes, of course, Maybel! I teased you about your kisses because I didn't want you to know I loved you. I was wrong to make you feel less than perfect. You know," Bernard's cheeks blushed, "I fantasized about kissing you on other parts of your body, too." His hand gently rubbed my back as I sat on his lap. My arms were wrapped around his neck and I played with his hair on the back of his head.

"Every time you have ever played with my hair has made me want to push you back and make love to you. My God, Maybel, you have a way with your fingers!" Bernard breathed deeply and closed his eyes while I continued running my fingers through his hair.

I kissed his lips lightly and he opened his eyes. I kissed him again and he breathed hard and placed me on my back on the sofa and laid beside me kissing me while he stroked my hair.

"I thought I annoyed you when I fidgeted with your hands and hair," I said.

"I couldn't tell you how much it turned me on!" he kissed me. "That's why I pushed you away so often when you touched my hair and held my hands. I wanted to kiss you so much. You have no idea!"

Bernard pushed his tongue gently into my mouth and kissed me. "Maybel, I love you so much. I'm so happy when we're together."

"Me too," I murmured. I reached my hand around his head and pulled him to me and I kissed him while I played with his hair.

Bernard breathed hard and I kissed his neck while my fingers slowly twisted and twirled his hair. I sucked his earlobe and pulled it with my lips and he moaned softly.

"Maybel," he sat up, still breathing hard. "I have to stop before I go too far with you."

Bernard stood up and pulled me up next to him. He paused then wrapped his hand around my neck and kissed me passionately. "I love kissing you," he breathed.

Bernard pulled back slightly. "Let's go do something. It's hard to lay with you and not tear your dress off."

"It is hard," I smirked, "very hard, indeed."

"Maybel," he blushed and kissed me again.

He pulled away again. "We have to get out of here. Come, Maybel," he took my hand and led me out of his family room and into his kitchen.

"Today is a beautiful day. Why don't we go for a walk down to the pond?" he suggested.

"That sounds nice," I smiled. "We can swim and make a campfire."

Bernard held my hand and we went out the kitchen door and there were Mr. and Mrs. Charleston sipping tea on their porch swing.

I quickly let go of Bernard's hand, but he just as quickly took my hand and held it again. I looked up at him nervously.

Bernard looked down at me. "I've finally got you. I'm never letting you go." He turned to his parents. "Maybel and I love each other. I'm going to marry her."

I stood stiff and weary of their reaction. I'd never been able to be with Bernard publicly until recently.

"It's about time, son. Proud of you," Mr. Charleston raised his glass.

"I've always known," Mrs. Charleston winked at me.

"We're going to the pond now," Bernard said.

"I'd like my first grandchild to be a girl, just as sweet and kind as Maybel; see what you can do, Bernard," Mr. Charleston chuckled.

Mrs. Charleston playfully slapped Mr. Charleston's arm. "Oh, stop it, sweetheart!" She then addressed Bernard, "But with all sincerity, honey, we want a granddaughter just like Maybel," she winked at me.

"We just started dating not long ago!" Bernard seemed exasperated.

"So, an autumn baby? Late autumn? Or are we thinking next spring?" Mr. Charleston laughed.

"Yes, dear, I don't mean to gloat, but I picked out a spot for our grandchildren's Life's Trees because, Maybel, as I've always told Bernard, I knew you were the one. See, the places I marked are right over there near Bernard's Life's Tree. You can of course choose different places as you wish. That tree over there I planted the day after you came here to repair Bernard's relationship with Catherine when you were a child. That's when I knew you'd be the mother of my grandchildren." Mrs. Charleston smiled proudly.

The tree she planted was an oak tree and was now tall and strong. I had seen it many times but never knew it was mine. "Thank you," I smiled happily.

"Ok, thank you mother and father, see you later!" Bernard's face was red from embarrassment.

Bernard's parents clinked their glasses and giggled like children. Bernard hurriedly pulled me away and out of sight.

"I'm sorry, Maybel! I didn't know they would be so forward about sex and babies! Are you ok? Are you upset?"

"No, I told you when I first met you that I was going to have a baby with you named Isabel, like Maybel, but a little different. Don't you remember?"

"I do remember," he sighed, "I was embarrassed and I felt awkward because you were eleven or twelve, and I was fourteen. I thought you were a baby and I didn't want to think about you sexually."

"But did you?" I asked curiously.

Bernard looked pained. "I liked you. I liked you a lot. Maybel, you were eleven, or twelve, I don't know exactly when I fell in love with you, but I know I loved you the day I met you. I never wanted to hurt you because I thought you were too young and innocent, and can we talk about something else because now I'm feeling panic."

"I'm sorry," I said, "What can I do to help you with your panicky feeling the way you helped me?"

"You told me to tell you happy things. What are some happy things you can tell me?"

"Susan and Paul are in love," I smiled.

"Yes, he seemed quite happy this morning at breakfast," Bernard snorted. He smiled as though he remembered something that was said to him.

"I really need to teach Paul how to sculpt a daisy, or something other than blooming roses and lilies."

Bernard laughed hard. "I have never in my life seen more attractive landscaping than when Paul gifted Susan five hundred vaginas." Bernard and I laughed so hard our sides hurt.

I loved Bernard's attention. We kissed and whispered into each other's ears and caressed each other's arms and backs. "Bernard, I'm going to go swimming." I stood up and took off my hot dress. "Do you want to come with me?"

I stood in front of Bernard in my undergarments, which were lightweight and didn't leave much to his imagination.

"Maybel," Bernard was laying on the tufts of clover, "I don't think you should go swimming." He stared at me, entranced.

"It's a warm day, Bernard! Come on!" I held my hand out to him.

"Maybel, the last time I saw you in wet clothes I became aroused and Catherine saw. The time before that, you drove me insane, and the time before that you hit me with pine cones and then I saw your beautiful body in wet, clingy clothing and I spent many a night in my bathroom thinking about those encounters. We just started being together as a couple. I don't want to hurt you by going too fast. Please just lay here beside me."

"Ok, but it's a warm day and I promise not to let you touch me.

"You won't let me touch you?" Bernard looked disappointed.

"No, I will not," I winked twice, very hard, so my dry delivery wouldn't escape him, as I walked toward the water.

"Maybel!" Bernard tore off his clothing and wore only his undershorts. "Wait for me!"

I swam out a way with Bernard following closely behind. I stopped swimming and waited for Bernard to catch up. "Ah! You finally made it!"

"I wasn't that far behind you!"

"You let me arrive first, like a true gentleman," I giggled.

"Ladies come first," he smiled.

I laughed. "Bernard," I wrapped my arms around his neck, "Kiss me."

"Always, Maybel," he held my waist under the water and kissed me.

"I've always wanted to marry you. I was always in love with you," I said.

"I thought you only liked me as a big brother. I didn't think you knew what love was."

"I knew I loved you." I kissed Bernard.

"I tried so hard not to love you, but I could never stop."

"I'm glad," I whispered. I kissed Bernard and felt his hands warm against my cold body.

"Maybel, when I see you in wet clothes, I want to rip them off and wrap your legs around my waist."

"When I see your chest, I want to touch you. I always wanted to feel your bare chest against mine. I used to hug you playfully just to feel you next to me and to smell your skin," I smiled and touched his bare chest.

"I let you hug me because I liked the feel of you against me when we danced and when you sat on my lap, though I thought you were only hugging me because you thought of me as a brother."

"Maybe sometimes I thought of you as a brother, in the beginning, but then I wanted you to kiss me and touch me," I confessed.

"I wanted to, Maybel, you have no idea how much I wanted to." Bernard began kissing my neck and sucking. I kissed his neck and sucked. His warm body in the cool water was a tantalizing contrast and made my stomach flutter.

"I felt so guilty, Maybel, for wanting you to touch me. I felt so guilty for holding you against me, feeling your waist as we danced, wondering what your legs would feel like wrapped around me. I didn't know you were attracted to me the way I was attracted to you," he said.

"Oh, I most definitely was attracted to you," I giggled. "I never wanted anyone to know though. I used to play wrestle with you just so I could accidentally feel your chest." I brushed my fingertips over his chest.

"I let you accidentally feel my chest," he smiled. "I just didn't realize you were doing it on purpose."

"There were likely plenty of things I didn't do on purpose," I said. "I really was quite naive looking back on things I did and said, however, yes, there were times I touched you on purpose."

"Maybel," I love you.

"I love you too, Bernard."

Bernard kissed me and then kissed my shoulder. He breathed deeply and smiled. "You have the most beautiful eyes."

"As do you," I kissed Bernard and his lips were warm and wet.

"Shall we dry off in the warm sun?" I smiled.

"Yes," he hesitated, "but I'll need a few minutes more of this cold water."

I giggled and began swimming to shore. I walked onto the shore followed closely by Bernard. I turned to take his hand. He was watching my bottom as I walked onto land and when I turned to him, his eyes were filled with lust as he admired my breasts and hips.

I wrapped my arms around his neck and kissed him. He pulled my hips tightly against his waist and I felt him hard against me. "Maybel," he breathed, "you're stunning!"

I touched his hard, wet chest. "This is what I wanted to do before," I whispered. I felt his skin and muscles. I kissed his chest as I touched him.

"Maybel," he breathed heavily, "I love the way you touch me."

"And now I finally get to touch you without you getting mad and pushing me away."

"I'll never push you away again," he pulled me into his arms. "You can touch me anytime you want."

"I like that," I said, and kissed his chest, letting my tongue play over his nipples.

I held his hand and led him to a grassy area warmed with sunlight. He laid down and pulled me on top of him. I straddled his waist and leaned down to kiss and suck his chest and stomach. His skin was smooth and soft and tasted like the sun. I became very aroused laying on his hard penis and kissing his hard muscles, bronzed by sun.

I let my hips very gently rub up and down his penis while I kissed and explored his shoulders and biceps down to his belly button and back up to his neck. When I began kissing down his body again, lightly brushing my waist against his very aroused penis, he moaned and I became wetter. I let my tongue play along the ridges of his abdominal muscles and licked around his belly button. I ever so lightly kissed his waist, and let my tongue explore just under the waistline of his underwear.

Bernard groaned and pulled me up into his arms breathing hard. "This is pure torture," he pulled my shirt off my shoulders and kissed my neck and then traced his tongue down to my shoulders. "Maybel," he moaned, "can I?"

"Yes, Bernard," I breathed heavily.

He pulled my shirt down further and kissed my bare breasts with increasing lust, ripping the rest of my shirt from my body and sucking my nipples until I moaned with anticipation. He laid between my legs kissing my breasts and caressing them. I rubbed myself against his hard stomach, rocking my hips back and forth, feeling an orgasm building.

Bernard came up beside me. He kissed my lips and put his thumb inside the waistline of my shorts. "Maybel, can I?"

"Yes!" I practically screamed.

Bernard pulled my shorts off with one quick sweep of his hand then kissed me, pushing his tongue inside my mouth while he pushed his finger inside me. I screamed out and bucked my hips wanting him to push harder. Bernard pushed into me harder and with such rhythm I grabbed his head and screamed into his neck as I orgasmed, my fingers digging into his back.

"Maybel," Bernard's face looked pained. "Please!" Bernard begged.

I reached for his shorts but he reached them first and yanked them off. He was thick and long and throbbing. I wrapped my hand around him and pulled up and pushed down gently, unsure of how Bernard wanted me hold him. "Bernard, help me."

He wrapped his hand around mine and squeezed, pumping up and down hard. After showing me the rhythm and pace he enjoyed, he let go and I continued while he pushed his finger back inside me.

We laid side by side touching each other and kissing. Bernard's face was becoming hotter and sweaty as I kissed him and stroked him. He pushed his finger inside me with the same rhythm and pace I used to pleasure him and soon I began screaming again as I felt myself getting closer to orgasming. Bernard watched me screaming as I orgasmed again and suddenly his body shook and he orgasmed all over my neck and stomach.

His body still spasmed as he moaned and kissed me. "Maybel," he moaned, "you're amazing!"

"As are you, Bernard!" I said breathlessly.

We laid side by side kissing and touching each other until our breath returned to normal. "Maybel, I think we need to go swimming again," he looked at my stomach.

I giggled, "Yes, I'm sticky."

"Sorry, sweetheart," he blushed.

"Don't be. I quite enjoyed myself," I laughed.

Bernard looked into my eyes for a moment then held my chin lightly and kissed my lips gently. "I love you," he whispered.

"I love you, too," I whispered back.

The sun began to lower and we were still kissing and whispering. "Maybel, I have kept journals over the years, and I wrote about when we first met and almost every day since."

Bernard suddenly looked like the way I felt when daddy lost me at the fourth of July parade when I was seven. I looked around and could not see in which way to begin walking. Every direction looked the same.

"I want to show you my journals. I want you to read them." Bernard still looked trepid.

"Well, that's an intriguing way to get me in your bedroom," I giggled.

Bernard looked shy suddenly, "I want you to read everything I've written."

"I didn't know you wrote."

"Sometimes I write in my journal about something interesting that happened that day," he held my hands and smiled.

"I do want to, but I also have to go home before my parents worry."

"Yes, of course." Bernard held me and kissed me and his tongue was probing, yet very gentle.

"You're making it really hard to say goodbye," I kissed him.

"You're making it hard too," he laughed.

I blushed.

Bernard kissed me again.

"Maybe just a couple entries before I return home." I returned his kiss.

Bernard smiled and kissed me again and again. "There's nothing holding me back from showing my love for you, Maybel. I want you to know how I've always felt about you, the good and the bad, and everything in between."

Bernard held my hand and led me to his room. He led me to a shelf with his prized possessions. "This is the teacup you made me the day we met."

"Yes, Bernard," I giggled, "I've seen it here before."

"But you haven't seen this." He handed me the teacup I made from the mud in my backyard. "Turn it over."

I turned it over and on the bottom of the teacup was scrawled, "I'm going to marry you, Bernard. Love, Maybel."

"I don't remember writing that!" I said, astonished.

"You did, Maybel. And I read it and teased you and you became angry and kicked me."

"I don't remember that!"

"I think you sense things too, Maybel, like my mother. Your intuition is true. That's why I want you to consider this note you wrote me when we were children."

I took the note from Bernard's hand. It read: "Our children will be happy."

"When did I write this?"

"Maybel, reread your stories. You have sensed things to come. When you write, when you day-dream, you open your mind and see things and write them down."

"I don't remember ever writing you, saying our children will be happy."

"You often scrawl out random things in the margins of your notebooks when you are deep in thought. You should go back and look through your journals. The writings you have let me read are quite interesting."

"I will," I said.

Bernard held my arm and led me to his bed. He sat on the edge and pulled me onto his lap. "I like holding you. I like when you sit on my lap." He kissed me.

"I have always wanted to sit on your lap. I always begged you to hold me."

"And I did hold you, until you got older, and I wanted to tear your dress off." Bernard kissed me. "Then I told you to stay away, and I was mean," he kissed my neck, "but what I really wanted to do was this...." He picked me up in his arms and laid me on his bed and straddled me while he leaned down and kissed me tenderly. Bernard laid behind me and kissed my neck. He handed me his journals from his nightstand.

I laid on Bernard's bed and began reading.

"You wrote about the day you met me and Catherine," I mused. Bernard laid beside me as I read, kissing my neck softly. He held my hand as I read.

"Catherine is beautiful and I want to date her. She has a little sister named Maybel. I wanted to kiss Maybel today, but she's too young, and anyway, I think Catherine returns my affection."

"You wanted to kiss me the day we met?" I asked Bernard, shocked.

"Yes," he blushed. "Maybel, I have always loved you and I want to show you just how much. Keep reading."

I continued reading Bernard's memories. He spoke of seeing Catherine for his dates but went into greater detail about playing with Catherine's little sister while waiting for Catherine to return from piano lessons.

"I go over early to Catherine's house so I have time to play with Maybel while I wait for Catherine. I like Maybel a lot. I wish she were older or I were younger."

As I read through Bernard's memories, I realized he focused mostly on me. He went on dates with Catherine, but he didn't say much about them except that they were boring get-togethers with Catherine's friends. He wrote about playing with me mostly.

"I danced with Maybel again. I always want to kiss her, but she still acts like a child, and I can't kiss a child. Today she cried because Catherine and I left her. I wanted to kiss her and tell her I was sorry we left her, but I told her to stop crying like a baby. She got mad at me for saying that. I wanted to hug her and say I was sorry, but I didn't."

"Maybel sat on my lap again today. I wish she wouldn't, because I really like it when she sits on me and plays with my hair."

I giggled. "Shall I play with your hair now?" I turned toward Bernard smiling.

"Always, sweetheart." Bernard smiled and took a deep breath and relaxed while I ran my fingers through his hair and whispered "I love you" in his ear. I lightly brushed my fingers over his cheeks and kissed his ear softly.

Bernard held me and I kissed his lips while my fingers twirled his hair. He kissed and sucked my neck gently.

Bernard's hand was on my waist and as he kissed my lips, he moved his hand slowly up my body. "Maybel?" His hand lingered just below my breast. He kissed my lips and pushed his tongue in my mouth, touching the tip of my tongue with his.

"Yes, Bernard," I breathed into his ear.

Bernard pushed his hand further up and over my breast and then pulled my dress down while he kissed me. His fingers gently tugged my neckline down to expose my breasts. His breath quickened as he touched my breasts and then kissed them.

"Oh, Maybel, you're beautiful!" He moaned in between kisses and suckles. His hands caressed both breasts as I laid on my back. Bernard straddled my legs as he hovered over my body, hungrily exploring my every curve.

"I want to feel your chest again, Bernard. I've always wanted to kiss your neck and chest." I pulled him down beside me and he smiled as I unbuttoned his shirt. His gaze into my eyes became more intense the further down toward his waist my hands went.

I unbuttoned the last button and slowly undressed Bernard. I pushed him back on his pillow and kissed his chest. My hands explored his chest and stomach as I kissed him and let my tongue play on his stomach muscles. I kissed and sucked his nipples while I squeezed his shoulder muscles and biceps.

Bernard played with my breasts and lightly rubbed my nipples as I tasted his skin. Bernard rolled me back and sat up. He looked down at me with lust and tucked his fingers into the waistline of my skirt and slowly pulled off the rest of my clothing while watching me closely to make sure I was ok.

I let Bernard undress me. He looked down at me with such hunger that just his gaze made my thighs tingle.

I sat up beside him and unfastened his pants. He stood up beside me and let his pants fall to the floor. I reached out and slowly pulled down his underwear to reveal his extremely hard penis. He was long and thick.

I looked up at Bernard. He laid back beside me in bed. He kissed me tenderly and stroked my hair, letting me relax again. He kissed my neck. His penis brushed against my stomach and it was hot and hard and my vagina became very wet and tingled deep inside.

I played with Bernard's hair while he suckled my breasts. Bernard came beside me and kissed my lips. His eyes searched mine, silently asking me for permission, and I held his hand and guided it down to my waist. He let his fingers play around my clitoris, massaging it until I moaned. I was ready for him and I wanted him. Bernard pushed his middle finger inside me and I moaned loudly. It felt so good. He pushed further and I moaned louder. I lowered my hand and touched his upper thigh and he kissed me urging me to continue.

I wrapped my hand around his penis and he moaned loudly and I felt his body shake. "Maybel!" he screamed, as I pushed and pulled. Bernard got on top of me and pushed my legs apart with his knees. "Maybel, I want to kiss you here," he rubbed my upper thighs.

"Yes," I breathed.

Bernard leaned down and rubbed my clitoris as he pushed his tongue inside me. I immediately orgasmed and Bernard sat up, breathing hard. "Maybel, I want to make love with you."

"I do too," I said breathlessly, as I reached up and pulled his neck down toward me.

"I want to pleasure you first though," I grinned.

I pushed him back and laid between his legs and kissed his chest. Bernard breathed hard. I felt him beneath me and he felt stiff. I kissed the top of his penis and he moaned. He grabbed the sheets with his fists and clenched them, and pulled them. I put him inside my mouth and he quivered beneath me. I held him while I pushed him further inside my mouth.

"Maybel," he pulled me up toward him and I felt his urgency. He rolled me onto my back and spread my legs. I wrapped my legs around his waist. He looked down at me for a moment and hesitated.

"I love you," he said. "I'm going to marry you and make you a mommy. By this time next year, you and I will be holding our baby."

I relaxed and smiled at Bernard. "I like that."

"I want to meet our children soon. I want them to look like you. I've loved you since the day I met you."

"I love you too," I said.

Bernard guided his penis to me and pushed inside me gently. I screamed out in pleasure and pain, and then he pushed himself deeper inside me.

I moaned as he gently pulled out and then slowly and carefully pushed himself inside me again. His gaze into my eyes was intense. He watched my every expression, making sure I felt more pleasure than pain. I began moaning louder and I arched my back slightly.

"Please stop moaning," Bernard begged. "I won't last if you moan."

"Stop making it feel so good," I breathed, "and I won't moan."

I orgasmed again and wrapped my legs around his waist as he screamed loudly with each push. I felt another orgasm building and grabbed his shoulders as he pushed himself harder into me. I screamed loudly as I orgasmed, and Bernard, with one more hard push, screamed and shook and I felt hot liquid pour into me.

Bernard kissed me again and again telling me how much he loved me. "Are you ok, sweetheart? Did I hurt you? How do you feel?"

"I feel so good, Bernard!"

He kissed me again.

"I love you, Maybel!"

"I love you too, Bernard!"

Bernard treated me like delicate porcelain. He gently caressed me, asking me if I felt alright and if I needed anything. "Maybel," he whispered, "don't leave yet. Stay here with me tonight."

"And what would I tell my parents? Mother, father, I know I've spent all day studying math, but I'm just so terrible at math that Bernard's going to tutor me all night now." I giggled.

"Or, we could tell them you were tired from the dinner party, that Paul and Susan were here, and you fell asleep in the study. Then you went upstairs to the guest bedroom to spend the night."

"If I don't return tonight, daddy will come looking for me with his gun. I have to go home." Bernard looked sad.

"I don't want to hide our love," I said, "I just don't want Catherine to find out until she becomes more comfortable with us spending time together."

"Maybel, we just made love for the first time. I don't want you to leave." He pulled me closer and kissed my lips.

"I don't want to come and go either, Bernard." I giggled, and Bernard laughed, then kissed me.

"I wanted to go slower our first time. I wanted it to last longer," he kissed my neck and caressed my breast. "I had in my mind the way our first time would go, but I wanted you so much that I skipped steps," he kissed me and let his tongue explore my mouth.

"We have the rest of our lives Bernard," I said gently.

"I want to make up for lost time," he kissed me and let his fingertips play with my nipples.

"You're making it hard to leave," I breathed into his ear.

"You're making it hard," he whispered into my ear.

Bernard pushed himself into me again and I arched my back moaning softly. He used his strong arms to hold his upper body up, and his strong stomach muscles to push into me deeply. I rolled my hips back and forth in rhythm with his thrusting, and suddenly grabbed his back, digging my fingers in and gasping as my body convulsed and contracted with intense orgasms.

Bernard watched me scream beneath him and his face and neck flushed red hot, then he screamed out loudly as he released himself into me.

"God, Maybel! Ah, God, you feel so good!" Bernard's body spasmed and he shook with pleasure.

"Maybel, I love you! Please don't leave tonight!" he kissed me and pushed gently into me as my orgasms faded.

"I'll stay here Bernard," I said. I was still catching my breath.

Bernard kissed me. "Stay here in my arms. I want to kiss you all night."

"Me too, honey, me too," I moaned.

"Call me honey again," he kissed me.

"Honey," I giggled.

"I like that," he kissed my shoulder.

"Sweetheart," I said, smiling.

"I like that more," he kissed my breasts.

"I love you so much," he said, as he kissed me all over.

The next morning, I woke up very early and kissed Bernard. He pulled me into him. "Not yet," he mumbled. "A little longer," he kissed me.

"I don't want my parents to worry," I whispered.

"Just a little while longer?" he pleaded.

Bernard let his fingers play between my legs until I moaned and writhed and then he spread my legs and entered me. He rocked slowly at first until I couldn't take it anymore and I cried out, "Please go harder and faster! Please!"

Bernard smiled down at me and pushed harder and faster until I screamed again and again. My orgasms were intense and I couldn't control my screams. He began breathing harder and moaning, as he pushed and thrusted, then orgasmed.

"I have decided that sex with you is my new favorite pastime, Maybel!" he laughed as he caught his breath. "I really, really like having sex with you!" he moaned into my ear and kissed me.

"It's my new favorite sport too," I breathed heavily.

"Bernard, I should really get home. I'm shocked my parents didn't show up here in the middle of the night."

"Can you tell them good morning then come right back here?" He continued kissing me and rubbing my legs. He cupped my bottom and pushed his tongue inside my mouth.

"Bernard," I moaned, "I'll come back soon."

"Come now, sweetheart," he smiled and kissed me. He pulled me on top of him and laid on his back.

I giggled. "I like this," I smiled down at him.

"I'm at your mercy, m'lady," Bernard smiled.

I liked being on top of Bernard. He was hard underneath me and I held him as I lowered myself onto him. I felt new sensations and pressures inside me, and I put my hands down by Bernard's neck and pushed myself all the way down his long and thick shaft.

Bernard moaned, "Maybel! Ah! Keep going!" he moaned louder.

I used my hips to buck up and down and I came hard. I liked being in complete control, and pushed and pulled myself up and down his long penis, feeling him deep inside me, throbbing and hard.

Bernard grabbed my wrists next to his neck and squeezed. "Maybel! I can't last much longer! It feels too good!" he moaned.

I bounced my hips up and down faster and harder, pushing myself down onto him. I ground against him with each push, letting his hard stomach muscles rub my clitoris. I screamed loudly and orgasmed and Bernard below me screamed and bucked his hips as he exploded inside me.

"Maybel! That was amazing!"

I fell into his outstretched arms. He was still inside me as I laid on top of him.

I pulled myself off him and laid, spent, next to him.

"As soon as I return, that's the first position I want to do again!"

"Yes, please!" Bernard laughed. "You're a tigress up there, Maybel! You really get passionate about your work!" he laughed.

"I was creating art," I giggled.

I climbed over Bernard and got dressed.

Bernard reached for me with both hands. "One more kiss please?"

I smiled, "Always, sweetheart."

When I arrived home, it was still early and everyone was still in bed. I tip toed upstairs and put my nightgown on then tip toed back downstairs to make breakfast. I figured it would be harder to yell at me with the smell of bacon and eggs awaiting my parents for breakfast.

Mommy was the first down for breakfast. "Good morning, dear," she kissed my cheek. "Breakfast smells wonderful!"

Daddy came down next. "Put an extra piece on my plate for your mother to steal please, Maybel."

"Yes, daddy."

"How is Mr. Charleston doing, honey? he asked.

"He asked about you. Why don't you play cards with him some night?"

"Will you be joining me for a round of poker?" daddy winked.

Mommy laughed, "You and your sense of humor!" she giggled at daddy. She didn't realize daddy was serious and enjoyed having me sit with him and win money for us both.

I winked back at daddy. "Oh, sure, daddy," I laughed, "You know how much I love gambling!" I joked.

"Oh Maybel!" mommy giggled, "You two are so funny!"

Daddy and I grinned at each other.

Catherine came downstairs. "Good morning," she said.

"Good morning," we three replied to her.

"How was your dinner with Paul?" Catherine asked me.

"Paul and Susan were there. We ate steak." I kept my answers vague.

"Sounds lovely. How is Bernard?"

"Fine," I said.

"Is Paul having dinner again tonight with all his family?"

"Yes. Lots of family visiting. Celebrating another one of his art shows," I answered.

"That's nice," she said.

Mommy and daddy listened to us, but were also playfully stealing bacon from each other.

"I can cook more bacon," I told them.

"Oh, no dear, then we wouldn't have anything to fight about," mommy winked at daddy as she broke off a piece of his bacon.

"Cupcake, come here for a kiss," daddy winked at mommy.

She giggled and leaned in for a kiss from daddy, and he reached over and stole a piece of her bacon.

She kissed daddy again, while slapping the bacon out of his hand. They both giggled and kissed each other again.

"Well, I'll let you two be alone," I said, and hurried upstairs before I saw something I didn't want to see.

I took a bath and washed away all the stickiness covering my body. I had bled a little from having intercourse for the first time. After thoroughly washing, I dressed and went to my room to brush my hair and get ready to return to Bernard. I was excited to see him again even though I'd just left him.

I felt giddy and utterly happy and excited to return to his embrace and his kisses.

I quietly opened my door and went downstairs. I didn't want to see Catherine or answer any questions. Mommy and daddy were holding hands and giggling about their first date.

"I'm going to the library and Susan's house. I'll probably be late getting home," I told mommy and daddy.

"Yes, dear," mommy said, and continued laughing with daddy.

I left and walked to Bernard's, thinking how easily it had been to stay out all night without them knowing, and wondering if Catherine had ever stayed out all night.

I passed Susan's house but didn't stop. I figured she was probably already at the library with Paul, holding his hand, kissing him, and discussing his vagina flower sculpture.

Paul wondered why that piece in particular was so popular. I deduced Paul, perhaps, had never seen a vagina, and had not realized how similar his flowers were to the shape of a vagina. I hoped I would be there watching his face as he looked at his flowers for the first time after having sex.

I went to Bernard's house, but instead of entering through the front door, I climbed the tree by his bedroom and tapped on his window. Bernard came out of his bathroom freshly bathed and wearing a towel around his waist.

"Maybel! You're back!" He pulled me inside and onto his bed. "You're stunning!" he kissed me.

"How do you feel?" He seemed concerned.

"I'm fine," I said.

"I noticed a little blood on the bed sheets when I was changing them. Did I hurt you?" He brushed my hair back and kissed my cheek.

"It was more pleasurable than painful," I said.

"Are you sore?"

"No," I answered.

"Then may I kiss you?"

I smiled. Bernard took my top and my skirt off, and smiled down at my naked body. I put my hand on his hip and gently tugged at his towel. He was already very aroused.

He began by kissing me, and then my neck and breasts, and down to my stomach. I eagerly awaited his mouth and kisses. He kissed my thighs, and then my upper thighs, where he lingered a painfully long time kissing my inner thighs until I begged him to kiss me between my legs. I gently pushed on the back of his head moaning, "Please, Bernard!"

He kissed my clitoris and I gasped. His tongue circled my clitoris and his hot breath made me shiver.

I moaned and craved release. He pushed his tongue inside me and I screamed. He felt so good. I pulled on his head to come up to me and make love to me but he resisted. Instead, he pushed two fingers inside me as he flicked my clitoris with his tongue. I arched my back and screamed. He pushed his fingers in deeper, and with a steady rhythm that made me shudder with intense orgasms.

I could hardly catch my breath. Bernard came up between my legs, and I eagerly wrapped my legs tightly around his waist. With frenzied lust, he pushed hard into me, so hard, I felt his scrotum smacking me with each thrust. I orgasmed again and could only moan breathlessly, as I'd long lost my breath. Bernard grunted and groaned with every penetrating thrust until he began shaking as he pumped and orgasmed deep inside me.

He laid on top of me moaning and I laid limply underneath him, catching my breath. I felt him slowly go limp as he continued shaking and moaning into my ear.

After finally catching our breath, he pulled himself out of me, and laid beside me kissing my neck and breathing hard.

We fell asleep in each other's arms. I felt so calm and happy when Bernard held me.

Bernard proposed to me atop the tree on my island, where I first kissed him. We wed shortly thereafter in a very, very small wedding because I began wheezing whenever mommy or Catherine mentioned guests, dress colors, food, and wedding invitations. Bernard and I were married and lived happily together. And that ends my retelling of how Bernard and I began our life together. Our journey and our love for each other is my soul's joy.